... the first time, the
from beginning to end ...
absolutely nothing stopping these books becoming little
steampunk classics in their own right.'
The Travelling Librarian

'Gosling is gifted in her world-building. Reminiscent of Sherlock
Holmes ... the book is full of intrigue.'
The Book Bee

'I flew through this book as Gosling uses her skill with prose and
plot to quickly pull in the reader, and I revelled in the multiple
plot twists ... It is a thoroughly enjoyable adventure story with a
pair of completely likeable protagonists, who you will find yourself rooting for almost from the very first page.'
Spreading UKYA

'Curious Fox couldn't have chosen a more exciting or involving
adventure story ... the story is so engrossing, the action scenes so
varied and full of drama.'
Books for Keeps

'A truly entertaining book that captured both my heart and
imagination and I for one cannot wait to read more books by
Sharon Gosling.'
Book Angel Booktopia

First published in 2016 by Curious Fox,
an imprint of Capstone Global Library Limited,
264 Banbury Road, Oxford OX2 7DY
Registered company number: 6695582

www.curious-fox.com

ISBN 978 1 782 02421 7
20 19 18 17 16
10 9 8 7 6 5 4 3 2 1

A CIP catalogue for this book is available from the British Library.

Printed and bound by CPI Group (UK) Ltd, Croydon, CR0 4YY.

In loving memory of Andy Sears, who always
looked good in a Royal Green Jacket.

The Sapphire Cutlass

SHARON GOSLING

Curious Fox

Contents

One

The Tiger and the Bird

The jungle fell silent.

A sudden hush dropped over the verdant foliage as if someone had trapped it inside a glass jar. The birds huddled closer to their branches, concealing their bright jewel colours beneath the sun-dappled leaves. The chattering hordes of black and white monkeys deserted their overhead perches, carrying their cries – and their babies – with them until the echoes faded into the distance. Even the insects ceased to buzz and skitter. The searing hot air of mid-morning became still and empty, a strange sense of expectancy hanging in it.

The chital froze and raised its head, the white dots that peppered the little deer's reddish brown flanks quivering as it sniffed the air.

Rémy cursed silently. Crouched beneath a bush just a few feet away, she was hot, cramped and tired of this hunt, which had been going on all morning without success. Whatever had scared the fawn at this crucial moment was in danger of depriving her of her dinner. The loop of rope that belonged to the makeshift trap she had set hours before lay just beyond where the creature now stood.

Go on, Rémy urged it, silently. *Just a little further…*

The chital turned, head still up, ears flicking this way and that, and took a step towards Rémy's hiding place.*No*, Rémy thought. *Not this way!*

The deer, oblivious and still afraid, took another step in the wrong direction. It looked as if it were preparing to bolt.

Sensing a last chance Rémy stood, but the deer was already moving. It leapt towards her, its small but powerful back legs kicking up the dust of the forest floor. Rémy lunged forward, arms stretched wide as if she could herd the creature in the right direction, but the chital flicked sideways in mid-air, black eyes wide with fright, nostrils flaring.

If, in those briefest of moments, Rémy had time to wonder why the deer had chosen to run *at* her rather than *away*, the question was swiftly answered. Something surged out of the undergrowth behind it, a flash of orange and white striped with black, massive and muscular with a gaping maw and yellowed teeth as large and sharp as carving knives. The huge creature scythed through the clearing, bathing Rémy in a wash of air that rolled over her as it passed.

The cat caught the chital, one massive bite from those fangs crushing the deer's neck before the beast rippled to a halt at the edge of the clearing, giant paws as silent as slippers on the jungle floor.

The tiger turned to look at Rémy Brunel.

The cat's head was enormous, almost half the size of the deer between its teeth. The tiger's body easily dwarfed Rémy's, and even now, from several feet away, she could see the rippling muscles beneath the bright beauty of its glossy tri-coloured coat.

Blood dripped from the tiger's razor-sharp teeth, peppering the earth with scarlet. Nothing else moved. The tiger watched her with huge, sepia-coloured eyes, as if waiting to see what she would do. Rémy herself didn't know. The tiger already had prey to occupy it, but the chital was small. She would make a bigger meal. If she moved, would it come after her? If it did, Rémy knew that as swift as she was, she'd never outrun a tiger in full flight.

The Little Bird was no match at all for a Big Cat. Not on the ground, anyway...

The tiger twitched, lifting one huge front paw and setting it down again. She could see its claws, shining like opaque, slivered jewels through the feathery white fur of its feet.

The tiger growled, the muscles along its nose wrinkling like waves on the ocean, its whiskers quivering. Rémy turned and ran. She made for the nearest tree, throwing herself at it and scrambling skywards up the parched bark at breakneck speed. She felt the tiger coming at her, its bulk disturbing the still air as it crossed the clearing in one leap. It thumped against the tree, shaking the trunk with its full weight so that Rémy almost lost her grip. She clung on, digging her nails into the bark, feeling it give under her fingers as she pulled herself up. The tiger leapt after her, paw outstretched and body extended, so big that she was sure she would feel its claws in her legs. Rémy kept going, scrambling higher and higher until she was out of the creature's reach. Breathing hard, she allowed herself a pause to look down.

The tiger was climbing the tree, using its needle-sharp claws to drag itself upwards. It snarled, the sound dispersing like the low rumble of thunder through the trees.

Rémy ran quickly along the narrow branch, balancing even as the tiger's movements shook and shuddered it beneath her booted feet. It began to bow beneath her weight, but by then she had lined up a jump. Taking a fraction of a second to centre herself, Rémy flung her body into mid-air, the colours of the jungle whipping past her like circus streamers as she reached for a branch of the neighbouring tree. Her hands gripped and held the rough bark like the bar of a trapeze and she swung there for a moment, testing its strength. To her relief it held. She bounced there for a second, then used the momentum to twist one hand over the other, turning to see what her hunter was doing.

The tiger snarled again and dropped back to the ground, too clever to follow her along the narrow branch. It moved to stand beneath her, instead. Rémy hung there, nothing but the strength of her arms and several feet of empty, hot jungle air between her and the angry cat. It hunched itself backwards on its hindquarters.

She swung out of the way as the tiger leapt, snapping its jaws around empty air. She hooked her legs over the branch and heaved herself onto her stomach, just as she would have done on the trapeze, then found her way to her feet. She moved higher, where the branches were thinner but out of the reach of the tiger's questing claws. Still the creature stood below her, those great yellow eyes watching every movement.

Rémy, out of breath, realised that she'd have to take the monkey's highway if she wanted to escape in one piece. *It's just as well,* she thought, as she scanned the trees around her for her next move, *that I have kept up my training, even though there has been no proper audience to watch me for months.*

She set off, zig-zagging from branch to branch through the trees, hands protesting at the rough nature of the holds she reached for over and over again. The tiger padded along beneath her for a long way, snarling every now and then, waiting for her to make a mistake. Rémy Brunel, however, rarely made mistakes – at least, not on the trapeze. She climbed, she jumped and she swung, as nimble and light as a bird – or a monkey.

Rémy didn't see the tiger go. One minute it was there, following below her like a flash of orange flame. The next it had melted back into the jungle. Most likely it was returning to the clearing to reclaim the chital before a pack of dhole came across it.

Still, she stuck to the trees. Just in case.

Puzzles

It took Rémy more than an hour to get back to the airship. Her crew had set her down in a small clearing that housed an ornate ruined temple. Rémy had been reluctant to take the swiftest route in case the tiger followed her and besides, she hadn't wanted to return empty handed. As it was, when she finally walked into the camp, Rémy carried over her shoulder a brace of rabbits – not quite the venison of the chital, it was true, but at least there would be something for the pot that night.

"Rémy!" Dita's voice danced out of the trees towards her. She looked up, just in time to see the little girl jump down from the lowest branch of the nearest tree. "You've been ages! I thought you were lost!"

"Lost? Me? Never!" Rémy told her with a smile. "Just a little waylaid, that's all."

"I have been practising," Dita said proudly, "while you

were gone. I can almost get all the way to the end without falling now."

Rémy looked at the taut rope that she and Thaddeus had strung between the two sturdiest trees that edged the clearing. It was four feet from the ground and at least eight feet long. "That's very good indeed," she said, genuinely impressed, making a mental note to adjust her next few lessons to accommodate Dita's apparently natural skill on the wire. "Especially since you've only been learning for a few weeks."

"Well, it is *wichtig*," said Dita, who still had the habit of peppering her English with words from her native German language. Her face took on a solemn look. "When we return home to Europe, I want a proper circus job." She wrinkled her nose. "No more sweeping up after the messy elephants. If I can walk a rope then I can do *anything*. Like you, *ja?*"

Rémy grinned, as much at the girl's enthusiasm as the compliment. "I'm not sure about *anything*," she said, pulling her catch from her shoulder and holding it up, "I'm still not too good at cooking."

"Pfft!" exclaimed Dita, her hands on her hips. "But that is a good thing! It means the boys have to do it. They have to be useful for something!"

Rémy smiled again and then looked around. The clearing was very quiet. "Where are they, anyway?" she asked.

Dita nodded towards the silent airship, at rest between two crumbling yellow walls with its balloon fully inflated. "J, he is hard at work on the ruby mechanism," she said, with a roll of her eyes. "He thinks it is not working quite as smoothly as it

13

should. Honestly, even if there were nothing wrong with it, he would find something to tinker with. Boys with toys, *ja?*"

"What about Thaddeus?" Rémy asked, walking to the area that had been designated as their 'kitchen' and dropping the rabbits in a heap beside the remnants of the previous night's fire.

"The other side," Dita said, indicating the airship again. She grinned wickedly. "He is an Englishman, no? He must hide from all this terrible sun!"

Rémy skipped quickly over a pile of fallen yellow wall, retrieved her bag from inside the airship, shouted a hello to the out-of-sight J and went to find Thaddeus Rec. He was sitting in the dappled shadows cast by the dense forest behind him, a large map spread out over his knees and his old policeman's notebook and pencil in one hand. His feet were bare, his trousers rolled up to his calves. His white shirt, although clean, was looking somewhat worse for wear after months of travel and was pulled up to the elbows and open at the throat. Rémy paused to watch him for a moment, smiling at the look of utter concentration on his face. Thaddeus's skin had darkened to a rich bronze tan in the sun that had followed them ever since they had reached the coast of India.

"Afternoon, *Monsieur*," Rémy said softly, as she approached. She knelt down beside him and kissed him on his cheek, which bore a prickle of dark stubble.

"Good afternoon, Miss Brunel," said Thaddeus, accepting the kiss with a smile. "I was beginning to wonder whether I should form a search party to come looking for you."

She shrugged with a grin, leaning against the tree beside

him and stretching out her legs beneath the map. "This little bird had an encounter with a big cat."

Thaddeus raised his eyebrows. "Oh?"

"A tiger. A big one, too – much bigger than me."

"A tiger? Good grief – are you all right?" He looked horrified, and she laughed.

"I am fine, as you see. Though tonight I think we should all sleep in the airship and seal the hatch. Just in case."

Thaddeus touched her cheek and nodded. "Good idea. I want to move on tomorrow, anyway – I don't like staying in one place for too long. It's too risky, with the airship."

Rémy glanced at the craft that had flown them all the way from Europe to the heart of England's colonial empire. They had been forced to dodge the curiosity of the British army a few times since they'd arrived, but that had mainly been near the coast, where their ships clustered in the teeming ports. Further inland, beyond the big cities, they had seen fewer colonial uniforms.

"Surely here, in the jungle, it is safe?"

Thaddeus frowned. "Perhaps. But I just have this feeling that it's better to keep on the move. The airship would be a rich prize for anyone, and without it we would be completely stranded."

Rémy nodded. "True enough. So, where to next, then?" she asked, indicating the map. "What has it told you, *Monsieur* Englishman? What are you looking for?"

He sighed. "I know we said we'd steer as clear as we could of the palace J remembers from his visit with Desai last year, but I think we're going to have to try there next. The trail has led us in that direction anyway. We can't be more than 20 miles from it now."

Rémy traced her eyes over the map and his open notebook, which was full of the notes Thaddeus had kept throughout their journey. The airship had been in this clearing for the past three days as her crew tried to work out where to take her next. They had followed every lead they'd been given and it had brought them here, to this lush jungle that reached up from the coast south east of them to cut a huge swathe through the centre of the massive continent of India. Now the trail had run cold.

"Have you asked J about what we can expect if we do go there?" she asked. "It would be good if we could prepare a little for what might greet us."

Thaddeus shook his head. "J says that Desai made the final journey to see the raja himself – he wouldn't let J or his friend Tommy accompany him."

Rémy frowned. "Why not?"

"J said Desai didn't think it would be safe for them."

She raised an eyebrow. "Not sure I like the sound of that."

"No, me either," agreed Thaddeus. "But what else are we to do? We've tried everywhere else."

"Perhaps we should visit the nearest town with a telegraph?" Rémy suggested. "Send one back to Desai's men in London, to ask if they can tell us anything else?"

Thaddeus shook his head. "We're a long way from anywhere big enough for that," he said, "and besides, I think they've told us everything they can. They don't know where he is any better than we do." He sighed, leaning back against the tree and shutting his double-coloured eyes. "It'd be easier if I could speak some of the languages and dialects, ask people more than just what Satu told me to write down. Perhaps we should have prepared better before we came on this trip."

Rémy rested a hand on his arm. "I do not think so," she said softly. "After all, we may already be too late. Delaying – that could not be a good thing."

It had now been some months since either Rémy or Thaddeus had seen their friend Maandhata Desai, who had been such an ally in their strange battle against Lord Abernathy and the war machines he had built beneath England's capital city. Desai had journeyed back to his homeland, leaving his network of operatives in London under Thaddeus' command and telling the then-policeman that he was returning to India to deal with something called the Sapphire Cutlass.

None of Desai's people had been able to give Thaddeus any more information about this curious name. Thaddeus, however, had a horrible suspicion that it was linked to the mad mechanical trail that had started in London with Abernathy and continued in France with the Comte de Cantal. While imprisoned in the Comte's monstrous volcanic dungeons, forced to listen to the man's ramblings about his power, the young man had seen for himself the peculiar tattoo that graced the Comte's chest – a short, curved sword with a glittering sapphire embedded in the hilt: a sapphire cutlass. How could something so strange be a coincidence? Thaddeus – and Rémy too, once he had explained it all – had been worried, not just for their friend, but also for the wider implications. If the Sapphire Cutlass – whatever it was – was behind the mania of the Comte de Cantal, where else did it have influence? The Comte's insanity had resulted in the destruction of an entire mountain that took with it a whole town, but if both he and Abernathy had had their way, things would have been much, much worse. If there was a driving force behind these desires, stoking them – what was coming next?

The problem was that Desai seemed to have disappeared completely. His men had given Thaddeus as much help as they could via telegram, whizzing typed messages back and forth across the vast distances from London to cities such as Bombay, Madras and Bangalore. They had suggested towns he might have visited, routes he might have taken, people he might have been to see, but each time the airship had arrived somewhere new, its crew full of expectation, their hopes had been dashed. No one had seen Desai or knew where he was.

Or at least, that was what they *said*.

Privately, both Rémy and Thaddeus had the sense that at least some, if not all, of the people that they had met along the way were hiding something. None of them wanted to talk about Desai or where he might be, as if they were scared of what might happen if they were overheard. As for the Sapphire Cutlass, well – mention those words and people might as well have turned to stone. Which, as far as the crew of the airship went, made the search even more important. It was unfortunate, then, that they had run out of ideas as to where to go next. India was a big, big place to search, even with the help of a device as miraculous as a ruby-powered airship.

Rémy absently opened her bag and took out her puzzle box, turning it around in her hands as she looked at the haphazard route they had followed to date. The last village they had visited, situated right on the edges of the jungle, had been so small that it had been immediately apparent that it wouldn't take them long to find out what they needed to know. The place had been made up of fewer than twenty small houses and, as far as Rémy could make out, was mostly populated by the very young and the very old. Perhaps anyone who was able to work was out in the fields, although the crops had seemed sparse and unkempt as the shadow of the airship had drifted across them.

The people had been terrified of the airship, which wasn't surprising. J had landed it a little way away and the group had walked in rather than touching down directly beside the houses. Desai was not there and, according to everyone they had shown Thaddeus' written questions to – the entire village – he never had been. Polite as they all were, it had been very clear that the people had just wanted them to go.

"So, have you had any more luck with that?"

Thaddeus' question jolted Rémy out of her thoughts and she found him nodding at the puzzle box.

"No," Rémy sighed, twisting one of its small outer panels so that a hinge folded in on itself. "Every time I think I have made progress, *voila*! Another hinge appears that I cannot open without undoing what came before." She made a sound of annoyance in her throat. "Truly, I am beginning to think that the old woman was just playing with me."

Thaddeus smiled, his fingers brushing hers as he took the puzzle from her and toyed with it. They had been trying to open it ever since they had left France, tantalised by the thought that whatever was inside might help Rémy locate her fabled lost brother.

"Don't give up," he told her. "Not that I think you ever would. Rémy Brunel always sees things through to the end, no matter how difficult the journey."

Rémy looked at him. Somewhere over the course of the past few months, things had changed between them. Perhaps it was just that she no longer had her opal to tell her his every thought, although Rémy somehow felt it was more than that. Things were easier between them. They were closer – they fit together better. They understood each other, and where they didn't, they at least tried to.

Maybe this is just what it feels like when you really love someone, she thought. *Maybe this is what happens when you find the person you should m—*

"What?" Thaddeus asked her with a laugh, as she continued to gaze at him, lost in her thoughts.

Rémy shook her head, a little shocked at where her mind had been leading her.

Thaddeus reached out and stroked his fingers along her jaw. "Come here," he murmured, pulling her gently towards him.

Her lips had almost touched his when there was a loud bang. A fraction of a second later, something thudded into the

tree behind them, just inches above Thaddeus's head, splinters
of sharp bark exploding from the impact.

Three

The Jewelled Man

Rémy and Thaddeus were on their feet in a second. Even as the sound of the explosion faded in their ears, another took its place, and this time Thaddeus felt the rush of air as a bullet whistled past his cheek. From somewhere unseen, Dita began to scream. The sound echoed around the clearing, reverberating off the yellow stone walls of the ruined temple. Primed for flight, scanning the edges of the forest, he saw movement and knew that something had found them.

"Soldiers!" Rémy gasped.

Men poured out of the jungle, lithe and quick, moving towards them like shadows – they were halfway across the clearing before Thaddeus and Rémy had even had a chance to react. Thaddeus set off for the airship at a flat run, knowing that Rémy was right beside him.

Thaddeus glanced over his shoulder. The men were still coming, rushing at them like a square-jawed tide. They were huge, with bronze skin; their chins were densely bearded, their shoulders broad. They wore blue and white: jewel-bright turquoise for the *pagris* wrapped around their heads and the loose trousers over their legs, purest white for the shirts that were fastened about their waists with wide gold cummerbunds. They moved in two waves: the first carrying huge, ornately curved swords, the second armed with rifles.

They were like no soldiers Thaddeus had ever seen, but that didn't make them any less terrifying.

From the corner of his eye, Thaddeus saw Rémy leap up one of the temple's crushed walls, scattering splinters of stone dust in her wake. Sunlight glinted on silver as a blade slashed after her, missing her by inches. Rémy jumped, twisting in the air as if on an imaginary trapeze, turning a somersault and then lashing out one leg to catch her attacker in the jaw before landing squarely back on two feet. Thaddeus didn't see what happened to the swordsman – he had his own worries as another of the soldiers lunged towards him, his vicious blade swinging directly for Thaddeus's head.

The Englishman threw himself forward, dropping to his knees and using the momentum to crash into his attacker's legs – nowhere near as elegant a move as Rémy's, but just as effective. Thaddeus was still no prize fighter, but he'd grown fitter during their journey in the airship. The craft was heavy and required muscle to keep her on course, muscle that he put to good use now. Their attackers were bigger than either Rémy

23

or Thaddeus, but Thaddeus wasn't intending to fight. All they needed to do was get to the airship.

He skidded under another blade that flew towards him, leaning backwards so that it passed over his chin in a curve that, had it been an inch lower, would have cut his throat. Thaddeus sprang back to his feet, glancing sideways to see where Rémy was. She'd vaulted the second wall, having levelled another swordsman. Thaddeus could see the huge man in the act of stumbling back to the ground even as Little Bird flew out of his clutches.

There came another scream from Dita.

"I will go for her," Rémy shouted, as she dodged another soldier.

"No – Rémy – wait!"

Thaddeus's shout came far too late to stop her – Rémy had already dropped out of sight over the far side of the temple wall. Thaddeus had no time to worry as another two soldiers came at him. Breathing hard, lungs burning with effort, he sidestepped them by feigning a lunge to the right before dodging left. By the time they had corrected their footing he was past them and almost at the airship.

"J," he bellowed, over the strange silence of the attack. "Get the airship up!"

"'Ere," said the boy, appearing on the ramp, "what's–"

"Attack," Thaddeus said, through gasping breaths. "Get her up!"

J saw the soldiers, his ruddy face paling. "Where's Dita?"

"Rémy's gone to get her. J – quickly!"

24

J, looking stunned, threw him the small axe they used to sever the airship's guide ropes. Thaddeus ran to the first one, swinging his arm and bringing the blade down across it, not even attempting to untie the knot. It cut cleanly, flicking into the air like something alive. The airship immediately began to lift. Thaddeus ran for the next tether.

"Wait," J cried. "We got to wait for the others!"

"We will," Thaddeus shouted back, already at the second rope, arm swinging back, "we'll pick them up, but we have to–"

Just like that, the soldiers were on them. Thaddeus dodged as one of them sliced at him with his sword, the blade coming so close that he heard the whistle as it only just missed him. He fought back, swinging the axe and cracking it into his attacker's jaw, but he might as well have been fighting a forest fire with a glass of water. He stumbled backwards, crashing into one of the temple's crumbling walls, the pain of connecting with hard rock jarring him badly. A second soldier came at him as the first regrouped, his face a cold mask of determination. Behind him were more men, surging closer by the second, all with their weapons drawn and ready. Thaddeus ducked another blade, swinging wildly at the airship's third guide rope. The rope came free as he parried a fresh blow and dived beneath yet another cruel blade.

The airship swung around above his head, nose still tethered to the ground but the rest of her straining towards the sky. Thaddeus had the sudden image of it leaving without them – drifting away into the sky without her crew, to sail the skies of the world alone. But that couldn't – must not – happen. If it did, it would mean the rest of them would all be captured or, worse, dead. He narrowly avoided another attack and then lunged forward, throwing all his weight at his nearest assailant. Caught off-guard for a split second, the soldier stumbled backwards, his head connecting with the brightly painted Union Jack emblazoned on the underside of the airship's hull. The man's eyes rolled back and he fell to the ground, unconscious.

Thaddeus hardly had time to take a breath before he was attacked again. This time he thought he was done for, but something dropped out of the sky, yelling like a banshee. It knocked his assailant to the ground and he scrambled away. Thaddeus's saviour was J, who had jumped from the airship's wildly tilting ramp onto the brute's back.

Thaddeus grabbed a handful of J's collar and dragged him away. "Get back on board!" he shouted. "I'm going to cut the last rope!"

"I ain't leaving Dita!"

"Neither am I! Rémy will get her!"

J squirmed away from him and then, before Thaddeus had a chance to stop him, had started running. Thaddeus, cursing, watched J dodge one of the men and realised he was out of time. They had to keep hold of the airship, or they were done for – it was their only advantage.

He'd left the guide rope closest to the ramp until last, but still – cutting it without anyone on board was risky. With no one to control it, the airship could drift away into the endless blue Indian sky, but Thaddeus had no choice. He severed the final rope and then heaved himself up onto the flapping ramp, kicking out at another soldier on his way.

The airship leapt into the air, free of the ground at last. Thaddeus dragged the ramp up and ran to the controls, bringing the craft around hard a-port to stop her nose smashing against the temple walls. For just a second, Thaddeus found himself face-to-face with a goddess as she smiled at him from the stone archway into which she'd been carved hundreds of years before. Then the airship turned, tipping away from the temple and towards the jungle.

Below him the men were watching, evidently awed by the sight of such a flying machine. Thaddeus ignored them, searching for signs of Rémy, Dita and J. With any luck he could whisk all of them from the ground – the guide ropes were still hanging below the ship, which was as close as he could get to a ladder at this moment.

Then he caught sight of Dita and J, and Thaddeus' heart sank. The two children had both been caught. They struggled in the clutches of their captors, but it was clear that neither of them would get away that easily. Of Rémy, though, there was no sign.

There was more movement at the edge of the clearing. The foliage moved, rippling as if disturbed by a breeze. Then it parted, and someone new emerged. Another man, who sat astride a grand white horse, which was dressed even more spectacularly than the soldiers. Jewels of every hue glinted in the creature's braided mane and along the leather of its harness. Its rider, though, outdid them all. He too was in silk of blue and gold, but the very fabric of his garments seemed to be spun through with diamonds so that he shone like a cut gem. His head was wrapped and adorned in a sumptuous array of jewels that glinted in the afternoon sun.

This man held his chin high, looking straight at Thaddeus through the window of the airship. He rode to meet it, urging his horse forward as if facing off with an enemy in battle, and the animal was so used to his command that he only required one hand on the reigns. With the other, he gestured to the two men holding Dita and J without even turning to look. The children were wrestled forward, still squirming, until they stood beside the horse. Then they were forced to their knees.

Thaddeus's blood ran cold as he saw the men's swords levelled at the throats of his two young friends.

"You will listen to me, commander of this ship of the air," came the man's faint voice, filtering through to Thaddeus, safe in the airship above. "You will follow me and my men, and you will surrender it to us. If you do not, the lives of your two companions here will be forfeit. Understand that I will cut their throats without hesitation should you fail to comply."

Without waiting for a reply, the man on horseback waved his arm again. Instantly, the soldiers formed up in a column of three lines. One more signed command from their leader and they all set off, the rider leading them into the jungle, dragging Dita and J along with them.

Thaddeus had no choice.

The airship followed.

Four

A Jungle Palace

The soldiers marched for hours, until the slivered moon was high in the sky and Rémy could barely see through the shadows that surrounded her. She kept her eyes on the airship, flying low above the treeline, blocking out a trail of stars as it went. She was beginning to wonder whether the jewelled man and his troops were planning to march all the way to Pondicherry when a shout echoed through the foliage – a sharp order sent back from the front.

Rémy realised with a start that they had obviously reached their destination. She'd been so focused on keeping track of the airship and not making sound over the uneven ground that she'd missed what was ahead of them. There, reaching above the dark mass of jungle, she could see walls looming into the sky, a luminous mass of white in the moonlight. They rose high above the forest – higher even, Rémy thought, than where the highest seat in the Cirque de la Lune's Big Top had been, though not as high as her trapeze had flown on those nights that she had performed in front of the crowds. The wall stretched for a long way in either direction. In the centre and on the ends of the wall were built large, square towers with domed roofs that were shining softly in the moonlight as if they were coated with silver. Beneath the domes, standing stiffly alert at their posts as they looked out over the forest, were soldiers armed with rifles.

Another shout, and the column halted so swiftly that Rémy almost walked into the back of the two men making up the rear. She darted behind the nearest tree, peering out as a loud creaking sound echoed into the night. Beneath the sentry post in the centre of the wall, illuminated in the yellow glow from two huge torches pinioned either side of them, were two massive doors. Rémy watched as they slowly opened, and even from where she hid she could see the glint of the metal spikes that studded the carved dark wood. There came another shout and the soldiers, led by the jewelled man on his magnificent horse, marched forward beneath the arch.

The airship lifted over the wall, and then dropped out of sight. The doors creaked again as they closed behind the last of the troops, shutting Rémy out – although not before she caught a glimpse of the airship, touching down amid the torrent of soldiers.

Careful to avoid drawing the gaze of the sentries, Rémy slipped closer. The jungle pressed right up against the walls, which seemed strange to her. Surely the best way of keeping such a place secure was to make sure that no one could approach without being seen, but as it was Rémy made it all the way to one cold, white wall. When she reached it, however, she realised that the walls were not as featureless as she had at first thought. They were peppered with holes and cracks of varying sizes; they pockmarked the surface of the wall with what looked like delicate lace in the moonlight, but that in daylight probably displayed themselves more like a series of ugly scars. They were the signs of fierce battle – each hole had been made by a weapon – by rifles, and in some cases, small cannon.

This place was old and crumbling. The troops that had attacked the airship's crew – whoever they were – were defending a relic that looked as if it should have been abandoned years ago. *Still*, Rémy thought, standing at the base of the wall and looking up it, *good for me…* She checked the sentries in their posts. They were still staring out over the forest, and the light cast by the torches at the gate did not reach far enough to her shadowed spot. Rémy took a breath and began to climb. Within minutes, the hand-holds provided by the wall's battle scars had helped her reach the top. Rémy crouched there, barely even out of breath, her black clothes as dark as the shadows around her, and looked down into a well of golden light.

She'd expected a fort of some kind – an ugly, bare patch of earth crammed with low barrack buildings for the soldiers. But what Rémy saw was anything but ugly, even though it was as crumbling and ancient as the walls on which she now crouched. Within stood a palace of white stone, gleaming in the moonlight like one of the gems on its owner's hand. Yes, some of the columns were crumbling with age, and there were signs of rifle strike among the ornate carvings that decked its windows and its many roofs. Its domes – far larger than the ones over the clueless sentries' heads – were dull grey instead of silver, but its beauty still took Rémy's breath away. She wondered how many rooms there were within its inner walls. From here she couldn't even count the windows, and there were at least four floors. It was magnificent, despite or perhaps even because of its age.

A sound drew her attention back to the vast courtyard in front of the palace's steps. The airship had landed in the centre, next to a carved stone fountain that must have run dry years before. Thaddeus was being dragged from the airship. He stumbled under his captors' grip, and was pushed to his knees, lined up in the dust beside Dita and J. Wordlessly, soldiers stepped towards each of them, drawing their curved swords and holding them at their necks. Anger swelled in Rémy's heart as she saw Dita flinch and tremble as the cold metal touched her skin.

The jewelled man had slipped from his saddle, handing the reins of his horse to a servant who bowed deeply before leading the creature away. The man then circled the airship thoughtfully, disappearing from Rémy's view as he walked around the front and then reappeared at the propeller end. She saw that he had something in his hand – he was throwing it from one and catching it in the other as he walked, and it glinted with the reflection of the flickering light from the torches on the walls. Rémy almost gasped as she realised what it was. Her puzzle box!

There was a brief commotion as a new man entered the scene, descending the steps of the palace at a slow, dignified pace. Dressed in pure white, this man was older, with wisps of grey-white hair escaping the *pagri* wrapped around his head. He held himself regally, and as Rémy watched she saw a ripple move through the assembled troops as he passed by – a straightening of the shoulders, a lifting of the chins. Clearly this man, too, held great power here, despite his lack of ostentatious jewellery. He stood before the airship's nose, his hands clasped behind his back. He did not seem in the least impressed, but instead regarded the craft with something like contempt.

The jewelled man completed his circuit of the ship and moved to stand with the man in white. They conferred quietly for a few moments, apparently disagreeing about something, though only mildly. The older man eventually brought his hands in front of him, spreading his palms in a gesture somewhat like a shrug.

The jewelled man nodded once, and then turned to the silent soldiers still standing to attention in the rows they had formed after entering the palace gates.

"This," he began, his deep voice echoing around the courtyard, "is a historic day, my friends. This – this!" he waved at the airship. "This magnificent ship of the air will change our fortunes and the fortunes of this great country forever. For too many years we have toiled without hope, dreaming of freeing

33

all of India from the foul grip of colonisation. Now, here, with the help of this marvellous contraption and the others like it that we shall build together – we will at last achieve our goals. Together, we will smite the British and their armies that ransack our land! We will take back our food, we will take back our cities and towns and villages! We will take back our sovereignty!"

A cheer rumbled up through the flickering torchlight, rolling over Rémy like a wave of thunder. The soldiers below all drew their curved swords, shouting and waving their weapons in the air until the glow of the glinting fire reflected in the blades was a blinding mass of light.

The man in white, Rémy noted, did not cheer. He stared straight ahead, his face impassive apart from, she thought, the slightest flicker of something that could have been fury, although it was gone before it had ever really been there at all.

The jewelled man raised his hands for silence, and it fell as quickly as it had in the jungle when the tiger had stalked the chital. Rémy dared not move a muscle, perched as she was atop the wall. If any of them were to see her, there were a thousand ways for her to die at the hands of these men.

"Go now, to your duties," the jewelled man ordered. "I must rest, for tomorrow is a new day, and it will dawn on a new era for us all."

The troops, as one, bowed low to their leader. They moved off, some taking up posts around the great courtyard, others disappearing through a large arch on the far side of the palace that Rémy couldn't see into but assumed was a barracks. Others still entered a smaller arch that framed a slope that led beneath the palace.

Rémy watched as Thaddeus, Dita and J were pulled roughly to their feet. Thaddeus tried to say something, but one of the soldiers clubbed him roughly about the face with enough force that Rémy winced, feeling a fresh surge of fury burst through her. Thaddeus, stunned, did not try to speak again, and a moment later the jewelled man waved a peremptory hand. The three prisoners were dragged in the direction of the small archway that led into the palace foundations. She watched as they disappeared through it and out of her sight.

The courtyard was almost empty. Besides the four guards that circled the airship, just the jewelled man and the man in white remained. The jewelled man looked proudly at his new acquisition before tossing Rémy's puzzle box into the air once more. He made a remark that made the man in white bow his head, as if in obeisance. Then he strode towards the palace steps, taking them two at a time and swishing through a door that opened for him as if by magic. After another moment of silent contemplation, the man in white turned and followed.

Five

Breaking In

Still crouched in the shadows atop the wall, Rémy looked down on the empty scene below her. Even with four guards, she could probably re-take the airship alone, but doing that would no doubt condemn her friends to death before she'd had a chance to ransom it for their return. She imagined them now, being shoved roughly into a dingy cell in the lowest part of the palace. No, she had to free them first. Which meant getting in unseen.

Now that most of the soldiers had left the courtyard, taking their torches with them, the light below her was far dimmer. There were still lights burning, though – two torches on each wall, like the ones beside the great wooden door. For Rémy not to attract the attention of either the guards on the wall or the four standing to attention around the airship, she needed a diversion.

Lying flat, Rémy slowly pried out a piece of the crumbling stonework. At first she didn't think it was going to budge –

the wall was sturdier than it looked – but her nimble fingers finally managed to pull free a chunk the size of her puzzle box. Puffs of chalky dust floated away into the hot night air as she lifted it carefully onto the wall before sitting up. She chose a spot in the forest – close enough to be of concern to the sentries but far enough away not to be easily inspected from their posts, drew back her arm and threw.

The piece of stone was swallowed by the night almost immediately, arcing in a smooth but invisible curve from Rémy's hand into the jungle outside the palace walls. By sheer luck she must have chosen the sleeping place of a family of monkeys, because there came a sudden and terrible cacophony of shrieks, followed by the shaking, not just of leaves, but of the entire tree.

As she'd hoped, both sentries on this side of the palace were suddenly instantly awake, fervently searching the forest for a sign of something coming towards them. They were so intent on what was happening below them that they didn't see her slip from her perch on the wall and descend into the shadows of the courtyard.

Once back on the ground, Rémy moved quickly, keeping to the edges, as far away from the sentries on duty at the airship as possible. She made for the archway she'd seen Thaddeus, Dita and J being dragged towards: the smaller one that led below the palace.

To get to it Rémy had to pass directly in front of the palace steps. She darted from one pool of shadows to another, stopping every few minutes to make sure she had

made no noise. The courtyard seemed even bigger now
that she was down on the ground – the fountain she had
dismissed as old and disused was, she realised now, almost
as big as the airship itself. The flagstones beneath her feet
were carved from large slabs of marble, white and veined
with lines of mineral that glimmered slightly even in the
darkness. The palace itself was built of the same marble,
carved and curved and in daylight, Rémy was quite sure,
very beautiful.

She reached the archway – which would be large enough to
take a cart and oxen without its driver having to leave his seat
– and slipped inside. The ground sloped down and away. Rémy
descended the path, a solid iron gate blocking her way just a
few feet inside. Beyond it, lights burned almost as brightly as if
it were day, and Rémy quickly flattened herself against the wall
as she realised there was movement there, too. Soldiers and
servants bustled about beyond the barrier, moving barrels and
sacks of food from one place to another – besides wherever her
friends were being kept, this level was obviously storage for the
rest of the palace, too. There was too much activity beyond the
gate for her to pick its lock without being seen.

Cursing silently, Rémy looked around. A flight of stone
steps curved upwards and out of sight to her left. Since she
seemed to have no other option, she dodged over and ascended
them quickly – if anyone happened to be coming the other
way, she'd definitely be caught, for the torch burning on the
wall meant here there were no shadows big enough to melt
into. Rémy sighed in relief as she made it to the next floor. The

stairway opened out into a wide corridor, off which led many small rooms and antechambers. It was cooler here, she noted – the marble of the palace walls helping to quell the incessant heat, at least a little.

Rémy headed along the corridor, hoping to find another way down into the lower levels. This floor seemed to be the servants' quarters. The rooms where doors were open showed her sparse, basic living arrangements of low beds and plain, dusty floors. Another room had rows of tables lined up almost like a schoolroom, except that each surface was piled with rich fabrics: silks and brocades, poplins and *charmeuse*. Rémy could imagine the room flooded with sunny daylight, filled with activity as the men and women who worked there sewed the jewelled man yet another extraordinarily beautiful outfit. For a split second she wondered whether any of the jewels they used to adorn his clothes would be kept in there, too, but despite the temptation to look, forced herself not to investigate. Rémy Brunel was a thief no longer, but sometimes… just sometimes…

With a silent sigh she moved onwards, past door after closed door. A sound echoed ahead of her – footsteps, coming closer. Panicked, Rémy looked around but there was nothing in the corridor to hide behind. She tried one door, turning the circular handle silently, but it appeared to be locked. Moving to another as the footfalls grew ever louder, she found that to be locked, too. She glanced over her shoulder, wondering if she could make it back to the flight of stairs, but realised that would be the height of folly – there was more light there, more chance that she'd be trapped between someone coming up and whoever this was, coming down.

Darting to the other side of the corridor, she tried another handle. This time the door gave and she slipped inside, finding herself in darkness. She leaned against the door, levelling her breathing as the person outside passed, footsteps echoing into the distance without pause. Rémy sighed in relief.

"Who's there?"

The voice behind her made her jump. Rémy's instinct was to drop to a crouch, and she did, staying near the door and hoping that the darkness was enough to conceal her. Rémy slowed her breathing – a circus trick she'd been taught long ago to help her calm herself on the wire – and prayed that whoever she'd stirred from slumber would drop off again just as quickly.

It seemed, however, that Rémy's luck was running low.

"I know you are there," said a man's voice, deep and low, melodic. "By the door. Show yourself, please."

Still Rémy said nothing. A strange sound echoed from the direction of the voice – a clank, followed by a rattle and the sound of something dragging itself through the darkness. Then the sound of a match being struck sent Rémy's heart plummeting. A pale, flickering light bloomed into the room as the owner of the voice lit a candle.

Rémy stood, swiftly, her hand already back on the door handle, ready to run. The figure on the bed was still moving, legs swinging over its low edge as the man's feet reached the stone floor.

"Wait," said the figure. "Don't go…"

Something about the voice and the figure made Rémy hesitate, just for a second. She turned to look at the man, taking in the long, unkempt hair and beard.

She gasped.

"Desai!"

Breaking Out

Desai, who was in the process of trying to stand up, looked up at her with sharply narrowed eyes that suddenly widened in recognition.

"Rémy Brunel! What in the name of Shiva are you doing here?"

Rémy was across the room in a second, standing angrily before her old friend as he got slowly to his feet.

"We came to look for you," she hissed furiously, "but we were attacked by the soldiers of this palace and the jewelled man that commands them. They have taken Thaddeus, J and Dita – they are here, somewhere below our feet even now. And now I find that you, our friend, the man we came to find, are in league with the monster that took them and stole the airship!"

Desai blinked at her with hooded lids. "Believe me, Miss Brunel, at this moment I am as much a prisoner as they." He raised his right arm, and the clanking sound Rémy had heard minutes earlier came again.

It was only then that Rémy saw the chain. It was thick and heavy, attached to a cuff that circled Desai's arm – an arm that, she noted, was far thinner than the last time she had seen him. The other end of the chain was fastened to a ring set fast into the stone floor.

Rémy glanced around in bemusement. This room was as bare as the others she had seen, with the exception that a small table stood close to the bed, on which was a pile of paper and an ink pen standing upright in its well. Desai's chain was just long enough to allow him to move between the bed and the table, but no further.

"What is happening here?" Rémy asked.

Desai gave her a faint smile. His hair had greyed even more since their last meeting. "The 'Jewelled Man', as you call him, is the raja of this palace and he wants what I have up here," he tapped his forehead with one thin finger. "Or rather, his right-hand man, Sahoj, does. They intend to keep me here until I give it to them."

Rémy fumbled beneath her shirt. She'd foregone her customary corset since reaching India – in the heat it was just unbearable – but wore her usual black shirt and the belt in which she still carried the tools of her former trade. She pulled out her pack of lock-picking tools, folded neatly in the small leather case that Gustave had given her a lifetime ago.

"Sit," she ordered, indicating the bed, and then as Desai did so, she knelt before him and took his right hand. The skin around the cuff was raw and she tried not to agitate it further as she worked on the lock.

43

"Tell me more about the jewelled man," she whispered, as she worked.

She glanced up to see Desai looking away into the shadows, a thoughtful frown on his face. Then he looked at her with a slight smile, as if to dispel what had caused the frown. "It will take a long time to explain. Perhaps it should wait…"

"Until we have escaped this place? *Mais oui*. Later, then… *voila!*" she whispered triumphantly, as the cuff slid undone under her fingers. "You are free, my friend. Now, let us see about the others, yes?"

Desai stood, rubbing his wrist. "There is another way down to the cells. We will need to go through the kitchens – they have their own access, so that the cooks may easily deliver food to the guards for the prisoners."

Rémy frowned. "There are still many people up and about. You are sure we will not be seen?"

"Oh, I am absolutely sure we will be seen," Desai said grimly, "but I have known this place for a long, long time. There are people who will be willing to help. But Rémy – getting to our friends, getting them out of their prisons, even, that is one thing. But getting out of the palace? That is quite another. As soon as the alarm has sounded, we will be trapped. And you my be able to scale the walls, my dear, but I guarantee you that such a feat is beyond me."

"Ah – but that is why we will re-take the airship," said Rémy. "In the air we will outrun them without any trouble."

Desai frowned again. "Airship. You used that word before. I have not heard of such a thing. What is it?"

44

Rémy grinned. "You will see. Another of the Professor's inventions, Desai, and one that meant we could follow you here, to this place. Now, are you ready? We are wasting time with all this chat!"

Desai turned and grabbed a sheet from the bed, holding it out to her. "Wrap this around yourself. Cover your head, also. My face is known here and prisoner or not I am not much to remark upon. But yours is not and will not go unnoticed." He nodded as Rémy did as she was told. "Good. Now, follow closely, and be alert."

Once out of the room, Desai walked quickly to the end of the corridor, and Rémy stayed as close to him as she could. They saw no one as they turned the corner and entered another corridor, this time where the doors were more widely spaced. Ahead, noise floated to them along with a glow that partially dispelled the night-time gloom. There came the rattle of what sounded like pots and pans, and the occasional shout of an order or the hiss of steam rising.

Rémy pulled her makeshift cloak more closely around her face as they entered the kitchens. There were people everywhere, working diligently as they chopped vegetables or stirred huge pots of richly scented sauces. Rémy's heart pounded, expecting one of the cooks to see them at any moment and raise the alarm. But when one man did look up and see Desai, his eyes merely widened for a moment before he bowed his head in what seemed to be a mark of respect.

Desai took no notice, hurrying through the kitchen, passing bench after bench of foods being prepared and spices being crushed. Despite their situation, Rémy's stomach rumbled – the brace of rabbits she'd caught earlier in the day had remained uncooked, and she was very hungry. She thought about slipping out a hand to snag a carrot as she passed, but thought better of it.

Her companion came to an abrupt stop as another cook stepped out in front of him. At first Rémy thought that Desai was about to be challenged, but instead the man offered the same nod of respect as the first had given. This time Desai responded in kind – they obviously knew each other. Desai leaned forward and spoke rapidly into the man's ear. The cook's gaze flicked to Rémy's for a second and then back to Desai before nodding quickly and turning. Desai looked over his shoulder at Rémy. Evidently they were to follow.

The cook led them to another circular flight of stairs, also lit with a burning torch. They descended quickly, and found themselves on the lower level, though this area was far darker than the one Rémy had failed to gain access to earlier. Passageways led in two directions, left and right, and both were lined with the sturdy doors of many cells. Silently, the cook pointed left. Desai clasped his arm firmly in thanks, and without another word the man had gone, vanishing back up the steps to resume his work.

Desai and Rémy moved quickly along the passageway. Rémy glanced in through each of the barred doors as they went, searching for Thaddeus, Dita and J. Some of the cells were empty, but others held pitiful-looking prisoners, thin men with protruding ribs and long, straggly hair who all seemed as if they had been there for a long, long time. Desai glanced left and right, seeing but passing on just as quickly.

They found their friends in neighbouring cells: the soldiers had separated Dita from Thaddeus and J and imprisoned her beside them. J and Dita were kneeling on the filthy floor, grasping each other's hands through the bars. Rémy, still concealed by her 'cloak', felt her heart leap in relief at the sight of Thaddeus with his back against the cell wall, his forearms resting on his drawn-up knees.

Thaddeus barely showed any interest as Desai and Rémy appeared in front of him. He merely glanced up at Desai before dropping his gaze briefly to Rémy and then looking away again. A second later, though, his double-coloured eyes flashed wide with recognition and he scrambled to his feet.

"My god! *Desai!* What are you–? How–?"

"No time, my friend, no time. Rémy, quickly, can you free this lock?"

"Rémy!" Thaddeus exclaimed again, as she threw off the sheet and stepped forward, once more reaching for her lock picks.

Rémy smiled at him through the bars. "You didn't think I'd leave you behind, did you? Where you go, I go, don't you know that by now?"

Thaddeus smiled back, fixing her with a look of such intensity that she found her heart leaping again, though for an entirely different reason.

"Can't you get Dita out first?" J pleaded, as Rémy turned her attention to the lock. "I 'ate 'er bein' in there alone."

"Better for us to get out first, J," Thaddeus said softly, moving to the bars and looking down the passageway. "That way if there's trouble, you and I can deal with it while Rémy frees Dita."

Rémy caught J's nod of agreement in the corner of her eye as she worked. These locks were more difficult than the one on Desai's cuff. She cursed under her breath as the barrel refused to turn.

"How long?" Desai asked, his quiet voice strained as he, too, kept an eye out.

"I will be as quick as I can," Rémy murmured calmly, keeping her concentration entirely on the lock.

"I'll be back," said Desai. "Be quick, Rémy. You must be the swiftest you have ever been, my dear."

He vanished up the passageway. Rémy half expected to hear the sounds of fighting echo out of the darkness that flowed into his wake, but there was nothing but silence. Still she worked, rotating the barrel again and again, until, at last–

Click.

She heaved a sigh of relief. The door opened, creaking on its rusted hinges so loudly in the quiet that she winced. Thaddeus grabbed the bars to hold it still, waving J out ahead of him as Rémy swiftly moved to the lock on Dita's cell. The little girl wrapped her hands around the bars, eyes wide as she watched Rémy's nimble fingers get to work.

Desai returned a few minutes later. "If we are quick now, we will have a clear route to the outer courtyard," he told them. "But we must be fast."

"I have to find the jewelled man – the raja you spoke of," Rémy said, her eyes fixed on the second lock.

"What do you mean?" Desai asked, appalled. "We have to leave, Rémy. We are vastly outnumbered, and–"

"He has my puzzle box," she told him, still concentrating, twisting the barrel, testing the lock. "I can't leave without it. I must get it back."

Desai made a sound in his throat, "Whatever he has taken from you, Rémy, I guarantee it is not worth the risk."

"It is to me," Rémy said. "I must have it back, Desai, I *must*. You take the others and go – get the airship. You said yourself, I can scale these walls. I'll follow once I have it."

"You must be joking," said Thaddeus. "Rémy, that's crazy. They weren't looking for you before – but once the alarm is raised…"

"I will not leave without it, Thaddeus," said Rémy, "I will not. Understand?"

"Then I will stay, too."

"No," she told him, "I will be faster – safer – on my own."

"You will be the death of me, Rémy Brunel," Desai muttered.

"Is that so?" she answered tartly. "And here I was thinking I had freed you once already tonight."

Desai sighed. "All right. Give me a moment. But we are running out of time!"

He vanished again, moving up the passageway and back towards the stairs that led to the kitchens.

"*D'acccord, d'accord,*" muttered Rémy, still working on the lock. It clicked suddenly, the door springing open more quietly than the first one. Dita slipped out, and J instantly clasped her in a brief, powerful hug.

Thaddeus was at Rémy's side as she straightened. He took one of her hands and squeezed it. "Please don't do this," he said softly. "Let it go, Rémy – let the puzzle box go. Only this morning you were saying you thought it was all a trick."

Rémy gave him a faint smile, and squeezed his hand back again. "But what if is *not* a trick? What if it really can tell me where my brother is?"

Thaddeus opened his mouth to reply but by then Desai was coming back along the passageway. He wasn't alone – with him was the cook Rémy had encountered earlier. He was carrying a silver tray bearing small bowls of food that smelled delicious enough to have Rémy's stomach rumbling, despite their plight.

"Go with Arund," Desai told her, picking up the sheet and thrusting it towards her, "he will help you. Now, the rest of us must go, or we will all be caught again."

Rémy squeezed Thaddeus' hand once more, and then let go. Seconds later, she was following the man she now knew as Arund. Rémy thought he was taking her back to the kitchen stairs, but instead they hurried past them, down another darkened passageway to a different set of steps entirely. Arund didn't pause as he led her up them. These went higher than the first two flights she had encountered, and when they emerged, it was on a very different type of floor. Where the servant's level had been dusty stone, this was a sparkling-clean mosaic of black and white marble tiles, spread with intricately woven carpets. The walls were hung with colourful tapestries and, unlike the empty corridors directly below, ornate furniture stood here and there against the walls: wooden cabinets carved with intricate scenes of the jungle, chairs draped with more of the rich fabrics Rémy had seen in the tailors' room on the floor below.

Arund moved quickly and silently with Rémy close in his wake, her cloak wafting in the breeze they created through the otherwise still and silent halls.

Then, suddenly he stopped and turned, picking up the silver jug from his platter and holding it out to her. Rémy hesitated for a second, confused, and then took it, careful not to spill any of the water contained within while still holding her cloak closed. They moved off again, turning a corner, and as she glanced up, Rémy saw a large door at the far end of the corridor, its hammered gold gleaming in the fiery lamplight, flanked by two guards.

At first Rémy thought the platter and jug were for the inhabitant of the room behind the door, but instead Arund greeted the two soldiers and held up the silver tray. It only took a brief glance for her to see the grins on the men's faces. Arund drew them away from the door until he could place the platter on an ornate table a few feet away. He beckoned to Rémy, taking the water jug from her when she moved closer and then waving her back.

Stepping away, Rémy found the guard's shoulders turned away from her, intent on their welcome mid-shift snack instead of on their posts. She knew it was the only opportunity she was going to get. Arund ignored her, laughing and joking in whispers with the guards as she moved silently until her back was against the door.

And then, in another moment, she was through it.

The room inside was dark, no light visible apart from the pale wash of moonlight through the large window at the far end of the room. Even so, Rémy could make out the shape of a huge bed at the centre of the space, its canopy hung with heavy, opulent cloth. Rémy crept closer, her eyes adjusting to the renewed dark. The room was airy, far bigger even than the kitchen she had seen downstairs. Compared to the servants quarters, this was a different world, full of beautiful wonders, the colours of which she could only imagine in the grey-toned hue of night.

Rémy crept towards the bed and the tangled mass of sheets that lay at its centre. As she moved closer, she saw that it was indeed the jewelled man – seeming, as such men so often did, far smaller and less significant in sleep than in life. But he wasn't what she was interested in. All Rémy wanted was her puzzle box.

Beside the bed stood a table, cluttered with trinkets that gleamed even in the faint light. And there, discarded like a toy, was her puzzle box. She picked it up, careful not to dislodge any of the other items on the tabletop, moving slowly and silently as her fingers gripped its whorled surface.

A sound echoed through the window – it was just one shout at first, but then it was a violent tide of noise: yells, screams, the echo of rifleshot cracking against stone, the sound of booted running feet pounding against the dirt.

The jewelled man's eyes flashed open, and they looked straight at Rémy.

Seven

Escape by Air

Thaddeus couldn't fathom how, but the gate they had been led through when they had entered the cells was open. Not only that, the passageway that led to it from the palace's lowest level was empty. Thaddeus looked around, wondering if he was mistaken and they were actually leaving by a different route, but Desai clamped a hand to his shoulder, urging him onward.

"Hurry, we have lost much time already," his friend muttered.

"But how–?" Thaddeus began, only to be cut off by a shake of Desai's grizzled head.

"I will explain later. For now, we must take full advantage of the lull. It will be only minutes before our time is up."

"There's four guards on the airship," J pointed out, as they approached the gate, "What do we do about 'em? We ain't armed."

"All we have is the element of surprise," said Desai, adding, "four of us, four of them. We take one each and do our best – this is our only hope."

"'Ang about," J protested. "You can't make Dita fight! She's half the size of any of 'em!"

Dita slapped J's arm, hard enough for the sound to ricochet off the stone walls around them. "Speak for yourself, dirty boy," she said in a loud whisper. "I will take mine down quicker than you will yours!"

"Pfft!" J spat back. "I'd like to see you–"

Thaddeus, already through the gate, turned on the two bickering youngsters. "Now is not the time!"

"Thaddeus is right," said Desai. "Do what you can, all of you – and do it… now!"

They burst from the archway, crossing the courtyard at a flat run. The moonlight bounced off the white flagstones beneath their feet, sending shimmering bursts of shadow undulating across the marble as their running bodies blocked its shine.

Desai was ahead, moving far faster than Thaddeus would have thought possible. They were lucky that the guards were positioned in such a way that only two were facing their position. Desai was on the first before he could even level his rifle and Thaddeus was close behind with the second. Their cries echoed across the courtyard, bringing the other two swinging around the airship, lifting their loaded guns as the sentries on the four corners of the palace walls turned to see what the commotion was about.

Thaddeus wasn't much of a fighter – he'd always avoided the brawls his fellow street children had revelled in when growing up – but there had been plenty of times he'd needed to be handy in a scuffle as a copper on the streets of London. The guard moved to discharge his rifle, but the weapon was too cumbersome to be useful in a close-quarters fight. Thaddeus swung his left arm in an arc that knocked the weapon far enough away that the shot, when let loose, flew wide, striking one of the palace walls in a shower of glinting marble dust.

Before the soldier could regain his balance, Thaddeus had punched him hard in the lower gut, finishing with a hard jab of his locked elbow to the man's chin. He went down and Thaddeus grabbed the gun as another shot echoed out of the dark. The sentries on the wall had seen what was happening and were responding accordingly, shooting down at them from above. Thaddeus swung around, trying to reload the rifle. He saw that Desai had downed his guard, too.

Together they ducked around the airship as more rifle bullets tore up the stone around their feet. Dita and J were struggling with their guards – Thaddeus felled J's with a blow to his solar plexus as the boy struggled to swing the rifle away from the airship. Dita writhed in the grip of the last man as he lifted her clear off the ground, her legs kicking out but too short to do enough damage. J dragged the gun around and slammed its butt into the final guard's knee. The man yelled in pain and dropped Dita. J lost no time in whacking him over the head and he slumped to the ground, out cold.

"Get her up, J!" Thaddeus rasped, struggling for breath.

J ran for the airship's ramp, pulling it down and scrambling inside just as more noise began to echo across the open courtyard. Desai fired another rifle bullet in the direction of one of the sentry posts and began to reload as Thaddeus turned to see more soldiers pouring out of the barracks towards them.

He hefted his rifle up and fired above their heads. The soldiers ducked for a second and then kept coming, wielding swords rather than guns. Thaddeus felt a movement and looked down to see Dita beside him holding another rifle, a look of grim determination on her face as she sent a bullet into the surge of men coming at them.

"Desai, there are too many!" Thaddeus yelled. "Dita, get inside..."

A rifle bullet whistled past his head from the wall again, narrowly missing Thaddeus and smacking into the wooden body of the airship. Thaddeus glanced at the damage – minimal, thank god – and then heard a hissing sound above him. He looked up to see the balloon filling, replacing the gas he'd released to land a few hours earlier. His heart pounded in relief as the craft, buoyancy restored, began to lift off.

Thaddeus, Desai and Dita leapt for the ramp, rushing up it and into the ship as she lifted away from the cold white marble. Within seconds they were rising, out of reach of the soldiers on the ground, although rifle bullets still thudded against the airship's wooden hull.

"One of those bullets hits the balloon and we're all done for!" J yelled, sitting at the airship's controls as he brought her about. "She'll go up like a firecracker!"

As if someone outside had heard him, a rough yell echoed from the palace. Thaddeus, in the process of pulling the ramp up, paused and, through the chink still left open, saw the jewelled man leaning out of a high window just above them, screaming at his men below.

"Do not harm the ship of the sky," he was shouting. "Death to any of you who damage her beyond repair!"

Thaddeus' blood ran cold, not at the man's commanding voice, but at the sight of who else stood at the window with him. It was Rémy, her throat caught in his crushing grip. She was struggling, gasping for breath.

"J," he shouted to the front of the cabin, "hold the ship still!"

"What?" J shouted back. "Are you mad?"

Thaddeus dropped the ramp. It fell back on its hinges, jerking the airship sharply to one side. The airship was still rising, the end of the open ramp just feet from the palace walls, almost close enough for anyone to reach out and grab them, but not quite. Thaddeus could see soldiers crowding against the lower windows, aiming to do just that – leaning out as far as they could but still unable to touch their fingertips to the escaping craft.

They were almost level with the jewelled man's window, his long fingers still digging into the moon-pale skin of Rémy's neck. Her struggles were becoming weaker, her knees buckling.

"Put her down," ordered the man, his eyes glinting cruelly in the moonlight. "Put the ship of the air back down or I will squeeze every last breath out of this whelp before you can turn away."

At that, Rémy forced herself around to face Thaddeus, her eyes defiant though she could clearly hardly breathe. She moved one arm and something sailed towards Thaddeus, dropping with a thump onto the airship's wooden floor.

Her puzzle box.

Thaddeus levelled the rifle in his hands at the jewelled man's head. "Let her go," he said, more calmly than he felt, "or I will take your head off, here and now."

The man grinned, showing his teeth in a show of hateful, swaggering arrogance. "You would not dare. You might hit her. Desperation, my friend. It is a sign that you have already lost."

Thaddeus moved the rifle just a fraction to the right and fired. There was an almighty sound as the bullet ripped into the stone window frame beside the jewelled man's head, shattering a hole in the white marble and filling the air with shards as sharp as razors. The jewelled man screamed and raised his arms to shield his face, letting Rémy go in the process. She sagged against the window, gasping for breath.

"Jump," Thaddeus shouted at her, the airship still rising. "Rémy, for pity's sake, jump!"

Rémy, still gasping, threw her legs over the window frame and leapt wildly at the ramp, which was now almost above her head. Her fingers slipped, grasping at the wood, searching for but not finding purchase. Thaddeus dropped the rifle and lunged for her, throwing himself down stomach-first on the ramp and grabbing at her wrists. The airship rose into the air, over the roof of the palace and away. As Thaddeus dragged Rémy to safety, the last thing they heard was the jewelled man.

"Follow them!" he screamed, leaning out of his window, his face bleeding where the splinters of his fine marble palace had struck him with a thousand tiny pinpricks. "Don't let them get away! Follow them! On pain of your deaths, *follow them!*"

"Are you all right?" Thaddeus sat on the floor beside Rémy, stroking her hair out of her face. "Rémy?"

She looked up at him, nodding faintly, still trying to catch her breath. There were red marks on her throat where the jewelled man's fingers had tried to choke her life from her body. "*D'accord*," she whispered hoarsely, "*d'accord*."

He pulled her towards him, wrapping his arms around her and holding her against his chest. "You have got to stop trying to get yourself killed," he told her, and had the vague idea that it wasn't the first time he'd told her such a thing.

He heard her laugh, her breath on his skin warm through his shirt. "You worry too much. Anyway, you say that as if it is always my fault."

He sighed and pulled back. "Well, that time was, wasn't it?"

Rémy shrugged and looked around for the puzzle box, still lying on the floor of the airship. "I had to get it back, Thaddeus. I had to."

She got to her feet and he followed. The airship bumped a little in a sudden breeze, and Thaddeus saw Desai grip the back of J's chair as he stared at the controls in wonder.

"This is – this is remarkable," Desai was muttering. "I have never experienced anything like it."

"She's a beauty, ain't she?" J said proudly, rubbing the airship's control panel with affection.

"It is a wonder," agreed Desai, and then looked a little wobbly as another puff of wind bumped against the airship. "Oh dear. I think perhaps this mode of travel takes some getting used to..."

"Don't worry," Dita assured him airily, "you will soon get your air legs, Mister."

Desai looked at her curiously and then held out one hand. "I do not believe we have met, Miss..."

"Dita," Dita told him, shaking his hand. "I am pleased to know you, sir."

Desai smiled. "And I you, Dita. Rarely have I seen someone so small acquit herself with such aplomb," he told her, and the little girl glowed in the light of such praise.

"Chit chat is all well and good," muttered J, "but would someone care to tell me where we're headed, like? If those fellers are comin' after us, it'd be nice to know, because I for one could do with somefing to eat and some shut-eye."

Thaddeus moved to look out over the darkened landscape. They were flying over dense jungle, the moonlight strong but not enough to show them any safe landing spots. "Our map is still back in that clearing where they attacked us," he said, "and I don't know this area at all. Desai, can you help?"

His friend frowned. "Well, let me see. What direction did we take out of the palace, J?"

J leaned forward and tapped the compass on the control panel. "I headed due north."

"North," Desai repeated thoughtfully. "In that case, yes – I have a very good place for us to head for. Turn her west, J, and follow that heading until you see a river. Once we see that below us, we follow it to its source. It shouldn't be far to fly in this magnificent machine."

"You think that'll be far enough to stop them finding us?" Thaddeus asked.

Desai smiled a little mysteriously. "They may find us, my dear Thaddeus. But I guarantee they will not be able to reach us."

The Past Resurfaces

Hours later, the airship flew towards a huge rock plateau. It rose out of the jungle, a monolith of rock that seemed to have been formed with one strike of an invisible hand. The dawn swarmed around it as the sun rose, vivid streaks of jagged pink and yellow reaching towards them from the horizon. The jungle clustered dense and dark around its base, but on top of the flat rock there was only scrub.

"There," said Desai, pointing. "That should do, don't you think?"

Thaddeus had taken over the controls from J some time earlier, and now he gently brought the airship into land. It bumped slightly on the uneven ground before coming to a rest, sitting on top of the world.

"Best let the balloon down for a bit," suggested J, leaning over Thaddeus' shoulder. "It's probably a bit windy out there, innit? Don't want 'er takin' off without our say-so, like."

"I don't suppose we are going to find any rabbits up here," Rémy said ruefully, absently rubbing her sore neck as she looked out at the sparse foliage that spread over the plateau. There was barely anything higher than a dandelion, and the grass was scrubby. "I am having trouble remembering the last thing we ate…"

"Don't worry," Dita told her, "I checked – we still have some rice left, and plenty of water. There's enough for all of us to have some breakfast, anyway. I will set the fire now, yes?"

"Rice for breakfast," J muttered. "It ain't right, I tell yer."

"All right then," shot back Dita, defiant hands on her hips in a pose they had all become used to over the months. "I suppose that means I can have your share?"

"'Ere, that's not what I said! Did you hear me say that? I didn't say that!" J called after her, as the girl helped Desai to drop the ramp and disappeared outside, ignoring him.

Rémy left Thaddeus and J to secure the airship and followed the others down the ramp. Outside, there was indeed a brisk wind whipping across the flat rock – to be expected of somewhere so high. Rémy walked to the edge of the plateau, looking out over the vast morass of jungle beneath them. The river they had followed glinted in the rising sun, the water tripping and jumping in flurries of sapphire blue and marble white as it rushed along its haphazard course. She rubbed her neck again – it was almost as if the ghost of the jewelled man's grip was still clamped around her throat. Rémy had underestimated him – she'd dismissed him as a dandy fop who was all glitter and no substance, easy for her to outwit or outrun.

But he had hidden speed and true brute strength beneath those elegant clothes. It had shaken her. She'd felt helpless, and she didn't like it. Little Bird was not used to feeling helpless.

"Penny for them?" Thaddeus's voice floated over her shoulder, and she turned to find him standing behind her. He held a shawl in both hands, reaching out to drape it around her shoulders.

"Oh, nothing," she said, pulling the woollen garment close around her. After the relentless heat it was strange to feel a chill. "Thank you."

Thaddeus rubbed a hand lightly across her back with a smile. He squinted slightly as he looked out into the bright beginning of the day. "What an amazing place. Desai's right: even if they manage to follow us, they'll never make it up here."

"It is a good place to regroup, for sure," agreed Rémy.

"Are you all right?" Thaddeus pulled her closer, running the fingers of one hand along her jaw as he cupped her face with the other and gently tipped her head back to better see the marks on her neck. "For a second there I really thought he might..."

Rémy reached up and grasped both his wrists. "Yes. But he did not. And you got me out of there, Thaddeus Rec. Something else for which I should thank you, yes?"

Thaddeus tugged Rémy against him and wrapped his arms around her, her head against his chest. They were silent for a moment, looking out at the landscape that was unfurling before them.

"What if," Rémy asked slowly, "they have something that can help them get up here?"

"What do you mean?"

She pulled back and looked at him. "The jewelled man. He must have the Sapphire Cutlass, must he not? It is too much of a coincidence, everything that has happened. We know that the Sapphire Cutlass, whatever it is, was somehow behind all those devices that the Comte de Cantal had in his mountain. So what if he has something similar here? What if they are on their way here, right now, with some insane machine that can climb mountains like a goat or – or fly, like the airship?"

Thaddeus frowned thoughtfully, the last shadows of dawn dancing across his face. "That's a good point. Although I don't think he can possibly have anything that flies or why would he want our airship? And that place seemed so dilapidated, when you got really close to it… It didn't seem as if he had much to show, let alone much to hide, did it?"

"True," Rémy agreed. She stood on tiptoe to look over Thaddeus's shoulder to where Desai was helping Dita cook the rice. "I think there's only one person here who can tell us what we want to know."

Thaddeus kept one arm around her as he turned to look in the same direction. "I think you're probably right."

Desai got to his feet as they approached, a faint smile on his face. "My friends," he said, his melodic voice dancing in the wind. "I owe you a great debt of gratitude for freeing me as you did – for being here at all, in fact. I still cannot quite believe you came here from England to find me, as Rémy said."

"Actually we came from France," Rémy told him and then, when a look of puzzlement passed Desai's face, added, "but that is a long story and I think we would all prefer to hear yours, first."

Desai smiled. "Yes, indeed. Let us sit here as a new day begins, and I will tell you everything. It, too, is a long story – longer than any of you will realise. Please sit."

Rémy took the shawl from around her shoulders and spread it on the ground so that she and Thaddeus could share it. J appeared from the airship, carrying bowls for the rice that was now bubbling steadily in a pot over the flames.

"Ooh," said J, "story time, is it? 'Ang on a tick, I want to hear this, too." The boy set down the bowls and sat beside Dita.

Desai stared at the flames, flickering in the pale light of the rising dawn. "Well, now. Do you remember, my friends, how we first met?"

"Come off it," said J, making a sound in his throat. "We ain't likely to forget somefin like that now, are we?" the boy shuddered. "Although I s'pose the Little Miss here wasn't there. We was all down in Lord Abernathy's tunnels, see," he told Dita. "Horrible, terrible place, that was. Right under London. 'E was using slaves to build an army to attack the city with. 'E 'ad contraptions down there you wouldn't believe, like."

Dita's eyes grew large and round as she listened mutely.

Desai smiled. "Indeed. But my question was really meant for Miss Brunel," he said softly, looking at her with eyes that were at once kind and full of more knowledge than she could possibly imagine. "Do you remember what I told you then, about the circumstances of your birth, and the curse that your parents passed on to you?"

Rémy nodded, feeling the familiar tingle that always passed up her spine when she thought about everything that

Desai had explained to her about her parents. "Of course," she said. "They stole a diamond, from a very powerful raja. He had his court magicians place the curse on them, and they passed it on to me when I was born. But what does that have to do with... Unless... Unless..." she trailed off, suddenly stunned as the implication of what Desai seemed to be suggesting sank in.

"Yes," the older man said, softly. "Did I not say then that it was strange, how the universe conspires to throw us all together, again and again? The man you refer to as the jewelled man is called Ikshuvaku. He was the owner of the diamond your parents stole, Rémy Brunel. The palace from which we have just escaped is where they performed for him, seventeen years ago."

Rémy stood, agitated. "But how can that be so? You said then that he was a rich and powerful leader," she protested. "This man does not seem that way, at all. He has jewels, yes – but the palace is crumbling around him, and most of his men are armed only with swords. They do not even have enough rifles to go around all their troops."

Desai was nodding before she had even finished speaking. "It is true. He is not the raja he once was, though he would still dearly love to think of himself as such – which is, of course, what makes him so very dangerous."

"Seventeen years ago: 1857," Thaddeus said thoughtfully. "Rémy had her seventeenth birthday as we journeyed here. I remember that you said she was an Indian baby – conceived here, if not born here. I didn't believe that you could know that just by looking at her, but..."

The older man smiled. "Ah, yes. So many significant things occurred in that year – for all of us."

"The Indian Rebellion," Thaddeus added. "That was 1857 as well, wasn't it? Is that why the palace looks as if it was in a great battle? Was this raja – this Ikshuvaku – part of the uprising?"

Desai looked at Thaddeus with amusement. "Again, you surprise me, Thaddeus Rec. I had forgotten what an excellently sharp mind you have behind those curiously coloured eyes. The Indian Rebellion took place much further north – but it sent ripples through the whole continent. It gave men like Ikshuvaku a reason to hope that the grip of the East India Company – and therefore the British Empire itself – could be shaken, and it gave the East India Company a reason to clamp down on anyone they considered troublesome, before they could indeed become so."

"You were here, weren't you?" Rémy said, sitting down again and feeling Thaddeus' hand stroke across her back. "So was Abernathy. You told us that you tried to be a go-between for the British and the raja, to keep the peace. That's why you knew the place and the people so well. Isn't it?"

"That is true indeed, Rémy Brunel. I made several trips to the raja's palace on behalf of the British government." Desai shifted a little uncomfortably, staring into the fire. "What I did not tell you was that during one of those visits, it also became my home."

"What do you mean?" Rémy asked.

"Sahoj sensed my powers – the ones I had kept hidden from the colonials. He knew my abilities could assist Ikshuvaku's cause. So they flattered me and over time I... allowed myself to be flattered. I chose to switch my allegiance. I stayed, and became one of the court's mystics, in Sahoj's circle. For a time it was wonderfully freeing to exercise skills that few others possess. For a time I was treated like royalty myself and, I am ashamed to admit, I revelled in it. But by the time the British attacked, I had been banished from the palace walls."

"Why?" J asked, listening closely even as he held out their bowls one by one for Dita to ladle rice into. "What did you do?"

"It was what I didn't do, young man, as much as what I did." Desai sighed, as if raking over the memories of those distant years was painful. "I told you the court mystics were ordered to put a curse on your parents, Rémy. I was one of them – and I refused. I did not think your parents or their unborn children deserved such a fate. Gustave was a different matter, and had that been the only order I would not have hesitated as I did.

"But in any case it made no difference. I was not the only mystic with such power, and no one else objected. The curse was set without me by Sahoj, who had always been more reckless with his powers than I, and less compassionate in the use of them. My disobedience was the start of my downfall.

"When Ikshuvaku began to make plans to rise up against the British, I knew I could not stand by or worse, help. I could see that it would be a disaster – Ikshuvaku always did overestimate his strength. An uprising would be crushed, and brutally, it was clear. The northern rebellions had had the advantage of surprise, but the Company was prepared now, and on the look out. He himself might survive, but the people – the poor, the desperate – that he planned to press into his army would not. I tried to convince him not to act, but by then I was an object of mistrust. They labelled me a traitor, and threw me out. By that time, relations between the raja and the British were completely sour anyway, thanks in part to Abernathy. The diamond he recovered from your parents was not the only one he stole. He took many of the raja's lesser jewels. Not that it did him any good – when the East India Company found out, they tried him as a looter because he had not turned his spoils over to the crown. He was thrown into jail."

"An' that's where 'e met the Professor!" J realised.

"Yes, J, that is where he met our hapless friend the Professor. And so our paths were set, all those years ago. The rest you know."

"Not everything," Thaddeus said. "How did you end up back there, and as a prisoner?"

Desai sighed. "A year ago, when I returned with the diamond in order to lift Rémy's curse once and for all, it was the first time I had approached Ikshuvaku since being banished. I was unsure of what reception I would receive, though I was sure he would welcome the return of the jewel, if nothing else. I knew from the eyes and ears I still had here that he had fallen on hard times – the uprising had indeed been stamped out with a harsh foot." He paused, spooning up a mouthful of rice and chewing silently, seeming to be miles away, his face lined with sadness.

After a moment he went on, "I found the place changed, but still recognisable. The intervening years had been difficult, but Ikshuvaku's spirit had not been extinguished. Once the seeds of rebellion had been drowned, the British had left him alone:

they rightly thought he was no longer a threat. He was older and – I thought, anyway – wiser… I left to return to London with my spirits buoyed. My only concern was the influence that Sahoj still seemed to hold over both Ikshuvaku and his court at large. I asked my eyes and ears at the palace to keep me apprised of proceedings. For a while all was well. Then I got word that Sahoj had persuaded Ikshuvaku to do something very stupid. So I came back once again, and tried to talk Ikshuvaku out of this insanity. And I have been a prisoner ever since."

"And what was that?" Thaddeus asked. "What was it that Sahoj had persuaded Ikshuvaku to do that was so stupid?"

Desai put down his bowl and rubbed one hand across his forehead. "Sahoj had decided," he said quietly, "to wake the Sapphire Cutlass."

"But what is that?" Rémy asked. "What *is* the Sapphire Cutlass?"

Desai turned, his eyes glittering with a dark light. "It is not a *what*, Rémy Brunel. It is a *she*."

Nine

A Sorry Tale

"Well, who is she?" Thaddeus asked. "How is it that you are so afraid of her? Is she a queen of some sort? With an army?"

"No, she is not a queen," said Desai quietly. "She is not even a servant. I have never seen her. Indeed, I do not believe she really exists."

Thaddeus frowned. "I think you're going to have to explain a little more," he told Desai, "because I'm sorry, but I for one just do not understand."

The older man smiled somewhat sadly. The dawn light was becoming almost blinding. The sun had risen over the horizon and was casting glaring rays across the landscape, silhouetting Desai where he sat. He looked into a glare for a moment, and then nodded.

"To truly explain," he began, "I must go back a long way. Back beyond the time, even, of the first men, back to when the Earth first came into being. There are many gods, great and small, some good and some not so good, and when they saw the beauty and bounty of India, they all wanted it for themselves. The gods dislike to war among themselves – why else would they make the Earth, if not to people it with beings that could fight amongst themselves in their place? And so the great gods divided it into pieces, amicably. And these pieces they gave to their foot soldiers: stewards they trusted to ensure that the affairs of Earth were kept in order. Spirits, some might call them. Angels, others."

"'Ang about a bit," J interjected, a look of puzzlement on his face. "Is this stuff all real now, Mr Desai? 'Cos I 'ave to tell you, I ain't never believed in angels, no matter what the Sally Ann tried to tell me."

Desai smiled at the boy. "That, my dear J, is something you will have to decide for yourself. I am merely telling the story the way I know how to tell it. How you decide to hear it is your own affair. Did you not learn of many things that caused you to wonder during our last visit?"

"Tha's true," admitted J. "Whenever I wasn't roastin' from the 'eat I was lookin' at somefing extraordinary, an' that's no mistake."

"Well then," said his mentor, "let us continue, and see what you make of this particular wonder. So the land was divided up into pieces, and populated accordingly. The land was bountiful and beautiful, and the foot soldiers of the gods found ways to provide amply for the people who found it their home – fish to the people near the seas and rivers, meat to those further inland, rice to the plains and hills in between. They created so much variety that the gods became jealous of their skill, and commanded them to cease. Whatever was in existence on that day would be the extent of creation. There must be no more. The gods decreed it. This caused no trouble for most of them – there had been such a flurry of invention that most sections of the land teemed with creatures of great beauty, and each place had been given something unique with which to trade for those things that they did not have.

"But for one of them, it was not enough. He had been given this land, here – this strip that stretches inland from the ocean, and he cared about the people who dwelt within the borders he had been commanded to protect. He had spent so much time perfecting the land that he had failed to provide anything unique with which his people could trade. They had some fish from the waters, and they had some game from the creatures that wandered across their land. But he wanted them to have something that was purely their own – something secret and valuable that would secure their future as long as they tended it wisely.

"He petitioned the gods for more time, but they were adamant. They would give no more. Creation was set, and the people must do what they could with what they had. The foot soldier must leave them be and return to his place with the gods. The people must fend for themselves.

"Angry and distressed, the spirit became a tower of sheer strength, a glittering giant who reflected the flawless blue of the sky. Incensed beyond reason, he stamped his foot, and in his rage he struck the nails of his toes against the great rocks of the land. They shattered, and the shards plunged into the ground, tearing it up into a mountain, hidden in a deep valley formed by the shape of his foot, far from any place that it could be easily reached or found. The shards of his nails, stained blue from the sky, became jewels buried in the Earth. And so, in his fury, the spirit had found a way to provide for his people. A single mountain, veined with stones the colour of a perfect sky, to be mined only by the people within his borders."

"Blue stones the colour of the sky," murmured Rémy. "Sapphires. You are talking about sapphires, are you not?"

Desai smiled. "Sapphires indeed, Rémy Brunel, oh great knower of gems. He gave his people the only sapphire mine in the south of this great continent, to be kept a secret for eternity, mined only by the villages that were in the valley around the mountain. They would take only what they needed in order to trade, and no stranger would ever be allowed within its confines."

"I suppose we know that that did not happen," said Dita. "Or you would not know about it now, *ja*?"

"You are quite right, of course, Miss Dita. For centuries the mine remained secret. The sapphires that were taken from it were flawless, peerless – more valuable, even, than the great diamonds of Golconda. Some rulers, over the years, did try to find their source, but they never succeeded."

"So what happened?" Thaddeus asked.

"The world came to India," Desai told them. "Hundreds of

years ago, when the Portuguese walked onto this land, a young man of their number decided to make a name for himself by uncovering sights that no person from his country had seen before. He travelled far and wide, and in doing so stumbled across the hidden valley of the sapphire mountain. The villagers, having never been visited by foreigners before, were curious and invited him to stay for a while.

"The family that took him in had a young daughter, Aruna. This daughter was beautiful and as bright as the jewels she worked with her father and brothers to mine. The young man was dazzled by her, and she by him. The village elders were careful not to tell this stranger of their mine, but soon he became curious as to where all the able-bodied went every day. He persuaded the girl to tell him, and thereafter became obsessed with the idea of the riches this mine represented, and the glory he would garner for revealing it to the outside world.

"He asked Aruna to be his wife, believing that as her husband he would be able to trade the sapphires in the mine more profitably. Aruna loved him, and believed his intentions to be pure. The village elders, though, were suspicious, and forbade the match. The Portuguese man left the village, telling Aruna that he could not yet afford to keep a wife, but that he would return for her when he could.

"Aruna, having begged and pleaded with the village elders to no avail, grew sick with longing. She loved her family and her village, but she loved the young man more. She feared that he would not come back – that he would forget her entirely.

And so she decided that if he could not afford to keep her, she would have to keep herself. She would steal from the mine – not a lot, just enough to pay her way through the world, and marry her love.

"The very next day, while deep in the mine, Aruna concealed two small sapphires in her mouth, so as to smuggle them out as she left that evening. She waited until that night, when her family was asleep, and then left the village. It was only when she reached the nearest town and tried to retrieve the sapphires to sell that Aruna realised she had swallowed one of the stones. Though an annoyance, she thought nothing of it – she sold the one remaining stone, which was enough to take her to Pondicherry, where the Portuguese man had told her he was headed when he left. On the journey, she began to feel a great pain in her stomach, but carried on, buoyed up by the belief that she was about to be reunited with her one true love.

"When she got to Pondicherry, she expected to be welcomed with open arms. But instead, she found her lover at the head of a garrison of soldiers, preparing as if for war. At the sight of her he shrugged, and told her she was no longer needed. Aruna was forced to watch as the garrison set off, by now too sick to follow.

"For days she was in pain and unable to move. She was taken in by a kindly couple who let her stay with them. There she remained, sick in heart and in body, until one day a great commotion rose to her sickbed from the street outside. Aruna dragged herself to the window, and saw below them the garrison led by the young man, returned. And each horse was laden with a sack, crammed with the most beautiful sapphires anyone had ever seen.

"At the sight, a rage overtook Aruna, for she knew exactly where these blue stones had come from. Her fury blotted out her pain, and she rushed from the house to confront the Portuguese man. He looked upon her with fear, and Aruna looked down to see that her nails had become talons of clear, pure sapphire. First she divested him of his curved sword, the cutlass that would later become her moniker and the symbol of her revenge. Then she tore him apart with her bare hands. Still enraged, she fled back to her home village.

"The village no longer stood. It had been razed by the Portuguese soldiers, every one of Aruna's family and friends put to the sword for refusing to give up the mountain. They were all dead, thanks to the love of one girl and the greed of one man.

"Aruna's fury mingled with a grief so potent that it drew storms from the sky. She stood, raging and hateful of the world, until a bolt of lightning struck the cutlass she still carried. Its energy surged through Aruna, finding the sapphire still within her belly, seeking it as surely as a plant seeks the sun.

"The stone within her, already woken by grief and shame and anger, came alive. It raged within her belly, pouring its ancient wisdom into the woman's body, flooding her veins with more than fury – filling her with a power so great that it rivalled the storms above her head. She turned on the Portuguese garrison who had come to avenge their comrades' deaths, tearing them apart, flaying their flesh to ribbons in the space of time that it would take a mortal to draw breath. Her rampage did not burn itself out – she flew onwards through the jungles, killing wherever she found life, so full of hatred that she was blind to her victims, seeing only her lover's face.

"Her fury was such that the gods themselves were woken from their slumber. They saw that with the power of the sapphire, this woman could become one of their number. They sent a group of wise men the means to subdue her into a sleep as great as their own. Aruna was placed deep inside the mountain from whence both her grief and her power originated, never again to walk the Earth. The valley of the mountain was cursed so that no one would ever again willingly set foot in its jungles. Over the years the story has changed shape, many times. There are people who admire Aruna for her strength, and worship her for her power. There are people who have made her a symbol of hope – a goddess for the downtrodden and mistreated. But no one has ever gone so far as to speak of waking her again."

"Until now," murmured Rémy.

"Yes," said Desai, with a sombre sigh that seemed to draw a thread of darkness through the bright tapestry of the new day. "Until now."

A New Cult

"But – but this is just a fable," protested Thaddeus into the silence that had fallen following Desai's tale. "It's just a story – it can't be true!"

"Surely by now you must realise, my dear Thaddeus, that what is true has far less importance than what is believed," said Desai. "Besides, do you doubt that gemstones can wield great powers? After what you saw in Abernathy's tunnels – after your means of travel from one side of the Earth to the other?" He gestured at the airship.

Thaddeus nodded. It was true – however rationally he thought about it, he could not deny the evidence of his own eyes. "And what do *you* believe, Desai?" he asked.

Desai looked back at him, his expression deadly serious. "That whatever the kernel of truth in the story is irrelevant. It is the cult that had grown up around the tale that is the true danger."

"A cult?" Rémy repeated. "You mean there are still people who worship the idea of Aruna and her power?"

"Absolutely there are," said Desai, "and as with all faith it only takes a clever mind to manipulate such devotion. For centuries these people have kept themselves secret – but now their numbers are swelling. They believe that Aruna is about to rise again, and they are flocking to serve her – or whomever has designated themselves her mouthpiece – while they still can."

"Someone is encouraging them?" asked Thaddeus, and was rewarded by a nod from Desai.

"Just so. This, I think, is Sahoj's most clever plan. Hidden away in Aruna's mountain he is building an army, and he has not even had to recruit them. They are coming to him."

"Sahoj," repeated Rémy. "When I was finding my way into the palace, I saw Ikshuvaku speak with an old man dressed in white robes. Is this who you mean?"

"Indeed it is," said Desai.

"He did not seem happy by the capture of the airship," Rémy observed.

Desai gave a brief smile. "I imagine the idea of the raja having any strength at his own command plays against whatever Sahoj is planning," he said. "It would suit him best to have the raja dependent on his power."

"But what could he be planning?" Thaddeus asked. "Another uprising against the British?"

Desai shook his head. "If that were all he were interested in, I would not be as concerned as I am. Unfortunately, even if the tale about reawakening the girl is false, the powers of the stones in those mines are true. If Sahoj has found a way to channel that power – as I believe he must at least *think* he has, or he would not be so audacious – then we must all fear the outcome, for I have no doubt his ambitions will extend far beyond these shores.

"But, most frightening of all is that he may believe he can control the power he has sought out – he may even succeed, for a time – but sooner or later he will fail. What is in that mountain was not meant to exist and its power cannot be safely harnessed, much less wielded. This is what the fable of the Sapphire Cutlass is intended to show. We must find a way to stop him, before the cult and its notoriety spreads, for the more it does so, the greater Sahoj's confidence will be."

Thaddeus and Rémy shared an uncomfortable look, which did not go unnoticed by Desai.

"What is it?" he asked. "My young friends, if you have something to say, I beg you – speak."

Thaddeus straightened his shoulders with a sigh. "I don't know how to tell you this, Desai, but I think it has already spread beyond India."

"Go on," the older man said.

"We told you we came here from France, yes?" Rémy said gently.

"Quite. I was going to ask you about that, in due course."

"You will remember that before you left on your journey here, you visited me in my office at the station and gave me a list of names," added Thaddeus. "On that list was the Comte de Cantal. It was he who took us to France."

As quickly as he could – and with help from Rémy, J and Dita – Thaddeus outlined the events that had surrounded the destruction of Mount Cantal. As the story unfolded – the kidnap of Claudette and Amélie, their discovery that the Comte's entire mountain had been turned into a factory for a huge mechanical army – Desai's face grew darker and darker. He stared into the distance, listening intently.

"The thing is," Thaddeus went on, almost hesitant to reveal the crux of the matter, "the thing is, Desai, that when he was leading me through that volcano, he revealed that he knew Abernathy. Or at least, if he did not know him personally, then he knew of him. He spoke of warning someone that Abernathy was not ready to receive the power he had obtained. And I saw, on his breast, a tattoo. It was of a curved sword, with a hilt inlaid with a sapphire embedded in his skin."

Silence reigned for a moment, punctuated by nothing but the dying crackle of the fire and the call of the jungle birds, waking into the day.

"It cannot be a coincidence, I think, what Thaddeus saw?" Rémy prompted, after a moment or two.

Desai shook his head. "No, it cannot. That motif matches the symbol of the Sapphire Cutlass. Their followers see it as proof of their devotion to tattoo themselves accordingly."

"Then," said Thaddeus hesitantly, "are we to assume – my god, Desai, are we to assume that all of those names on the list you gave me are members of this cult? They were spread all over the world, weren't they? I remember names from as distant as the Far East on that piece of paper!"

Desai nodded, his mouth a thin, hard line. "From what you have told me, and what you have discovered, I fear you must be correct."

He got to his feet, agitated, and began to pace. "I have tarried too long. I have been arrogant. I came to India imagining that I could deal with this problem on my own – that it was a thing I could contain by myself, as if Ikshuvaku and Sahoj were merely errant children. But I am too late. Perhaps it was too late before I even set foot on my homeland again. If the cult of the Sapphire Cutlass has already spread throughout the world, then perhaps there is nothing more to be done. Perhaps there never was."

Thaddeus stood, dusting his hands off on his trousers. "That can't be true, Desai. I won't accept it. We defeated both Abernathy and Cantal. Perhaps we still have a chance to do something, if we act now. Do you have any idea what might stop this?"

Desai spread his hands. "My young friends, I do not. But whatever is to be done – if anything can be – the doing of it must take place within that mountain."

"Where is it, then?" J asked. "Is it a long way away, like? Cos I'm willin' to wager that this beastie has been further, Mr Desai." He waved proudly at the airship.

The older man smiled and said, "In some ways, it is very close, J, and in others it is a lifetime away." He raised his arm and swept it out over the horizon, which now glowed in the bright yellow sunlight of an Indian day. He pointed, and there in the distance, silhouetted against the light, reached the

85

jagged tip of a twisted mountain. Its lower reaches plunged into a valley so deep and so clogged with jungle that even as high up as they were, it was impossible to see from whence it sprang.

"There," said Desai. "There is the mountain created by the angry stamp of a lesser god, and there lies the answers to the questions we have posed for ourselves."

"Right then," said J, getting to his feet and slapping his hands against his thighs. "Well, what are we waiting here for then? Places to be, things to do. Let's be 'avin' you, eh?"

"J, it is not that simple," cautioned Desai.

"Why ain't it? There it is, right there, and you's said that's where we got to go to work this fing out. So I say we hop to it, quick like, before this Sahoj and his Sapphire wotsit 'as a chance to see us comin'."

"J, I know what a brave soul you are. I know what brave souls you all are," said Desai, his words encompassing the whole of their small assembly. "But this is not what we found in Abernathy's lair. It is not even what you encountered in France. This is on a different scale, and what we find there... What we find there could well be the end of everything we know. Think of the legend of Aruna. Think of those soldiers, torn apart by the bare hands of an unarmed young girl. Think what sort of power could induce such events as that."

There was a brief silence, which Thaddeus broke in a soft, but firm voice. "Well then," he said, "that's all the more reason for us to hurry. Wouldn't you say, Desai?"

Desai looked at him, and then at each of their faces in turn. Something passed through his eyes – an emotion so large that even their dark depths struggled to contain it. He seemed to struggle to speak for a moment, and when he did his voice was thick. "My young friends. Your courage and loyalty are lessons for all. And, if you are our future – then perhaps it is in better hands than we even deserve."

"So tha's settled, then," said J. "We're all going. And I say we don't lose any more time chin-wagging, or it'll be time for lunch and frankly, I ain't missing another one o' those unless the sky is fallin' in."

Dita nudged him in the ribs with an elbow. "Be careful what you wish for, eh, dirty boy."

"I keep *tellin'* you," J said, "I ain't–"

"There is one thing," said Desai, his voice cutting through the children's squabbling, "that we must address first."

Thaddeus frowned. "Oh? What's that?"

Desai turned to Rémy with a soft smile. "Your knowledge of the Sapphire Cutlass is not the only thing you brought with you from France, am I right?"

Thaddeus watched as Rémy's face passed from confusion and into realisation. "Oh," she said. "Do you mean the puzzle box? But – but that is of no importance, Desai. It can wait."

Desai raised an eyebrow. "Of no importance? This trinket that you risked your life to reclaim from the raja's palace is of no importance?"

"I mean, it is not as important as everything else," Rémy amended. "Anyway, I am not sure the thing works at all. We have all tried for months to open it and we cannot."

Their friend smiled. "My dear, I am inclined to believe that where you are concerned at least, there is very little that is not important. In this case, I am sure of it. May I ask what you believe it to contain?"

Rémy sighed. "An old woman, in France – a medicine woman – she gave it to me. She told me it would take me to the truth. She was also the one who told me that I had a brother: a twin, born just before me. I thought she meant the truth about my brother. But maybe I'm wrong about what she meant. Or she may just have been crazy – and anyway, if I have never known him yet, it cannot matter if I never do at all."

"Do you really believe that?" Desai asked.

Rémy shrugged, twining her fingers together restlessly. "*Monsieur*, what can it matter that I may have a brother if the fate of the world is in the balance?"

Desai smiled. "What indeed? May I see it?"

Rémy hesitated for a moment and then crossed to where her leather bag sat on the ground. Pulling it open, she fished in its depths for the cube, and then passed it to Desai. He turned it around in his hands, watching the play of sunlight dance across the intricate whorls and patterns on each surface. Then he looked up at her.

"You trust me with this?"

"I – yes, of course. I trust all of you. I would not have shown it to anyone but Thaddeus, otherwise."

Desai nodded with a slightly sad smile. "It is a balm to a weary soul such as mine, Rémy Brunel, to find such optimism in one who has endured such hardships as you."

Rémy blinked. "I am not–" She trailed off as Desai gripped

the box in both hands. Instead of attempting to open the stubborn hinges, as they had each tried in turn, he held it out in front of him and twisted, one hand moving right and one hand moving left.

Rémy watched, astonished, as the box realigned itself, shearing smoothly along the new angle offered it by Desai. Still the hinges did not open, but they did fold on themselves. A moment later, where once the box had been a perfect cube, now it was a sphere formed of triangles. Desai held out his hand, the newly formed sphere resting on his palm. As they all watched, a feature appeared on its uppermost curve – a button, clicking out of the whole.

"It is yours to press, Rémy Brunel," said Desai quietly.

Holding her breath, Rémy stepped forward and hesitantly reached out a hand. The box was gleaming as if lit from inside, which she knew to be nonsense – it was merely the gold of its outer shell refracting the sun's bright rays. The sphere felt warm to the touch, as if it had been woken, somehow, from a deep, deep sleep.

She pressed the button. It pushed in with a sharp click, and then – almost before Rémy could move her hand away – the sphere began to react. Each of the triangles that formed one half of the sphere flicked outwards, until they stood open like the petals of a flower.

Inside was a compass. With trembling fingers, Rémy reached in and lifted it out.

Eleven

The Puzzle Undone

The others all moved closer to see. The compass seemed very old – a hand-painted dial set in a glass-faced gold case with two filigree hands pointing north and south that looked almost too delicate for their task. Rémy held the device in her hand, and as she did so, something on the dial began to move. A tiny flap opened and a fold of gold popped up through it. It didn't seem to be affixed to anything, but instead wavered for a few seconds, whisking up and down the arc that represented north and south. Then it stopped, turned around on itself once and began to unfurl. As they all watched, a third hand, smaller than the first two and even more delicate, unrolled out of itself like the frond of a new fern. It wriggled for a moment or two in its new state, before setting firm.

"Cripes," said J, after a moment of silence as they all continued to watch the compass, waiting to see if it would do anything else. "I ain't never seen nothin' like that."

"Do you know what this is, Rémy?" Desai asked quietly.

Rémy shook her head, still staring at the compass in her hand, transfixed. "No, *Monsieur*. Like J, I have never seen such a thing. I am sure that none of us have. Except maybe you, of course?"

Desai nodded and then, being careful not to touch the compass, pointed to the new hand. "You see this? This is your direction, Rémy. This is the direction you must follow."

She looked up at him with a frown. "What do you mean?"

"You will find your truth – and possibly, with it, your twin brother – on this bearing. Moreover, you must follow it immediately, for the third arm will lose its direction as the sun sets on the day it is activated." He paused and looked up at the sky, into which the new sun was gleaming joyfully. "You are lucky, Rémy Brunel. Today will last a long time."

"But – wait," said Rémy, her mind spinning, "I – I cannot follow it now. We – we must help you deal with the Sapphire Cutlass first."

Desai smiled at her gently. "No, my dear girl, I do not believe that is your true course. If it was, the hand would point towards the mountain, would it not? And see here – it points to the south east, which is very nearly in the opposite direction."

"But – no," said Rémy, still perplexed. "I cannot follow it, then. Not now."

"If you don't, you will lose your chance to know the truth."

"I – I will take a note of the new heading, and follow it another time," said Rémy, shrugging with a nonchalance she didn't feel. Her stomach was churning, her heart beating in an unsteady patter. "*D'accord?* I have promised to help you, Desai, and Rémy Brunel does not abandon her promises so easily."

Desai smiled again and reached out to take her arm in a firm but gentle grip. "There is a reason the heading only lasts for a day, Rémy. Tomorrow the truth – or at least where it is situated – will be different. If you do not follow it, you may never find it at all."

"But – but I don't even know if this is about my brother!" Rémy exclaimed, frustrated and infuriated, though she didn't really know why. "It could be about anything!"

"Indeed, that could be true," Desai said, a gentle smile still in his eyes. "But somehow, I think not. Boxes such as these are rare, Rémy, and to find them gifted even rarer. Be honest with me now. What do you think most about these days? What have you thought most about since you arrived here, in India, the place where you know you were conceived?"

Rémy couldn't help looking at Thaddeus. He was watching her with eyes that, though they were shadowed with worry, were still full of the gentle reassurance she always saw there when she took the time to look.

He smiled at her, and she wanted to say that she had spent most of her time thinking about him – which was almost true, or would have been if something else hadn't always been lurking in the back of her mind.

"To find out about my family," she said softly, still looking at Thaddeus. "To – to find out if I really do have a brother."

"Quite," said Desai, dropping his arm with another smile. "This is enough to tell me that the truth you seek – the truth that is indicated along that heading – is about exactly that."

"You knew," she said. "You knew what was going to be inside the puzzle box. Why would you get me to open it now, when there are so many more things to worry about? How can I go and follow my own path when there is so much that needs to be done?"

"You imagine that these things are unconnected, Rémy Brunel," Desai told her. "But you are the common thread that has run through this story from start to finish, and I cannot believe that your twin is not a similar part of the weft and weave. If we are nearing this tapestry's completion, it seems to me that if you can find him, it is of as much importance to the pattern as anything else we may encounter from here on."

"He's right," Thaddeus said softly, stepping closer. "After all, if you do have a brother and if he's even half as wonderful as you are, Rémy Brunel – well, I for one would like him by my side in whatever fight may be coming."

Rémy looked down at the compass, still resting patiently in her palm. "How far will I have to go?" she asked Desai, her voice rasping against her suddenly dry throat. "How long will it take?"

"I don't know," Desai told her. "These, too, are truths that will only be revealed along the way."

"Take the airship," J piped up. "You've sailed it yerself enough to know 'ow to handle 'er, Rémy. That'll speed things up, eh?"

"I can't do that – if everything you have told us is really so, Desai, you will need it, yes? You will need to be able to escape, quickly."

Desai shook his head. "Arriving by air will draw too much attention. We must use stealth from here on. Besides, Sahoj has seen it, has he not? He'll be looking for it. Better that he does not see it coming. You can fly us as far as the furthest reaches of the valley and drop us there. That way we may even fool him a little – make him think we have contemplated entering the valley and turned back out of fear, as many a person has before. Any small advantage we can garner will be a help of incalculable worth."

"But – but–" Rémy looked from one to the other, until her gaze rested on Thaddeus who, with a smile, reached out to pull her into a soft embrace. Rémy turned her head so that it rested against his chest. The others moved away, leaving them to it.

For a few minutes they said nothing, only held each other. Then Thaddeus pulled back slightly and Rémy raised her head to look at him.

"You have to go," he told her. "You know you do, Rémy."

"I'd be leaving you again," she murmured. "I promised myself last time that I would never do that again."

"I told you – I'll come with you. Whatever's out there, Rémy, we'll face it together."

She shook her head. "You can't come with me, Thaddeus. You heard what Desai said, about what could be waiting in that mountain. He will need all the help he can get – J and Dita won't be enough, you know that. If I really am to go – then you must stay."

Thaddeus thought for a moment, his eyes scanning the horizon over her head.

Eventually he sighed and nodded. "You're right, of course."

"I wish I'd never opened the box," Rémy said miserably. "I wish I'd left it to the raja, and good riddance. I don't want to leave you. I don't want to leave any of you, but you most of all, Thaddeus Rec."

Thaddeus smiled, and pressed a kiss to her forehead. "You'll be back. You and I – we're like a compass ourselves," he said, nodding to where she still held it in one hand. "You're my north, Rémy, and I'm the arrow that points to you. We'll always swing back towards each other in the end."

He kissed her again, this time on the lips so that her words died away amid a blur of happiness tinged with worry and guilt. They parted after a moment, and Thaddeus rested his forehead against hers.

Eventually Rémy looked up at him, still hesitating even as the sun rose higher and higher on her back. As usual, time seemed to be running out, and she wondered how it could always be the case that, however old the universe was and however long it had existed, whenever something important had to be decided, it actually turned out there was no time at all.

"Go," Thaddeus whispered. "There's no choice to make, Rémy. Find this brother of yours and bring him back to help us."

She nodded reluctantly, and then, before he had a chance to move away, pushed herself up on tiptoe and kissed him, deeply. Thaddeus took her hand as they broke apart, turning to Desai, J and Dita.

"Let's go," he said.

Desai nodded, striding forward. "It is the right decision, Rémy. The only decision, truly. But now I must ask you for a favour."

"Of course," said Rémy, "I will do anything I can."

"I must ask you for the loan of your opal," said Desai. "I know that it is precious – the only memento you have of your parents. But it is possible that if we are to defeat the Sapphire Cutlass, the stone may be able to help."

Rémy put her hand to her neck, a reflex reaction returning her to an old habit she'd harboured for years. Until just a few months ago, the opal necklace given to her by her mother had been her constant companion, always hanging on a thin gold chain at her throat. But now, beneath her black shirt, her neck was bare.

"I'm so sorry, Desai, but I do not have it. I have not had it for months. I gave it to Claudette, so that she might speak to Amélie…"

Desai's face clouded with fresh worry for a moment, before he dispelled it with a wide smile. "Ah, well. It was just a thought. Come, my friends, we must be about our business, and let Miss Brunel be about hers."

Dita and J kicked dust across the remains of the fire as Thaddeus and Rémy readied the airship for flight. Rémy was at the controls as the ship rose into the air, turning its nose to head for the one patch of jungle that steadily refused to be lit by the sun — a valley so steeply banked and so densely packed with foliage that it gave off a darkness greater than that of the night they had so recently left behind.

Far below, weaving swiftly through the thick undergrowth, a group of soldiers left the great shadow cast by the huge rock monolith. They had followed all night and waited a long time for the airship to leave its safe harbour.

Their patience, it seemed, had finally paid off.

***

With fresh gas in the airship's balloon, the journey towards the mountain was a swift one. Desai told Rémy to put down before they reached the valley that stretched away from its foot. It would attract too much attention and be too dangerous, he said, to fly directly into the cult's lair. They chose a small clearing quite some way from the valley's furthest reach, where the sun still dappled the ground instead of refracting off the dense jungle leaves. Desai, Dita and J took the scant equipment they had chosen and left the airship.

Then all that was left was for Thaddeus to bid Rémy goodbye.

"I hate this," she muttered, as he pulled her against his chest. "I should be coming with you."

Thaddeus kissed the top of her head. "Everything will be fine," he told her.

She pulled back and looked up at him. "You cannot possibly know that!"

He smiled. "Don't be such a pessimist."

"Don't be such an idiot," she retorted.

He grinned. "If I wasn't, I don't think you would love me quite as much."

Her eyes gleamed for a second and Thaddeus knew she'd thought of a sharp comeback. He leaned forward and kissed her before she could say it. Rémy wound her arms around his shoulders and when they broke apart, they lingered there, their foreheads touching, until Desai's voice broke the silence.

"My young friends, it pains me to separate you, but we should all be on our way," he said, his gentle voice floating to them from the airship's ramp. "If the landing of the airship was noticed, we do not want to be in the vicinity when someone comes."

Rémy pushed out of Thaddeus' arms with a nod. "Go," she said, "and I will too – the sooner I follow this heading, the sooner I will come back for you all, yes?"

Thaddeus smiled. "Fly safely, Little Bird."

"Do not lose your way, little policeman."

They looked at each other for another moment, and then Thaddeus turned and left. He stood on the jungle's soft earth and watched as Rémy winched the airship's ramp back into place, hiding her from his view inch by inch until she disappeared completely.

Desai placed a hand on his shoulder. "You will see her again, Thaddeus, and soon. I am sure of that."

The airship began to lift off as Thaddeus turned with a smile. "I know I will."

He looked up to see that the airship – and Rémy with it –
was already high above the treeline, sailing away into the blue,
blue sky.

Twelve

Ambush

It had yet to reach nine o'clock in the morning, but the air was already hot. It beat down on the thick, silent jungle, turning the air into a heady, humid soup of smell and sensation. Thaddeus could feel his pack sticking to his back, his shirt already drenched in sweat, though they had barely begun their trek towards the valley. Below his feet, the soft ground was slowly beginning to slope up into the steep pass that marked the valley's entrance from the direction they had chosen. Ahead, he could see the jagged lines of the rise they would have to navigate. It formed a landscape the Englishman had never seen before – a line of cracked earth through which grew a line of trees so dense that their leaves seemed to gather darkness against their trunks. The trees stood like sentries at their posts: still, impenetrable, forbidding.

The legend was right about one thing. It wasn't anywhere Thaddeus would have chosen to go willingly.

The sombre air seemed to have had a similar effect on his companions. J trailed behind Desai, who had taken the lead. The boy's head was down and his shoulders were slumped. Even J's usually rambunctious hair was subdued, plastered against his scalp in the haze of heat that surrounded them. Dita was quiet for a change, too – no sign of the constant bickering that usually typified her conversations with J. The little girl stared around her, her eyes flicking anxiously here and there as if trying to keep watch on the whole forest around them.

Desai, meanwhile, toiled stoically on ahead, and not for the first time Thaddeus wondered at the man's endurance. Desai must have reached his sixtieth year, and actually had probably surpassed it, but he showed no signs of fatigue or physical distress. Although, the younger man reflected, perhaps that had more to do with what he knew was ahead for them.

Thaddeus, making up the rear, had spent much of his time thinking about Rémy. Her absence now was the first time they had been apart in all the months since their exodus from France, and even though he knew full well where she was and what she was doing, even though they had said goodbye just an hour or so before and he had seen the airship depart, Thaddeus still found himself, in those split seconds between one thought and the next, looking up and expecting to see her. Her absence simply felt wrong. His body and his mind could not absorb it.

Things had changed between them over those past months. They had become easier, less fraught with misunderstanding and argument. They had got to know each other better, they had become accustomed to each other's moods and daily routines, each other's likes and dislikes. They fitted together better – they fitted together *well,* which wasn't something either of them thought would be possible for two such disparate people.

What did it mean? If they fit so well that even an hour apart felt unnatural and strange, at least at first – what did that *mean?* Affairs of the heart, he reflected, were so much more difficult to navigate than a police investigation.

Yet he thought he knew. Thaddeus reached into his pocket, finding the tiny object that he had put there weeks ago and frequently taken out to look at since, without ever finding the right time to give it to its intended recipient.

Thaddeus pulled his fingers away from the trinket with a sigh. Of course, being apart may not feel at all odd to Rémy, who was quite possibly the most independent person he knew. It was one of the many things he loved about her, partly because he thought it boded well for him. She didn't need anyone at all, really, and yet still she chose to stick with him.

The snap of a twig brought Thaddeus out of his reverie in a second. The sound had come from behind him and he turned, surveying the forest for any sign of movement. He could see nothing, but a renewed sense of unease poured fresh tension into his shoulders.

"Desai…" he called, keeping his voice low. "I think…"

The attack was upon them before he even managed to finish his sentence. Four men clad in the raja's colours appeared from the undergrowth, teeth bared and fists clenched. Thaddeus backed up, keeping his face to them, realising with a jolt that none of them had drawn their swords.

"They want to take us alive!" Desai shouted. "Do not let them get close enough – make for the valley, as fast as you can!"

Thaddeus saw J grab Dita's hand and together the two children made a run for it. He hung back, hoping to give them a chance to get a head start, but two of the men peeled off from their group and followed them.

Thaddeus began to run himself, dodging under the lowest branches he could find in an attempt to slow down whomever might be on his trail. He saw Desai a little way to his left, doing the same. The men pursuing them were fast and nimble, but one-on-one, even if it came to a fight, they had a chance. He wondered why there were not more of them, and where their horses were. If the raja had sent them, they must have been following the airship and to do that would need–

Of course, he thought, darting around the thin trunk of a tree mid-stride, *the airship. That's what the raja really wants. If there were more men like these, they will have gone after it. Godspeed, Rémy...*

He felt a hand clamp on his shoulder, heavy breathing just behind him as the touch spun him around. Thaddeus ducked under his attacker's arm, swinging left and then dodging right around the man before kicking out one leg at his calf. The raja's soldier was too fast, sidestepping the blow before it could connect and then aiming a swift hook at Thaddeus'

jaw. Apparently wanting to take them alive didn't mean
they had to arrive at the raja's feet bruise-free. Thaddeus
avoided the punch and then clasped both of his hands around
the man's slicing fist, bending his knees and throwing his
weight back onto the forest floor. The momentum took his
attacker by surprise and he went sailing over Thaddeus' head,
disappearing into the jungle undergrowth with a grunt and
a rustle. Thaddeus was on his feet and running again in a
second.

He could see Desai ahead of him, his own pursuer so close
on the older man's heels that it could only be seconds before
he was caught. Of Dita and J – or the two men who had chased
after them – there was no sign, which at least gave Thaddeus
the breathless hope that they were still free. Perhaps they had
even reached the valley and found somewhere to hide there. Its
lip leered at them from just a few hundred yards away, its dusty
jagged edge tantalizingly close.

Thaddeus kept running, not even turning to see whether
the man he had downed had recovered himself as yet. As he
ran he ducked to scoop a handful of the soft, dry forest dirt
into his hand. Clutching it, he made straight for the man on
Desai's tail, his lungs burning with the effort.

He saw the soldier glance over his shoulder as he heard
Thaddeus' footsteps. Thaddeus lunged forward, narrowly
avoiding a tree root that reared up to snag his leg and then
shoved the fistful of dirt into the man's face. He howled as the
dust scratched against his eyes, immediately dropping back and
doubling over with both hands to his face.

"Thank you, my young friend," Desai called over his shoulder breathlessly. "Keep going – we are almost there!"

"And then what?" he shouted back. "Will there be somewhere to hide?"

"You will see!"

The ground was sloping sharply upwards. Thaddeus' legs ached with the renewed effort it took to climb the incline. There was a commotion ahead of them. Thaddeus brushed the sweat out of his eyes to see the two men who had followed Dita and J skittering back down the slope. One of them fell, rolling against a tree trunk before dragging himself up again. Thaddeus thought the two men would launch themselves towards them, but instead they simply seemed intent on getting back down the slope as fast as possible.

One of them passed him close enough for Thaddeus to see the look on the soldier's face.

It was full of terror.

A New Heading

The compass was set on a south easterly heading, which took the airship back along the river they had been able to see from the plateau. It cut through the jungle like a pure blue line, its waters far clearer than any river Rémy had ever seen before. Through the airship's window she could see it twisting and turning through the trees as if it would never stop. Hours passed and still all that Rémy could see below her were trees, punctuated by the rushing billow of that pure blue water. Several times she reached out to issue a sharp tap against the glass case of the compass, wondering whether perhaps it was broken. Or perhaps, she thought, since she didn't know what she was supposed to be looking for, she could have missed something below her on the ground. But then, surely, the compass would have done something – changed, somehow – to tell her so?

She had no one to ask, and so she and the airship flew on. Rémy wished that Thaddeus were there with her – or rather, that she was back there with him. It seemed terribly wrong to be leaving him to deal with whatever he would have to face alone. It was only Thaddeus' own words convincing her to go that kept her on her course. Otherwise she may have turned back, the puzzle box and its cryptic gift be damned.

As the day grew ever older, the landscape changed. Jungle gave way to open pasture that was dotted by only a few trees. Pasture gave way to more and more villages, all surrounded by neatly cultivated fields instead of unruly jungle. Then she saw towns and then, eventually, even a great walled city. Still there was no indication from the compass that Rémy had reached where it was taking her. It stayed resolutely on its south easterly heading, not changing, not moving. As the shadows began to creep across the ground below her, Rémy grew impatient.

"Come on!" she exclaimed, picking up the compass and looking at it closely as if it might suddenly tell her something new. "Is this a trick? Hmm? If Desai had not believed in you, I would have tossed you over the side of that plateau! Perhaps I should have anyway! Where are we going? Why aren't we there yet?"

The compass merely rocked slightly in her palm, its north and south hands shivering against her anger but the third hand holding firm to its course.

With a sigh, Rémy replaced the compass on the control panel and looked up to see a vast line of blue tinting her horizon. White flecks danced on its rolling peaks as it crashed towards her before breaking against the shore.

The airship had reached the ocean.

"Agh!" she cried, throwing her hands up in the air. "Now what? I am supposed to leave this place altogether? I am supposed to just fly out over the water? What?"

The compass refused to tell her anything at all.

From the position of the burning bright sun and the shadows casting across the hot ground, Rémy thought it must be about four o'clock. Days were long here, and the sun would not set until at least eight. Four more hours to find whatever the compass was trying to show her.

Rémy sat down with a sigh and rubbed her hands over her face. "Well, I have come this far, yes?" she muttered to herself.

She flew on, planning to continue until sunset before turning back. If she kept on a reverse heading she'd find her way back to the valley in time for tomorrow's first light. She'd be a day behind the others, but Rémy was fleet of foot, especially when the occasion called for it.

Rémy had given up hope that she'd actually find anything out here on the ocean. Below her the waves bobbed and splashed against each other, stretching on and on in what seemed to be an endless body of water. There were no islands on the horizon, no curves of land unexpectedly showing from the sea. There was nothing and no one.

"Well, old woman," Rémy muttered, leaning back in the chair and raising her shabby booted feet to rest against the lip of the control panel. "You have played me for a fool, yes? I wonder where you are now, and how often you laugh at that lost little French girl who so wanted to believe you, eh?"

A sound pulled her attention back to the compass. It was vibrating against the airship's control panel so hard that it skittered between the knobs and dials, bouncing slightly on the hammered metal surface.

Rémy picked it up, and saw that the third hand was folding back into itself, returning to the tiny slot it had appeared out of that morning. In another moment or so, it was impossible to tell that it had been there at all. The compass was just a compass once again, with two hands telling her which way was north and south, and nothing at all out of the ordinary besides.

Rémy's heart gave a slight judder and leaned over to look out of the window. This must be it. She must have reached her destination – the place the compass wanted her to find. But how could there be anywhere out here? Then, squinting into the glorious glare of the setting sun, she saw it.

Bobbing on the waves was a ship – three-masted, all of its sails proudly set out to catch the wind whipping across the churning waves that were burnished in amber as the sun sped towards sunset. Rémy flew towards it. Was this, finally, what the compass had wanted her to see?

As she neared, Rémy could see movement as the sailors realised what was coming towards them. Their shouts brought more men from below, until the deck was awash with them. None of them wore uniforms, Rémy noted – instead, they were dressed in a vast array of styles that seemed to mix everything from coat tails to shabby cut-off trousers. It looked, Rémy thought, like an odd kind of circus, though what a circus would be doing out here on the ocean instead of performing in a town or city somewhere she couldn't imagine.

Putting down the compass, she flew around it in an arc, leaning forward to see what was happening below. The people on deck were shouting at her in a rather unfriendly way. She saw two of them run for the main mast and begin to haul on a rope there, hoisting a flag up its length, their huge muscles straining with the effort.

The flag unfurled quickly, the wind catching its roll and whipping it out to stand proud against the prevailing wind.

It was dark – black, in fact, with a skull and crossbones tattooed in white across it.

A Jolly Roger.

Rémy's stomach clenched sickly and she fumbled for the controls. Pirates! She had to get out of there. There was no telling what–

Something hit the hull with a sharp *thunk* and instantly the airship began to list to the side, pulling the nose around towards the pirate ship's bow. Rémy almost slid out of her chair as the airship juddered and she fought to pull her straight again, but without success. A moment later there was another *thunk* – this one hit towards the airship's tail, and suddenly Rémy felt herself being hauled in, pulled lower and lower towards the ship that bobbed below her on the waves.

In a panic, Rémy fought with the controls – the airship bucked and weaved like goat caught in a rope, but to no avail. Another thunk followed, and then another, and with each came an extra tug that pulled the airship closer and closer to the pirates' boat.

She could hear them now, roaring as the airship got ever nearer. Rémy had no idea what to do. The controls were all but useless, whirring hopelessly under her hands.

"Heave!" came a shout from outside, followed by a roar made up of many voices, *"Heave! Heave! Heave!"* Each jolt that brought Rémy lower was timed with a cry of *Heave!*, until the rhythm was as impossible to escape as the ship's inexorable journey downwards.

Rémy leapt up from the controls – they were useless for now anyway. She ran for the airship's ramp and the small axe that hung beside it. If she could sever the tethers that were drawing the airship in…

The sight that greeted her as the ramp came down was terrifying. The airship had been pulled so low that the hull was almost level with the pirate ship's deck. A dozen ropes with climbing spikes had been hurled towards her craft, embedding themselves into the hull as easily as a bare foot presses into wet sand. Each rope was held in the grip of two pirates – they had looped the other ends of their ropes securely around their ship's guardrail and were now straining as they pulled the airship in, inch by inch. More stood by, screaming encouragement at their fellows. They were all terrifying to behold – scarred and tattooed, painted and bejewelled; they bared their teeth, screaming and shouting, caught up in a bloodlust meant purely for Rémy and the airship they were claiming as their prize.

Rémy edged as far out onto the ramp as she could, knowing she only had a matter of seconds. Raising the axe, she aimed for the furthest rope and swung, severing the thick cord in one heavy strike. The pirates that held the other end lost their balance as their weight suddenly had nothing to counter it. They sprawled backwards, ending up on the deck in a pile that briefly filled the air with bellows of laughter instead of murder.

She swung for the next rope and did the same, scrambling backwards as it flicked free and then immediately swinging for the next. The airship's nose twisted away as the tethers loosened their grip. For a moment Rémy felt a surge of hope – it was working! Then she felt a vibration shaking the ramp and turned. Over her shoulder she saw one of the pirates climbing nimbly towards her up the ropes that still tied the airship fast.

It was a woman. Her white teeth were bared in a terrifying grimace, the blade of a *talwar* clamped between them. Her hands, bedecked with spiked rings, gripped the twanging ropes as she surged towards Rémy, her brown eyes sparking fury. Rémy could see another long-bladed sword strapped to her back. In a second she was on the ramp, grabbing the sword from between her lips with one hand and grasping Rémy's shoulder with the other, hauling her back up the ramp and into the airship, knocking the axe from her hand.

The pirate woman dragged Rémy upright, her sword coming up to press viciously against Rémy's neck as she stared at her, seeming transfixed by her face.

"Who are you?" the pirate demanded. "Who sent you?"

The airship juddered again and another pirate – a man, this time – appeared in the open doorway.

"Bring her down," he said, dipping his head to fit his bulk into the small cabin. "He wants to–" the man broke off as he looked up and saw Rémy. Surprise burst across his face, creasing the ugly jagged scar that bisected his left cheek from ear to mouth. A second later suspicion settled where the surprise had been a moment before. "He wants to see her."

"You," said the woman, hissing sharply into Rémy's ear, "are wanted below."

"What about the ship?" Rémy gasped, feeling the bite of the cold blade against her neck with every struggle. "I can't just leave it."

"It's secure," the man that Rémy named to herself as Scar Face growled. "We will tow it behind us."

"But–"

There came another shout from outside, but this one was different. It was urgent, full of warning, and came from the bird's nest at the top of the main mast.

"Ship ahoy!" bellowed the voice, "Look lively, lads! They've got their cannon–"

There was the sound of a huge crash, like thunder rolling in the distance, followed by a low, swift whistle. The woman holding Rémy swung around, looking out of the open ramp. Below them on deck the pirates scattered, yelling, running for their posts as the whistle grew louder.

A second later a cannonball broadsided the pirate ship with a force that caused the entire vessel to buckle. It crashed through the second deck, sending wave after wave of splintered wood into the air, carried by the wind. Pandemonium reigned above – pirates wielding rifles and pistols, huge spiked metal balls on chains and all manner of swords. Then they let loose their own cannon, two at once – one from forward and one from aft, the recoil shaking the ship almost as badly as the strike had done a moment earlier. The airship slewed sideways, buffeted by the force as she strained against her tethers.

"Incoming!" bellowed the lookout in the bird's nest. Another rolling crash of cannon-thunder echoed over the melee. The sails of the pirate ship flapped and shuddered and as they dipped, another ship came into view, swung sideways and with all her cannon gates open.

"It's the British," cried one of the men. "They've found us. That infernal air-boat has led them to us!"

"Listen to me," Rémy cried. "If one of those cannonballs hits the airship, we will all burn – your ship, and mine! It's not like your ship, it cannot take a single strike – it will explode!"

The pirate shook Rémy like a rat. "You lie!"

"No! I don't! You have to–"

The second cannon caught the pirate ship a glancing blow forward, smashing into its nose. Flames licked along the guardrail and there were shouts for buckets and water.

"I swear," said Rémy, "I am not lying. Just one flame like that one and we're all done for."

The female pirate snarled with anger and released Rémy, flinging her away so that she crashed against the airship's control panel and stumbled against the chair. Just as she did so another cannonball fired from the British frigate crashed into the ship below. Rémy couldn't see what was happening, but from the frantic cries of the people below she knew it must have been a hard hit.

"He's going to have to run for it," exclaimed Scar Face. "We're no match for their firepower, but the Black Star can outrun their bucket of bolts! We're not at anchor! Why isn't he *running?*"

As if someone below had heard him, a shout echoed up from below. "Cut it loose," came the cry, "the air beastie is dragging us back. The British have got us like sitting ducks! Cut it loose!"

The woman pirate leaned out of the window, "We cannot lose this prize!"

"Take it to the cove at Maginapundi," came back the answering shout. "Do it now!"

With a curse, the woman raised her sword and slashed at the tangled ropes still holding the airship fast to the deck. With a jerk the airship was free. It rose away from the pirate ship, soaring into the air like a freed bird. Rémy leaned over the controls, yawing the craft around as she almost tangled with the pirate ship's sails. She swung the airship toward the coast as the pirates dragged up the ramp and secured it shut.

A second later Rémy felt the bite of a blade at her neck once more.

"Now," hissed the woman, into her ear. "I have had to abandon my ship for you, *anukarana*. So one wrong move and I will not hesitate to part your head from your shoulders. Understand?"

Into the Valley

They crested the stony ridge, and fell into a different world.

Unexpectedly soft earth dropped away from him and Thaddeus stumbled, fetching up against the rough trunk of a tree that barred his descent. He crashed to his knees, feeling a stab of pain in his shoulder where the tree's harsh bark had scraped the skin. He shook his head as if to clear it – convinced for a moment that he had gone deaf. Ahead of him, further down the slope that careened sharply into the valley's dim depths, he could see J helping Dita to her feet. Thaddeus heard the crackle of twigs as the two youngsters regained their footing, and realised after all that he hadn't lost his hearing. It was just that the valley had sucked them into the kind of ringing, noisy quiet that stuffed the ears as surely as scraps of rag. After the chaos of their fight with the raja's men, the sudden cease of sound was doubly confusing and distinctly unsettling.

He got to his feet, looking around for Desai. The older man was gingerly making his way down through the trees towards him. Of the raja's soldiers there was no sign. It was as if they had disappeared into thin air.

"What happened?" Thaddeus asked. He spoke in a whisper but his words still sounded loud in the valley's cloying quiet. "The soldiers – where did they go?"

Desai paused, turning to glance back up the ridge. Then he looked at Thaddeus with a slight smile. "They are afraid to enter the valley. More afraid than they are of disobeying their master's orders."

Thaddeus looked around, feeling a deep prickle of unease move across his shoulder blades. "Why? Just because of the legend?"

"Yes. It is superstition, mainly."

He looked back at Desai with one eyebrow raised. "Mainly?"

Desai clapped him on the shoulder. "Courage, Thaddeus. I know you have such a quality or you would not be here at all. Come – night will fall early here, and we should cover as much ground as we can before then."

Thaddeus watched as his friend went ahead to Dita and J, who were looking as troubled as he felt. Then, quietly, slowly, they all began to move – Desai in front leading the way, Thaddeus making up the rear.

"Stay close," Desai counselled them all, in a whisper that would have carried like a leaf on a breeze anywhere else, but here cracked like a dry twig, "and stay alert. We are in strange country now."

It was true. Even the foliage looked different. The trees squatted fatly over their heads with large leaves far thicker than the ones Thaddeus had grown used to seeing over the months of their journey through India. The greens were deeper, darker, tinged with purple and veined with faint silver lines that glittered in the gloomy afternoon light. The ground was thickly clogged with dead leaves that shifted under foot as Thaddeus walked, rippling as if he were walking across a serpent's patterned spine.

But there was no life here, save for the trees. No creatures rustled in the dull branches as they passed beneath, no insects skittered from the wake of their footfall. The valley felt abandoned – and if so, Thaddeus would not blame those who had chosen to flee. He wasn't so far off doing so himself, however courageous Desai thought him to be.

Still, Thaddeus thought to himself, *this awful quiet does give us one advantage – we'll hear any attackers coming a mile off.*

They walked on, deeper and deeper into the valley. The light here was mediocre – fading as if the sun was setting, although it could barely be 4 o'clock in the afternoon. Thaddeus looked up and saw above him a dense roof made from the overlapping leaves, so thick that it stopped almost all light from filtering to the ground.

Mist twisted through the trees, weaving around the trunks like snakes. The air grew colder, as if the heat of India herself had been siphoned from the valley.

"I don't like this," muttered J.

He and Dita were walking with their hands clasped tightly

in each other's, shoulders bumping as they huddled close together.

Dita said nothing, staring fearfully around her as the mist seeped towards the group, growing denser by the second.

"We must move faster," said Desai, his voice echoing to Thaddeus as if from a great distance, even though he was only a few feet away. "And try to stay out of the mist."

"How?" J protested. "The stuff is everywhere! It's like wading through cold treacle, an'–"

Dita emitted a sharp scream that made them all jump. She clutched J even closer, her thin fingers bunching into his top as she peered wildly through the mist.

"What did you see?" Thaddeus exclaimed, his heart pounding.

"I – I don't know," Dita cried. "A – a face, I think. A face without eyes, only black holes where the eyes should be, and… and…" her voice faded to a whisper and Thaddeus could see that she was shaking.

"And what?" he probed gently, trying to sound calm even though he felt as terrified as the girl looked. "What else, Dita?"

"Teeth," she whispered, so quietly he had to lean forward to hear her despite the silence around them. "Rows and rows of sharp white teeth."

"Come," said Desai, "we must keep walking. This mist – it pulls strange tricks on the mind. Do not believe everything you think you see."

"What should we believe then, eh?" cried J, as Desai waved them on. "If we can't believe our own eyes?"

"We'll be fine, J," said Thaddeus, trying to tell himself that it was true. "We'll stick together and keep moving, all right? Everything will be fine."

They followed Desai, but Dita was still shaking like a leaf. With every snap of a twig beneath their feet or fresh billow of mist reaching out at them as bony fingers would, she flinched, her thin face pale.

"We 'ave to go back," said J. "Whatever's down 'ere, we ain't ready for it. There ain't enough of us, fer a start!"

Dita raised her head from his shoulder. "No," she said, firmly. "We must go on, *ja*? We must."

"But you—"

"You stay close to me," she said. "You stay close to me and I will be – how do you say it? Right as rain, dirty boy. *Right as rain.*"

J hugged her and they stumbled on, although by now the mist was so thick that it was hard to see more than a foot or two in front of them. Thaddeus stumbled over a gnarled tree root protruding like a broken limb from the leaves under foot. In the second that it took him to right himself, he'd fallen behind enough to lose the others. A spark of panic burst through his heart.

"Desai!" he shouted. "J, Dita! Wait!"

The mist rushed in around him, sheets of thick grey coldness as palpable and heavy as blankets left out in the rain. Thaddeus batted it away from his face and arms, shouting for his friends again, trying to stem the panic as the mist touched his face and slid along his hair.

Ahead of him he heard noises – another piercing scream from Dita, shouting from J and, he thought, even from Desai, too. Thaddeus stumbled forward, trying to head for the sounds – it felt as if he were forcing his way through a heavy curtain as he battled against the mist. He could hear other noises now, too – a strange, low chanting, rising around him like another wave of fog. It was impossible to make out the words – if they even *were* words – but they rolled closer before snapping away sharply, as if whoever was speaking them was darting in close to his ear and darting away again before Thaddeus had a chance to turn and see them.

Then, as quickly as it had enveloped him, the mist rolled back. It was as if someone had opened a window and pulled it out – as he watched, it drew back in columns that looked disturbingly like tentacles – coiling, curling, sinuous it crept back between the trees to wherever it had come from.

Thaddeus found himself out of breath, as if he'd been running. He spun around, looking for his companions. They emerged from the mist like statues – Desai, J... but no Dita. J looked around wildly, searching the forest as it came into view.

"Dita!" J shouted, frantic. "Where are you?"

There was no answer. The forest was a silent as it had been when they first rushed over the ridge. Thaddeus went to J and grabbed his arm.

"What happened?" he asked, but the boy shook his head miserably.

"I don't know! She were here one minute – holding on to me, like, and then... and then... she were gone. She told me,

Thaddeus, didn't she? She told me to stay close, and she'd be fine. But she wasn't fine – she wasn't..."

Thaddeus hugged him. "We'll find her, J. Don't worry. We'll get Dita back."

Desai moved to Thaddeus' shoulder, although he was looking out into the darkness, which seemed even deeper than before.

"We must go," he said. "The power of the Sapphire Cutlass has already grown stronger than I realised. They will not stop until they have us all, and if we want to save Dita then we must stay free."

J sniffed and wiped the back of his hand under his nose. "All right. Which way is it then? I'm all turned about after the mist."

Desai paused for a moment, looking around. Then he gestured. "It is this way."

"You sure?" J asked defiantly. "Because it all looks the same to me and I don't want to end up wasting time going in the wrong direction, right?"

Desai looked at the boy steadily. "J. Trust me. I know where we're going."

J stared back again for another moment. "All right then. Let's get on wiv it." He turned and stomped off.

"J," said Thaddeus, catching up with him and laying a hand on his shoulder. "Calm down."

J shrugged him off, his face a picture of anger. "I said we shoulda turned back. Didn't I? Didn't I say so, Mr Rec?"

"Yes, J, you did. And Dita said no, didn't she? She wanted to carry on, because she knows how important this is. So that's what we're going to do. We'll carry on, we'll get her back, we'll get out of here and we'll do it together. All right?"

J didn't have a chance to answer. There came a warning shout from Desai, and Thaddeus turned to see the mist rushing in again. It came faster this time, a grey wall that swallowed them up almost before they'd even seen it coming. He reached for J, standing right next to him, and felt the boy being pulled away even before he heard him yell.

Thaddeus heard Desai shout, too, and heard a commotion that could only mean the older man was fighting an attacker. Thaddeus felt solid shapes moving around him, had the fleeting impression of faces in the mist, darting in and darting away again. The chanting returned – louder, he thought, this time, but it could also just have been that it was closer.

Desai's shouts stopped as suddenly as they started, leaving only the dull roar of the chant, roving closer and closer. Thaddeus spun around, listening for any sign that his friends were still nearby, but heard nothing.

He felt something slide down his arm – fingers. Thaddeus jerked himself away, backing into the mist, but doing so bumped him into something else – something grasping, pulling at his shirt, drawing him in. He pulled away again, spinning to face his attacker, but there was nothing but the infernal grey blankness and the endless, endless chanting.

A feeling of hopelessness washed over him as he saw ghostly faces peering out of the mist. The others were gone, he knew that – their silence was as loud as the chant that droned on and on like some kind of drug. He would be taken, too, and who only knew where – somewhere that none of them would ever be found, much less where they could hope to stop whatever the Sapphire Cutlass had planned beyond this valley of terrors.

The chanting stopped. Thaddeus knew he was out of time.

As one, the figures lunged towards him. Cruel hands reached for him, grasping his arms, his legs, tightening around his neck.

Anukarana

The waves lapped at the dark shoreline. Rémy shivered in the breeze that whisked across the pale sand. Now that the sun had set – had been set, in fact, for an hour or so – the air had chilled again. In fact, it was becoming so cold that the two pirates holding her captive were in the process of building a large fire. Flames licked at the dry wood they had collected from the shore, the orange flickers growing by the second, their crackle and fizz filling the restless salt air.

Rémy sat on the sand with her back against a rock, her hands and feet tied so that she could not move even to rub her cold arms. The fire had been constructed in the sheltered shadow of a spit of stone that jutted out from the even taller cliffs around them. It would be invisible to anyone looking towards the shore from the ocean, and indeed to anyone looking from inland, too, unless they happened to lean directly over the crumbling cliff edge and look down. It was a good spot to hide – one that her captors were obviously very familiar with, judging from the remains of old fires dotted about the shore.

The airship stood behind them where Rémy had been forced to land it, a safe distance from the growing fire. The balloon was almost completely deflated – the ruby exhausted from its long two days of flight.

Rémy rolled her shoulders, hating being so helpless. As she watched, the female pirate moved slowly in Rémy's direction, her attention on the fire as she rubbed her hands together. Rémy watched her profile with interest. She didn't think this girl was much older than she was. Her face was built of sharp and elegant angles – a proud forehead, a pointed nose pierced with a tiny diamond that glinted like a star against her skin. Her eyes were large and clear, even in the darkness. The girl's long black hair swept back from her face in a thick, unfussy plait that fell almost to her waist. There were scars, too – almost as many as Rémy had noticed on the men – slashes that patterned her arms and neck, a testament to a hard life. The girl's clothes were shabby and functional – a cropped green top without sleeves, baggy brown trousers bound with a belt at the waist and what looked like strips of leather at the calves, where they were pushed into scuffed tan boots that laced almost to the knee. The *talwar* hung in a leather scabbard from her belt, her hand hovering near its hilt as if ready to draw it at a moment's notice.

"How long have you been a pirate?" Rémy asked quietly.

The girl started as if she'd forgotten Rémy was even there, looking at her for a second before setting her mouth in a line and looking away.

"I used to be part of a circus," Rémy went on, trying to find something that they might both have in common. "My master made me steal almost as soon as I could walk. It's not a great life, is it?"

The girl turned and looked at her again, her eyes piercing and disdainful in the firelight. "Speak for yourself, *anukarana*," she said, in a low voice. "I have a very good life. I am my own master."

"You called me that before," said Rémy. "*Anu... Anukarana?*"

The girl stared hard at the fire, her eyes glittering in the flickering light. "Yes."

"What does it mean?"

The girl was silent for a moment, her shoulders hunched against her knees. Then she looked at Rémy, her face expressionless. "In my language it means 'imitator'."

"Why do you call me that?"

She turned back to the fire. "You know."

"I don't," said Rémy. "I promise you, I don't. Please tell me."

The girl didn't look at her again, or speak another word, as if the fire was telling her secrets that she had to strain to hear.

"I can't explain how I found your ship," Rémy said quietly. "I don't think you would believe me if I told you. But I had a reason – a good one. I was looking for my brother. My twin."

Rémy saw the girl's shoulders tense and knew that she'd heard what Rémy had said.

"Is there someone aboard your ship that looks like me?" Rémy asked. "Is that why you called me an imitator? Is that why you all look at me," she indicated Scar Face, sitting on the other side of the fire, "as if you have seen me before?"

The girl turned to look at her again. "Who sent you?" she asked. "Your ship bears the Union Jack. Have the British paid to put a curse upon Kai's soul? Is that why you are here, *anukarana*? To trick us into betraying him because they can find no other way to catch him?"

"Kai?" Rémy asked, her heart speeding up. "Who is that? Does he – does he look like me?"

The girl smiled, though the gesture was far from friendly. "If you truly do not know, you will find out soon enough. When he comes with the others."

"Do you mean your ship?" Rémy asked. "How do you know they'll make it? They took heavy damage. What if they were destroyed?"

The girl put back her head and laughed. "Impossible, *anukarana*. Kai leads a charmed life. He will survive, no matter what you or his other enemies throw at him."

"I'm not – I'm *not* his enemy," Rémy said, frustrated, and then stopped as a thought occurred to her. "He – Kai – you say he has a charmed life. Does he have a talisman? Perhaps a precious stone – an opal, maybe – that he wears around his neck?"

The girl looked at her sharply, eyes narrowed and fingers flexed. The she relaxed a little and looked back to the fire. "I am Upala," she said softly. "I am his opal, and his talisman. I will always keep him safe."

Rémy was about to ask her what she meant when a mighty yell echoed against the cliff walls and reverberated around the beach. At first Rémy thought it was the wind playing tricks, but then it came again, closer this time. She twisted around, looking towards the water as Upala stood.

The pirate's vessel crested the waves as it rounded the cliff to enter the cove. It was battered and scarred, but it was whole – and on its deck stood every one of Upala's shipmates, apparently unharmed.

The ship dropped anchor and the pirates began to jump over the side, splashing into the shallows and wading through the water like a tide of their own making. They were singing and dancing, swaggering as they drew nearer, evidently pleased with themselves.

The pirates rushed up the beach towards the fire, scattering sand into the breeze around them. All around her, they moved in flurries of colour and sound. It felt unreal to Rémy, as she was watching everything from very far away, atop one of the cliffs that served as their shelter. Gone were the terrifying cries that had greeted the airship, replaced now by laughter and wild yells of celebration.

For a second, the mass of bodies parted, like two tides drawing away from each other. Rémy looked through the gap and saw a pirate striding up the sand against the wind. He was thin and wiry, dressed all in black – black boots, tied up to his calves, black breeches, black shirt. On his head was a black tri-corn hat.

Rémy felt her heart judder as he turned, knowing what she was about to see even before she had actually seen it. And suddenly, there he was. It was like looking in a mirror where everything is recognisable, although very slightly skewed. This man, this pirate dressed in black – he looked like her. He looked like Rémy.

He didn't even glance in her direction. She watched him stride across the sand, weaving around his carousing shipmates with complete determination. Rémy realised that he was making for Upala. A smile burst across her face as she saw him – the first genuine one Rémy had seen her give in all the hours they had spent together this day. The two pirates walked towards each other and Rémy expected them to embrace, but instead they stopped a pace or so in front of each other, seeming suddenly awkward. Upala dipped her head, nodded and then shrugged at something he said. Then she looked in Rémy's direction, said something and pointed.

The man turned. He looked straight at Rémy with a look sharp enough to pierce stone.

Her heart began to thump as he strode towards her, no trace of surprise on his scarred face. The pirate walked until he stood a hair's breadth away, his face a mirror that Rémy could easily have pressed her nose to.

"Well, well," he said softly. "So here you are at last, Rémy Brunel."

Rémy opened her mouth, but found it impossible to get any sound past the lump that had unexpectedly formed in her throat. In any case, what was she to say? It seemed that this pirate knew her, and of course she should know him, but she did not.

The face before her – so familiar and yet so completely unknown – studied her carefully. The pirate's eyes narrowed slightly.

"My name is Kai," he said, softly. "Do you not even know that, little sister?"

The Reunion

The pirates' celebratory mood continued long into the night. The fire burned brightly, and they danced on the sand in the light of the flames as they roasted fish freshly caught from the ocean for their supper. Rémy sat on the sand beside the pirate captain – her brother, and not only her brother, her true twin. Together they looked out at the shenanigans before them.

Upala had left them to talk, and was now dancing with one of the largest men Rémy had ever seen, even accounting for all her years of travelling with the circus. Rémy glanced at Kai, and saw that her brother's gaze was fixed on the fierce female pirate. Upala had removed her boots and was dancing barefoot with such carefree abandon that it was easy to forget just how fearsome she could look with a sword in her hand and a scowl on her face. Kai watched her with an expression that softened the hardest lines of his face, too, and seeing this Rémy looked away, a slight pang piercing her heart. Kai's regard for Upala was obvious, and it made her think of Thaddeus. She wondered how he and the others were, and wished she were with them. The sooner she could follow their trail, the better. Which meant she shouldn't merely be sitting here, watching this celebration.

"You did not seem surprised to see me," she began, leaning closer to Kai so that her voice carried over the noise of the party.

Kai offered a slight smile, but his gaze remained fixed on the festivities. "Oh, I was surprised – to see you *here*, anyway."

"I never even knew I had a brother," Rémy told him. "Not until a few months ago. But you knew you had a sister, all along?"

The pirate turned to look at her at last, a dark light in his eyes. "I knew about the curse that hangs over our family. I knew what part the raja and that rat Gustave had in it and I knew, yes, I knew, that I was one half of a twin. But life is difficult enough, Rémy, without dwelling on those things you cannot change. If you are waiting for me to apologise for not searching for you, you will wait a long time. I have had hard enough work just keeping myself alive."

Rémy looked away, pained. "That's not what I meant," she said, blinking hard as she stared at the flames. "I just do not understand why you knew when I did not."

Kai leaned forward to pick up a piece of driftwood at his feet and turned it in his hands. "When our parents separated, they took one of us each. Our mother took you. Our father took me."

"And brought you back here? To India?"

Her twin shrugged. "He died before I was old enough to think to ask him why. Maybe he thought he could find a way to lift the curse himself. He always talked of you – you and our mother. He loved you both. They just… could not be together, all the time that the curse was in place. And he never found a way to break it."

"It is broken now," Rémy told him. "You know that, don't you?"

Kai stopped twirling the stick, but he didn't look up. His face took on a frown. "What do you mean?"

"I have a friend. His name is Desai. He is from here, but he has spent many years living in London. The diamond that our parents stole from the raja all those years ago – I found it, Kai. Desai brought it back here, to lift the curse. We are both free."

Kai slowly lifted his head and looked out at the dancers again. The tune had changed, but the music was still just as fast. Upala weaved in and out of the other dancers, laughing as she twisted and turned, her bare feet scattering flurries of sand into the air. Kai's eyes found her in the crowd, as Rémy suspected they always would. "The curse… is *broken*?" he repeated slowly.

"Yes, thanks to Desai."

"He must be a great friend, indeed."

Rémy saw her chance and seized it. "He is. He is a great friend and a great man. At this moment he is trying to save this place from a terrible danger."

Her brother turned to look at her. "A danger? What danger?"

Rémy took a deep breath. "It is called the Sapphire Cutlass. Have you heard of it?"

Kai stared at her from a moment, and then gave a bitter laugh. "Your friend has been selling you fairy stories, little sister. There are far worse dangers here than a fable like the Sapphire Cutlass. Monsters that you, in your soft little circus life, could not possibly imagine."

Rémy prickled at that. "Dangers such as running into a band of marauding pirates, for example?"

Kai shook his head. "We are not the people to fear here – not for good, ordinary folk, in any case. We do what we do to help the people of this country, not to hurt them. The British take everything from these people and give nothing back. They take their land, their crops, their jewels, their sons. What can be more monstrous than that? So the people turn to the person they think can help them – the raja, who is even worse. He forces them to fight against all his enemies in an army that has no firepower, no training – no hope of winning at all."

Rémy thought of the villages that the airship had stopped in before the jewelled man had attacked them – how in many of them there had only been the very young and the very old and the very sick. Suddenly it seemed obvious where the able-bodied had gone, and why the crops had gone untended.

"We take from both sides, and we do what we can to help with what we steal," Kai went on. "So you see, little sister, we have plenty of monsters already without making more up out of children's stories."

"What if it isn't a children's story?" she pressed.

Kai laughed scornfully. "A woman made of sapphire with the power to tear whole armies asunder with her bare hands? How could it be anything but?"

Rémy shrugged. "Some people believe, yes? There is a cult, so Desai told me."

Kai threw the chunk of driftwood away. "So there is, he is right. A cult made of superstitious old men and women with nothing else to do with their time and nothing better to put their faith in."

"Desai says it is more than that – that the cult has been growing, becoming more and more powerful," she said, thinking it better to leave out, at least for the moment, her friend's belief in the supernatural powers of the mountain and its sapphires. "He thinks someone is using the myth of the Sapphire Cutlass as a way to recruit more people."

Her brother looked at her thoughtfully. "Does he now? And what would be the good of that?"

Rémy shrugged. "People will do anything for something they believe in, isn't that right? Terrible things. Bad things. Desai thinks they are preparing for war."

"A war? Who with?"

"He doesn't know, but he thinks it is the raja's mystic, Sahoj, behind it. And if that's the case and the British find out, there will be a war."

Kai raised his hands. "Well then, I say let them fight. If they wipe each other out, so much the better, eh?"

Rémy put her hand on his arm, leaning closer. "Really? You would want that? You would let those people you care so much for be caught in the middle of such a war?"

Her brother set his jaw and did not answer, staring at the
fire with dark eyes.

"I have seen things, Kai. The airship I brought here – it is
nothing compared to the machines of war that I know are out
there. Metal soldiers with no feeling and no heart that can
march for days without food and will fight without mercy;
ships that can sail beneath the water so that no one will see
them coming – powered by the earth itself and by gem stones
like the one that our parents stole, all those years ago. You
don't have to believe me – I can show you the ruby that makes
my ship fly. I have seen things you wouldn't believe, brother,
and they have all led us here, to this place – to the Sapphire
Cutlass. Perhaps the story is just a story, but whatever is
happening in the name of that story should terrify us all."

"And say I were to believe your words, little sister? Say I
were to feel myself as afraid as you – what would you have me
do about it?"

"Help us. The people I travelled here with – good people,
four of them – they are journeying into the valley of the
Sapphire Cutlass as we speak. Come with me – you, and your
pirates. Come with me to find them – to help them, with
whatever they find."

Kai turned to look at her. "Four people?" he said
incredulously. "This man Desai believes you must fight an army
– and he brought only three people with him?"

Rémy looked down at her feet. "He didn't bring us. He was
imprisoned by the raja. We came looking for him and freed him."

"So… these people you brought with you," Kai said. "They are soldiers? Fighters of the first order? Fearsome warriors, able to fell armies as easily as the girl in the story. Yes?"

Rémy shifted uncomfortably on the sand. "Not exactly."

"Oh?" She could feel Kai watching her with sharp eyes. "Tell me, then. Who are they, these people who will defeat a supernatural army?"

Rémy shut her eyes. "One is a policeman. His name is Thaddeus Rec, from London. He is a brave and honourable man who will stop at nothing to do the right thing."

"A policeman," Kai repeated, his voice flat. "Well, I hope you are starting at the bottom and working your way up, Rémy Brunel."

"Then there is J," Rémy went on, her heart sinking at her brother's unimpressed tone, but carrying on regardless. "He is swift and brave – I met him in London, too. He was a pickpocket then, but–"

"A pickpocket?" Kai interrupted her, his disbelief growing further. "This man Desai must be a fool. Who else but a fool would bring other fools with him to a battle?"

"J built the airship," Rémy said. "He built it from nothing but a book of words and scraps he found around Limehouse."

That shut her brother up. His eyebrows rose in surprise and he looked over her head towards the craft sitting silently on the shore.

"Appearances can be deceptive," Rémy told him, "and I would have thought that a pirate, of all people, would know that."

Kai looked at her and grinned, his teeth straight and white apart from a single, black gap where he had lost one. The absence made him look fierce and reckless, and she longed to hear of the life her brother had led. Maybe they would have time, one day, to swap stories – of her life on the road, of his on the ocean.

But not now. She could tell that despite his interest, Kai was far from convinced by her story. She decided not to let on that two of Desai's party were children. Let him find out for himself if he agreed to help. And if he didn't – well, there would be no need for him to know in any case.

"And the final member of your little fighting force?" Kai prompted, as if he could read her thoughts. She wondered briefly if he could, but his question seemed genuine enough.

"Dita," Rémy said, scuffing her toes in the sand. "Small, wiry and quick. She speaks many languages, has a head for heights and is as brave as they come."

Kai looked out at the dancing pirates, once again finding Upala in the crowd. "Could she have a hope of bettering Upala in a fight?"

Rémy smiled privately at the thought of little Dita, who would barely reach Upala's waist, clashing blades with the pirate woman. And yet…

"She would do her best," Rémy told him truthfully, "and she would fight with her whole heart."

Kai nodded. "As Upala does," he said. "As it should be." Her brother sighed. "I admire you and your friends, little sister. It takes courage and spirit to go up against something with so few hands, especially with so little knowledge of what you may encounter."

"Then help us," Rémy urged. "If you truly live your life to help others, help us – and in doing so, help all of India. All of the world, perhaps. Help us before it is too late."

Kai shook his head. "Even if I thought it would make a difference – my people are fighters on water, not on land. On the ocean I can keep them safe, but on land they will be easy prey before we even reach the valley you speak of. Every one of them has a bounty on his head, put there by the British, who will kill them if they are caught. I will not lead them to certain death on the basis of a story," he held up a hand before she could interrupt, "and a story is all you have, Rémy. Can't you see that?"

Rémy was silent for a few minutes. Then she said, "What if I gave you the airship?"

Kai looked surprised. "What?"

"Help us, and afterwards, I will give you the airship. That would give you an advantage over the British, would it not?"

The pirate threw back his head and laughed. "Oh, little sister – look around you. If I wanted your ship, I could take it from you in a flat second."

"But you wouldn't now how to fly it," Rémy countered. "Help us, Kai, and when it's over I'll give you the airship – and I will teach you how to use it, too. You have my word."

Kai looked at her as if he were sizing up the truth of her statement. "And what about this J, who built it? Won't he be rather upset that you've given away his contraption?"

"Desai sent me to find you, Kai. I see that now. He knows we need your help. J will understand if it is the only way to secure it."

Kai looked over to the airship, rubbing his chin thoughtfully. He stood up, and Rémy followed as he crossed to where it waited patiently in the sand.

Her brother ran his hands over the wood of the hull, and she could tell he was interested. What pirate wouldn't be? To be able to attack from the air – it would make Kai the undisputed king of the ocean.

Rémy heard a noise behind her and turned to see Upala approaching, her dark cheeks flushed pink from dancing. She stopped beside Rémy and put her hands on her hips, watching Kai as she caught her breath.

"What are you thinking?" she asked him, over the noise of the party continuing behind them.

"That this would give us the advantage we so desperately need," Kai said, as he continued to contemplate the airship.

Upala nodded, crossing her arms. "Then it's fortunate we have the *anukarana* to teach us how to use it."

"I'll teach you, if you help me," Rémy said firmly.

"Help you do what?" Upala asked, looking between the twins suspiciously.

Kai turned and walked back towards them. "Upala. You and the rest of the crew take the ship back to our safe harbour. I'll join you there – with the airship – when I can."

"Why?" Upala asked. "Where are you going?"

"To see whether what my sister had told me about the Sapphire Cutlass is true."

"I believe it is," said Rémy, "and if it is we need more help than just you, Kai."

"Well, I am all you're getting, little sister. I'll not drag anyone else along for what could be a one-way trip."

"You're going with her?" Upala looked appalled. "It could be a trap!"

"Yes," agreed Kai, watching Rémy steadily, "it could be. But somehow I don't think so. Or if it is, it's not one set by her. So I will go with her and find out."

Rémy held her brother's gaze, feeling her heart flood with relief. It wasn't what Desai had been hoping for, she was sure of that – one extra pair of hands against whatever they would have to face. But it was better than nothing – and if they could be on their way immediately, then so much the better.

By now the rest of the pirates had realised that something was afoot. The music and dancing had stopped, and Kai's crew had formed a semi-circle around them, quietly watching what was going on.

"I'm coming with you," Upala declared. "I will not let you go alone."

"It'll be safer if you–"

"Safer!" Upala scoffed, cutting him off. "What do I care about staying safe?"

"I care," Kai told her, the quiet, clipped words seeming to kill all other noise around them save for the crackle of the fire. The two pirates stared at each other, and Rémy realised that something significant had happened in that one, small moment. She had assumed they were a couple, but perhaps she was wrong. She remembered, then, her brother's reaction when he'd learned they were no longer cursed. Had he been holding back? Had he kept his distance from Upala because he knew about the curse?

"I am coming with you, Kai," Upala said, into the quiet. "If you don't let me travel with you, I will follow on foot. Do you understand?"

"If we are going to go at all," Rémy said, into another silence. "Then we should go now."

Inside the Mountain

He was on a trapeze, and he didn't like it.

Thaddeus could feel himself swinging in mid-air – back and forth, back and forth – but around him was only darkness. He couldn't see the ground, or even the contraption that was holding him up. He felt queasy and wrong, but he didn't know how to stop the swinging. Back and forth, back and forth…

Thaddeus!

A voice soared to him out of the darkness. He had heard it before, he realised as he heard it again, but it was further away this time. Or perhaps he was the one that had been further away – perhaps they were both on a trapeze.

Thaddeus!

Who did he know that would be comfortable on a trapeze?

Thaddeus!

Rémy Brunel! It could only be her up here, swinging with him in the darkness. Wherever 'here' was – at the moment he couldn't tell, because everything was so dark, and the trapeze just would not stop moving… He tried to twist around and see what was behind him, but in doing so, he almost slipped from the swing completely. He flailed with his arms, clutching at anything he could. His hands found cold, hard rungs and he held on.

"Thaddeus!"

The voice shouting at him suddenly got much louder. Thaddeus frowned. It wasn't Rémy after all. It was–

"Mr Rec! Would you please just bleedin' well WAKE UP!"

J!

Thaddeus jerked awake and immediately wished he hadn't. Pain smashed into his temple as if someone had cracked it hard with a rock. He clutched his head, wondering for a split second if he'd been in The Grapes the previous night, before remembering that he hadn't been at the Limehouse drinking spot for months.

"Thaddeus!"

"All right, all right," he mumbled back, "I'm awake, I'm–"

He turned around, and slipped, falling. He cried out before something abruptly broke his fall a second later, or rather, two somethings that were part of a larger something altogether. Thaddeus blinked, trying to clear his head enough to focus. He could feel his legs dangling into thin air, and there was that infernal swinging again – back and forth, back and forth – through chilled air.

Even with his eyes open, it was dark, although not quite as dark as it had been in his dream. There was a faint light coming from somewhere – yellow, like a burning torch. It gave enough of a glow to show him where he had fetched up.

Thaddeus Rec was in a cage.

"What the–"

"Are you all right?" he heard Dita's voice call, from behind him. Thaddeus turned his head and saw that she was in a cage, too, hanging beside him, her small hands clutching at the golden bars that imprisoned her as she stared anxiously at him.

"Thaddeus? Are you hurt?" That was Desai, on the other side of him, in another cage, peering through the dim light and the obstruction of yet another barred prison, this one holding J.

Thaddeus looked down at himself, still dazed from the pain of whatever blow his head had encountered. His legs had fallen between two of the rungs of his prison and he was dangling out of the bottom of it – their cages were suspended, apparently hanging above the ground, which he could not see through the darkness.

He struggled, pulling himself up and balancing his feet on two of the rungs – crouching, as the others were. It wasn't comfortable, but then presumably whoever had built the cages hadn't been very concerned about the comfort of their prisoners. They hung there in a line: Desai, then Dita, then J, then Thaddeus, in four cages each just large enough to hold a person, cubes made of golden bars not quite far enough apart for agile little Dita to squeeze between them. Thaddeus looked up to see that the roof of his cage bore a hatch, and beside the hatch was a sturdy ring, through which had been threaded a hook, and from this hook led a chain as thick as Thaddeus' arm. It led up to a large metal track set in the roof of the cavern that stretched away into the gloom around them. It instantly reminded Thaddeus of what they had found in the Comte de Cantal's mountain catacombs.

"Where – where are we?" he managed, his voice rasping. His mouth felt as dry and dusty as the floorboards of the professor's workshop.

"Where'd you fink?" J asked. "Looks like it didn't turn out to be as 'ard to get into the ruddy mountain as Mr Desai thought it were going to be, eh?"

Thaddeus put a hand to his head as he looked up again. The throbbing was diminishing a little, but he'd give his best trousers for a cool glass of water.

"Are the rest of you all right?" he asked. "None of you are hurt?"

"It looks as if you got the worst of it, my boy," said Desai.

Thaddeus looked around again, trying to see where they were. Their voices echoed as they spoke, he noticed – wherever it was that they had ended up, it was large.

"Have you shouted for anyone?"

"Other than you, you mean?" J asked. "Yeah, we've shouted. Nuffin doin'. No one's come to see us at all since they stuck us in 'ere. But I suppose they don't need to, do they? Not seeing as there's no way any of us can get out."

Thaddeus looked up at the roof of the cage again.

"Makes you wish Rémy were here, don't it?" J added. "She'd be up there picking that lock in no time. As it is, none of the rest of us can manage it."

"I have tried," Dita said softly. "I'll keep trying, but I'm just not as good as Rémy is."

"Don't you worry, Miss," J soothed. "It ain't your fault. No one is, are they?"

Thaddeus looked over at Desai, whose face he could only just make out in the darkness pressing in on them. "Any ideas, Desai?" he asked. "You haven't got… I don't know, anything hidden in those robes of yours that might get us out of here?" Several times in the past Desai had surprised them all by producing potions capable of amazing feats – the ability to melt metal being one of them.

Desai shook his head. "My apologies, Thaddeus. After so many weeks in captivity at the raja's behest, I am afraid my supplies have been well and truly plundered."

Thaddeus nodded slowly, and then wished he hadn't. He shut his eyes briefly, trying to close out the pain, but doing so just made him more aware of the gentle swing of the cage. J was right – Rémy would be in her element here. Little Bird, the girl who could fly without wings, and that no cage had yet managed to enclose – at least, not for long.

"All right," he said. "Well, let's look at this rationally and see what we can come up with. It's reasonable to assume that we're still inside the valley, isn't it? And we've most likely been taken by the Sapphire Cutlass. Which means we're probably inside the mountain – in the mines themselves. Yes?"

"I would say that is a reasonable deduction," agreed Desai.

"Fat lot of good that does us," J muttered loudly.

"J," Thaddeus sighed. "Look – I know you're angry, but–"

"Damn right I'm angry!" J burst out, his knuckles white where his hands gripped the rungs. "I told yer – didn't I? I said we should turn back, and now look where we've ended up! You can be rational all you like, Mr Rec, but we ain't getting ourselves out of 'ere in a hurry, are we? We're stuck, and gawd only knows what the people who put us in 'ere 'ave got planned fer us!"

"J," cried Dita, "don't say that!"

J looked past Thaddeus to the girl, his face softening. "Sorry," he said. "Sorry. We'll be all right. Course we will. It's just…"

A noise swelled below them, quiet at first, but growing. Thaddeus felt the hairs rise on the back of his neck as he realised what it was. It was voices, chanting – the same chant that had surrounded them out on the fogged valley floor was rising to them again from somewhere below their cages, a collective murmur growing louder and louder, the sound of too many voices to count united in one repeated mantra.

"Where the bleedin' 'eck 'ave they come from?" J cried. "'Ave they been down there all along, just being really quiet, like?"

For some reason, the thought made Thaddeus shiver. Then, somewhere off to his distant right, there came a noise like the sound of a giant match being struck: a harsh rasp, a fizz as a new flame added more light to the darkness. They all scrambled to the other side of their cages, stepping clumsily from one rung to another, careful not to slip into the spaces between as the motion jerked and shuddered their dangling prisons.

A large wooden torch had been lit. It burned brightly in the darkness, illuminating a yellow circle around itself. It had been pinned to hewn grey stone above a narrow walkway cut from more of the same rock. Another torch was lit further along the same wall, and then another and another, tracing a route that circled where Thaddeus and his friends hung in their cages.

"If we ever get out of here," came J's plaintive voice, as their surroundings slowly came into view, "I ain't never going anywhere near a mountain again. You hear me? Not a mountain, not a cave, not an underground bleedin' tunnel. Never again. I's seen enough of 'em to last me five lifetimes!"

They were in a large cavern. J was right – it could have been Lord Abernathy's submarine base beneath London, or the one housing the Comte de Cantal's metal army in France. It made sense, Thaddeus supposed. If one were drawn to nefarious deeds, it was natural to find somewhere such as this to hide them. Although, he reflected for a moment, there was nothing natural about any of the things they had found in such places. He felt exactly as J did – that if they made it out of this particular predicament, he had had enough of dark places to last him a lifetime. Give him sun, blue sky and a beach that stretched for as far as the eye could see…

If they got out of here. Which, as he looked around, Thaddeus realised would be nigh-on impossible.

The cavern was a rough oval shape, so large that even with the torches burning their brightest, there were parts of it that were still in darkness. Into its walls had been hewn huge, curved alcoves – eight in total, Thaddeus counted – and in each alcove stood a massive, intricately carved statue. Each one of the huge stone figures depicted the same woman, her face contorted into a terrifying grimace of abject rage. Her fingers bore talons instead of nails, and around her feet wove stone snakes. The carving was so detailed that despite her inhuman size, Thaddeus could almost believe that at any moment, the carved woman would step out of her resting place.

The cages in which Thaddeus and the others were trapped hung from large iron hooks in the ceiling, giving him a good view of the whole place. Thaddeus looked around carefully, fixing it in his mind as he searched for a way out. The cavern was on four levels. Below them was a pit, its depths hidden from view by shadows. This pit had been carved beside a raised stone stage that formed one end of the cavern. A narrow channel had been sunk into the raised rock, leading from near the front of the stage and disappearing back through an archway in the cavern wall at its rear. Opposite where the prisoners swung, at the far side of the stage, a wide, sloping stone path led up to another archway that stood between two of the massive statues.

Squinting through the flickering gloom, Thaddeus realised that the chains from which their cages dangled fed through the hoop above them and ran across the cavern's ceiling to a winch beside this archway. The winch meant that the cages could be raised or lowered, so if they wanted to get down safely, that was what they needed to reach.

From the mouth of this smaller arch, a narrow ledge circled the cavern, where the burning torches had been lit to flicker at the feet of the huge statues. Thaddeus turned awkwardly, following where it went, and saw, at the opposite end of the cave, another smaller entrance with a narrower sloping path. This path led down to the cavern's main level.

Thaddeus finally let his eyes drop to what filled the space between them and any hope of freedom. Arranged in tight rows that edged the pit and stretched from one side of the cavern to the other were hundreds of people. They all stood, chanting, swaying slightly as if in some kind of trance as they stared wild-eyed at Thaddeus, J, Dita and Desai. Their faces were the fearsome ghosts that had circled them in the mists: black around the sockets of their eyes, white in the hollows of their cheeks. The men were naked to the waist, wearing loose trousers in a pale, shimmering blue. Each wore a belt that seemed as if it were made of metal that encased his hips and stomach like armour, and into each of these was mounted the sheath of a curved, wide-bladed sword. On these men's chests was a tattoo – a cutlass just like the ones they carried in their belts, crossing over the left nipple where a hard blue stone glittered as it reflected the light of the burning torches. Their arms, all as thick and strong as tree-trunks, were clad in impenetrable armour right up to the elbows.

The women – there were as many as there were men – were clad in armoured breast-plates and wore the same trousers. They too had swords, and each of them bore a tattoo on her left arm, the sapphires glinting and winking, blinding Thaddeus with a thousand pinpricks of starlight until he felt utterly mesmerised by the sight.

The cult of the Sapphire Cutlass.

Eighteen

A Journey by Night

The airship scythed through the night, passing swiftly over the dark landscape like a cloud pushed by the winds of a storm. Rémy was impressed with how easily Kai and Upala had become comfortable with the motion of the craft in the air, but then they spent most of their time bobbing up and down in a ship on the ocean. Perhaps, after all, sailing through the air did not feel so very different.

Upala, apparently too restless to sit down, roamed about the cabin, opening cupboards and sifting through what she found there. Kai sat up front beside Rémy. He seemed to be fascinated with the airship's controls, watching closely as she made each adjustment. She wondered whether her brother had half a mind to learn its workings on his own so that he could discard her without keeping to their bargain, but she tried to push the thought away. After all, if you couldn't trust your own kin, who could you trust? And, advisable or not, she couldn't help but want to trust Kai. There was something about him Rémy had warmed to, despite his splinter-sharp glances and occasionally harsh tones. Here on the airship, for example, he was more of a boy than a bloodthirsty pirate, simply fascinated by everything around him. It made Rémy wish even more than she already did that she'd known him as they had both grown up.

"So, Rémy Brunel," Kai said, leaning back in his chair and crooking one leg to rest his foot on the edge of the control panel. "How did you end up travelling the world with a policeman instead of a circus?"

Rémy smiled. "Thaddeus isn't a policeman any more."

Her brother raised his eyebrows. "Even so. A thief and a man of the law? Seems a union most would think unlikely to succeed."

She lifted her chin, staring out into the darkness. "I'm not a thief."

Kai leaned forward to look at her more closely, elbow on his knee. "Perhaps not *now*," he said, "but I still remember the stories of the circus our father told me as a child. No one could work under that cur Gustave for so long without being put to work."

Rémy grimaced. "Well. That was a long time ago."

Kai leaned back again with a shrug. "Perhaps. So. This Thaddeus Rec. You trust him?"

"With my life."

"It's not your life I'm concerned about. It's your freedom. And mine. I'm a wanted man, little sister. How do I know this isn't some trap to finally put me into the hands of the British?"

"If you really thought that, you wouldn't be here," Rémy retorted.

"Perhaps I like a challenge?"

"Thaddeus is *not* working for the British."

"So he's come all of the way here to India to search out an evil that may or may not exist, simply out of the goodness of his heart?"

Rémy leaned forward to make an adjustment to their heading, feeling her brother's piercing gaze on her back. "He came because he knew it was the right thing to do. And... because I asked him to."

"Ahh," Kai said. "Now we reach the crux of it. Did you lure him away from his good principles, little sister?"

"Thaddeus would never abandon his principles," Rémy retorted. "He is too good a man for that."

Kai raised an eyebrow. "Is that so. How did you two meet?"

Rémy didn't say anything for a moment, and then was forced to admit, "He was trying to protect a jewel that I was trying to steal."

Kai laughed softly. "And yet here you are, little sister. Free as a bird."

"I helped him return it, in the end, and I haven't stolen anything since." Rémy turned and looked at him. "I will never steal anything again, because of him. I will never *want* to steal anything again, *because of him*. Which actually makes him a rather good policeman, don't you think?"

They stared at each other for a moment. Rémy detected something in Kai's eyes, just a for a moment – something like a flash of sadness that was there for no more than a second before melting beneath a wolfish smile.

There was a clatter behind them. Rémy turned to see that Upala had wrenched most of their meagre belongings out on to the floor.

"What are you looking for?" she exclaimed. "We don't have anything worth stealing, you know."

Upala made a scornful noise in her throat and kicked a pile of clothes out of her way. "I do not want your rags," she growled. "We need weapons! Where are your *weapons?*"

"We don't have any. We can't afford them."

"Agh!" Upala threw up her arms in exasperation. "Well, don't expect me to give you one of my swords," she said. "You can use those little hands and feet of yours, for all I care, *anukarana!*" With that, Upala threw herself down on one of the small bunks at the back of the cabin, her arms crossed dramatically over her face.

Rémy turned to look at Kai, who was watching Upala with another grin on his face.

"I wish she wouldn't call me that," Rémy said quietly.

Kai flicked her a glance, accompanied by a slight shrug. "It is as close to a term of endearment you can expect from Upala."

"Oh?" Rémy said. "In that case, what does she call you? 'The Ugly Real One'?

Kai threw back his head and laughed. "Perhaps she should, at that."

Rémy couldn't help but smile at her brother's laughing face. "And you two?" she asked, a moment later. "How did you two meet?"

Kai spun back to the control panel, looking out into the darkness as his smile faded. "I found her in the wreckage of a village plundered by the raja's men," he said. "She'd never held a sword before that day. She picked one up and fought like a tiger, but still she couldn't save her family or her friends. She stood in a ring of blood and bodies, some the raja's men, the rest the people she loved. She thought we were there to take more from her, and she would have killed us too. I asked her to join us instead. That was four years ago. She's been with us ever since, and that tiger has never left her, not in all that time." He lifted one hand to his temple, rubbing at an imaginary spot there. "I don't think it ever will. She is all tiger now. She is all terror."

"Not all," Rémy observed. "I have seen the way she looks at you."

She saw a brief flash of red colouring her brother's neck as he glanced at her from the corner of his eye. "Don't let her hear you say that," he advised. "She'd have your guts for garters. Besides, there is no time in the life of a pirate for that kind of nonsense."

Rémy was about to point out that you have to make time for such things, when something loomed out of the darkness ahead of them. It was the huge, jutting rock promontory where the airship and her original occupants had stopped for the night.

"We are not far away now," she said, leaning forward as they flew over the outcrop. "We will reach the valley soon enough."

Kai leaned forward alongside her, cursing under his breath at the night outside. "When I meet your friend J, I shall ask him why he did not put lights on the outside of this thing."

Rémy grinned. "Ach," she said, "where's your sense of adventure, big brother?"

He glanced at her, amused. "I am saving it for when I need it most."

Rémy's smile faded as she banked the airship and headed for the valley, which even in the darkness surrounding them, showed up like a slash of deeper black on their horizon. At its head, the mountain pricked the night sky, its jagged, rocky edges as immortal as the legend that told of its creation.

"When I left the others, I landed outside the valley for fear of alerting its inhabitants," Rémy told Kai, "but now…"

Kai nodded at her unspoken words. "Now, speed is our best advantage, not secrecy. Perhaps you are right. And perhaps the night will conceal us for long enough to land."

"Assuming," came Upala's dry voice, speaking so unexpectedly close to Rémy's ear that it made her jump, "that we can see well enough to find a spot to land."

Upala has crossed the cabin floor in complete silence, and Rémy found herself wishing for that kind of stealth. "I will do my best," she muttered, as the valley edge grew ever closer.

The pirate woman dropped something small but heavy into Rémy's lap. It was the little axe that usually hung beside the ramp to sever the airship's guide ropes. "It is not a sword," Upala shrugged. "But it is better than nothing. Stick it into that belt of yours, *anukarana*."

Rémy did as she was told, taking her eyes off the controls for a moment as she slipped the axe into her utility belt. When she looked back up at the darkness again, something caught her eye.

"What's that?" she asked, pointing.

Through the window, moving from the west, was a line of yellow lights. They were headed for the valley, just as the airship was – a procession of flaming torches, moving as if they were being carried on horseback.

Kai stood and leaned over the controls, peering out to get a better look. "Soldiers, perhaps?" he asked. "The raja's men?"

Rémy bit her lip. "They did follow us when we fled the palace. He wanted the airship."

Kai looked at her over his shoulder with a frown. "Well, he's not getting it. It's mine."

"Don't worry," Rémy told him. "They can't reach us up here, and we'll be far ahead of them by the time we land."

Kai still seemed troubled, watching the progress of the lights as they wove through the jungle. Rémy stayed on course for the valley, noting that a thick fog seemed to be lying amid the trees enclosed within its walls. Upala leaned close to her.

"You think you will be able to find somewhere to land in all that?" she asked. "You had better be good at this flying thing, eh, *anukarana*?"

"I will try my best," said Rémy.

"Your best may not be good enough. Perhaps we should set down outside the valley and walk in. If we don't, we risk damaging the ship – and ourselves – on the trees as we come down."

"If we land before we get to the valley those men down there will find us, or the ship, or both," Rémy pointed out. "Better that we fly into the valley. The fog is a good thing. It'll hide us. And that is what we want, yes? To get as close to the mountain without being seen?"

Upala turned to Kai. "Captain? What do you think? Land here, or land there, in the fog?"

Kai turned, a frown on his face. He was about to speak when, behind him, a light arched into the frame of the darkened window behind him. It burst towards them in a shooting star of flickering yellow flame.

"*Mon dieu!*" Rémy cursed, wrenching the airship's control around, trying to pull it out of the way. Kai and Upala stumbled against each other as the ship jerked and bucked. "They are shooting at us!"

The men below were firing at them with burning arrows. Another lit the night sky, curving past briefly illuminated trees and hurtling towards the airship like man-made comets.

"I thought you said the raja wanted the airship!" Kai shouted, gripping the back of the chair as Rémy swung them this way and that. "Why would he try to destroy it?"

"Perhaps these are not the raja's men after all! Or perhaps he has changed his mind. Whoever they are, they want us to burn," shouted Rémy, as the night sky lit up with a myriad of burning arrows. "I cannot dodge them all – there are too many!"

"Bring her down," Kai ordered, his voice shaking as the airship juddered with the effort of avoiding the flames. "Get us out of the air!"

Rémy gritted her teeth and put the airship into a fast plunge. They were nearing the valley's edge and she aimed straight at the fog beyond – if they could reach it and land, there was still a hope that the men pursuing them might not be able to find them there.

The ground came up fast, the darkness giving way to a dense floor of treetops, cut asunder by the valley's sharp edges.

"We'll make it," Kai hissed. "Just a few metres more…"

Something hit the glass in front of them – a bulge of flame that glanced off the hard surface and spun away, back into the night. For a second Rémy was relieved – that was the closest any of the arrows had come and it wasn't close enough – but then a light bloomed, bright as day against the hull.

"What is it?" she cried, fighting to hold the airship steady in her swift descent. "Are we burning?"

Kai lunged forward, trying to see out of the window as the glow grew. "It's the ropes holding the balloon," he told her, "That last arrow must have lit them. They're going up like fuses!"

There came a vicious jolt that pulled the airship to one side. Rémy felt the control lever under her hand slacken, spinning uselessly against her hand. The ground was coming up, faster and faster, and she could hear the flames now, roaring in their wake as they ate more and more of the hull.

They were a comet, burning across the sky. They were a meteorite, plummeting to earth.

Taken by Spirits

The airship caught the top of a tree, branches cracking and crunching as they broke and scraped against the underside of the burning hull. There was a roar, a rushing bellow of movement from above, and Rémy knew the flames had reached the balloon.

"We have to get out!" she screamed to Kai and Upala, even as the ship careened onwards, smashing over the top of another tree, the glow from the inferno they carried turning the dense, rising fog they rode into a strange kaleidoscope of refracting colours.

"We're still too high! If we jump now we'll die," Kai shouted.

"If we don't jump, we'll burn!" she shouted back over the noise of the airship tearing itself apart around them. Lurching out of her chair, Rémy wrestled her way across the bucking floor towards the hatch. "Help me!"

Upala was by her side in an instant, wrenching on the wound ropes that held the hatch shut. Kai made his way towards them, stumbling to his knees as another tree slowed their troubled descent by smashing itself against the airship's nose. The window shattered, shards of glass piercing the air along with a wash of fierce heat.

Rémy pulled at the ropes, ignoring the slicing pain as the glass splinters peppered her back. Upala turned away, hiding her face from the worst of the shards, but Kai caught one full in the cheek, a nasty blow that opened a fresh wound on his scarred face.

The hatch came open, flinging itself away from them as if in a fury all of its own. It tore itself from its hinges, smashing against another tree top, catching against the branches and wrenching itself loose from the hull. The airship followed, twisting around as it lost another part of itself.

The crackle of flame burst from behind them anew, and Rémy turned her head to see fire seeping through the walls as the planks burned through.

"Go," she shouted to Kai and Upala. "We have to go now! Go!"

Upala leapt, disappearing into the smoke and fog swirling outside just a second before Kai followed her.

Rémy battled her way across the airship's heaving floor, clinging to the doorframe as the craft bucked and juddered. Its bones were showing now, the planks fracturing, separating, turning to cinders. Rémy thought about the ruby, still in its mooring, but it would have to rest in the ashes, for she'd never be able to reach it without burning herself alive. Outside the fog was so thick it was impossible to tell how far she would have to jump.

The airship smashed into another tree, groaning as if it were in pain, and the cabin split in two.

Rémy jumped.

The fog swallowed her whole, cold and cloying as if she had leapt into a roiling ocean. She tried not to tense up – the only way to survive a plunge from the wire was to let every muscle and bone relax – but not knowing how far she had to fall made that difficult. Branches hit her first, scratching at her face and legs, but mercifully slowing her down.

And then, the ground.

She crumpled, ankles folding to her knees, knees folding to her hips, arms just managing to stop her head smashing hard against the earth. The breath was knocked from her lungs as surely as if she'd been punched in the stomach. Rémy lay on her back, staring up into a mess of swirling grey, lit from above by the flames of the dying airship. They bloomed yellow and orange and red like a sinking summer sun, the colours diffusing through the mist until it felt as if they filled the sky.

Winded and unsure of how badly she'd been hurt, Rémy realised she had to move. The airship was disintegrating above her, raining fire through the fog. A clod of burning plank thudded into the ground just inches from her head. She dragged herself up, feeling a sharp pain in her ankle but ignoring it. Rémy pushed through the mist, stumbling into tree after tree, blind in the grey-white gloom.

"Kai?" she shouted, crunching into yet another tree. "Upala?"

Her voice seemed to echo against the thick mist. Something brushed against her – not a branch, this time. Something else. A hand? She spun, trying to follow the movement, but it disappeared before she could fix on it.

"Kai?" she shouted, again. "Are you there? Upala, can you hear me?"

A hand clamped over her mouth from behind. She was dragged to the ground, falling against somebody who held her firmly from behind.

"Ssh," hissed a woman's voice, into Rémy's ear. "Be quiet, *anukaruna*. They will hear."

Upala! Rémy struggled against the pirate's hand until the woman let her go. Rémy scrambled away, turning to face her. Upala held a finger up to her lips and then moved the same hand in a circling motion, indicating the fog around them.

"They are out there," she said quietly. "They are coming for us. They took Kai."

"What? Who? Where–"

A look of irritation flashed across the pirate's face. She leaned forward and clamped her hand over Rémy's mouth, eyes flashing fire as surely as the airship through the fog. Then she froze.

For a second neither woman moved at all, until Upala slowly turned her head. Rémy followed her motion with her eyes, and saw a movement through the gloom, illuminated by the flames from the still-burning airship. It was barely there – a hint of a shape through the mist, the lithe movement of limbs disappearing into the fog. Upala looked back at her, then removed her hand.

"I saw them take Kai," she mouthed, her voice barely there. "One moment he was beside me as we looked for you, the next…" she flicked her fingers. "We will be next."

Rémy glanced around, detecting more shapes in the mist. And was that a face, there, in the shadows? She reached for the axe and found it gone. It must have slipped from her belt as she fell. Rémy, dismayed, looked at the ground around her feet in case it was there – without the axe she was entirely defenceless. There was nothing. It was gone.

The shapes crowded towards them, closer and closer. There were so many of them, too many to fight, but that wouldn't stop Rémy trying. She'd be damned before they took her too easily. She pushed herself slowly to her feet, feeling Upala move with her and hearing the sound of metal sliding against metal as the pirate drew both her swords. A second later Rémy felt something brush against her right hand. She jerked her fingers away, imagining a creature from the mist grasping at them.

"Take it," Upala hissed.

Rémy looked down to see the woman's hand outstretched, holding out the same blade she had offered her on the beach.

"We will fight them together. Yes, *anukaruna*?"

Rémy didn't need telling twice. She grasped the hilt of Upala's sword. "Yes," she said. "Together."

166

"Back to back," Upala murmured, turning slowly so that their shoulders were touching. "Keep your head up. Do not let them see your fear. Understand?"

The light from the airship was dimming, but even so it was enough to let the two women see what was coming for them. There were figures in the mist, many of them, a circle of bodies joining around them, layer upon layer of them all slowly moving forward. Rémy's heart beat hard – even with Upala's sword in her hand she could see no way of fighting off so many attackers.

Then, above the crackle and spit of the airship's dying throes, another sound grew into the air. At first Rémy thought it was just her heart, beating so hard and so fast that it had set the air alight. But the beat slowly grew: *louder, faster, louder and faster.*

Drums. It was the sound of drums.

The sound thundered through the forest, echoing between the trees and glancing off the mist. At the sound of them, the figures in the mist began to slink away. It was hard to tell at first, so hidden were they by the fog, but one by one, they vanished like wraiths into the forest.

"They've gone," Rémy said, speaking over the sound of the drums.

"Yes," agreed Upala. "But where?"

The two women turned to look at each other, listening to the sound. It felt as if it were beating through them, vibrating the very ground on which they stood, filling their veins as surely as any rhythmic chant.

"They were following that noise," Rémy said. "The drums were calling them somewhere. *To* somewhere."

Upala nodded, her eyes glittering. "Then we must follow. Don't you think?"

Rémy nodded. "Yes," she said. "I do think."

They took off through the trees, staying close to one another and allowing the beat of the drums to pull their blood in its direction.

Desperate Times

Over the sound of the incessant drone of chanting came
another noise: the clang and rattle of metal. Thaddeus turned
to see that down on the stone ramp below them, another cage
was being readied for use. There came another shout: angry,
indignant. A ripple of movement was passing through the
rows of swaying cult members – someone was being dragged,
kicking and fighting, to the cage. That someone had short dark
hair and was dressed all in black. Thaddeus stared hard.

The new prisoner fought hard, but whoever it was seemed
to be hampered by an injured leg. In the end, the cult was too
strong – four grabbed an arm and a leg each. They carried the
struggling figure the rest of the way to the cage and threw it
inside. The cage was immediately winched into the air, jerking
the prisoner around inside with each pull as it gradually rose to
meet the others.

"'Ere," said J, "is that Rémy? 'As she got 'erself caught 'an all?'"

Thaddeus had been wondering the same thing, but as the prisoner drew nearer he saw that though the incarcerated may be a Brunel, it definitely wasn't Rémy.

The cage slid into place beside the rest of them. It could have been Rémy, Thaddeus thought. It was most certainly her twin. The man swinging beside them would have been her mirror image if not for the square stubbled jaw and the faint scars criss-crossing his weather-beaten face. He was bleeding from a shallow cut on his dirt-smeared cheek and his trousers were ripped, showing a nastier gash in his thigh. Breathing hard, the prisoner got gingerly to his feet and looked at them each in turn. Then he shook his head and busied himself by tearing a strip of cloth from his ruined trousers and using it to bind his wound.

"An old man, two children and a sunburned, threadbare vagabond," he said, with a bark of unimpressed laughter. "I should have known."

"Who are you?" Thaddeus asked

The man finished tying his bandage and put his hands on his hips. "Can't you tell, Thaddeus Rec?"

"You must be Rémy's brother," Thaddeus replied, "but beyond that you have the advantage over me, Mr...?"

The man stared back at him with eyes that were disturbingly similar to Rémy's. "Kai," he said. "My name is Kai."

"Where is she?"

Kai glanced around with narrowed eyes, taking in the room. "On her way here, I would think."

"As a prisoner? Or free?"

Kai's eyes met his again. "That's to be determined. For our sakes we'd better hope that both she and Upala are still the latter."

"Upala?" It was Desai who asked the question, this time.

Kai flicked his glance towards Desai with a serious look on his face. "Upala. She's a gem, that one. If they're both still free, then we may have a chance."

"Wot about the airship?" J piped up. "Is she bringing that, too? I 'ave a feelin' we ain't getting' out of 'ere without it."

Kai looked at him seriously. "You're J," he said. "She told me you built it. Was she lying?"

J puffed his chest out, scowling. "No, she ain't lying. I got it to work."

Rémy's twin smiled. "I'm impressed." Then his smile faded. "I'm also sorry to report that the airship is no more. We were brought down by fools with flaming arrows. The very last of it is probably still burning out there now."

J's face turned pale and his shoulders slumped. "Burned?"

"Aye. We came in like a sack of rice hurled from a cargo ship. We're lucky any of us survived the crash at all."

"But – but you all did?" Thaddeus asked, fear curling like smoke around his heart. "Rémy wasn't hurt?"

Kai looked at him thoughtfully. "Actually, now you come to mention it… I didn't see Rémy leap from the ship. But surely you know by now that she has more lives than a cat?" He grinned. "She and I, we both do. She'll have made it."

Thaddeus rubbed a hand over his face, trying to swallow his

distress. He felt Kai's curious eyes on him, but Thaddeus didn't meet his gaze again. A moment later, Kai turned his attention to Desai.

"So you are the one who filled their ears with children's stories, are you?"

Desai raised an eyebrow at the implied accusation and then lifted one arm and swept it out to indicate the rows of swaying cult members below them. "Children's story or not, I would say my prediction of trouble was accurate, wouldn't you, Mr Kai?"

Kai followed his gesture and narrowed his eyes again. "It's just Kai," he said. "I'm no English *gentleman* and I won't be treated as such." He thrust his chin at the men and women below. "That armour. Its not just armour, is it? There's something... strange about it."

Thaddeus had to agree. "I think it's grafted to their bodies," he said, pushing his worries about Rémy to one side. "Look at where the rivets have been placed at their joints. I don't think they can take it off."

"What's the good o' that, then?" J asked. "Won't their skin just be all manky underneath, like? Why wouldn't they want to take it off?"

Thaddeus didn't have an answer for that, except... "We saw something similar in France. And in England, come to think of it. Mechanical soldiers."

"But these ain't mechanical," J reasoned. "They's people. Ain't they?"

"Maybe they are at the moment." Thaddeus looked up at Desai with a frown. "But maybe they won't be for long."

Desai's face was serious as he nodded thoughtfully. "There is alchemy that can turn men to stone," he said, "but as for turning them into metal…"

"Why turn men into metal," Kai asked, still looking out at the mass of people below, "when you can simply cover them in it?"

"Metal men have no thoughts of their own," Thaddeus pointed out. "They'll do whatever they're ordered to, however terrible the order. They are automatons."

Kai looked down at the chanting army below with a shrug. "Are you trying to tell me that they won't obey any command they are given?" he said scornfully. "Whatever minds of their own they once had are long gone. They are already automatons, Thaddeus Rec. And I bet real people are a damned sight cheaper to find than metal men."

"Then whose command are they taking?" Thaddeus wondered. "They look like worshippers, not like soldiers. Desai, I've been thinking, and if you're still telling me this is all for the raja and his mystic… I don't think I believe it. Not now I've seen them."

Desai smiled at him thinly. "Ever the detective, Thaddeus Rec. I confess, I was thinking the same thing."

"Well, what then?" Dita's voice made them all look towards her. She was pale, her face fearful. "What is happening here? And what are they," she nodded in the direction of the people below, "going to do with us?"

The rest of them had no answer for that. No good one, anyway. Below them, the dull droning of the chant went on and on. It felt like a drug, flooding Thaddeus' mind until he couldn't even think clearly.

"Well, there's no sense waiting around to find out," Kai said, his voice cutting through the fog of noise around them. "We've got to find a way out of here."

As they watched, he climbed quickly and easily to the top of his cage. Thaddeus was reminded of Rémy again – Kai was almost as graceful in his movements as his sister. He shook the hatch at the top of the cage, but to no avail – it was locked fast.

"Anyone got something I can pick this lock with?" Kai called down to them. "I suppose that would be too much to hope for, wouldn't it?"

"Pity Rémy ain't 'ere," J observed. "She's always got that sort of fing on 'er."

Kai smirked. "And there she was trying to tell me that she was a reformed character…"

The end of his sentence rang into silence.

The chanting had stopped. Just like that, as if someone had snapped their fingers or flipped a switch, the noise ended. Every one of the hundreds of people below them fell silent in one single breath.

The change sent a prickle up Thaddeus' spine. The new quiet was so absolute that he could hear his heart thumping in his chest. Slowly he turned and looked down. No one moved. No one said a thing. The cult of the Sapphire Cutlass had lifted their chins and now stared up at the five prisoners in complete and utter silence, their wild eyes wide and unblinking as if they were nothing more than posed dolls on a child's shelf.

A drumbeat began to sound. It reverberated around the cavern in a rumble like thunder. Low at first – slow at first – it grew louder and faster with each stroke.

Thump thump thump thump

Thump-thump-thump-thump

Thump-thump-thump-thump

Thumpthump-thumpthump-thumpthump

Thumpthump-thumpthump-thumpthump...

Their cages began to move. They rattled along the track set into the cave roof above them, inching towards the raised stone stage set with the throne that Thaddeus has spied earlier.

"Oi!" J yelled. "Now what?"

Thaddeus looked up at the track above them, illuminated in a way it had not been before the torches were lit. It wasn't leading to the stage, he realised. It stopped short before that. It ended above the darkened pit sunk in the cavern floor, but he still wasn't close enough to see what it held, though whatever it was moved restlessly in the dim light.

"Desai," he shouted, along to the front of the line of cages. "What is that? What's down there?"

Desai didn't have a chance to answer. A piercing scream shattered the air, loud enough to drown out the drums.

It was Dita. In the cage beside Desai, she was almost as close to the pit as he was. She pointed at what was below them.

Thaddeus peered down as his own cage finally reached the lip of the pit.

Snakes.

The pit was full of thousands of writhing, squirming snakes.

Dita had stopped screaming and slumped to the bottom of her cage, her knuckles white where they gripped the bars.

"Don't you worry," J shouted to her, his voice almost lost beneath the sound of the drums, "Dita, we'll get out of here before – before anyfin' 'appens wi' those snakes. You hear me? Dita? We're all right fer now, ain't we? They can't get us up 'ere. Can they, eh?"

The little girl didn't answer – perhaps she hadn't heard. She was still staring down into the pit as her cage came to a stop above it with the others sliding into place beside her.

"This is getting worse by the minute," said Kai. "We have to do something."

"Like what?" Thaddeus asked.

Kai looked around. Then he threw himself to the other side of his cage. It swung wildly on its chain, bumping into the one in which Thaddeus was trapped.

"Hey, watch it!"

Kai took no notice. He scrambled to the other side of the cage just as it was swinging back into place, forcing it into further motion. This time it avoided bashing into Thaddeus' prison, arching into a wider swing. Thaddeus saw Kai grin as he leapt to the other side of the cage again. The cage swung even more.

"What are you doing?" Thaddeus asked.

"What do you think? Use your brain, copper! Why else would they put us over this pit unless they intend to drop us right into it? If you ask me, we've got until those infernal drums stop their racket."

176

"So? What is dashing about like a lunatic going to achieve?"

Kai didn't look at him, still moving swiftly from one side of his cage to the other, rocking it wildly. "We can't stop them dropping us. The only thing we can do is try to change where we're going to land."

Thaddeus watched as Kai's prison swung again. The chain rattled harshly, pulled as taut as it would go as the cage hovered, just for a moment, over solid ground rather than over the pit. If the chain had snapped then, the cage would have crashed to the floor of the cavern rather than down into the writhing mess of snakes.

"He's right!" Thaddeus exclaimed. "Everyone – do what Kai's doing. Do it now!"

Twenty One

Desperate Measures

The drums led Rémy and Upala to a ruined temple, an intricate stone façade cut straight into the base of the mountain. They crouched in the shadows of the jungle leaves, watching for signs that anyone was standing guard. There was no movement anywhere. The place seemed deserted, though both women knew better.

Creepers had grown into every crack and crevice of the temple's facia. They wound around the carved pillars like snakes.

"Better not go in the front door," Rémy whispered to Upala, pointing up to a high window. "Do you think you could climb up there?"

The pirate woman flashed her a sharp grin and before Rémy knew it, Upala was half way up the wall, using the creepers to reach the window. Rémy followed, impressed by her fearlessness and stealth.

Within minutes, both women were standing inside the temple. The sound of the drums was even louder here, echoing through the dim torchlight that could be seen beyond the open door of the window-room. They moved towards it together, checking this way and that before beginning to traverse the passageway outside. There was no sign of anyone at all.

They moved quickly and quietly, pausing at each room to search for any sign of their people. They found none. Instead, the temple was bedecked with all manner of marvels: stone carvings of what looked like a goddess depicted in several terrifying warlike poses. There were piles of precious stones, too – the sapphires from which Aruna had drawn her fame and fable. They glinted in the meagre light, calling to Rémy as surely as if they had spoken, but she resisted the temptation to take one.

Upala showed no interest in any of the rooms they passed at all – a strange pirate indeed, Rémy thought, who was not in the least distracted by such unattended wealth. She thought of Kai's story about her, and wondered what kept Upala going – what interested her now that her life was so empty of family. Although, Rémy reflected, her own life wasn't so different so long ago. They had both made families out of the people around them.

The drums pounded on, faster and faster. The two women followed them, seeking their source. It couldn't be much further – the sound was like a summer storm now, close and cloying, hovering right overhead.

They turned a corner, and the tunnel they were in ended so swiftly that Upala almost walked straight out into the open. Rémy caught the other woman by the arm and pulled her backwards, out of sight. Together they dropped to a crouch beneath a narrow arch that formed the end of the passageway, staring at the scene playing out in the vast cavern below them.

Rémy found it difficult to take everything in at once. The first things she saw were the huge carved statues standing in alcoves hewn out of the rock around the walls of the cavern. They were massive and as intricately carved as the furniture and rooms she and Upala had found on their way through the mountain. These, though, were many times the size, standing on spindly legs and looking for all the world as if they would lurch forward into life at any moment.

The second thing she became aware of was the people. Hundreds and hundreds of people, mercifully all standing with their backs to where she and Upala hid – there were too many to count easily, but their number was dizzying. She felt a hand grip her arm and glanced at her companion to find Upala pointing at something in the room below them.

Five golden cages were swinging unevenly from the ceiling, each filled with a figure that Rémy instantly recognised. Her heart sank. They had found their friends, all right – but how to reach them? Upala squeezed her arm again and nodded with her chin at the great pit they could see in the floor.

"Snakes," she whispered in Rémy's ear. "It is full of snakes. They are about to become a sacrifice."

"A sacrifice?" Rémy asked, horrified, "Who for? What to?"

A movement across the cavern caught their eye. A figure appeared through the archway at the top of the slope that led down to the stage. He took up position beside the winch fixed in the wall. Rémy realised that the chains fixed to it led to the cages and her heart clenched. A second later, the drums stopped. The silence filled the space, expanding with the final drumbeat, and in it the new arrival spun the winch.

"Swing harder!" Kai's voice shouted, echoing through the cavern. "Harder!"

The cages dropped. Four missed the pit entirely, crashing instead onto the raised stone platform. The fifth, though, had not swung far enough. It swung back again and crunched down onto the very edge of the pit. Its bars folded around the ledge so that it rested there. A thin, high scream of terror echoed from it.

"Dita!" Rémy cried.

"Go!" Upala hissed. "Go, go, go!"

The two women ran along the narrow ledge between them and the winch. Below them, Dita's screams rose higher as the cult members rushed forward and tried to dislodge her cage. The man beside the winch saw the two women coming and pulled his blade from his waistband, but it was Rémy who launched the first sally. She parried his sword with a kick, spinning her shoulder into his chest. Upala followed with a slash of her talwar that knocked him off balance and also off the ledge.

Together they grabbed at the winch, trying to turn the wheel that would lift Dita's cage. It was heavy and stiff, so much so that Rémy thought it wasn't going to move at all.

Below her she could see more of the cult members surging forward, some joining the cause to push Dita's cage into the pit, others clawing their way up the stage wall like ants. Thaddeus, Kai, Desai and J had squeezed out of their damaged cages and J was leaning over the edge of the pit as if he could reach Dita himself, while the others tried to keep the rest of the cult at bay.

The winch gave just as Dita's screams reached a crescendo and the cage toppled into the pit. Rémy and Upala spun the wheel, rushing to take up the slack as it thundered over the edge. In truth, Rémy thought they were too late. The cage disappeared from view, and she imagined it crashing to the bottom, snakes writing up and around Dita in a slithering morass. But then the chains pulled taut and the winch bit back, raising the cage precious inches.

"There's no time," Upala managed, through gritted teeth.

She was right. Some of the cult members that had made it onto the stage were ignoring Thaddeus and the rest in favour of heading for the slope. Upala threw the winch lock and grabbed her discarded sword, turning to Rémy.

"You go help them," she hissed. "I'll find a diversion – a way to stop the rest."

"How?"

But Upala had already spun away, and another scream from Dita drew Rémy's attention back to the pit.

Kai, Thaddeus and Desai were trying to hold off the cult horde by kicking back as many as they could before they made it up onto the stage, but it was hopeless. Kai was already grappling with one and many more were behind.

Rémy looked around. There was no way she'd be able to fight her way down to them. She'd have to help some other way. She looked at the chains that had held the cages in place. They formed a bridge right over the heads of the army below. She couldn't walk them like a tightrope: they were at too much of an angle. But she could climb.

She leapt onto the winch and leaned forward, gripping one of the chains with both hands and pulling herself up, hand over hand, foot over foot. Rémy moved as quickly as she knew how. As she got higher, Dita's cage came into view, swinging slightly as it hung low in the pit. It hadn't touched bottom, but it was very close, just a few inches from the base. Dita had clawed herself as high up the bars as she could up and was clinging to them, trying to keep her legs above the snakes that writhed and slithered just below.

The drums started again as Rémy reached the hook in the ceiling. The beat inspired a surge in the cult members, as if the sound had renewed their energy. They climbed onto the stage doubly fast. Rémy could see her friends backing away, herded into a smaller and smaller space with their broken cages at their backs.

Dita or Kai – who should she go to first? Rémy felt Upala's sword in her belt and knew the answer. Taking a deep breath to steady herself, she wrapped her booted feet around one of the chains that led to the ground. Then, keeping her hands loose and wishing they were gloved, she slid down it. The clang as she landed on the downed cage was loud enough to make Kai and Thaddeus turn towards her.

"Rémy!" they both shouted.

Rémy leapt to the stone floor and drew Upala's sword from her belt, thrusting it towards Kai as she passed him. He seemed to be limping but, even injured, her brother would know how to use it better than Thaddeus could.

Rémy ran towards where J was still leaning over the pit. Rémy didn't even pause before she jumped, soaring past him and landing on top of the cage. The girl was still holding on, but she wasn't high enough. The snakes were winding themselves around the bars, slinking higher and higher.

Rémy dropped to her knees above the girl, tugging at the locked hatch to no avail. "Dita," she urged, "climb! Climb higher!"

"I can't!" Dita sobbed. "My arms aren't strong enough!" She was pale, tears streaking her face.

"You can do it," Rémy told her. "You must!"

"I can't!" the girl wailed again, too terrified to make herself move.

"All right, all right," Rémy soothed. "I will help you. You can do this. *D'accord?*" She quickly undid her belt and then climbed down the side of the cage herself to loop it through the bars and around the girl.

"Remember what we have been learning, Dita," she said to the terrified girl, as they faced each other and Rémy fastened the belt. "A little at a time, yes? I am here. You're not going to fall. Take it slowly. Do what I do. We will climb back up together, *d'accord?*"

Dita nodded through her tears. Then she took a deep breath. Rémy began to move, slowly and purposefully, her

184

feet braced against the bars, one hand holding on to the belt, the other grasping at the cage. She moved one foot and then another, a few centimetres at a time before pausing to let Dita do the same. When they got to the corner of the cage, Rémy had to undo the belt, but Dita clung on until she'd done it up around her again.

"You've done it!" Rémy shouted, over the maelstrom of noise around them. "You're at the top. Look, Dita! The snakes can't reach you here!"

Dita smiled and hugged her through the bars, hard. It was only a temporary solution and the belt wouldn't support the girl forever, but it was something.

Rémy looked up to see Thaddeus struggling with a woman who looked as if she could snap him like a twig. As Rémy watched he dodged backwards as the woman swung her razor-sharp cutlass. For a second she thought he'd been sliced through the stomach, but then Rémy saw that it was only his shirt that had been a victim – this time, anyway.

Come on, Upala, Rémy thought. *Whatever you're going to do, do it!*

"You have to help them," Dita shouted to Rémy, through the bars. "I can hold on now. They need–"

Dita's words were swallowed by a sound so loud that it even drowned out the noise of the drums. It was the crash of thunder trapped inside a room, accompanied by the creak of a tree big enough to hold up the world falling to its death. The noise drowned out everything else that was going on around them, and the crash that followed shook the ground.

Rémy, still holding fast to Dita, twisted around to see that one of the huge stone statues had toppled from its alcove. The colossus had smashed into the stone slope and had begun to roll down it, crushing everything in its path – cult worshippers and pieces of the cavern alike. Rémy watched open-mouthed as another statue began to fall just like the first, rocking in its alcove for a moment and then, as if in slow motion, toppling forward into the cavern.

A Diversion

When the sound came, it was so loud that at first Thaddeus thought the roof was caving in. His momentary distraction was enough for the woman in front of him to smash him to the ground. He had to scramble back to avoid the blade that followed the blow.

As he fought his way back to his feet, Thaddeus saw one of the huge stone figures set into the walls around the cavern toppling forward, its limbs crumbling into chunks of rock the size of boulders as it went. It crashed to the ground, cracking the surface of the slope before what was left of its body began to roll down towards the platform. As he watched, another of the statues began to fall, smashing into the first. At this impact the second statue fractured, limbs cracking and splintering into stone dust and shrapnel as the two colossal forms battled for space as they rolled. They picked up speed despite their size, crashing against each other, urging one another on as they hurtled down the slope.

At first the cult worshippers seemed entirely oblivious, too intent on their human foes to notice what was happening behind them. The woman struggling with Thaddeus battled on, regardless. But then something began to happen. One by one, the soldiers turned towards the approaching statues. They raised their arms and walked forward, armoured limbs outstretched before them even as they stood in the path of the immense stone tide.

The woman trying to kill Thaddeus abruptly abandoned her attempt. She turned away, walking back to the edge of the platform and quickly descending it. Joining the other cult members she raised her arms and began to walk towards the statues.

"What's happening?" Kai shouted, and Thaddeus realised that he, Desai, and J had also all been left alone.

The cult members began to chant again. They stood, most of them three-deep in a row that blocked off the end of the slope from the platform. The first row dropped to their knees, arms outstretched, the second leaned over the shoulders of the first, their arms also outstretched. The soldiers in the third row, made of the tallest of the masses, remained upright, reaching out over the heads of the first two rows, also with their arms outstretched. The statues continued their journey down the slope, each smash of their stone bodies sending more and more dust and sharp chips of rock into the air. The cavern was full of it, as thick as the mist had been out in the forest.

"Look!" J shouted, pointing through the smog at the wall where one of the statues had previously stood. "Who's that? She ain't dressed like the rest of 'em!"

A lithe figure slipped out of the now-empty alcove, making back up the stone slope. It was a woman, Thaddeus could make out that much, but no one he recognised.

"That's Upala!" Kai exclaimed with distinct relief. "She's still alive. Where is she going?"

"I have no idea, but I believe," came Desai's voice, over the sound of crushing, careening stone, "that this is intended as a diversion to help us out of our predicament. In which case we should take advantage of it while we still can. We have to find the source of the power. We have to stop it, *now*."

"What about Dita?" J cried. "We can't just leave 'er 'ere!"

Thaddeus looked over to the cage, still dangling low in the pit. Rémy was working at the lock while Dita clung to the top of her prison for dear life.

"She's all right, J," said Thaddeus. "Look – Rémy's with her."

"She ain't all right!" J cried. "She's still stuck in that thing!"

As if she'd felt their eyes on her, Rémy glanced up and met Thaddeus' gaze.

"Go!" she shouted, her voice only just carrying above the sound of disintegrating rock. "Get out of here while you can! I know how to get us both out of here. I'll take care of her, J. I promise."

"An' who's going to take care of you?" J yelled back. "Eh, Rémy? Who's going to take care of *you*?"

Thaddeus grabbed J's arm, dragging the boy around to face

him. "I don't want to leave them either, J, but staying isn't going to help them. If we can work out why this is happening and stop it, then maybe we'll all be saved. We have to go."

"You go," J said, trying to wriggle out of Thaddeus' grip. "Go on. Go. But I ain't going *nowhere*."

"J, you have to. Do you want Rémy to have to rescue you, too?"

"She won't 'ave ter—"

Thaddeus was through arguing. Every second they tarried in the cavern was a second lost for escape. He bodily dragged J away from the pit, though the boy did his best to resist. Kai grabbed his other arm and together he and Thaddeus practically carried J out of the cavern, heading for the dark recesses beneath the arch at the far end of the platform. Kai was still limping, but if he was in pain the pirate seemed not to feel it. Desai followed behind them.

As they reached the archway, a new sound reached them: a rumbling scrape like the magnified screech of chalk scraping over slate. Thaddeus turned to look back, feeling Kai, J and Desai do the same beside him.

"Bleedin' 'eck," muttered J.

The carcasses of the statues had reached the bottom of the slope. Rather than crushing the rows of cult members, however, they had been forced to a stop by the collective strength of those outstretched, armoured arms. As Thaddeus watched, the second statue crashed into the back of the first: an impact great enough to shake the ground on which they all stood. And yet the cult members still stood firm, arms braced against the first statue. They barely even shook.

The chant began again – a rhythmic blend of incomprehensible words rising into the dusty air. Then, so slowly that at first it was impossible to see at all, the statues began to shift. The cult members were forcing the stone monuments to move, rolling their damaged bodies back up the slope.

"Each of those things must weigh as much as my ship with a fully loaded hold," Kai muttered. "How can they possibly be strong enough to move two of them with their bare hands?"

"Their hands ain't bare though, are they?" said J grimly. "They've got that armoured nonsense all over 'em."

"I'm afraid J's right," agreed Desai. "It would seem that their strength is being enhanced already, and I would wager it is not by natural means."

"How we can fight these people?" Kai asked, as the sound of stone scraping inexorably against stone went on. "The British Army itself couldn't, rifles and cannon or no. What can we do, with nothing of the kind?"

"We locate the source of this power and we stop it," Desai said, grimly. "Now, before it has a chance to grow further."

Kai shook his head with a brief laugh. "As easy as that, eh?"

"You said it yourself, Kai," said Desai, "this is nothing but a children's story – and what is there to be afraid of in that?"

"I'm not afraid," Kai told him. "I just know when I've met my match. So I plan on finding Upala, getting out of here and taking my ship far, far away where none of this nonsense can find us. The rest of you can come if you want. Or not – it's up to you."

"Wherever you go, be it to the ends of the earth or even beyond, it will not be far enough," Desai told him. "Once this power reaches its zenith and escapes this place, there will be no stopping it."

"I don't know what it is you're looking at, old man," said Kai, "but I'm telling you, there's already no stopping it."

"And I am telling you that you are wrong," said Desai. "Sahoj is behind this, and he may be a mystic but he's still a man and at this moment he can still be stopped. Trust me, if not we would all be dead already. So this moment is all we have. If we do not act now, *then* all will be lost."

Kai stared at Desai for another moment, as if weighing a mess of odds in his head. Thaddeus could almost see the cogs working in the man's mind as his dark eyes flickered in the gloom.

"You came with Rémy to help," Thaddeus said softly. "No sense in leaving a job half done, is there?"

Kai glanced at him. "Actually I came because she promised me the airship," said the pirate. "And a fat lot of good that thing turned out to be in a fight."

"Well, then I suppose you have a choice to make," said Thaddeus. "Leave your sister behind and try to make a run for it, or stand up for something. I already know what Rémy would do in your place, however hopeless the situation. She's already doing it, trying to save Dita instead of just her own skin."

For a moment Thaddeus thought Kai might swing the sword he was holding in his direction, but then the pirate shook his head. "You're all fools." He looked at Desai. "All right. Lead on, old man. You'd better know what you're doing, that's all I can say."

Thaddeus paused for a moment, looking back to where Rémy still laboured with the lock on Dita's cage. Then he followed, too.

Twenty Three

A Brief Reprieve

The lock just wouldn't give. Rémy cursed under her breath and glanced down at Dita. The little girl was holding onto the bars, her knuckles white where they gripped the metal.

"You can't do it, can you?" Dita asked, her face a brave mask despite the fear in her eyes. "You can't get me out."

"I'll get you out," Rémy told her firmly. "I promised I would, and I will. I'm going to open this lock, and we're going to use the chain to go back the way I came. All right? Simple. Everything will be just fine, you'll see."

"But–" Dita stopped, and bit her lip.

"What?"

"The belt," said Dita. "I can feel it slipping…"

Rémy glanced down to see that the ancient leather was beginning to split with the strain of holding Dita's entire weight. She held in another curse and tried the lock again.

It wasn't like any mechanism she had ever seen before – it seemed to have cogs within cogs, as if it were operated not by a key but by something else entirely.

"I don't think I can hold myself up," Dita told her. "Not if it breaks. I don't think I'm strong enough."

"Hey," Rémy told her, "don't worry. I'll have you out of there long before that happens, *d'accord?*"

Dita nodded and tried to smile. Rémy smiled back, hoping that the gesture met her eyes well enough to hide the worry that must be lurking there. Even if Rémy did get her out, where were they to go? The statues dealt with, the pit was once again becoming surrounded by the soldiers of the Sapphire Cutlass. It would take a miracle to get them out of there at all, let alone in one piece.

A shriek from below her brought Rémy's attention back to Dita. With a ripping sound, the belt tore in two. Dita clutched herself closer to the rungs, forcing her feet through the bars so that she could use her ankles as hooks. Rémy flung herself down and reached through the bars for the girl, clutching her tightly to her chest. A split second later Rémy saw something plunging down through the cage, a cascade of tiny silvery implements catching the light as they fell, bouncing against the metal and spinning one by one down into the pit. Her lock picks. Too late to worry about them now.

"I can't hold on," Dita sobbed.

"It's all right," Rémy shouted, over the noise of the cult. They had started to chant again, a dull, droning echo that got inside the skull. "I've got you."

Rémy tried to sound more confident than she felt. With every passing second she could feel Dita slipping from her grasp. Rémy readjusted her hold, and felt Dita's grip on her shoulders weakening.

"I'm going to fall!"

"You're not!"

"It's no good, Rémy, I can't..."

Dita's sentence was cut short as they both felt the cage move. She heard the chain fastened to the hook not far from her face rattle. Lifting her head, Rémy saw it moving. A few seconds later, she felt the cage swaying as it was lifted slowly from the pit.

"Do you feel that?" Rémy cried. "Dita? I told you we'd get out of here!"

Dita sobbed again, tears escaping the little girl's eyes.

Rémy twisted around and looked up the slope. Through the murk she could just see the figure of Upala, using the winch at the top of the stone slope to lift the cage. Rémy's muscles were tiring fast – she could feel Dita's weight growing heavier and heavier below her, but the cage still wasn't clear of the snakes.

Just a little longer, she prayed silently, *just let me hold on a few more minutes and she'll be safe...*

The cage jerked to a stop, the jolt hard enough for Rémy's remaining grip to fail completely. Dita screamed, scrabbling for something to grab onto as she fell. She crashed to the bottom of the cage, hitting her head against one of the rungs.

"Dita!" Rémy screamed.

Then she realised that there were no snakes to writhe around the little girl's body. The cage had lifted just clear enough of the bottom of the pit. She was safe, after all – still imprisoned, but safe all the same.

Rémy, breathing hard, jumped to her feet on top of the cage and turned to see Upala battling one of the cult members. Sword to sword they fought along the narrow walkway, until the pirate woman bettered her opponent and sent him plunging back down to the cavern floor. More cult members poured past the fallen figures of the statues, kicking up stone dust in their wake as they charged after Upala. Pausing, she turned to look at Rémy across the chasm of space between them.

"Go!" Rémy urged her, pointing one arm in the direction that their friends had fled. "You can't help us now. Go!"

Upala can't have heard her over the noise rolling around the room, but she understood Rémy's gesture well enough. She hesitated again, as if loath to leave Rémy and Dita alone. But the soldiers were swarming towards her, just as they were towards the pit in which the cage now swung, gently, on its chain.

The pirate woman raised one hand towards Rémy – a gesture of both apology and goodbye – and then fled through the archway, the cult members surging after her like dogs chasing a fox.

Rémy looked down at Dita, struggling to her feet in the bottom of the cage, and then at the cult members who had come to stand around the edge of the pit.

There was no way out, for either of them.

"Rémy," Dita called up to her, with a shaky voice. "What are we going to do now?"

"Don't worry," Rémy said. "Everything is going to be—"

A sudden yelp of pain cut her words short.

"What?" Rémy asked, worried. "Dita? What happened?"

Dita shook her head. "I don't know. Something…" she reached down into her skirts and her face grew pale as she drew something out of the folds of fabric. It writhed and wriggled in her hand until she dropped it through the bars of the cage.

A snake.

"Dita!" Rémy cried. "Have you been bitten?"

The girl looked dazed. "I… yes… I think…" She glanced up at Rémy, her face white and her eyes glassy as they lost focus.

"Dita!"

The girl slumped to her knees.

Twenty Four

A Familiar Device

Thaddeus, Kai and Desai moved along the wide stone corridor as quickly and as quietly as they could.

"How do you know we are going the right way?" Kai asked Desai, glancing back the way they had come, the sword in his hand primed for trouble.

Desai indicated the narrow channel in the floor that had run beside them ever since they left the cavern. "This must lead somewhere, must it not?"

"That's all you've got?" Kai asked, incredulous. "I was hoping for a little more."

"Such as?"

"I don't know – you're supposed to be the mystic!"

"What is that, anyway?" Thaddeus asked, indicating the channel.

"Looks like it's been made to move somethin', if you ask

me," said J. "Whatever it is fits in the channel and gets tugged along, like."

"Indeed," agreed Desai, "exactly what I surmise too, J. And since whatever it is seems to lead straight into that cavern – the meeting place of what seems to be the cult's core…"

"…then whatever we're looking for is probably at the other end of it," finished Thaddeus.

"Exactly."

"Give yourselves a pat on the back, lads," muttered Kai. "With any luck you'll be able to think us all out of our graves, too."

They reached a fork in the corridor. The channel in the floor led down an avenue in the rock that curved out of sight some way ahead. There seemed to be a glow emanating from beyond this curve, a vague light illuminating the route. The other passageway had burning torches on its walls, spaced far enough apart to cast the rest of the route into deep shadow.

"I says we keep following the channel," said J.

"Agreed," said Desai.

"Seconded," said Kai, "but I–" He stopped suddenly. "Footsteps," he hissed.

He was right. Echoing towards them was the sound of running feet. Kai listened again and then pointed at the fork without the channel. "It's coming from there."

"What do we do?" J asked.

Thaddeus nodded to the other corridor. "If we keep going we can be out of eyesight before they get here."

"But then what if they comes down 'ere too?" J asked.

Kai held up a hand for quiet and then listened with a frown. "That's just one person – there's only one pair of feet," he said. "I say we bring down whoever it is. Maybe they can tell us what we need to know. You go ahead – get out of sight if you can."

They did as they were told as Kai took a few steps towards the second passageway. Positioning himself in the centre of the corridor, he assumed a fighting stance with his sword at the ready. The footsteps echoed closer and closer as the rest of them moved swiftly away from the fork, heading for the curve and the light that glowed beyond.

Thaddeus heard a cry of surprise behind him. He turned, afraid that Kai had been overrun. The pirate grappled briefly with someone in the shadows, but there was no sign of him raising his sword.

"Kai!" Thaddeus hissed, starting back up the corridor in the hope of being able to help.

"It's all right," Kai's voice came back. Then he appeared with someone else by his side – the young woman Thaddeus had last seen across the cavern amid a blur of stone dust. "It's Upala."

The woman striding towards Thaddeus beside Kai was impressive – tall, dark skinned, dark haired, with eyes as bright as stars and wielding a sword as sharp as any he'd ever seen. Upala looked him up and down briefly, issuing a nod and a curve of her lips that could almost pass as a smile.

"You are Rémy's policeman," she said. "From England."

"I am."

Upala's clear eyes bored into his. "She is a brave one, that girl."

"Yes, she is. Is she– Where–"

"I lifted the cage. It was all I could do. The rest is up to her."
She turned to Kai. "There are more men behind me – I heard
them. We should not linger here."

Thaddeus looked back down the passageway. At the
point where it vanished, J was standing, waving his arms.
Desai was nowhere to be seen. The two men and Upala
hurried towards him.

"You ain't going to believe this," the boy hissed, when they
reached him.

They turned the corner, and he was right.

The room they found themselves in was pure blue, as if they
had walked into the sky itself. The stone around them glittered
with a faint internal light, revealing layer after layer of facets
stacked one upon the other. The entire room seemed to be one
huge gemstone, still in its natural state.

"Sapphire," Upala whispered, in awe.

"It looks as if we've stepped inside one of those fings
the Professor had knockin' around his warehouse, don't
it, Thaddeus?" J asked. "The crystal fings that looked like
boring old stones on the outside, but when you smashed 'em
open…"

"Geodes," Thaddeus finished for him. "This looks like the
inside of a huge geode."

"Tha's the one," agreed J, his tones still hushed.

Kai moved further into the sapphire cavern, stooping to
reach for a pile of loose gems that were scattered across the
ground.

"No," Desai told him sharply, from where he had been silently contemplating the room. "Do not touch a thing. Do not *take* a thing."

Kai looked up at him. "You bring a pirate here and you expect me not to pocket at least one tiny stone?" he asked. "It's not as if this place can't spare one, is it?" He crouched to pick up one of the loose sapphires, a large oblong gem that almost filled his palm with its uneven cut. "Just one of these would pay for the repairs to my ship."

Desai moved to him quickly, knocking the stone from Kai's hand so that it skittered across the ground, chinking quietly as it rolled. Kai stood quickly, facing the older man with squared shoulders.

"Kai," Upala said, her voice soothing, stepping forward quickly to put her shoulder between the two men. "I think we should listen to him, Captain. This place... it is so strange..."

Kai brushed his hands off on his breeches with a shrug. "True enough. Come on then, mystic. What do we do now? Upala says there are more men coming. We need to act or find somewhere to hide."

"'Ere," came J's voice, echoing from some way off. Thaddeus realised that he'd wandered deeper into the stone room. The boy was looking past a towering crystalline formation of sapphire that masked whatever he was staring at. "You lot might want to come and take a look at this..."

The rest of them moved to where J stood. Beyond him was another, larger cavern of pure sapphire, but it wasn't the sheer amount of the stone that had caught the boy's attention. It was what was suspended at the middle of it.

"I don't know about you," J said, to the collected group. "But that thing there gives me the right willies."

In front of them was a large sphere, formed of metal filaments – thin arms of gleaming silver twisting against and around each other to create a pattern of abstract, many-cornered shapes. These shapes fitted together like the delicate segments of a stained glass window, though the space between each metal twist was empty. At the centre of the sphere was a plinth, and from the base of the plinth it was possible to see conduits of similar metal plunging into the rock below. Another series of tubes led further into the depths of the sapphire cave, twisting and tangling around each other.

"I have seen something like this before," said Thaddeus. "Desai, this is what Abernathy used to power his contraptions. It's why he stole the Darya-ye Noor in the first place. What is it?"

Desai's face was the most troubled that Thaddeus had ever seen it. "It's a Sakhi sphere," he said, his deep voice sombre. "I have never seen one, only heard the theory of them."

Thaddeus stepped forward, looking at the empty plinth. "Rémy had to remove the diamond from it to stop it working," he said, turning to Desai. "But there are no gems in this one."

Desai shook his head. "Look around you, Thaddeus Rec," he said. "Why would you need to place gems inside it when you can place it inside a gem?"

"What's it for?" J asked. "What's it do?"

"It is designed to harness the natural power of ancient stones," Desai told them. "More than that, it will amplify them."

Thaddeus looked around. "Abernathy only had the diamonds – the Darya-ye Noor and the one that Rémy's parents stole from the raja," he said. "He knew that would be enough to power his entire army. If this one is connected to all the sapphires in this room… it would be enough… enough to power…"

"Yes," said Desai. "It would generate enough power to mobilise an army big enough to march the world."

A new fear bloomed in Thaddeus' heart. "Desai, if there is one here, and if Abernathy had one, too…"

"Did you see one at the castle of Cantal?"

Thaddeus shook his head. "No, but that doesn't mean there wasn't one there somewhere. I only saw the main cavern. Abernathy had his secured away – we had to cross a chasm to get to it, remember? Desai, if every one of the people on that list of names you gave me in London has one of these… They are all over the planet, on every continent!"

Desai nodded, his face becoming grimmer by the minute. "Just so."

"I might not have any idea what the two of you are talking about," said Kai, "but I don't like the sound of it. Tell us what to do, mystic, so that we can do it and get out of here."

Desai shook his head. "It is not activated."

Thaddeus knew what he meant. "Abernathy's had power flowing all over it, through the sphere's filaments, feeding from the diamonds. This one – this one seems to be dead. So where is the power that the cult already has coming from?"

Desai was examining the sphere with narrowed eyes. "Something is not right…"

J huffed a half-laugh. "You're tellin' me."

"If this is the heart of everything, why is it not better guarded?" Desai asked. "They surely cannot be so confident, even here, that they would not post a guard?"

"I am liking this less and less by the minute," Kai muttered. He turned to Upala. "I want you to go. Get out of here – I know you can, you'd be able to find your way anywhere. Get back to the ship and tell them to sail as far away from here as possible. Sail east – I hear the pickings can be good in the South China Sea."

A frown like a cloud passed over Upala's face. "And you? What will you do?"

"I've promised to help these people. To do whatever needs to be done. But I'm beginning to feel it's going to have a price I don't like. A price that I wouldn't ask anyone else of my crew to pay."

"You expect me to leave you here?" Upala asked. "With these strangers, to face Shiva knows what?"

"I expect you," Kai said evenly, not dropping her gaze, "to follow orders."

"We're not on deck now, Kai."

"I'm still your Captain. I want you to leave."

"Why? I can help. You *know* I can help. Why would you tell me to leave before I am able to?"

Kai's gaze flickered over her face. "The men will need a new Captain. I always intended that it should be you if it ever came down to it."

Upala made a scornful sound in her throat. "You talk as if you are dead already."

"Maybe I am, Upala, and—" Kai paused, a twinge of something painful passing over his face. "I don't want you to die with me."

"You're not going to die, and neither am I," the pirate woman told him, reaching up with one hand to pull a chain from beneath her shirt. On it glinted a milky white stone, laced with ribbons of colour – an opal. "I am your talisman, remember?"

Desai made a surprised sound and sprang forward, reaching out to gently grasp the pendant around Upala's neck. "You have an opal!"

Upala backed away and Desai let the gem fall back against her chest. "Kai gave it to me. After the *last* time I saved his life. Because I am opal, myself, yes?"

"Yes," Desai breathed a look of realisation on his face as he turned to Kai. "*Upala* – opal."

Kai shrugged. "I told you she was a gem, did I not, old man? Did you think I was just using a term of endearment? Do I seem like the type, to you?"

"This is wonderful," said Desai, his face ebullient with hope. "My friends, I knew there was a reason that Rémy was given that compass – why it was important she found you, Kai, now of all times. Now we do indeed have a chance."

"A chance?" came a drawling voice from behind them. "A chance to do what?"

The sapphire room filled with soldiers. These were not wild-eyed, armoured cult members but liveried, rifle-bearing men with nervous faces and *pagri*-wrapped heads. In front of them stood a man they had all seen before but only one of them had the misfortune to know of old. Sahoj stepped forward, looking at Desai with a lazy smile and a raised eyebrow.

"Forgive me if I speak out of turn," he said, with exaggerated courtesy. "But, Desai, I do believe your chances have just run out."

Twenty Five

The Sapphire Cutlass

"Sahoj," Desai said, his voice echoing around the sapphire chamber. "What have you done?"

"Done?" asked the mystic, walking towards his old colleague as if he were merely taking a stroll in the park. "Why, nothing at all."

Desai waved at the Sakhi sphere, still standing dormant behind them. "Then what is this? And those people out there in the cavern – the cult of the Sapphire Cutlass?"

"Ah ha," said Sahoj, waving a finger. "You should be more accurate with your words, Desai. You question should have been, 'What am I *going* to do?'"

Thaddeus could see the tension in his friend's jaw as Desai gritted his teeth. "Don't play games with me–"

In a flash, Sahoj had stepped directly into Desai's space, grasping at the other man's throat with a strong hand. "I will play games," he hissed, "with whomever I choose. You, Desai, are no longer a person of authority. Here, or, I would wager, anywhere at all." Sahoj abruptly let go of Desai and stepped back, a sly smile spreading across his face as Desai struggled for breath. "It really is such a pity. You could have joined me, had you been less obstinate. But now… Well, now it is far too late. The Sapphire Cutlass has chosen her cohorts, and you are not among them."

"What do you mean?" Desai asked hoarsely.

"Enough talk," Sahoj declared, turning to the soldiers behind him and waving at Desai's group. "Bring them. Let them see for themselves."

The soldiers' gazes flickered to Desai. They seemed reluctant to move, the fear clear in their eyes. Thaddeus watched as they shifted nervously, remembering how their pursuers had fallen back once their prey had crossed into the valley. It seemed that him that these troops had no more desire to be here than he himself did.

"Do it, you lazy curs," Sahoj barked, "or I'll see to it that you suffer for your disobedience. Do you understand?"

At his words, the soldiers hurried forward, levelling their weapons at the prisoners. Sahoj swept ahead as they herded Thaddeus and the others before them, back through the chamber and beneath another sapphire archway. Thaddeus became aware of noise ahead – the chink and skitter of tools against stone echoing faintly in the eerie blue glow that flickered around them.

Beyond the archway was another sapphire room, though this one was not as deserted as the first they had encountered.

Indeed, it was a hive of activity. Two more lines of soldiers – this time the distinctive, closely-armoured figures of the cult – were working steadily, cleaving chunks of precious stone from a point in the room's wall hidden from Thaddeus' sight by their activities.

Sahoj waved the prisoners and their guards to a standstill, surveying the scene before them with a smile on his lips.

"What is this?" Desai asked.

Sahoj turned to him, his smile broadening. It gave his face a distinctly sinister aspect, Thaddeus thought. "Well you see, my dear Desai, when I first found my way into the mountain, I at first thought of it only as the perfect place from which to restore the raja's power. After all, have you ever seen such gemstones? Such quality, such power? But then after I had spent months visiting its hidden corners, I discovered–"

"Sahoj? What is the meaning of you summoning me like some... commoner?"

The voice echoed from the archway behind them, interrupting the mystic's words. Thaddeus saw a flicker of irritation pass over Sahoj's face, quickly replaced with an obsequious smile as he turned in its direction.

There stood Raja Ikshuvaku, imperious as ever, his hands on his hips and flanked by more of his men.

"Ahh, Raja," said Sahoj, opening his hands in greeting and striding towards the jewelled man. "I am glad you are here. Your men had no trouble finding their way?"

Ikshuvaku was surveying the room with interest, reaching out to run his fingers down the sapphire walls.

"Once I had impressed upon them the foolishness of their superstitions under pain of instant death, they had no further problems," the raja murmured. "Well, well, so this is the place that has taken you from my side so often during these last months. I must say, Sahoj, that you have done well."

Sahoj bowed deeply as Ikshuvaku's gaze caught on his prisoners. "What are *they* doing here?"

The mystic glanced at Desai. "I believe *he* has been looking for a way to thwart your efforts, Raja. I suppose we should have expected as much. No matter. As you see, he has not succeeded."

The raja grinned, placing both hands on his hips as he strolled towards Desai. "No, indeed Sahoj, I see that he has not."

"Raja," Desai began, moving forward as far as his captor would allow. "You must listen–"

Ikshuvaku raised one hand, flicking his fingers towards Desai as if brushing a bug from his tunic. "I must do nothing, traitor. Other than kill you, of course. I should have done it years ago – I always have been too merciful for my own good. Why is he not dead yet, Sahoj? Why are they all not dead yet?"

Sahoj bowed again, so deeply that the sash of his cummerbund brushed the azure floor. "I wanted him to see your final triumph, my raja. I wanted him to witness the futility of his attempts to oppose your return to your rightful place."

"Whatever he has told you, whatever he has promised you," Desai said, his voice echoing into the cavern along with the chink of the men still working the stone, "it is a lie, Ikshuvaku, of that I am certain."

"Come now, Desai," Sahoj's tone was coldly haughty. "It is simply because you cannot conceive of anything but betrayal that you can see nothing but the same in anyone else." The mystic turned to look at the raja. "Ignore him, my lord. He is merely twisted with jealousy and bitterness for your wisdom and wealth."

"Quite so," agreed the raja. "It is so sad to see, Desai. You could have shared in the glory and riches as I return to my rightful place – as I return all *India* to her rightful place – and yet instead, here you are, pursuing your own agenda."

"I assure you, Ikshuvaku, *I* am not the one doing that," Desai spat. "Listen to me–"

"Enough," commanded Sahoj. "Raja, I asked you here to see the crowning glory of our achievements come to fruition. To see the moment that my– that *our* plans are put into action."

The raja clapped his hands together with genuine delight. "Wonderful!"

"First, there is something I must show you," said Sahoj. He looked towards Desai, and Thaddeus saw something pass across the hard planes of the man's face that was hard to read. There was triumph there, it was true, but there was something else, buried deep. Fear, perhaps? It was gone in a second as Sahoj turned and addressed the cult members, still working feverishly at the sapphire. "It is time," he said, raising his voice until it boomed against the gemstone walls. He raised his arms, and at the gesture, every worker ceased their movements, turning towards him. "It is time. Prepare," Sahoj commanded.

The cult members turned as one and stepped away, their

movements slow but purposeful, as if sleepwalking. As they did so, what they had been working on was revealed.

The air in the room seemed to become unbearably hot. Thaddeus couldn't breathe. He simply stared wordlessly at what stood before him, every hair on the back of his neck standing up in nameless and abject fear.

"Bleedin' 'eck," he heard J mutter.

Desai, standing at Thaddeus' side, drew in a sharp and fearful breath.

Kai spat a word Thaddeus had only ever heard on the docks at Limehouse, but at this moment found himself heartily agreeing with.

Before them had been revealed a young woman of perhaps 18 or 20. She was standing half inside a column of pure, clear sapphire that reached from the floor of the room to the ceiling above. The workers had evidently been chipping her out of her resting place, as if she had been entirely encased in the jewel itself. She had been freed as far as her waist and stood, arms slightly raised as if in the process of stepping forward. The woman's eyes were shut and to Thaddeus she seemed to be in slumber, but she was clearly alive – her chest rising and falling as she breathed. She was naked to the waist, the dark skin of her arms and shoulders reflecting the tint of the sapphire. It wasn't until Thaddeus looked lower that he realised with shock that where her legs should be seemed to disappear into the remainder of the sapphire column. Below her hips, there was nothing at all, as if something had rubbed the remainder of her being out of existence.

"What is this?" breathed Ikshuvaku.

"This, my raja," said Sahoj, his tones hushed and reverent, "is the Sapphire Cutlass."

There was a pause, and then Ikshuvaku threw back his head and laughed. "This? This child is the dread warrior of the old story? This is the power at which armies tremble? Half a girl-child I could snap between my finger and thumb? You take me for a fool, Sahoj!"

A black look flicked across the mystic's face, quickly replaced with another of his smiles. "Trust me, oh great raja. Once you have seen her true power, you will no longer doubt it."

For a moment, it seemed as if Ikshuvaku would move to touch the woman in the sapphire, but Sahoj blocked his way, an apologetic look on his face. "Please, raja, let us finish our work. She is... still at rest, as you see."

As Sahoj spoke, the cult members he has sent away returned from several directions. Some bore armour, which they proceeded to strap onto the woman's chest and arms. Others came bearing coils of filament similar to those that made up the Sakhi sphere, unrolling lengths of it to that it reached into the room from somewhere else – somewhere, Thaddeus felt with uneasy certainty, that would join up directly with the sphere itself. He turned to look at Desai as these men reached the woman and began connected the ends of the filaments to aspects of the armour she now wore.

"Sahoj," Desai said, watching with a pale face, his voice tight. "This is foolishness in the extreme. Stop this, now, before it is too late."

"Too late for what, Desai?" the raja asked.

"Too late for him to rescind his traitorous ways," Sahoj cut in, before Desai could answer. "Too late to stand at your side as the Sapphire Cutlass bends her power to your will, my raja."

"Ahh," said Ikshuvaku knowingly. "Of course, of course. Desai, I think I have been patient enough with your various deceits. With this creature's power I will retake my rightful place, with or without your approval."

"Is that what he's told you?" Desai asked. "That he is releasing this power for your benefit? It's a lie, Ikshuvaku. No one can control such power as this place – this woman – possesses. No one! What else has he told you? That once this is done, you will reign supreme? That he is only acting in your best interests? Tell me, Raja, if that is the case, then why did he keep this," Desai gestured at the living statue, "a secret until now?"

The raja raised an eyebrow at Sahoj. "It is a valid question, Sahoj."

Sahoj smiled and bowed deeply. "Master, I would not bring you something I could not be sure would work."

The raja nodded. "*Now* you are sure?"

Sahoj moved into another gesture of obeisance. His voice echoed back at them from somewhere near the floor. "Oh yes, my raja. I am very, very sure."

"And why is that, Sahoj?" Desai asked. "What have you done to ensure your own survival? What have you promised the Sapphire Cutlass in order to keep your own life?"

Sahoj straightened to look at his former friend with a look of utter contempt. "You bore me, Desai, as much as you ever did. Now it is time to be quiet." He raised one hand in a dismissive gesture flicked towards their guards.

Desai lunged as the men moved forward. He reached for Sahoj, tearing at the mystic's loose white tunic. It ripped in two, the sound echoing slightly against the blue gemstone around them. The guards wrenched Desai back, but it was too late. The mystic's chest had been exposed.

"That's it, isn't it?" Desai said breathlessly, struggling in his captor's grip. "You see, Raja?" he asked. "Do you have one of those? I am willing to bet on my very life that you do not."

There, on Sahoj's exposed chest, was a tattoo. It was of an ornately curved short sword, and where it crossed over his nipple was embedded a glittering stone as blue as the fractured walls around them all.

"Enough!" bellowed Sahoj, clutching closed the ruined garment with one hand and making a violent, slicing motion with his other. "Get them out of here. Take them to the throne chamber. There they will bear witness to what they most fear and are helpless – helpless! – to prevent."

"His plan does not include you, Raja!" Desai yelled, as he and the others were dragged away. "If it did, you would have the tattoo as well! Only those that have it will survive! She will only recognise those who have it as her followers!"

Ikshuvaku took no notice. A new drumbeat began.

Twenty Six

A Poisonous Transformation

Rémy was still crouched on top of Dita's cage, the little girl
slumped across the bars at the bottom.

"Dita!" Rémy cried. "Stay awake! Can you hear me? Try to
stay awake!"

The drums began to sound again. They echoed through
the cavern, louder than ever before. The cult members began
to move. They abandoned the pit and some left the raised
stone stage, dropping back down to the ground level to resume
their previous formation. Others remained on the platform,
separating into two silent, impenetrable lines. One by one
they all turned to face the centre of the platform, a fresh chant
beginning, droning on endlessly beneath the beating drums.

There was movement behind the stage, too. Out of the
darkness of the archway came another cascade of cult members,
walking in two slow, solemn lines on either side of the channel

etched in the stone floor. Each of these carried a drum, fastened around their necks with a cord woven of blue thread, beating it rhythmically as they walked slowly out of the gloom.

Between them, apparently moving of its own accord within the channel in the floor, was a huge stone throne, patterned with ornate carvings. It was turned away from the cavern, its back so high that Rémy couldn't see who was sitting in it. It slid smoothly in time with the drumbeat, tugged forward by invisible hands. To its left walked a lone man not dressed in the colours of the Sapphire Cutlass, but in white, with a golden cummerbund at his waist and a turban wrapped around white hair – Sahoj. His white tunic had been torn to reveal the tattoo of the cult, etched across his chest. He stared straight ahead, walking calmly in time with the throne until it reached the end of the channel. When it stopped, he stepped aside, turning to face it, a movement echoed by the drummers. They, too, turned inwards to face the throne, still hammering out a slow, hypnotic beat.

Rémy's saw movement to her right, this time at the tunnel entrance near the winch. She looked over to see her friends being herded back into the cavern. Behind them were more soldiers, not wearing the colours of the cult, this time, but those of the raja. Her friends were trapped, outnumbered and surrounded, and Rémy's heart sank. Surely, now, all hope for them – for everything – was lost.

The drumbeat ceased, although the chanting went on. She looked back towards the stone stage just as the throne began to rotate, swinging on an invisible pivot.

Rémy felt her breath run still in her chest.

On the throne sat a woman clad in gold, her eyes shut as if she were sleeping. Her chest was encased in a breastplate that reached over her shoulders to end in spikes as sharp as a church's spire. Her armour was etched with intricate patterns – whorls and loops like the waves of a churning ocean so that it seemed to ripple even though she was as still as the statues around her. Her waist was encompassed in a wide belt, also of gold, edged by strands of blue silk that fringed her thighs.

The woman's legs were bare, though at first it seemed as if they were clothed in the same blue silk as worn by her followers. But then, as they caught the light from the flaming torches on the walls, Rémy realised the truth. Her legs were not covered, but transparent, formed of a stone so clear and so blue that it would match the sky of a high summer's day over Paris. Even from this distance, where she clung on top of Dita's cage, Rémy could see how they distorted the shape of the throne behind them, refracting the image of the carved stone as if through a prism.

Slowly, deliberately, the woman raised her hands and then lowered them to the armrests of her throne. She tipped back her head, opening her eyes.

Rémy shivered. Behind the woman's lids there was nothing but pure, bright sapphire, faceted to glint and shine the same unnatural, transparent blue as her legs.

The Sapphire Cutlass pressed her palms into the stone arms of her throne. Rivulets of power began to dart from her form into its carvings, tracing from where her heart should be along the patterns that circled her armoured torso and into the throne, as if the chair was part of her. She lifted her chin, and Rémy realised with dread that the supernatural woman was looking straight at the cage on which she crouched. The Sapphire Cutlass moved her head with one tiny flick and the cage instantly began to move. Rémy felt it judder beneath her feet and then lift clear of the pit before swinging towards the throne and descending, just as smoothly, to land at the woman's feet.

Dita lost consciousness completely as the cage touched the stone. The Sapphire Cutlass stepped from her throne with silent, menacing grace. Rémy flexed her arms and rotated her shoulders, ready to fight. The goddess seemed not to notice her at all, her attention fixed on Dita instead. Rémy sensed her chance and leapt from the cage, left foot extended in a move she would usually use to mount a moving pony in the circus ring.

She was knocked from mid-air by the metal-clad arm of one of the woman's attendants. Rémy crashed to the ground, a forest of legs closing in around her. She sat up, her head ringing painfully from the impact, and rough hands grabbed her shoulders, dragging her to her feet.

The Sapphire Cutlass seemed oblivious to the disruption. She raised one hand towards the cage, and two of her soldiers moved forward to grasp the bars. Another fluid movement of her hand, and they were pulling the metal apart, bending the rods, prying open Dita's prison as if it were made of nothing more than paper. One of them reached in and lifted the little girl out, laying her at the foot of his goddess.

"Dita," Rémy shouted, struggling against the arms that held her. "Dita, wake up!"

The girl didn't move at all and Rémy feared that she was already dead. The Sapphire Cutlass looked down at the lifeless pile of rags that was Dita, examining her with cold blue eyes. Then, slowly, she crouched at the girl's side and extended one hand to place it on Dita's forehead.

"Stop it!" Rémy cried, still struggling and still trapped. "Leave her alone!"

She saw a tiny lick of blue flame dance around the woman's arm. It circled the limb from shoulder to elbow, from elbow to wrist, from wrist to palm, before flickering out of sight. The Sapphire Cutlass withdrew her hand from Dita's head and stood up. She remained at the girl's side, looking down with her impassive, terrifying blue gaze.

The drumbeat went on and on, crashing and echoing around the cavern. Rémy's head ached and the flames from the ever-burning torches were beginning to hurt her eyes.

Dita moved. She turned her head left and right. She sat up. She opened her eyes.

They were of the purest, purest blue.

They were sapphire.

Twenty Seven

A New Jewel

Thaddeus struggled to hold on to J, who was fighting against him with everything he had.

"Dita!" J cried. "What's that monster doing to 'er?"

Thaddeus felt helpless, watching as Rémy was held fast by two of the goddess's guards. There was fresh movement behind him and Ikshuvaku appeared, his terrified soldiers parting to let him through. As he looked down into the cavern, the smug look on the jewelled man's face turned first to shock and then to fear.

"What devilry is this?" The raja's horrified voice was so hushed that it was almost lost beneath the pounding beat of the drums.

"What's the matter, Raja?" Desai asked quietly. "Not entirely how Sahoj described it when he spoke of the Sapphire Cutlass?"

The jewelled man opened his mouth to say something else, but no sound was forthcoming. After a second he shook his head and tried again. "He told me she would become another servant," Ikshuvaku murmured. "That once she was awake, she would do my bidding and none other's."

Desai's mouth twisted into a grim smile. "Does she look as if she's likely to take your orders, Ikshuvaku? Does she look as if she would take the orders of any mere man?"

The raja tried to say something, but managed to stutter, "This... this power..."

"It should not exist," Desai finished for him.

The raja fell silent again, continuing to watch as the Sapphire Cutlass turned her attention to Sahoj. The mystic stepped forward with a deep bow, and appeared to say something to the woman.

"Are her legs truly made of sapphire?" Thaddeus asked, somewhat mesmerised by the play of flame-light that danced through the strange woman's transparent limbs. This all felt unreal, somehow, and he wondered whether that was the point of the never-ending drumbeat, which now almost felt as if it were coming from inside his own skull.

"She is becoming the stone," Desai answered. "See the power that radiates from her even now? When the transformation is complete... she will be unstoppable."

"Surely you exaggerate, as always, Desai," said the raja, his tone straining to achieve its usual languid mockery. "Sahoj clearly thinks she can be controlled, or he would not be so close to her."

Desai cast the raja a pitying look. "He does not seek to control her. He seeks to join her – to stand at her side and feed from her fortunes, even as he did with you all these years. Your power is almost spent, but hers is rising and it will be greater than the world has ever seen. What better place to enjoy such power but at its right hand?"

"The tattoo," Kai spoke up. "Is it really so important? They all have them."

"It is how she will recognise her followers and bestow her power upon them," said Desai. "Any without it will serve as slaves – or perish."

"The Comte de Cantal had one," said Thaddeus. "So we have to suppose that all those other people on the list do, too."

"Indeed," Desai agreed. "They have been planning this for years. Decades, perhaps. It seems her followers are spread throughout the world, awaiting this awakening and the power of her true strength. With it, no mortal will be able to stand in their way. They will own the world."

"What do we do?" The words were spoken by the raja. When the eyes of the group turned to him, he squared his shoulders and set his jaw. "I do not have the tattoo. I will not serve and I refuse to die," he spat.

"The only chance we have now is in the opal," Desai said, turning to look at Upala. "It may be the only thing that can stop the transformation."

Upala pulled her opal pendant from beneath her shirt as she looked down at what was happening below them. It glowed faintly in the dim light of the cavern. "What do I have to do?"

"Nothing," Kai said forcefully, as he stepped forward. "Whatever has to be done, I will do it." He held out his hand to Upala. "Give me the stone."

"No," said the pirate woman. "You gave it to me. It is mine."

"I will return it to you," Kai told her, gesturing with his hand at the opal. "When this is done, you can have it back."

Upala looked at him steadily. "You are injured," she pointed out. "Whatever has to be done, I am sure it will need to be fast. Tell me, old man," she said, her gaze still fixed on the pirate captain even as she addressed Desai. "What must I do?"

"The opal must drain her power," Desai told her. "To do that you must press it to her forehead and hold it steady. For as long as it may take."

Kai spun to look at him. "You have got to be joking."

Desai shook his head. "I am afraid not."

"You are not doing it," Kai said, turning back to Upala. "I am your Captain – it's my responsibility. Give me the opal."

Upala took a step back. "I will not," she said calmly. "The gem is mine. You gave it to me. I accepted it and now I accept the responsibility for using it."

"But I didn't know!" Kai burst out. "When I gave it to you, I didn't know all this. I just wanted… just wanted to…"

Upala moved closer. "You wanted to… what?"

Colour sprang into Kai's cheeks. He looked away, putting his hands on his hips and adopting a swaggering stance. Upala lifted one hand and ran her fingers lightly along his jaw. He reacted quickly, reaching up to grab her wrist and clutching it tightly against his chest.

"You are my Captain," Upala said softly, "and I am your talisman. I will do this. It is my duty. It is my right."

"You'll never make it," Kai said thickly. "They'll kill you before you even reach the demon."

"Have a little faith, Captain Kai."

He tugged her a little closer. "If I have ever had faith in anything, then I have it in you."

Upala smiled, a spark of bright beauty against the backdrop of nightmare playing out below them. She stepped away from Kai, turning to face the rest of them as the Captain's hand released her wrist and slid down to grasp her fingers, instead.

"I will need a diversion," she said. "Or Kai's right, I will not make it. Fight like tigers, my friends, and we may still prevail."

"What about Dita?" J asked. "We can't just leave 'er like that! We've got to 'elp 'er."

"Go for the girl first, if you can," Desai told Upala. "Her transformation is new, and you may still be able to reverse it entirely."

Upala nodded. "All right. Now, enough talk. It is time for action." She let go of Kai's hand and drew her sword. "Carve a path that will make them think we are launching a full-on attack."

"And you?" Thaddeus asked. "What are you going to do?"

Upala smiled at him. "I shall take a stealthier route."

She went to move away, but Kai reached out and pulled her back, spinning her towards him. They stared at each other for a split second, and in it Thaddeus felt his stomach drop. He knew that look – he had looked at Rémy that way so many times that it was impossible to count them all.

"Don't die," Kai told Upala, quietly. "That's an order. *Don't. Die.*"

Thaddeus looked away as their lips met. His eyes sought out Rémy instead, her black-clothed figure drowning in the impossibly huge sea of gold and blue that flooded the cavern below, and his heart turned over. These past days and hours had been about the fate of the entire world, and yet in the few seconds of yearning he had felt radiating from Kai and Upala, Thaddeus recognised a simple truth.

None of it mattered to him without Rémy.

Twenty Eight

Last Chance

Rémy found herself firmly trapped between two lines of the cult's soldiers.

"Dita," she shouted, trying uselessly to push between the bodies in front of her. "Can you hear me? Look at me!"

The little girl was on her feet now, her back to Rémy, her hands hanging loosely at her sides. The Sapphire Cutlass was walking back to her throne, and on her back was a new bloom of stony blue, creeping up towards her shoulders from beneath her armour, turning her flesh transparent. The stone in her nature was spreading steadily through her form.

The unnatural woman sat down, more little arcs of blue electricity snaking from her form to hiss across the stone. She lifted her chin as if surveying the room, and for a moment Rémy thought she was going to say something. Instead, she lifted one hand and held it out to Dita, who began to move towards her.

"No!" Rémy shouted. "Dita! Wait!"

She struggled forward, trying to force her way between the soldiers. They were an impenetrable wall. Hands dragged her back, one arm twisted up and around her neck until she felt the breath struggle to reach her lungs. Rémy kicked out, aiming for her captor's shin and hearing a sharp intake of breath somewhere near her ear. She'd obviously caused some pain, because the grip on her throat lessened a fraction – enough for her to take a lungful of the cavern's musty, stale air.

Rémy dropped her centre of gravity, becoming a dead weight as the soldier who had her in his grip tried to regain his composure. She slid further out of his grasp, dropping to her haunches as his hands scrabbled to pull her back up. That was all the time Rémy needed. She twisted, flicking her hips into a spin just as she would on the trapeze, bringing her lead leg around so fast that the force was enough to pull even further on her captor's upset balance. For a second, she was free, pivoting quickly to bring her left leg up and punch it forward into his unprotected sternum. She felt the crack under her foot as his bones gave way, but it didn't give her pause. She lunged forward, dragging his cutlass from his belt as he slumped to the ground.

Wheeling with a wild yell, she sliced the curved sword around her in a circular motion, sending more of the soldiers out of alignment. The drummers faltered, unable to defend themselves as Rémy leapt towards them. She didn't try to go through them – instead she took a running jump, launching herself at tallest of the line and planting one foot against his drum as she soared skyward. The leverage gave her enough momentum to take her over his head in a curling twist that landed her several feet in front of him more quickly than he had time to react.

"Dita," she cried again, but the girl acted as if she heard and saw nothing at all but the strange woman seated on the great carved throne. Rémy ran forward and grabbed Dita's shoulder, spinning her around.

Where Dita's eyes had once been there was only the transparent blue of stone cold sapphire. The rest of the girl's face was entirely expressionless. Then she smiled, a gesture as chilling as the sight of her eyes.

"Dita," Rémy begged. "You must be in there somewhere. You must be! Whatever this is, fight it – I'll get you out of here. I promised, didn't I? And Rémy Brunel does not break her promises."

A roar echoed around the cavern. Rémy turned to see a commotion thundering down the stone slope towards them – a whirling rush of faces she recognised, together with some she did not. Thaddeus and Desai led the charge, running headlong towards the platform, side by side. She could see J and Kai doing the same but taking a different route, down onto the cavern floor. There, too, was the jewelled man and some of his soldiers, their faces contorted into the screams and yells of battle as they surged towards the far greater force of the Sapphire Cutlass. Of Upala, though, there was no sign.

Around Rémy, the atmosphere instantly changed. The drumbeat became chaotic as some of the drummers abandoned the rhythm. The men who had been charging towards Rémy faltered, looking up at these new attackers. The Sapphire Cutlass turned in her throne, her attention captured by the noise as Thaddeus and Desai piled into the first row of soldiers. Sahoj, standing at her right hand, raised his arm, and just as if he had issued a silent order, the cult members around them began to run towards the fight, eager to protect their goddess from the onslaught.

Rémy saw a chance at once – with the attention of the cult and its leader elsewhere, a gap had opened up behind her. She grabbed Dita by the arm.

"Come on," she said urgently. "Dita, we have to go…"

Rémy managed to drag the girl a few steps. Then she felt something clamp down on her arm. Rémy looked to see that Dita had grabbed her and was squeezing so hard that Rémy's arm was turning white.

"Dita, you're hurting me," she said. "Let go."

Dita ignored her, staring at her with those transparent blue eyes, a sly smile plastered across her face. She squeezed tighter and Rémy yelped in pain. She tried to twist herself free from the girl's grip, but Dita held fast. Her strength was phenomenal – no matter how Rémy bucked and wove, the girl stood firm. Rémy dropped the cutlass, using her free hand in an attempt to pry Dita's fingers loose, but it was no good. Dita clamped her other hand over Rémy's wrist, drawing her arms together so that they were useless.

Rémy couldn't help but cry out as the pain in her arms grew sharper. Her fingers were tingling, cold – rainbowing from red to blue where the blood supply had been cut off. It felt as if her bones were being crushed under the pressure.

"Dita," she begged, "please… stop…"

The girl ignored her. Eyes blurred with pain Rémy kicked out, trying to use her legs as weapons, but Dita parried every blow she struck with impassive ease. Rémy sank to her knees and saw, over her shoulder, her friends waging a losing battle. *It's almost over,* she thought desperately. *We can't win this…* Almost as if the Sapphire Cutlass had heard her thoughts, she turned away from the scrum to look at Rémy. Dita looked up at her new mistress, their blue eyes flickering with an unnatural common knowledge. The sapphire had crept to the woman's neck, already tracing its thick lines of stone up her veins to her face. She glittered as she moved, a human body being slowly swallowed by a living, livid gem.

Rémy felt herself tugged forward, her knees scraping against the rough ground as Dita pulled her towards her mistress. Resisting was impossible – Dita's supernatural strength was overpowering. The Sapphire Cutlass raised herself out of her throne once again, this time with all her attention focused on the woman trapped in Dita's clutches.

A flurry of movement surged across Rémy's now-blurred vision. It emerged out of the dimness behind the throne, from the direction of the tunnel from which the Sapphire Cutlass herself had been brought. Rémy, struggling with the rising pain, only realised it was Upala when the pirate woman arrived in front of her, dropping the sword she had been wielding to clamp one hand to Dita's forehead and wrapping her other arm around the girl's waist.

Dita screamed and released her hold on Rémy. The girl's cry was a howl of pain and anguish. She writhed in Upala's grip, but the woman held on. The Sapphire Cutlass bellowed too, the strange sound of rock grating against rock. The blue bloom of stone had now mottled her face – her lips were pure, undulating blue, her cheekbones were sketched in true sapphire. Upala backed away from Rémy, pulling Dita with her and turning to face the goddess.

Rémy struggled to her feet, grabbing Upala's sword and throwing herself between the Sapphire Cutlass and the pirate woman. She traced the air between them with swift slashes, but the Sapphire Cutlass barely seemed to notice. Her forehead, now almost entirely gem, wrinkled as she frowned, her mouth open in a roar of anger that showed teeth and tongue of solid, moving stone. She dashed away Rémy's sword with nothing more than the back of her hand, as if she were swatting away a fly in the midday heat. She advanced, one firm stride at a time, and Rémy found herself forced back, still aware of Dita's weakening cries behind her.

The Sapphire Cutlass moved swiftly, glittering a trail of light like bursts of fireworks as her hard heels sparked off the stone beneath her feet. Rémy heard a soft thud behind her, and a moment later Upala was at her side.

"Take the girl," she said breathlessly, "I will deal with this."

Upala grabbed the sword and Rémy let it go. In the fraction of a second before she turned away, the pirate woman fixed her with a fierce look.

"Make sure Kai leaves," she said. "He will want to stay. Make sure he understands – I do not want him to."

Rémy had just enough time to nod, and then Upala was gone, her hair whipping out behind her as she wheeled towards the fight.

Dita was lying on the ground, her eyes closed, her face impassive. In two steps Rémy was standing over her, wary of being caught again.

"Dita?" she asked, but got no answer.

She looked over her shoulder to see Upala and the Sapphire Cutlass facing each other. Upala raised her sword and spun into a slicing blow that glanced off the woman's armoured upper arm, casting sparks into the musty air. The Sapphire Cutlass merely reached out and grasped the blade, closing her gemstone fist around it as if it were nothing more than a blade of grass. She pulled Upala towards her, gathering her into a deadly embrace.

Upala did not resist. Instead she took the goddess by surprise. She hurled herself forward, straight at the once-woman's chest, so quickly that the Sapphire Cutlass had no chance to defend herself. Upala raised her free arm and opened her palm, slamming it against what had once been the woman's forehead.

The sound the Sapphire Cutlass made was more of a bellow than a scream. It roared out of her, sharp and deep, the noise of sheering stone, of an avalanche. A movement shot through the stone of the cavern itself, rippling the air like a flame. The scream went on and on, and Rémy watched, open-mouthed, as the gemstone figure began to shudder and convulse.

A sudden hush fell as in one single, charged second, every member of the goddess's cult realised what was happening. The change was instant. They no longer cared about the men they were fighting. All they saw was their goddess in pain.

"Go," Upala shouted at Rémy, her voice vibrating as the shaking of the Sapphire Cutlass juddered through her being. "Get out!"

The tide of cult members turned. Roaring, screaming, yelling, they all rushed back towards the platform – towards Upala and their stricken goddess.

Rémy spun towards Dita and saw the girl's eyes were open. The sapphire hue had gone.

"Dita," she said, crouching at the girl's side. "You've got to get up. Can you move?" She tugged the child upright and into her arms. Dita's head lolled against her shoulder, and if not for the fact that her eyes were open, Rémy would have thought she was alseep. "Wrap your legs around me, and hold on."

She staggered upright, taking Dita's weight with her, and ran. Behind her, the sound of pounding, running feet echoed along with the war cries of the cult and the screams of the Sapphire Cutlass. She felt Dita lift her head.

"Don't look," Rémy told her. "Dita, don't look."

Twenty Nine

Done For

Thaddeus saw Rémy scoop Dita into her arms. Between them, the worshippers of the Sapphire Cutlass were separating, scattering in their confusion and fear.

"Rémy," he shouted, cupping his hands to his mouth to make himself heard over the din.

At the sound of his voice she looked up, their eyes meeting across the distance. A smile bloomed on Rémy's face, blotting out the exhaustion that had shadowed it a moment before. They ran towards each other, ignored by the last straggling cult members that had not converged on the throne.

Rémy staggered under Dita's weight as she reached him.

"Let me take her," Thaddeus shouted, hefting Dita from Rémy's arms.

"What's happening?" she shouted back. "What's Upala doing?"

"She has an opal," Thaddeus told her. "She's our last chance to stop Aruna's transformation."

They struggled back up the slope as Kai made his way towards them, limping badly. The fight had worsened his injury and now blood was seeping down his leg, drops of it rolling in the dust of the cavern floor as he moved. He didn't seem to notice – his gaze was fixed on the fight below. Upala was still locked against the Sapphire Cutlass, her grip refusing to waver even as Sahoj attempted to pry her away with his bare hands and the cult members swarmed her like ants. Blue sparks were exploding in the air above the two women, fizzing and spinning as they arced away from where Upala's brave hand ground the opal against the goddess's sapphire skull.

The ground began to shake. For a second Thaddeus thought it was just the chaos around him, the weight of a thousand pairs of frantic feet pounding on the cavern's floor. But then came another tremor, then another and another, each greater than the last.

"An earthquake," Desai shouted. "It is the power being released from their struggle."

The tremors increased. A tearing sound ripped through the cavern. Below them on the cave floor a split appeared, zig-zagging through the rock, a black void opening into the ground. One by one the burning torches fizzled and spat their last, until the only light left spun from the blue trails of electricity thrown from the Sapphire Cutlass.

"We have to go," said a voice. "This place is tearing itself apart!"

It was the raja. The jewelled man looked dishevelled. He was breathing hard and his tunic had been slashed by the blade of a sword. Blood ran down his arm from a cut across his bicep. Behind him, his men were fleeing into the darkness, swallowed up by the mouth of the tunnel they had driven Thaddeus and his friends through earlier.

Another rumble of cracking rock and a split appeared in the cavern's ceiling, sending chunks of stone plummeting down into the cavern.

"I'm not leaving without Upala!" Kai shouted over the din. "Go. Go on, all of you. Run. But I'm not leaving her."

Rémy grabbed his arm, turning him to face her. "She wants you to leave," she told him, voice shaking with the vibration of the earthquake. "Upala knew you would want to stay. She wanted me to tell you – she doesn't want you to."

Kai frowned, "I can't just leave her. Not now. Not here – not like this."

"She wants you to live, Kai. She's doing this so you can *live*. We can't save her. You know that. But if you live – so will she. In here. Yes?" Rémy moved one hand to place it on Kai's chest, right over his heart.

Kai wrenched himself away as the others fled for the archway. Rémy waved Thaddeus away as he tried to pull her away.

"I will follow," she said. "I promise. Get Dita out of here."

"We've gotta go, Mr Rec," J yelled. "We've got to go NOW!"

Thaddeus turned and ran, cradling Dita against his chest as chunks of grey rock rained down on them. When he reached the archway, Thaddeus chanced a look back. To his relief, Rémy and Kai were following.

***

They staggered along the corridor, straggled out in a wide line behind the raja and Desai, Thaddeus carrying Dita with J by his side and Rémy with her arm around the hobbling Kai. They made their way through the mountain, shuddering along with the stone itself as the earthquake went on around them. They passed room after room of antiquities that were being shaken like dust from their places.

"I tell you," said Kai, breathless, "if I had known this place was here, they would have lost all of these years ago. What a waste."

Rémy tugged him onwards. "Don't even think about it."

Kai stumbled as a tremor shuddered the ground beneath their feet. He braced himself against the wall, casting a grim look at Rémy.

"Think about what?" he asked. "The fact that there's no way we're going to get out of here alive?"

"Don't say that," Rémy ordered him, forcing him onwards.

"I should have stayed with her," Kai said, his dark eyes angry, though Rémy sensed the rage was mostly aimed at himself. "We're going to die in here anyway. I should have died with her."

"We are not going to die," Rémy hissed, her own anger surging as she struggled to keep them both moving forward. "And Upala wouldn't thank you for staying."

Kai gave a bark of laughter. "She rarely thanks anyone for anything. She doesn't have much to be thankful for."

"She has you," Rémy observed.

Kai said nothing to that. Rémy twisted her aching neck to glance at him. The look on her brother's face was closed. There was something excessively sad about it.

He loves her, Rémy thought to herself. *I wonder if he ever told her so?*

Kai looked up and met her eye. He opened his mouth to say something, but whatever the words were, they were lost in the catastrophic rumble of another huge tremor. The force was enough to jolt them apart – Rémy lost her grip on Kai's arm and fell back against the rough rock wall of the corridor hard enough to knock the back of her head against the stone. She slipped to the floor, jarring her tailbone as she blinked, trying to clear the sudden blur in her vision. Kai ended up on his knees, his sharp cry echoing along the passageway as the impact tore at his already-injured leg. Blood spattered from the wound and Rémy saw him clamp one hand over it in an attempt to stop the bleeding.

Another huge tremor immediately followed, shaking Rémy like a dog shakes a rat, until her teeth rattled against each other. Ahead of them, Thaddeus was struggling to keep his balance while he held on to Dita, shielding her head with his hands as he tried to brace himself against the shuddering, shaking wall. J had fallen at his feet and was on all fours, trying to get back up. Rémy did the same, but every time she made it to her feet, another seismic wave sent her off kilter again. Kai had curled into a foetal position, one arm trying to protect his head from reverberating off the rock floor while the other clamped uselessly against his wound.

Rémy shut her eyes. The noise was deafening, as if they were standing inside the barrel of a cannon at the second that its fuse connected with the gunpowder. It rolled around and around, combining with the shaking of the mountain until Rémy no longer had any idea whether she was on her feet or on her back.

Then: nothing.

The quake stopped. In the space of a whip-crack, the world went so still and so dark that Rémy thought she must be dead – dead, and floating in the void between whatever comes between now and after.

Seconds that felt like hours stretched into the void as Rémy's hearing slowly returned. At first she thought she was surrounded by silence, but then she realised she could hear breathing – and not only her own.

"R-Rémy? Are you there? Are you all right?"

Thaddeus' voice floated to her out of the darkness. The sound of it flooded her with relief.

"I'm here." Rémy realised she was lying on her side, her cheek against the dirt floor. There was dust in her nose and her cheekbone throbbed with a dull ache – she must have cracked it against the rock as she fell. Coughing, she slowly sat upright, testing her body as she would if she had fallen from the wire. "I'm not hurt."

Beside her there was the sound of fabric scuffing against stone, then a groan that resolved itself into a cough.

"Kai?"

"I'm all right," he said.

There was more sound of movement as they all began to pull themselves upright.

"J?" asked a faint voice.

"Dita!" there came the sound of a match being struck, and flame-light flared in the darkness, illuminating J's eager face. It lasted a few seconds before dying. "Are you all right?"

"Yes," said the little girl, her voice barely above a whisper. "What– what happened? I– I can't remember…"

"Don't you worry none about that for now," J soothed. There was the sound of tearing fabric, and then of another match being struck. The flame flared again as Rémy got to her feet, her eyes searching for Thaddeus. The light lasted longer this time – J had torn a strip from his shirt, setting fire to it.

Rémy reached Thaddeus as he got to his feet. She pulled him to her, and he tucked her head under his chin.

"Are you hurt?" she asked.

"No, just winded. Desai," Thaddeus asked, raising his voice and turning slightly to look at the older man, "is it over?"

Desai was looking past them with a frown, down the dark passageway through which they had fled. "Possibly. I suggest we keep moving, just in case."

"I agree," said the raja. "We should not wait around to find out."

"Well," Kai said, dragging himself to his feet though his leg was still bleeding. "The quake seems to be done with. I'm going back. Upala might still be alive."

"Don't be ridiculous," said Rémy, pushing herself out of Thaddeus' arms to turn to her brother. "You can't, Kai. Even if the Sapphire Cutlass is dead, not all of her followers will be."

Her brother gave her a steady look. "Then I'll take them on. Now that the ground's stopped shaking, it'll be easier. Besides, with their goddess gone, they will be leaderless."

"There's still Sahoj," said Thaddeus.

Kai made a disdainful sound in his throat. "That fat old man? He's nothing but flesh and blood. I'm not afraid of him." He pulled his sword free from its scabbard and turned, bracing himself uncertainly against the wall.

"Do not be so sure that the Sapphire Cutlass has been defeated," Desai said softly, his gaze searching the shadows lurking in the passageway behind Kai.

The pirate turned. "What? What are you saying?"

"That we really should go," the old man said softly. "Before we find out that Upala and her opal were not as strong as we hoped."

Kai's face convulsed at that. He gripped the hilt of his drawn sword so tightly that his knuckle glowed white against its golden tint. "With those words you prove what a fool you are, old man," said the pirate, through gritted teeth. "Upala's spirit is stronger than that of any goddess."

Desai lifted his hands in appeasement. "I meant no disrespect. Upala has proven herself to be of brave heart and noble mind. No fault lies at her feet. I merely meant–"

A noise swelled out of the darkness, a cacophony of sound rolling along the tunnel towards them like a tidal wave. It was

244

a piercing scream, made not just of one voice, but of many – a war cry, high and grating, full of abject fury and bile.

J pulled Dita against his side, wrapping his arms around her as a look of fear spread across his face. "What the bleedin' 'eck is that? Sounds like a ton of pigs havin' their necks cut wiv a razor blade."

A light appeared at the end of the tunnel, a blue glow that grew even as they watched it. Black shadows flickered at its heart, drawing closer and closer by the second as the light swelled ever brighter. By the time that any of them realised what they were seeing, the tide was almost upon them.

"We have failed!" Desai cried, as the shadows solidified into the forms of the Sapphire Cutlass's foot soldiers, howling their insane fury as they charged. "Run. *RUN!*"

Thirty

A Sapphire Tide

The tide of running, thrashing fury was on them before they could move more than a few steps. Bodies surrounded them, a sea of armour spoiling for the final fight. Rémy found herself alone, marooned as Kai was torn away from her, buffeted by the eddies of an ocean that had once been human, but was now pure rage. Thaddeus and the others were drowning somewhere ahead of her, already out of view. Rémy found herself spun this way and that, turned and tumbled until even her legendary sense of equilibrium found it hopeless to tell which way was up.

A muscled, metalled hand clamped around her throat. Choking, she was drawn against the chest of a colossus whose vengeful eyes were rimmed with pure blue. His mouth screamed at her, the noise lost in the maelstrom's entirety. Rémy fought, gasping for breath, but he lifted her from the ground as if she were nothing more than a struggling bug.

Through the sound of dying blood rushing in her ears, Rémy became aware of something else. The blue glow had reached them too, along with a fusing, cracking sound. The bright sapphire hue washed along the passageway, colouring the stone – no, not just colouring it, changing it: turning it into pure gem. Electricity traced the air, sheer power dancing with the oxygen that she couldn't pull into her lungs. Around them, above them, below them – all was the pale, glittering blue of sapphire, moving past where Rémy fought for life, past where the supernatural army fought a battle they were sure to win.

The hand on Rémy's neck loosened. The rage in her attacker's eyes turned to fear. He dropped her and she fell to her knees in the dirt, hands grasping at her neck as she struggled to gulp great drafts of air into her lungs. Looking up, Rémy watched in fascinated horror as he began to clutch at his own chest. The sapphire embedded in his skin was vibrating as it glittered with a fierce glow.

Screaming, the soldier dropped to his knees. He would have crashed into Rémy if she hadn't scrambled backwards. Around them, all the men and women of the Sapphire Cutlass were doing the same – screaming in fear and pain, writhing their armoured fingers against their chests and arms – anywhere they had fastened a sapphire into their skin.

The stones were growing, transforming the human flesh around themselves from skin and fat and bone to rock-hard sapphire. Rémy saw it radiate from the tattoo, swallowing the black lines of the drawn cutlass as if it had never existed, opening up a transparency in the man's chest that looked like a void. He kept screaming until the gem's growth had spread to his throat, where his cry strangled and died. The last thing to go were his eyes, which looked at Rémy with a pitiful plea, as if the woman he had been trying to slaughter a second ago could somehow be his saviour now. A moment later, there was nothing before her but a shape cut out of sapphire that had once been human.

Around her, the horror was being played out over and over again as the foot soldiers of the Sapphire Cutlass were turned to stone – not animated, moving stone as she had been, but dead, inert crystalline structures with no life apart from what glinted in them as light glanced from the unnatural angles of their surfaces.

Something grabbed her arm – Kai, who had battled through the dying cult members to her side. She couldn't hear what he was shouting at her over their horrible screams, but he waved one arm and she turned her head to see the others, urging them to run. The passageway, ahead and behind them, was now made of sapphire, and the stone was continuing to spread, turning what had once been the darkness ahead of them into a tunnel of prismatic blue light. The only part that had remained untouched was the dirt path beneath their feet, a grey ribbon leading them through the vivid blue.

Rémy, still stunned, found it difficult to move. Kai wrapped his arm around her waist and staggered forward, pulling her onwards despite his own injury. Thaddeus must have seen her hesitate, because he passed Dita to Desai and started back towards them.

"Come on," he bellowed into her ear once he reached them, squeezing her arm with one hand. "We have to hurry."

Thaddeus hooked Kai's other arm over his shoulder and together they hoisted him up, carrying him between them.

"What's happening?" Rémy shouted, not even sure her voice could carry to Thaddeus' ears over the din. *Is this it?* she wondered. *Can the Sapphire Cutlass only destroy? Will the entire world turn to stone?*

Thaddeus hadn't heard her, but he was trying to tell them something anyway.

"Don't touch," he yelled. "Desai says, whatever you do, don't try to take one of the sapphires."

For once in her life, Rémy had absolutely no interest in owning a gemstone.

They ran, dodging transforming and transformed cult members, trying not to touch the human statues that littered their path. Rémy saw one such statue topple, falling against another pure sapphire form as it fell, shattering into a cascade of smaller jewels. Kai, answering some kind of reflex, tried to bend to pick one up, but Rémy and Thaddeus stopped him.

Ahead of them, Rémy saw the raja do the same. He paused for a moment, as if mesmerised, before snatching up handfuls of sapphire. Desai realised what he was doing and tried to yell a warning, but it was too late.

The raja started to scream. He opened his palm and tried to shake the jewels from his hand, but they had already fused with his skin. They burrowed like insects into his very being, and in a second his veins were flooding with a blue light that tore through his body like fire. His hand became sapphire. The once-proud raja held it out to them as they passed, as if somehow one of them could do something to help him. The jewel spread up his arm to his shoulder, exploded into his chest, then rose up his neck to his gaping, screaming mouth. He fell silent, enveloped in stone.

The sound of the terror receded as they left those horrors behind them. The sapphire was still spreading – the rooms through which Upala and Rémy had crept with wonder were all now a uniform blue, simple and cold in its purity. They stumbled out of the entrance to the mountain and saw that both the statues and the carvings were all also transformed.

Rémy was relieved to see, though, that the sapphire had apparently reached the extent of its growth. The creepers that grew in elaborate tangles over the surface of the mountain temple were still alive, and still wore the green and tan hues of their true selves. The jungle outside was still there as well – brighter, lighter and greener, somehow, than it had been when they had first began their sojourn inside the mountain.

The group stumbled out into the open and collapsed a few paces away from the temple's entrance. Kai grunted with pain as he hit the ground. They all sprawled out on the warm earth, exhausted and gasping for breath.

"What in the name of blazes were that?" J rasped, Dita's hand clutched tightly in his. "I thought we were done for, good and proper!"

Desai began to laugh, a deep, rumbling sound that Rémy realised she'd never heard before.

"What's so funny?" J asked, irritated as he sat up.

The older man sat up, too, and reached out to clap J on the back. "My dear, dear J – I thought we were done for, too. I thought the Sapphire Cutlass had won." He looked over to Kai with a smile. "But it seems that Kai was right. I underestimated Upala's strength."

"You mean, what happened just then, that was the opal working?" Thaddeus asked, looking up at the pure sapphire of the mountain.

Desai followed his gaze. "I think it was more than that. My guess is that the power of the Sapphire Cutlass was actually too great for the opal to contain. The energy released – the power it tried to drain from her – had to be absorbed by something else. So the mountain took it back. The mountain reclaimed its power and, in doing so, finally regained what had been stolen from it, so many years ago."

"So that's it?" Kai asked. "It's all over?"

Desai nodded, his exhaustion beginning to show on his face. "That would be my hope, yes."

"You can't be sure?"

The older man lifted his palms in a humble shrug. "One can never be sure."

Silence fell around them as they all contemplated Desai's words. In it, somewhere in the depths of the jungle valley, a bird sang a happy song.

"Listen to that," said Thaddeus, raising his head and shutting his eyes under the sun's golden rays. "There were no birds here, before we went in to the mountain. The valley seems different. It feels different. More... alive, somehow."

"Well," said Desai. "Nature has a way of reasserting herself over man's folly."

"Can I go back in?" Kai asked. "I need... I need to find Upala."

Rémy felt her heart twinge in sympathy. She laid a hand on his arm. "Kai... I don't think there is any hope that she–"

"I know," Kai cut her off gruffly, looking at his feet. "She's dead. I know that. But... I feel like I have to see her. I have to... pay my last respects."

Rémy looked at Desai, who seemed troubled. "Would it be safe?" she asked. "The earthquake has gone. There... doesn't seem to be any more... transformations... happening. Is it over?"

Desai paused before answering. "I think it would be prudent to wait. I really have no way of knowing what is happening inside the mountain. Wait, Kai, until the morning. Until you have rested and I have seen to the wound in your leg. I think... that Upala can wait for you."

Kai nodded. Rémy watched her brother's face for a moment, until she saw that his eyes were filling with tears. Then she turned away.

***

They collected wood for a fire as the shadows lengthened in the valley, turning the sky overhead from azure to indigo before eventually fading into darkness completely. Thaddeus helped J and Rémy gather the wood, reflecting silently on the events of the past few days. The valley's natural life was, as

Desai had said, reasserting itself. Night creatures crept around them, skittering in the undergrowth. Of the mist that had concealed their attackers, there was no sign.

Thaddeus watched Rémy. They hadn't spoken much yet, besides holding each other close in a brief reassurance that they were indeed both still whole. There had been a moment there, when he'd left her on top of Dita's cage surrounded by hundreds of murderous acolytes, that Thaddeus had really thought he might never see her again. He wondered what it meant that he'd left anyway. Kai had wanted to stay with Upala, even though he knew it would have been hopeless.

Thaddeus hadn't wanted to leave Rémy there. Of course he hadn't. It was just that they had spent so long weathering such dangers together that he knew how she would have reacted if he hadn't gone to help Desai instead of staying with her. She wouldn't have thanked him for it. She probably would have resorted to one of the old insults she used to use back before they were together, in London, and called him stupid. It wasn't that Rémy didn't need protecting. Everyone needed protecting in one way or another. It was just that she wouldn't allow it. And he loved her. What was love if it wasn't accepting what the person you loved wanted, even if it wasn't what you would choose for yourself?

They built the fire and lit it, settling around it quietly as it crackled and sparked in the dark. Thaddeus found himself staring quietly at the flames, sitting with his elbows on his knees as Desai fixed up Kai's leg with Rémy's help.

"Penny for them?" she asked, coming to sit beside him a few minutes later, close enough to lean her head against his tired shoulder.

Thaddeus turned and kissed the top of her head. "Just… taking it all in, I suppose. What happened back there… it could easily have been the end of the world, which is just… staggering, really."

Rémy pressed herself closer to him and he sat back, wrapping one arm around her shoulders to pull her against his chest.

"We couldn't have done it without Upala and Kai," she said, quiet enough that her voice would not carry over the flames. "He is so upset, Thaddeus. He's trying to hide it, but… I think he's heartbroken."

Thaddeus buried his nose in her hair and looked over the flames to her twin. Kai held his bandaged leg stiffly out in front of him, staring into the middle distance as if he didn't see any of it at all. *There but for the grace of God go I,* Thaddeus thought to himself. *If I lost Rémy now…* he pushed the thought away and shut his eyes for a moment, feeling the rise and fall of her breathing as they sat twined together, almost as close as it was possible for two humans to be. It seemed impossible to imagine that they didn't belong exactly as they were now.

"He's determined to go back into the mountain," Rémy continued quietly, oblivious to Thaddeus' train of thought.

"I suppose there's nothing we can do to stop him," Thaddeus murmured.

"No, there isn't. So I am going to go, too."

Thaddeus felt a sick twist of worry knot itself into his

stomach. "Rémy, no – we don't know what you'll find in there. We don't know for certain if its safe. We don't even know–"

She pulled gently out of his arms and straightened up to face him. "Thaddeus, I can't let him go alone. He is my brother – my true twin. I've only known him a few days. I can't leave him to do something like this alone, now. Especially not when it's my fault that–"

Thaddeus moved to cup her face in both his hands. "It's not your fault."

"If I hadn't gone to find them – if I hadn't convinced them to help us, then…"

"It is not your fault, Rémy Brunel. I won't allow you to think that. It's Sahoj's fault, it's the raja's fault, it's Aruna's fault… I don't know, it's that legendary Portuguese man who lived hundreds of years ago's fault. But it is not yours, no matter what you might think."

Rémy's lips curved in a watery smile. "You are too nice to me, Englishman."

Thaddeus kissed her gently, warmly. "You deserve it." He pulled her to him again, settling her head against his chest. "You're still going to go though, aren't you?"

Rémy tightened her arms around him. "I have to. Does that make you hate me?"

Thaddeus laughed quietly. "Of course I don't hate you. I love you, Rémy Brunel. I always will, no matter what crazy, hare-brained situations you drag me into. Don't you know that by now?"

Thirty One

Opals and Bones

The mountain stayed silent all night, no unpleasant echoes of the events that had taken place in its depths drifting out of its transformed mouth. In the morning a new sun rose over the valley, casting its rays against the biggest sapphire Rémy had ever seen. She stood, her feet damp with early-morning dew, and watched as the dawn light refracted against the ancient carvings, now as blue as the sky over her head. The jewel itself, though, seemed quieter, somehow, as if whatever peculiar electricity had animated it had gone.

"Ready?" Kai asked, stepping to her side. He was still limping, but his stride was stronger than it had been the night before. Behind them stood the others: Desai, J, Dita and Thaddeus, waiting for them to set off back into the mountain.

"Yes," she told him. "Are you?"

Kai looked up at the mountain, squinting in the already-bright sunlight, his face impassive. "As ready as I will ever be, little sister. Let's go."

He moved off, his pace slow to accommodate his injured leg. Rémy hung back, turning to Thaddeus with a smile. He walked towards her, leaning down to kiss her gently.

"Don't be long," he said softly.

She kissed him back. "We won't be. Don't get sunburn while I'm gone."

Thaddeus smiled and let her go. Rémy followed Kai, up the sapphire steps, through the great archway, and into the mountain.

The sunlight, so bright outside, faded away once they had gone just a little way. They had been prepared for that, bringing torches that had been wrapped with cloth donated from their clothes. Whatever happened next, once all this was done, Rémy told herself, they would all need new things to wear. It was amazing that the ones they had still held together, they were so tattered. She thought of the silks and embroidered drapes that adorned the inner chambers of the raja's palace, and wondered what the chances were of being able to get hold of them. Slim, most likely. She couldn't imagine that, in the absence of both the raja and Sahoj, the place hadn't already been ransacked, and she couldn't blame the people for doing that. They deserved to take back what had been taken from them over so long.

With a torch each, it was easier to see the way. The flame-light haloed against the sapphire walls, reflecting back over and over until it seemed as if they were walking through a hall of mirrors. There was no sign of movement, save for them. The stone was as dead as the cult members they came across – or rather, what was left of the cult members, who remained where they had been standing when the transformation overcame them, frozen for all eternity in twisted, ice-cold sapphire versions of themselves.

Rémy tried not to touch anything. The stone seemed to be dead, but after witnessing what had happened to all these people – not to mention to the raja, whose transparent, invaluable carcass they passed – she was in no hurry to test the theory.

At length they passed into the cavern. Their torches were not strong enough to light the entire space and flickered and died beyond a circle around them both. But it was enough to illuminate more bodies of pure jewel, all caught in poses of flight as they had tried to outrun the explosion of power behind them.

"The torches on the walls," Kai whispered, sending sibilant echoes into the dark void that answered back, over and over again. "We should light them."

"Will they not have been turned to sapphire, too?" Rémy asked, disturbed by the echo of her own voice rolling around them.

Rémy's supposition was right. Every fixture, from the wooden shaft of each torch to the metal rivets that had held them in place, had been transformed into gemstone. There was nothing for it but for them to feel their way, slowly, with the light they had.

As they walked deeper into the cavern, they came across more and more sapphire corpses. In some places, they were so close together that it was almost impossible to find a way through. Their limbs tangled together like a climbing rose bush, so impenetrable that at last Kai, frustrated, drew his sword and before Rémy could raise her voice to stop him, had smashed it down, cutting through a mess of crystalline arms and legs.

Rémy froze as the gems shattered, listening with a pounding heart as the broken stones tinkled against the sapphire floor. She was convinced that something would come rushing at them from the jagged dark beyond their torchlights – something ravenous with anger. But there was nothing but the echoes of the skittering gems. Kai pushed onwards through the path he had made as a new feeling of misgiving flooded through Rémy.

"Kai – wait," she urged, ignoring the incessant echoes of her own words. "Please. Listen to me, just for a moment."

Her brother turned to face her, his weather-beaten face taking on the reflections of blue stone and orange flame.

"I just…" Rémy took a breath, wondering how to say what was worrying her. "It's Upala. Kai, the same thing has happened to everything inside this place. Everything. Upala – she's going to look just like this now. She is going to *be* just like this. Do you really need to see that? Don't you want to… remember her as she was, not as she is now?"

Kai glanced around him at the carcasses of the cult. He took a breath, a look of unutterable sadness fleetingly crossing his features. It was gone in an instant, replaced by a clenched jaw and a familiar look of determination.

"I have to find her," he said. "I have to."

Rémy looked at him for another second, and then nodded. They moved on, past the pit of snakes that no longer writhed but instead were frozen in permanent curlicues. They forced their way between more death, and finally up onto the stone stage. Rémy could see the tension radiating from Kai's shoulders, knowing that Upala must be somewhere close. He stalked forward, his limp almost indistinguishable beneath the forceful movement of his steps.

He stopped.

"Rémy," he said, his voice thick – and remarkably, there was no echo. *"Look."*

She moved to her brother's side, and looked up at what he had found. Rémy drew in a sharp, amazed breath.

In front of them was the throne of the Sapphire Cutlass. In it was seated Aruna, the girl-goddess who had turned against the world itself. She was slumped backwards, arms outstretched along her arm rests, eyes closed as if she were merely asleep – and she was flesh and blood.

Gone was the taint of sapphire that had so poisoned her body, gone was the pure blue transparency of her legs and arms. Instead there was only burnished skin, as human and as fallible as that of Rémy's own.

"I… don't understand…" Rémy muttered, awestruck.

Then Kai moved his torch, lifting it to his left. Beside the throne was pillar of pure sapphire – not formed in the shape of anything but itself, a large tablet of glittering jewel. Inside was the perfectly preserved form of Upala. She stood as if on tip-toe, arms by her side, head raised and eyes open. She looked as fierce and beautiful as ever, and so unharmed that at first Rémy thought she was still alive. But there was no rise and fall in her breast and no space for air between the limits of her being and the sapphire that surrounded her. She was dead. Beautiful, eternal – but dead.

Kai stepped up to the pillar and dropped his sword, placing both hands on Upala's magnificent tomb. Rémy could see tears running down his face, and it was clear that, for now, he did not care if she saw them. He stood there, silently, looking up at Upala for a long time. Rémy looked away, wanting to give them privacy, somehow. Her eye was caught by something lying on the ground. She stooped to pick it up, recognising it at once.

"Kai," she said gently, holding it out to him.

It was a pendant fashioned from opal, hanging on a gold chain. Within the opal's milky whiteness shone a thick band of iridescent blue. Kai took it from her and coiled the necklace in his palm as a tear fell from his face to glide across the stone's surface. He passed his thumb across it.

"She always wanted to know where it came from,' Kai muttered thickly, staring at the gem in his hand. 'The opal, I mean. She knew it wasn't from anywhere on this continent. I told her it was from Australasia – so far away and so dangerous a place that it's where the British send their criminals. She wanted to go and I told her…" he trailed off, and then started again. "I told her that one day, we'd go. One day, I'd sail her all the way there, just because she wanted to go. I thought that was as good as telling her I loved her. But it wasn't. I loved her, and I never told her. Why didn't I *tell* her?"

Rémy put a hand on his arm. "She knew, Kai. And she loved you, too. You knew that, didn't you?"

Kai looked up at Upala, suspended forever in her magnificent jewel. "It's not the same," he said, his voice cracking. "Life's too short, little sister. Life's too short not to say what you mean."

Rémy wrapped her arms around her brother. After a moment, he held her, too. Two lost twins, finally reunited.

At length Kai gave a big sniff and pulled away. "We should go," he said. "There's nothing more we can do here."

Rémy nodded, and then looked at Aruna's curiously unmarred human corpse. "What should we do with her?" she asked.

Kai gave the body a long look. "Leave her there," he said. "Her bones belong to the mountain. Let it keep them."

Epilogue

"You know what would be really useful right now?" said J, as they made the journey out of the valley. "An airship. Didn't we have one, once? Oh yeah – we did. And someone crashed it."

"I did *not* crash it, J," Rémy sighed. "We were hit by a flaming arrow."

"Yeah," grumbled J, "an' *then* you crashed."

"Hush," said Dita, who was walking beside him. Desai was a little way ahead of them, leading the way. "The walk will do us good."

"Hrumph," J muttered. "What we just went through, we need sleep, not bleedin' exercise."

"Oh yes, I was forgetting," said Dita, her voice caustic, "what a hard time you had back there, dirty boy. All that running around was terrible, *ja*? Far worse than getting bitten by a snake and being turned into a monster."

"I *ain't* dirty, an' that wasn't what I meant," J protested, "and you wasn't a monster! Not even close!"

"What was I then?" Dita asked, slipping her hand into his. "A freak? Like one of those poor beardy women you see in a circus?"

"Bearded women," J corrected. "And no, you wasn't a freak, neither."

They carried on bickering as they walked, their chatter fading into the background with the chirrup of the crickets as Thaddeus tuned them out. They had been walking for a long while already, and it would be longer still before they reached the valley's edge and moved out of the mountain's shadow. Thaddeus was tired, but happy – relieved to be leaving this place behind, and also at Rémy's reports of what had happened inside. That Upala was truly dead was a tragedy, but knowing that the rest of the cult had been similarly subdued was a cause for relief.

Thaddeus became aware that Rémy was no longer at his side. He turned to see that she had dropped back, putting space between herself and the rest of the group. Thaddeus slowed his pace, falling into step with her.

"Everything all right?" he asked, anxious when he saw the thoughtful look on her face. "What's the matter?"

"Nothing's the matter. I've just been thinking, that's all."

"Oh? What about?" Thaddeus glanced up the slight hill they were climbing to where her brother Kai soldiered onwards, stoic despite his grief and pain. No doubt Rémy was thinking about him. What must it be like, to think you're alone in the world and then to come face-to-face with your twin? It must be–

"Will you marry me?" Rémy asked.

Thaddeus stopped dead in his tracks, looking at her in astonishment. "What?"

Rémy stopped beside him and shrugged. "I've been thinking about it for a while, but... something that Kai said, back there, made me realise that I should just go ahead and ask," she said. "So do you want to? Get married, I mean?"

Something fierce and hot radiated out from Thaddeus' heart as he caught her arm and pulled her to him. "Do I *want* to? Rémy – of course I want to! But I thought – I wasn't sure that you..." He took a breath and willed his heart to calm down as he stepped back and looked at her, smiling widely. "Rémy Brunel. Nothing would make me happier than to be your husband, and to call you my wife. In fact..."

"What is it?" Rémy asked, puzzled, as he pulled away and reached for one of the pockets in his trousers.

Thaddeus found what he was looking for. Pulling out a small twist of paper, he unwrapped a small ring. It had been formed of two thin bands of gold, twisted together in a wreath to hold a tiny diamond. He hesitated for a moment, and then reached out to take Rémy's left hand. He looked at her face and saw the delight spreading across the features that he had come to love so well. Smiling, he slipped the ring onto her finger. It fit perfectly.

"I know it's only tiny, but I thought," he said quietly, "that you deserved to have a diamond that you didn't have to steal."

Rémy stared at the ring, holding it up so the little stone could catch the light. "It's beautiful," she whispered. Then she cast him a look. "How long have you had this in your pocket?" she demanded. "And where did you get it from?"

"Ahh," said Thaddeus, holding up both hands. "That would be telling. I've got to have *some* secrets."

Rémy grabbed his hands, laughing. "What, even as my husband?"

Thaddeus laughed with her, wrapping her up in his arms and kissing her soundly. "Well, perhaps not *then*..."

"Why did you never ask me?" Rémy said. "If you had the ring..."

Thaddeus shrugged. "I could never work out how."

Rémy rested her forehead against his. "I find that simply usually works."

"Yes," Thaddeus laughed. "Apparently so."

"The only thing is," Rémy added, "I am not sure I could ever be 'Rémy Rec'. It just doesn't..." she trailed off with a grimace.

Thaddeus made a face. "Ugh. No, I can see what you mean. I'm not sure you could ever be anything other than Rémy Brunel anyway. Maybe I should take your name instead."

Rémy looked up at him. "Really?"

Thaddeus shrugged. "Why not? Thaddeus Brunel has a bit of a ring to it, don't you think?"

Rémy raised her eyebrows. "It's a very French name. I am not sure you could be sufficiently French to own it. For a start you would have to drink less tea."

"Oh, god." Thaddeus stopped, a look of mock horror on his face. "I can't do it, Rémy. I love you, but I just can't."

She punched him lightly in the arm as they both laughed. "Stupid man."

266

"What are you two laughing about?" asked a voice.

It was Kai, watching them with a slight, subdued, smile. Thaddeus and Rémy parted, still holding hands. Thaddeus saw Kai's gaze drop to the little ring on Rémy's finger.

"Ahh," he said, with a smile that managed to be both wider and sadder at the same time. "I see that congratulations are in order."

"Kai, I am sorry," Rémy said, faltering over the words. "I know – I know that you... that you..."

Kai stepped forward and grasped his sister's hand. "There is no need to be sorry for anything, little sister," he said softly. "I am glad that you have more sense than me – in some things, anyway. I am very happy for you both."

Rémy let go of Thaddeus to hug her brother fiercely. "Thank you, brother. That means so much to me."

When they parted, Rémy took Thaddeus's hand again and the three of them started to walk, following the others once more.

"So," Kai asked, "what are you two going to do now? Besides tying the knot, I mean. Will you go back to England?"

Thaddeus glanced at Rémy, who looked back with a shrug. It was a good question, and one that neither of them had considered at all.

"There's not much for me in England," Thaddeus admitted. "They'll never make me a policeman again."

"Are you sure?" Rémy asked, looking up at him with concern etched on her brow. "You were the best they had, Thaddeus. You might be surprised – I bet they would be glad to have you back."

"I doubt it," he sighed. "Besides, after all the things we've seen, all the places we've been, knowing what else is out there in the world... well, I'm not sure I want to go back, really. What about you, Rémy? It's not just about what I want – what do you want to do next?"

Rémy's gaze drifted towards her brother. "I don't know," she said, "although I would like a chance to get to know the only family I have..."

Kai gave her a smile and then a smirk. "Well," he said slowly. "You know, I do have need of more good hands aboard my ship. I always told Upala that if she left me I'd have to find two to replace her. I wasn't lying." He shrugged. "You could join my crew. I'd be glad to have you – both of you."

Thaddeus grimaced in answer to Rémy's raised eyebrows. "Look... I may not be a policeman any more... but I don't think I could be a pirate."

"Really?" Rémy teased. "And there I was thinking you were looking quite piratical these days, what with your torn shirts and your constant tan."

Thaddeus laughed, squeezing her hand. "I'm sorry, Rémy, but I couldn't."

She smiled at him softly. "I know. You're just too good a man for thievery and plunder, whatever the cause. I'm sorry, Kai," she said, addressing her brother, "but I think we have to say no."

Kai nodded with a grin. "I expected as much. Pity. Although..." He trailed off, looking thoughtful.

"What?" Rémy asked.

Kai shrugged. "I think I might be over the pirate life, too, at least for now. I have another ship – smaller than the *Black Swan*, but just as seaworthy. The *Silver Cygnet*. I could take her and sail anywhere I wanted to – as long as I had a crew to help me, of course."

"A crew?" Thaddeus asked. "How big of a crew?"

"Not many. Four should do it, with me besides." Kai's gaze drifted ahead, to where J and Dita were still bickering merrily as they walked along, their feet kicking up trails of dust that flurried in their wake.

Rémy frowned. "And where were you thinking of taking this ship of yours?" she asked.

"I've not decided yet," Kai said quietly. Then he pulled Upala's opal from his pocket and held it up so that it swung in front of him. "Perhaps I will simply trust the wind to take me wherever it wishes to go."

Thaddeus looked down at Rémy, who looked back with a question on her face. He felt like laughing, and wondered how it could be that since he'd met her, life didn't seem to have even taken a breath, let alone stood still.

"What do you think Dita and J want to do next?" she asked him.

Thaddeus raised her fingers to his lips and kissed them. "I don't know," he said. "Let's ask them and find out."

towards nullifying her geographical advantage: zinc concentrates and wolfram ores, produced in Australia, had to be smelted in Germany; Australian lead and the bulk of the Indian mica mines were controlled by German financial interests. The attempts made to remedy these deficiencies were modest ones. Opening the National Physical Laboratory in 1902, the Prince of Wales described it as 'almost the first instance of the State taking part in scientific research'. In the same year the Government took over the Imperial Institute, which sponsored some scientific research related to industry, and in 1907 the Imperial College of Science and Technology was founded. By 1914 the National Physical Laboratory was getting the distinctly un-mammoth grant of £7,000 per annum, with an additional grant for aeronautical research. A little-noticed subsection of the 1911 National Insurance Act made provision for a medical research fund, and it was out of this that, just before the war, the Medical Research Committee began to take shape.[4]

Great Britain, comprising England, Wales and Scotland, governed since 1707 by the same Parliament, was one island. Ireland was another. Together, in 1914, they formed the United Kingdom of Great Britain and Ireland, governed since 1800 by this same Parliament at Westminster. Britain was prosperous and heavily industrialized; Ireland, lacking the mineral bounty with which Britain was blessed, was poverty-stricken and, save for the Belfast area, almost entirely agrarian. Her population was in decline, and stood, in 1911, at just over four millions; the population of Britain, 40·8 millions, that is to say about ten million families, was still increasing, though the rate was less healthy-looking than it had been in the nineteenth century. Britain's two strongest commercial rivals, Germany and the United States, had populations of 64·9 millions and 91·7 millions respectively.

Forty million people crammed into a small island meant that Britain was markedly an urban country. The location of coal had determined the direction of the population flow provoked by the industrial developments of the eighteenth and nineteenth centuries: thus in Lancashire, Northumberland, Yorkshire, the Midlands, South Wales and the Scottish lowlands, big towns had erupted like boils, surrounded by an unsightly rash of smaller towns and villages. Birmingham, like a number of other towns, expanded its boundaries shortly after the 1911 Census, giving administrative recognition to the growing urban sprawl: it then comprised a total of 840,202 inhabitants. Glasgow had 784,496, Liverpool 746,421, Manchester 714,333, Leeds 445,550, Newcastle 266,603. In 1914 the basic industries associated with these areas – iron and steel, textiles and coal – were prospering, though in every case Britain's position was being strongly challenged. It was as futile to lament over this as it was to believe that by some magic incantation Britain could somehow freeze other countries at a level of development which left her supreme. None the less, there was a disquieting lack of flexibility and amenity to new ideas in British industry; and for a country which had called herself the workshop of the world the growing dependence of her export market on a primary raw material, coal, was ominous.

Only 21·9 per cent of the population of England and Wales lived in what the Census, somewhat inprecisely, termed 'rural districts', and since the depression of the 1870s farming had become a rather neglected craft. The slight revival of the Edwardian era could not stand comparison with the conscious German policy of creating farm out of forest, marsh and sand dune.[5] On the eve of the war Britain was dependent on imports for four-fifths of her wheat and 40 per cent of her meat.

The country's ballast, then, was in the north, southern towns like Bristol (population in 1911, 357,048) and Bath having lost much of their former importance. But there was one tremendous make-weight. Irrespective of all other population trends, London, since Roman times, had advanced steadily and far ahead of its nearest population rivals and it now mustered in what was officially termed the Greater London area $7\frac{1}{4}$ million inhabitants. London was the centre of the far-flung Empire, the seat of government, and the control point for business and the professions. As such it had already been invaded by the germs of one of the major afflictions of twentieth-century urban society, the special care of the London Traffic Branch of the Board of Trade, which reported of the year 1913:

Among the various phases of the London traffic problem, one most important feature is the daily movement of a very large section of the population from their residences within an area of 30 miles round London to places of business in Central London and back again. . . .

There can be no longer any doubt about the gradual withdrawal of a large amount of traffic of all sorts from the railways to the roads, owing to the development of the motor vehicle. The convenience of the mechanically propelled vehicle for passenger purposes very rapidly asserted itself, and today it accounts for fully 94 per cent of the passenger vehicles met with on the roads round London. . . .

Street accidents are an unfortunate phase of the traffic problem and there is no hope that they can ever be entirely eliminated. . . .[6]

London was the geographical focal point for the élite of British society. That Edwardian and early Georgian Britain was a very rigid class society is abundantly clear from a wealth of contemporary material, even if the same material does not furnish evidence for any very precise analysis of the class structure. In his highly perceptive *The Condition of England,* published in 1909, C. F. G. Masterman distinguished three major classes, the 'conquerors', the 'suburbans', and the 'multitude', with a fourth depressed class, the submerged proletariat, whom he called the 'prisoners' tacked on to the underside of the 'multitude', or working class.[7] Leo Chiozza Money, concerned more with inequalities of wealth and income, limited himself to three classes, which he preferred to call rich, comfortable and poor, rather than upper, middle and lower.[8] There were forces at work which were blurring the more rigid and more complicated hierarchy which had obtained in mid-Victorian times: a rise in money incomes had brought classes and gradations within classes closer together; direct progressive taxation, which got steeper and steeper on higher incomes, had 'compressed the whole scale of disposable incomes'; and, most important, technological advance had brought to the less well-off material circumstances not in character far different from those of the better off.[9] The main consequence was not so much a mixing of classes as the creation of a greater homogeneity within the working class, a tendency assisted by the expansion of trade unionism among the unskilled workers. At the same time it was still true in 1914 that a skilled artisan earned double the wages of the unskilled labourer.

Yet within the same historical period the growth of a suburban white-collar lower-middle class, associated with the rise of large-scale industry and its ancillary developments in insurance and accountancy, had added a new subtlety to the class structure. It is almost entirely from this class that Masterman drew his picture of the 'suburbans', who lead

a life of Security; a life of Sedentary occupation; a life of Respectability; and these three qualities give the key to its special characteristics. Its male population is engaged in all its working hours in small, crowded offices, under artificial light, doing immense sums, adding up other men's accounts, writing other men's letters. It is sucked into the City at daybreak, and scattered again as darkness falls. It finds itself towards evening in its own territory in the miles and miles of little red houses in little silent streets, in number defying imagination. Each boasts its pleasant drawing-room, its bow-window, its little front garden, its high-sounding title – 'Acacia Villa' or 'Camperdown Lodge' – attesting unconquered human aspiration.[10]

'The rich,' says Masterman, 'despise the Working People; the Middle Classes fear them.'[11]

The major social fact of the day remained the great and accepted gulf which existed between the working class and the whole of the rest of society, a gulf very apparent in the attitudes of the Schlegel sisters towards the self-improving artisan, Leonard Bast, portrayed by E. M. Forster in *Howards End*. So certain are people of the existence of this separate working class that it is rather difficult to find a definition of it, the implication being that to meet a member of the working class was to recognize him at once, by his smell if not by his garb. Bowley, in introducing the valuable surveys he conducted in 1913, did make the attempt:

The definition of 'the working class' cannot be exactly drawn on pre-conceived lines. Of course, in the great majority of cases included in our Tables the principal occupant of the house was working for weekly or hourly wages, and in the great majority of houses in our samples treated as non-working class the occupier was professional, commercial or living on income from property. The necessity for less obvious discrimination arose in houses rented at from 7/6 to 12/- a week. If the principal occupants were clerks, travellers, teachers, shop managers or employers in a small way they were excluded from the working class Tables. Shop assistants were included in the working class if working for butchers or grocers. The great majority of shop assistants are, of course, not householders but living with their parents. The working class householders include among their supplementary earners a not very large number of persons who would, if principal occupants, have been excluded.[12]

In effect he is really doing little more than elaborating upon what might be called definition by instinct; an instinct at its most sensitive in its appreciation of the special proletarian attributes of butchers and grocers. In the last sentence Bowley reveals, incidentally, that there is little in the way of social mobility out of the working class.

There is one administrative line of division in society which is worth a little attention, the income-tax line. It is a striking fact that on the eve of the war there were less than $1\frac{1}{4}$ million income-tax payers, that is less than seven per cent of the occupied population. Payment of income-tax is scarcely a highly sought-after social privilege, yet it is a measure of a man's respectability as a financial pillar of society, and an indication of his positive stake in the community. The figure of £160 per annum, the lowest upon which income-tax was assessed, is too high to be taken as the upper boundary of the working class, but it is a useful pivotal point to bear in mind. The actual size of the pre-war working class can only be estimated very roughly, though it is at once evident that it is very large. The grand total of wage-earners, men, women, boys and girls, as revealed by the 1911 figures, was 15·6 millions, or three-quarters of the occupied population; this is the main core of the working class as understood by contemporaries. However, to this we should, almost certainly, add the 1·2 million men and women employed as small shopkeepers, hawkers, dressmakers, etc., whose earnings were not more than those of most wage-earners, and, less certainly, a proportion of the 1·2 million salaried men and women earning less than our pivotal £160 per annum;[13] following Leo Chiozza Money, we would call these last, at least, the lower-middle classes rather than part of the working class. Included in this debatable group we have the elementary school-teachers, almost all working-class in origin and outlook.

Moving into the middle class proper, we have 400,000 salaried men earning over £160 per annum[14] (the number of women in this elevated station was negligible), a professional group of 330,000 (this includes clergymen, doctors, lawyers, engineers, writers, artists, entertainers, law clerks, but not teachers, who go under the salaried classification), and a proportion of the 580,000 farmers (some of whom might more properly be accounted lower-middle, or even working-class owing to their lowly earnings). Finally, among the occupied classes there are 620,000 employers, ranging from the shopkeeper with one assistant, the small provincial businessman who is quite definitely middle-class, to the owner of a large national concern who might be regarded as belonging to the uppermost class in society, the London-based élite. Among the unoccupied in 1911, 60,000 stated that they had 'independent means'. Class lines at the top of the social scale are rather harder to define than at the bottom, unless one unjustifiably restricts the uppermost class to the old landed aristocracy. There is a self-evident difference in status between John Dewar, the Perth whisky manufacturer, elevated to the peerage as Lord Forteviot, and a small Lancashire businessman like Elijah Sandham, whose only political outlet was in the local organization of the Independent Labour Party.

The uppermost class, characterized by its wealth, status, and, above all, political power, was an amalgam of top business and professional men and the landed aristocracy, who still enjoyed a social and political primacy in town, and a feudal dominance in the countryside.[15] The way to the heights for the man not born with aristocratic connexions was through an apprenticeship in politics; the looser conventions of the Edwardian era had made great wealth itself a possible passport to high society, but not to high politics. Masterman and Money seem to have a large rather than a small group in mind for their uppermost class of 'conquerors' or 'rich'. Bowley in a more recent study[16] has given various random figures relevant to 1913–14 upon which a computation of the total upper class might be based – 13,850 people with incomes over £5,000, 47,000 with over £2,000, 75,000 private dwelling-houses with an annual value of over £150 per annum in London or £100 per annum in the provinces, 151,000 motor-cars on the roads. Or one could limit the upper class to that 2·5 per cent of the population which, according to Bowley, held two-thirds of the country's wealth.

Before attempting a complete proportional picture we must turn again to Bowley's 1913 survey: before giving his attention to his sample of 2,150 working-class households, Bowley creamed off 480, which he described as middle and upper class[17] – just over 20 per cent of the total. This accords fairly well with the occupational figures given above: very roughly, then, we could divide the country on the outbreak of war into 80 per cent working class, anything from 10 to 18 per cent middle class depending on definition, and the remainder upper class. However, we can see again where the really important divide lay, when we reflect that the average wage for the adult male industrial worker on the eve of war was about £75 per annum, whereas the average annual income of the salaried class was £340.[18] In terms of human relations the class divide was most clearly expressed in the enjoyment by every middle-class household of the amenity of one or more servants. It was most obviously buttressed by the educational system: though some secondary schools had as many as 25 per cent free places, few working-class children ever progressed beyond the rudimentary disciplines acquired in the free elementary schools. All in all, there were only 200,000 secondary-school pupils in 1914. Political equality was much more widely diffused than social or economic equality. Every adult male householder had the Parliamentary franchise – that is, out of about 25 million adults, 8 million had the vote. Attempts to rationalize local government – where some women did have the vote – had been made in the nineteenth century; but before the formation of borough councils and urban and rural district councils there had been a great proliferation of *ad hoc* bodies which gave the middle classes opportunities both for service and for a demonstration of their social status. Since 1902 the trend had been towards the elimination of these bodies, but the Boards of Guardians for administration of the Poor Law and a number of minor educational authorities still existed.

Poverty among the working class was the main theme of the various social surveys. Leo Chiozza Money put it dramatically when he pointed out that the five-million-odd people whose principal bread-winners (or caviare-winners, Money implied) were above the £160 line had half of the total national income at their disposal, whereas the remaining 39 million had to make do with the other half. Bowley, using the very bare definition of the 'poverty line' adopted by Seebohm Rowntree in 1901, found 16 per cent living in what he called 'primary' poverty, as distinct from the 'secondary' poverty brought about by unwise disposition of available income. His vigorous conclusion was that 'to raise the wages of the worst-paid workers is the most pressing social task with which the country is confronted today'.[19] Poor dieting gave many members of the lower orders yet another characteristic which distinguished them from the rest of society: their small stature. In 1914 the Board of Trade's 'average family' – reckoned as equivalent to 3·84 adult males in calorific requirements (4·57 units would actually have been a more realistic figure) – spent about 23s per week on food (the larger, and more usual, family, taken as including 1·2 supplementary earners, would spend about 25s), including 7 lb of meat at from around 6d to 8d a pound, 1 lb of bacon at 1s a pound, 6 four-lb loaves at 5d each, 9–10 pints of milk at 2d a pint, 10 eggs at 1d each or more, and less than 2 lb of butter and 1 lb of margarine.[20]

Bad housing came second to malnutrition as a social evil. Asquith, the Prime Minister, estimated the shortage of houses in 1913 at between 100,000 and 120,000. Bowley described conditions in the Northumberland mining village of Stanley as 'horrifying'. In Carmarthen, the Medical Officer of Health reported that there were houses 'that may aptly be described as squalid hovels and hot-beds of diseases'.[21] Industrial Scotland had an especially notorious reputation for bad housing; a Royal Commission on Housing in Scotland had already been appointed and its report was to explode with maximum effect bang in the middle of the war. The provision of working-class housing was, and was expected to be, very largely the job of private enterprise,[22] though there were in existence a number of modest local-authority schemes. The 1913 plans of the Invergordon burgh council reveal the limits expected of working-class domiciliary ambition, and take account of the existence of an upper- and lower-working class:

The houses, which are built of stone and slated, have gardens in front and behind, and are of two sizes. The larger house is rented at £19 per annum without taxes, and consists of parlour, kitchen, scullery with sink and tub, coal place, and press on the ground floor, with two bed-rooms, bathroom and napery press on the upper floor. Only one block of four houses of this type is being built. Four blocks – each containing four houses – will be built of the smaller house. Each house on the ground floor contains a kitchen, parlour, bedroom, scullery with sink and tub, water-closet, press and coal place; each house on the upper floor contains a kitchen, parlour, two small bedrooms, scullery with sink and tub, water-closet and coal place. The rents for these houses are £11.10 without taxes.[23]

Being in Scotland, these proposed rents are rather on the low side for the United Kingdom as a whole; existing working-class housing in England varied in rent from about 4s to 7s or more a week.[24] Some large companies built housing estates for their workers, the Coltness Iron Company building to the following specification: 'one room, kitchen, scullery, water-closet and coal cellar.' Only 19 per cent of working-class houses in York, Rowntree had reported in 1901, had a separate water supply, let alone baths, which, throughout the Edwardian period, were not considered a necessary adjunct to working-class housing. A miners' village in Dumfriesshire was so far in advance of its age that the Local Government Board officials noted 'with pleasure . . . the provision of baths in the later houses.'[25]

While housing was on the whole bad, there were elsewhere continuous signs of improvement in social welfare and the amenities of living. Out of the previous eight years of Liberal rule had come free school meals and free school medical services, old age pensions at five shillings a week, and the National Insurance Act of 1911, of which the Health provisions, covering practically everyone (unless self-employed) earning under £250 per annum, were the more important; the Unemployment Insurance was much more restricted in scope and, in particular, applied only to the 2¼ million members of the building, shipbuilding, and iron and steel trades, the ones most affected by fluctuations in employment. Over the whole span since the turn of the century public health had shown a steady improvement: to compare the figures for 1912 with the average experience in the last decade of the nineteenth century, infant mortality had declined 38 per cent, the death-rate from measles 16 per cent, from scarlet fever 66 per cent, from whooping cough 40 per cent, from diphtheria and croup 57 per cent, from enteric fever (a special affliction of those among the poor who ate quantities of cheap and suspect shellfish) 75 per cent, from tuberculosis (all forms) 32 per cent, and from pulmonary tuberculosis 25 per cent. Up to 1911 the decline in the death-rate from puerperal diseases was 28 per cent, from pneumonia 15 per cent, and from bronchitis 45 per cent. The death-rate from all causes declined 27 per cent between 1891–1900 and 1912.[26] There were, none the less, in the latter year more than ninety deaths from starvation or privation due to destitution.[27]

It was not, however, the issues of social reform which disturbed British society in the years immediately prior to the outbreak of war: attention rather was concentrated on Ireland, where civil war between Ulstermen and Irish nationalists seemed imminent, on the repeated outbreak of serious strikes, often accompanied by bloodshed, and on the arson and disorder created by the suffragettes. Before the passing of the 1911 Parliament Act, which curbed the powers of the House of Lords, there had also been the unedifying last-ditch demonstrations of the peers. These issues had their separate roots, but they were covered by a common hot-house blossom of violence. British society in 1914, having enjoyed since 1898 a long golden cycle of rising prices which yet opened no escape from the insistent industrial challenge of foreign powers, which cosseted the wealthy in their lust after conspicuous consumption but left the real wages of the working classes at a standstill and bypassed the many pools of misery and depression, was demonstrating an unmistakable urge towards bellicosity. 'Beneath an outward prosperity so brilliant', there was, said Sir Michael Sadler, the famous Civil Servant and educationist, 'a deeply felt unrest of heart and mind'.[28] Britain, said another commentator, was in a condition of 'moral chaos' in which her 'inner state' was 'marked by profound unrest'.[29]

War had been talked of as a possibility all through the early years of the century. The most-used argument to confute suffragette claims had been that women were incapacitated from voting by their inability to participate in the military defence of the community, a curious line of thought when few men really expected that they would be called upon to handle a rifle, but symptomatic of the orientation towards the prospect of war. One of the most popular of all socialist agitators, Robert Blatchford, was an open and vigorous Germanophobe. That the British, given any sort of a lead, were a belligerent and jingoistic lot was apparent in music-hall songs,[30] in the doggerel cry for more battleships, 'We want eight and we won't wait', and in the hysteria which had accom-

panied the Boer War, when one particular outburst of patriotic
jubilation had brought a new word, 'Mafficking', into the language. There was a school of thought which saw a new war as a
necessity if the Empire were to prove that in the bloated years of
peace lasting from the Crimean War, and interrupted all too
briefly by the Boer War, it had not forfeited its honour. Idealists
like William Archer in his *The Great Analysis,* published in 1911,
reckoned that some 'great catastrophe' might be the prerequisite
of the establishment of a happier world order. To say that the
country as a whole consciously looked forward to war would be to
say too much; but there can be no doubt that there was abroad in
the land a spirit which made war, when it came, intensely welcome.

Turning our attention to the more articulate expressions of the
wish for war, we can distinguish two strands of thought, frequently in practice intertwined. What we might call the realists
felt that in a world in which 'war is a fact of life that cannot be
ignored',[31] and, more specifically, a world in which Germany was
challenging British commercial and naval supremacy at every turn,
a great trial of strength, regrettably or otherwise, was inevitable.
But there was also a strong strand of idealism, going no further in
many cases than the conventional calls of patriotism, love of
country, service of King, service of God, but stemming too from
young radicals and reformers, out of sorts with panting Georgian
Britain and anxious to take a new broom to Britain and to the
world. Both strands are to be found in a tract of 1906 advocating
national military service. Conscription, the writer says, is necessary 'if England is to be saved from the grave dangers which now
threaten her'. The writer of a separate introduction declares that
'there is a very real need for some new note, for some clarion call,
as it were, which shall inspire us to march forward under new
auspices to a new destiny.'[32] Moving forward to 1909, we hear
the older generation, in the person of Lord Rosebery, speaking
directly to the younger, as represented by the boys of Wellington
College, whose responses we can also detect:

The stress that patriotism will have to bear in days not distant, and
perhaps imminent, will be greater than has yet been known in the
history of this country (*Hear, hear*). There never was a time when men
were more needed to speak and act up to their faith (*Cheers*). I think
that men will have to be more universally armed in the future than they

are now (*Hear, hear*). . . . There are encroaching opinions which threaten patriotism, menace our love of country, and imply the relaxation, if not the destruction, of all the bonds which hold our empire together (*Hear, hear*). I would urge that so far as possible the study of patriotism should be promoted (*Cheers*).[33]

There is an even clearer response in a school prize-winning poem of 1911 or 1912 which ran:

> England, narrow seas divide thee
>   From the foe.
> Guard the waves lest ill betide thee;
> Lest the foe that lurks beside thee
>   Lay thee low.[34]

After 1910 and up till the summer of 1914 there was less open hostility towards Germany. Events then plumbed the currents flowing just below the surface. As *The Times* journalist, Michael McDonagh, wrote in his diary on 3 August:

Germany has always been disliked and distrusted for her bullying policy of sabre-rattling, the mailed fist, the goose-step, and the spiked helmet – symbols of violence and brute force. Indeed she has been suspected for years of looking forward to a war with Great Britain.[35]

The source for the patriotic poem quoted above is a disapproving pamphlet by Arthur Ponsonby, who is representative of another important section of articulate British opinion, those who, strongly aware of the militaristic currents of the age, were as strongly determined to resist them. From 1911 such Liberals as Ponsonby and C. P. Trevelyan were increasingly critical of a Liberal Government which appeared to be swinging the wheel of policy further and further round on collision course, and they had powerful support from two daily papers, the *Daily News* (edited by A. G. Gardiner) and the *Manchester Guardian* (edited by C. P. Scott), and from the weekly *Nation* (edited by H. W. Massingham). Pacific liberal opinion veered between a belief in internationalism and a simple desire for isolation. The City of London and many businessmen believed that war would be an unmitigated disaster.[36] They had the intellectual reinforcement of Norman Angell's *The Great Illusion* (1910), which sought to show that not even the victor could profit economically from war.

Apart from one or two individual, but highly popular, figures, the Labour movement was strongly pacifist in inclination. Formally it was committed to the resolution passed at the 1907 International Socialist Conference:

If war threatens to break out it is the duty of the working class in the countries concerned and of their Parliamentary representatives, with the help of the International Socialist Bureau as a means of coordinating their action, to use every effort to prevent war by all the means which seem to them most appropriate, having regard to the sharpness of the class war and to the general political situation.

Should war none the less break out, their duty is to intervene to bring it promptly to an end, and with all their energies to use the political and economic crisis created by the war to rouse the populace from its slumbers, and to hasten the fall of capitalist domination.[37]

The class-war emphasis of this resolution was rather out of keeping with the atmosphere of the British Labour movement, but the anti-war sentiments which are at its centre were reinforced in Britain by the strong moralistic flavour of the native movement. As we move to the actual outbreak of war we shall see that anti-war sentiment was momentarily almost as demonstrative as pro-war sentiment.

[II] EXCITEMENT AND EMERGENCY

Summarizing what has been said in the final part of the previous section, we might say of British opinion, both militant and pacifist, prior to August 1914, that war was widely expected as an eventual probability, but it was scarcely visualized at all as an immediate contingency. This explains why the breaking of war brought both a sense of long-sought release and an atmosphere of panic and untempered emergency. The immediate excitement and panic evaporated pretty quickly; the emergency legislation of the last days of peace and the first days of hostilities endured throughout the war, being constantly added to and consolidated.

Although the alarums and excursions of world politics from the assassination of the Archduke Franz Ferdinand on 28 June onwards were reported in the British newspapers, they scarcely succeeded in driving the impending civil war in Ireland from the main headlines. On the whole, Conservative newspapers showed a greater awareness of the implications of the international situation than did their Liberal counterparts.[38] But by the end of July it was common knowledge that Britain might be involved in a European war. On the last day of the month *The Times,* repository of worldly wisdom about national security and the balance of power, produced a very prosaic appeal for an immediate British declaration of war on Germany:

A German advance through Belgium to the north of France might enable Germany to acquire possession of Antwerp, Flushing, and even of Dunkirk and Calais, which might then become German naval bases against England. That is a contingency which no Englishman can look upon with indifference. But if it is merely a contingency why should England not wait until it is realized before acting or preparing to act? Because in these days of swift decision and swifter action, it would be too late for England to act with any degree of success after France had been defeated in the North. . . . Even should the German Navy remain inactive, the occupation of Belgium and northern France by German troops would strike a crushing blow at British security. We should then be obliged alone and without Allies to bear the burden of keeping up a Fleet superior to that of Germany and of an Army proportionately strong. The burden would be ruinous.[39]

The appreciation that the technology of modern war had put a premium on speed was shared by the military commands in the various European countries, and helps to explain the inexorable massing of the forces of doom once the first fatal hesitant steps had been made. After that, decisions were fudged, and action, to the confusion of all military experts, was the opposite of swift.

As Bank Holiday Monday (3 August) approached, greater folk prepared for the worst and lesser for the best, the wealthy concerned for the security of their savings, the less wealthy concerned to make their annual spree go with a swing: together they created a run on the banks and a great strain on the Bank of England.[40] Bank Rate, which stood at four per cent on Thursday, 30 July, was doubled the following day, and pushed up to ten per cent on Saturday, 1 August. The Government further girded up its loins for battle with a series of Royal Proclamations. On 1 August the use of wireless telegraphy by merchant ships within the harbours or territorial waters of the United Kingdom was prohibited, as was the flying of aircraft over the United Kingdom (2 August), and the export of a certain specified list of warlike materials (3 August). Putting into force an Act of 1871, the Government took over control of the railways. To give the Bank of England the breathing space which was its greatest need, the payment of certain bills of exchange was postponed for a month, the Bank Holiday was extended right up to Thursday, 6 August, and postal orders were made legal tender. The excitable and unpatriotic rushed off to lay in stores of food and on 3 August there was a sharply marked rise in food prices. While railway stations and coastal resorts were besieged over the week-end, crowds also gathered in central London, where there was shouting of 'Down with Germany.'⁴¹

Germany declared war on Russia on 1 August, and on France on 3 August. The British Cabinet had to give consideration to two immediate issues, apart from the broader threat which a possible German conquest of France would present: her ties of friendship and moral obligation to France, and the likelihood of a German violation of Belgian neutrality, which Britain had a *right* rather than an *obligation* to defend. Grey, the Foreign Secretary, persuasively expounded these points to the House of Commons on the afternoon of the Bank Holiday. The following day news came through of a definite German invasion of Belgian territory, and the Prime Minister, Asquith, announced that an ultimatum expiring at 11 p.m. (midnight in Berlin) had been served upon the Germans calling upon them to withdraw from Belgium. As the time-limit approached, a great concourse of people gathered in Trafalgar Square and Whitehall waving Union Jacks, singing patriotic songs and displaying 'marked tendencies towards Mafficking'; when the British declaration of war upon Germany was issued at the Foreign Office it was greeted with 'round after round of cheers'.⁴²

The patriots did not have things all their own way. On Sunday, 2 August, there had been a Labour demonstration against war addressed by Keir Hardie, H. M. Hyndman, George Lansbury and Arthur Henderson, Secretary of the Labour Party. On Monday, 3 August, pleas for neutrality from a group of distinguished Cambridge Fellows and from a couple of bishops were published and a Neutrality Committee, which included Lord Courtney of Penwith, Gilbert Murray, the classical scholar and advocate of international arbitration, Basil Williams, the Oxford historian, Ramsay MacDonald, the Chairman of the Parliamentary Labour Party, and a number of prominent Liberal publicists, announced itself.[43] In Trafalgar Square on the fateful 4 August anti-German demonstrators had competition from an organized anti-war demonstration.[44] That evening a women's protest against war in the Kingsway Hall had as principal speaker Mrs Fawcett of the National Union of Women's Suffrage Societies. A body calling itself the Neutrality League was wealthy enough to take out, too late, a full-page exhortation against war in the *Daily News* of 5 August. In the daily press the lead to the opposition to British involvement was given by the *Manchester Guardian* and the *Daily News*, the latter being little moved by the Belgian issue: war, it said, commenting on Sir Edward Grey's Bank Holiday speech, would quite probably lead to the absorption of Belgium by France, while at the same time opening the way to the creation of 'a dominant Russia' – something which Liberals constantly feared.[45]

This opposition to the war was striking, but no more striking than the speed with which the bulk of it dissolved. On the morrow of the war the *Daily News* still felt bound to record its conviction 'that a mistaken course of foreign policy, the departure from our traditional policy of splendid isolation, has led us to the terrible conflict in which we are now engaged', but it agreed that the major task now was 'to win'. After Asquith's speech of 5 August, declaring that Britain was fighting 'for the principles whose maintenance is vital to the civilized world', and the publication of the Blue Book showing the avenues the Government had explored and the stones it had turned in the pursuit of peace,[46] this grudging acceptance of war gave way to wholehearted enthusiasm for it. There were many other thirteenth-hour conversions. The Labour Party and the trade unions swung their weight behind the war effort so that Ramsay MacDonald, who maintained his anti-war views, had to resign from the chairmanship of the Parliamentary Labour Party. Mrs Fawcett invited the members of the National Union of Women's Suffrage Societies to put their organization at the disposal of the nation in its hour of need.[47] The prophet of Edwardian nonconformism, the Reverend Dr John Clifford, a bearded Old Testament figure, former President of the National Free Church Council and leader of the pacifist opposition to the Boer War, returning in the last days of peace from a conference of the Churches' Peace Alliance, held in Germany, had drawn up a statement 'in favour of a rigorous abstention from joining in the war'; but becoming convinced 'that our Government had done everything that could be done to allay the storm and preserve the peace of the world . . . that Prussia had launched an ultimatum to Russia . . . had violated Luxemburg', and then, 'deliberately and of express purpose and according to long prepared plans, had broken into Belgium, flung to the winds as veriest chaff her solemn treaty obligations, flouted public law, and trampled under foot with ineffable scorn the rights of small nationalities as not even the small dust of the balance', he held support for this war to be as much a religious duty as ever opposition to the Boer War had been:

The path of duty shone out in clearest light, and wherever it might lead us we had to go. It was the pillar of cloud by day and the pillar of fire by night. We must follow.[48]

These conversions, we shall discover, were not achieved without mental suffering. There remained an important cluster of socialists, Liberals, philosophical pacifists, unflinchingly committed against the war. But by and large the country, on the surface at least, was united and enthusiastic: F. S. Oliver, businessman, social-imperialist, and political *éminence grise,* sent a number of reports to his brother in Canada: 'England is already a different place than it has been for years past.' . . . 'I had not conceived it possible that a nation could be born again so quickly. This war even now has undone the evils of a generation.'

The ordinary man's belief is – even Radicals and Socialists, for the opposition to the war is more nearly 'nil' than I have ever known it to be to anything – that Germany has made this war to impose a military supremacy over the whole of Western Europe, including Britain, and that it is better to be beaten than to submit. Also there is a feeling that since the Kruger telegram, eighteen years ago, things have been working up to this issue, and a sense of relief is experienced by the ending of it.[49]

Less exhilarating was the rise in prices of ordinary food-stuffs: imported meat rose by one penny a pound; bread rose more drastically from 5½d for the 4-lb loaf to 8d or more.[50] Greater increases in the cost of imported goods were contained by the Government's introduction of a State insurance scheme to cover war risks. After consultation between Government and shopkeepers, a scale of maximum retail prices was drawn up but never properly operated.[51] High prices, unemployment, general distress, that was what serious observers expected. On 4 August a Cabinet Committee on the Prevention and Relief of Distress had been established and the Local Government Board, in a circular to the local authorities, had warned:

The outbreak of war upon the Continent of Europe may involve a considerable dislocation of trade in this country, and in consequence, there may be a serious lack of employment in certain industries.[52]

An appeal for a National Relief Fund was issued by the Prince of Wales on 6 August, and the administration of this was at once taken over by an Executive Committee which contained three members of the Cabinet.

The Labour movement made its own preparations. On the initiative of Arthur Henderson a special conference of all organizations affiliated to the Labour Party was held on 5 August and a Workers' National Committee set up to watch over the special interests of the working classes during the War Emergency.[53] Where there was distress in the first months it was very acute: in patriotically turning their minds from dress to higher things, women of the middle and upper classes helped to throw more than 40 per cent. of their labouring sisters out of work or on to short time.[54] Yet it was one of the lesser ironies of the war that, after all the preparations for unemployment, it was in the end to furnish an unprecedented demand for labour.

Shortly before war broke out, the Liberal Secretary of State for War, Colonel Seely, had resigned, and his duties, pending a fresh appointment, had been taken over by the Prime Minister. The military colossus of the age was Lord Kitchener, Commander-in-Chief of the British forces in the latter two years of the Boer War, presently British Representative in Egypt, and described by the *Observer* as 'Cromwellian':[55] a strong campaign was waged in the press calling for Kitchener, who was on leave in Britain, to be seconded to the War Office. The Government vacillated, but finally, when Kitchener was on the point of re-embarking, he was summoned back to have the secretaryship thrust upon him. A non-political figure, Kitchener added the right quality of national solidarity to the Ministry; large in stature as in military reputation, he was undoubtedly a hero in the eyes of the public, concentrating upon himself the imperial longings of the little man, which had now burst out in joyous flood; but at sixty-four, he was past his best; much had changed in the dozen years since the South African War; he was ignorant of politics and caused laughter upon his first appearance in the Lords as War Secretary by seating himself upon the episcopal bench.[56]

Kitchener's appointment was taken as an earnest of the Government's good intentions in regard to the prosecution of the war. On 6 August Parliament authorized an increase in the Army of 500,000 men; the first recruiting appeal appeared the following day:

YOUR KING AND COUNTRY NEED YOU

A CALL TO ARMS

An addition of 100,000 men to His Majesty's Regular Army is immediately necessary in the present grave National Emergency. Lord Kitchener is confident that this appeal will be at once responded to by all who have the safety of our Empire at heart.

TERMS OF SERVICE

General service for a period of three years, or until the war is concluded.

Age of enlistment, between 19 and 30.[57]

The terms of service show that Kitchener at least did not share the widely held belief that the war would be over within six months. Because of the confusion and ineptitude of the authorities, the first 100,000 was not obtained till 25 August,[58] though recruiting offices were thronged with eager volunteers. A call for a further 100,000 was issued on 28 August; the age-limit was raised to thirty-five, and a special appeal was made to married men. By 15 September, after a further increase of 500,000 had been authorized there were already more than 500,000 recruits – half a million of the country's bravest and most idealistic young men, heroically committed to a cause greater than themselves. Rupert Brooke, poet, former President of the Cambridge Fabian Society, to whom 'Honour has come back, as a King, to earth', spoke for all of them; many came from respectable Evangelical backgrounds, and to them duty to God and duty to King and Country were sufficient call; others were atheistic or pantheistic social reformers, like F. H. Keeling, who wrote, 'I may possibly live to think differently; but at the present moment, assuming that this war had to come, I feel nothing but gratitude to the gods for sending it in my time;'[59] miners from South Wales were as much in evidence as the sons of the prosperous middle and upper classes. These men were first crammed into inadequate, overcrowded camps, so short of basic amenities that recruits were told to bring their own blankets and toilet articles. Soon they would be required across the Channel, for the professional British Expeditionary Force, after helping to bring the German advance to a halt on the Marne (6 to 9 September), was shortly wiped out at Ypres. An increase in the Army of another million was authorized in November, and by 21 December 1915, a third and then a fourth million had been sanctioned.[60]

The culmination of the first burst of emergency legislation was the Defence of the Realm Act of 8 August. 'D.O.R.A' – the widely used name conjured up in the public mind the image of a cruel and capricious maiden who at the snap of her fingers could close down a newspaper, requisition a ship, or prohibit whistling for cabs – will be so often referred to in the course of this book, that it is worth quoting the original act in full:

An Act to confer on His Majesty in Council power to make Regulations during the present War for the Defence of the Realm.

Be it enacted by the King's most Excellent Majesty by and with the advice and consent of the Lords Spiritual and Temporal, and Commons, in this present Parliament assembled, and by the authority of the same, as follows:

1. His Majesty in Council has power during the continuance of the present war to issue regulations as to the powers and duties of the Admiralty and Army Council, and of the members of His Majesty's forces, and other persons acting on His behalf, for securing the public safety and the defence of the realm; and may by such regulations authorize the trial by courts martial and punishment of persons contravening any of the provisions of such regulations designed –

(*a*) to prevent persons communicating with the enemy or obtaining information for that purpose or any purpose calculated to jeopardize the success of the operations of any of His Majesty's forces or to assist the enemy; or

(*b*) to secure the safety of any means of communication, or of railways, docks or harbours;

in a like manner as if such persons were subject to military law and had on active service committed an offence under section five of the Army Act.[61]

Additions were made by a second D.O.R.A. of 28 August, and there were amendments and revisions in the Defence of the Realm Consolidation Act of 27 November, further modified by Acts of 1915 and 1916. Trial by court-martial for civilians was possible under the original D.O.R.A.; the Consolidation Act of November went so far as to authorize the death penalty in the case of offences 'committed with the intention of assisting the enemy'. Protests in the House of Lords produced the amending Act of 16 March 1915, which largely restored the right of trial by jury, though this could still be suspended in case of invasion or other military emergency: it was under this dispensation that the executions after the Irish Easter Rising of 1916 were carried out. In the later stages of the war there would be a constant stream of orders and regulations from many different ministries, covering lighting, early closing, food control, and so on, all issued under the umbrella of D.O.R.A. The lights of London – a vulnerable target for German air attack, the authorities feared – were lowered for the first time on 11 September, and as a further precaution the distinctively shaped lake in St James's Park was drained.

During the Napoleonic Wars the British scientist Humphry Davy had been able to leave the country to collect a medal in France from 'the enemy'. In this war there could be no charity, let alone enthusiasm, on either side, for aliens. Anti-German sentiment was pretty spontaneous, though helped along by the popular press; attacks on people with German-sounding names were at first probably motivated as much by fear of espionage as by hatred. Many people with German names made haste to change them; *sauerkraut* and liver sausage appeared in shop windows labelled simply 'good English viands'.[62] The first Aliens Restriction Act was introduced on 5 August and subsequent legislation required that enemy aliens of military age should be interned and others repatriated. From 28 November it was decreed that everyone, British or foreign, must register with the police when moving into hotels or boarding-houses.

Nor could the press be left untrammelled. To begin with, a clumsy double censorship of war news was carried out by the Admiralty and the War Office acting independently, with the result that newspapers had practically no war news at all. An Official Press Bureau was therefore set up which itself doled out highly uninformative official communications to the newspapers, and to which editors were supposed to submit all controversial news items; it was still possible for the press to circumvent the Bureau, but it would then, of course, invite prosecution under D.O.R.A.[63]

Young men flocked to the colours, but not fast enough for the old men, often, like the novelist Arnold Bennett, stirred out of the pacifism of a lifetime:

When one sees young men idling in the lanes on Sunday, one thinks: 'Why are they not at war?' All one's pacific ideas have been rudely disturbed. One is becoming militarist.[64]

Women were not behind in their enthusiasm, which showed itself in two traditional responses: bandaging and knitting. 'I spend my time . . .' a schoolboy reported to his mother, 'being bandaged and unbandaged by the girls who want to be V.A.D.s'. If some of them ever manage to get into a hospital, Heaven help their patients.'[65] Mrs C. S. Peel recollected that:

We knitted socks (some of them of unusual shape), waistcoats, helmets, comforters, mitts, body belts. We knitted at theatres, in trains and trams, in parks and parlours, in the intervals of eating in restaurants, of serving in canteens. . . . It was said that such a stock of knitted goods flooded into the trenches that men cleaned their rifles and wiped their cups and plates with their surplus socks and comforters.

Arnold Bennett, at least was gratified: 'This instinct to do something on the part of idle young women or half-idle is satisfactory to behold.'[66]

Excitement and enthusiasm for the war bordered upon derangement, as is seen most strikingly in the story which began to circulate at the end of August, that Russian reinforcements 'with snow on their boots' were passing through Britain on their way to the Western Front. Even the hard-bitten McDonagh fell for the story and played his part in circulating it; the *Daily News*, anxious still for an easy ending for a war it had swung behind so late and so unhappily, was highly credulous; the *Daily Mail*, which was already taking a lead in insisting on the seriousness of the war, on the other hand, was highly satirical about the whole affair. The rumours were not formally denied till 16 September. Whether they originated from a misunderstood report that a consignment of Russian *eggs* was on the way, or from the bearded soldier who declared from the window of a train that he came from *Ross-shire*, is immaterial; they are the heady froth upon the first bubbling month of war.[67]

[III] BUSINESS AS USUAL

While the legislation for war continued to be extended and refined, the panic and excitement subsided, though it was never completely subdued. Businessmen were well aware that their best interests would be served by a continuance of normal trading habits. As early as 11 August, H. E. Morgan of W. H. Smith and Son, in a letter to the *Daily Chronicle* suggested that the country would do well to follow a policy of 'Business as Usual'. Harrods, the top department store of Edwardian England, took up the phrase in a display advertisement which, two days later, announced their policy for the war. Later in the month a crowded meeting of advertisers and traders resolved that, together in unity, they would fight the war on the slogan 'Business as Usual'.[68] Tom Bruce Jones, a Scottish economist of erratic views, published a tract on *The Danger of Britain's Invasion, And How It May Be Met Whilst Carrying On 'Business as Usual'*. The phrase, then, was not, as has been said, coined by Winston Churchill, but by the big shopkeepers, anxious to unite duty with profit; once coined, however, its velocity of circulation was enthusiastically boosted by the Government.

Official endorsement of Business as Usual was shown most obviously in the first war budget, introduced by the Chancellor of the Exchequer, David Lloyd George, on 16 November.

Income-tax was already calculated on an elaborate graduated scale: at the outbreak of war the ordinary wage-earner was, as we have seen, totally exempt; salaries between £160 and £500 paid at the rate of 9d in the pound, above £500 the rate was 1s 3d, and incomes above £3,000 paid an additional supertax. In doubling the ninepenny rate to one and six, Lloyd George cast before him the faintest shade of things to come. The tea duty was raised from 3d per pound to 8d, and the tax on beer put up by the equivalent of a penny a pint, raising the price to 4d. And that was about it – no new taxation of any sort. If *The Economist* praised the Government for having boldly faced an 'unprecedented emergency by calling upon the nation to make an unprecedented sacrifice',[69] that just showed how far orthodox opinion was out of touch with the needs of the hour.

Politics were much as usual as well. Asquith, treading warily as ever, decided to enact his Irish Home Rule Bill, but with the proviso that it would not become law till the end of the war, when there would be an amending act to make possible the exclusion of the six Ulster counties where Protestant sentiment was strongest. None the less, the Conservatives were deeply angered, and after a bitter speech Bonar Law led his followers out of the House of Commons, giving the Prime Minister the opportunity to mock them as 'middle-aged gentlemen trying to look like early French revolutionaries in the tennis court'. Party government, therefore, continued, qualified only by the presence in the Cabinet of Lord Kitchener, by the loyal restraint which Conservatives put on their criticisms of the conduct of the war, and by such smaller instances of collaboration as the consultation between Lloyd George and Austen Chamberlain over the preparation of the first war budget.[70]

One slight change there was in the technique of government. On 5 August there came into existence a War Council, in effect a development of the pre-war Committee of Imperial Defence. In November the former Conservative Prime Minister, A. J. Balfour, was invited to its meetings, but the body had an advisory function only.[71] Executive power stayed in the Cabinet, where the three leading figures were Asquith, intellectually powerful but not readily given to speedy decision-making, Winston Churchill, impetuous and full of daring schemes, and Kitchener, a god in the eyes of the public, but already shown to be out-of-date in his strategic thinking and utterly lacking in the organizational gifts required in a war of the new scale.

The military aspects of the war were turning out to be altogether different from what had been expected. As Sir John French, the Commander-in-Chief of the British forces, plaintively put it:

No previous experience, no conclusion I had been able to draw from campaigns in which I had taken part, or from a close study of the new conditions in which the war of today is waged, had led me to anticipate a war of positions. All my thoughts, all my prospective plans, all my possible alternatives of action, were concentrated upon a war of movement and manœuvre.[72]

So, too, not unnaturally, had the war been misunderstood by the younger generation:

War to my generation implied campaigns on the Indian frontier, in Egypt or in South Africa. My ideas of European war were derived from panoramas of the Franco–Prussian conflict to be seen in continental cities. It was the war of tradition. Cavalry charged at the foe. When death came, it was a heroic death brought about by heroes on the other side.[73]

Instead, the same writer continues, there came 'war atrocities' and 'frightfulness'. Worse, wholesale slaughter became a commonplace. As early as 24 October the editor of the *Daily Express*, R. D. Blumenfeld, was noting in his diary:

One would have thought, before the war began, that the single report of the killing or disablement of any friend or acquaintance would be terribly disconcerting. So it was, at the beginning. The first eight or ten casualties had as much publicity as all the rest put together. People discussed deaths of young second lieutenants with bated breath. Gradually the familiarity of the thing became apparent. You receive the news of the death of your friends as a matter of fact.[74]

The fighting was still being waged as of yore by a Regular Army augmented, admittedly on an unprecedented scale, by volunteers, not in any real sense by a nation in arms. Where industrial distress and disruptions of trade had been expected, stay-at-homes found that trade was booming. These two facts, added to this warty defensiveness in face of news of death, account for the widening rounds of giddy social pleasures found among the upper classes in the last months of the old year and the first months of the new. Described as 'desolate and dreary wastes' shortly after the outbreak of war,[75] theatres were in January said by a prominent actor-manager to be 'booming'.[76] Two months later, according to Blumenfeld, social activity had not abated in the least.[77] There were exaggerated tales of the working classes 'warming themselves in the sun of affluence', buying pianos, 'that coveted proof of respectability', gramophones, and motor-bikes.[78] More in evidence than affluence was the further privation caused to the lower-paid workers and their families by the sharp price rises. Labour members forced the issue in debate early in February 1915, when it was claimed that many labourers were getting only one good meal a week. The Prime Minister admitted that, compared with February 1914, prices of flour had risen 75 per cent, home meat 6 per cent, imported meat 12 per cent, sugar 72 per cent, coal 15 per cent, but he justified Government inaction on the grounds that these rises were no worse than the ones brought by the aftermath of the Franco-Prussian war of 1870.[79] 'Business as Usual' could hardly be taken to more absurd lengths.

Ruling opinion was still strongly against Government interference in the free play of the market, and, indeed, against too much Government action in any direction once the necessary emergency measures of national self-defence had been taken. The period of 'business as usual' was marked by a last great flowering of grand-scale private charity of a type more suited to the world of Blandings Castle than to the waging of modern war. Allowances and pensions for the dependants of men on active service were an obvious first charge upon the nation, but the only official organization at the outbreak of war for administering such benefits was the Commissioners of the Royal Hospital for Soldiers at Chelsea, and the actual rates paid had not changed since the Boer War. Any supplementation had to come from charitable funds channelled through the Soldiers' and Sailors' Families Association or from the National Relief Fund. It was the Executive Committee of the latter body which took the decision to raise allowances from 11s 1d per week, with

1s 9d for each child, to 12s 6d with 2s for each child; these rates, with a further slight increase in the child's allowance, were officially adopted by the Government on 1 October. As it was discovered that in a large number of cases soldiers were not in fact married to the women they were living with, the Executive Committee decided that 'where there was evidence that a real home had been maintained allowances should be made to unmarried mothers and their children'.[80] In this way there was, despite many earnest protests about the licensing of sin, admitted into the well-defended regions of nineteenth-century middle-class morality a first spy from the earthier realms of working-class *mores*.

Even when allowances were established as due there were often outrageously long delays before payment was made. So great was the outcry against the muddle and mismanagement that the voluntary societies concerned were forced to conduct an investigation into their own affairs; confusion, if anything, was worse confounded, and eventually the Government had to appoint its own Select Committee.[81] From the deliberations of this Committee came, in November 1915, the Naval and Military War Pensions Act, still, in essence, an attempt to integrate private charity and public appeal into Government action.

The readiest opportunity for private philanthropy was provided from the very beginning of the war by the Belgian refugee problem. As the Germans marched into Belgium a full million of the rightful inhabitants sought refuge outside the borders of their country, over a hundred thousand embarking at once for Britain.[82] To cope with this influx, three august and public-spirited personages, Lady Lugard, the Hon. Mrs Alfred Lyttelton, and Viscount Gladstone, formed on 24 August a War Refugees' Committee; Lord Hugh Cecil became Chairman. From the public at large there came at once offers of hospitality for a hundred thousand refugees. From 9 September the whole business was taken over by the Local Government Board, but the treatment received by individual Belgians continued, naturally, to depend very much on the reactions of individual Britishers. On the whole it can be said that, in the early stages at least, the British people rallied magnificently to those felt to have suffered unjustly in a common cause, giving a sign both of timeless human generosity and of the moral idealism of the first part of the war. But as the months wore on many an unfortunate Belgian found himself in the position of the much-adored kitten which has grown into an unwanted cat.

The first rude shaking of domestic complacency into a new sort of awareness that war was no longer just something that other people fought came when on 16 December a German cruiser force shelled the Hartlepools, Whitby and Scarborough on the east coast. As the censorship had not yet quite grasped the idea of suppressing all news which might affect civilian morale, the episode, with its 110 dead (more careful counting brought the total to 137 killed and 592 injured),[83] was given a large spread in the press, pointed up by graphic photographs of the destruction wrought to buildings on the sea-front. Actually the censorship should perhaps be credited with wisdom as well as restraint, since the British sense of outrage expressed itself palpably in the next few days in the first marked rush to the recruiting stations since the palmy days of August.[84] So lacking in Christian feelings were the Germans that on Christmas Eve they sent an aeroplane over Dover and the following day another one over Sheerness. These incidents, however, merely became a further matter for complacent self-congratulation, since the one bomb unloaded on Dover had done no hurt to anyone, and the inhabitants of Sheerness had had their Christmas celebrations enlivened by the exciting spectacle of British planes in hot pursuit of the raider.[85] After these pioneer efforts by aeroplane, the Germans devoted themselves in the New Year to aerial attack by Zeppelin, a raid of 19 January over Yarmouth and Sheringham killing four. Further raids caused much damage, but little loss of life: business could still continue much as usual.

[IV] EMOTIONAL ATTITUDES

Propaganda, as a facet of war, was well understood by the military authorities. In the British Expeditionary Force routine orders for 24 September 1914, mention was made of the Kaiser's alleged description of the force as 'the contemptible little army'. Though without factual foundation, the phrase was exploited to the full and had fantastic success in encouraging recruiting.[86] Yet it was through private enterprise that the first body devoted to the dissemination of propaganda for domestic consumption was established – the Central Committee for National Patriotic Organizations, of which the Prime Minister became Honorary President with Lord Rosebery and A. J. Balfour as Vice-Presidents. From its headquarters at 8 Carlton House Terrace, the Committee invited prominent individuals to lecture or write upon the causes of the war with a view to justifying 'both historically and morally England's position in the struggle'.[87] The approach was almost Victorian in the weight it placed on men of intellectual and academic standing, and in the way in which their efforts were directed, not towards the ignorant masses, but to educated doubters. From six members of the Oxford Faculty of Modern History the Committee secured *Why We Are at War, Great Britain's Case,* which was followed by the 'Oxford Pamphlets', which, while never descending into downright mendacity, did not, of a set purpose, maintain the highest standards of objective scholarship.

Among the reams of distressful special pleading, the distressed *How Can War Ever be Right?* by Gilbert Murray, signatory to the plea for British neutrality published on the first day of war, stands out. For him, as for Dr Clifford, the Belgian issue was the immediate occasion for his change of heart. Aware as ever that 'as far as the rights and wrongs of war go, you are simply condemning innocent men, by thousands and thousands, to death, or even to mutilation and torture', he none the less proceeded now to argue that war could not be judged as 'a profit-and-loss' account, leaving 'out of sight the cardinal fact that in some causes it is better to fight and be broken than to yield peacefully'.[88] The causes Gilbert Murray had in mind were those of 'honour';[89] in elaborating this, the argument veers towards the quaint, the path being all the sadder for the writer's tortured awareness that for a high intellectual he is on dangerous ground:

A deal of nonsense, no doubt, is talked about 'honour' and 'dishonour'. They are feelings based on sentiment, not on reason; the standards by which they are judged are often conventional or shallow, and sometimes utterly false. Yet honour and dishonour are real things. I will not try to define them; but will only notice that, like Religion, their characteristic is that they admit of no bargaining. Indeed we can almost think of honour as being simply that which a free man values more than life, and dishonour as that which he avoids more than suffering or death. And the important point for us is that there are such things.[90]

Moving from the abstract to the present European situation, Murray continues:

Great Britain had, by a solemn treaty more than once renewed, pledged herself to maintain the neutrality of Belgium. Belgium is a little state lying between two very strong states, France and Germany, and in danger of being overrun or maltreated by one of them unless the Great Powers guarantee her safety. . . . Germany suddenly and without excuse invaded Belgium. . . . Our answer was: 'Evacuate Belgium within twelve hours or we fight you.'

I think that answer was right. . . . For my own part, weighing the whole question soberly and without undue passion, I feel that in this case I would rather die than submit; and I believe that the Government, in deciding to keep its word at the cost of war, has rightly interpreted the feelings of the average British citizen.[91]

'So much,' then says Murray, 'for the questions of honour, pure and simple.'[92] He now argues with great cogency that even without the Belgian issue, national security would probably have demanded British intervention to prevent an all-powerful Germany dominating the European continent, concluding triumphantly with what he admits is 'one of the old optimistic beliefs of nineteenth-century liberalism': 'our interest coincides with our honour'.[93]

Most illuminating of all, both for its perceptive analysis of the war enthusiasm shown by the first volunteers and for its revelation of the way in which this enthusiasm has affected an academic opinion-former like Murray, is his final answer to his agonizing question, 'How can war ever be right?' Again Murray's scrupulous personal honesty permits points of doubt to penetrate through the glossy surface of the page:

War is not all evil. It is a true tragedy, which must have nobleness and triumph in it as well as disaster. . . . This is dangerous ground. The subject lends itself to foolish bombast, especially when accompanied by a lack of true imagination. We must not begin to praise war without stopping to reflect on the hundreds of thousands of human beings involved in such horrors of pain and indignity that, if here in our ordinary hours we saw one man so treated, the memory would sicken us to the end of our lives. . . . But when we have realized that, we may venture to see in this wilderness of evil some cases of extraordinary good.

These men who are engaged in what seems like a vast public crime ought, one would think, to fall to something below their average selves, below the ordinary standard of common folk. But do they? Day after day come streams of letters from the front, odd stories, fragments of diaries, and the like; full of the small intimate facts which reveal character, and almost with one accord they show that these men have not fallen, but risen. . . . I think again of the expressions on faces that I have seen or read about, something alert and glad and self-respecting in the eyes of those who are going to the front, and even of the wounded who are returning. 'Never once', writes one correspondent, 'not once since I came to France have I seen among the soldiers an angry face or heard an angry word. . . . They are always quiet, orderly and wonderfully cheerful.' And no one who has followed the war need be told of their heroism. I do not forget the thousands left on the battlefield to die, or the groaning of the wounded sounding all day between the crashes of the guns. But there is a strange deep gladness as well. . . .

Human nature is a mysterious thing, and man finds his weal and his woe not in the obvious places. To have something before you, clearly seen, which you know you must do, and can do, and will spend your utmost strength and perhaps your life in doing, is one form at least of very high happiness, and one that appeals – the facts prove it – not only to saints and heroes but to average men. Doubtless the few who are wise enough and have enough imagination may find opportunity for that same happiness in everyday life, but in war ordinary men find it. This is the inward triumph which lies at the heart of the great tragedy.[94]

Once this sort of idea had been enunciated by men of intellect, it was easily perpetuated by countless mushy stories in book and newspaper; long after the first enthusiasm of the early volunteers had evaporated, their decimated ranks replenished with less enthusiastic conscripts, people at home went on believing in the 'happiness' of the men in the trenches.

In admitting that once war had broken out Britain's task was 'to win', the Liberal *Daily News* had added the flat proviso that in so doing she should try to *avoid* ruining 'European civilization and European liberty'; but soon the pulse quickened – Britain was fighting *for* European civilization, *for* 'the emancipation of

Germany' as well as *for* the 'liberties of Europe'; the war was seen as 'the last supreme struggle of the old dispensation against the new'.[95] In arguing thus the Liberals contributed to the concept of the war as a high crusade; but in justifying their abandonment of the anti-war position they were also placing a heavy emotional mortgage upon the future world dispensation. Nor could they forget their existing commitment to European civilization: news of German atrocities might strengthen their belief in Britain's holy cause, but what would ultimately affect them most, unless the outcome of the war proved all to be supremely worth while, would be the blows rained by civilized man upon civilized man. The reality of the doubt behind the enthusiasm for the war is revealed in a reference to German atrocities made by Dr Clifford in a speech of January 1916:

The effect of this revelation of the German mind on ourselves is many-sided, deep, disturbing and yet strengthening. In its presence the last shred of doubt as to the righteousness of our cause has gone. We were sure of our ground in 1914; we are a thousand times more sure to-day. Doubts that haunted us a year ago have been swept to the ends of the earth; and questions we discussed with seriousness then are no longer put.[96]

Conservatives, on the whole, felt less need to garb their patriotic sentiments in the flowing robes of ideal objectives, though it was J. L. Garvin, editor of the Conservative *Observer*, who on the day war was declared coined the words which eventually were to become wounds:

We have to do our part in killing a creed of war. Then at last, after a rain of blood, there may be set the greater rainbow in the Heavens before the vision of the souls of men. And after Armageddon war, indeed, may be no more.[97]

H. G. Wells took the idea up and became the great phrasemaker of Liberal pro-war idealism, writing of 'The War that Will End War' and of how 'in the hour of victory' Britain would 'save the liberated Germans from vindictive treatment'.[98] For his contribution to the Oxford pamphlets, A. D. Lindsay, the great educationist and political philosopher, chose the title, *The War to End War*. Although Wells, through his articles and his novels, particularly

Mr Britling Sees it Through, reached a wide audience, few to begin with paid much attention to such notions as fair treatment for the German people; it was enough that he and other eminent authorities should confirm that this above all wars was a war on behalf of righteousness.

'Duty' and 'honour' were the emotional moulds within which British attitudes set. Each class, each group, each individual then added the trimming of whatever precise ideal he had most at heart. In explanation of the attitude of the Parliamentary Labour Party, the joint spokesmen of the Trades Union Congress, the General Federation of Trade Unions, and the Labour Party, declared that the Party 'recognized that Great Britain, having exhausted the resources of peaceful diplomacy, was bound in honour, as well as by treaty, to resist by arms the aggression of Germany'; they then added their conviction that the war was being fought for 'the preservation and maintenance of free and unfettered democratic government'.[99]

Of the mood of the inarticulate public it is difficult to say more than that its most obvious features were an intense hatred of the German Kaiser and people, and a mighty sense of righteous exaltation, the one clearly reinforcing the other. It must be stressed that the exaltation was based on a deeply felt sense of moral purpose: it is this which, despite the unexpected grimness of the test, held aloft British enthusiasm till nearly the end of the war, then plunged it into a well of emptiness. Lloyd George, the supreme demagogue, put this sense of moral purpose into words of fire and velvet in his first speech on 'the Great War' (the title was already universally recognized), delivered at the Queen's Hall on 19 September 1914:

There is something infinitely greater and more enduring which is emerging already out of this great conflict – a new patriotism, richer, nobler, and more exalted than the old. (*Applause*). I see amongst all classes, high and low, shedding themselves of selfishness, a new recognition that the honour of the country does not depend merely on the maintenance of its glory in the stricken field, but also in protecting its homes from distress. (*Hear, hear*). It is bringing a new outlook to all classes. The great flood of luxury and sloth which had submerged the land is receding, and a new Britain is appearing. We can see for the first time the fundamental things that matter in life, and that have been obscured from our vision by the tropical growth of prosperity. (*Hear, hear*.)[100]

'He personifies our War aims and emotions', McDonagh wrote in his diary, seeing Lloyd George now as second only to Kitchener as a 'War Minister'.[101]

There were other types of response, some overtly sexual or sadistic in origin. A girl in Dumfriesshire began an atrocity story by forging a letter which purported to describe how her sister, a nurse in Belgium, had had her breasts cut off by the Germans.[102] Before August was out young women in Folkestone were handing out white feathers to young men still to be found skulking in civilian clothes (the instigator of the original scheme, however, was said to have been a certain Admiral Penrose-Fitzgerald).[103] For puritanical zealots the war came as a token of heavenly encouragement to renewed endeavours. Drink, gambling, professional football – here in the extreme was the conspicuous consumption of the energies of young men eminently eligible for the trenches – came under very heavy fire. Posters and sandwich boards outside football grounds which once had read 'Are you prepared to meet your God?' or 'Repent, for the time is at hand' were replaced by 'Are you forgetting that there's a war on?' 'Your country needs you', or 'Be ready to defend your home and women from the German Huns'.[104] For all that, despite the evangelical thunderbolts of the leader of the campaign, Frederick Charrington, football, like other activities, continued as usual and before large crowds. The Reverend Spencer H. Elliott thundered against football pools:

The war found us with forty thousand bookmakers in our country, with an annual turnover of at least eighty millions. The law did not touch them. Football coupons flooded the country, offering odds that were utterly unfair, and working men, women, lads, and even girls, emptied their pockets into those of anonymous scoundrels.[105]

Racial hatred, which went far beyond anything that the Government can have possibly desired or welcomed, was kept going by a number of charming messages, all prominently boxed and heavily leaded, carried by the *Daily Mail*. One declared:

REFUSE TO BE SERVED BY AN AUSTRIAN
OR GERMAN WAITER.
IF YOUR WAITER SAYS HE IS SWISS
ASK TO SEE HIS PASSPORT.

At the end of October the First Sea Lord, Prince Louis of Battenberg, was forced out of office because of his German origins. In accepting the resignation, Churchill as First Lord of the Admiralty placed the situation perfectly:

This is no ordinary war, but a struggle between nations for life and death. It raises passions between nations of the most terrible kind. It effaces the old landmarks and frontiers of our civilization.[106]

The first Government venture into the world of propaganda was the secret War Propaganda Bureau established in Wellington House, the offices of the National Health Insurance Company, under the direction of C. F. G. Masterman, the social commentator and Liberal politician.[107] Given the attitudes of the various voluntary agencies we have already discussed, there was no need for complete control of opinion. The popular press, though subject, as were all newspapers, to a strict censorship of overseas news and to the provisions of the Defence of the Realm Acts, otherwise approached the issues of wartime in much the same way as it had been in the habit of approaching the issues of peacetime, following current attitudes rather than leading them, going in for stunts and sensationalism rather than calculated brainwashing. Headlines got bigger and bolder, effecting a permanent change in newspaper presentation, but the patriotic rubbish printed remained the invention of proprietors and editors rather than of governments.

Where the Government did have to engage itself from the start was in such mundane problems as the promotion of enlistment in the Army and in the war industries, the launching of relief work, and the encouragement of economy in the purchase of food and extravagance in the purchase of Government bonds. Towards the end of 1914 the Parliamentary Recruiting Committee, also something of a do-it-yourself propaganda body, gave commissions for more than a hundred posters, all of them of rather low quality save for Alfred Leete's distinguished 'Kitchener', which has secured immortality for the War Minister and whose accusing finger must have directed many a wavering young man towards the nearest recruiting office. Acting on its own account, the London Electric Railways Company began to commission posters of greater aesthetic distinction, as, indeed, in its various guises, the

Company has continued to do ever since.[108] In January there appeared a number of posters aimed directly at women, inciting them to send their menfolk to the trenches. Among the most famous of all was the one picturing a little girl asking her father in the post-war years, 'Daddy, what did you do in the Great War?' ('I tried to stop the bloody thing, my child,' is what Bob Smillie, the Scottish miners' leader, said his reply would be.) Local recruiting committees throughout the country kept up the pressure.

On 18 February 1915, Germany imposed a submarine blockade on the British Isles; this was widely accounted a further piece of German 'frightfulness', and it enabled the Liberal press to over-come the qualms aroused by Britain's own naval blockade of Germany.[109] Ultimately the domestic repercussions of the sub-marine threat were to be enormous, though for the time being the tendency in high places was to take the threat rather lightly. A recruiting notice published on 17 February and addressing 'Five Questions to Patriotic Customers', did ask, 'Have you realized that we cannot have "Business as Usual" whilst the war continues?' But 'Business as Usual' ended, not with the whimper of a recruit-ing poster, but amid the bangs of the Battle of Neuve Chapelle. Neuve Chapelle was fought to the same basic plan as practically all the other offensives on the Western Front throughout the war. First of all a heavy bombardment was launched to smother the enemy's artillery, cut his barbed wire, and kill the inmates of his front trenches; then the guns lifted to targets farther back, and the infantry leapt out of their own trenches and into the fire of his machine-guns. This simple two-point strategy lost lives in thous-ands but gained ground only in yards.

First dispatches from Sir John French, however, were couched in glowingly optimistic terms. But by late March news of enormous losses was seeping through, elaborated by horrifying tales of men hung up like washing on German barbed wire which faulty British shells had failed to cut. Sir John French's final dispatch[110] was markedly less ebullient than earlier reports had been, and was the signal for a prolonged bout of heart-searching in the British press. It was Neuve Chapelle which jerked society to an awareness of what was involved in this most beastly of wars. The politicians continued to be happily insulated from the changing currents of

opinion for another month, but already, well before the first
Ministerial reconstruction, a new phase of the domestic war had
begun.

NOTES TO CHAPTER ONE

1. *Hist[ory of the] Min[istry of] Mun[itions]*, Vol. I, 1922, p. 7.

2. R. H. Tawney, 'The Abolition of Economic Controls, 1918–21,' in *Economic History Review*, 1943, p. 1.

3. L. C. Money, *Riches and Poverty*, 1905; 1913 edn., p. 202.

4. *Report of Committee of Privy Council for Scientific and Industrial Research for 1915–16;* P.P., 1916, VIII, Cd. 8336, pp. 3–8. *1st Annual Report of Medical Research Committee, 1914–15;* P.P., 1914–16, XXXI, Cd. 8101, pp. 3–5.

5. B. H. Hibbard, *Effects of the Great War upon Agriculture, in the United States and Great Britain*, New York, 1919, p. 173.

6. P.P., 1914, XLI, Cd. 7190, pp. 6–8.

7. C. F. G. Masterman, *The Condition of England*, 1909, *passim*.

8. *Riches and Poverty*, p. 49.

9. T. C. Marshall, *Citizenship and Social Class*, 1950, pp. 46–7.

10. *Condition of England*, pp. 57–8.

11. ibid, p. 58.

12. A. L. Bowley and A. R. Burnett-Hurst, *Livelihood and Poverty*, 1915, p. 176.

13. A. L. Bowley, *The Division of the Product of Industry*, 1919, pp. 8–13.

14. ibid, on which the next sentences are based.

15. See F. M. L. Thompson, *English Landed Society in the Nineteenth Century*, 1963, pp. 292–326.

16. A. L. Bowley, *Studies in the National Income*, 1942.

17. *Livelihood and Poverty*, p. 46.

18. *Division of the Product of Industry*, p. 18.

19. *Livelihood and Poverty*, pp. 46, 42.

20. A. L. Bowley, *Prices and Wages in the United Kingdom, 1914-20*, 1921, p. 34. *Report of Working Classes Cost of Living Committee, 1918*; P.P., 1918, VIII, Cd. 8980.

21. *Annual Report of Local Government Board, 1913-14;* P.P., 1914 XXXVIII, Cd. 7610, p. xii.

22. ibid, pp. xxxvi–xxxvii.

23. *Annual Report of Local Government Board for Scotland, 1913;* P.P., 1914, XXXVIII, Cd. 7327, p. lxxviii.

24. *Livelihood and Poverty*, p. 18.

25. Cd. 7327, pp. lxxxi, lxxxii. B. S. Rowntree, *Poverty, a study of town life*, 1901, p. 187.

26. *Annual Report of Local Government Board, 1912–13 – Report of Medical Officer;* P.P., 1914, XXXVII, Cd. 7181, p. v.

27. *Annual Report of Local Government Board, 1913–14;* P.P., 1914, XXXVIII, Cd. 7444, p. liv.

28. In A. P. Newton (ed.), *The Empire and the Future*, 1916, p. 3.

29. *New Republic,* 11 September 1915.

30. See e.g. C. Booth, *Life and Labour of the People in London,* Final Vol., 1902, p. 53.

31. Quoted in R. B. McDowall, *British Conservatism, 1832–1914,* 1959, p. 95.

32. T. C. Horsfall, *National Service and the Welfare of the Community,* 1906, pp. 71, v.

33. Quoted in D. Newsome, *Godliness and Good Learning,* 1961, p. 202.

34. Quoted in A. Ponsonby, *Social Reform versus War,* 1912, pp. 4–5.

35. M. McDonagh, *In London during the Great War,* 1935, p. 5.

36. R. C. K. Ensor, *England 1870–1914,* 1936, pp. 492–3.

37. *Labour Year Book 1916,* p. 15.

38. I. Cooper Willis, *England's Holy War,* New York, 1928, pp. 16–42.

39. *The Times,* 31 July 1914.

40. F. L. McVey, *The Financial History of Great Britain, 1914–18,* New York, 1918, p. 10.

41. *Annual Register 1914,* p. 184. *Labour Gazette 1914,* p. 323. *The Times,* 4 August. 1914.

42. *Daily News,* 5 August 1914. *Daily Mail,* 5 August 1914.

43. *Daily News,* 3 August, 4 August 1914.

44. McDonagh, p. 5.

45. *The Times,* 5 August 1914. *Daily News,* 4 August, 5 August 1914.

46. H.M.S.O., *Great Britain and the European Crisis,* 1914.

47. *Common Cause,* 7 August 1914.

48. J. Clifford, *Our Fight for Belgium and What It Means,* 1917, p. 7.

49. S. Gwynn (ed.), *The Anvil of War: letters from F. S. Oliver to his brother,* 1936, pp. 30 (12 August), 42 (6 September), 37 (19 August).

50. *Labour Gazette 1914,* p. 323.

51. E. V. Morgan, *Studies in British Financial Policy 1914–25,* 1952, p. 36.

52. *Memorandum on Steps taken for the Prevention and Relief of Distress;* P.P., 1914, LXXI, Cd. 7603, pp. 3, 29–32.

53. War Emergency: Workers' National Committee, *Report, August 1914–March 1916,* p. 3.

54. I. Andrews and M. Hobbs, *Economic Effects of the War upon Women and Children in Great Britain,* New York, 1918, p. 23.

55. *Observer,* 16 August 1914.

56. McDonagh, p. 18 (25 August 1914).

57. *The Times,* 7 August 1914.

58. J. A. Fairlie, *British War Administration,* New York, 1919, p. 84.

59. F. H. Keeling, *Keeling Letters and Reminiscences,* 1918, p. 209.

60. Fairlie, pp. 18, 84.

61. *Public General Statutes* (4 & 5 Geo. 5), Ch. 29.

62. McDonagh, p. 11.

63. *Memorandum on the Censorship;* P.P., 1914–16, XXXIX, Cd. 7679. *Memorandum on the Official Press Bureau;* P.P., 1914–16, XXXIX, Cd. 7680.

64. A. Bennett, *Journal 1896–1926,* 1932, p. 98 (10 August 1914).

65. C. S. Peel, *How We Lived Then,* 1929, p. 27.

66. Bennett, p. 95 (6 August 1914).

67. See esp. A. Ponsonby, *Falsehood in War Time,* 1926, pp. 63–66. For other examples see C. E. Playne, *Society at War 1914–15,* 1931, pp. 255–81.

68. *The Times,* 26 August 1914.

69. *Economist,* 21 November 1914.

70. F. W. Hirst and H. Allen, *British War Budgets,* 1926, p. 15.

71. J. P. Mackintosh, *The British Cabinet,* 1962, pp. 329 ff. Lord Hankey, *The Supreme Command, 1914–1918,* 1961.

72. Lord French, *1914,* 1919, p. 11.

73. E. Wrench, *Struggle 1914–20,* 1935, pp. 112–3.

74. R. D. Blumenfeld, *All in a Lifetime,* 1935, p. 17.

75. ibid, p. 7 (22 August 1914).

76. *Daily Mail,* 13 January 1915.

77. Blumenfeld, p. 20 (9 March 1915).

78. See esp. *Daily Mail,* 1 February 1915.

79. *House of Commons Debates,* 11 February 1915.

80. P.P., 1914–16, XXI, Cd. 7756, pp. 4–5.

81. Fairlie, p. 158.

82. P.P., 1914–16, VII, Cd. 7750, p. 4, XXV, Cd. 7763, on which the remainder of this paragraph is based.

83. *The Times,* 17, 18 December 1914.

84. *The Times,* 30 December 1914.

85. *The Times,* 26 December 1914.

86. See Ponsonby, *Falsehood in War Time,* pp. 84–7.

87. *Report of the Central Committee for National Patriotic Organisations,* 1914, p. 3.

88. G. Murray, *How Can War Ever Be Right?,* 1914, pp. 5–6.

89. p. 7.

90. pp. 7–8.

91. pp. 13–15.

92. p. 15.

93. p. 22.

94. pp. 24–7.

95. *Daily News,* 5 August, 8 August 1914.

96. J. Marchant, *Dr John Clifford, Life, Letters and Reminiscences,* 1922, p. 100.

97. Quoted D. Thomson, *England in the Nineteenth Century,* 1950, p. 219.

98. *Daily News,* 14 August 1914. *Daily Chronicle,* 8 August 1914.

99. *British Labour and the War,* 1915.

100. D. Lloyd George, *The Great War,* 1914, p. 14.

101. McDonagh, pp. 28–9 (19 September 1914).

102. Ponsonby, *Falsehood in War Time,* pp. 67–70.

103. *Daily Mail,* 31 August 1914.

104. McDonagh, p. 44 (16 December).

105. Society for the Propagation of Christian Knowledge, *The Enemy Within,* 1915.

106. *The Times,* 1 November 1914.

107. J. D. Squires, *British Propaganda at Home and in the United States from 1914–1917,* Cambridge, Mass., 1935, pp. 26–7.

108. M. Hardie and A. K. Sabin, *War Posters,* 1920, pp. 9–10.

109. Willis, *England's Holy War,* pp. 201–2.

110. *The Times,* 15 April 1915.

CHAPTER TWO

Changed Men: 1915–1916

IF THE weaknesses now revealed in the British armoury were to be remedied, the first problem to be dealt with must be that of manpower; in a 'war of machines' it was at least as necessary to look to the supply of machine-makers at home as to the supply of machine-users on the fields of battle. It is this problem of labour which is the flash-point for many of the major changes in social status, relationship, and environment which are apparent from early 1915 onwards. The process was a fairly simple one. To get the most out of the existing labour force the Government had to cajole and bargain with trade union leaders, giving them a status they had never possessed before; to combat the inefficiency allegedly caused by alcoholism they remodelled the country's liquor licensing system; to surmount labour shortages they upgraded unskilled labour and encouraged women to take on new tasks; as women flexed their muscles on behalf of their country they found that they were at the same time winning the battle for emancipation so long fought by their pioneers; all in themselves of outstanding importance, these developments reacted and interacted to create an immense range of ramifications and side effects.

The first great hindrance to the war industries was the indiscriminate recruiting of the early days of the war. Statistics compiled after a year of war showed that almost a quarter of the employees in the chemicals and explosives industry had enlisted, as had a similar proportion from electrical engineering; over a fifth had gone from coal-mining and almost as many from the metal trades.[1] The private armaments firm of Vickers was the first to sense the danger of too much patriotism and, in September 1914, suggested a system of badges which could be worn by men on vital production and thus protect them from the attentions of the recruiting sergeant and the young women with their white feathers.[2]

The idea of badging as a defence against badgering ~
up by the Admiralty in December and, finally, in March the ~
Office, with great show of reluctance, introduced a similar scheme
into its own ordnance establishments. By May the War Office had
become aware of the need to look beyond the walls of its own factories and it issued a circular to recruiting officers telling them to
keep their hands off men in certain specified occupations. At the
same time efforts were made to bring back some of the skilled men
already enlisted. Thus, after a sharp drive at the beginning of the
war to get men into the trenches, there followed a more spasmodic
movement to keep certain men out of the trenches. Later in the
war, as military strategy continued to demand that men must be
hurled against machines, it was necessary to start debadging some
of these men, to conduct a 'comb out', as the charming phrase
had it, of the reserved occupations.

There were other obstacles to the maximizing of labour power.
The most important of these was the elaborate structure of trade
union rules and restrictions built up over the years of struggle with
the employing classes. Immediately after the outbreak of war a
number of private firms, acting independently of the Government,
entered into negotiations with the unions in the hope of securing
the abandonment of restrictive practices; conferences were held
on Clydeside and on Tyneside and a rather vague 'industrial
truce' was offered on behalf of labour.[3] A more positive step was
the meeting in November between the Engineering Employers'
Federation and the unions, which produced the so-called Crayford
Agreement whereby it was established that, though female labour
was not to be employed in place of skilled men, such labour could
be employed on purely automatic machines, these machines being
set up by fully skilled mechanics.[4] This was no great advance from
the aspect of increasing productivity and the little the agreement
did achieve was vitiated by a series of disputes in the engineering
industry throughout the winter. It was this state of affairs, together with the unfavourable military situation, which made
Government intervention necessary.[5]

The crying need was to secure trade union approval for 'dilution', the introduction of semi-skilled, unskilled, or female labour
into jobs, or parts of jobs, hitherto reserved for skilled craftsmen.
This was the main problem considered by a special Government

committee (shortly called the Committee on Production) set up in February 1915; but for the time being the Government confined itself to a policy of exhortation. The first big agreement on dilution was again a private one, the Shells and Fuses Agreement of early March 1915 between the engineering unions and the Employers' Federation. Confined to the duration of the war, the agreement laid down that in return for the acceptance of some dilution the employers would avoid any permanent restriction of employment in favour of semi-skilled or female labour, and that at the end of the war, or before, the 'dilutees' would be the first to be dismissed.[6]

It was at this stage that the Chancellor of the Exchequer, Lloyd George, depressed by the set-backs of the war, and already feeling himself to be the strong man at his leader's elbow if not yet the eager man breathing down his leader's neck, stepped in. Upon his initiative a conference was held at the Treasury from 17 to 19 March between Arthur Henderson and a number of other trade union leaders on the one side and Lloyd George and Walter Runciman, President of the Board of Trade, on the other. Henderson and his colleagues gave an undertaking that unions engaged on war-work would forgo the right to strike, that disputes would go to arbitration, and that there would be a relaxation of 'present trade practices'; it was understood that these concessions were for the duration of the war only, and that the Government for its part would see to it that the permanent standards of trade unionists were not endangered.

The miners were the only major grouping to stand aside from this agreement, for, although the representatives of the Amalgamated Society of Engineers declared that they had no authority to sign the first agreement, a further special agreement was concluded with them on 25 March.[7] On the surface the outcome of these negotiations was scarcely favourable to the labour movement; but already the point had been made that if the war were to be fought to a successful conclusion the co-operation of labour leaders must be enlisted. This point was driven home by the appointment of the labour representatives at the Treasury conference as a standing National Labour Advisory Committee to the Government, though in the event this body was to prove of symbolic rather than practical importance.

The Treasury conference showed Government awareness of the

problem of manpower; but awareness was no substitute for firmness. Without legal sanction, the agreements soon proved themselves inadequate. While this was becoming apparent the Government itself was rocked by two separate crises: a sharp conflict at the Admiralty between Winston Churchill and Lord Fisher, which resulted in the latter's resignation, and a scandal over the shortage of shells on the Western Front. Either alone would probably have been sufficient to force a change of Goverment. Historians have tended to follow too uncritically Lord Beaverbrook's insistence that the Admiralty crisis alone brought the downfall of the Government:[8] it certainly made a Ministerial reshuffle an immediate inevitability, but without either crisis the general disparity between social and military needs and Government action would have brought change before very long.

In the present context greater interest attaches to the shell shortage, which became a crying public issue with the publication in *The Times* of a dispatch from its military correspondent, Colonel Repington, which read in part:

We had not sufficient high explosives to lower the enemy's parapets to the ground, after the French practice. The infantry did splendidly, but the conditions were too hard. The want of an unlimited supply of high explosives was a fatal bar to our success.

This article appeared on 14 May; that same day Lord Fisher resigned. Five days later Asquith announced that he was proposing to reconstruct his Ministry and on 21 May there was a debate in the House of Commons on the munitions crisis. In the new Ministry established a few days later the Conservatives took their places as partners in a war coalition. Even more significant was the inclusion in the Cabinet, as President of the Board of Education, of the Secretary of the Labour Party, Arthur Henderson; this was the first time a member of the Labour Party had held Government office. Two other Labour M.P.s attained minor office: William Brace, a South Wales miner, became Under-Secretary at the Home Office, and G. H. Roberts, a printer, became a Government Whip.

One of the first major acts of the new Government was the creation of a Ministry of Munitions, with a Minister in the person of David Lloyd George. Almost at once, a Munitions of War Bill, which sought to put the Treasury Agreement on a legal footing, was presented to the House. Its first part was concerned with the avoidance of industrial stoppages: strikes and lock-outs in all industries covered by the Munitions Act were prohibited, and all labour differences were, if the Board of Trade so decided, to be resolved by compulsory arbitration. In the second part of the Act provision was made for the Ministry of Munitions to take over direct control of certain factories concerned in war production. In these factories all trade union practices were to be suspended, though, as in the Treasury Agreement, it was made clear that this was for the duration of the war only, and that wage rates would be safeguarded; any changes in wage rates, however, had to be vetted by the Ministry. As a sop to the workers it was at the same time enacted that there would be a limitation of profits within the controlled establishments.

That Government control, in the sense of a constant watchfulness over discipline, time-keeping, and the achievement of a reasonable level of output, was intended to be a reality is demonstrated by the following clause:

The employer and every person employed in the establishment shall comply with any regulations made applicable to that establishment with a view to attaining and maintaining a proper standard of efficiency with respect to the due observance of the rules of the establishment.

There was at least a rough justice in this, even if it did carry overtones of *1984*. The one clause which was manifestly unjust was the following:

A person shall not give employment to a workman who has within the previous six weeks ... been employed on or in connexion with munitions work ... unless he holds a certificate from the employer by whom he was last so employed that he left with the consent of the employer.

The evil this clause was intended to deal with was that of employers bidding against each other for the limited supply of skilled labour; but in binding the employee hand and foot to his employer it substituted a worse one, for there was no equal restriction upon the employer's right to dismiss the employee. The 'leaving certificate' was a standing grievance for the next twelve months.

The second part of the Munitions of War Act also dealt with another labour problem which we have not so far touched on – the problem of mobility. In the early stages of the war it had been left to the employment exchanges to exhort men to move to the jobs where they were most needed. At the end of the year the town of Middlesbrough took the initiative in forming what was called the 'King's Squad', a volunteer group of skilled workmen who undertook to go wherever their work was required. By May 1915 this had developed into an official War Munitions Volunteer Scheme and by June it had taken the shape typical of the transition stage of the war: men all over the country were invited to volunteer, but once they had done so they were expected to go unquestioningly wheresoever the Government sent them. Legal sanction for this was provided by Clause 4(6) of the Munitions Act. This amalgam of initial voluntaryism and final compulsion, the traditional basis of the armed forces, was not in the result very successful in increasing the mobility of labour. The third part of the Munitions of War Act, as it finally passed into law, was an addendum brought in by the Government to meet criticism in Parliament that the ordinary courts should not be left to deal with the offences created by the Act: it was now enacted that these offences should be dealt with by specially created Munitions Tribunals.[9]

It is in the months following the creation of the Ministry of Munitions that the movement to keep useful men out of the forces by giving them badges reaches its apogee and is overtaken by the contrary movement to get as many men as possible into the forces by depriving men of their badges. To cut through the entanglement of the many schemes then in force and to resolve the opposing needs of the home front and war front, the Government hit upon the bold stroke of compiling a National Register of all persons, male or female, between the ages of fifteen and sixty-five. The necessary Act of Parliament received the Royal Assent on 15 July 1915, and Sunday, 15 August, was the day set aside for the populace to provide particulars of age and occupation. Left-wingers and liberals stirred uneasily as they felt the cold chill of conscription in the air,[10] but it would seem reasonable in view of the economic and industrial difficulties we have been discussing to take at its face value Lord Lansdowne's explanation of the Government's intention:

that every member of the community should bear not merely a part in the national task but the part which he is best qualified to take.[11]

If there was anything sinister to be read between the lines of this, it was not simply military conscription, but conscription for all aspects of the war effort. For the time being, however, the Prime Minister denied that there was any intention of introducing military conscription.

As the National Registration forms came in, those of men of military age were copied on to pink forms (the Civil Service having a most inept sense of colour values), and a star was placed against the names of those in essential occupations. But attention had by this time turned from the shell shortage, now being handled with unquiet confidence by Lloyd George, to the shortage of men on the Western Front. The first stage in the new recruiting drive which was, in the end, to culminate in the imposition of conscription, came with a conference on 28 September between the Government and the unions. In face of the inflexible opposition to conscription expressed by the latter it was agreed that one further great voluntary effort should be made. This was followed by the appointment on 11 October of Lord Derby in the new office of Director-General of Recruiting.[12]

[II] LIQUOR

Describing the England in which he lived for a time in the mid-eighteenth century, Benjamin Franklin tells of a printer who 'drank every day a pint before breakfast, a pint at breakfast . . . a pint between breakfast and dinner, a pint in the afternoon about 6 o'clock, and another pint when he had done his day's work'.[13] Alternative amusements certainly were scarce in the eighteenth century, but what is perhaps most significant is that the beer was clearly regarded as a necessary adjunct to work. In Edwardian times heavy drinking of an evening was still an important leisure activity of a big section of the people, and for many heavy manual workers it was felt to be an essential support to the earning of their daily bread by the sweat of their brows.

That alcoholic liquors stood on a slightly different footing from other food and drink had long been recognized by British Governments: Acts regulating the drink traffic had been passed in 1495, 1551, at the height of the Gin Age in the eighteenth century, and during the burst of Gladstonian piety in the nineteenth century. The total effect was that all premises selling alcoholic liquors had to seek a licence year by year from the local magistrates, and that, in 1914, there was in all areas a legally imposed closing time: in London this was half an hour after midnight (the pubs opened again at 5 am); in other towns the opening hours were 6 am to 11 pm and in country districts 6 am to 10 pm. Scotland suffered a harsher régime, the open hours being from 10 am to as early as 9 pm in some areas, 11 pm in others; on Sundays pubs in both Scotland and Wales were closed. England treated her Sabbath in the more complicated fashion which has now become standard for every day of the week: the pubs were open for a couple of hours in the middle of the day, then were closed in the afternoon, to open again at six for a further four or five hours.[14]

When war broke out, therefore, there was ample scope for the indulgence of patriotic feeling. The civilian, perhaps, could harm no one by himself; but the War Office and the Admiralty perceived at once the undesirability of recruits coming on parade, or on board ship, suffering from heavy hang-overs. Thus one of the earliest regulations under the Defence of the Realm Act[15] declared:

The competent naval or military authority may by order require all premises licensed for the sale of intoxicating liquor within or in the neighbourhood of any defended harbour to be closed except during such hours as may be specified in the order.

The regulation itself is of no great importance: it was purely military in purpose, and it was soon superseded. But as the indulgence of patriotic feeling hardened into a pattern of 'ribald songs, dancing and quarrelling'[16] each evening at closing time, the Government opened its massive onslaught upon traditional British drinking habits. By the terms of the Intoxicating Liquor (Temporary Restriction) Act of 31 August, the Chief Officer of Police in any licensing district or the licensing justices for any licensing district, acting upon the recommendation of the Chief

Officer of Police, were empowered to impose such restriction upon the hours of sale of alcohol as might seem desirable for the maintenance of order or the suppression of drunkenness. The Act was to be valid till a month after the end of the war.

By the end of 1914 nearly one half of the one thousand licensing authorities in England and Wales had made use of the Act to stipulate an opening time of 8 or 9 am. In London a new closing hour of 11 pm was introduced on 4 September; it became 10 pm on 19 October. Many good consequences flowed immediately, so that even the ranks of the brewing trade could scarce forbear to cheer:

A transformation of the night scenes of London has followed from the closing of the public-houses at 11. Great traffic centres, like the Elephant and Castle, at which immense crowds usually lounge about until 1 o'clock in the morning, have suddenly become peaceful and respectable. The police, instead of having to 'move on' numbers of people who have been dislodged from the bars at 12.30 at night, found very little intoxication to deal with, the last hour and a half being responsible for much of the excess of which complaint is made. Many of the public-houses were half empty some time before closing time.[17]

This, however, was not enough for the sanctimonious watch-dogs of manners and morals, for whom the war provided a glorious field-day in which they paraded, fangs bared and tails wagging. Led by Lord Kitchener at the top and fuelled by the various abstinence societies, there was a powerful campaign against drinking generally and against, in particular, 'treating' – the traditional custom of buying drinks in rounds, aggravated into a clear nuisance when many a man saw an easy way to doing his duty vicariously by buying drinks for his fellows in uniform. Kitchener, in a 'Message to the Nation' of 24 October 1914, issued through the Press Bureau, appealed

to the public, both men and women, to help the soldiers in their task. He begs everyone to avoid treating the men to drink, and to give them every assistance in resisting the temptations which are often placed before them.[18]

All that happened, however, was that the 'business as usual' budget put the price of beer up from 3d to 4d a pint.

Lloyd George had once been the great rabble-rouser of Welsh nonconformity; he was now in process of developing into one of the greatest war statesmen in British history. The merging of the one into the other can be seen in two speeches of 28 February and 29 March 1915. In the first he concluded a blistering attack on the 'small minority of workmen' given to drunkenness with the cry: 'Drink is doing us more damage in the war than all the German submarines put together.'[19] A month later the threat had assumed even more serious proportions: 'We are fighting Germany, Austria and Drink, and, as far as I can see, the greatest of these deadly foes is Drink.'[20]

One man who was clearly impressed was the King, who on 15 April 'took the pledge', and was rather hurt by the failure of other public figures to follow his lead despite the efforts of a teetotal organization specially founded to canvass businessmen and politicians.[21] But the Government took the drastic action which has left permanent scars, first preparing the ground with an investigation into bad time-keeping in shipbuilding, munitions and transport areas. The main conclusion of the Report, presented on 29 April 1915, was that, although there were no doubt many reasons for loss of time, the most important was the ease with which men now enjoying high rates of wages and abundance of employment could obtain beer and spirits. From the Clyde, however, it was reported that no noticeable increase in drinking had taken place since the war began; whether this was because the men of the Clyde were a particularly sober breed, or whether it was because no increase upon the amount consumed before the war was humanly possible, the Report does not make clear; elsewhere it is stated that the influx of Scotsmen into Barrow 'has led to the greater sale of spirits'.[22] Taken along with what has already been said about drinking habits in 1914, the Report is substantial evidence of the prevalence of heavy drinking, given the opportunity, among the working classes. But its conclusions were too sweeping, and in many cases unconvincing. It failed to bring out prominently that the basic evil really was that a very tiny minority of drunkards could hold up the labours of entirely sober mates. It said nothing of other classes in the community, who, to judge from the lack of response to the King's pledge and from the widespread stories about London night-clubs and drinking dens, were no less fond of their liquor. By the activist section of the working classes the Report, rightly, was regarded as an unjustifiable slight.

But the Government had secured its verdict. The Defence of the Realm (Amendment No. 3) Act was passed on 19 May 1915; by an Order in Council which followed on 10 June the Defence of the Realm (Liquor Control) Regulations were promulgated, and these in turn led to the establishment of the Central Control Board (Liquor Traffic).[23] The Central Control Board was not intended to impose its rule on the entire country indiscriminately, but rather to take over control of liquor-licensing in those areas where excessive drinking could be held, in some way or another, to be impeding the war effort. By 1 October control had been taken of fourteen such areas, and, among other limitations, an important general order restricting sale, whether for consumption on or off the premises, to two and a half hours in the middle of the day and to three (or, in some cases, two) hours in the evening was put into force. The sale of alcohol, that is, was prohibited before midday and throughout the afternoon after 2.30 pm.

The Board's other main measure was the prohibition of the controversial 'treating'. The police were enthusiastic: from Bootle the Chief of Police expressed the hope that the prohibition had come to stay:

It has in my opinion been largely instrumental in almost entirely wiping out what is locally known as the public-house 'bummer'.[24]

Everywhere reductions in the incidence of drunkenness were reported. This, however, was the negative side of the Board's work. More positively it made itself responsible for the provision of canteen facilities in the new munitions areas, and its attempts to foster 'model pubs' did much to eradicate the sordid image of the British pub as a mere drinking den.

From early 1916 the Board was in a particularly strong position to carry out these reforms in three areas, for in them it was decided that the State should itself acquire all licensed premises. The areas concerned were Enfield Lock in London, where there was an important munitions factory; the march lands embracing Carlisle in England and Gretna in Scotland, where the enormous influx of munitions workers had created a state of drink-sodden

chaos; and Invergordon and Cromarty, where there were important naval establishments. These experiments in State control have
endured, but although there were many pressing recommendations, particularly from the Board itself,[25] for total nationalization,
this was never accomplished. Rather, the Board proceeded by
piecemeal extension of control: by March 1916 its regulations
applied to twenty-seven areas and 30 million people; by March
1917 to 38 million people out of a total population of 41 millions.[26]
At no stage in the war was the entire country under control: when
the Armistice came it was still possible in the more desolate,
rustic parts, far from the madding crowds of war workers and
military personnel, to drink without a break from dawn till dusk.
It was left to the Licensing Act of 1921 to remove this dire
anomaly.

The other main lines of attack on heavy drinking lay through
increasing prices, decreasing potency, and introducing special
restrictions on the sale of spirits. In its first series of orders the
Board laid down a maximum of seventy degrees proof for all
spirits, the figure which still obtains widely today; it forbade
spirit sales by the bottle on Saturdays and Sundays, and otherwise
limited such sales to the midday opening hours – even then, by a
curious process of reasoning, it was stipulated that sales must be
made only in quart bottles, the working men being more regu-
larly in the habit of purchasing smaller quantities for speedy
consumption.[27] In some areas where the favourite tipple had been
a glass of spirits followed immediately by a 'chaser' of beer, the
rather difficult task of preventing such simultaneous purchases
was imposed upon publicans.[28] Successive budgets throughout
the war placed punitive taxation on spirits: from being, at 3d a
glass, on a par with beer in 1914, spirits now soared into the
luxury class and were being sold at four or five times that price
by 1920.

Reductions in output and strength of beer, which were enforced in 1916 when the acreage under hops was reduced by more
than half and supplies of grainstuffs were severely curtailed, were
as much designed to conserve essential food supplies as to combat drunkenness.[29] Scarcity conditions brought sharp price rises
up to, in some areas, as much as 10d a pint. Weak beer – 'Government Ale' – and high prices became a standing grievance – one

member of the drinking classes was heard to remark darkly as news filtered in from Russia in March 1917, 'Russia was never troubled by revolution till she went teetotal.'[30] In October 1917 the Government were forced to introduce price-control, at 4d and 5d a pint, for beer. In April 1918 the gravity of beer was again reduced and by 1919 the permitted price – depending on strength – was anything up to 9d a pint: from $\frac{1}{4}$d on the average pint costing 3d, taxation had risen to $3\frac{1}{2}$d on the average pint costing 7d.

Whatever criticisms may be made of certain of the utterances of rhetorical bigots there can be no question that the liquor restrictions of the First World War brought about a salutary change in one of the most important social habits of the people of Britain. From being a melancholy but inescapable feature of the British scene, drunkenness became a limited and manageable problem: in 1914 average weekly convictions for drunkenness were 3,388 in England and Wales; by the end of 1918 they had fallen to 449. In Scotland the weekly average fell from 1,485 immediately before October 1915 to 355 in 1918. As female drunkenness was affected too, the figures could not just be written off as due to the absence of men at war.[31] Drink was no longer, from morning to evening, an indispensable adjunct to the work of many; money was conserved for the more essential commodities of a healthy life. One Scottish Chief Constable reported:

Non-licensed grocers and other shopkeepers say that they have never done so good business amongst the working classes on Saturdays. This they believe to be due to the fact that working men get home with their wages, which they hand over to their wives, and partake of a proper meal prior to the opening of licensed premises.[32]

All of this is directly traceable to the regulation and reduced supply brought about by the necessities of war; but that is not to say that controls which were highly desirable in Edwardian conditions are necessarily desirable today.

[III] RED CLYDESIDE AND OTHER PLACES

When we talk of the labour movement, we can mean either or

both of two things. Speaking generally, we are referring to all attempts, however haphazard, whatever the philosophical motivation, of the working classes to better their lot politically and economically; to anything in fact where there are both labour and movement, whether that movement be forward, backward, or circular. Speaking more specifically, we mean the broad advance under organized leadership of the working classes towards the present high slopes occupied, on the one side, by the Labour Party, and, on the other, by the trade unions. The period of the First World War is distinctive in recent labour history for the way in which, despite superficial appearances, the disorganized sporadic outbursts of labour protest meshed with the formal organized movement to the great advantage of the working class as a whole. In entering into industrial bargains and political coalitions the official leadership in some degree put themselves out of commission as frontline defenders of the local interests of working men: the defence of these interests now fell to unofficial agitators or to those minor union officers, the shop stewards, whose one main function before 1914 was to supervise the piece-work arrangements in their own shops.[33]

That these interests were often in need of defence is an obvious concomitant of the stringent labour regulations we have already discussed. But the first outbreaks of discontent after August 1914 must not be attributed entirely to the new situation created by the war. All of them owed something to the ideas of syndicalism and industrial unionism which had been disseminated in previous years. Syndicalism presented the doctrine that through a universal strike the workers could create for themselves the opportunity to seize power. Industrial unionism concentrated on the proposition that the workers could greatly strengthen their position by organizing themselves in large unions based on whole industries, rather than in small, sectional, craft unions: ultimately the objective was the creation of one vast industrial union which would be a centre of political as well as industrial power. Accepted in whole or in part, these theories fostered a definite militance in the trade union world and created a current favourable to 'workers' control' – a thesis most persuasively argued by the exponents of guild socialism, itself in part an offshoot of syndicalism. For a few double-dyed syndicalists and neo-Marxists, the war was at once a final demonstration of the follies of capitalism, to be resisted at all costs, and a glorious opportunity for the workers to press home their advantage. All this apart, the first open industrial troubles are directly attributable to the normal expiration of various trade agreements towards the end of 1914.

War-time events in the Clydeside area of the west of Scotland are of especial interest both because the informal labour movement here was at its most colourful and cohesive, and because 'Red Clydeside', possessing an enduring quality of its own, wrote itself into history long after the noise of wartime struggles had died away. The Clyde movement can, as it were, be examined both horizontally and vertically: horizontally in the sense that, for a comparatively limited period of time, it was part of a wider phase of working-class discontent which affected all parts of Britain; vertically in the sense that it had a specific local quality which made it an influence long after the wider movement had died away.

Much of what is distinctive about the labour history of Glasgow can be explained by the way in which over the half-century before 1914 the city, like a vast dirty blotting paper, had sopped up the flow of immigrants from the Scottish highlands and from Ireland; Celtic fire and spirit, and, be it said, Celtic parochialism, coexisted with lowland Scottish caution and rationality. Here there had been sympathetic ears enough for the industrial unionism propagated by the Irish republican, James Connolly, whose party, the Socialist Labour Party, though numerically tiny, had important leaders in the Clyde engineering shops, men like Arthur McManus, J. W. Muir, and David Kirkwood, the last-named the prototype of the hard-headed lowland Scot.[34] The Socialist Labour Party was the twin child of Britain's first Marxist political party, the Social Democratic Federation (founded 1884). The other twin was the British Socialist Party, whose most active members in the Glasgow area were William Gallacher (son of a highland father and an Irish mother) and John McLean, a schoolmaster who did more than any other single person to spread the fundamental doctrines of Marxism throughout the west of Scotland. At the same time there was a strong tradition of democratic socialism stemming from Keir Hardie's Scottish

Labour Party of the 1880s, merged in 1893 into the Independent Labour Party (I.L.P.). The I.L.P., itself the most important component part of the ramshackle structure which the Labour Party then was ('the Labour Party is a jelly-fish, the I.L.P. its backbone' was a later and less kind metaphor), was also the most important Labour political organization on Clydeside, despite the fact that it drew most of its membership from the craftsmen, small tradesmen, schoolteachers and white-collar workers rather than from the engineers and more characteristic industrial workers.[35] The most important figure in the Glasgow I.L.P. was an Irish-born Catholic, John Wheatley, a chubby owl behind his pebble-lens spectacles, who, after working in the Lanarkshire coal-pits as a boy, had built up a small publishing business of his own. Although the different sects slanged each other in public, there was a deeper inter-dependence. One of John McLean's pupils, James Maxton, spent a lifetime in the I.L.P.; Kirkwood, shortly after the outbreak of war, was persuaded by Wheatley to leave the B.S.P. for the I.L.P.[36] Coherence was given to a movement which might otherwise have been fragmented among the different factories and workshops by the existence of vigilance committees whose prime function was to maintain a high level of trade union membership, but which tended to be staffed by the more politically conscious figures.[37]

On the first Sunday after the outbreak of hostilities there were, in the Glasgow area, big demonstrations against the war as a purely capitalist venture. But what really affected the main body of working men was the demand made in June by the local committee of the Amalgamated Society of Engineers for an advance of twopence per hour to take effect in January 1915, when the three-year agreement then in force was due to terminate. Negotiations took place from November onwards, but the most the employers would offer was an hourly increase of three farthings. A disputed wage claim combined with syndicalist agitation against the war created a likely situation for a rank-and-file revolt against the executive of the Amalgamated Society of Engineers, which was in favour of acceptance of the three farthings.[38] But there was one new, almost fortuitous circumstance, which reveals much about the working class on Clydeside, always in the final analysis touched by a near and real issue rather than any hypothesis about the final collapse of capitalism: in February the firm of Weir's of Cathcart, on the outskirts of Glasgow, engaged, at higher pay, a number of Americans. Within days 5,000 engineers were out on strike.[39]

It was a spontaneous strike, but it was also very efficiently organized. From being minor cogs in the official trade union machinery the shop stewards in the various factories affected became the major wheels of unofficial discontent; joined together, they became a mighty conveyor-belt of working-class action, the Central Withdrawal of Labour Committee, which demanded that it, and not the A.S.E., should be responsible for negotiations with the employers. The strike ended, however, when, on a ballot vote, the men decided by a small majority in favour of arbitration and were finally awarded a penny an hour increase, with 10 per cent on piece rates.

These increases, half of what had been asked for, left a sense of injury; insult was added when there appeared on 1 May the report, referred to in the previous section, which blamed bad time-keeping on heavy drinking, a slight which men like Gallacher and Kirkwood, who were life-long teetotallers, must have found hard to bear. The waters, then, were already pretty troubled when the Munitions of War Act, with its leaving certificates and provisions for dilution and the total abolition of strikes, was launched. The members of the Withdrawal of Labour Committee determined upon full-scale resistance to the Act and 'for the purpose of concentrating the whole force of the Clyde area against it' formed itself, along with others interested, into the Clyde Workers' Committee.[40] President of the Committee was Gallacher, secretary an engineer, James Messer, treasurer Tom Clark, shortly succeeded by Kirkwood, who acted as a channel of communication with the political genius in the background, John Wheatley.[41] Its first manifesto declared:

The support given to the Munitions Act by the officials was an act of treachery to the working classes. Those of us who have refused to be sold have organized the above Committee. . . .[42]

It is only towards the end of this manifesto that anything is said about the theory of industrial unionism. A later article in the weekly paper which the Committee established, *The Worker*, brings out the same point: the main purpose of the Committee was the limited and practical one of dealing with the infringement of traditional rights felt to be involved in Government policy; the question of establishing 'one big industrial union' is relegated to the end of the article and defined as 'an ultimate aim', the words being heavily leaded.[43]

A wider objective, which the Committee did put in the forefront of its demands, was that of 'Workers' Control' – that, as it was put in the first issue of *The Worker*, 'organized labour' should have 'a direct share in the management down through all departments'; again there was a certain stern practicality in that the proposals for the reorganization of industry were all extremely carefully elaborated. Two incidents in the months following the passing of the Munitions Act revealed to the Government the seriousness of the Clyde movement. Resistance at the firm of Lang's of Johnstone forced the withdrawal of the Ministry's dilution circular of August 1915, and a strike at another firm resulted in three strikers who refused to pay the fines imposed by the Munitions Tribunal being sent to prison. A general Clydeside strike seemed a possibility until the unions of the men concerned solved the problem by paying their fines for them.[44]

Meanwhile there were rumblings of discontent throughout the trade union movement over the working of the Munitions of War Act. The Government appointed a two-man Commission of Investigation, which took a special interest in Clydeside.[45] Hard on its heels came the great prince of industrial peace, Lloyd George. The Minister of Munitions first addressed a mass meeting in the St Andrew's Hall on Christmas Day, but in that chill un-Christian assembly Lloyd George's Welsh wizardry for once fell completely flat – so flat, indeed, that the press was prohibited from publishing any report of the meeting save a small official hand-out. For printing a full and circumstantial account, the Glasgow socialist weekly, *Forward*, was suppressed. The report began:

The best paid munitions worker in Britain, Mr Lloyd George (almost £100 a week), visited the Clyde last week in search of adventure. He got it. . . .[46]

Never a man to be deflected from his set purpose, Lloyd George now insisted upon meeting the shop stewards from the whole area at the Parkhead Forge, where Kirkwood was chief shop steward. Dull egoist though Kirkwood in many ways was, he managed, in introducing the Minister to his fellows, to hit upon words which deservedly became famous:

I can assure him that every word he says will be carefully weighed. We regard him with suspicion, because every action with which he is associated has the taint of slavery about it.[47]

Considering the series of slaps in the face to which Lloyd George was subjected, he comported himself very ably. Kirkwood informed him that he and his fellow shop stewards were not opposed to dilution as such, but that 'dilution must be carried out under the control of the workers'.[48] Responding with great sensitivity, the Government dispatched three further commissioners to Glasgow to work out with the shop stewards a mutually acceptable scheme of dilution. The man who drafted the scheme which in the later stages of the war worked to the satisfaction of both sides was John Wheatley.[49]

Before the *via media* was established, there was another big strike, whose causes appear remarkably similar to those of the strike of February 1915. While unskilled workers and women were being steadily brought in, the management at the Parkhead Forge, in a strange and ill-considered reversal of tactics, suddenly banned Kirkwood from checking on the conditions under which the dilutees were employed. Of the strike which broke out on 17 March and lasted till 4 April the careful official Labour Party inquiry reported:

We do not think that the Clyde Workers' Committee as a collective body was responsible for the strike which occurred. . . . In our opinion, that strike was a *spontaneous outbreak* of the general body of workmen employed there, and was intended as a protest against what they regarded as the unfair restriction of facilities which had previously been allowed to the chief shop steward.[50]

Drastic Governmental action followed, ten of the leaders, including Kirkwood, being deported to other parts of the country. Ironically this helped to speed up something which was taking place already, the spread of the Clydeside pattern of industrial action to other areas.[51] At the same time it brought to an end the first and most important phase of Clydeside activity. For the next two years the various leading figures, Gallacher and the shop stewards as well as Wheatley, the lawyer dandy Rosslyn Mitchell, and the members of the I.L.P., devoted themselves to precise, practical campaigns, of which the one against increased rents was the most important. While men from the industrial side of the movement turned towards non-industrial social objectives, such an eminently political figure as James Maxton, schoolteacher and member of the National Administrative Council of the I.L.P., showed his sense of identity with the industrial side of the movement by having himself arrested and imprisoned for a speech advocating further strike action.[52] Bound thus tightly together, the threads of industrial action and of political agitation made a strong rope.

Before examining the way in which the Clydeside pattern spread we must look at another troubled area where extreme discontent, canalized in pre-war days by the South Wales Miners' Unofficial Reform Committee,[53] arose concurrently with, and independently of, the first disturbances on Clydeside. Just as the engineers on Clydeside had had a three-year agreement with the employers which was due to expire six months after the outbreak of war, so the South Wales Miners' Federation had a five-year agreement with the mine operators which was due to expire on 1 April 1915. Before April came round, however, the miners throughout the country had successfully pressed their claim for a war bonus, and through the arbitration of the Prime Minister a national agreement involving definite increases had been arrived at.[54] In Wales the coal-owners insisted that this national agreement should take the place of the new local agreement due to be concluded in April. This was not acceptable to the miners in Wales, who were anxious to secure a permanent rise rather than a war bonus which might well terminate with the conclusion of hostilities.

When negotiations between the miners and the South Wales coal-owners appeared to have reached an impasse, the Government, aware of the serious effects a coal strike would have on the war effort, took a hand; in this case its attempts at mediation were unsuccessful, and it was announced on behalf of the miners that the strike would begin on 14 July. Before that date the Government found itself armed with the provisions of the Munitions of War Act, and on the day before the strike took place it issued a proclamation threatening the miners with the pains and penalties provided in the Act. This merely heightened the sense of grievance of the miners, for they claimed that in the previous negotiations with the Government Lloyd George had given an undertaking that no such coercion was contemplated. Thus, despite the opposition of the Miners' Federation itself, the strike began on the appointed day. Five days later, so serious was the cessation of coal supplies from South Wales that Lloyd George, in company with Runciman and Arthur Henderson, Labour's first Cabinet Minister, had to scuttle down to Cardiff and there agree that the miners' demands should be met in full. Work began again on 20 July; a further brief interruption in August merely emphasized that the workers in this industry had the Government at their mercy, so that it was better to accept their demands rather than risk a prolonged coal stoppage.[55] The successes of the South Wales miners provided the encouragement for rebel movements in other areas, but it was Glasgow which provided the method.

The big organizational change which emerged from the Clydeside struggles was the conversion of the shop stewards from minor trade union officials into major spokesmen of rank-and-file discontent who derived their strength from the fact that they served with and were elected by the men on the shop floor. In some cases the change was an immediate one; in others there grew up first of all unofficial shop stewards alongside the official ones, till eventually the unofficial ones got *de facto* recognition as the true powers in the workshop.[55] This new machinery was to furnish a valuable outlet for working-class action in the later stages of the war when the official leadership, suffocated in the Governmental embrace, was unable to function properly, especially when the workings of the Conscription Acts brought new grievances.

[IV] CONSCRIPTION

Lord Derby was Lord Kitchener's answer to the shortage of manpower in the trenches. Lord Derby's answer to Lord Kitchener was the Scheme for which his name will always be celebrated, one of those shot-gun weddings between the fair maid of Liberal idealism and the ogre of Tory militarism of which recent British history has not been entirely innocent and for which Asquith's last ministry provided peculiarly efficient brokerage. At the base of the scheme was the continental practice of dividing the adult males of the country into annual classes, each class in turn to become available for military service with the changing of the calendar.[57] The one refinement was the pledge that no married men were to be considered until there were no longer any unmarried men available. For this curious theory that, although all men are eligible, bachelors are more eligible than others, there was no moral or legal sanction, save perhaps loyalty to the ideal of the family unit; the suspicion that the main intention was to set the one group of men against the other seems well founded.

The Derby Scheme, then, provided some of the groundwork of conscription on the continental plan, but there was no compulsion – liberal principle was still strong enough to see to that. Instead, by a mixture of suasion and blandishment, men were pressured into 'attesting', that is to say undertaking to serve if and when called upon to do so. Every man was to attest, but those who were found to have good national (skilled work in a munitions factory, say) or personal (single-handedly running a sweet-shop and supporting an aged mother and five maiden aunts on the proceeds, say) reasons were to be given exemptions. It was for the purpose of determining these exemptions that a Local Government Board circular of 19 November 1915 announced the establishment of tribunals throughout the country, with a central tribunal under Lord Sydenham in London.[58]

As it affected society the Derby Scheme was a gigantic engine of fraud and moral blackmail, but, given that the Government had to find soldiers somehow, it was a very astute piece of political tactics. If it succeeded, well and good – the sanctity of voluntaryism had been maintained; if it failed, the case for conscription would be well-nigh irresistible. Opinion on conscription was still very divided in the autumn of 1915. In the years before, it had been advocated by a small group of right-wing imperialists, and it had had an able supporter in J. L. Garvin, editor of the influential Sunday newspaper, the *Observer*. Realizing that the bulk of the country still disliked the very notion of

conscription and believing national unity to be of greater importance than the principle of universal military service, Garvin, very
laudably, had donned velvet gloves to restrain the iron hand of
Lord Northcliffe, whose pro-conscription campaign had begun
in August 1914, and the other extreme conscriptionists. Liberal
newspapers like the *Daily News* and the *Manchester Guardian*
carried strongly worded editorials against conscription and, in
order to lay the dreaded shadow, were forced to praise the substance in the Derby Scheme. The Labour movement, partly
because of the industrial implications, maintained its opposition.

The Derby Scheme had been in operation for only just over a
fortnight when Asquith put his finger up to the wind. 'If', he said

there should still be found a substantial number of men of military age
not required for other purposes, and who, without excuse, hold back
from the service of their country, I believe that the very same conditions which make compulsion impossible now – namely the absence
of general consent – would force the country to a view that they must
consent to supplement, by some form of legal obligation, the failure
of the voluntary system.[59]

Another six weeks elapsed before the results of the Scheme were
put to statistical test: in his *Report on Recruiting*, published as a
White Paper at the beginning of the following year, Lord Derby
announced that of 2,179,231 single men shown by the National
Register to be of military age only 1,150,000 had attested; the
proportion of married men was not greatly different – 1,152,947
out of 2,832,210. His conclusion was that, in view of the pledge to
take single men first,

it will not be possible to hold married men to their attestation unless
and until the services of single men have been obtained by other means,
the present system having failed to bring them to the colours.[60]

The 'other means' appeared within days in the Military Service
Bill introduced on 5 January 1916, by the Prime Minister. Its
main clause declared that all single men (including widowers
without children) would be deemed to have enlisted and to have
been transferred to the Reserve, whence they could be called up
as required. The Liberal newspapers were most unhappy about
this, even if it could be simply represented as the necessary

redemption of the pledge to the married men, but only one Liberal Cabinet Minister resigned – Sir John Simon, who thereafter made no further attempt to fight the issue. While Sir John Simon resigned because of his opposition to the Bill, the Labour representatives in the Government, who believed its provisions to be necessary, were expected to resign in order to be free to support it; the T.U.C. had just voted against the Bill by over two million votes to less than half a million. But in the end the Labour members withdrew their resignations, and criticism from the Party outside was stayed until a formal conference could meet and thrash out the problem.[61]

Semi-conscription was inadequate to the ever-mounting demands of the trenches and on 25 April a second Conscription Bill was presented to a secret session of the House of Commons: so fumblingly did the measure try to reconcile present needs with past promises, however, that the Government found itself faced with a storm of opposition which blew the Bill back into their own faces. At the beginning of May a new universal conscription Bill, which soon became law, was introduced. Again the resignations of the Labour Ministers were announced; again, after a more seemly interval had elapsed, they were withdrawn. The real hub of the hostility of the Labour movement to military conscription had been the fear that it would be followed by industrial conscription, that conscript labour would be set to work in the home factories and workshops at army pay and under army discipline; the seeming inconsistency of Arthur Henderson and his colleagues can be justified on the grounds that, for the time being, there was no hint of this.

The imposition of universal conscription was an event of central importance in the social history of the war. It implied a definite swing in Government policy from the careful hoarding of its skilled labour to a prodigal casting of copper, silver and gold into the lottery of the trenches; it meant that the highly controversial 'dilution' which had been designed to maximize the domestic labour force now became 'substitution', the attempt to release the able-bodied by the employment of the less able-bodied. By greatly exacerbating the labour shortage, it marked the lowering of the remaining barriers of prejudice to the full-scale employment of women. Above all it brought first-hand experience of the horrors of war, not just to a couple of million volunteers and horny-handed professionals, but willy-nilly to twice as many ordinary unadventurous civilians – one in three of the adult male population. Of the experience in wait for them we have already said a little, and there are whole libraries of books which say the rest. Life in the trenches was a life lived in a new dimension of foulness, a tunnel life lived in a troll kingdom in which immobility never brought peace, and activity scarcely ever brought mobility. Once upon a time the putrefaction of war could be concealed in the salt of glory and conquest. Now conquest seldom extended beyond a few hundred yards of mud or the desolate stones of a shattered village: the salt had lost its savour.

The imposition of conscription did not silence opposition to the war. A group of Liberals and Socialists in December 1914 had founded the Union of Democratic Control (U.D.C.) dedicated, in the immediate view, to the securing of an early negotiated peace, and ultimately to the adoption by British Governments of an open, democratically-controlled foreign policy which would avoid the errors which had led to war.[62] In the same month, Fenner Brockway, Clifford Allen and C. H. Norman founded the No Conscription Fellowship (N.C.F.) for young men of military age:[63] this body fixed careful eyes on the various manœuvres of the Government which seemed to presage conscription. From November 1915 the N.C.F. was in a full state of preparedness, with a complicated mesh of communications holding together the branches which spread throughout the country. Modelling itself partly on the Irish Sinn Fein movement and partly on the suffragettes, it provided each of its officers with a 'shadow' to carry on his duties if he himself were arrested. It was ready to act as an open pressure group upon Parliament, as a semi-legal organization disseminating its propaganda under the shadow of D.O.R.A., and as a clandestine conspiracy maintaining contact among its members as they disappeared into prison.

It was partly due to the pressure of the N.C.F., which could count on the good offices of a handful of friendly M.P.s, that the first Conscription Act directed that the tribunals, set up by the Derby Scheme, under which they considered appeals for exemption on economic and personal grounds, were now also to hear appeals based on 'a conscientious objection to the undertaking of combatant service'. A new term (usually of abuse), 'conscientious objector', had entered the English language. But the N.C.F. was not satisfied: 'it is not fighting in particular which revolts us', it declared; 'it is war itself that we will not assist'. Again it had some success in that in the Second Conscription Act it was made clear that in certain cases absolute exemption from all duties connected with the national effort could be granted to conscientious objectors.

Made up of solid local worthies, the tribunals could scarcely be expected to treat the claims of conscientious objectors with sympathy: hatred, fear and horror at the mounting slaughter on the Western Front could be vented vicariously on such 'shirkers', the exposure of whom seemed a patriotic duty. A few tribunals did comport themselves with scrupulous attention to the letter and spirit of the conscience clauses of the Military Service Acts, but all found great difficulty in comprehending the attitude of the young man who declared he could play no part at all in the national effort and demanded absolute exemption. To begin with, as conscientious objectors had their applications rejected by the tribunals, they were passed on to the military authorities. Three groups, deemed to have enlisted in the Non-combatant Corps, were smuggled out to France: there sentence of death was read out to thirty-four men, commuted (after a pause) to ten years' penal servitude.

The information service of the N.C.F. had already got wind of this and at once alerted its friends in Parliament, who secured from Asquith, who was undoubtedly appalled by the action of the military, a statement that no executions would be carried out. A further triumph for the anti-conscription movement was the issue on 25 May 1916, of Army Order X, which laid it down that after being court-martialled conscientious objectors should be handed back to the civilian authorities for incarceration in one of His Majesty's prisons. In June the Government, to its credit seriously disturbed by the problem of the conscientious objector, set up the Pelham Committee, which was charged with finding alternative national work for men who were prepared to take it. A Central Appeals Tribunal was to consider all cases of men already in prison held to be 'genuine' and to direct them towards the Pelham Committee. Those who were willing were released from prison and employed under what was called the Home Office Scheme.[64] Altogether there were about 16,000 conscientious objectors: about 3,300 accepted service in the Non-combatant Corps, somewhat under 3,000 did various forms of ambulance work or work under the direct supervision of their tribunals, around 4,000 accepted work forthwith from the Pelham Committee, and rather more than 6,000 went to prison at least once. Of these, 3,750 were subsequently employed under the Home Office Scheme, leaving 1,500 intractable absolutists whose challenge to the authority of the State the Government simply could not comprehend.[65] Shortly after his translation from the War Office to the Ministry of Munitions, Lloyd George delivered himself of a resounding denunciation of the absolutists:

I do not think they deserve the slightest consideration. With regard to those who object to the shedding of blood it is the traditional policy of this country to respect that view, and we do not propose to depart from it: but in the other case I shall only consider the best means of making the lot of that class a very hard one.[66]

That these sentiments in regard to all types of conscientious objectors were shared by most members of the community, there can be little doubt. There are many reports of I.L.P. or U.D.C. peace demonstrations being broken up, of Quaker meetings being disturbed, and of conscientious objectors serving the national interest in such innocuous occupations as felling trees being molested by local inhabitants.[67] For the absolutists the Government provided only a dismal treadmill of arrest, court-martial, imprisonment, release, arrest, court-martial, and so on. Clifford Allen, Chairman of the No Conscription Fellowship, was imprisoned thrice before becoming so seriously ill that the Government, reluctant to have him die on their hands, gave him a conditional – that is, conditional upon his remaining seriously ill – release. Allen's case was typical of many; about seventy men actually died from their prison treatment.[68]

The organized resistance to military conscription of the First World War is of importance because it added a draught of physical action to the internationalist theorizing of the U.D.C. As more and more people, in the years after 1918, began to see the whole war as a ghastly mistake, the men who at the time had suffered persecution for that same belief emerged as leaders of public opinion. More important than that, the 16,000 conscientious objectors and, above all, the 1,500 unshakable absolutists were standing for the right of individual protest against the demands of the State and of the majority. Whether they were right or wrong – wrong, obviously, in their underestimation of the war-lust of the Prussian military caste, right, perhaps, in their realization that war would not remove militarism but only harden its yoke upon the peoples of the world – they were helping to safeguard that most precious of man's possessions, his right of individual judgement. Mention must be made of the many Liberals, so out of touch in many ways with the needs of the hour, who did defend this right: F. W. Hirst, Gladstonian editor of the *Economist*, Philip Morrell, husband of the great Edwardian society hostess, Lady Ottoline Morrell, Dr John Clifford, whose abandonment of a former pacificism has already been noted. Though a whole-hearted supporter of Britain's cause against Germany, Clifford was a wholehearted opponent of conscription, as is shown in his address to the second national convention of the No Conscription Fellowship:

The Military Act has imposed Conscription upon this country. Let us remember how it came upon us. It was a fraud. It does not express the matured judgement of the people. . . . I know something about the Tribunals. I am ashamed of my country. These Tribunals are a disgrace to our name. . . . Let us go forward; we are fighting for human well-being; we are fighting for the most precious possession of the British people. Conscience is the best asset a nation can possess.[69]

Lord Hugh Cecil, in pre-war days more often found inhabiting last ditches than leading the humanitarian vanguard, strongly denounced the bad treatment of conscientious objectors, and even *The Times* 'confessed' to 'considerable sympathy' with them, though it thought, using the same argument upon which it has always based its opposition to votes for women, that they ought to be disfranchised.[70] The war showed British mass hysteria at its worst; in flashes it showed British individualism at its best.

Leaving the philosophical and political opponents of the war, we must turn again to the attempts of the Government to 'comb out' skilled labour for service in the trenches. This too, of course, made good rabble-rousing material for the popular press. 'Probably there are very few of our readers who do not know at least one case of men who should be serving but have escaped,' declared the *Daily Mail* in the black lead it reserved for its frequent spasms of patrio-sadism.[71] There had been, in connexion with the Derby Scheme, a Reserved Occupations Committee in existence since October 1915; its functions were taken over in March 1916 by a Central Cabinet Committee, which, by an administrative development typical of the war, was replaced later in the year by the Manpower Board.

A proposal of this board to nullify the exemptions of all men under twenty-six brought to straining point the tensions which had been developing between the unions and the War Office in the latter part of 1916. The wrongful enlistment of a Sheffield engineer, called Hargreaves, an incident analogous in its personal quality to the banning of Kirkwood from the workshops at Parkhead, brought an unofficial strike organized by the shop stewards, among whom there was in J. T. Murphy a leading proponent of 'workers' control'. So serious was the strike, which lasted from 9 to 17 November, that the Amalgamated Society of Engineers had to take the matter up formally with the Government. The outcome was a signal victory for labour, the conclusion of the Trade Card Agreement, by which decisions in the matter of exemptions from military service were to be left in the hands of the union itself.[72] For all that the individual workman might still feel his disabilities and grievances, this victory must be accounted a powerful symbol of the power and status enjoyed by labour at the end of 1916. This was confirmed by the Cabinet changes of December. Arthur Henderson held down a seat in the new small War Cabinet over which Lloyd George now presided, John Hodge of the Steel-smelters became Minister of Labour, G. N. Barnes of the Engineers became Minister of Pensions, and three other Labour M.P.s, William Brace, G. H. Roberts and James Parker, all got minor posts. One of the first acts of the new Government was to appoint a sub-committee under J. H. Whitley, M.P., on the 'relations between employers and employed'. Reporting early the following year, it recommended the appointment throughout industry of councils representative of both employers and trade unionists.[73] The 'Whitley Councils' never amounted to much, but the mooting of them at this stage in the war is again symbolic of the Government's desire to recognize and meet the claims of labour.

NOTES TO CHAPTER TWO

1. *Board of Trade Report on State of Employment in United Kingdom, July 1915.*
2. H. Wolfe, *Labour Supply and Regulation,* Oxford, 1923, p. 19.
3. N. Dearle, *Economic Chronicle of the War,* Oxford, 1929, pp. 5–15.
4. G. D. H. Cole, *Trade Unionism and Munitions,* Oxford, 1923, pp. 53–4.
5. *12th Report of Proceedings under the Conciliation Acts;* P.P., 1919, XIII, 185, p. 5.
6. *Hist. Min. Mun.,* Vol. I, pt. 2, p. 110.
7. P.P., 1919, 185, pp. 11–12.
8. Lord Beaverbrook, *Politicians and the War,* I, 1928, pp. 100–3.
9. Wolfe, pp. 107, 196, 110.
10. J. W. Graham, *Conscription and Conscience,* 1922, p. 52.
11. *House of Lords Debates,* Vol. XIX, Col. 336.
12. P.P., 1914–16, XXXIX, Cd. 8149.
13. Quoted by E. N. Williams, *Life in Georgian England,* 1962, pp. 115–16.
14. A. Shadwell, *Drink in 1914-22, A Lesson in Control,* 1923, p. 1.
15. Regulation No. 7 of 12 August 1914.
16. *Brewers' Gazette,* 26 September 1914, quoted by Shadwell.
17. ibid.
18. H. Carter, *The Control of the Drink Trade,* 1918, p. 24.
19. *The Times,* 1 March 1915.
20. *The Times,* 30 March 1915.
21. C. Addison, *Politics from Within,* I, 1925, p. 80. *Observer,* 11 April 1915.
22. *Report of the Committee on Bad Time-Keeping;* P.P., 1914–16, LV, 220, pp. 3, 24.
23. *1st Report of Central Control Board;* P.P., 1914–16, XXV, Cd. 8117, p. 4.
24. *2nd Report of Central Control Board;* P.P., 1916, XII, Cd. 8243, p. 29.
25. *Memorandum of Central Control Board;* P.P., 1917–18, XXVI, Cd. 8613.
26. *2nd Report of Central Control Board,* pp. 15–17. *3rd Report,* p. 5.
27. Shadwell, pp. 41–2.
28. P.P., 1916, XII, Cd. 8243.
29. Shadwell, pp. 83–4. W. Beveridge, *British Food Control,* Oxford, 1925, pp. 101–2.
30. *Daily Mail,* 2, 3 April 1917.
31. *Report of War Cabinet for 1918;* P.P., 1919, XXX, Cmd. 325, p. 293.
32. Quoted by Carter, p. 264.
33. G. D. H. Cole, *Workshop Organization,* 1923, pp. 1–25.
34. W. Gallacher, *Revolt on the Clyde,* 1936, pp. 26–7. D. Kirkwood, *My Life of Revolt,* 1935, pp. 1–32.
35. A. Marwick, 'The Independent Labour Party, 1918–32', unpublished Oxford B.Litt. Thesis, 1960.
36. Kirkwood, p. 87.

37. Labour Party, *Report on Clydeside Deportations,* 1917.

38. W. R. Scott and J. Cunnison, *The Industries of the Clyde Valley during the War,* Oxford, 1924, pp. 139–41.

39. Gallacher, pp. 38–9. Kirkwood, pp. 88–9. Scott and Cunnison, p. 141.

40. *The Worker,* 29 January 1916.

41. Kirkwood, pp. 84, 87, 128.

42. Quoted in Labour Party, *Report on Clyde Deportations.*

43. *The Worker,* 29 January 1916.

44. Scott and Cunnison, pp. 144, 150.

45. G. D. H. Cole, *Trade Unions and Munitions,* p. 117. P.P., 1914–16, XXIX, Cd. 8136.

46. *Forward,* 1 January 1916.

47. Scott and Cunnison, p. 144.

48. *The Worker,* 8 January 1916.

49. Kirkwood, pp. 117–18.

50. Labour Party, *Report on Clyde Deportations.* My italics.

51. Cole, *Workshop Organization,* p. 33. Scott and Cunnison, p. 151.

52. A. Marwick, 'James Maxton', in *Scottish Historical Review,* April 1964.

53. Cole, *Workshop Organization,* pp. 107–8.

54. M. B. Hammond, *British Labour Conditions and Legislation During the War,* New York, 1919, pp. 231–4.

55. ibid.

56. Cole, *Workshop Organization,* pp. 38–47, 76–84. B. Pribicevik, *The Shop Stewards' Movement and Workers' Control 1910–1922,* 1959, p. 35.

57. *Report on Recruiting;* P.P., 1914–16, XXXIX, Cd. 8149, p. 3.

58. *Annual Report of Local Government Board,* 1915–16; P.P., 1916, XX, Cd. 8331, p. 21.

59. *House of Commons Debates,* 2 November 1915.

60. Cd. 8149, pp. 5, 7.

61. Labour Party, *Report of Annual Conference 1916,* p. 8.

62. See H. H. Hanak, 'The Union of Democratic Control in the First World War,' in *Bulletin of Institute of Historical Research,* November 1963.

63. See Graham, *Conscription and Conscience,* pp. 171–204, and A. Marwick, *Clifford Allen: the Open Conspirator,* 1964, pp. 20–45, on which the next paragraphs are based.

64. *Annual Report of the Local Government Board 1915–16;* P.P., 1916, XX, Cd. 8331, p. 24. *Ibid 1916–17;* P.P., 1917–18, XVI, Cd. 8697.

65. Graham, pp. 344–52.

66. *House of Commons Debates,* 26 July 1916.

67. B. Russell, *Portraits from Memory,* 1956, pp. 32–3. McDonagh, p. 91. *Manchester Guardian,* 16 February 1916. *Daily Mail,* 27 April 1917. *Observer,* 29 April 1917.

68. Graham, pp. 312 ff.

69. J. Marchant, *Dr John Clifford,* p. 154.

70. *The Times,* 17 October 1916, 6 July 1916.

71. *Daily Mail,* 30 March 1917.

72. Wolfe, *Labour Supply and Regulation,* pp. 38–40, 44–5.

73. P.P., 1917–18, XVIII, Cd. 8606.

CHAPTER THREE

New Women: 1915–1916

BEFORE THE War, women of the lower classes were the industrial drudges of the community, earning an average wage of 11s 7d per week, about one third of the male average. For women of the upper classes it is true that professional opportunities were beginning to open, but by and large it could with equal literalness be said that these women were good for nothing – educated only sufficiently to grace a leisurely life. The first effects of the war were disastrous for the women in the 'sweated' and dressmaking trades. But before the end of the year the first attempts at dilution in munitions and ordnance factories had brought an expansion and change in the work done by female factory workers. It is easy to exaggerate the importance of this and forget that hard industrial work had been a commonplace in the lives of very many women since before the industrial revolution; however, while for some only a very slight change in job was involved, there were other cases where large numbers of girls and women had been drawn in who had never previously worked in a factory or workshop, including girls hitherto entirely engaged in their parents' homes, waitresses, shop assistants, clerks and domestic servants, as well as unemployed women from miscellaneous women's industries.[1] These developments were confined to munitions and ordnance factories and were on such a small scale that a mere restoration of the pre-war level of employment was not achieved till April 1915.[2]

Many women of the middle and upper classes showed from the start great anxiety to contribute to the patriotic cause. Indeed one of the most interesting psychological phenomena of the war is the way in which the suffragettes, who for ten years had been waging war on the Government and the community, now outshone everyone in their patriotic fervour and stirring appeals for national unity and endeavour. The moderates of the National

Union of Women's Suffrage Societies (led by Mrs Fawcett, who had been opposed to war till the very last) were prepared for the time being entirely to submerge their campaign for women's suffrage. As Mrs Fawcett expressed it in the suffragist paper, *Common Cause*, two days after the outbreak of war:

In the midst of this time of terrible anxiety and grief, it is some little comfort to think that our large organization, which has been completely built up during past years to promote women's suffrage, can be used now to help our country through the period of strain and sorrow.[3]

Mrs Emmeline Pankhurst, matriarchal head of the famous suffragette family, swung the extremist Women's Social and Political Union sharp right into fervid nationalism, to the disgust of her radical daughter, Sylvia, who turned left, establishing her own Workers' Suffrage Federation, which maintained a resolute opposition to the war. It must also be recorded that the No Conscription Fellowship was only kept in being through the devoted resourcefulness of the young women who took over as the male members disappeared into prison. In a famous trial held in March 1917, an anarchistic second-hand-clothes dealer from Derby, Mrs Alice Wheeldon, whose real crimes were the sheltering of deserters and conscientious objectors and a vociferous general hostility to the Government, was accused of plotting with her daughters and son-in-law to kill Lloyd George and Arthur Henderson by means of poison darts. It is clear from reports of the case that the police had made use of *agents provocateurs*, and it was on the most dubious evidence that Mrs Wheeldon was sentenced to ten years' penal servitude, her married daughter to five years, and her son-in-law to seven years; the other daughter, Harriet, was discharged.[4]

Upper-class Amazons, who, for months prior to the war, had gasped in admiration at photographs of the women Volunteers of Ulster preparing to defend the integrity of British Ireland, in February 1915 established the Women's Volunteer Reserve.[5] Women who sought a more constructive part in the war effort found that, while the knitting of garments and comforts for the troops was welcomed, more ambitious efforts were treated with extreme reserve: when, for instance, the distinguished Scottish medical woman, Dr Elsie Inglis, offered to form a women's ambulance unit, she was rebuffed at the War Office with the words, 'My good lady, go home and sit still.'[6] In March, coincident with the general abandonment of 'business as usual', the Government announced that it was compiling a register of women willing to do industrial, agricultural or clerical work.[7] Although there was an immediate and enthusiastic response, little work was in fact found for the applicants;[8] as with so many other pieces of early Asquithian war legislation, the motivation seemed to be no more than some sort of vague desire to do the right thing. There was no sense of the intrinsic value of the possible contribution women might make.

In Glasgow, where dilution was already being successfully applied in the engineering shops, the municipal tramways, with Scottish intrepidity, took on two women conductresses on a week's trial; the experiment was soon extended, the women being fitted out with natty uniforms in Black Watch tartan.[9] The opening of a new Tube station at Maida Vale in July gave the London Electric Railway Company the opportunity to bring in from the outset an all-female staff.[10] For the convenience of its middle-class readership, the *Daily Mail* in June listed 'some of the new occupations for women': they were, tramway conductors, lift attendants, shopwalkers, bookstall clerks, ticket-collectors, motor-van drivers, van guards, milk-deliverers, railway-carriage cleaners, window-cleaners, dairy workers, shell-makers. The implication that these were jobs for middle-class women with time on their hands and not suggestions for the working-class housewife was borne out by the placing of the most proletarian job last, and reinforced by an article two days later describing the Women's Police Force as an occupation for 'gentlewomen'.[11] But the overall picture was one of willing women finding no outlet for their desire to serve. This was more than could be borne by the flesh and blood of Mrs Emmeline Pankhurst and the W.S.P.U., who, on Saturday 17 July, organized in the centre of London a procession and demonstration of 30,000 women on behalf of women's 'right to serve'.[12]

But the first large-scale exploitation of the services of women and the revelation of the adaptability of female labour to tasks long believed to be beyond their powers, which came in the late

summer and autumn of 1915, owed far more to economic
necessity and the dilution clauses of the Munitions of War Act
than to feminist agitation. Already in August we find a trade
magazine commenting a little incredulously that by no means all
of the work being done by women

has been of the repetition type, demanding little or no manipulative
ability, but much of it ... taxed the intelligence of the operatives to a
high degree. Yet the work turned out has reached a high pitch of
excellence ... It may safely be said that women can satisfactorily
handle much heavier pieces of metal than had previously been dreamt
of.[13]

Before the year was out the new use of female labour was being
extended to industries other than those directly involved in the
manufacture of munitions, and the Board of Trade had increased
its strength of women factory inspectors by 50 per cent. These
developments in the main were limited to working-class women,
although when the Ministry of Munitions' recruitment of
'munitions girls' got under way many of the delicate products of
middle- and upper-class homes were found to possess a remarkable
toughness and resilience.[14]

Society, like a pub full of bachelors, was from the start very
conscious of the feminine intrusion, and contemporary accounts
tended greatly to exaggerate it; for the press, starved by the
censorship of most hard news, articles on the new role of women
were highly marketable and served the patriotic purpose of
encouraging women as yet without employment to follow the
example of their sisters. It was, furthermore, easy to argue from
the odd encounter with a female shop-assistant or ticket-collector
that a whole liberating army of women was on the march when in
fact only a few outposts had been established. The London
General Omnibus Company was not converted to the use of
employing women as conductresses until February 1916;[15] in
March there were still only one hundred bus conductresses in
London, though training schemes were by then on hand to
provide another five hundred within a month. As late as July
1916 *Women's Industrial News* commented sharply on popular
misconceptions as to the extent of the employment of women
in agriculture:

Most of the press paragraphs referring to the replacement of men by women upon farms have been calculated to give an erroneous impression to the unknowing public. The demand for female labour in agriculture during 1915 was not very great and large numbers of girls who offered to take up such work failed to find employment.[16]

The fact was that quite apart from their innate conservatism, farmers preferred to hire the cheap labour of school children rather than pay an adult wage to women workers.

The event which began the second and definitive growth in women's employment and determined that the changes involved should go far beyond a limited expansion and upgrading of industrial labour, made a trifle more dramatic by the entry for the first time into hard physical work of a few adventurous members of the upper classes, was the introduction of universal military conscription. On 8 June, two weeks after the passing of the Act, the Government launched its first concerted national drive to fill the places vacated or about to be vacated by men. Only now did the war-time pattern of women's employment begin to assume its final shape.

In July 1914 there had been 212,000 women employed in what were to become the munitions industries. The figure for July 1915, 256,000, shows only a relatively small increase; but the great expansion of later 1915, combined with the impact of compulsory military service in early 1916, is seen in the next July figure, 520,000, an increase of over one hundred per cent. There was still a great deal of slack, so that by July 1917, when the National Service scheme introduced by the Lloyd George Ministry had had six months to bear fruit, the figure was 819,000;[17] in the last year of the war there was a further increase of well over 100,000.

In industry as a whole the total employment of women and girls over ten as between 1914 and 1918 increased by about 800,000, from 2,179,000 to 2,971,000.[18] Narrowing our range again to a field we glanced at before, we find that by February 1917 the total number of bus conductresses leapt from the timorous handful of the previous year to about 2,500, some half of whom, it was said, were former domestic servants. Over the whole war it is transport which shows the biggest proportionate increase in women's employment – from 18,000 in 1914 to 117,000 in 1918. And it is domestic service which is the one industry which shows a decline – from 1,658,000 in 1914 to 1,258,000 in 1918:[19] the decline is substantial (400,000) but, as can be seen, domestic service was far from being wiped out, as is sometimes suggested. Contemporaries were well aware of what was happening. Describing to a correspondent the way in which housemaids were flocking into the munitions factories, R. D. Blumenfeld added his conviction that they would never come back.[20]

After transport the biggest proportional increases were in clerical, commercial, administrative and educational activities. In banking and finance there was a fantastic rate of growth – from a mere 9,500 female employees in 1914 to 63,700 in 1917. Taking the entire span of the war, the number of women and girls employed in the whole of commerce and its allied occupations rose from 505,000 to 934,000. In national and local government, in which education is included, numbers rose from 262,000 to 460,000.[21] It is in these arid statistics that we traverse a central theme in the sociology of women's employment in the twentieth century, the rise of the business girl, taking the term to cover the whole range from executive secretary to shorthand typist. The growth of large-scale industry and bureaucracy would undoubtedly have brought this development eventually, but it was the war, in creating simultaneously a proliferation of Government committees and departments *and* a shortage of men, which brought a sudden and irreversible advance in the economic and social power of a category of women employees which extended from sprigs of the aristocracy to daughters of the proletariat.

The new economic power was noted as early as mid-September 1915. 'No woman worker is in greater demand than the shorthand typist,' reported the *Daily Mail*, adding that wages had in a year risen from £1 to 35s per week. The social development was described under the heading 'Dining Out Girls':

The wartime business girl is to be seen any night dining out alone or with a friend in the moderate-priced restaurants in London. Formerly she would never have had her evening meal in town unless in the company of a man friend. But now with money and without men she is more and more beginning to dine out.[22]

The writer further noted the public smoking of 'the customary cigarette'.

More than half a century before the Great War, Florence Nightingale had established the right of the respectable young lady to the role of ministering angel, and it was to nursing that young ladies had most readily turned in the early stages of the war. By July 1917 there were 45,000 of them thus occupied.[23] For all that the nursing of wounded heroes was accepted as a reasonably natural task for girls of the middle and upper classes, the figure does none the less represent the fact that these girls were for the first time doing hard and rewarding work, and were in many cases doing it under conditions of unprecedented freedom. Despite the rebuff administered to the more ambitious project of Dr Elsie Inglis, this intrepid lady, in fact, proceeded on her own initiative to establish her Scottish Women's Hospitals in France and in the Balkans, so becoming a legend of the courage and resourcefulness of women all the more potent since she herself died in harness. Shortage of male doctors at home very quickly opened new opportunities for the few women who possessed the necessary qualifications: there was the rub – there were so few that already in November 1915 the demand for women doctors was greater than the supply.[24] By the end of 1916 a fair variety of women's paramilitary organizations had sprung up, consolidated by the Government at the beginning of the following year into the Women's Auxiliary Army Corps (WAACS); there followed the WRENS and the WRAFS, all providing for adventurous women an opportunity for overseas travel and service hitherto denied them.

Given the rigidities of the Edwardian class structure, there are difficulties in the way of summing up the consequences of the war for women as an entire sex. In the business, medical and military functions which have been mentioned, the women concerned were very largely women of the middle and upper classes. Yet the major section of these women had been in pre-war years a depressed class, tied to the apron-strings of their mothers or chaperons, or to the purse-strings of their fathers or husbands. Now that they were earning on their own account, they had economic independence; now that they were working away from home, in some cases far from home, they had social independence. Above all, in their awareness that they were performing arduous and worthwhile tasks, were living through experiences once confined only to the most adventurous males, they gained a new self-consciousness and a new sense of status.

Upper- and middle-class women learned that they could perform hard physical work, if only in their own deserted kitchens. This was no news to women of the lower classes; yet the ultimate experience for working-class women was remarkably similar to that of upper-class women, save that the former were less well placed to defend the gains of the war period than were those of the classes above. Most important for women of the lower classes was the escape from ill-paid life-diminishing drudgery as dressmakers and domestic servants or low-grade industrial labour into work which gave both economic status and a confidence in the performance of tasks once the preserve of skilled men. Even those women who were unable to free themselves from the swamps of the worst-paid trades were able to command at least £1 a week as opposed to the 9s of pre-war days. By the last year of the war the female munitions workers were pulling in well over £2 per week, and other women factory workers could count on about 25s a week.[25]

For the consequences of this upon the social character of working women we have the thoroughly reliable evidence of the Chief Factory Inspector in his report for 1916, in which he refers to 'the new self-confidence engendered in women' by the new conditions of work.[26] The *New Statesman,* too, reported:

They appear more alert, more critical of the conditions under which they work, more ready to make a stand against injustice than their pre-war selves or their prototypes. They have a keener appetite for experience and pleasure and a tendency quite new to their class to protest against wrongs even before they become 'intolerable'.[27]

Obviously, then, women of all classes shared in a similar kind of emancipation. The suffragette movement before the war had, for whatever sophisticated motives (the main one being that 'votes for women' must come on its own merits, not as a part of a general extension of the franchise), aimed simply at the same limited franchise for some women as was enjoyed by some men. The Women's Movement from 1915 onwards is a more unified movement than ever it had been previously.

[II] WINNING THE VOTE

Upper-class women in the eighteenth century enjoyed a certain rough equality with their men-folk, though in politics they were limited to the right to own the property on which all political power was based. One bemused foreigner said of them:

> They do whatsoever they please and do so generally wear the breeches
> . . . that it is now become a proverb that England is the hell of horses
> and the paradise of women; and if there were a bridge from the island
> to the continent, all the women in Europe would run thither.[28]

The middle-class society at the end of the century, however, very firmly thrust women into a subordinate position; almost at once the Women's Movement came into being, and over the ninety years from the 1820s to the outbreak of the Great War a great deal was achieved in the way of social and political emancipation: married women's property acts were secured; the local government franchise was won; medical degrees were wrested from the guardians of hallowed privilege; at discreet distances from the ancient universities women's colleges were founded. The preliminary question one must ask before discussing how votes for women were achieved in the war period is not what had women so far achieved, but why had they not achieved more. On several occasions favourable majorities had been secured in the House of Commons for private members' bills to give women the franchise, but the feminists never managed to get up the head of steam which automatically forms itself behind a measure sponsored by a government firmly established in power, or which can be directed behind a measure if there is an organized public opinion strong enough and intense enough.

For all their valiant propagandist work, the feminists still had against them two fortresses of prejudice: the prejudice of men, and the prejudice of women, who feared to be thrust out from cloistered femininity into the harsh male world of politics. Within Parliament the feminists, who had influential supporters in both Liberal and Conservative parties, fell victims to the party structure. As Mrs Fawcett neatly put it: 'The Liberals were an army without generals, the Conservatives generals without an army.'[29]

In this particular impasse the women were especially helpless – excluded from Parliament, it was impossible for them to argue a parliamentary case. As *Punch* made a suffragette explain, 'We could not get the vote because we had not got the franchise.'

In the first light of the social and economic advances made by women in the war years, it would hardly seem necessary to explain in detail how each obstacle to women's suffrage was overcome. There are, it can be argued, great subterranean currents in history of which political changes (the winning of the vote, say) are simply surface manifestations; but, more often than not, the time and the form of these manifestations depend on individual whim, accidents of circumstance, or confluence with another separate movement of change: these, singly or together, are sometimes powerful enough to distort or submerge. So it was with the Women's Movement. Before considering how the suffrage question, to the surprise of the women as much as anyone else, suddenly became a pressing issue half-way through the war, the precise manner in which the two great fortresses of prejudice were reduced must be examined. Before the war the feminists had had to contend with the apathetic indifference of the vast mass of British womankind, and with the active hostility of one or two leading women, such as Miss Violet Markham or the novelist Mrs Humphry Ward. The war brought unity in the higher ranks and a dissipation of apathy in the lower: men were quick to heap praises on the women's war effort, but scarcely any quicker than the women themselves. Inflated by the wind of patriotic romanticism purveyed by the press, the women of Britain became a gigantic mutual-admiration circle; now that they knew their worth, they knew that they were worthy of the vote. Having leapt on the band-wagon of adulation for women's contribution to the common effort, Miss Markham and the others could not suddenly jump down again when the question of the suffrage came up. By 1916 the female anti-suffragist was a negligible figure.

Behind the weakening of male bigotry lay a number of considerations. On the margin of importance was the disappearance of suffragette militance, which had certainly been an irritant in pre-war years, but which had probably served to confirm masculine prejudice rather than to create it. Mrs Fawcett, who was herself biased against the militants, quotes one humble member of the Liberal Party as referring in the middle stages of the war to the way in which 'the women had made good their cause by their services where they had formerly spoilt it by their threats'.[30] More important is the relationship of the theme of post-war reconstruction – a phrase which was on all articulate lips from 1916 onwards – to the woman question. In demonstrating their talents, women also demonstrated the gross national wastage implied in not exploiting these talents to the full, politically as well as economically. As early as October 1915 the National Union of Women Workers held a conference to stress the importance of the role women would have to play in reconstruction after the war.[31] This concept of not wasting women's talents merges into the larger one of women's place in the national defence, which most men had by 1916 and 1917 to accept as clearly established; some even went further and declared that in courage and martial valour women had shown themselves capable of equalling men. One way or another the foundations beneath the old premise about the non-military role of women being sufficient reason to debar them from the vote were thoroughly mined. Lloyd George, as in so many other topics, opened the floodgates of rhetorical affirmation of this truth when he greeted Christabel Pankhurst's procession of July 1915 with the words: 'Without women victory will tarry and the victory which tarries means a victory whose footprints are footprints of blood.'[32]

When that confirmed opponent of women's suffrage, Walter Long, President of the Local Government Board and a man who concealed a fine brain and a humane heart behind the externals of an old-world country squire, introduced National Registration he explained that any exclusion of women would be taken by them 'as a serious rebuff wholly unjustifiable in face of the splendid services which they had rendered already to the prosecution of the war.'[33] Speaking to the Women Workers' Reconstruction Conference, a noted feminist, Mrs Henry Morgan, exposed the naked heart of the male argument:

There is the much-discussed question as to whether women are able to take any part in the defence of their country and thus prove themselves worthy to have a voice in its reconstruction. This oft-debated question has at last been settled by actions rather than words.[34]

The national defence idea was clearly apparent in Churchill's remark that without the women it would have been impossible to
win the war, and also in the maiden speech of Lloyd George's
successor at the Munitions Ministry, E. S. Montagu, who declared that 'our armies have been saved and victory assured by the
women in the munition factories'.[35]

Fatuous as were most of the statements about women's martial
valour, they were not more fatuous than the military theory of
men's supremacy which they helped to destroy. One of the most
senseless of all the senseless acts of German militarism was the
execution of Nurse Edith Cavell. Working with the Red Cross in
German-occupied Belgium, Edith Cavell had nursed British, Belgian and German soldiers, but because she had helped Allied
soldiers to escape, she was court-martialled by the German authorities, and, despite the valiant endeavours of the American Embassy,
hastily shot. Technically the Germans no doubt had a case, but
it was a case which signally failed to commend itself to world
opinion. Asquith, again with an enforced glance at the suffrage
issue, expressed British civilian opinion when he declared:

She has taught the bravest man amongst us a supreme lesson of courage;
and in this United Kingdom and throughout the Dominions of the
Crown there are thousands of such women, but a year ago we did not
know it.[36]

Great prominence was given in the press to the work of Dr Elsie
Inglis and the Scottish Women's Hospitals, now combating the
military and climatic rigours of Serbia with quite fabulous courage
and resourcefulness. One remark by the Prefect of Constanza was
very widely quoted:

It is extraordinary how these women endure hardships; they refuse
help, and carry the wounded themselves. They work like navvies. No
wonder England is a great country if the women are like that.

No one was churlish enough to point out that the women were
Scots. Heroism was to be found nearer home. In one nasty shell
factory explosion in the North of England the behaviour of the
women employees was considered so exemplary that it was announced that Sir Douglas Haig was to be asked to let the men at

the front know of the courage and discipline of their womenfolk.[37]

Thus the last philosophical argument against giving women political rights was destroyed. Journals such as the *Morning Post* remained firmly unconvinced; politicians like Asquith (till the end of 1916, at least) remained not entirely convinced; other politicians, such as Lord Curzon and the last-ditch elements in the House of Lords, never would be convinced. But on the whole late 1916 and early 1917 were marked by a number of prominent conversions. Sir Arthur Stanley, Chairman of the British Red Cross, could scarcely resist the evidence of women's contribution to his own organization; his brother, Lord Derby, agreed with him; so did Winston Churchill; so did Sir Arthur Conan Doyle. In the newspaper world, *The Times,* the *Observer* and the *Daily Mail* swung round. J. L. Garvin pronounced a formal recantation:

Time was when I thought that men alone maintained the State. Now I know that men alone never could have maintained it, and that henceforth the modern State must be dependent on men and women alike for the progressive strength and vitality of its whole organization.[38]

In 1916 a similar tide of conversions swept through the North American continent, and many states in both Canada and the U.S.A. extended the franchise to women. There is, however, little evidence to warrant any suggestion that Britain was fired by the transatlantic example.[39] More worthy of study is the experience of France. France with its tradition of conscript national service had from the outbreak of war extended welcoming arms to the women participants in the nation's business, and full political emancipation for women was being freely predicted as early as 1915.[40] In fact French women had to wait another generation and endure another world war before they secured the vote. In Britain the women benefited from a rather fortuitous concatenation of political circumstances. Among the minor points, the establishment of two coalition Governments created a parliamentary situation in which there were no longer hard-and-fast party alignments inimical to the interests of the suffragists: Mrs Fawcett's pre-war armies now had generals, the generals now had armies. Personal changes, too, were important. The formation of the first coalition meant the disappearance of one or two bigoted anti-suffrage Liberals, and the entry of well-disposed politicians like Arthur Henderson and open-minded ones like A. J. Balfour, Bonar Law, Lord Robert Cecil and Lord Lytton.

Balfour, indeed, in 1892 had made a pregnant utterance:

If any further alteration of the franchise is brought forward as a practical measure, this question will again arise, menacing and ripe for solution, and it will not be possible for this House to set it aside as a mere speculative plan advocated by a group of faddists. Then you will have to deal with the problem of women's suffrage, and deal with it in a complete fashion.[41]

The British electoral franchise was at that stage, and was still in 1916, governed by the Reform and Redistribution Acts of 1884 and 1885. The Reform Act of 1884 had extended to the country householder the right to vote which, since 1867, had applied to his counterpart in the towns. To qualify as a householder it was necessary to prove unbroken occupation of the house in question for twelve months prior to the previous 15 July; that is to say, qualification was essentially one of physical occupation rather than of mere residence. In 1914 about seven million men were entitled to vote by virtue of the householder occupation qualification: additionally there were about a further million voters based on various qualifications, of which the most important were the historic forty-shilling freehold franchise and the lodger franchise.

By the terms of the Parliament Act of 1911 the normal life of any one Parliament was limited to five years; there should, therefore, at the very latest have been an election in January 1916. Quite apart, however, from the question of the wisdom of holding a general election in time of war, there was the problem that by going overseas to fight, or to other parts of the country to make munitions, several million men had lost their occupation qualification, and hence disfranchised themselves; moreover, there was a strong current of feeling that, purely as it affected men, the old register was insufficiently democratic, and that men in the forces, whether householders or not, had a strong claim to enfranchisement. In November 1915 there were a number of rumours that the Government was proposing to clean up the franchise muddle with a new Registration Bill. The N.U.W.S.S. at once threatened that if the political truce, which the suffragists took to imply an embargo on all political innovations, were thus broken, suffragist activity would be resumed.[42] What the Government did finally do in December was to produce a Bill which would prolong the existing Parliament beyond the date when a general election was legally due, but which left the existing register in force.[43]

Once aroused again, however, suffragist suspicions did not die easily. The following May, Mrs Fawcett felt impelled to send a letter to Asquith on the implications of the obsolescence of the present register and the necessity for a revised one:

When the Government deals with the franchise, an opportunity will present itself of dealing with it on wider lines than by the simple removal of what may be called the accidental disqualification of a large body of the best men in the country, and we trust that you may include in your Bill clauses which would remove the disabilities under which women now labour. An Agreed Bill on these lines would, we are confident, receive a very wide measure of support throughout the country. Our movement has received very great accessions of strength during recent months, former opponents now declaring themselves on our side, or at any rate withdrawing their opposition. The change of tone in the press is most marked ... The view has been widely expressed in a great variety of organs of public opinion that the continued exclusion of women from representation will ... be an impossibility after the war.[44]

In reply, Asquith denied that alteration of the register was being contemplated by the Government, but added that if such an alteration should become necessary Mrs Fawcett's points would be 'fully and impartially weighed without any prejudgement from the controversies of the past'.[44]

Whatever Asquith's intentions may or may not have been at this stage, his elbow was given a sharp jog in the House of Commons by a back-bench M.P. who raised the question of the compilation of a new electoral register.[45] Four weeks later the Government produced its proposals, or rather, for what it was worth, its one proposal. In the course of a long meandering speech, characterized by the Ulster Unionist leader, Sir Edward Carson, as a piece of opera bouffe, the Home Secretary, Sir Herbert Samuel, indicated that, the old register being now useless, something would have to be done, but that to draw up a new register on the old basis, still leaving many fighting men without the franchise, would be nearly

as bad; thus all sorts of other complicated problems such as redistribution, plural voting, adult suffrage, and votes for women would
have to be faced. The Home Secretary therefore proposed that,
the matter being too complicated for the Government, it should
be thrashed out by a Select Committee of the House of Commons.
Falling like stale tea into a choked sink the proposal was at once
withdrawn, though not before Sir Edward Carson had given a
thorough airing to his own proposal for a franchise based on
national military service.[46] The curious fact that the suffragists at
this stage themselves believed that emancipation was still a long
way off is brought out by an article in *Common Cause* which admitted that the question of franchise reform was, as Charles James
Fox had put it in the analogous circumstance of parliamentary
reform at the height of the Napoleonic Wars over a hundred years
before, 'a sleeping question'. An almost unbelievably quaint foot-
note added, 'This article was written before the answers about a
possible Redistribution Bill *threatened* to bring the question of the
Suffrage into the sphere of immediate practical politics.'[47] Two
N.U.W.S.S. deputations followed: one received by Asquith on
25 July, the other by Bonar Law and Robert Cecil on 3 August
1916. The main point made by the women, illustrating well their
own diffidence about plunging boldly into a suffrage struggle at
this stage, was that, provided there were no proposal to alter the
basis of the old register (as opposed to the modifications necessary
to enable voters who had enlisted to maintain their qualification)
and no intention of holding a general election, they would not
press their own claims: they would, however, force the suffrage
issue if the male vote was to be democratized, or if it was proposed
to consult the electorate on the vital topic of reconstruction.[48]

Since the House of Commons had refused the Government's
invitation to grasp the problem of franchise reform it was
essential that the Government should produce definite proposals
of its own. Accordingly on 14 August 1916 Asquith introduced
his Special Register Bill, designed to prolong once again the
length of Parliament, and, furthermore, to make it possible for
householders who had lost their occupational qualification to
retain the vote. Clearly, however, this was intended only as a
basis upon which more drastic amendments might be built, as
indeed the Prime Minister implied when introducing the Bill:

Have not the women a special claim to be heard on the many questions which will arise directly affecting their interests . . . ? I cannot think that this House will deny that, and I say quite frankly that I cannot deny that claim.[49]

With this piece of ponderous Asquithian thinking-aloud booming in their ears, the N.U.W.S.S. leaders gathered at the House of Commons to concert tactics with sympathetic M.P.s,[50] of whom the most prominent was the same Sir John Simon who had been a bit of a broken reed in the anti-conscription movement, but who was to be the stoutest of oaks in the final stages of the suffrage struggle. For the student of the political pressure group there is an obvious similarity between the parliamentary activities of the N.C.F. and the moves now made by the N.U.W.S.S.

But any jubilation was premature, for the following day the Speaker, Mr J. Lowther, ruled out all amendments designed to extend the franchise, whether to soldiers or to women, to abolish plural voting or to introduce proportional representation. Above the ensuing clamour there floated the rational suggestion of Walter Long that all of these delicate problems should be referred to a committee drawn from all parties and from both Houses of Parliament, to sit under the chairmanship of the Speaker. The idea was enthusiastically accepted; for many politicians with axes of their own to grind, the inclusion of the topic of women's suffrage was a rather minor detail.

The Speaker's Conference held its first meeting on 12 October. All of its deliberations were secret, and the request made by the N.U.W.S.S. to be allowed to give evidence was declined. Instead, a memorandum putting the women's case was circulated among members of the Conference, and a series of feminist resolutions from political associations, town councils, trade unions, and women's societies was forwarded to the Speaker, himself believed to be an anti-suffragist.[51] Now there began, in a manner familiar in recent British experience, a period of waiting upon the pronouncements of the oracle; the Government tacitly recognized this by dropping, in early November, the idea of a Special Register Bill.[52]

The accession to power of Lloyd George a month later augured well for the women and it is during his period of office that the story is completed. Reporting on 30 January 1917, the Speaker's

Conference unanimously supported three basic propositions and a host of lesser ones. The three proposals were that the unsatisfactory occupational basis of the existing franchise should be replaced by a simple residential qualification, that proportional representation should be introduced, and that there should be a simplification of the local government register. Unanimity was lacking on Section VIII of the Report, the one which dealt with women's suffrage. It read as follows:

The conference decided by a majority that some measure of woman suffrage should be conferred. A majority of the conference was also of opinion that, if Parliament should decide to accept the principle, the most practical form would be to confer the vote in the terms of the following resolution:
'Any woman on the Local Government Register who has attained a specified age, and the wife of any man who is on that register, if she has attained that age, shall be entitled to be registered and to vote as a parliamentary elector.'[53]

For the 'specified age' the report suggested thirty or thirty-five. The theory behind this projected age-bar was that the country could not risk having an electorate in which women were in a majority; absurd vestige of prejudice though this was, the moderate suffragists were prepared for the time being to let it pass in the belief that once women had been exercising the vote for some years the prejudice would die – as indeed it did.[54]

The next move was a highly astonishing one. Asquith, ousted Prime Minister, bastion of the resistance to the women's claims in pre-war days, reluctant conceder of women's value in time of war, now moved a resolution calling for an early Bill to implement the recommendations of the Speaker's Conference. 'Some of my friends may think,' he said contritely, 'that . . . my eyes, which for years in this matter have been clouded by fallacies and sealed by illusions, at last have been opened to the truth.'[55] It was a graceful retraction; the motion was passed by 341 votes to sixty-two. The following day Lloyd George played host to a deputation of women war workers organized by the N.U.W.S.S. The women successfully insisted that the promised Bill must embody women's suffrage from the start, avoiding the pre-war device of a general Bill to which women's suffrage could be tacked on as an amendment. The Bill, which settled upon thirty as the minimum voting age for women and gave the vote to all adult males but ignored proportional representation, had a fairly easy passage through the Commons, the largest minority against the women's suffrage clause being fifty-five.[56] The House of Lords, which still had the power of delay, seemed likely to be a tougher proposition. A full-dress debate on the final reading, which contained some unconscious humour, as when Lord Chaplin declared that the whole country looked to the Lords in such times of peril, culminated on 11 January 1918. Much interest attached to the line Lord Curzon would take in winding up the debate. The word was passed on to a group of suffragists by a policeman, who is recorded as saying, 'Lord Curzon is up, ladies. But 'e won't do you ladies no 'arm.'[57] The policeman was right. Curzon recommended abstention, to avoid an open clash with the Commons. The Bill anyway secured a clear majority of 136–71, and passed into law on 6 February 1918.

[III] MANNERS AND MORALS

The historian of sexual *mores* faces difficult, though intriguing, problems, and in paying attention to surface changes, to the clamour of bigots or the calculated indiscretions of fops, almost inevitably underestimates the basic constancy of human behaviour. Shakespeare describes youth as a time of 'getting wench with child'; the close-knit rural society of pre-industrial revolution England seems to have had a humane and tolerant attitude towards the illegitimate child born within its midst; to the eighteenth-century aristocrat 'gallantry' was one of the most important of the do-it-yourself pastimes of that age; and as a corrective to taking the sanctimonious protestations of the Victorians at face value one need only glance at the institution of child prostitution which catered especially for the Victorian businessman.[58] But if behaviour does not essentially change, attitudes do; and in a patriarchal society such as that of the Victorians the received attitude will also be the actual reality for the female members of that society.

In middle- and upper-class Britain in Victorian times, therefore, a double standard obtained: the male, ashamed of his sexual desires, for which he might find outlet outside the pale of respectable society, enforced his ideal standard upon his women-folk.

Most feminists in the nineteenth century had no desire to free themselves from this ideal standard; what, for example, Josephine Butler, who conducted a courageous and successful campaign against licensed prostitution in garrison towns, was aiming at was rather a raising of the secret male standard up to the feminine ideal.

Ironically, it was already becoming clear before 1914 that, if anything, the opposite process was taking place. One important factor was the spread among the upper classes after about 1880 of efficient methods of mechanical contraception. In his evidence before the National Council of Public Morals in 1925, Sir William Beveridge declared that:

1. The revolutionary fall of human fertility in Europe since 1880 is due mainly, if not wholly, to deliberate prevention.

2. The sudden spread of the practice of prevention after 1880 cannot be connected with any change of economic conditions, including the need for restricting families, and must be attributed to the invention of more effective means of prevention.[59]

An earlier report, published in 1916 and based on what was admitted to be rather bare evidence drawn from the immediate pre-war years, found grounds for 'a strong presumption that, among the middle and upper classes, conscious limitation of fertility is widely attempted.'[60] This growth in the use of contraceptives was almost entirely within the framework of normal family life, but obviously for women of *avant-garde* inclinations it did provide for the first time the opportunity for secure extra-marital relationships. Stimulus to such experimentation was provided, within the limited circle familiar with his works, by the theories of Sigmund Freud, loosely interpreted. The Edwardian chapters of Richard Aldington's *Death of a Hero* give a good picture of the puzzled growth of the 'New Woman', of whom H. G. Wells's Ann Veronica is the prototype.

There is no need to look for parallel developments in the lower orders of society. As Mary Agnes Hamilton perceptively put it:

Of necessity, female 'delicacy', in any of its forms, was the prerogative of the relatively well-to-do, as was the ignorance that was part and parcel of it. The village girl and boy, and the girl and boy who grew up in dense industrial areas, of necessity knew a good deal more than was once thought proper in their better-off sisters.[61]

The problem of dependants' allowances, we have seen, was to reveal a whole underworld of irregular conjugal relationships. The best way of summarizing the position on the outbreak of war would be to say that, for the upper and middle classes, Victorian conventions still stood (Aldington brings this out beautifully when his 'hero's' mistress collapses back into all the nineteenth-century formulae at the first hint of pregnancy), but that effective methods of birth-control – the euphemism was coined by an American, Mrs Margaret Sanger, just in time for the outbreak of war[62] – were available; for the lower classes there had never been any such conventions, but they did not have easy access to contraceptives. What the war did was to spread promiscuity upwards and birth-control downwards.

'When I left England in 1911,' commented Sir Robert Bruce Lockhart, 'contraceptives were hard to buy outside London or other large cities. By 1919 every village chemist was selling them.'[63] In the last year of the war Marie Stopes, the great propagandist for the use of contraception, published her classic, *Married Love*.

First *frisson* of the storm was the discovery in April 1915 of 'War Babies' (contraception obviously had not got very far yet). In a letter to the *Morning Post*, which was extensively quoted and added to in the rest of the press,[64] a Conservative M.P., Mr Ronald McNeill, announced that throughout the country, in districts where large numbers of troops had been quartered, 'a great number of girls' were about to become unmarried mothers. The topic was a godsend for journalists and for the letter-writing public. Mrs Wannop, the literary woman in Ford Madox Ford's war tetralogy, keeps pestering the hero, Tietjens, for material for an article on War Babies. For two weeks even the *Observer* devoted a great deal of space to it, but on the third week the editor peevishly snapped that the 'whole matter had been grossly exaggerated' and that despite the masses of letters still pouring in the correspondence must be discontinued.[65] There was justification for the *Observer*'s embarrassment: the year 1915 actually presented the highly moral combination of an exceptionally low illegitimate birth rate and a phenomenally high marriage rate. Next year the illegitimate rate did go up and by the end of the war it was about thirty per cent up on pre-war.[66]

The 'War Babies' episode is important, not for an exact estimate of increased promiscuity, but for the illumination it throws on public attitudes. Although one young woman of breeding (she read the *Observer*) felt strongly that young men should have been sent to the trenches with 'something more noble and helpful than lowering the whole standard of womanhood',[67] McNeill's thesis, which was widely upheld, was that no shame should attach to 'the mothers of our soldiers' children', nor to the children themselves. 'Suffer the little children to come unto me' was the *Sunday Pictorial*'s proud quotation.[68] In time the war was to destroy the conventional belief in the sanctity of private enterprise and free trade; already it was loosening the belief in conventional purity. There was a charming naïvety about McNeill and his fellow enthusiasts. Later in the war a more sophisticated argument was raised against a too rigid maintenance of conventional canons: by hook or by crook, as it were, the country needed births to mitigate the slaughter of the war.[69] The rise and fall of newspaper campaigns, or interest in the wider trend in sexual behaviour, should not, as Sylvia Pankhurst pointed out, be allowed to obscure the misery and misfortune which fell upon many girls of the poorer classes deserted by their soldier lovers.[70]

The exact reality behind the stories and the statistics is difficult to determine, but obviously it sprang from two related circumstances: changed conditions at home, especially for women, and the new awareness, in face of the slaughter on the battlefields, of the transience of human life. Something has already been said of the new economic and social freedoms women derived from their war-work, of the way in which young girls travelled daily long hours from home, or, in many cases, left home to live in hostels or lodgings of their own. Explaining the 1916 upsurge in the illegitimacy rate, the Registrar-General referred to 'the exceptional circumstances of the year, including the freedom from home restraints of large numbers of young persons of both sexes'.[71] Concerning the second circumstance the words of two women historians who themselves lived through the war cannot be improved upon:

Life was less than cheap; it was thrown away. The religious teaching that the body was the temple of the Holy Ghost could mean little or nothing to those who saw it mutilated and destroyed in millions by Christian nations engaged in war. All moral standards were held for a short moment and irretrievably lost. Little wonder that the old ideals of chastity and self-control in sex were, for many, also lost ... The great destroyer of the old ideal of female chastity, as accepted by women themselves, was here. How and why refuse appeals, backed up by the hot beating of your own heart, or what at the moment you thought to be your heart, which were put with passion and even pathos by a hero here today and gone tomorrow.[72]

If these young men, alive today and dead tomorrow, if these young women who, as they read the casualty lists, felt fear in their hearts, did not seize experience at once, they knew that for many of them it would elude them for ever. Sex became both precious and unimportant: precious as a desired personal experience; unimportant because it had no implications – except to mothers of 'war' babies.[73]

Gone too were those pillars of Edwardian upper-class virtue, the chaperons. They were, as one young lady explained in a letter to Mrs C. S. Peel, 'hard at work canteening and so on, and people who gave parties didn't want to feed and water them. And if they were elderly they didn't feel like having to walk home after late nights'.[74]

Allied to all this, the horror and austerity of war produced a hedonism more powerful than that denounced in Edwardian times by C. F. G. Masterman and other social critics. Degraded cinema pictures, immoral night-clubs and theatres purveying 'exhibitions of scantily dressed girls and songs of doubtful character' were denounced by clerics, magistrates and generals.[75] More relevant to our present theme:

'Give the boys on leave a good time' was the universal sentiment at home, and the good time consisted to a very large extent in consuming alcohol and enjoying sex. As a popular song of the period had it, 'There's a girl for every soldier'.[76]

Just as the Victorians had concealed the suggestive legs of their tables behind elegant draperies, the Edwardians still wrapped the question of venereal diseases in a web of guilt and ignorance. Victims who could afford it avoided their respectable family doctor by going to expensive quacks, and the poor often found that evidence of one of the diseases could be sufficient excuse for the Poor Law Guardians to refuse outdoor relief, or, more cruelly absurd, to debar them from receipt of Health Insurance benefits.[77]

It was a great tribute to governmental and administrative concern with a serious problem rendered more intractable by evasions and secrecy that in 1913 a Royal Commission on Venereal Diseases was established.

The Battle of the Somme was at its height, the moral climate in Britain was warm and mild, when the Commission published its final report, which, in calling for wider public knowledge and education and for 'a franker attitude towards these diseases',[78] set the keynote for subsequent discussion. When Sir Malcolm Morris declared, 'Before the war it would have been practically impossible to have held a Commission on Venereal Diseases, on which there had hitherto been a conspiracy of silence',[79] he was wrong on a point of actual fact (the Commission having been established in 1913), but right in contrasting the present roar of frankness with the previous silence.

Much of the work of the Commission had been taken up with the evidence and examination of prostitutes. Many a sex-starved Edwardian youth had had a romantic image of the prostitute as the emblem of glorious femininity scornfully shaking her buttocks in the face of social conventions by which he, apart from one or two guilty escapades, felt himself to have been rigidly confined. Further acquaintanceship during the war must have done much to weaken this image in any case, but it was the Commission on Venereal Diseases which most convincingly stripped away the romantic aura of the fallen woman, leaving a stark picture of a pox-ridden, money-grubbing harridan. Now, just when sweethearts who had formerly been cherished and guarded until the wedding-night were beginning to show a readiness to anticipate that ceremony, men began to find resort to a prostitute definitely unsatisfactory. However one interprets matters which are by their very nature insubstantial and conjectural, it is certainly true that there has been a decline in the number of prostitutes in Britain since the years before the First World War;[80] better economic standards for women and for the lowest strata of society as a whole are obviously also an extremely important cause of this.

Human behaviour, we have said, does not change much. There seem, as between men and women, to be certain ingrained differences of approach towards sexual questions. Kingsley Amis's Patrick Standish, in *Take a Girl Like You,* written fifty years later,

is still fighting a very hard battle over the virginity of Miss
Jennie Bunn, and he is reduced to the taunt that the kind of man
she craves for died out in the early months of the First World
War, a statement which many of Mr Amis's male readers may well
have resented. All the historian can do is to note the more obvious
changes. The safest generalization about the First World War
would be that it was a time of powerfully heightened emotional
activity and responses. Often this just meant earlier and hastier
marriage, reflected in the fantastic 1915 figure of 19·5 marriages
per thousand inhabitants.[81] But even this, in an earlier age, would
have smacked of a lubricious disregard of the requirements of
social security. Marriage in haste often meant divorce at leisure:
there was nearly a threefold increase in the number of divorces
'made absolute' between 1910 (596) and 1920 (1,629).[82] Whatever
the subtle differences in sexual standards among individuals, this
did represent a fundamental cracking in the cement of conventional society as the Victorians understood it. Women who were
deserted by their 'war husbands', or who were unable to obtain a
divorce, helped to swell the scrap-heap of unemployed in the
1920s.[83]

In considering the other ways in which the new-found freedoms
of women showed themselves, we move away a little from what, in
the limited usage of today, we call 'morals', towards what can best,
perhaps, be described as 'manners'. The unabashed ordering of
restaurant meals, the public smoking of cigarettes, the much publicized invasion of the public-houses, made light of by Shadwell as
merely a return to the Middle Ages, when public-houses were not
only frequented by women but were generally kept by them[84] –
these features were all part of the new manners. Most striking of
all was the change in women's dress; for, however far politicians
were to put the clocks back in other steeples in the years after the
war, no one ever put the lost inches back on the hems of women's
skirts. The shortened dress-length is usually attributed to the
obvious need while engaged on war-work for a garment unham-
pered by trailing skirts. Actually the first fashion changes anticipated any wide use of women's desire to serve: the *Observer*'s
Woman's Page is talking of 'short full skirts' with 'more than a
suspicion of ankle visible' in the first December of the war,[85] of the
'extravagantly short skirt' at the beginning of January, and of

'skirts six inches off the ground' in February. The very desire itself, however, combined, one would think, with a shortage of
luxury dress materials, may well have been the crucial motivation
in the adoption of a style of dress readily adapted to active service.
The growth of women's employment certainly consolidated the
development.

The Northcliffe press fought a bitter rearguard action against
the new fashions. 'Just now our young and pretty girls are pushing
the craze for short skirts to the utmost limit,' the *Daily Mail*, three
months behind the times, declared in May 1915. 'But even now,' it
added snidely, 'these ultra-remarkable models are regarded with
suspicion by women of good taste.' A day or two later it returned
again to 'the walking skirt that is absurdly short' and which 'is not
worn by the best-habited woman'. In June it was still sounding
off against the 'extraordinarily short skirt' . . . 'revealing, as it does,
the feet and ankles and even more of the stockings.'[86] But shorter
skirts were not the whole of it. Girls engaged on farm-work took
naturally to the wearing of trousers during their labours, and by
an easy stage to the wearing of trousers even while off duty. In at
least one case the County Women's Field Labour Committee, one
of the *ad hoc, noblesse oblige* committees typical of the early stages of
the war, attempted to insist upon the resumption after work of
'ordinary feminine dress', but was overruled by the Government-
sponsored Country Agricultural Committee.[87] The growth of the
women's para-military organizations with their 'trim short ser-
viceable skirt' gave a further impetus to the shortening of skirt-
lengths.[88] *Punch*, as so often, summed it all up neatly in a post-war
cartoon in which a little girl looking at an Edwardian beauty asks,
'Mummy, hasn't she got any legs?'

Towards the end of the war Arnold Bennett noted in his diary,
more as a piece of social reportage than as a hostile criticism, the
prevalence of 'painted women .[89] Self-adornment in all its forms
was an age-old custom of women, but in prim Victorian Britain
the use of powder and paint had died away.[90] In the Edwardian
era the foundations of the modern beauty trade were laid but it
needed the stress and excitement of war, the affluence among the
lower classes and the greater spending money available to middle-
class girls, to bring a return to the heavy use of cosmetics. This
was deplored by the older generation, though Joyce Cary's ageing

Sally in *Herself Surprised* readily went with the fashion, and it was too readily assumed (mainly by men) that the basic object of the exercise was sexual. Mary Agnes Hamilton made a good point when she suggested that the new preoccupation with 'Beauty' was 'self-absorption' rather than 'sex-absorption'.[91] The new pride in personal appearance, especially among a class of women who had formerly become ill-kempt sluts by their mid-twenties, if indeed they had ever been anything else, was one of the pleasantest by-products of the new female self-confidence remarked upon by the Chief Factory Inspector. Small wonder if women performing long arduous tasks, covering long journeys in crowded trains and trams, facing the unremitting stares of their fellow human beings for whole days on end with scarcely the briefest interlude of privacy, felt the need of rouges and creams.

One other beauty aid whose boisterous career really begins with the war is the brassière. Advertisements for this garment, it is true, are to be found in pre-war papers, but it is only from about 1916 that they seem to be successfully ousting what their manufacturers contemptuously refer to as 'the old-fashioned camisole'.

[IV] WOMEN, WELFARE AND CHILDREN

One by-product of the entry of women into factories and industries where they had not previously been employed was the development of what the Chief Inspector of Factories and Workshops described as 'a striking degree of solicitude on the part of the managers for their welfare and comfort'.[92] Welfare facilities were by no means completely lacking in British factories before the war. An enthusiastic young research student from Australia, drawing her evidence from the last year of peace and the first year of war, before the influx of women had had time to make itself felt, was able to compile a three-hundred-page tome on British welfare work. In a preface to the book, which was published in 1916 when the topic was becoming one of pressing interest, Lloyd George stressed that great and important changes had taken place since the completion of the text; in particular the modest private initiatives in the matter had been bolstered by the inception of a Special Welfare Department at the Ministry of Munitions.[93]

Before the war, factory inspectors had for many years been

pressing upon employers the advisability of the provision of qualified medical services, of the setting aside of canteens and rest-rooms, of the supervision of women factory workers by women welfare officers, and of the need for hygienic lavatory and washroom facilities, expecially where there were employees of both sexes in the same workshops.[94] It was on the last point that complaints were most prevalent. The lady Inspector for the North-west reported in 1913:

It is impossible to describe in a public paper how low the standard has been and still is in many places, where in other respects the conditions are not only not noticeably bad, but are quite good.[95]

The more intelligent factory-owners were becoming dimly aware of the correlation between output and the physical condition of their workers, so that 'dining-rooms and restaurants' were 'slowly becoming more general, more especially in the modern and most up-to-date factories, and in those so situated that the workers cannot return home readily for their meals'. But it was in 1915 that a 'great advance in welfare work' was noted, with arrangements for dealing with sickness and injury appearing, as well as canteens and mess-rooms.[96] The reasons were various. The employment of women where no women had been employed before, and the employment especially of the delicate flower of the middle and upper classes, were definitely the starting point at the personal level of individual employer-employee relationships,[97] though its importance must not be over-stressed. Britain had a long tradition of factory acts designed to protect women and children, but qualified by the persisting belief that to attempt to legislate for the adult male was to reflect upon his manhood.

The hectic conditions of the home front created new needs. The concentration of labour in a munitions centre brought a heavy pressure on available accommodation, so that it became not unusual for the same bed to be in use day and night, first for a night-shift worker, then for a day-shift worker. In other cases the worker, man or woman, might have long distances to travel each day, which, when added to the overtime hours frequently worked, might leave barely six hours available for sleep.[98] Attention was therefore directed to problems of fatigue, sickness and nutrition;

in the case of girls living, or daily travelling, far from home, there was felt to be an especially strong case for the establishment of welfare supervisors. Women working on T.N.T. ran grave health risks and were nicknamed 'canaries' as they developed a yellow discoloration of the skin: for them a free daily pint of milk was provided.[99]

It was perhaps something of a natural reaction on the part of the wealthy Briton, steeped in the Victorian ideal of the charitable soup-kitchen, to reach, in time of stress, for the soup-ladle. 'Canteening' was an activity of elderly chaperons in the first stages of the war. There was a touch of the same austere charity in the anti-drink campaign and the establishment of the Liquor Traffic Central Control Board, one of whose most valuable achievements was to foster the growth of restaurants and canteens as an alternative calorific source to unadulterated alcohol. At the same time the dim stirrings of a few advanced factory-owners became merged in a 'new general awakening to the dependence of efficient output on the welfare of the human agent'.[100] Where private employers remained asleep the Government was prepared to act as knocker-up.

Some innovations were less well received than others by the factory workers. Canteens, in time of food difficulty, performed a welcome task in providing cheap, if not exciting, food. A typical menu is as follows:

Sausage and Mash, 2½d. Mince and Mash, 2d. Patties, 1d. Beans, 1d. Stewed Fruit, 1d. Milk Pudding, 1d.[101]

But rebellious working-class spirits of Clydeside calibre and independent-minded women were frequently resentful of welfare supervision, which with shrewd cynicism they saw as merely a paternalistic attempt to maintain their efficiency as so many units of labour in the total sum of production.[102] Nevertheless, when the Chief Factory Inspector, in his report for 1915, suggested that the war-time welfare schemes would be 'likely to be felt and to spread long after the war has ended, and to leave behind a permanent improvement in factory life',[103] he was making an eminently sound prediction which subsequent industrial history has more than vindicated.

Concern for the welfare of working women soon broadened into concern for the welfare of working men. But, important for immediate survival as was the maintenance of the morale and efficiency of the domestic labour force, there was a yet more serious long-term problem to be faced:

In no direction are the ravages of war more serious or more difficult to replace than in the loss of human lives. Whatever degree of success may attend the nation in the present European war, the cost in life must inevitably be heavy.

'Consequently,' the Chief Medical Officer of the Board of Education argued, 'the question of the preservation of the rising generation, and care for its physical fitness and equipment, is of more than ordinary importance.'[104] School meals and school medical services in some areas dated back to the turn of the century: as national institutions they were products of the first burst of social reform legislation of the 1906 Liberal Government. The Chief Medical Officer's Reports for the pre-war years are a sorrowful indictment of the community's manifest failure to interest itself in the preservation of the generation rising in the working-class, elementary-school background. All reports are agreed that children were better fed, better clothed, and in better health during the war years than ever before. But this had nothing to do with the calculated piety of the Board of Education's desire to make good the loss of life in the war; it was a consequence of high wages and the heavy demand for labour. After 1916 the school medical services were in fact very drastically curtailed, and the number of children medically examined dropped by 28 per cent.[105]

The plans for the development of a national education system drawn up by the Liberal Government in 1914 were stifled by the outbreak of war. Even the total amount of the bare and inadequate instruction which was the main business of the existing elementary structure was allowed to fall away in face of demands that the national cause required the physical services of children rather than the development of their minds. The laws governing school attendance and child employment in 1914 had the appearance of wishing to be all things to all men, a strange medley of firm and laudable principles vitiated by exceptions and qualifications. Children were required to attend school until the age of fourteen, with the exception of those who at thirteen had secured a certificate of 'proficiency' or of regular attendance. Children could not work in factories until their school attendance was completed, unless they were 'half-timers', girls and boys of twelve or over who might work not more than thirty-three hours a week and were compelled to go to school half the time. Children under eleven might not sell articles in the street and boys under fourteen might not work in coal-mines. Local authorities might if they liked (not many did) forbid all work by children under the age of fourteen. Working conditions for children over fourteen were governed by laws similar to, but more stringent than, those applicable to the employment of women. Well intentioned in their various ways as these provisions no doubt were, they were already becoming paving stones for the road to a hell of national ignorance and educational deficiency.

Before the first year of war was out the Board of Education found itself under heavy pressure from local authorities desirous of suspending the school attendance by-laws. County magistrates were especially anxious that children should be released to undertake 'national work' (i.e. work on the farms of the county magistrates). A sad letter from the secretary of one County Education Committee to the Board of Education explained the importance of paying heed to 'influential persons, including magistrates, chairmen of district councils, and so on' and the danger of alienating the 'sympathies of magistrates and employers of labour'.[106] More humane motives played a part too. For all that wages and living standards began to rise during the war, some families were placed in a serious plight when the one wage-earner was on active service overseas; pleas for the release of school-children based on straitened family circumstances were not easy to resist. Over all the wastage was enormous. In August 1917 H. A. L. Fisher, the responsible minister, admitted in the House of Commons that during the first three years of war 600,000 children had been put 'prematurely' to work;[107] this figure did not include the hundreds of other children set to work in total violation of the law.

Juveniles over the age of fourteen did very well out of the war boom; it was possible for both boys and girls to earn from £1 to £2 a week in the munitions factories. In fact it was among boys and girls under eighteen that the wartime rise in wages was most marked. As with the trend towards economic status for the female secretarial worker, this was a socio-economic movement which has never been reversed. The war as a whole brought a revolution in the age-sex earning pattern in Britain, and marked the beginning of the trend leading to the affluent teenager of the 1960s.

Affluence, disruptions in the educational structure, and the social upheaval and flux of wartime Britain, brought a serious increase in juvenile delinquency,[108] especially among children between eleven and thirteen. Referring to the attitudes and policies of the war period, the Secretary of the Howard Association of London, Cecil Leeson, asked bluntly and rhetorically, 'Had we set out with the deliberate intention of manufacturing juvenile delinquents, could we have done so in any more certain way?'[109]

But among magistrates and local dignitaries the most favoured scapegoat for delinquency was the cinema. Certain incidents, such as the appearance in court of nine boys calling themselves the Black Hand Gang of St Luke's, seemed to lend justification to this. In its investigation of the cinema, the National Council of Public Morals recorded:

It is very strongly alleged and widely believed that the picture house is responsible for the increase in juvenile crime, and that boys are often led to imitate crimes (larceny and burglary) which they have seen in the pictures, or to steal money that they may pay for admission.

The evidence, the committee reckoned, was largely against these two theories, overwhelmingly so in the case of the latter. Increased crime by young offenders, they declared, must be considered in relation to wider social and economic questions; statements as to the extent of this increase in crime were probably inflated, for, as a Westminster probation officer pointed out:

There has been a tendency in recent years to increase the variety of offences with which children may be charged. For instance, children are now charged with wandering, with being without proper guardianship, with being 'beyond control'. Our streets are now more rigidly supervised than ever before. There is a large and increasing army of officials whose duty it is to watch over child life. In many cases it has seemed to me that the zeal of those officers was not always tempered by humanity and expediency.[110]

These qualifications were less valid for the latter stages of the war when the manpower shortage began to affect policing and officialdom.

Youth, being central to every discussion of post-war developments, was a topic which received in full measure its wartime quota of extrovert bombast and sentimental fustian. One turns with relief to the Final Report of the 1917 Departmental Committee on Juvenile Education.[111] After a model exposition of the deplorable situation obtaining at the outbreak of war, it proceeds, eyes unclouded by romantic optimism, throat unchoked by patriotic fervour:

Upon this educational and industrial chaos has come the war to aggravate conditions that could hardly be made graver, and to emphasize a problem that needed no emphasis. Many children have been withdrawn at an even earlier age than usual from day schools, and the attendances at those evening schools which have not been closed show a lamentable shrinkage. We are not prepared to say that much of the work which is now being done by juveniles in munition factories and elsewhere is in itself inferior to the work which most of them would have been doing in normal times, but there can be no doubt that many of the tendencies adversely affecting the development of character and efficiency have incidentally been accentuated . . . Parental control, so far as it formerly existed, has been relaxed, largely through the absence of families from their homes. Wages have been exceptionally high, and although this has led to an improved standard of living, it has also in ill-regulated households induced habits of foolish and mischievous extravagance. Even the ordinary discipline of the workshop has in varying degrees given way; while the withdrawal of influences making for the social improvement of boys and girls has in many districts been followed by noticeable deterioration in behaviour and morality. Gambling has increased. Excessive hours of strenuous labour have overtaxed the powers of young people; while many have taken advantage of the extraordinary demand for juvenile labour to change even more rapidly than usual from one blind alley employment to another.[112]

NOTES TO CHAPTER THREE

1. *Report of Chief Inspector of Factories and Workshops, 1914;* P.P., 1914–16, XXI, Cd. 8051, pp. 32–3.

2. I. O. Andrews and M. A. Hobbs, *Economic Effects of the War upon Women and Children in Great Britain,* New York, 1918, p. 24.

3. *Common Cause,* 7 August 1914.

4. Marwick, *Clifford Allen,* p. 34. McDonagh, *In London During the Great War,* pp. 180–1. *The Times,* 9, 10, 12 March 1917.

5. *The Times,* 10 February 1915.

6. F. Balfour, *Dr Elsie Inglis,* 1918, p. 144.

7. *Manchester Guardian,* 18 March 1915.

8. *Suffragette,* 14 May 1915. *Common Cause,* 24 September 1915.

9. *Daily Mail,* 30 March 1915. *Suffragette,* 16 April 1915. Scott and Cunnison, *Industries of the Clyde Valley during the Great War,* p. 65.

10. *Observer,* 6 June 1915.

11. *Daily Mail,* 4 June 1915.

12. *The Times,* 19 July 1915.

13. *Engineer,* 20 August 1915. Quoted by Andrews and Hobbs, p. 33.

14. *Report of Chief Inspector of Factories and Workshops, 1915;* P.P., 1916, IX, Cd. 8276, p. 14. M. Cosens, *Lloyd George's Munitions Girls,* 1916. L. Yates, *The Women's Part,* 1918.

15. *Manchester Guardian,* 16 February 1916.

16. Quoted by Andrews and Hobbs, p. 35.

17. *Report of the War Cabinet for 1917;* P.P., 1918, XIV, Cd. 9005, p. 69.

18. *Report of Committee on Women in Industry, 1919;* P.P., 1919, XXXI, Cmd. 135.

19. *Daily Mail,* 24 February 1917. Cmd. 135.

20. Blumenfeld, *All in a Lifetime,* p. 61 (8 May 1916).

21. Cmd. 135.

22. *Daily Mail,* 14 September 1915, 17 April 1916.

23. Cmd. 135.

24. *Observer,* 14 November 1916.

25. Bowley, *Wages and Incomes,* p. 192.

26. P.P., 1917–18, XIV, Cd. 8570, p. 7.

27. *New Statesman,* 23 June 1917.

28. Quoted by E. N. Williams, *Life in Georgian England,* 1962, p. 52.

29. M. Fawcett, *The Women's Victory and After,* 1920, p. 125.

30. *Ibid,* p. 118.

31. National Union of Women Workers, *Report of Reconstruction Conference, October 1915,* 1915.

32. *Suffragette,* 23 July 1915.

33. *House of Commons Debates,* 5 July 1915.

34. National Union of Women Workers, *Report of Reconstruction Conference,* 1915, pp. 15–16.

35. *House of Commons Debates,* 15 August 1916.

36. *The Times,* 3 November 1915.
37. Fawcett, *Women's Victory,* p. 116.
38. *Observer,* 13 August 1916.
39. Fawcett, pp. 118–19.
40. *Suffragette,* 15 April 1915.
41. *House of Commons Debates,* 27 April 1892.
42. *Common Cause,* 20 October 1915.
43. *House of Commons Debates,* 9 December 1915.
44. *Common Cause,* 19 May 1916.
45. *House of Commons Debates,* 22 May 1916.
46. Ibid, 16 August 1916.
47. *Common Cause,* 30 June 1916. My italics.
48. Ibid, 4, 11 August 1916.
49. *House of Commons Debates,* 14 August 1916.
50. *Common Cause,* 18 August 1916.
51. Fawcett, p. 138.
52. *House of Commons Debates,* 12 November 1916.
53. *The Times,* 30 January 1917.
54. Fawcett, p. 142.
55. *House of Commons Debates,* 28 March 1917.
56. Ibid, 19 June 1917 (col. 1751).
57. Fawcett, p. 149.
58. See generally, I. Clephane, *Towards Sex Freedom,* 1936.
59. National Council of Public Morals, *The Ethics of Birth Control,* 1925, p. 168.
60. National Council of Public Morals, *The Declining Birth Rate,* 1916, p. 21.
61. In R. Strachey (ed.), *Our Freedom and its Results,* 1936.
62. Clephane, p. 209.
63. R. Bruce Lockhart, *Your England,* 1955, p. 79.
64. *Morning Post,* 17 April 1915. *Daily Mail,* 17 April 1915. *Observer,* 18 April 1915, 25 April 1915. *Sunday Pictorial,* 18 April 1915.
65. *Observer,* 2 May 1915.
66. *Annual Report of Registrar-General for 1916;* P.P., 1917–18, V, Cd. 8869, p. xix. *Annual Report of Registrar-General for 1915;* P.P. 1917–18, V, Cd. 8484, p. vii.
67. *Observer,* 25 April 1915.
68. *Sunday Pictorial,* 18 April 1915.
69. See e.g. Sir A. Conan Doyle in *Observer,* 14 October 1917.
70. S. Pankhurst, *The Home Front,* 1932, pp. 182–3.
71. Cd. 8869, p. xix.
72. M. A. Hamilton, in *Our Freedom,* p. 251.
73. Clephane, p. 196.
74. C. S. Peel, *How We Lived Then,* p. 70.
75. *Observer,* 27 August 1916, 17 September 1916.
76. Clephane, p. 197.
77. *Final Report of the Royal Commission on Venereal Diseases;* P.P., 1916, Cd. 8189, pp. 62, 2, 43.
78. Ibid, p. 62.
79. *The Times,* 10 March 1917.

80. *Our Freedom*, p. 223.
81. Cd. 8484, p. vii.
82. G. Heard, *Morals Since 1900*, 1955, p. 113.
83. Scott and Cunnison, *Industries of the Clyde Valley during the Great War*, p. 171.
84. Shadwell, *Drink in 1914–22*, p. 108.
85. *Observer*, 13 December 1914.
86. *Daily Mail*, 25 May 1915, 31 May 1915, 2 June 1915.
87. Ibid, 30 August 1916.
88. T. Meech, *This Generation*, 1928, Vol. II, p. 77.
89. Bennett, *Journal*, p. 229 (28 April 1918).
90. V. Ogilvie, *Our Times*, 1950, p. 91.
91. *Our Freedom*, p. 273.
92. P.P., 1916, IX, Cd. 8276, p. 14.
93. E. D. Proud, *Welfare Work*, 1916, pp. ix–xiii.
94. Cd. 8276, p. 15.
95. P.P., 1914, XXIX, Cd. 7491, pp. 9–10.
96. Ibid, p. 8. Cd. 8276, p. 10.
97. See esp. M. Cosens, *Lloyd George's Munitions Girls*.
98. P.P., 1914–16, LV, Cd. 8151, p. 3.
99. Andrews and Hobbs, *Economic Effects of the War upon Women and Children*, p. 133.
100. Cd. 8276, p. 15.
101. Cosens, p. 78.
102. Andrews and Hobbs, pp. 138–9.
103. Cd. 8276, p. 10.
104. *Annual Report of Chief Medical Officer of Board of Education*; P.P., 1914–16, XVIII, Cd. 7730, p. v.
105. *Report of Board of Education for 1916–17*; P.P., 1918, IX, Cd. 9045, p. 5.
106. Board of Education, *Correspondence relating to School Attendance 1915*; P.P., 1914–16, L, Cd. 7803, p. 9. See also Cd. 7881 and Cd. 7932.
107. *House of Commons Debates*, 10 August 1917.
108. *Report of Board of Education for 1916–17*, Cd. 9045, p. 4.
109. Andrews and Hobbs, p. 159. See C. Leeson, *The Child and the War*, 1917.
110. National Council of Public Morals, *The Cinema*, 1917, pp. xxxiv–xxxvii, 204–5.
111. P.P., 1917–18, XI, Cd. 8512.
112. Ibid, p. 5.

CHAPTER FOUR

Gentlemen in England Now Abed:
1915–1916

[I] AN AFFLUENT SOCIETY?

SURVEYING SOCIETY as a whole in 1915 and 1916, Government inspectors and newspaper reporters were agreed that there was a widespread diffusion of affluence. Most obvious in the case of war profiteers, it touched all classes. 'Profiteering' was one of the emotional corrosives of the war period, eventually in compound with other acids of discontent to eat away at social ideals till many people could see only the bitter contrast between those who had fought and suffered and those who had stayed at home and waxed fat. Working-class leaders, labour politicians, and a sizeable section of the press kept up a constant denunciation of high profit margins and luxury spending. It is a topic worth lingering on for a moment.

In August 1917 the *Spectator* took it upon itself to deplore the popular denunciations, insisting that high prices were not due to profiteering.[1] But the *Spectator* protested too much: although there was little evidence of new monopolistic rings being set up, there was no doubt at all that industrialists and traders were using their existing economic power to exact the highest possible terms from the community. The not untypical case of the South Wales millers, Spillers and Bakers, was one of the first to attract attention. According to *The Times* report of 3 May 1915, the company, after paying dividends on preference and ordinary shares (preferred and common stock), disbursed extra dividends to the tune of £80,165, or 17½ per cent on the ordinary shares: there then remained from the year's earnings the sum of £248,419, which represented an added return of 54 per cent on the ordinary shares. The big profiteering debate in Parliament on 17 October 1916 brought out many other examples and instances.

The industries which were completely indispensable to the nation's survival in time of war were shipping and coal-mining, and they took care that the nation knew it. In his evidence before the Sankey Coal Commission at the end of the war, A. Lowes Dickinson, Financial Adviser to the Coal Controller, produced evidence to show that coal profits in 1916 were 'just treble those of the average of the five pre-war years'.[2] For the high ransom exacted by the shipping firms we need look no farther than the budget statement of 2 May 1917 made by Bonar Law, then Chancellor of the Exchequer and a shareholder in the shipping industry. A man of rigid principle, Bonar Law described his own sense of shock at the high returns that his own investments were yielding willy-nilly.[3] A later parliamentary statement put shipping profits at $33\frac{1}{3}$ per cent *after* payment of excess profits duty[4] (introduced for the first time in September 1915, and in itself a good indication of the high profit level).

For the wage-earning classes constant employment, longer hours, and war bonuses meant an upward movement in earnings, clearly noticeable from February and March 1915. Over the whole year there was an average rise of 3s 10d per week.[5] A year later the *Labour Gazette* was commenting:

No complete account can be given at this time of all the changes in rates of wages which have been made since the beginning of the war, as amongst unorganized work people many changes escape attention, but so far as reported it appears that up to the end of December 1916, nearly six million work people had received some advance. The amount varied, but on average the weekly increase to these work people was about six shillings per head, and in some of the industries directly concerned with the supply of war requirements ranged from ten shillings to twelve shillings per week.[6]

Relatively the gains were most marked among the submerged workers of pre-war days (Masterman's 'prisoners'), those in casual or sweated employment, and those who had been pretty well constantly out of employment. In 1915 and 1916 there was a very sharp decline in the incidence of pauperism, and in the autumn of the latter year it was confidently reported that there was 'less total distress in the country than in an ordinary year of peace'.[7] The Glasgow figures for underfed and ill-clad school-children are instructive: there were 209 such children in the last year of peace; the number rose to 264 in the first year of war, before rising employment had made itself felt; in 1915–16 it had dropped to 150, and it was down to 68 in 1916–17.[8]

Till the end of 1915 the popular press was full of stories of lavish spending both on the part of the working classes and the profiteers. 'There are no poor in Newcastle-upon-Tyne,' reported the *Daily Mail* in one of a series of articles on working-class affluence.[9] Reliable evidence as to working-class purchases of what Mr Wemmick called 'portable property' and what we would call status symbols is not lacking; sale-rooms in the first months of post-war depression were to be tragically saturated with fur coats and less portable, but more status-giving, cottage pianos.[10] At the other end of the social scale the *Draper's Record* noted increasing expenditure on women's clothing. Whether this was entirely due to the *nouveau riche* is less certain. One West End shop manager was reported as describing 'our luxury women' as

Rather a different clientele than before the war ... and hardly so discriminating, but certainly more free with money. Many of our regular West End clients are economizing, but evidently there is a new and prosperous section of the community taking their places. This new section is so well-off that no article is approved unless it is costly.[11]

From the beginning of 1916 newspaper references to the condition of the working classes concentrated on the high cost of living rather than affluence. Actually, apart from a brief plateau immediately after the first excitement and emergency had subsided, prices had been showing a constant upward movement, so that in June 1915 food prices were about 32 per cent up on those prevailing in July 1914. Butter was up by 2½d, bacon by 3d or 4d, cheese by 3d, pork sausages by 2½d and cooked meat by 4d to 6d (all per pound). If the standard working-class budget in 1914 is taken as 25s 8d per week, the equivalent figure was now 33s or over. By September 1916 the increase (weighted by the Board of Trade in order to reflect actual spending habits) was 65 per cent. Price increases in towns with more than 50,000 inhabitants were noticeably greater (68 per cent) than those in small towns and villages (62 per cent). The highest increase of all was in the price of sugar, 163 per cent up. Otherwise increases were highest in the case of imported meat, as high as 123 per cent in the case of breast of mutton in town shops. Alternative sources of protein also rose steeply in price; fish, only 70 per cent up in country areas, was 103 per cent up in towns; eggs, on average, were 82 per cent up.[12]

High earnings, the British *penchant* for sweetstuffs, and the failure of the Government to channel the short supplies of sugar away from the sweet manufacturers, combined to produce a situation in the early months of 1916 in which the ordinary Britisher was eating more sweetmeats than ever before.[13] However, it was clear that it was only through the working of longer and more regular hours by more of its members that the ordinary family managed to keep a seat on the unbroken bronco of price inflation. The 1915 Government report, whose phrase about 'less total distress than in an ordinary year of peace' was widely quoted, actually went on to point out:

Certain classes normally in regular employment, whose earnings have not risen in the same proportion as the cost of living – for example, the cotton operatives and certain classes of day-wage workers and labourers – are hard pressed by the rise in prices, and actually have to curtail their consumption, even though the pressure of high prices may have been mitigated, in some cases, by the employment of members of a family in munition works, and by the opening of better-paid occupations to women. Many people in receipt of small fixed incomes necessarily also feel the pressure; and it is obvious that while the total receipts of families past school age may have greatly increased, a family of the same class in which children are within school age may suffer exceptionally.[14]

In the summer of 1916 there were several important protests and demonstrations against the high cost of living, including one organized by the National Union of Railwaymen and held in Hyde Park on 27 August.[15]

One of the most resented facets of war-time domestic economy was the rise in house rents. Bad and inadequate housing was a serious cancer in 1914: the war brought a general cessation in house-building and a slackening in the activities of Local Government Board inspectors. A number of measures early in the war, adapting to military exigencies the ideas of the great 1909 Act and foreshadowing the definitely collectivist approach of the post-war years, did little in practice to remedy the overall deficiencies. An Act of 10 August 1914 authorized local authority assistance to building societies prepared to limit their own profits to five per cent, and gave the Commissioners of Works power to acquire and dispose of land and buildings, and to build dwellings for Government employees. On 16 March 1915, the Government took powers under D.O.R.A. to take possession of land for housing, and later on the Ministry of Munitions assisted directly in the building of working-class housing.[16]

Essentially the problem remained one of an expanding and, more important, a moving population being crammed into houses whose condition was steadily deteriorating, of munitions workers crowding into small towns like Carlisle, workers of all types bumping up the already appalling density of large towns like Glasgow, and office workers for the new bureaucracy pouring into the centre of London. Landlords naturally took advantage of heavy pressure on limited space to put their rents up. Resistance was so strong on Red Clydeside that the Government was forced in 1915 to appoint a special Departmental Committee on Rent Increases in Scotland. Once again John Wheatley was the chief spokesman on behalf of the Clyde working man, and the upshot was the passing of the Rent and Mortgage Interest (Rent Restriction) Act of 1915. Pressure from all classes of society upon space in the centres of the great towns, London especially, combined with heavier taxation and shortage of servants, meant that small houses and flats were at a premium, whereas large houses were often empty.[17] The First World War was the master interior builder which turned the rambling town houses of a more spacious age into the cramped flats and bed-sitters of the contemporary world.

Working-class advances in the years 1915 and 1916, taking the rising cost of living into consideration, owed as much to longer hours and increased employment as to war-time bonuses and higher wage rates. In truth the working classes did, in the long view, make very real gains in their material standards; but for the ordinary working man the long-term reality tended to become lost in the welter of immediate hard-felt grievances. What of the middle-class man who did not enjoy a war bonus and was neither one of the charmed élite for whom 'social activity had not abated in the least'[18] nor a profiteer? The statistics are tenuous and hard to interpret. By the end of the war the class portrait of Edwardian Britain had changed to comprise a rather smaller working class and a slightly larger middle class. This could imply that over the war years the old middle class had done badly in that it was being threatened by newcomers to its ranks. At the same time, after the war, sections of the middle classes, professional people in particular, were taking a bigger share of the national income than they had done before it; this could again in part be attributed to new recruitment. Lawyers did well from the confusion of D.O.R.A. regulations, and were kept happy disentangling the exact legal status of British firms which were offshoots of larger German companies. In so far as some members of the middle classes, being on fixed salaries, were not as readily able to secure rises as, for instance, the Welsh miners, they clearly suffered from rising prices. On the other hand, growing bureaucracy opened new opportunities of social and material advancement to the salaried classes, and small businessmen were often the ones to cash in most obviously on the war boom.

In October 1915 a middle-class reader in the £400 per annum bracket, stung by loose talk of extravagance and tight talk of economy, submitted his own budget[19] which showed no obvious evidence of extravagance and no apparent margin for economy:

Food, laundry, cleaning, etc.	£130
Rent	40
Servant	18
Education (2)	12
Rates	14
Coal	12
Light	7
Water	4
Clothes (4)	50
Season ticket	12
Holiday	None
Insurance	14
City expenses, lunch and tobacco	40
Income-tax	25
Others (doctor, repairs, etc.)	10

The first war budget had made little difference to the relative economic positions of the different social classes. The second war budget, still the responsibility of Lloyd George, did little that was new, save impose greatly increased duties on alcoholic drinks: the ample warning provided by the Chancellor's own bombastic pronouncements and the King's pledge had enabled the wealthy to lay down extensive cellars in good time.[20] The great buoyancy shown by existing taxes is indicative of the prosperity being enjoyed by the middle and upper classes. Whatever else Lloyd George was, he was not a great wartime Chancellor of the Exchequer, and it was necessary for his successor, Reginald McKenna, to bring in a supplementary budget in September. McKenna raised the income-tax by 40 per cent, and increased the supertax on incomes above £8,000 per annum. The first was of greatest importance socially in its effects on the middle classes; both measures, together with the new excess profits duty, accelerated the equalization of incomes. More significant, the great engine of income-tax was for the first time directed towards working men who were earning more than £2 10s per week. On the obvious level this added to working-class grievances; on a more subtle level it meant the beginning of a new process destructive of the rigid line between the Edwardian classes and masses. Other measures, such as the 50 per cent increase in the tea and tobacco duties, and the abolition of the halfpenny postage stamp and the sixpenny telegram, fell on the poorer rather than the wealthier elements in society.

McKenna's next budget continued the movement towards a progressive, equalizing tax structure: at the same time, among the handful of new or increased indirect duties the imposition for the first time of an amusements tax added a new element to the rising cost of living, already blatant in the case of the necessities of life. Thereafter there were no striking alterations in the tax system, for the burden of the war, in fact, was financed out of borrowing. This traditional method of war finance had in the past had the effect of fostering inequalities of wealth, since it was only the rich who could afford to lend, and it was these same rich who had in succeeding years become richer as they raked in their interest payments. For the middle years of the war the traditional practice was largely maintained: two long-term loans were floated with suitable *éclat* in November 1914 and June 1915, and the last of the same type was launched in January 1917. Immediate needs were met by various expensive short-term devices which were very much to the liking and profit of the financial and banking world. But the 1915 loan did represent a nod in the direction of democracy, for it made it possible for the humble to subscribe through five-shilling, ten-shilling, and one-pound vouchers, obtainable at post offices.[21] The Montagu Committee, appointed in November 1915, further examined this aspect, and as a result of its deliberations there appeared early in 1916 the eminently democratic War Savings Certificate, holdings of which were limited to a total of five hundred; there had been some idea of enforcing a means test on would-be purchasers, but the War Savings Committee decided that to do so would be to introduce undesirable class distinctions.[22] There was no one-way trend in the economic developments of 1915 and 1916 as they affected the different social classes, but on the whole sentiment and fact were combining to weaken the sturdy barriers of Edwardian days.

[II] RIPPLES FROM THE WAR

A journalist's description of the first Easter of the war shows how far away 'business as usual' now was:

Twelve months ago lamps blazed in the London streets at night. Theatres were full. The West End was glittering and full until midnight ... And now! Although Brighton is reported to be nearly full for Easter, although some of the South coast hotels are booked up, although passenger boats are running to the Continent and Ireland, and although one hears of excursions into Wales by motor char-à-bancs, the general atmosphere of the seaside resorts is one of reconciliation to their lot. We see khaki everywhere. Military searchlights send staggering gleams across the sky, taking the place of the flickering advertisements which did so much to make London look gay by night.

Hundreds of thousands of men – colliers, shipwrights, munition makers, and the like – will be at work who in normal times would be at play. There will be few visitors to Scotland and the north, for on these long journeys the ordinary fares are more than double the excursion fares. For the normal holiday traffic to the Continent, all brightness and new frocks and motor-cars and golf-clubs, is substituted an exodus of a different kind. True the Folkestone boats are full; but there is very little joviality and holiday tackle. People go quietly, with grave faces, to visit wounded friends in hospital.[23]

Almost at once there followed an incident which severely shook public sentiment still inclined to underplay the German submarine menace. Early in April, the Cunard liner *Lusitania* was sunk off the West Coast of Ireland by a German torpedo. Two thousand passengers were drowned, many of them children, who were later pathetically washed up on the beaches of Shannon where, looking like a McTaggart seascape gone horrifically out of control, they were photographed for the gratification of righteous British war-lust. The immediate reaction was an outburst of rioting and pillaging on the night of 12 April; in the East End of London many a harmless shopkeeper who had the misfortune to have a German name had his property wrecked. This was the most serious test yet for the Special Constables: insufficiently distinguishable by their armlets, many were inadvertently coshed by the Regulars, with the consequence that the Specials were henceforth given a proper uniform of their own.[24]

The *Lusitania* incident shows well the relationship between popular hysteria and official propaganda. The riots, following so quickly upon the news of the disaster, have every appearance of a spontaneous outburst of hatred which grew on a diet of harrowing sensationalism and righteous indignation. However, Lord Newton, head of Foreign Office propaganda, improved the shining hour by having large quantities of the medal said to have been issued by the German Government to commemorate the occasion reproduced for circulation in Britain and abroad; actually the medal (one of a series struck by a Munich craftsman) was intended as a satire on the Anglo-American cupidity which had allowed the *Lusitania* to sail despite German warnings that she would be sunk. Within weeks quantities of leaflets illustrating the medal and featuring the phrase, 'another triumph for our glorious Navy', torn from context so as to appear to apply to the *Lusitania* incident, were distributed.[25]

So far the secret propaganda department at Wellington House, concentrating its energies on enemy and neutral countries, had not done much to influence domestic opinion. Its most brilliant stroke was the choice of Lord Bryce, who had for many years been a well-loved and much-respected ambassador in Washington, to chair a committee appointed in December 1914 to investigate alleged German outrages. With access to the flimsiest of uncorroborated evidence the Committee none the less reported unhesitatingly that the Germans were guilty of deliberate and systematic massacres of civilians, violation of women, the use of civilians as a shield for advancing armed forces, and calculated looting, incendiarism and destruction of property as part of a policy of general terrorization. 'Murder, lust and pillage,' the Committee declared, 'prevailed over many parts of Belgium on a scale unparalleled in any war between civilized nations during the last three centuries.'[26] As hoped, the Report had a powerful effect on American opinion.[27] Masterman also showed a touch of genius in his awareness that the cinema could be exploited for propaganda purposes. At first he encountered great opposition from the War Office and the Admiralty, where it was believed that there was something vulgar and disreputable about this new-fangled contraption, but eventually the first British propaganda film, *Britain Prepared*, was completed and given its première at the Empire Theatre on 27 December 1915;[28] in retrospect this occasion can be seen as a pointer towards the metamorphosis of the great music hall of the naughty nineties into the luxury cinema of today. Again the target was American and other neutral opinion rather than the British cinema-goer. The effect was spoiled in certain parts of the United States where exhibitors of German sympathies exhibited the film as *How Britain Prepared*.[29]

While distinguished ambassadors and Oxford dons as well as barons of the press were giving a lead to anti-German sentiment, the voice of organized religion was not silent. In *On Forgiving our Enemies,* one of a series of 'Wartime Tracts for the Workers' published by the Society for the Propagation of Christian Knowledge, the Reverend Prebendary Burn touched the central moral dilemma:

The challenge is flung at us. Can I forgive the unforgivable? To the question thus expressed a Christian can answer 'No' with a clear conscience. Divine Love is revealed as wrath against all unrighteousness. Our Lord Jesus Christ showed at times the most terrible wrath which can be imagined against foul injury to the weak and helpless, against that lie in the soul which betrays a man into calling evil good and good evil. What the Bible calls the wrath of the Lamb is the righteous anger of the meek and gentle flaming into fury for the sake of others.[30]

Even science added its mite. Addressing the British Association meeting at Manchester in September 1915, Professor Arthur Schuster, moved by 'the shadow of a great catastrophe' to talk on 'the Common Aims of Science and Humanity', concluded with the following words:

Happy were the times when it could be said with truth that the strife of politics counted as nothing before the silent display of the heavens [Professor Schuster was an astronomer]. Mightier issues are at stake today; in the struggle which convulses the world, all intellectual pursuits are vitally affected, and Science gladly gives the power she wields to the service of the State. Sorrowfully she covers her face because that power, acquired through the peaceful efforts of the sons of all nations, was never meant for death and destruction; gladly she helps, because a war wantonly provoked threatens civilization, and only through victory shall we achieve a peace in which once more Science can hold up her head, proud of her strength to preserve the intellectual freedom which is worth more than material prosperity, to defeat the spirit of evil that destroys the sense of brotherhood among nations, and to spread the love of truth.[31]

Popular fury flamed again at the execution of Nurse Edith Cavell and later at that of Captain Fryatt, a British merchant seaman who had turned defence into attack by ramming a German submarine. In July 1916, the Secretary for War, Lord Kitchener, set off on a mission to Russia, but got no farther than Scapa Flow, where his ship was sunk. To Kitchener's colleagues, long aware of his gross deficiencies as a war minister, this was a blessed release, but for the country as a whole it was the tragic loss of a beloved hero. To everyone capable of adding two and two (but little beyond that) it was obvious that Kitchener was the victim of a dastardly spy-plot, and there was a spasm of spy-scares and hunt-the-alien campaigns more intense than at any time since the first months of the war. The death of Lord Kitchener was an occasion for national grief, but by the end of 1916 there were few families untouched by personal grief. Each day at Charing Cross station a double line, mostly of women, waited patiently for disembarking troop trains; each day the newspapers carried a list of about 4,000 casualties. Yet the universal numbness and the patriotic fervour kept private grief from becoming national outcry. One diarist echoes the sentiments expressed eleven months before by R. D. Blumenfeld:

The very multitude of names of killed, wounded or missing does something to blunt the sharpness of sympathy. Death on the battlefield has become so much a matter of course as to deprive it of some of its terrors.[32]

On the evidence of letters to the press and of the continued breaking up not just of pacifist but of internationalist meetings, enthusiasm for the war, for all the slaughter it entailed, had not abated by the end of 1916. Most famous of all demonstrations of this is the 'Letter of "a little mother" ' quoted by Robert Graves in *Goodbye to All That*:

To the man who pathetically calls himself a 'common soldier', may I say that we women, who demand to be heard, will tolerate no such cry as 'Peace! Peace!' where there is no peace. The corn that will wave over land watered by the blood of our brave lads shall testify to the future that their blood was not spilt in vain. We need no marble monuments to remind us. We only need that force of character behind all motives to see this monstrous world tragedy brought to a victorious ending. The blood of the dead and the dying, the blood of the 'common soldier' from his 'slight wounds' will not cry to us in vain. They have all done their share, and we, as women, will do ours without murmuring and without complaint. Send the Pacifists to us and we shall very soon show them, and show the world, that in our homes at least there shall be no 'sitting at home warm and cosy in the winter, cool and comfy in the summer'. There is only one temperature for the women of the British race, and that is white heat. With those who disgrace their sacred trust of motherhood we have nothing in common. Our ears are not deaf to the cry that is ever ascending from the battlefield from men of flesh and blood whose indomitable courage is borne to us, so to speak, on every blast of the wind. We women pass on the human ammunition of 'only sons' to fill up the gaps, so that when the 'common soldier' looks back before going 'over the top' he may see the women of the British race on his heels, reliable, dependent, uncomplaining.[33]

There was one potent intoxicant which helped even intelligent men to accept 'the indescribable suffering and sorrow which have been imposed upon millions of our fellow creatures'[34] long after the sentiments of honour and duty were becoming tarnished. This was the feeling that here indeed was *the* Great War, a time of historical intensity such as had never been lived through before, a time when what was old and bad must inevitably be consumed, and what was good and new triumph. In part this was merely a development of the wishful thinking of the idealist reformers who had hailed the outbreak of war so enthusiastically; in part it was a mistaking of the first swallows, women conductresses, say, for the whole summer; in part it was a perceptive appreciation of the deeper implications of the social changes that were in truth taking place. Writing in August 1916, Sir Michael Sadler saw the war as a time of 'gestation of a new social ideal'.[35] Blumenfeld had already noted, 'The war has simply turned the whole world topsy-turvy';[36] in October 1917 he was writing, 'That horrible ogre, Tradition, lies in the dust.'[37] McDonagh was most struck by the effect of the war on poverty; by December 1917 he had concluded that 'there is now no such word as "poor" in our social vocabulary'.[38] For Professor G. C. Henderson, whose description of the war is quoted at the beginning of this paragraph, the 'silver lining' was that 'the upheaval of existing habits and traditions' caused by the war had aroused the British nation from 'its state of apathy towards science' to a realization that its future prosperity was 'ultimately dependent on the progress of science'.[39] Official reports and commissions nearly all have somewhere a touch of optimism: change *is* taking place. The historian W. H. Dawson, writing in late 1916, expressed the whole mood very well:

We are living at a time when days and weeks have the fulness and significance of years and decades. Who does not feel that since August 1914 England has in many ways broken with her past and entered an entirely new epoch in her history, marked by transformations of every kind, so that when the day of peace arrives, be it soon or late, we shall be confronted at home by an altogether altered situation?[40]

What people at home heard of the fighting man's war was only a confused murmur. They knew the statistics of death – nearly 20,000 killed on 1 July, the first day of the Battle of the Somme[41] – but not the foul horror of it; they saw the glory, but not the sordid filth of trench life. Fighting men, appalled at the nature of the war in which they found themselves, were unable to convey the unbelievable substance (any success in this line that they did achieve was doubtless frustrated by the censorship). 'There are some things better left undescribed . . . Perhaps in the afterwards when time has deadened matters, you will hear of them,' wrote one young soldier.⁴² 'Everyone out here,' wrote another, 'considers it only fair to one's womenkind to hush up the worst side of the war.'⁴³ Wellington House sponsored films of the Somme fighting, which played to packed houses, but the horror was carefully left out; occasional flashes of truth and terror, as the *Manchester Guardian* film critic remarked, were completely subordinated to the spectacular.⁴⁴

Government attitudes towards British soldiers imprisoned in Germany, of whom there were 37,000 by the end of March 1917, caused much heart-searching and bitterness. The first British schemes, resulting in the establishment of the Prisoners of War Help Committee, were entirely voluntary, and the War Office, though invited to do so in June 1915, refused to take over responsibility for this body. From September of that year the Committee did have the co-operation of the Home Office but it was only in September 1916 that the War Office established an official Central Prisoners of War Committee; by this time better treatment had been secured for some prisoners by the agreement of May 1916 that British and German wounded and invalided prisoners should be transferred to Switzerland. Finally the War Office Committee did decide to undertake the provision of all British and Indian prisoners of war with a supply of food and clothing, causing much resentment among voluntary workers and private donors, who wanted to earmark their gifts for specific recipients.⁴⁵

By the summer of 1915 people at home were beginning to feel that in the German air threat they had a considerable problem of their own. Small and rather ineffective night-attacks took place throughout the spring; on 1 June the press presented a most uninformative account of a Zeppelin raid on 'outlying London', no details being given for reasons of 'public safety'; in fact ninety bombs, mostly incendiary, had been dropped, causing much damage and twenty-four fatalities.⁴⁶ Another raid on 7 June rubbed in the seriousness of the situation, so much so that on the 18th the police, for the first time, published a list of suggestions as to the appropriate behaviour during an air-attack. Raids continued on all parts of the country (the south-east took most punishment) at a rate of roughly two a month, with occasional lulls and periods of intensive raiding. Under regulation 12 of the Defence of the Realm Regulations it was open to the local military authorities to impose some form of black-out. Early in April 1915, the Chief Constable of Middlesbrough took the initiative in bringing together the Garrison Commander, Tees and Hartlepools Garrison, and the local ironmasters to discuss the best means of obscuring ordinary lighting, and, more particularly, the glare from the blast furnaces, in the event of an air-raid. There was as yet no question of a perpetual black-out. The scheme eventually perfected allowed for the dowsing of all light and glare within twelve minutes of receiving a code warning of the approach of the enemy.[47]

During the sleeping hours between 12 October and 13 October 1915 there came the most severe raid of the middle period of the war, when Zeppelins over Norfolk, Suffolk, and the Home Counties and London, inflicted a casualty list of 199. A crescendo of protests over the absence of an advance-warning system followed. It was at the same time pointed out that the introduction of lighting regulations had led to an increase in street accidents. Early in 1916 clocks, believed to be a gratuitous navigational gift to the night-fliers, ceased to chime, and the comprehensive London lighting orders were extended to the Midlands and the West. In Middlesbrough the Chief Constable encountered strong resistance from the public and from the Watch Committee when he attempted to introduce a more general black-out. Yet resistance to the lighting regulations existed side by side with criticism of their ineffectiveness, which the *Manchester Guardian* attributed to the lack of a common policy among the various local authorities charged with enforcing them;[48] the Government even lost a by-election to an independent candidate campaigning for a more vigorous air policy against the raiders. By late 1916 it was coming to be believed again that inconvenience rather than danger was to be expected from air-raids. Travellers into Waterloo after night-fall might find that their train suddenly stopped, the lights went out, and a wait of several hours in cold and darkness ensued, enlivened only by distant flashings and rumblings.[49]

Even without the attentions of airships and aeroplanes, night-time was the distinctive time in war: total darkness (after mid-1916) where once there had been a constellation of light; sounds of steam-hammers and factory machinery where once there had been silence; rumbling convoys of armoured vehicles where once there had been only the occasional errant drunk; long ominous trains packed with munitions or carrying the shattered bodies of soldiers direct to the sidings at military hospitals. Day and night were stood upon their heads: where once the forenoon streets had been filled with breathless bustle, now they were deserted, for all had work to do, be it in a munitions factory or at the local forces' canteen. Unmitigated darkness at sunset brought an awareness of the good daylight going to waste in the hours before many families rose from their beds. In the autumn of 1915 a few small businesses tried to wring the last ounces of light out of the shortening days by starting work earlier in the morning. The idea of organizing this sensible husbanding of the natural bounty of light on a national scale through the simple device of putting all clocks forward by an hour had been advanced in 1908 by a Mr William Willett, F.R.A.S. The first Bill embodying his idea had been introduced into Parliament in February of that year, and a subsequent Select Committee reported favourably; but despite a further series of similar Bills, all of which got considerable support, nothing was done at Government level.[50] As the days lengthened into the summer of 1916 the matter came up again in Parliament, and a motion in favour of the institution of Summer Time, introduced by Sir Henry Norman, was passed on 8 May by 170 votes to two. On 21 May the Summer Time Act became law, so that from 21 May till 30 September 1916 all British clocks ran one hour in advance of Greenwich mean time, giving longer and lighter evenings. A committee appointed to investigate the effects spoke enthusiastically of increased efficiency and more healthful recreation, and, although it admitted the parental problem caused by children staying up later at night, it wholeheartedly recommended Summer Time as a 'permanent insititution'.[51] It was in fact introduced again in 1917, and has been every year since, save for the 'Double Summer Time' of the Second World War.

One of the reasons for the ignorance of people at home of the true nature of life in the trenches was the censorship; it also served to keep people unaware of the extent of German air-attacks. The official attitude was explained in the following censorship order issued by the Press Bureau:

It is undesirable that too much space should be given to describing Zeppelin raids.

The actual military damage that has been done is slight, but at the same time so long as the Germans think that the raids have great effect they will be continued, and long accounts tend to produce an impression both in England and Germany that they are of greater importance than they are in reality.[52]

The temporary suppression of journals like *Forward*, the *Labour Leader,* organ of the I.L.P., and *Tribunal,* the organ of the No Conscription Fellowship, need cause no surprise, but the Conservative *Globe,* too, fell under the censor's interdiction in November 1915, and the Liberal *Nation* was not allowed to travel beyond the confines of the British Isles. Even *The Times*, revealing under the ownership of Lord Northcliffe some of the old nineteenth-century thunder, incurred a D.O.R.A. prosecution.

D.O.R.A. could impinge upon people in all walks of life: negligent citizens could find themselves facing stiff fines for showing lights at night; from August 1916 the Londoner was deprived of the normal liberty of whistling for a cab; the Government could requisition private land and property for military purposes. That such requisitioning was, to begin with, done under the prerogative power of the Crown is sometimes cited as illustration of the tremendous control over the liberties and property of the subject exercised by the State, in this case by reference to its figurehead, the monarch; actually the resort to forms more appropriate to the Tudor age, and the absence of any machinery of control adapted to the requirements of the twentieth-century constitution, show rather how exceptional this control was, and how little the State was expected in normal times to interfere with the individual. In the spring of 1915 the Government appointed a permanent commission to adjudicate upon claims for compensation made by individuals who felt they had suffered loss from Government action under D.O.R.A. In its decisions the Commission showed a consistent lack of generosity, though it must be said that many of the cases brought before it showed great triviality and lack of public spirit on the part of the claimants.[53]

In financial transactions of a lesser sort the distant presence of the war made itself felt: gold sovereigns continued to circulate side by side with paper money till the autumn of 1915; thereafter they rapidly disappeared.[54] The implacable casualty lists apart, these intimations that the nation was at war were far from calamitous. But preparations were on hand in case of calamity. A hand-book for civilians described among other things the correct behaviour should the country be occupied by the Germans. In various areas arrangements were elaborated to be put into practice in the event of the Germans attempting to land an invading force: they involved the dismantling of all machinery and rolling stock, the collection of all tools likely to be of use to the enemy, the immobilizing of motor vehicles and carts, the slaughter of animals, and the evacuation of the population and preparation of food supplies.[55] No invasion came, but, as 1916 passed away, the community began to savour more sharply the realities of modern total war.

[III] LIFE AND LEISURE

More people at work, and each person working longer hours, meant less total time available for leisure pursuits. The balance was restored by the greater spending money accumulated by many of those in domestic employment, and by the presence of soldiers on leave with little to do but sample the pleasures of civilian life. The type of entertainment for which there was the highest demand was of the lowest quality: everyone desired to escape from present reality.

The Edwardian era had been a great age of the theatre. But since the time when Queen Victoria set her personal seal of respectability on the drama, theatres had been largely the preserve of the middle classes, a fact which Charles Booth confirmed in his researches at the end of the century. Certainly suburban and provincial music-halls had derived much of their support from the lower classes, but for the poor anything more than the very occasional visit was out of the question. It was the advent of the cinema, of which there were 3,000 in 1914, which did most to bring dramatic or musical entertainment of a sort within the reach of the poorer members of the community. As the chairman of the London branch of the Cinematograph Exhibitors Association pointed out:

The cheapness of this form of amusement has created what is really a new type of audience. Over half of the visitors to the picture theatres occupy seats to the value of threepence or less. In the main, the vast majority of picture house patrons were not in the habit of attending any other places of amusement. The picture house is emphatically the poor man's theatre.[56]

The picture palace, also, was the theatre of the young, 'being attended by a larger number of children than any other form of public amusement'. If the cinema did nothing else, it at least provided a strong counter-attraction to street hooliganism and to the public house. In the years of war-time liquor legislation it was almost an enforced alternative and so played its part in the enduring modification of the alcoholic basis of working-class leisure.

As early as 1911 objections raised against the moral tone of certain imported films had opened up the question of a film censorship. In October 1912, with the approval of the then Home Secretary, Reginald McKenna, a Board of Censors was established, with a Mr Redford as president. He, in collaboration with four censors, began work on 1 January 1913, dishing out 'U' certificates to films suitable for viewing by all types of audience including children, and 'A' certificates to those suitable for adult audiences. It was at first intended that the Board of Censors should deal direct with the cinema-owners, but it soon became clear that the latter felt no strong inclination to adhere to the Board's rulings; accordingly the local authorities were brought in as middlemen. Redford was regarded, even by his own colleagues, as being rather too lenient, about 97 per cent of all films submitted being allotted certificates. When T. P. O'Connor succeeded him, there was a perceptible tightening up.[57]

Puritans and busybodies were very sensitive to the moral danger of a form of entertainment, freely attended by members of both sexes, which took place in the dark. Pre-war cinemas had employed specially trained supervisors to watch for offences against public pudency, but they were withdrawn during the wartime labour shortage. The National Council of Public Morals was very concerned that there should continue to be 'adequate supervision' and, if possible, 'sufficient light'. In dismissing the many complaints of the prurient, a Mr Goodwin, representing the London Cinema Exhibitors, coined a fine phrase. 'When investigation is made,' he said, 'it is usually found that the alleged misconduct is nothing more than the privileged manifestation of affection between the sexes.'[58] More to the point were complaints, despite the

best attentions of the censor, about suggestive films which portrayed desperate struggles between members of the opposite sexes
and scenes of rape which were only faded at the very last instant.
Most of the press agreed with the National Council of Public
Morals that a stricter censorship was required, and the *Daily Mail*
expressed its horror of 'objectionable, unwholesome films'.[59] Good
wines need no bush, but bad films have always needed their bare
bosoms:

The posters advertising the films are often much more objectionable
than the films themselves, when they emphasize the sensational or sensual
aspects.[60]

That films could join the ranks of creative art, and could produce entertainment of high quality, was recognized by intelligent
critics;[61] Charlie Chaplin and the American film-maker D. W.
Griffith were showing in their various ways what could be done
with the medium. But on the whole the emphasis during the period
of the First World War was on escapism, whether sensual or
spectacular. In referring to this the National Council of Public
Morals remarked:

It has been insisted again and again by representatives of the trade that
exhibitors can only provide profitably what the public will take. They
state, for instance, that the public does not to any extent want the
educational film. This contention cannot be allowed absolutely; the
danger of the position of the purveyor of public amusements is that it
inclines him to rate both the intelligence and the conscience of his
patrons lower than they actually are, or at least can possibly be made.[62]

Nine-tenths of the films shown in British picture houses were
American. This situation was partly caused by Britain's technological backwardness, but it was exacerbated in the days when
films were still made out of doors by her execrable climate. The
film is a mass medium, designed to sell to a mass audience and
financed out of a budget to match. America with her large population had the mass audience ready made; British film-makers were
less agreeably placed financially. While Britain was only a fraction
of the American film-maker's market, the British producer found
the greatest difficulty in selling his films in America. The final
twist to the American stranglehold was provided by the fact that

in time of war national energies and scarce resources had to be directed away from the non-essentials such as films. The growing demand, which had been given a certain respectability by the exploitation of the cinema for national purposes, could only be met by more and more American imports.[63]

The empty leisure pursuits of the 1920s are often seen as part of a reaction against the war. Yet just as the basic pattern of a Hollywood-dominated cinema was consolidated in the war, so, too, many of the other features associated with the high life of the twenties were born in the fevered atmosphere of 1915 and 1916. There was, said Mrs C. S. Peel, reporting on the upper-class life with which she was familiar, a great craze for dancing[64] – with chaperons absent on other business. The syncopated rhythms of ragtime and jazz had filtered into Britain in pre-war years; now sophisticated and complicated dances, such as the fox-trot, were fabricated upon them. It was due to the difficulties of the new dances, a dancing master declared, that couples spent entire evenings together rather than hazard their toes to an untutored outsider;[65] the older convention that one should never dance twice successively with the same partner was broken, though a more potent reason was the brevity of civilian reunions when dances were held on the brink of a departure for the front.

Dancing was still essentially the recreation of the wealthier set; as was the much-discussed new growth from the fertilizations of war, the night-club. Wartime hedonism, wartime darkness and dullness and wartime liquor restrictions created the appetite; young officers on leave provided the material upon which it could feed and multiply. By all accounts they were unconscionably dull places, these wartime night-clubs. Their main function was the provision of alcohol, sold as 'ginger ale' or 'tea' and astronomically priced; the one other main activity practised within the precincts was gambling, and the press was full of harrowing stories of young officers ruined through being tempted into uttering cheques they could not honour. One way or another the First World War put that quaint and dingy area of London known as Soho on the map; mainly in fact as a conveniently central shopping area with the added attraction of exotic foods unobtainable in the bigger West End shops.[66]

Theatres, after a few bare first days, prospered throughout the war. Visiting Edinburgh in the summer of 1918, Clifford Allen, the pacifist leader, noted in his diary the difficulties of getting a seat at any of the city's several theatres.[67] Further comments of his suggest that the audience was drawn from a wide cross-section of the community. Undoubtedly the intellectual content of almost all the theatrical productions of the period was minimal: there was a plethora of musical revues, garnished with the scantily-dressed dancers to whom angry old men took such exception, but grounded on a witless patriotism which could incorporate into songs phrases like 'Your king and country need you'. An enterprising management did cash in on the interest aroused by the Royal Commission on Venereal Diseases to revive the French play *Damaged Goods*, which in feeble and cumbersome manner dealt with this problem. Ibsen enjoyed a revival, and the Old Vic, a theatre still almost as genuinely proletarian as its geographical setting, had crowded houses at its Shakespearian productions.[68]

Most people, it might be said, wanted frivolity and *ersatz* excitement, but there were stirrings of seriousness. Ernest Newman, the distinguished music critic, expressed his amazement at the popularity of serious music:

Taking the country as a whole, audiences have been larger than they were in pre-war days; and it is all the more amazing when we remember that every town has been denuded of many hundreds of the men who used to be the most regular attendants at concerts.[69]

In part, Newman thought, 'the demand not merely for plenty of music but for plenty of good music' could be attributed to what he called 'the keener psychosis of the nation'. But he was prepared to give most credit to the personal efforts of Sir Thomas Beecham, the daring young conductor, whose supply of good music created a new demand: 'had there been no war, Sir Thomas Beecham's activities would have had practically the same results.' Ernest Newman's opinions are ones which the historian must treat with the utmost respect, as he must treat Sir Thomas Beecham's labours with the admiration he would, in another sphere, accord to Lloyd George. Without Beecham, as without Wood, Elgar, Bax, Vaughan Williams and Elgar, there would have been no British musical renaissance; none the less, with the experience of the 'keener psychosis' of the Second World War to refer to, the conclusion that a deeper interest in good music was a side-product of the emotional upset of the war is inescapable. Beecham offered the following explanation of the success of his English Opera, which performed extensively in the provinces as well as in London:

The combination of a high mood of idealism in the public and of economic stringency in the musical profession was effective in enabling me to create and develop the finest English singing Company yet heard amongst us. In wartime the temper of a section of the people for a while becomes graver, simpler, and more concentrated. The opportunities for recreation and amusement are more restricted, transport is limited, and the thoughtful intelligence craves and seeks these antidotes to a troubled conscience of which great music is perhaps the most potent.[70]

Through the Hallé Orchestra Beecham was able to introduce concert works by French, Russian, Italian and, above all, English composers to audiences prepared on patriotic grounds to lend an ear where once they would have turned and fled. There were strong pressures in favour of the banning of all German music, but these, fortunately, were successfully resisted.[71]

Visiting art galleries was not the ordinary Briton's distinctive leisure pursuit. But the statistics of admissions at the principal London museums and galleries, though clearly useless as absolutes, do seem to suggest a trend for the early twentieth century: a growth in the appeal of the two major art galleries, the National and the Tate, and a decline in the appeal of the two major museums, the British Museum and the Victoria and Albert;[72] a growth, to push generalization to its most dangerous limits, in aesthetic interest, if not appreciation, at the expense of mere antiquarian curiosity. The excitements of war brought a slight drop in attendances in 1914 as against 1913. The Director of the National Gallery, however, found 'healthy' and 'gratifying' signs in

the growing interest on the part of the British public in the National Collections, as demonstrated by attendance at the galleries, the interest shown by the Press and Parliament in the acquisition or presentation of important pictures, the increasing sensitiveness at the loss of national treasures, and the formation of a powerful and representative society to resist the prevailing exodus.[73]

Attendances further declined during 1915. In 1916 the Government took the incredibly obscurantist decision to close for reasons of economy the London art galleries and museums. There were such strong protests from the *Observer*, the *Nation*, the *New Statesman*, and the *Manchester Guardian*[74] that the decision was at once partially rescinded. Later in the war, so great was the crush of visitors to the National Gallery that on certain days the turnstiles had to be put out of commission.[75] If visiting art galleries is a minority pursuit, patronage and purchase of works of art are very much more so. Something of that war psychosis which called for satisfactions of the mind and spirit, apparent in the world of music, seems to have shown itself in the British art market. Certainly there was a boom in works of art, as in many other commodities,[76] though doubtless this can in part be written down as a reflection of the increased affluence of the wealthy, of the bid of the profiteer for social acceptability, or of general price inflation.

When we turn to sport, and, in particular, the great spectator sports which originated in Victorian Britain, we come to the very marrow of working-class and lower-middle-class leisure activity. After a winter of failure Frederick Charrington secured total success for his campaign for the abandonment of professional football in the spring of 1915. Everything else went by the board: 'no cricket, no boat race, no racing', Blumenfeld lamented in August of the same year.[77]

With the lights of simple pleasure going out all around him, the ordinary man had as consolations home and reading. The war coincided with some important developments in the newspaper press. The Canadian businessman, Sir Max Aitken (shortly to become Lord Beaverbrook), had taken over the *Daily Express* and launched it on a colourful and successful career. Rudimentary forms of the tabloid already existed in the *Daily Mirror* and the *Daily Graphic*; on 14 March 1915, the *Sunday Pictorial* appeared for the first time, aimed rather at the lower middle class than the working class, to judge from the pseudo-intelligent nature of its features. In fact it is clear that the working classes were not yet a powerful enough advertisers' market for it to be worth while designing newspapers specifically for them. At a time when much of the colour was diluted out of the news by the censorship, pictorial features were at a premium, and the war gave a boost to those papers which orientated themselves in this direction. The war also brought new freedoms in the use of banner headlines and cross headings: with glorious advances (or retreats) taking place every day it became essential to have some means of distinguishing the occasional really important headline from the routine ones. The majority of papers, including the *Daily Mail*, continued, however, to print their news inside, leaving the front page for advertisements.

The two most popular novelists of the war period, Nat Gould and Victoria Cross, were without pretensions to literary quality. Even so, the lower classes probably sought such creative writing as they desired from the *feuilletons*, the serial sob-stories of romantic love printed in the popular newspapers. Gramophone sales were booming, and records were extensively advertised in the press. Popular patriotic songs, or songs like the nostalgic 'Tipperary', which was written just before the war, seized upon by the first British troops, and praised for its aesthetic qualities by the distinguished composer Ethel Smythe,[78] accounted for the bulk of the records pressed during the war.

For members of the upper classes, especially those with religious affiliations, the opportunities for canteening as a genteel leisure activity increased as the war progressed. There was a healthy rivalry between the nonconformist churches and that of the establishment. In Middlesbrough the former got off their mark first, establishing Free Church Canteens for Soldiers and Sailors in 1916: the Church of England Canteen for Sailors and Soldiers appeared early in 1917.[79] The quaint period quality of canteening can be gathered from a contemporary account of the work of the Free Church organization:

The Refreshment Room in the Park was put at the disposal of a special Committee by the Lessee (Mr Dent), and, with the hearty co-operation of the Colonel, the Secretary organized a group of lady workers under the general management of Mrs Gaines, and every parade morning during a long and bitter winter supplied the men with a mug of hot coffee and a cake or biscuit. The Officers of the Battalion cordially assisted by so arranging the drilling of the companies that in turn the men fell in for refreshments.

The cost, which was heavy, was borne by voluntary subscriptions. Frequently over a thousand men daily partook of the Town's hospitality in this way.

Both Officers and men expressed the deepest gratitude and shared equally in the fare provided. The R.S.M. said, 'I believe you have saved lots of these lads' lives.'

Another branch of work largely organized by the Secretary was the securing of homes to which men were invited on Sunday afternoons and evenings. This spread through most of the Churches and hundreds of men in this way found homes and friends which helped to make their stay in the Town pleasanter and safer than it could otherwise have been. The Troops at Maron Hall were included in this hospitality in the homes. Each Christmas and New Year the men were entertained to parties and suppers free of charge and many scores of concerts were given.[80]

Soldiers were not the only lonely people in Britain during the war. Organizations were formed, too, to bring together the wives, mothers and sisters of soldiers. The ladies of the Tipperary Rooms in Middlesbrough furnished their own description of their activities:

The rooms provide for our comfort in every way. There is a book-lending library and savings bank. There is also a nursery for our children to play in. For the small sum of $1\frac{1}{2}$d we can get the eatables with the cup that cheers but does not inebriate. On Wednesday evenings we are entertained with a splendid musical programme. We do not feel that we are wasting our time, as we have already knitted and sent socks to our soldiers and sailors, also made sandbags, and we are now knitting mufflers. The materials are supplied by the ladies who so kindly try to make our lives brighter while our men are doing their duty.[81]

The war brought a re-knitting of community life, even in the intractable territories of rural Scotland, where prior to the war 'the greatest defect ... considered from the standpoint of the working population, has been the almost complete absence of community and social life'. The war years, the same writer continues, 'brought to rural Scotland a welcome increase in associated effort ... building up the much needed ... social interest' and giving 'confidence and a sense of value to the community'.[82]

NOTES TO CHAPTER FOUR

1. *Spectator*, 4 August 1917.
2. *Report of Coal Industry Commission*, Vol. I; P.P., 1919, XII, Cmd. 359, p. 4.
3. *House of Commons Debates*, 2 May 1917.

4. ibid, 24 May 1917.

5. *Labour Gazette,* 1915, pp. 67, 105, 142, 354–5.

6. ibid, 1916, pp. 4–5.

7. Board of Trade, *Report of Departmental Committee on Prices;* P.P. 1916, XIV, Cd. 8358, p. 5.

8. Scott and Cunnison, *Industries of the Clyde Valley during the Great War,* p. 172.

9. *Daily Mail,* 27 December 1915.

10. Scott and Cunnison, p. 184.

11. C. S. Peel, *How We Lived Then,* p. 68. *Daily Mail,* 8 December 1916.

12. *Labour Year Book 1916,* p. 212. *Daily Mail,* 24 May 1915. Cd. 8358, p. 4.

13. *Board of Trade Journal 1916,* pp. 388, 457.

14. Cd. 8358, p. 5.

15. *The Times,* 28 August 1916.

16. Hammond, *British Labour Conditions and Legislation During the War,* pp. 221–2.

17. *The Times,* 29 September 1915.

18. Blumenfeld, *All in a Lifetime,* p. 20 (9 March 1915).

19. *Daily Mail,* 19 October 1915.

20. Blumenfeld, p. 23 (17 April 1915).

21. *National War Savings Committee 1st Annual Report;* P.P., 1917–18, XVIII, Cd. 8516, p. 1.

22. ibid, p. 7.

23. *Daily Mail,* 2 April 1915.

22. ibid, p. 7.

24. Peel, pp. 34–5.

25. Lord Newton, *Retrospection,* 1929, p. 50. Ponsonby, *Falsehood in Wartime,* pp. 121–5. L. Masterman, *C. F. G. Masterman,* 1939, p. 280.

26. *Report of Committee on Alleged German Outrages,* 1915, p. 48.

27. J. D. Squires, *British Propaganda at Home and in the United States,* Cambridge, Mass., 1935, pp. 27 ff.

28. L. Masterman, p. 284.

29. D. Brownrigg, *Indiscretions of the Naval Censor,* 1920, p. 37.

30. S.P.C.K., *Tract No. 15,* 1915.

31. *Report of British Association for the Advancement of Science 1916,* p. 23.

32. H. Lucy, *Diary of a Journalist,* 1922, p. 218 (24 September 1915).

33. R. Graves, *Goodbye to All That,* 1929, pp. 283–6.

34. Professor G. C. Henderson addressing Chemistry Section of British Association, 8 September 1916. *Report of the British Association 1916,* p. 366.

35. In A. P. Newton (ed.), *The Empire and the Future,* 1916, p. 4.

36. Blumenfeld, p. 51 (18 April 1916).

37. ibid, p. 95 (14 October 1917).

38. McDonagh, *In London during the Great War,* p. 237 (16 December 1917).

39. *Report of British Association 1916,* p. 366.

40. W. H. Dawson (ed.), *After War Problems,* 1917, p. 7.

41. J. E. Edmonds, *Short History of World War I,* 1952, p. 182.

42. J. Hendrie, *Letters of a Durisdeer Soldier,* n.d., p. 84.

43. Quoted in L. Housman (ed.), *War Letters of Fallen Englishmen,* 1929, p. 30.

44. *Manchester Guardian,* 29 August 1916. L. Masterman, p. 286.

45. *The Organization and Methods of the Central Prisoners of War Committee;* P.P., 1917–18, XVIII, Cd. 8615, pp. 2–6.

46. *The Times,* 1, 2, 24 June 1915.

47. W. Robertson (ed.), *Middlesbrough's Effort in the Great War,* n.d., p. 126.

48. *Observer,* 17 October 1915. *Daily Mail,* 1 February 1916. *Manchester Guardian,* 9 February 1916. *Middlesbrough's Effort,* p. 126.

49. Blumenfeld, p. 70.

50. *Report of Summer Time Committee;* P.P., 1917–18, X, Cd. 8471, p. 3.

51. ibid., p. 18.

52. Quoted by Blumenfeld, p. 130.

53. *Defence of the Realm Losses Commission 1st Report;* P.P., 1916, VII, Cd. 8359.

54. Blumenfeld, p. 67 (18 November 1916).

55. Robertson (ed.), *Middlesbrough's Effort,* p. 127.

56. National Council on Public Morals, *The Cinema,* 1917, pp. 5–6.

57. ibid, pp. lxxx–lxxxi, 114–15, 216.

58. ibid, pp. 267, xxv, 83.

59. ibid, pp. 134, 143, 240, xxx. *Daily Mail,* 26 January 1916.

60. National Council on Public Morals, *The Cinema,* p. xxxi. See also pp. 18, 24, 26, 85, 135, 208.

61. *Manchester Guardian,* 28 March 1916.

62. *The Cinema,* p. xxi.

63. Commission on Educational and Cultural Films, *The Film in National Life,* 1932, p. 46.

64. Peel, *How We Lived Then,* p. 68.

65. *Daily Mail,* 4 September 1918.

66. Peel, p. 67.

67. Marwick, *Clifford Allen,* pp. 50–1.

68. Meech, *This Generation,* II, p. 176.

69. *Observer,* 12 December 1918.

70. T. Beecham, *A Mingled Chime,* 1944, p. 152.

71. ibid, pp. 133, 156–7, 161–2.

72. *Report of the Director of the National Gallery for 1913;* P.P., 1914–16, XXIX, 116, p. 60.

73. ibid, pp. 4–5.

74. *Manchester Guardian,* 22 January, 23 January 1916. *Observer,* 30 January 1916. *New Statesman,* 28 January 1916. *Nation,* 28 January 1916.

75. *Report of Director of National Gallery for 1919;* P.P., 1919, XXI, 21, p. 6.

76. *Manchester Guardian,* 18 August 1918.

77. Blumenfeld, p. 27 (20 August 1915).

78. *Observer,* 25 October 1915.

79. Robertson (ed.), *Middlesbrough's Effort,* p. 169.

80. ibid, p. 170.

81. ibid, pp. 184–5.

82. J. S. Duncan, in W. R. Scott *et. al., Rural Scotland During the War,* Oxford, 1922, pp. 218–19.

The declaration of war: crowds gather outside the House of Commons.   *Radio Times Hulton Picture Library*

The aftermath of anti-German riots in the East End of London,
June 1915.   *Radio Times Hulton Picture Library*

Taking the Oath: recruits at the White City, June 1915.
Radio Times Hulton Picture Library

Damage from a Zeppelin raid on London, September 1915.
Imperial War Museum

Replacing men: a woman worker in an engineering shop.
Radio Times Hulton Picture Library

Recruiting fervor: Miss Olga Nethersole addresses a meeting in Trafalgar Square, August 1915. *Radio Times Hulton Picture Library*

'Patriotic' women raise the white-feather flag. White feathers were
presented to men in civilian clothes.
Radio Times Hulton Picture Library

In March 1915 Glasgow municipal tramways boldly took on two conductresses on a week's trial. Here, later, are a driver and a conductor wearing their natty Black Watch uniforms.

Imperial War Museum

A grocer's shop run by women, Bedford Park, London, August 1915. *Radio Times Hulton Picture Library*

'High' society supports the war effort by patronizing a Russian exhibition at Hampstead, January 1917.
Radio Times Hulton Picture Library

Scouts help with the harvest: pulling flax, August 1918. Children's war work helped the economy, but not their education.
Radio Times Hulton Picture Library

The art of disenchantment: 'La Mitrailleuse' by C. R. W. Nevinson. *Reproduced by permission of the Trustees of the Tate Gallery, London*

Handing in rifles and equipment at Wimbledon, December 1918. Only the fortunate were demobilized as early as this: delays caused much discontent. *Radio Times Hulton Picture Library*

CHAPTER FIVE

The Challenge to Laissez-Faire

[1] SACRED PRINCIPLES

LAISSEZ-FAIRE as a complete and coherent economic and political philosophy was evolved in the early stages of the Industrial Revolution. It was born at a time when ancient limitations and restrictions and the current belief in the necessity of tariffs and bounties seemed to be holding back the natural progress of industrial growth; its proponents, of whom the earliest one of importance was Adam Smith, author of *The Wealth of Nations*, published in 1776, argued that ideally there should be no state interference in economic and social matters, that individual initiative and unfettered private enterprise were the keystones of prosperity, and, by logical extensions made by the followers of Smith rather than by Smith himself, that if it resulted in the grinding of the faces of the poor, this, though no doubt regrettable, was unavoidable. Overseas trade, said the classical political economists (often justly described by their opponents as 'the dismal scientists') should be freed of all tariffs, restrictions and bounties. Their third point of substance was that the Government should not meddle with the country's currency, which should be securely based on the actual amount of its gold reserves.

These theories were most nearly (but never completely) put into full practice in the middle decades of the nineteenth century, but were very shortly challenged by a countervailing philosophy, that of collectivism. The advocate of laissez-faire (or individualist) argues that by leaving the individual to his own devices the best interests of the community will be served. The collectivist argues that such a system, in stimulating excessive competition, is often inefficient and that, under its sway, many of the weaker members of the community will go to the wall: he therefore favours collective action, which, in effect, usually means State action, on behalf of the interests of the community as a whole, or of major sections of it. Up to a point economic theories are the product of prevailing economic conditions: the early and mid-nineteenth century was a time of small business enterprises competing with each other in the unsullied conditions of the free market; the later nineteenth century saw the beginnings of large-scale industrial combination with the element of free competition sensibly diminished. Even so, there was still a basic philosophical divergence between the individualist who was prepared to allow amalgamations on the part of individual businessmen on the grounds that they were thereby increasing economic efficiency, and the collectivist who saw such amalgamations as possible threats to the community as a whole. Industrial combination, then, could be a stimulus to developing the theory of collectivism, but was not itself a part of collectivism.

In any event it is too easy a temptation to talk of individualism, collectivism, progress, reaction, as broad impersonal, ineluctable forces, forgetting that the theories behind them are the theories of particular men, the measures that implement them the measures of particular men, and that these men, as often as not, are struggling with the events of fortuitous circumstance. The hard-boiled Marxist has an elegant circular argument to deal with this, but the greatest Marxist playwright, Bertold Brecht, gets nearest to the point. His Galileo, ageing, conscious that he has betrayed his great scientific discoveries, is being comforted by one of his former pupils, who tells him that the forces of reason are none the less steadily triumphing: 'the triumph of reason,' Galileo breaks out bitterly, 'is the triumph of reasonable men.' Leaving aside the meaningless question of whether, in the abstract, the collectivist or the individualist solution is the more reasonable, I hope here, and in a later chapter, to bring out from the shadows of historical inevitability some of the individuals who participated in the challenge to laissez-faire which is one of the salient and enduring features of the domestic history of the First World War.

In 1914 the three principles of free trade, free currency, and free enterprise, were still sacrosanct to the vast majority of politicians, businessmen, and civil servants; though a small group of Conservatives, led at the turn of the century by Joseph Chamberlain, had attempted to controvert the first. The existence of a highly elaborate system of direct taxation was a modest infringement of the second, and the collectivist social reforms enacted since the 1870s a qualification of the third. Almost everyone accepted these reforms, which were aimed, not at the reorganization of society, but at filling in the more glaring gaps where the existing system failed to provide the barest necessities of social well-being.

Among the tiny minority who were prepared to go far beyond this in the direction of collectivist intervention it is possible to distinguish five groupings. At the centre stands the Fabian Society, founded in 1884 and committed to seek by propaganda and political activity the progressive socialization of Britain. Here we rub against another word which presents problems of definition: in the nineteenth century and later, people often used 'socialism' as a synonym for collectivism, perfectly correctly since the emphasis in the word itself is on putting the interests of society as a collective unity before the ambitions of the individual; it is in this sense that the Liberal Chancellor of the Exchequer, Sir William Harcourt, could in the 1890s make the famous declaration, 'We are all socialists now.' However, it is a good rule in the use of language that where two distinct words exist they should be used according to the separate nuances which they have attached to them, rather than as loose synonyms. There can be no precise definition of socialism, a word which is highly emotionally charged, and which is used by the body of its adherents rather as the adolescent girl uses the word 'nice', but, as distinguished from collectivism, it connotes a more positive egalitarianism; being the philosophy of the have-nots, it is associated with the conscious working-class movement, and it implies that in the desired reorganization of industry and society the worker will have managerial and political power, whereas collectivism alone could result in former employers continuing in exactly the same jobs, only as highly-salaried employees of the State. All socialists, then, are collectivists (though some, for example the guild socialists, would desire the collective unit to be very small); but not all collectivists are socialists. None the less, throughout our period of study we shall find people using the terms as pretty well interchangeable.

The Fabians, among whom the most consistently important was Sidney Webb, the small, egg-headed author of weighty treatises, were a society of intellectuals, and tended to stress the collectivist rather than the egalitarian or working-class aspects of their beliefs. Although formally affiliated to the Labour Representation Committee (which took the title Labour Party after 1906), the society continued to believe in the possibility of 'permeating' the major parties with its ideas. By 1914 the commitment to the Labour Party, partly because of the agitation of the younger generation of Fabians, was becoming more pronounced, and most Conservative and Liberal sympathizers had flown from the Fabian aviary to their own political cages, often, however, taking Fabian ideas with them. Just before the war the Fabians founded a new organ of intellectual and political opinion, the *New Statesman*, edited by Clifford Sharp, which in February 1914 published the first part of a meticulous report on the problems of nationalization, compiled by the Fabian Research Department; the second and third parts followed in May 1914 and May 1915 respectively.[1]

The Labour Party in 1914 was scarcely a party at all: rather was it a loose alliance between confirmed socialists who demonstrated their socialism through being members of the I.L.P. or Fabian Society, and hard-headed working men whose main interest was in the immediate bettering of their industrial lot, and whose first thoughts centred on their trade union. Only one side of this alliance was necessarily socialist, for many trade unionists had little interest in the philosophy of socialism and saw the Labour Party merely as a means to limited ends. The Labour Party as an entity, therefore, had not committed itself to a complete socialistic programme. Most of its most active members, however, were convinced socialists, and they make up the second of our five groupings.

At Labour Party conferences resolutions calling for the nationalization of basic industries had already become something of a formality, though there was an awareness that nationalization (or collectivization) would not itself bring Utopia. This is apparent in a resolution carried at the 1913 conference of the T.U.C. and repeated in 1915:

This Congress expresses the opinion that nationalization of public services, such as the Post Office, is not necessarily advantageous to the employees and the working classes unless accompanied by a steadily increasing democratic control, both by the employees and the representatives of the working classes in the House of Commons. It, there-

fore, pledges itself to work steadily to develop public opinion in both
these directions.[2]

During the war there was a sharp divergence between the trade
union side of the Labour alliance, which was firmly behind the
war effort, and the political and socialist side as represented by
the I.L.P., most of whose important figures were against the
war (Fabians, however, on the whole supported the war); yet
the two sides could unite at the 1916 Labour Party conference in
calling for the nationalization of railways, mines, shipping, banking and insurance.[3]

A third group of collectivists was to be found on the radical
wing of the Liberal party, where the most vociferous personality
was Sir Leo Chiozza Money, a former Fabian (this illustrates
the central position of the society), and author of *Riches and
Poverty*. In May 1908 a number of radicals had formed themselves
into the Railway Nationalization Society, of which the president
was the barrister and Liberal M.P., Clement Edwards.[4] Money
himself had brought in a Bill for the nationalization of the railways in the last months before the outbreak of war.

The Conservative Party is not readily thought of in connexion
with collectivist social reform, yet in the later nineteenth century
it was often more progressive in this respect than the Liberal
Party, which was wedded to Gladstonian ideas of private enterprise and free trade. If the Conservatives hankered after a static,
paternalistic society with the rich man in his castle and the poor
man at his gate, it was part of the paternalism that the poor man
at the gate should not die of starvation. Ideas of imperial grandeur
fostered by Benjamin Disraeli went hand in hand with a desire to
make the British a strong and healthy people. At the domestic
end of the rope labelled 'constructive imperialism' and thrown to
the underdeveloped colonies by Joseph Chamberlain was 'Tory
radicalism'. The collectivist process is often taken as beginning
with the Artisans' Dwelling Act of 1875, passed by a Conservative ministry under Disraeli. Although, on the whole, Edwardian
Conservatives went no further than the filling-the-gaps type of
social reform, there were a number of extreme right-wing
Conservatives whose interest was primarily in war and empire,
who were favourable to State action in the form of military

conscription, and who were not unaware that German military potential owed much to her social welfare schemes.

Here we come up against another of the complications of the problem: members of the Conservative élite were prepared to talk in terms which sounded favourable to the idea of State interference, but there was always the unvoiced reservation that the interference should always be with other people, never with the élite. In other words, when Conservatives said 'the State', they often simply meant themselves, an attitude which Bernard Shaw had pinned down with one of his barbs in 1884 when he remarked that the Government had no more right to call itself the State than the smoke above London had the right to call itself the weather. Yet historians have rightly stressed the 'social imperialism' – that is to say, the buying of working-class support for imperial and militaristic policies with social welfare legislation – of both Conservative and Liberal ministries at the beginning of the twentieth century.[5] Although historically ends are more important than means, so that one can draw a distinction between the militarist who desires happy and healthy cannon-fodder, and the collectivist who desires a better and more humane society, it is necessary in discussing collectivism to keep the 'social imperialist' element in view. The strength of Conservatism as a political philosophy, furthermore, is its empiricism and adaptability, and Conservatives, presented with the unique circumstances of the war, were often far more ready than their political opponents to adopt the collectivist solution.

The fifth grouping included various administrators and technically non-political figures, many of whom had at one time or another been influenced by the Fabians. The overwhelming mass of the permanent Civil Service, especially at the Treasury, the War Office and the Local Government Board, was strongly laissez-faire in outlook, but in pushing through their social insurance legislation in 1911 Lloyd George and Winston Churchill had made use of a small storm corps of civil servants led by Sir Hubert Llewellyn Smith and W. J. Braithwaite,[6] and Churchill had, at the suggestion of Beatrice Webb, the female half of the great Fabian partnership, brought in a young journalist, William Beveridge, who was thereafter to lead a brilliant career in the public service.[7] With the growth of factory and public health legislation there had, too, grown up a tradition of enlightened bureaucracy, many of whose servants, on grounds of efficiency alone, were not averse to seeing it farther extended. The Board of Trade had become quite a hot-bed of eager young bureaucrats, of whom U. F. Wintour, shortly to take himself and a new broom to the Contracts Department of the War Office, was one. However, there can be no doubt that to the Liberal Government, to the Conservative opposition, and to right-thinking people everywhere, the three sacred principles stood unshaken when war broke out.

[11] MEASURES OF SELF-DEFENCE

In the interests of national self-defence even the most confirmed Liberal was prepared to concede some sacrifice of principle, and self-defence is the key to the first steps along the road to collectivism. The emergency measures of August 1914, particularly the limitations on trading and contraband, were obvious and rather unimportant examples. The requisitioning on 3 August of all shipping in waters adjacent to the United Kingdom, in practice about one-fifth of the total merchant tonnage, was essentially a military move, and had the effect of creating a greater free-for-all, and more opportunities for profiteering, among the owners of the remaining ships.[8] More important was the Defence of the Realm Act, the very embodiment of the theory of national self-defence: it did not itself, in its original form, involve any solid collectivist experimentation with industry or society, but it was, as it were, the unsubstantial awning under which the bits and pieces of collectivist organization could be built up.

In 1914 Britain's railways were a skein of tangled threads compared with Germany's well-knit pattern based on sound military design; but by the time Prussia had completed her lightning conquest of France in 1870, authority in Britain was alerted to the fundamental strategic importance of efficient railway organization. Accordingly the Regulation of the Forces Act of 1871 provided that in the event of war the railways would be put at the disposal of the Government, and in 1896 a Railway War Council was established.[9] On 4 August 1914 the railways passed into the control of the Government, to be run as a unified system by the

Railway Executive Committee, of which the official chairman was the President of the Board of Trade. The individual railway companies were guaranteed the same level of profits as they had enjoyed in 1913; receipts were pooled and the Government, instead of making separate payments for troop movements, from time to time put into the pool the amount by which it fell short of the earnings of 1913 – in 1916, for instance, about £6 million.[10] Since, furthermore, the Railway Executive Committee consisted of the general managers of the principal lines, and since the President of the Board of Trade scarcely interfered with the acting Chairman, who was Herbert Walker of the London and North Western Railway, this measure could not be called nationalization as understood by the committed socialist. Looking back on a year's working, this is how the arrangement was seen in a resolution unanimously adopted by the Trades Union Congress:

That in view of the fact that to meet the great national emergency with which the country was faced in August last it was found to be necessary to place the whole railway system of Great Britain under unified Government control, and having regard to the admitted success from the military point of view, which has attended this step in the interests of the community, this Congress reaffirms its conviction that the complete nationalization of British railways would prove to be in the interests of the community generally. Further, in view of the partial, vague and unsatisfactory character of the present arrangements between the railways and the State, this Congress calls upon the Government before relinquishing its present control to introduce legislation having for its object the effecting of complete national ownership of the railways, to be administered with the aid of an advisory Committee (upon which the employees shall have elected representatives), under a Minister of Railways responsible to Parliament.[11]

The railways were administered 'not by the government, but for the government'.[12] None the less, the theory of private enterprise had taken a knock in that profits to shareholders were pegged far below what they would have been had the companies been free to cash in on the war situation, and in that free competition had been superseded by unified control. The measure passed into effect without a murmur from the most confirmed

Liberal; the real decision, after all, had been taken in 1871.

Contemporary military thinking was, naturally, as alive to the value of certain strategic materials of war as it was to the value of effective rail communications. Much of the near-hysteria which surrounds international politics in the pre-war years was caused by the feeling that technology had so speeded up war as to make a quick trigger-finger essential. Shortly before the outbreak of war the British Army had adopted the new explosive, tri-nitrotoluol (TNT), the other standard explosive being picric acid.[13] The way in which the potential advantage in supplies of strategic materials which Britain derived from an empire on which the sun never set was diminished by her lack of the scientific expertise necessary to exploit them has already been discussed. Of tin and mica she had such abundant supplies that these commodities could, if necessary, be used as media of exchange with the United States and other neutral countries. Coal and steel, normally, were also in abundance, but in time of war had to be carefully husbanded. For iron ores, nitrates, copper and aluminium, Britain relied heavily on North America, and here she would be governed by shipping capacity and availability of credit. The quest for ferro-chrome and certain special steels and irons took her even farther out of the comforting rays of the imperial sun: there was a real danger that the principal sources, Norway and Sweden, might fall under the dominion of the enemy. Optical and chemical glass, potash, spelter and tungsten, and a range of scientific instruments and electrical goods came from the land of permanent darkness.[14]

Between 3 and 5 August 1914, the War Office leapt into action, prohibiting the export of benzol, coal-tar toluol, phenol, nitro-toluene, and other chemicals essential to the manufacture of high explosive. In November all supplies of toluol in the country were requisitioned, but to mollify continuing laissez-faire sentiment a very generous price was paid. At the same time the Defence of the Realm Consolidation Act (which became law on 27 November) gave the Admiralty and the War Council the right to take possession of factories employed in war production or of their output. A more direct, though extremely minor, piece of Government interference in a section of industry not covered by this Act came in December, when distillers were compelled to recover all toluene in excess of three per cent before marketing benzol or naphtha. By this time there was already tremendous competition in the United States for American nitrates and metals: the timorous War Office expedient of appointing an American banking firm as its purchasing agents had all the effectiveness of one little dyspepsia pill combating a perforated ulcer, for British manufacturers continued their own ruthless competition for raw materials, mercilessly bidding up prices against each other. The War Office at the same time put great trust (with some reason, it should be said) in the skilled purchasing ability of the large private firms with which it had had a long association.[15] By the end of 1914, however, it was apparent to the clear-sighted, of whom there were few, that the only way of ensuring that British factories got the necessary materials at reasonable prices was for the Government to assume responsibility for purchase, supply, and distribution. Its own agents kept pressing the War Office to adopt a system of advance bulk purchase and, soon after his appointment on 26 September as Director of Army Contracts, U. F. Wintour circulated a memorandum which to a remarkable degree anticipated the measures which eventually, through sad experience, had to be implemented.[16] Sir Hubert Llewellyn Smith of the Board of Trade referring in an important note of 23 January 1915 to the domestic manufacture of munitions, raised even wider issues:

It is ... probable that we shall ultimately find some form of compulsion necessary in order to ensure both that effective priority shall be given to Government work on existing contracts and sub-contracts, and also that new Government contracts (and sub-contracts) shall be accepted and given priority as compared with private orders already booked. Nothing but compulsion could relieve the contractors from the obligations of their private contracts, and in many cases they would welcome such compulsion. It should, therefore, be carefully considered whether the matter can be dealt with by existing regulations under the Defence of the Realm Act or whether new legislation or new regulations would be necessary for this purpose.[17]

The increasing difficulties of the early weeks of 1915 necessitated more and more direct buying abroad and stimulated spectacular action at home in connexion with one commodity in which supply suddenly ran desperately short: sandbags. All new sacking from the Dundee mills and all old sacks were requisitioned, the usual generous prices being paid. Nevertheless, old-guard resistance to wider governmental control, or even to a general policy of buying ahead, remained unsurmountable.[18] The upshot was the great shell crisis.

The near-monopoly of the German chemicals industry meant that, in addition to explosives, Britain ran dangerously short of dye-stuffs. It was because of this that the Government, acting on the advice of a Committee on Chemicals which it had set up at the outbreak of war, decided upon the ambitious scheme of floating a national joint stock company to manufacture aniline dyes. Itself a somewhat half-baked compromise between Government sponsorship and private shareholding, the scheme very nearly failed in face of the resolute opposition of private manufacturers; a complete fiasco was enthusiastically anticipated by the *Economist*, which, under the editorship of F. W. Hirst, was a bastion of economic orthodoxy. Through Government subscription of £1,700,000 British Dyes Ltd was kept in being till the end of the war, when it was amalgamated with Messrs Levinstein Ltd.[19]

Before the war two-thirds of Britain's sugar supply came in the form of beet sugar from Germany and Austria. In this case Government intervention, in the form of the appointment of a Royal Commission on Sugar Supply with executive powers to purchase and distribute sugar on behalf of the community, was rather more successful than it had been with dye-stuffs.[20] Here, in theory, was a great advance on the nervous fumblings of the War Office in face of a similar problem, and in practice it was highly successful in that, though prices did rise, domestic supplies of sugar were remarkably well maintained. The arrangement, however, was as much in the interests of the sugar traders, otherwise threatened with a loss of their livelihood, as of the community at large. A leading article in the Labour Party newspaper, the *Daily Citizen*, read the lesson of the Sugar Commission and preached another one:

Thus in the hour of its supreme need does the nation turn to the collectivist experiments urged for so many years by the Labour movement. And the experiments are not found wanting. They are abundantly and brilliantly vindicated. Is it too much to hope that the experiment will now be extended from sugar to wheat? Is it too much to hope that these experiments will still be remembered when these dark, anxious days are at an end? If it be necessary for the State to guard the poor from exploitation now, will it not be sound policy to continue the experiment during what we hope will be the long years of un-broken peace?[21]

Leaving the long years of unbroken peace aside, the *Daily Citizen* was justified in showing concern for the problem of wheat supply. For fifty years the British had been turning their backs on arable farming, so that in 1914 four-fifths of the wheat consumed had to be imported from abroad. Although there was as yet no truly serious interference with shipping, bread prices had shown an alarming rise in the first days of war, and the possibility of a flour famine was not one to be lightly dismissed. The War Emergency Workers' National Committee suggested to the Board of Agriculture that the entire home wheat crop should be com-mandeered. Contemporary opinion in Government and Civil Service circles is admirably summed up in the reply from the Assistant Secretary of the Board:

Having regard to all the circumstances of the case, the Board think that so long as the price of wheat remains moderate it would be unwise to interfere with the free play of competition.[22]

In fact, although the Government left the domestic market to its own devices it did interfere in the international market, purchas-ing between November 1914 and February 1915 three million quarters of wheat in the United States and Argentina.[23] So strong was the continuing prejudice against the Government under-taking business activities that the whole transaction was carried out in total secrecy.

Government interference in the world sugar market was in the interests of the sugar traders; its interference in finance was, as much as anything, in reply to the demands of the financiers. As a precedent the infringement of the principle of free currency was important, but in reality what the Government was trying to do was to restore to free working a fiscal mechanism which had jammed up under the impact of war; its policy was 'less an inter-ference with the economic system than an attempt to restore a damaged part to normal working'.[24] The war hit the financial world in the solar plexus. The normal flow between Central Europe and the West abruptly halted; city men suddenly found themselves called upon to meet unexpectedly heavy commitments, or else found that they were stuck with fistfuls of bad debts, while, at the same time, the normal sources of loans had dried up. What was needed was a quick transfusion of liquid cash, and this was what the Government provided in the Currency and Bank Notes Act of 6 August.

According to classical political economy the amount of currency circulating in the country should be governed strictly by the amount of gold held in the country, but it was accepted that, since some proportion of the currency would be constantly in use and could not therefore be presented for conversion into gold, the Bank of England could safely issue notes which exceeded by a strictly defined amount the total value of its gold deposits; this strictly defined amount, issued, as it were, on trust, was called the fiduciary issue. The Bank of England was now given permission to increase the fiduciary issue at the same time as the Treasury began the printing of its own £1 and 10s notes. Theoretically Britain remained on the Gold Standard; the new currency notes were legally convertible into gold, and there was no prohibition upon the use of gold for payment of external debts. But so little did holders of currency notes avail themselves of their legal right, and so big were the practical difficulties of transferring large-scale gold payments in time of war – virtually impossible without Bank of England or Treasury assistance, which naturally was not forthcoming – that the traditional working of the Gold Standard was effectively suspended.[25]

Closed as an emergency measure, the Stock Exchange did not open again until January 1915, and then only under very restricted conditions. Yet orthodox opinion seems to have been more impressed by the Stock Exchange being open at all than by the limitations imposed upon it. It was left to the Fabian *New Statesman* to stress the importance of the innovation of Government control of capital issues and direction of investment towards projects believed to be in the national interest.[26] The Government farther imposed restrictions and even prohibitions upon foreign lending. All this is central to the theory of the collectivist planned economy, yet at the time it passed, save in the eyes of a few shrewd socialistic observers, as an *ad hoc* defensive policy upon which no long-term construction should be placed.

There is one other very obvious way in which the war challenged orthodox political economy, and that was through the prodigious expenditure which it involved. Very early on, the Government gave up any attempt to make separate allocations to military or naval expenditure, but simply asked Parliament to make farther grants in aid of the total war effort: such lax prodigality would have brought shudders to Cobden, Bright and Gladstone, pillars of an earlier and more careful era. By July 1915 the war was costing £3 million a day, and over the entire war period national expenditure multiplied sixfold. The National Debt, about the abolition of which the younger Pitt, first prime ministerial disciple of Adam Smith, had once had some deluded notions, rose from £650 millions in 1914 to £7,435 millions in 1919. None the less, over a year of warfare elapsed before any onslaught was made on the old tax structure.

The various scarcities of the early months merge into the associated problem of high prices. Hoarding had been a feature of the early days of the war; in reply the Board of Trade armed itself with the power to requisition at reasonable prices foodstuffs 'unreasonably withheld'.[27] It also went so far as to draw up, in collaboration with the grocers, a list of recommended maximum prices. But the two measures signified no more than an amiable intention, if even that, since little or no attempt was made to put them into practice. By the beginning of 1915 Labour organizations and newspapers were strongly voicing demands for Government control of basic foodstuffs and their prices. The *New Statesman* remained icily detached from its proletarian fellows: the remedy for high prices, it said, with breath-taking perspicacity, was peace, or else, possibly, an extension of the co-operative movement, but certainly not centralized control. It showed no special enthusiasm for the panacea humbler socialists were advocating, Government control of all shipping, though it did favour more energetic organization and control of internal transport: 'more drastic measures,' it agreed, 'may presently be called for.' All such hints and proposals merely aroused the hearty contempt of *The Times*.[28]

The whole question boiled up into the important House of

Commons debate of 11 and 17 February 1915. J. R. Clynes and other Labour speakers pressed the Government at the very least to institute control of prices. Asquith, it will be recalled, defended Government inaction on the highly unimpressive ground that present conditions were no worse than those prevailing in the aftermath of the Franco-Prussian war. The President of the Board of Trade, Walter Runciman, followed him with an unequivocal defence of the doctrine of private enterprise.[29] One might almost suspect them both, were they not such earnest believers, of parodying the laissez-faire cause. The Government's rejection of the nostrum of price control again got the hearty approval of *The Times*.[30]

Most interesting of all was the speech made by the Conservative leader, Bonar Law. It was a difficult speech to follow, the speech of a man not quite clear about his own attitudes. At times he seemed to upbraid the Liberal Government for not going far enough in its modest measures of State interference, yet in conclusion he seemed, for the time being, to be against such interference. A brief aside during the last sentences of the speech suggests that Bonar Law had at least been reflecting that Toryism did not have quite the same organic association with laissez-faire as Liberalism:

British-owned ships are under British control, and we have just as much right – I do not know whether this is good Tory doctrine or not – to seize this part of the national organization as I believe we have, if the necessity arises, to seize every able-bodied man in the country. From that point of view I am not in disagreement with the hon. gentlemen opposite. But I do say that no such case has arisen yet, and that until the evil becomes much greater than it is any attempt to exercise control in that way would be found perfectly futile. It would be very different in any case. But I repeat that there is a limit to the profit which we can allow to be made out of this war, and if that limit is reached, I would be at one with those who say that the House of Commons ought to step in.[31]

This wondrously vague piece of Tory soul-searching stands as a good example of how little progress the ideas of collectivism, despite isolated successes in exceptional instances, had made by February 1915. However, many of the basic issues which take us on beyond the universally accepted demands of self-defence had been aired, and the one major consequence of this House of Commons debate was the setting up of two Committees of Investigation into Coal Supply.[32] The reports did not come till April, but they then carried farther the challenge to laissez-faire.

[III] THE PRESSURES OF NECESSITY

One of the major sources for the history of the development of State control during the First World War is the massive *History of the Ministry of Munitions* written up from the inside at the end of the war. It prints many valuable memoranda and other original documents which give a particularly good picture of the attitudes of leading Civil Servants: parts of the *History*, indeed, were withheld from the public until after the Second World War. At the same time much of the commentary is written in the mood of extreme economic orthodoxy which characterized the Lloyd George ministry in the years immediately after the war. Necessity, it is insisted again and again, was the mother of State control. Talking of the State factories set up under the first Munitions Act, it declared that they 'owed their inception not to any definite plan or policy of State monopoly but to the immediate stress of practical necessity'.[33] It shrewdly explained the way in which State control increased by what it fed on:

Once any measure of control had been undertaken the forces pressing for complete control became stronger and were ultimately irresistible. Partial control was unjust as well as unsuccessful, and control of supply created monopolies which had to be met by controlling prices.[34]

The overall attitude of the writers is revealed on the first page of the seventh volume when they say, 'It appears probable that experience of State control during the war has retarded rather than hastened the spread of State socialism.'

The basic and non-polemical trend of the argument of the munitions historian is supported by a distinguished contemporary economic historian , who has written:

There was no one at this time to present the theoretical case for direct State action, and the controlled economy was not seen and planned as a whole, but allowed to grow, regulation upon regulation, as specific needs arose.[35]

With the second, and more important, part of this statement there can be no quarrel whatsoever; the first part requires slight amendment. From March 1915 to December 1916 more and more publicists put forward with strengthening conviction what might not unfairly be called 'the theoretical case for direct State action', until one could say that in the autumn of 1916 there was probably, in informed public opinion, a majority to be found in favour of such action. Admittedly newspaper leading articles are particularly difficult source materials to deal with: one has always to reckon with the possibility that some of the most pungent ones may have been written by a junior sub with a hangover, and it is quite often impossible to derive any sense at all from the less pungent ones. Fluctuations in opinion are especially discernible in the *Manchester Guardian*, edited by one of the greatest Liberal radicals of the generation, C. P. Scott; these may well have been a genuine expression of the Liberal dilemma. As the war wore on the *Guardian* spoke more and more strongly and consistently in favour of State control. In *The Times*, which was given wide editorial freedom, though owned by the first of the great Tory press Lords, Lord Northcliffe, the fluctuations can be explained as part of the Tory duality already mentioned. The historical value of *The Times* does not reside so much in its leading articles – too often an uncommunicative blend of balance and bigotry – as in the authoritative articles by eminent outsiders which it carried. A Liberal line more old-fashioned than that of the *Guardian* was followed by the *Daily News* (edited by A. G. Gardiner), the *Nation* (edited by H. W. Massingham) and the *Economist,* the last-named being essential to an understanding of the direction in which received economic attitudes were blowing.

By the third month of 1915 the inadequacies of British war production held the field of public discussion. The champion of collectivist radicalism, Leo Chiozza Money, contributed a shrewd article to the *New Statesman* entitled 'Power of Production First':

Opinions are very much in the melting-pot at this time, and all sorts of queer things are bubbling up to the surface in our United Kingdom.

We may excuse the appearance during the process of no small amount of froth. There are hasty concessions to Conscription, to Protection, to Big Navies, to Railway Nationalization, to the Control of Supplies, and even indeed to the rankest Socialism. So many cherished opinions, whether right or wrong, are without stable foundation that there may be plenty of surprises in store for all political parties when the Great War has at last come to an end, and the nation dissolves its organization for war to resume the disorganization of peace.[36]

In writing thus, Money was both premature in suggesting that there was as yet any real organization for war and undeceived in his forecast of the final outcome after the war.

The Defence of the Realm (Amendment) Act (No. 2) of February 1915 put into practice the suggestions made two months previously by Sir Hubert Llewellyn Smith, and involved a revolutionary extension of the Defence of the Realm Consolidation Act of November. It was possible for economic traditionalists to swallow the powers granted to the Admiralty and the War Office in connection with firms which were already in the munitions business; but the application of these powers, as necessary, to all other factories and workshops capable of conducting war-work was altogether a much larger mouthful. *The Times* gave its blessing to what it headlined as 'A Step in Government Control', but the *Manchester Guardian*, talking of 'Socialism in War', and 'another great advance towards the temporary nationalization of industries', expressed uneasiness. Nine days later the *Manchester Guardian* published a more favourable leading article, entitled 'War Socialism', which called for the further step of control of profits.[37] Limitation of profits was in fact a bait which, from the time of the Treasury Conference, the Government began to dangle in front of the Labour movement.

An atmosphere of crisis overhung April and May; there was universal anxiety over the shell shortage after the publication in the middle of April of Sir John French's long and factual dispatch on Neuve Chapelle, and anger after the publication of Colonel Repington's *Times* report on 14 May. The appointment of a special Munitions' Committee under Lloyd George was welcomed by *The Times* as a solution 'for which *The Times* has repeatedly pressed'. The *Manchester Guardian* called for 'some of the discipline and organization of Germany',[38] and other papers made much of the shining example set in this respect by the enemy country. From both *The Times* and the *Mail* there was much heated agitation for 'mobilizing the whole nation' or for 'national service'.

Growing pressure of opinion and the failure of the existing Government to come to grips with the problems of war would almost certainly have brought a change in ministry within months; the immediate shell scandal blown up by Colonel Repington made it inevitable within weeks; the violent and irreconcilable quarrel at the Admiralty over the ill-fated Dardanelles expedition between the First Sea Lord, Admiral Fisher, whom the Conservatives admired, and the First Lord of the Admiralty, Winston Churchill, whom they loathed, pinned it down to days. Only the back-bench Liberals seemed to be taken by surprise. On Monday 17 May the 'lobbies and smoke-rooms' were 'full of dismal prophecies', and two days later, when the decision to bring in the Conservatives had been announced, there was an indignant meeting of Liberal M.P.s, who were mollified, however, within twenty minutes by Asquith.[39] Too much should not be made of the change in personnel involved in the construction of a coalition ministry. It is true that Asquith's closest political friends, men like McKenna and Runciman, were the most zealous upholders of private enterprise, and that, on the whole, the new Conservative ministers were more prepared to approach war-time difficulties empirically, but the real boost that the Coalition gave to the forces of collectivism was that as an all-party ministry, and manifestly a war ministry, it could with much greater impunity pass measures which were in violation of beliefs previously firmly held by most Liberals and Conservatives alike.

As a symbol of the intention to grapple firmly with the munitions problem a new ministry was created, the first appearance of the most typical, and often the most fruitless, by-product of the collectivist process. There followed the Munitions of War Act, described by an American contemporary as 'perhaps the most decisive step in the state control of industry taken during the war'.[40] Primarily the Act dealt with the labour shortage, but State control of labour was paralleled by State control of profits. Most important of all, the new ministry went straight ahead with the establishment on its own account of National Factories, of which there were sixteen by the end of July and 250 by the end of the war, most of them built during 1915 and 1916.[41]

The sight of the Government at last rolling up its sleeves was hailed with delight in most of the press, though the *Manchester Guardian* hankered after something at once more radical and more tender towards the susceptibilities of the business classes:

We confess we should have thought it simpler and better for the Government to have dealt with munition works as they did with the railways, taking over the entire concern and allowing to existing owners a handsome income as owners and remuneration as managers.[42]

The Times canvassed another proposal for dealing with both the labour shortage and the demands of the Western Front, the compilation of a National Register. Although the *Economist* countered with a trumpet blast of individualism, the Government took up the suggestion at the end of June, and National Registration Day was duly held early in August. To the *New Statesman* this was a turning point, bringing an end to the four months of repentance and good resolutions which had followed upon the utter disorganization of the first stages of the war.[43]

We have concentrated, rightly, on the munitions crisis and the labour problem associated with it, for this was the first great force which pushed politicians, reluctant to go beyond the obvious provisions for national self-defence, towards positive collectivist action. But at the same time as the dramatic changes were being heralded with all the pomp and circumstance of which Lloyd George was master, discontent with high prices was bubbling away and slowly working its own change in the alchemy of administrative activity. Scarcity of labour had caused the setting up of the Committee on Production, but the Committee's own Fourth Report makes it clear that fear of profiteering was a strong motive for turning the thoughts of its members towards ideas of State control.[44] The Committee of Investigation into Coal Prices, which consisted of Mr Vaughan Nash, C.B., Professor W. J. Ashley, Mr A. W. Flux, and three M.P.s, declared resoundingly in its April report that the ordinary capitalist distribution 'has broken down in the extraordinary circumstances of the present winter'; that immediate direction and control were essential, and that it might even be necessary for the Government to

assume direct control of the output of the collieries of the United Kingdom, with a view to regulating prices and distribution in accordance
with national requirements during the continuance of the present
war.[45]

The more conservative reports of the other coal committees reinforced the Government's own prejudices in the matter, and it
went no farther, even after the ministerial reconstruction, than
imposing domestic price control, although there were calls from
many camps, including that of the extreme suffragettes, for
nationalization.[46]

   Agitation over food prices brought a modest but growing governmental response. In April 1915 all the insulated spaces on
British steamships on the Australian and New Zealand sea-routes
were commandeered; in December all insulated spaces, irrespective of the sea-route served, were taken over; and at the close of
the year a Requisitioning Committee was set up with powers to
requisition entire ships.[47] Comment in the press varied between
vague advocacy of a national policy on food purchase and distribution and very firm rebuttals of any such thing. Government
spokesmen still continued openly to extol the virtues of the un-
regulated market, though agitation over high rents had also
brought the Increase of Rent and Mortgage Interest (War Restrictions) Act, which in effect pegged rents of houses with rateable values not exceeding £35 in London, £30 in Scotland and
£26 elsewhere to their 1914 level.

   None the less, it is in the summer of 1915 that the long discussion of the rising cost of living blends with the second great
positive force of necessity which eventually pushed the country
a long way farther along the road to State control: the physical
shortage of food, and the need to maximize home production.
In June 1915, a Committee on Agriculture was set up under the
chairmanship of Lord Milner, right-wing die-hard and enthusiastic social-imperialist. Its first report, published in July, put forward
a number of sensible recommendations amounting to a national
agricultural policy. Unhappily the Government, believing that it
had now mastered the submarine menace, made no attempt to
put them into practice. The second report, presented in October,
suggested the creation of County War Agricultural Committees
to give directives to farmers in the locality as to the most efficient

use of their available resources.[48] The Committees were duly appointed; but, lacking clear leadership from the Board of Agriculture, then headed by Lord Selborne, outstanding among the covey of incompetent administrators which was the parting gift from the old world of Edwardian England to the new world of total war, they achieved very little. The theories which, when put into practice eighteen months later, gained great praise for the Lloyd George ministry were actually fully hatched by the autumn of 1915; there lacked only the political will to set them to work.

Late 1915 and early 1916 are a time of stalemate as far as the growth of collectivism is concerned. Attention was concentrated on the National Register, the Derby Scheme, and conscription. It was for these topics that the *Economist* reserved its individualist fire, demonstrating incidentally that if Liberals were out of touch with the economic needs of the war, they were also heroic in their defence of the rights of conscience, now beginning to suffer in face of the aggrandizement of the State. There was, too, the breach in the dyke of classical political economy opened at another point by the budget of September 1915: it was a breach no bigger than a man's finger, but the waters, once let through, would not easily cease. In prefacing his budget proposals, McKenna expressed the fear that they would 'satisfy neither the strict Free Trader nor the scientific Tariff Reformer'; the natural working of free trade, he said, had in any event been spoiled by the war. The sentences which marked the first swing in British policy towards protectionism since the Repeal of the Corn Laws in 1846 sounded pretty innocuous – an effect which was heightened by the highly humorous interjection of the Labour member, Will Crooks, faithfully recorded in the *Hansard* report:

I put forward now, however, a list of articles the importation of which may properly be restricted by means of duties, in time of war, on both the grounds I have mentioned, namely foreign exchange and luxuries. So far as the duties do not put an end to importation, they may be a source of revenue not to be neglected. The articles to which I refer are motorcars and motor-cycles, and parts thereof, cinema films ⌐ (Mr W. Crooks: 'Poor old Charlie Chaplin') – clocks, watches, musical instruments, plate glass, and hats. . . .

On each of these articles I propose an *ad valorem* duty of 33⅓ per cent, or its equivalent, in the form of a specific rate, that is to say, on weight instead of on price.[49]

Only one back-bench Liberal, Thomas Lough, a former junior minister and chairman of a prosperous grocery concern, put up a spirited defence of the divine right of free trade. A concurrent breach in the principle of free currency was involved in the Treasury decision, in face of the fall in value of the pound to 4·50 dollars, to support the rate of exchange by the purchase of British-held American securities.[50] Early in 1916 the free trade hole was enlarged by the introduction of 'safeguarding', further protectionist tariffs said to be necessary to safeguard essential British industries.

The continued extravagance of the War Office and its reluctance to make use of its compulsory powers gave rise to the sick joke: 'No price is too high – for the War Office to pay – when honour and freedom are at stake.' But the direction in which opinion was swinging can be seen in the report of a Board of Trade Departmental Committee on Prices appointed in June 1916, a key document in the study of collectivism during the First World War.[51] The full report was extremely conservative in tone, going no farther than the recommendation that, if necessary, there should be farther Government requisitioning of shipping, and that bulk buying of meat by the Government (originally conceived as part of the programme of feeding the vast armies) should be extended. But an actual *majority* of the Committee (seven out of twelve) added the following memorandum:

... The present circumstances, being altogether exceptional, lend themselves readily to the inflation of prices and the making of large profits, and we think the evil cannot be effectively checked short of Government action, which must be wise and well considered, but at the same time far-reaching. The Government, we think, should more and more enlarge its purchases of meat and bacon from outside sources, and, where possible, become the sole purchaser, and should insist upon the purchasing public getting the full benefit of advantageous buying.

We think the recommendations should also have dealt with the home supplies of meat, bacon and milk. In many cases far too much profit is being made by the home producers, and we are of opinion that reasonable prices should be fixed. There is no new principle in this. The

Board of Trade, which has taken wide action in respect to the price of coal, is now extending its powers. There has been legislative action affecting the rents of houses. The Government has taken over the whole woolclip of the United Kingdom at a price determined by reference to the prices of the previous year. We know of no adequate reason why the public control of prices should not embrace the primary foodstuffs produced at home. In regard to the milk industry, for instance, a Committee of men and women acquainted with the conditions of the trade might be appointed to regulate prices, taking all the factors fully into account, and endeavouring to act fairly as between farmers, the distributors and the public.

We believe that machinery could be set up by Parliament which would eliminate from milk prices any element of extortion and encourage more efficient organization in distribution.[52]

Among the seven who signed this memorandum there were two Labour M.P.s, W. C. Anderson and J. R. Clynes (who were both, in addition, members of the I.L.P.), one trade union leader, Tom Shaw, and a member of the executive of the Fabian Society, Mrs Pember Reeves; but the other three, Sir Gilbert Claughton, Chairman of the London and North Western Railway and a director of Barclays Bank, D. Drummond Fraser, a banker and economist, and Thomas Brodrick, were all men who had heretofore held economic opinions of unimpeachable orthodoxy. As nearly as such things can be calendared, the summer of 1916 was the time when, as far as intelligent opinion is concerned, the tide of collectivism was definitely in flood.

[IV] INTELLIGENT OPINION

From the later decades of the nineteenth century, industry had been combining into larger units than would have been thought proper in mid-Victorian times. If in some respects the growth of industrial combinations was halted by the war, the value of large-scale production and minimized competition was at the same time made abundantly clear to capitalists. In 1915 the five main London transport undertakings decided to pool their resources, and this was given the sanction of Parliament. It was in the same year that the main London milk distributors linked themselves together in the United Dairies Limited.[53] The most important sign of the co-operative, if not combinative, impulse among businessmen was the founding in the summer of 1916 of the Federation of British Industries, which described itself as:

the latest and most important development of the Trade Organization movement in the United Kingdom. For many years past the manufacturers in many of the leading industries of the country have experienced the advantages to be gained by co-operation and association for the protection of their common interests in organizations devoted to their particular trades. The exigencies of wartime conditions added impetus to this movement and led to a large increase in the number of trade associations, with the result that practically every industry and the majority of trades within each industry, now have associations to assist and to foster the manufacture of British goods.

For this scheme of organization to be complete it was seen that British manufacturers and producers required the co-ordinating assistance of a National Association, which would concentrate and weld together the efforts which each trade exerted through its trade associations so that manufacturers might be enabled to speak and act in a manner commensurate with their strength and importance. The national needs during the war, and still more, the problems which would have to be faced when the war was over, necessitated the formation of a strong central organization representative of British manufacturers and producers as a whole.[54]

In time of war the impulse towards combination, co-operation, and rationalization helped to reinforce the movement towards State collectivism. Although at the end of the war the literature of the Federation of British Industries burst into a chorus of hatred against collectivism and all its works, for the period of war there was no hint of this attitude in F.B.I. publications. Other writers used the need for industrial rationalization as an argument in favour of State action. At the same time the glories of war gave a great stimulus to the theories of social imperialism. The two lines of thought form the basis of an interesting series of articles published in *The Times* during July and August 1916, and shortly republished, with an introduction by Lord Milner, as *The Elements of Reconstruction*. 'Reconstruction' is the theme word and the two anonymous authors are looking forward to a solution, after the war, to the problems of industrial organization: they claim that in that solution must be combined the experience gained in both the wartime national factories and the new private trusts and combines, and the lessons of German State socialism tempered by elements of British guild socialism.[55]

The amalgamation which had just taken place of the two great chemical firms, Brunner Mond and Co., and Castner Kellner and Co., is referred to approvingly, and the writers suggest that there should be 'a still more comprehensive crystallization', with 'the British Empire itself as an active and contributory partner in the ultimate combination'. *The Elements of Reconstruction* goes on to insist on the necessity of 'one national plan', and to contrast the old 'chaotic world of individualistic business run for unchecked private profit' with the proposed new 'system of amalgamated businesses in which the public interest is the controlling share-holder'.[56] The whole approach is well summed up in the following passage:

Without any preachment or propaganda we all find ourselves today drifted into a virtual agreement upon the reasonable course of economic development. It is a development towards nationalization; so far we go with the Socialist, but it is a development not by the Socialist's panacea of 'appropriation' at all, but by amalgamation, by co-ordination and co-operation, and by bringing the State into partnership, and an increasing partnership, in the big businesses that result from these amalgamations, by developing the crude beginnings of the 'controlled establishment', by the *quid pro quo* of profit-sharing and control in the national interest in exchange for the national credit and a helpful tariff.

It is not one of the least of the compensations for this war that it has necessitated experiments upon an otherwise impossible scale in the handling and rationing of the people's food and drink, and upon the conversion of private into quasi-public businesses.[57]

The writers were obviously impressed by, and sympathetic towards, guild socialism, which they say has done valuable work in 'preparing the minds of large masses of workers for industries upon a national scale'. Among the wilder proposals, that for parliamentary constituencies drawn on an occupational rather than a geographical basis (firmly stepped on by Lord Milner in his preface) has guild socialist overtones. If there are also about the whole programme faint shades of an incipient fascism – there must be an end, the authors say, to 'the pitiful old struggles' in the labour world⁵⁸ – the basic impression is of men of high intelligence and right-wing sympathies who have arrived at a considered rejection of all the old dogmas of laissez-faire.

Meanwhile, W. H. Dawson, the historian, was compiling a collection of essays on *After War Problems*, which, because of wartime delays, was not published till 1917. In his introduction Dawson talked of 'the deadly doctrine of laissez-faire'.⁵⁹ None of his contributors was quite so forthright, though Sir Joseph Compton-Rickett, Free Churchman, Liberal M.P. and former coal-owner, in a chapter on 'Organization of the National Resources' called for the cautious extension of collectivism. 'The growth of communal control and of State ownership,' he concluded, 'will probably secure the best of Socialism for us without its inherent weakness.'⁶⁰ A chapter on 'National Efficiency' by William Garnett emphasized the necessity for State encouragement of science. While thinkers of the political right and centre were becoming converted to some kind of collectivism, spokesmen of the left were consolidating their prepared positions. At the 1916 Labour Party Conference all sections of the movement united behind Philip Snowden's resolution on the financing of the war, which called for nationalization of railways, mines, shipping, banking and insurance.⁶¹

It is necessary now to turn again to the very practical and pressing problem of food shortage and food prices, another matter governed by a vital development in the outside war: the German resumption in October 1916, after an interlude designed to appease American sentiment, of submarine warfare. Now a 'decisive step'⁶² was taken with the appointment of a Royal Commission 'to inquire into the supply of wheat and flour in the United Kingdom, to purchase, sell and control the delivery of wheat and flour on behalf of His Majesty's Government, and generally to take such steps as may seem desirable for maintaining the supply'. An important parliamentary debate on food prices took place on 16 October. Barnes, for the Labour Party, accused the Liberals of a 'mournful, lingering feeling of regret' for laissez-faire, which he said was 'as dead as Queen Anne'. Runciman, for the Government, had already poured derision on the idea of a Food Controller or Minister of Food, but he got no praise from the *Economist* which, with the departure of F. W. Hirst, had switched to the new tunes. 'The advocates of stricter control and stronger measures,' it said, in reporting the debate, 'had the best of the argument.' Turning to prophecy, it forecast that in a year's time nine-tenths of the country's food would be under Government control.[63]

Poor Runciman was shortly eating his words: on 15 November he had to announce that the Government had decided to appoint a Food Controller. 'We have been driven bit by bit, against our will,' he explained, 'to suspend the easy flow of purely voluntary action.'[64] The problem was to find someone to take on the job, but that was not easy, as the Government visibly shook before a number of thunderous onslaughts, the most telling of which was that of Winston Churchill:

It has been a question of driving bit by bit, inch by inch driving the Government along the path which necessity in the end has forced them to enter upon . . . I believe that before the end of this War, unless it comes to an unexpected end, all shipping will certainly be taken over by the Government and regulated in one form or another, no doubt through its existing owners. I believe that all important employment will be regulated by the State for the purposes of the War. I believe that ration tickets for everything that matters will be served out to every one of us. I believe that prices will have to be fixed so as to secure to the poorest people in this country who are engaged in fighting this War as comrades with us, the power of buying a certain modicum of food sufficient to keep up physical war-making efficiency, at prices which are not outside the scope of the wages they receive, whatever those wages may be . . . All this will come. It can all be avoided quite easily. We have only got to send across and say we want to give in and all these difficulties can be avoided. But . . . all this kind of thing will undoubtedly be done, and more than we can think of now will be done, by the desperate resolution of the British nation not to be balked of its object. But why not do these now? Why not do them now while there is time? No one is stopping the Government except themselves.[65]

The Government food policy had got no farther than the Order of 21 November, which enforced price control for milk, when recurrent trouble in the South Wales coalfield forced its hand in another direction. Various proposals for control of the coalmines had been canvassed in the press throughout the autumn though *The Times* put it about that the Government was restrained by a tenderness towards coal-owners who were generous contributors to Liberal Party funds.[66] However on 29 November a new Defence of the Realm regulation made provision for the taking over of the South Wales mines on 1 December. The regulation specifically envisaged the extension of this control, if and when necessary, to other mining areas. The ideas of collectivism, then, were very much in the air in December 1916; but there was a strong feeling that the Government was showing laxity in failing to channel them into definite action. It is in this atmosphere that the great political crisis breaks; to it we must now, briefly, turn.

[v] THE UNDERTONES OF POLITICS

According to one economic historian, the political crisis of December 1916, and the replacement of Asquith by Lloyd George, 'formed a watershed in the conduct of the war'.[67] E. V. Morgan puts the matter more circumspectly:

The turning point, so far as there could be any single one, was the resignation of the Asquith Ministry and the accession to power of Mr Lloyd George.[68]

As shorthand statements these serve well enough, though they cry out for the obvious qualification that strong pressure for collectivist action had been building up for many months before December 1916, and had, indeed, already achieved many striking successes. Furthermore, in many of its policies the new ministry was as ham-handed and inadequate as its predecessor. Asquith, in fact, was in greater degree an obstacle to the type of centralized control the war made necessary than Lloyd George was an instigator of it. It is tempting, none the less, to see the vanquishment of Asquith solely as a victory for the forces of collectivism. There is more truth in this than the old-fashioned historian with the blood of political battle pounding in his ears would have us believe, but it is a truth that must be integrated into the complicated background murmur of politics.

The new Cabinet of May 1915 contained twelve Liberals, eight Unionists, one Labour member and Lord Kitchener; the Irish Nationalists had been offered, but declined, representation. It was

bigger by two than the old Cabinet: there was a Minister of Munitions (Lloyd George), and Lord Lansdowne, aristocratic heir to
the great Whig tradition of liberal rationalism though an ultra-
Conservative in his hostility to Irish Home Rule, was included as
Minister without Portfolio. In February 1916, the further addition was made of a Minister of Blockade. To counterbalance
this growing cumbrousness of the Cabinet machine, one important
step was taken towards modernizing the parliamentary system: a
temporary Act was passed freeing ministers from the eighteenth-
century requirement that upon appointment they must resubmit
themselves to the electorate. As a token recognition of the need
to reorganize the political control of the war, the War Council was
reconstituted in June as the Dardanelles Committee: the name itself
expresses the significance of the Dardanelles expedition – pressed
by Churchill, Lloyd George and Hankey (Secretary of the War
Council), resisted by Sir John French and the generals on the
western front – as the major military storm centre of the period.
Yet the executive decisions remained in the hands of the large and
unwieldy Cabinet, an arrangement which *The Times*, calling for 'a
smaller cabinet sitting every day', attacked as early as September
1915.[69] In November the Dardanelles Committee became the
War Committee of six leading politicians, organized on a more
formal basis; the Cabinet was still the ultimate authority. As there
was no place for him in the six, Churchill resigned from what he
called 'well-paid inactivity' and joined his regiment in France.[70]
Then Sir Edward Carson, who advocated a more vigorous attempt to open up an eastern front at Salonika in the Balkans,
resigned on policy grounds. As a violent Ulster Unionist, he had
never been very well disposed towards Asquith, and he now
became a powerful opponent.

Ministerial woes had been greatly increased by the incompetence
of Sir John French and of Lord Kitchener: Arnold Bennett, dining
at the McKennas', was informed 'that nobody *could* be worse at
the War Office than Kitchener. He wasn't even a brute.'[71] Asquith's solution was to divest the War Secretary of his additional
Staff functions, to give them, along with the title of Chief of the
Imperial General Staff, to Sir William Robertson, and to replace
French as Commander-in-Chief by Sir Douglas Haig. While these
changes marked clear gains in the British military potential

against the German, they also strengthened the military at the expense of the politicians. Asquith could not, however, escape as easily as this from the mounting criticism of his political leadership. Between the introduction of conscription for single men and universal conscription, there was a first-class crisis, when the provisional Conscription Bill introduced by the Government had to be withdrawn because of the hostility it met in a secret session of the House of Commons. In March 1916 Christopher Addison, Liberal M.P. and crony of Lloyd George, noted in his diary:

There appears to be a movement among the Conservatives to try and get L. G. to take a strong line and they are even prepared to go the length of recognizing him as P.M.[72]

From outraged Ireland came further slings and arrows when the Dublin Easter Rising made it clear that the more excitable Irish patriots were not prepared to wait upon the parliamentary game at Westminster. The incident was a shattering one for British Liberalism, and it brought the resignation of the Irish Secretary, Augustine Birrell, who had clearly been taken entirely by surprise. After an ill-conceived spell of repression (including fourteen executions), Lloyd George was sent to negotiate. He showed great skill in a difficult situation, though also, his enemies said, more than a dash of his proclivity for being all things to all men; be that as it may, many Liberals *believed* that Lloyd George had produced a viable settlement, and that it was the fault of Asquith that it was not put into effect.

In May *The Times* was calling for a reconstruction of the Government.[73] Kitchener's death necessitated a slight Cabinet reshuffle: Grey was recruited to the House of Lords, and Lloyd George, after some misgivings over the diminished powers now enjoyed by that Office, became War Secretary; E. S. Montagu took Lloyd George's place at the Ministry of Munitions, and Lord Curzon was added to the War Committee. On balance Asquith's position was weakened, for Kitchener, if stupid, had been loyal, and Grey had been a valuable right-hand man in the Commons. Public criticism of military strategy was muted, but within the innermost circles of politics men like Carson, Churchill and Lloyd George were genuinely uneasy about the way the war was going, particularly over the failure to open up an effective eastern front. According to Christopher Addison the last straw for Lloyd George was the way in which Rumania, unsupported by the Allies, was allowed to fall under German dominion.[74] That there was a good deal of overt criticism of the weakness of Asquith's control of domestic policies we have already seen. The actual issue which provoked the final crisis, that of a reform in the executive machinery of war government, was both a banner behind which the two lines of criticism could march without appearing disloyal or subversive, and a matter of substance in its own right; it was also a useful lever by which Lloyd George could apply the pressure of personal ambition. In September Asquith had tried, unsuccessfully, to appease the critics, by experimenting with a pair of Cabinet committees – one for war, one for finance. In an earlier period – in the middle of the Crimean War, say – the situation would have been resolved by an open vote in the House of Commons. Now that the war emergency had set the seal on the long process whereby such decisions were steadily being removed from the direct purview of Parliament, this was practically out of the question. To that extent denunciations of the backstairs intrigues which took place at the beginning of December are anachronistic. In any case the Government was a coalition, and bound to collapse if it lost the support of its Conservative members, though the Conservatives could not withdraw their support till they saw a viable alternative.

It is on this point that the coming-together of Lloyd George and Bonar Law is crucial. The two had nothing in common but their faults; in their virtues – Lloyd George's greatest was his warmth and generosity of spirit, Bonar Law's his austere honesty – they were poles apart, and for years Bonar Law had nursed a cordial detestation of the man he regarded as a ranting demagogue. The first mediating figure was Carson, but the man who did most to bring about the vital juncture was Sir Max Aitken, the owner of the *Daily Express*. In bringing together two men who had a basic common purpose by overcoming the prejudice of one of them, there was nothing very sinister. Less agreeable was the way in which Aitken's *Express* as well as Northcliffe's *Mail* helped to whip up a crisis atmosphere in a manner unfavourable to Asquith. Even so, these powerful organs of mass communication were not really going far beyond what many intelligent commentators believed to be necessary; they were in fact acting, in however distorted a form, as the agents of a change necessary to the safety and well-being of society at a time when the normal electoral process had been disrupted.

Lloyd George made his move on Friday, 1 December, proposing to Asquith that the war should be run directly by a reduced War Committee, which would take day-to-day decisions without reference to the larger Cabinet; Asquith would continue to have the name and forms of the Prime Ministership, but he would be excluded from this committee, of which Lloyd George would be the chairman. Lloyd George was without doubt chiefly motivated by a concern for the successful prosecution of the war; at the same time he cannot have been unaware that his proposal in effect meant the supersession of Asquith by himself. Asquith was not keen on the idea, but the impression he derived on Sunday, 3 December that the Unionists would not back him made him decide that evening to give way. The next day, accordingly, Lloyd George began making his plans, while The Times raised Asquith's temperature with an article saying that in the new arrangement he would be a complete nullity. Had this been channelled by Lloyd George through Lord Northcliffe (the owner of The Times), as Asquith believed, there would be more validity in the accusations often levelled against the press lords and against Lloyd George. In fact the article was written by Geoffrey Dawson, editor of The Times, who had seen Carson the day before; if anyone comes badly out of the incident it is Carson (not to mention Asquith, who demanded that Lloyd George should denounce the article). The article is best viewed as a reasonably independent-minded commentator's attitude to the crisis.[75]

Asquith might well have been more disturbed by the same morning's Manchester Guardian, which in the course of a vigorously anti-Asquith leader said of his ministry: 'Nothing is foreseen, every decision is postponed. The war is not really directed – it directs itself.'[76] In supporting Lloyd George's scheme, C. P. Scott could see as clearly as Dawson that it effectually meant the eclipse of Asquith. The Guardian's final remedy was in keeping with its high ideals, though not with the dire necessities of war: it suggested a general election.[77]

Asquith, indignant with Lloyd George, indignant with *The Times*, and misadvised by McKenna and his laissez-faire friends, informed Lloyd George that his projected system was unworkable. Lloyd George replied with his resignation. The following day (Tuesday 5 December) the Conservative members of the Cabinet pressed Asquith either to resign or to accept their own resignations. Asquith, therefore, went to the King with his own resignation, his friends telling him that, since none of his rivals was strong enough to form a ministry, he would soon be back. In fact Bonar Law, Lloyd George and their close associates were now concerting their final moves. Though Lloyd George was clearly going to be the dominant figure in any alternative ministry it was agreed that, if strategy demanded it, Bonar Law (who was summoned by the King that evening) should become Prime Minister. Bonar Law endeavoured to persuade Asquith to join a new Government, preferably as Lord Chancellor. After a first refusal on Tuesday evening, Asquith seemed more amenable the following afternoon when a meeting was held in the King's presence between Asquith, Bonar Law, Lloyd George, Balfour and Henderson; but later in the day Asquith stated categorically that he would not serve under Bonar Law or indeed under anyone else. Obviously a ministry headed by a Conservative (Bonar Law) and lacking the support of the Liberal leader (Asquith) would be weaker and less viable than one led by a Liberal (Lloyd George) and supported by the Conservative leader (Bonar Law). On Bonar Law's advice, therefore, the King on Thursday 7 December invited Lloyd George to form a ministry, and he, after his famous 'doping séance' with the leaders of the Labour Party, in which he got their support in return for a series of more or less extravagant promises, accepted the King's commission that evening.[78]

The final political consideration in Lloyd George's triumph was the support he got from Labour, and, more important, from a large section of the Liberal Party. It was here that Asquith and his friends miscalculated. On the Monday Addison and a fellow Liberal M.P., Kellaway, had initiated a canvass on behalf of Lloyd George, which revealed that Lloyd George had forty-nine out-and-out supporters, and that 126 others would support him if he could form a Government.[79] The potential patronage of the prime ministerial candidate was clearly an important influence, but the figures, taken in conjunction with the opinions expressed by the *Manchester Guardian* and the *Economist,* are also of interest in showing the existence, prior to the final *dénouement,* of a substantial body of Liberal discontent with Asquith's leadership. One of the reasons for this was certainly the Irish issue. Criticism was put in its most extreme form by the *Manchester Guardian* in the following words:

Mr Asquith permitted the Home Rule agreement negotiated by Mr Lloyd George to be torn up along with Government's pledges on which it was based.[80]

But the main reason turns us again towards the basic explanation of the change of ministry as the political summation of changes in economic and social attitudes which had already taken place. The *Guardian* expressed the belief that the new Government in contrast to the old, would not shrink from State control of mines, shipping, and 'any other industry vital to the war . . . or to the food of the people':

Who shall say that, if mightily conceived and boldly carried out, such a mobilization of our national resources may not be decisive in its effects on the war? At least such an attempt will be well worth making, and we have good hope that it may be made.[81]

The *Economist*'s epitaph on the Asquith ministry was that 'the country was always ahead of the Government'.[82] Lest the *Guardian* be thought a naïve and uncritical supporter of Lloyd George, it is worth noting that on 6 December it had forecast that Bonar Law would be the new Prime Minister, and that it kept up its advocacy of a general election long after Lloyd George was solidly ensconced in power.

Asquith, having rejected the attempts to include him in the new ministry, retired with his followers to the Opposition benches: they, not Lloyd George, had split the Liberal Party, though it was Lloyd George who confirmed the split by perpetuating his coalition with the Conservatives at the end of the war. The Liberal dichotomy between laissez-faire absolutists and radical social reformers had been apparent before the war, though it had been cast into relative obscurity by Asquith's brilliance as a parliamentary tactician; the war exposed it ruthlessly. Had there been no war the Liberals might have been left with enough time to adapt themselves to the needs of twentieth-century society, to trim their outdated dogmas, and open their ears to the aspirations of the working classes. But time was just what they did not have in 1916; the war had blown the bottom out of the hourglass. Labour, which had seemed so insignificant that up to 1916 the *Liberal Year Book* lumped Liberal and Labour Members of Parliament together in one biographical section of, as it were, 'goodies', and Conservatives and Irish Nationalists in two separate sections of 'baddies',[83] was now showing its mettle as a party whose collaboration was essential to the success of the war effort, a party, therefore, which was in a position to profit to the utmost from Liberal divisions. Sadly recognizing hard facts, the *Liberal Year Book* for 1919 (the first since 1916) put Liberal and Labour Members in separate tables.[84] Looked at through the telescope of the historian of broader social movements, the advance of the Labour Party and the retreat of the Liberal Party represent the gains of collectivism at the expense of laissez-faire. But for the war the process might have been somewhat different; as it was, by the time Liberals were in a position to cry 'Keynes' or 'Beveridge' at the trifling follies of the other two parties, it was too late.

NOTES TO CHAPTER FIVE

1. *New Statesman*, 14 February 1914, 30 May 1914, and 8 May 1915.
2. Trades Union Congress, *Annual Report 1915*, p. 287.
3. Labour Party, *Annual Conference Report 1916*, p. 35.
4. *The Times*, 22 May 1908.
5. For a brilliant analysis see B. Semmel, *Imperialism and Social Reform,* 1960. Semmel, however, grossly exaggerates when on page 234 he attributes working-class enthusiasm for the war in 1914 to gratitude for the social reforms given them by the imperialists.
6. See W. J. Braithwaite, *Lloyd George's Ambulance Waggon,* 1957.
7. See W. Beveridge, *Power and Influence,* 1953.
8. H. L. Gray, *War Time Control of Industry,* New York, 1918, p. 140.
9. S. J. Hurwitz, *State Intervention in Great Britain,* 1949, p. 156.
10. L. C. Money, *The Triumph of Nationalisation,* 1920, pp. 120–1.
11. Trades Union Congress, *Annual Report 1915,* p. 79.
12. *The Times History of the War,* Vol. VI, pp. 183–4.

13. *Hist. Min. Mun.*, Vol. VII, pt. 1, p. 5; Vol. II, pt. 4, p. 11.
14. ibid.
15. ibid., Vol. VII, pt. 2, p. 6.
16. Quoted in Vol. I, pt. 1, p. 70.
17. ibid, pp. 58–9.
18. E. V. Morgan, *Studies in British Financial Policy, 1914–22*, 1952, pp. 38–9. *Hist. Min. Mun.*, Vol. VII, pt. 1, pp. 6–7.
19. *Economist*, 23 January 1915. J. M. Rees, *Trusts in British Industry, 1914–21*, 1922, pp. 160–1.
20. *Board of Trade Journal, 1914*, p. 808.
21. *Daily Citizen*, 5 October 1914.
22. War Emergency: Workers' National Committee, *Report 1916*, p. 3.
23. P.P., 1915, LXXXVI, Cd. 8438.
24. Morgan, pp. 36–7.
25. W. Ashworth, *An Economic History of England, 1870–1939*, 1960, pp. 266–7.
26. *New Statesman*, 23 January 1915.
27. Morgan, p. 36.
28. *New Statesman*, 16, 23 and 30 January 1915. *Times*, 18 January 1915.
29. *House of Commons Debates*, 11 February 1915.
30. *The Times*, 12 February 1915.
31. *House of Commons Debates*, 11 February 1915.
32. Gray, *War Time Control of Industry*, p. 61.
33. *Hist. Min. Mun.*, Vol. VII, pt. 1, pp. 6–11 and *passim;* Vol. VIII, pt. 1, p. 34.
34. Vol. VII, pt. 1, p. 9.
35. Morgan, *Studies in British Financial Policy*, p. 35.
36. *New Statesman*, 6 March 1915.
37. *Hist. Min. Mun.*, Vol. I, pt. 2, p. 57. *Times*, 10 March 1915. *Manchester Guardian*, 10 and 19 March 1915.
38. *The Times*, 12 May 1915. *Manchester Guardian*, 12 May 1915.
39. C. Addison, *Politics from Within*, 1924, Vol. I, p. 58.
40. Gray, p. 30.
41. L. C. Money, *Triumph of Nationalisation*, p. 49. *Hist. Min. Mun.*, Vol. VIII, pt. 1, pp. 40–8.
42. *Manchester Guardian*, 2 July 1915.
43. *The Times*, 24, 26 May, 23 June 1915. *Economist*, 5 June 1915. *New Statesman*, 14 August 1915.
44. *Hist. Min. Mun.*, Vol. II, pt. 2, pp. 68–70.
45. P.P., 1915, X, Cd. 7866.
46. *Suffragette*, 10 September 1915.
47. Gray, p. 144. See generally, A. Salter, *Allied Shipping Control*, Oxford, 1925.
48. P.P., 1915, X, Cd. 8048, Cd. 8095.
49. *House of Commons Debates*, 21 September 1915.
50. Morgan, p. 41.
51. P.P., 1916, XIV, Cd. 8358.
52. ibid, p. 17.
53. *Report of Advisory Committee on London Traffic;* P.P., 1920, XXI, Cmd. 636, p. 10. Departmental Committee on Prices; P.P., 1916, XIV, Cd. 8358, p. 12.

54. Federation of British Industries, *What It Is and What It Does*, n.d. (1923 ?), p. 1.

55. *The Elements of Reconstruction*, 1916, p. 38.

56. ibid., pp. 38–9, 43.

57. pp. 47–8.

58. pp. 66–71, 57–8.

59. W. H. Dawson (ed.), *After War Problems*, 1917, p. 10.

60. ibid., pp. 116–20.

61. Labour Party, *Annual Conference Report 1916*, p. 135.

62. Gray, p. 205.

63. *Economist*, 21 October 1916.

64. *House of Commons Debates*, 15 November 1916.

65. ibid., 16 November 1916.

66. *The Times*, 22 November 1916.

67. S. Pollard, *The Development of the British Economy, 1914–50*, 1960, p. 42.

68. Morgan, *Studies in British Financial Policy*, p. 91.

69. *The Times*, 1 September 1915.

70. ibid., 13 November 1915.

71. Bennett, *Journals*, p. 156 (11 March 1916).

72. Addison, *Politics from Within*, p. 246.

73. *The Times*, 2 May 1916.

74. Addison, *Politics from Within*, p. 268.

75. On this paragraph see T. Jones, *Lloyd George*, 1951, pp. 83–7, and the sources cited there.

76. *Manchester Guardian*, 4 December 1916.

77. ibid., 6 December 1916.

78. On this paragraph see Jones *loc. cit.*

79. C. Addison, *Four and a Half Years*, 1934, p. 274.

80. *Manchester Guardian*, 7 December 1916.

81. ibid., 8 December 1916.

82. *Economist*, 9 December 1916.

83. *Liberal Year Book 1914*, pp. 39–76; *1915*, pp. 40–77; *1916*, pp. 41–78.

84. *Liberal Year Book 1919*, pp. 42–73.

CHAPTER SIX

Seasons of Discontent: 1917–1918

[I] SOCIETY AND SHORTAGES

1917, IN a war of ironic equivocation, was the most equivocal year of all. American entry ensured ultimate victory for the West, but for some who were that way inclined it later stirred the bitter reflection that Britain could no longer win a European war without external subvention;[1] although a great moral and, in time, economic boost for the Allies, its immediate effects were to increase Allied difficulties in that America now required her shipping for her own transport purposes, and directed her resources towards her own newly forming armies. President Wilson brought with him a firm and sincere moral ideal, which gave great comfort to troubled liberal consciences in Britain; but it also provided ready-made cant for British politicians of the older balance-of-power tradition. It can even be argued that American entry prolonged the war, giving the West European statesmen a blank cheque upon which they obediently pencilled President Wilson's ideals (elaborated in 1918 as the Fourteen Points), adding, in small writing, their own objective of un-conditional surrender. The Russian Revolutions sent tremors of excitement through the Left, but their upshot was dissension in the Labour movement and a hardening of the reactionary influence of the Right. Allied co-operation – the Supreme War Council was established in November – did help to strengthen the call for international action as a post-war safeguard to eternal peace; but Anglo-French relations were never in reality completely free of jealousy and suspicion.

Old economic theories were abandoned, indelible outlines for future social reform drawn, yet working-class discontent and industrial unrest reached a peak. Real care and attention were for the first time lavished on industrial and scientific reconstruction and much was written on the need for Britain to be economically competitive at the end of the war; but as she fought the war, former customers, cut off from supplies of British manufactured goods, developed their own industries and ceased to be customers even of the most competitive-minded British manufacturer. The old heavy industries were enjoying their last frantic burst of prosperity: soon they would be depressed industries. By the spring of 1917, Germany's submarine campaign was hitting British shipping hard, so that in addition to trying to speed up her own ship-building programme she appealed to America and Japan to increase theirs. At the end of the war the world had too many ships for its needs: Britain's unchallenged naval supremacy was gone for good, and her ship-building industry was becalmed in economic doldrums. Sir Maurice Hankey and a number of the younger naval officers put it to Lloyd George that the submarine challenge could be met by sending British ships out in convoy: Lloyd George was enthusiastic, but Admiral Sir John Jellicoe and the top naval brass said that the suggestion was out of the question. When the Prime Minister insisted on trying the new expedient there was a steady fall over the summer of 1917 in the loss of shipping tonnage.[2] By the end of the year the new investments in scientific and technological research had paid dividends in the form of submarine detection by high-frequency sound-waves and destruction by depth-charges and paravanes,[3] so that the running danger was under control; the major damage, however, had already been done. If Jellicoe and his colleagues had wished to burlesque themselves as obscurantist fuddy-duddies denying the younger generation the leadership it deserved, they could scarcely have been more successful.

The remark is even more desperately true of the Generals on the Western Front. The year's campaigns opened with the French spring offensive led by the youthful Nivelle (no shining example to his elders, it must be admitted), which brought such a disastrous burden of casualties as to provoke mutinies along the French front and permanently scar French morale. Sir Douglas Haig resolved that the year so badly begun should end in a blaze of definitive glory to be achieved by what was officially known as the Ypres Campaign of 1917 (the third Ypres Campaign of the war), but what became emotionally lodged in the British mind as 'Passchendaele'. The rights and wrongs of Haig's strategy need not detain us here; if he has been unfairly savaged by his opponents, his reputation has not been completely salvaged by his apologists, the most recent of whom admits the emptiness of one of most favoured defences of the General: that he was trying to take the weight off the French.[4] What is certain is that the campaign was fought over territory which was nothing less than a swamp, low-lying land which had been subject to unusually heavy rainfall and whose normal drainage system had been shattered by constant shelling, that it cost 244,897 casualties[5] and achieved microscopic military gains. The new year, despite Russia's virtual withdrawal from the war at the end of 1917, began rather better with a dramatic British break-through at Cambrai, which brought the ringing of bells from church steeples at home; unfortunately the resources needed to follow this up had been squandered at Passchendaele. In March the Germans completely reversed the picture by achieving a forty-mile penetration into the Allied lines; a second offensive in April opened a thirty-mile breach and at its direst moment it was the occasion of Haig's famous Order of the Day of 11 April. There was a further German advance in May. All of this, while never properly exploited by the Germans because of exhaustion and difficulty in maintaining communications, added up for the British to three months of anxious tension which not even the censorship could muffle. From May the war news got steadily better and in the summer the tunnel war at last broke out into a war of movement.

At no time during the First World War was there any widespread privation in Britain, and what might justly be called 'shortages' were only really apparent in 1917, when scarcity of sugar, potatoes, margarine (butter was often quite unobtainable) and coal brought a new phenomenon on the civic scene, the queue. (Beveridge in the study of *British Food Control* which he wrote later for the Carnegie Foundation was out by over six months when he declared that the first food queues, 'due to exceptional circumstances', appeared in October[6] – the proud Civil Servant has here got the better of the impartial historian.) Here is an account from the *Observer* of 8 April 1917:

The usual week-end potato and coal scenes took place in London yesterday. At Edmonton 131 vehicles were lined up at the gates of a coal depot at nine o'clock in the morning, while the crowd numbered several hundreds. There were also bread and potato queues of such a length that the police had to regulate them, and newcomers had to inquire which was the particular queue that they wanted. During last week the Edmonton District Council sold over fifty tons of seed potatoes.

In South London trolleymen with coals were besieged by people who had requisitioned all types of receptacles, including perambulators, wheelbarrows, go-carts and trucks, while others brought sacks, baskets and boxes. At a railway coal-siding the would-be purchasers assembled soon after seven o'clock in the morning and the queue of waiting women and children extended to a great length within an hour or so. Several policemen regulated the crowd, who first had to secure tickets at the coal merchant's office and then make their way to the siding, where the coal was served out to them directly from the railway trucks.

At Wrexham a big farm-wagon laden with potatoes already weighed into shillingsworths was brought into the square by agriculturalists who at once proceeded to sell them to all comers. The wagon was surrounded by hundreds of clamouring people, chiefly women, who scrambled on to the vehicle in the eagerness to buy. Several women fainted in the struggle, and the police were sent for to restore order.

Farnborough, Kent, was yesterday besieged by people who heard that a farmer named Staples had a large quantity of potatoes for sale at 1s. per gallon . . .

Although Lloyd George, succeeding where Asquith had failed, had appointed a Food Controller in the person of Lord Devonport, formerly H. E. Kearley, a self-made magnate of the retail trade, and had established a Food Ministry in Grosvenor House, where the lavish pink flesh of the Rubens murals was covered up to avoid offence to the young girls recruited as typists, any temptation to attribute a magical quality of reform to the Lloyd George Ministry, or to see the change of Government as the inevitable expression of a general will towards more efficient conduct of the war, is easily dispelled by a consideration of Lord Devonport's record. His egregious incompetence is a standing testimony to the influence of personality in history. Devonport had a fixation about what he called 'flaunting', and his first efforts were directed against the display in shop windows of luxury foodstuffs. There followed prohibitions against the feeding of game and the consumption of crumpets and sugar icing, and restrictions upon the kind of food that could be eaten in tea-shops between 3 and 5.30 pm. At times, according to Beveridge, the Food Ministry chiefs would sit in inquisition upon specimens of bakery and confectionery, solemnly deciding whether or not they conformed to the law's demands, the specimens later providing a sumptuous tea for the typists of the sugar department.[7]

As prices rose (to a shilling for a quartern loaf in the case of bread) and shortages developed, Government control of distribution appeared more desirable than ever. The new Food Controller's response was to publish on 3 February 1917 an appeal for voluntary rationing; by what was in effect a sort of Derby Scheme for food, each citizen was to restrict himself to four pounds of bread (or three pounds of flour), two and a half pounds of meat, and three-quarters of a pound of sugar per week:[8] as with the Derby Scheme compulsion was held in the background as a threat which could be applied if necessary, and supervisory powers were vested in local food committees. The scheme, apart from its reliance on public good will, had no basis in reality; the poor still ate far more bread and far less meat than provided for here – it was not uncommon for an agricultural labourer to consume up to fourteen pounds of bread a week – and sugar was already almost unobtainable in many places. At the beginning of May a Royal Proclamation on the saving of grain was read on successive Sundays in churches and chapels throughout the land, and a food economy campaign directed by a leading Conservative extrovert, Kennedy Jones, and assisted by Harry Lauder, was launched.[9] The entire effort more resembled a gigantic music-hall act than a serious effort to deal with the country's food problem.

Lord Devonport's one other contribution was the introduction, followed shortly by the abolition, of a system of meatless days; neither he nor the Government had the stomach for compulsory rationing. On 30 May he resigned; as neither Bob Smillie, the miners' leader, nor Addison, who since Lloyd George's accession had been at the Munitions Ministry, was willing to take on the job,[10] Lord Rhondda was summoned from the Local Government Board. Rhondda was a man of entirely different mettle, 'spare, dark, sensitive, with the look of a mystic' where Devonport had been 'well-fed, florid, grumpy and gruff'.[11] He forthwith secured from the Cabinet approval for the principle of registration for sugar: the country was divided into 2,000 districts, each with a local food office to which the householder sent in an application form for a card which would entitle him to half a pound of sugar a week, though he could have more if it was available in his locality. Imperfect the scheme undoubtedly was, but it was not even put into practice until the end of the year; the fear was that the introduction of even so rudimentary a form of rationing would damage civilian morale and give encouragement to the enemy.[12] When it was finally decided to implement sugar registration, there was, as might be expected, the urbane opposition of *Punch*. In a cartoon entitled 'David in Rhonddaland', David (who looks a little like Lloyd George) is having a trying conversation with the Mad Grocer (who looks a little like Lord Rhondda):

David: I'm often away from home. How do I get sugar?
The Mad Grocer: You don't: you fill up a form.
David: But I *have* filled up a form.
The Mad Grocer: Then you fill up another form.

Government action had in various places been anticipated by private and local initiative: the Birmingham Co-operative Society, for instance, introduced its own system of sugar cards in July 1917. Lord Rhondda's directive of August setting up statutory Food Control Committees throughout the country gave a further stimulus to progressive local authorities, such as those at Gravesend, Pontypool and Birmingham, to go ahead with their own rationing schemes.[13] Imports of tea, which had been maintained at about 15,000 tons per month between 1913 and 1916, fell drastically to about 6,000 in the summer of 1917, causing more queues and local rationing. Even with local schemes it was still possible for the footloose shopper to amass considerable quantities of scarce commodities. Sympathy for a woman who fainted in a tea-queue in Cardiff soon evaporated when it was discovered that she already had half a stone concealed about her person.[14]

The Times of 10 December 1917 listed the following as in short supply in London: sugar, tea, butter, margarine, lard, dripping, milk, bacon, pork, condensed milk, rice, currants, raisins, spirits, Australian wines. A week later it reported:

The food queues continue to grow. Outside the dairy shops of certain multiple firms in some parts of London women begin to line up for margarine as early as 5 o'clock on Saturday morning, some with infants in their arms, and others with children at their skirts. Over a thousand people waited for margarine at a shop in New Broad Street in the heart of the city, and in Walworth Road in the south-eastern side of London the queue was estimated to number about 3,000. Two hours later 1,000 of these were sent away unsupplied.[15]

In some areas workers were taking time off to relieve their wives who had been queueing for long spells. The biggest grievance of all was the high price of bread, already a shilling for a four-pound loaf (more than twice the pre-war price) in the spring of 1917. In September the Government, with the assistance of a subsidy, fixed the price at ninepence; from November there was also a subsidy for potatoes.[16]

Christmas 1917 was heralded by appeals from the new Director of Food Economy, Sir Arthur Yapp, for austerity, and was succeeded by stories in the press of a 'meat crisis' or even a 'meat famine'. Provision had been made for retail price control in September 1917, and many butchers were said to be closing their shops in protest at the prices decreed by the local food committees. The Government brought a new word into everyday language when, at the end of February, it imposed upon London a system of rationing for meat depending upon the clipping of 'coupons' from the customer's ration card. From 7 April meat rationing of this type was applied to the whole country, and in May the weekly ration was reduced to three-quarters of a pound. Universal rationing (by registration card, not coupon) followed for tea and butter.[17]

In December 1916 and January 1917, domestic rail services were slashed, and prices increased by as much as 50 per cent; newspaper prices doubled in February (*The Times* from one penny to twopence, the *Daily Mail* from a halfpenny to a penny). But food remained the principal item in the vastly increased cost of living: the average weekly food bill for the 'standard' working-class family (4·57 units and 1·2 supplementary earners) had risen in June 1918 to 47s 3d, the average weekly total bill to 75s 5d. With the emphasis on essentials, increases were proportionally greater for unskilled than for skilled workmen. The Board of Trade reckoned on an 81 per cent increase in the cost of living for the unskilled workman's family as between July 1914 and June 1918; for the skilled workman's family, the figure was 67 per cent.[18] Prices of meat (about double pre-war prices in the summer of 1917), bread and potatoes flattened out somewhat with Government regulation from the autumn of 1917, but other items, bacon for instance (1s 8d per pound in July 1917), continued to rise steeply. Bread, from December 1916, was 'Government Bread', which at first meant no more than that it contained a high (and beneficial) quantity of husk. Later all sorts of foreign substances, such as potato flour and bean flour, were introduced; certain combinations were found to go 'ropey' in warm weather.[19] Upon this bread the civilian, from late 1917 onwards, spread margarine manufactured under the direction of the Ministry of Food, and with it he drank the anonymous blend, Government Control Tea.

Shortages and standardization of available foods contributed to the process of communizing social experience and telescoping class; on the whole, however, it would seem that the much-advertised culinary innovations, such as haricot-bean fritters, savoury oatmeal pudding, barley rissoles, and nut rolls[20] were aimed at those middle- and upper-class households where protein consumption in pre-war days had been high. Mrs Peel in her *Eat-Less-Meat Book,* published in 1917, pointed the contrast between the pre-war menu of a modest middle-class household and that of a labourer. The middle-class menu ran:

FRIDAY. *Breakfast:* fish cakes, sardines, fried bacon, bread, butter, marmalade, tea, coffee. *Dinner:* rabbits, potatoes, gooseberry tart, rice pudding, cream, sugar. *Tea:* bread, butter, jam, cakes, tea. *Supper:* cheese, biscuits, bread, butter, cakes, cocoa.

SATURDAY. *Breakfast:* fish, sardines, fried bacon, bread, butter, marmalade, tea, coffee. *Dinner:* beefsteak, potatoes, cauliflower, queen of puddings, rice pudding, cream. *Tea:* bread, butter, marmalade, cakes, tea. *Supper:* cheese, biscuits, bread, butter, cakes, cocoa, milk, coffee.

SUNDAY. *Breakfast:* bacon, poached eggs, bread, butter, marmalade, tea, coffee. *Dinner:* roast beef, Yorkshire pudding, roast potatoes, rice pudding, gooseberry tart, cream, sugar. *Tea:* bread, butter, jam, cakes, tea. *Supper:* cheese, biscuits, bread, butter, cake, cocoa, milk.

MONDAY. *Breakfast:* bacon, sardines, bread, butter, marmalade, tea, coffee. *Dinner:* cold beef, salad, potatoes, sponge cake, custard pudding, rice. *Tea:* bread, butter, cakes, marmalade, tea. *Supper:* eggs, biscuits, bread, butter, cakes, cocoa, milk.

TUESDAY. *Breakfast:* fried bacon, poached eggs, bread, butter, marmalade, tea, coffee. *Dinner:* cold beef, salad, hashed beef, potatoes, stewed fruit, rice pudding. *Tea:* bread, butter, cakes, marmalade, tea. *Supper:* cheese, biscuits, bread, butter, cakes, cocoa, coffee, milk.

WEDNESDAY. *Breakfast:* fried bacon, sardines, bread, butter, marmalade, tea, coffee. *Dinner:* roast mutton, jelly, potatoes, cabbage, gooseberry tart, pancakes. *Tea:* bread, butter, cakes, jam, marmalade, tea. *Supper:* cheese, biscuits, bread, butter, cakes, cocoa, milk.

THURSDAY. *Breakfast:* chicken and tongue mould, bread, butter, marmalade, tea, coffee. *Dinner:* cold mutton, potatoes, salad, curry, rice pudding, stewed fruit. *Tea:* bread, butter, cakes, jam, marmalade, tea. *Supper:* cheese, biscuits, bread, butter, cakes, cocoa, milk.

Wealthier middle-class families, Mrs Peel added, would, for the adults, have had a late dinner. The trend during the war was for more and more people to have their main meal in the middle of the day.

The labourer's pre-war menu read as follows:

FRIDAY. *Breakfast:* bread, cheese, tea. *Dinner:* potatoes, bread, tea. *Tea:* bread, butter, tea.

SATURDAY. *Breakfast:* 'dip', bread, butter, tea. *Dinner:* sausages, bread. *Tea:* bread, cocoa, jam, tea.

SUNDAY. *Breakfast:* bacon, bread, toast, tea. *Dinner:* meat, potatoes, Yorkshire pudding. *Tea:* bread, pie, tea cakes, tea.

MONDAY. *Breakfast:* bacon, bread, tea. *Dinner:* bacon, bread, tea. *Tea:* bacon, bread, tea.

TUESDAY. *Breakfast:* bread, meat, tea. *Dinner:* meat, bread, tea. *Tea:* meat, bread, tea.

WEDNESDAY. *Breakfast:* bacon, bread, tea. *Dinner:* meat, bread, tea. *Tea:* eggs, 'dip', bread, tea.

THURSDAY. *Breakfast:* bread, butter, tea. *Dinner:* meat, bread, 'dip', tea. *Tea:* meat, bread, butter, tea.[21]

For all classes the hardships of austerity, such as they were, were made grimmer by the intensification of German bombing raids. The worst raid of the whole war came on 13 June 1917, when 162 people were killed and 432 injured, and the autumn that followed was so full of menace that Londoners took to the practice of sheltering in the Tubes, while some of those who could afford it moved to the safer locations of Bath or Bournemouth. The last raid took place over Kent on 17 June 1918, when there were no casualties. Altogether, between January 1915 and April 1918 there were 51 Zeppelin raids, causing 1,913 casualties, and between December 1914 and June 1918 there were 57 aeroplane raids, causing 2,907 casualties. Total civilian casualties were 5,611, including 1,570 fatalities, of whom 1,413 were killed in air attacks.[22] The town which suffered most of all was Dover, especially in the autumn of 1917 when the attacks came in waves lasting twenty to thirty minutes. Dug-outs were constructed and the caves at each end of the town developed into shelters, so that by the end of the year there was accommodation for about 25,000 people. House-holders who so desired were supplied with materials for building shelters in the chalky slopes of their own gardens.[23]

For air-raid victims in all parts of the country a dribble of assistance was provided by the National Relief Fund, which also continued to make payments to unemployed boarding-house keepers in the East Coast resorts.[24] Attacks by air and sea apart, some domestic employments were not without risks of their own: deaths from poisoning were not uncommon among those handling explosives, and there were occasional explosions, the worst being that of January 1917 in a munitions factory at Silvertown in east London, which resulted in considerable loss of life:

Looking down the Thames I saw a high column of yellow flames rising, as I thought, from the river ... The sky ... became overspread with the loveliest colours ... The phenomenon lasted, I should think, several seconds. Its disappearance was accompanied by a terrific explosion, rising and shattering and dying away with an angry growl.[25]

Nerves were frayed, tempers tried; discontent mounted. Yet, even discounting press stories of working-class affluence, real gains were made. It is difficult to discern a clear pattern of earnings at this stage of the war, but by its end wages had doubled, had, in other words, kept ten or twenty per cent ahead of the rise in cost of living. At the same time wage rises often lagged well behind the most recent rise in the cost of living, and households with a large number of non-wage-earners were extremely hard hit. When the Working Classes Cost of Living Committee reported in 1918 that the working classes, as a whole, were in a position to purchase food of substantially the same nutritive value as in June 1914, this was perhaps almost as much a condemnation of pre-war conditions as a tribute to wartime reorganization. The Report comments fairly cautiously:

Indeed our figures indicate that the families of unskilled workmen were slightly better fed at the later date, in spite of the rise in the price of food. This conclusion is more than confirmed by the reports we have obtained from the Medical Officers to the Education Authorities in the great cities. From London it is officially reported, after inspection of all the children entering the school, that 'the percentage of children found in a poorly nourished condition is considerably less than half the percentage of 1913'. A similar improvement is shown by the figures furnished by Birmingham, Bolton, Bradford, Bristol, Glasgow and Nottingham. The general impression, especially of the poorer children, is favourable, and the view that parents are now better able to give their children the necessary food is borne out by the information we have received as to the number of meals provided to 'necessitous children' by the local education authorities. It is only in very exceptional cases that education authorities are supplying anything like as many meals as before the war; in most places the number has fallen to about half (Nottingham, Stoke, and Sheffield) and a quarter (London and Bolton), and in some places (as in Birmingham and Liverpool) it is hardly necessary to provide meals at all. The last available figures for England and Wales, those for 1917, compared with the estimated number for 1914, show a decline by about four-fifths in the country as a whole.[26]

Other evidence accumulated by the Board of Trade and the Ministry of Food cuts various ways. Even when the meat ration was at its most exiguous, it was found that 'a certain part of the population, especially in Scotland and in some country districts, did not choose, or could not afford, to purchase the full amount to which their ration entitled them.'[27] On the other hand the reluctance of purchasers in other areas to take such lowly products of the butcher's art as black pudding, a traditionally North-country and Scottish dish, soon meant that they were released from rationing. There is a similar implication, and perhaps there are other more dubious ones, in the Ministry of Food circular of 26 June 1918:

In order to utilize to the best advantage imported meat which may not be suitable for issue to the public in its original form, the sale of beef sausages has been permitted without any coupon.[28]

The warning for the historian is an old one: that it is dangerous to take British society, whether in eating habits or anything else, as geographically homogeneous. Certain areas of Scotland, with a long history of hard times, were still almost medieval in their austerity. However, the wartime pressures of rationing and State control were towards greater uniformity among classes as well as regions. Under State-directed distribution, prime home-killed joints for the first time found their way to poorer areas, where price control made them accessible to local housewives; a proportion of frozen meat ended up in the West End.

For the rich there were other interferences with normal pleasures. Petrol was very strictly rationed, and restrictions were placed on restaurant meals. The first Public Meals Order of 5 December 1916 limited day meals to two courses, and evening meals to three courses – not at all harsh considering that cheese did not count as a course, and soup only as half a course. In April 1917 rationing by weight was introduced in restaurants, and in the last stages of the war coupons were clipped in restaurants as well as in shops. 'The profiteers . . . are still with us,' Blumenfeld noted in his diary in March 1917. One notorious instance, brought about by the search for substitute foodstuffs, was the great wave of profitable speculation in beans and peas at the beginning of the year.[29] Conspicuous consumption was still apparent, much jewellery on view, and dress sales higher in 1917 than in 1915. Theatres continued to prosper famously, and not just in London.

Gilded upper-class life, strikingly depicted in the war novels of Ford Madox Ford, continued remarkably unchanged. Colonel Repington entered some interesting confidences in his diary:

Lady Ridley and I discussed what posterity would think of us in England. We agreed that we should be considered rather callous to go on with our usual life when we were reading of 3,000 to 4,000 casualties a day. But she said that people could not keep themselves elevated permanently on some plane above the normal, and she supposed that things around us explained the French Revolution and the behaviour of the French nobility.[30]

Upper-class life continued, but there were changes. The two

most obvious developments were the blows struck by wartime taxation at the landed interest, and the intrusion of businessmen into the political élite. The first interpretable figures after the war show a decline in the proportion of wealth and income held by owners of land,[31] and an acceleration in the breaking up of the great landed estates.[32] In neither case was the process new, but war deaths had multiplied the burden of death duties. The mass entry of the businessmen can very precisely be pinned to the change of Government in December 1916.[33] Certain organs of the press had for some time been calling for 'a businessman's government', and the social climate, as with other changes associated with Lloyd George, was favourable to his innovations in governmental personnel. There was nothing new about the businessman in politics: politics from Victorian times to 1914, we have seen, had been very much the politics of a class welded out of the old aristocracy and the newer aristocracy of industrial wealth; but to reach high office the businessman had had to climb a political ladder. If the first distinctive characteristic of Lloyd George's ministerial businessmen was their numerical strength, the second was that in a large number of cases they had served little or no political apprenticeship at all. In this category were Sir Albert Stanley, manager of the London Underground and General Omnibuses Combine, Joseph Maclay, a Glasgow shipowner who refused to take a seat in either House of Parliament, Lord Rhondda, a coal-owner, Lord Devonport, an ennobled shop-keeper, Sir Alfred Mond, a chemicals manufacturer, Sir Frederick Cawley, Albert Illingworth and R. E. Prothero. Two further considerations enhance the significance of this new recruitment to government office: first, it coincided with a great extension in the powers and functions of government, and secondly, it was bolstered and consolidated by the great patriotic prestige which businessmen had acquired in this war of machines and industrial systems.

The other striking, though numerically slight, modification in the composition of the political élite was one which has been touched on already in a different connexion, the rise of the Labour politician. Clynes, Barnes, Roberts, Henderson, all came from un-impeachable working-class origins, though it is perhaps more important to note that they had all, in contrast to many of the new

businessmen, served a very definite apprenticeship in politics. The
political Labour movement since the end of the nineteenth century was the obvious vehicle for the ambitious member of the
working classes. Arthur Henderson, the first to reach Cabinet
office, had done sterling work as general secretary of the Labour
Party. The new infusion did not necessarily strengthen the
country's political leadership – in some cases it manifestly weakened
it – but it did publicize the ideal of the professional: Maclay was
made Shipping Controller because he knew about ships, Devonport Food Controller because he knew about the buying and selling of food, Barnes Minister of Pensions because he knew about
working-class hardship. An older principle had prevailed when in
the general shuffle of May 1915 Asquith had appointed Henderson
President of the Board of Education, for which he had no obvious
qualifications. The ideal of the professional extended from
parliamentary politics into administration and the Civil Service.
As ministries and government departments expanded, Lloyd
George again drew upon industry for his top personnel.[34] This
specific movement, designed for the purposes of waging war,
interacted with a much greater one: the rise within industry of the
managerial class. At the end of the war the salaried segment of the
community had greatly expanded.

On the whole the wartime trend was towards increased central-
ization of power, though there was much local initiative in such
matters as Air Raid Precaution and food rationing. One of the
commonest administrative devices of the war was the local committee or tribunal, with powers over matters varying from the
determination of the genuineness of a young man's claim to have a
conscientious objection to war, to the ploughing of pasture land.
Representatives of labour and the odd *nouveau riche* tradesman
figured on these committees, but by and large their régime marked
an Indian summer of power and glory for the traditional local
bigwigs. Otherwise the war certainly did create a strong breeze of
egalitarianism. In the hustle of wartime living many of the more
formal symbols of position were quietly abandoned: top hats and
butterfly collars disappeared.[35] Many of the more tangible products of position became unobtainable: petrol rationing after
August 1916 steadily drove that luxury toy, the motor-car, out of
sight. In the Army the badges of officerdom made too obvious a

target for enemy snipers, so officers adopted a uniform not very dissimilar from that of their men. The Army did its best to maintain the rigidities of hierarchical distinction, but could not destroy altogether a unity kindled in upheaval and shared danger. More positive were the self-confidence and sense of purpose engendered in a working class which waged many successful battles against authority, and which had its sons lauded as saviours of their country. A decline in the numbers of servants, and of sempstresses and workers in the women's luxury trades, meant a deflation of one of the main bolsters of class-distinction. Political recognition of the rise of the working class and of the female sex was embodied in the Representation of the People Act of 1918, which as well as giving women householders and wives of householders the vote – provided they were over thirty – gave the vote to all men over twenty-one.

[II] THE TEMPER OF LABOUR

The reasons for the extreme working-class discontent of 1917 were varied, and differed in emphasis from place to place; among them were the Conscription Acts, and the manner in which they were applied by over-zealous military authorities, the Munitions Acts, with 'leaving certificates' still a special grievance, the attempts by private employers to extend dilution, high prices, bad housing, and the resentment of skilled workers who found themselves overtaken in the wage race by unskilled. It was in 1917 that the method of working-class action through shop stewards and unofficial representatives, developed on Clydeside and elsewhere in the earlier years of the war, began to react positively with rapidly growing working-class resentment. First news of the Russian Revolution in March 1917 caused great excitement in all corners of the Labour movement, but above all to the advocates of workshop organization. Stress and strain of war, and the sight of much affluence, often just out of reach, were other less tangible agents of unrest.

A hundred years of British history seem to have taught that while the poor are steadily diminishing in numbers, slums are always with us. Since 1913 when it was estimated that the country required a hundred or a hundred and twenty thousand houses, not only had very little been done to meet this requirement, but, with the suspension of much normal building activity, and the congregation of hordes of people in the munitions centres, the situation had actively deteriorated. Thus, although the problem was not a new one, it now came into sharp focus, a grim contour running strongly or faintly across every chart of domestic grievances, a manifest evil when politicians were calling for sacrifice in the name of a better order. It so happened, as with the Royal Commission on Venereal Diseases which, though appointed before the war, delivered its pronouncements into the receptive wartime atmosphere, that the Royal Commission on Housing in Scotland, appointed in October 1912, reported in 1917. Its words on Glasgow need no gloss:

In the older tenements or 'lands', the passages are often dark, narrow, and foul-smelling. Some passages are T-shaped, and at the farther end it is necessary to light a match in the daytime in order to distinguish the doors. Those doors and the partitions are so poorly constructed that there is no privacy even within the houses.

In other cases there is a single long passage traversing the tenement, with doors on either side giving access to different houses (in certain 'back lands' in the Cowcaddens Ward in Glasgow there are as many as ten or twelve houses opening off one passage). With this arrangement through ventilation is impossible.

There is one instance in the Anderston district of Glasgow in which a whole street of high tenements, with damp and dark sunk flats below the level of the street (which is only 19 feet wide), has been wedged into a V-shaped space between two important converging thoroughfares. One witness described the area as follows: 'The sunk flat houses even in a hot dry summer remain damp and unwholesome. The stairs down to these houses are almost invariably dark and dirty, the passages pitch dark on the brightest day, so that only by feeling along the walls can one discover the doors. The bulk of the houses are of the made-down type, very dark lobbies (now lighter by night than day owing to the Corporation's recommendation that incandescent burners be put on the stairhead lamps) . . . In all these closes the stairs are filthy and evil-smelling, water-closets continually choked, and foul water running down the stairs, sickly cats everywhere spreading disease. . . . One street is known as 'The Coffin Close', so bad is its repute – narrow stairs, and dark twisting lobbies, with no light and absolutely no air.[36]

The Commission of Enquiry into Working Class Unrest of June 1917 remarked on bad housing conditions in other parts of Britain. Those at Barrow, a munitions centre where population had expanded greatly, were described as 'a crying scandal':[37] of such new houses as had been made available since the outbreak of war, almost half had been built by the armaments firm of Vickers. In Wales and Monmouth, it was reported:

. . . the workers feel deeply discontented with their housing accommodation and with their unwholesome and unattractive environment generally. The towns and villages are ugly and overcrowded; houses are scarce and rents are increasing, and the surroundings are insanitary and depressing. The scenery is disfigured by unsightly refuse tips, the atmosphere polluted by coal dust and smoke and the rivers spoilt by liquid refuse from works and factories. Facilities for education and recreation are inadequate and opportunities for the wise use of leisure are few.[38]

Housing was a background cause of the rising ire of the working classes.

In the foreground stood the more obvious wartime problems. Before its fall the Asquith Government had been negotiating for official trade union support for the extension of dilution to work other than that connected with the manufacture of war materials, but had failed to win over the Amalgamated Society of Engineers. The desire to maximize national productivity in all commodities was now inextricably bound up with, and overshadowed by, the desire to release as many fit men as possible for service in the armed forces. When, therefore, the new Government again proposed dilution for private work in March 1917, it followed this up on 3 April with the withdrawal of the 'trade cards' scheme, which had been a great triumph for the Amalgamated Society of Engineers, in giving them control of the call-up of their own skilled men. In place of the 'trade cards' scheme the new Ministry of National Service operated a 'schedule of protected occupations', and began to accelerate the release of skilled men for military service; greater use was made of the substitution schemes of September 1916, which had established yet another set of special local committees, this time charged with the task of finding unfit substitutes for militarily fit men.[39]

Before any enactment had been made in regard to the dilution issue, a Rochdale engineering firm saw fit to cash in on what it believed to be the Government's intention, and began to introduce dilutees into its own private work: an immediate strike followed (3 May). But while the mailed fist of military authority at once punched some of the strikers into the Army, the gloved hand of government extracted a fine from the firm, a recognition of the justice of the strikers' case. Meantime national and local grievances throughout the country produced the unofficial 'May strikes' which began on 10 May and lasted for a fortnight. The gloved hand predominated this time, for although eight leaders were charged under the Defence of the Realm Acts the charges were dropped, and the Government agreed that all outstanding complaints would be dealt with by negotiation between Government and trade union leadership; again unofficial action had brought a formal gain.[40]

On 13 June the Government appointed a series of Commissions of Enquiry into Industrial Unrest in eight separate areas in Great Britain. The problem was so urgent that reports were to be furnished within three weeks, though in fact the eight reports and separate summary were not published till 17 July. In the northeast, the commissioners found high food prices the most general cause of complaint. Any image of working-class affluence in this part of the country is severely shaken by their report:

The high prices of staple commodities have undoubtedly laid a severe strain upon the majority of the working classes, and in some instances have resulted in hardship and actual privation. It is no doubt true that in some industries wages have risen to such an extent as largely to compensate for the increased cost of living, but there are workers whose wages have been raised very slightly, if at all, and some whose earnings have actually diminished, and on these the high food prices have borne heavily.[41]

Resentment was aggravated by the belief that high prices were largely due to profiteering and a lack of courage on the part of the Government in dealing with the matter. Leaving certificates and other aspects of the Munitions of War and Defence of the Realm Acts also aroused hostility.[42]

In the north-west area the investigators reported that high food prices were the main cause of unrest: the cost of living, they said, had gone up by 70 to 75 per cent, and the cost of food by 102 per cent, while wages at the most had risen by 40 to 50 per cent, and in some cases not at all. Other sources of anger and irritation were bad housing, military bumbledom, and weak beer which, to make matters worse, was available only at inconvenient hours.[43] The Commissioners for Yorkshire and the East Midlands found food prices and profiteering the basic grievances. They also reported a marked distrust among ordinary working men of the Government and of the official trade union leadership; the latter, the commissioners said, helped to explain the strength of the shop stewards. As a remedy they recommended a programme of social legislation, to which one of the investigators, J. J. Mallon, socialist warden of Toynbee Hall, added a rider calling for higher taxation of the wealthy.[44] In the west Midlands, London and the south-east, the south, the west and Scotland, where there was a strong conviction as to the prevalence of profiteering, food prices were again the chief grievance. While a rather wordy report by the commissioners for Wales elaborated upon the poverty of the whole texture of Welsh social and economic life, the London report contained specific references to a sense of 'inequality of sacrifice' and want of confidence in the Government, and the Midlands report to anger over the leaving certificates' system.[45] The only true note of optimism was that contained in the Scottish report which declared that 'on the whole, the aggregate weekly incomes of industrial workers keep pace with the cost of living.'[46]

The squabble between the Amalgamated Society of Engineers and the Government over the extension of dilution to private work was meantime continuing. Since the revelations of the Commissions on Industrial Unrest suggested that Addison, though undoubtedly a man of progressive sympathies, might be better employed elsewhere than at the Ministry of Munitions he was, in October, moved to the new post of Minister of Reconstruction, while Churchill returned to front bench politics as Minister of Munitions; almost immediately he dropped the contentious proposal for private dilution, and abolished the equally contentious leaving certificates. Free mobility of labour was not thereby restored: D.O.R.A. Regulation 8B of April 1915, which had been designed to prevent employers from enticing workers from one factory to another, remained in force, and a new regulation was introduced prohibiting a worker engaged on one class of work from changing to a different class.[47] None the less there were real concessions to working-class sentiment. Labour's belief in itself and its determination to voice its grievances and aspirations were well demonstrated at the 1917 congress of the T.U.C., which, the *Observer*[48] commented, marked the beginning of a change of mood throughout the entire Labour movement. Arthur Henderson and Sidney Webb completed their draft of a new constitution for the Labour Party, which, while retaining something of the old federal quality, sought by making provision for the establishment of local constituency parties to give it a more homogeneous national basis, turning the ramshackle structure into something more like the efficient mass electoral machine necessary, if Labour were to compete successfully with other political parties. The new constitution which, in addition, committed the Party to a clear socialist objective, came before the Labour Party conference in January 1918, and, after a second conference, was finally adopted.[49]

The new Labour Party constitution marked a consolidation in the strength of the formal, political, and official aspect of the Labour movement. The informal, unofficial and mainly industrial aspect had further successes of its own, which, once again, involved the official industrial leadership. On 26 November 1917, a strike broke out at Coventry over the non-recognition of shop stewards; the trade union leadership was forced to intervene, and in December the position of the shop stewards was recognized in the 'National Shop Stewards Agreement'.[50] Although the worst governmental restraint on mobility of labour, the leaving certificate, had been abolished, the employers in July 1918 developed on their own account a system of 'embargoes' designed to avoid a costly bidding among themselves for scarce labour: further unofficial strikes, again beginning in Coventry and spreading through Birmingham to most of the Midlands, culminated successfully in the withdrawal of the 'embargoes'.

For the Government, the essential problem was to 'comb out' yet more men for the armies of the western front, so drastically depleted in the Passchendaele offensive. The problem was put before the leaders of the Labour movement at the 'Man

Power Conference' which sat between 3 and 5 January 1918; so great was the need for the complete sympathy of the Labour movement, and so strong the muddled aspirations which President Wilson had kindled, that on the last day of the conference Lloyd George made a formal pronouncement of his war aims. On 6 February there came a new Man Power Act which made a bonfire of most of the remaining exemptions from military service. A national conference of shop stewards condemned this measure out of hand, and the trade union leadership kept the Government engaged in delicate negotiation, but the news of German victories in March crumbled away resistance, even among unofficial agitators. A more drastic Military Service Bill of 9 April which brought a further cancelling of exemptions had no effective opposition to face, but, when in June, the Government attempted to extend the War Munitions Volunteer Scheme, which came very close to industrial conscription, trade union resistance was so great that the proposals were withdrawn.[51] The distinction between military and industrial conscription may, philosophically, be a nice one: if men at the front are forfeiting liberty and life, is it morally just that men in the factories should have freedom to strike, and to push up wages? Some of those who resisted military conscription gave as one of their reasons the likelihood that military conscription would lead to industrial conscription. Matters would undoubtedly have been simpler for the Government if it could have gone even farther than the harsh and bitterly contested restrictions which it introduced, and it is, above all, a tribute to the growing strength of the British Labour movement that nothing which really resembled industrial conscription was introduced in this country. At a time when so many sawdust ideals were collapsing, it was as well that the substance of industrial freedom was not irreparably damaged.

Beneath the surface discontent, for which there were real enough reasons, there were equally real, and more enduring, achievements. Most obviously eye-catching was the success in office of leading members of the Labour Party, though even this could serve to unsettle disgruntled spirits. G. N. Barnes was modestly competent as Minister of Pensions, till he replaced Arthur Henderson in the War Cabinet; J. R. Clynes won many plaudits, first as Under-Secretary at the Food Ministry, then as

Food Controller. In politics a revolution was taking place akin to that in seventeenth-century England, when by cutting off the King's head and running the country themselves the Parliamentarians made nonsense for ever of the Stuart claim that there were mysteries of State which only a King could deal with; so too had Henderson, Clynes, Barnes and Roberts made nonsense of the tale that, good as Labour chaps might be on wages and hours of work, they were not fit to govern. The *Observer*[52] predicted that in ten years time Clynes would be Prime Minister of a Labour Government; actually there was a Labour Government in six years, and Clynes just missed being Prime Minister.

[III] CHANGING MINDS

The propaganda techniques of the First World War were afterwards the subject of many exhaustive and more or less hostile studies. In one of the best of these Professor H. D. Lasswell offered the following definition:

It refers solely to the control of opinion by significant symbols, or to speak more concretely and less accurately, by stories, rumours, reports, pictures and other forms of social communication. Propaganda is concerned with the management of opinions and attitudes by the direct manipulation of social suggestion rather than by altering the conditions in the environment or the organism.[53]

From the start propaganda had to be directed at the fairly routine tasks of recruiting, saving, economizing and so on. When the Ministry of National Service was founded one of its main functions seemed to be the purchase of space in the press from which to exhort the older members of the community to offer their services for domestic war work: in one advertisement a young soldier addresses one of his elders in a familiar phrase which had now taken on an admonitory connotation: 'It's a business of blood for me; it's business as usual for you.' To boost the War Savings Campaign of the latter part of the war, use was made of Whistler's 'Portrait of the Artist's Mother': however, to make sure that people got the message, it was felt to be necessary to ruin the painting by printing across it the words, 'Old Age Must Come'.[54]

But beyond these relatively innocuous matters, propaganda was required, in the words of Professor Lasswell,

to mobilize the animosity of the community against the enemy, to maintain friendly relations with neutrals and allies, to arouse the neutrals against the enemy, and to break up the solid wall of enemy antagonism.

It was to the last three objectives rather than the first that the Secret Propaganda Bureau at Wellington House devoted most of its energies; for mobilizing the animosity of British society, there was from 1914, right through 1916, a plethora of preachers, politicians, and pressmen, who scarcely needed the encouragement of the Governmental agencies. Till late 1916 the propaganda machine practically ran under its own steam, churning out a miscellaneous array of slogans, both idealistic and vicious; after 1916 the Government had deliberately to prime the machine by feeding these by-products back into it.

How deep a change there was in the attitudes of ordinary men and women towards the war in 1917 is impossible to determine. From the start there had been stories of working men – apart from articulate syndicalists and shop stewards – who declared that, since society had never done anything for them, the war was no cause of theirs.[55] Yet even in the I.L.P., the strongest of all pacifist and anti-war organizations, patriotic enthusiasm, moral pressure, and conscription were strong enough to ensure that the majority of the eligible members of the party went into the army: in Bradford, historic birth-place of the party, the absent membership in 1918 was accounted for as follows – 429 in His Majesty's Forces, nineteen in His Majesty's Prisons, with, in addition, twenty-nine conscientious objectors on Alternative Service.[56] Even the Glasgow socialist paper *Forward* ran a weekly column of extreme jingoism by 'Rob Roy' (Dr Stirling Robertson). On the whole, therefore, it would seem that almost everyone was touched by war fever. 1917 was not so much marked by disillusionment as by discontent. But there was a touch of despair too, as the scale of the terrible bleeding of the war began to seep into the national consciousness: diarists who had once been full of cheery predictions as to the early end of the war are now wondering if it will ever end at all.[57]

Control of propaganda was undoubtedly one facet of warfare to which the Lloyd George ministry was temperamentally better suited than the Asquith ministry. Lloyd George's innovation was a Department of Information whose function it was to supervise four subdivisions: Wellington House, which continued to provide material for domestic and for neutral consumption; a Cinema Division devoted to the exploitation of this first of the twentieth-century mass media; a Political Intelligence Division charged with ascertaining the state of public opinion throughout the world; and a News Division which was responsible for filtering war news through to the British public. The head of the Department of Information, first C. H. Montgomery of the Foreign Office, then Colonel John Buchan, had the assistance of an Advisory Committee containing three leading newspapermen, Lord Northcliffe (later, when he went on a mission to America, replaced by Lord Beaver-brook), Robert Donald (editor of the *Daily Chronicle*) and C. P. Scott; just as Lloyd George believed that for shipping control you needed a ship owner and for food control a shopkeeper, he saw that for propaganda you needed newspapermen. Subsequently, as a further step in the co-ordination of government policy and propaganda, a member of the Cabinet, Sir Edward Carson, was given supervisory powers over all propaganda matters, and further reorganization in February and March 1918 resulted in the creation of a Ministry of Information under Lord Beaverbrook.[58]

These developments came none too soon as discontent and war weariness began to temper hysterical enthusiasm. A special War Aims Committee, on which Asquith served along with the man who had displaced him, was formed to combat the growth of pacifist sentiment;[59] almost at the same time the most famous propaganda achievement of the whole war was launched, the story that the Germans were converting the bodies of dead soldiers into lubricating oils, pig-food, and manure. Credit for this invention again belongs to private enterprise – that of *The Times*. For the Government Lord Robert Cecil merely contributed the remark, when questioned about the story, that *The Times* 'is a reputable newspaper'. Dummies of a leaflet designed to circulate the story were considered by Wellington House and, according to Mrs Masterman, rejected. None the less *someone* in the Department of Information must have acted, for very shortly just such a leaflet was available. Headed, *A 'Corpse-Conversion' Factory*, and subtitled 'a Peep behind the German Lines', it began:

Out of their own mouths, the military masters of Germany stand convicted of an act of unspeakable savagery which has shocked the whole civilized world, including probably, now that the truth has come out, many of the German people themselves. Attila's Huns were guilty of atrocious crimes, but they never desecrated the bodies of dead soldiers – their own flesh, as well as the fallen of the enemy – by improvising a factory for the conversion of human corpses into fat and oils, and fodder for pigs.

That is what the autocrats of Prussia have done – and admitted. 'Admitted' is too mild a word. They have boasted of it. It is an illustration of their much-vaunted efficiency! A sign of their pious Kultur! Proof of the zeal to waste nothing! Further evidence of the Kaiser's self-imposed deification! 'There is one law, mine!'

How was the discovery made? Quite simply. Herr Karl Rosner, the Special Correspondent of the Berlin *Lokalanzeiger* on the Western front, made the announcement in his published dispatch of 10 April.

The pamphlet then gave a reproduction of the dispatch in the original German, followed by an English translation. One or two oddments of circumstantial evidence were added, and various expressions of horror from such notabilities as the Chinese Ambassador in London.[60] Actually if the German dispatch meant anything it meant that the corpses of horses were being utilized, and the whole story was finally and formally exploded in the House of Commons in 1925. It made a great impression at the time, and it left its odour behind it: when tales first came through early in the Second World War of Hitler's gas chambers, Fleet Street would not print them, saying that it wanted no more corpse-conversion stories.

One of the most notorious of the Ministry of Information propaganda films, *Once a Hun, always a Hun*, was much criticized in Parliament by Mr Leif Jones, for too nakedly revealing the economic interests of many of the businessmen employed at the Ministry. Two German soldiers are first shown in a ruined French town meeting a woman with a babe in arms whom they strike to the ground. The two soldiers gradually merge into two commercial travellers now seen in an English village after the war. One enters a small general store and shows the shopkeeper a pan. The shopkeeper is at first impressed, but his wife enters and reveals the 'Made in Germany' inscription underneath. She calls in a policeman who orders the German from the shop. The final words on the screen point up the message, 'there can be no trading with these people after the war'.[61]

In the changed atmosphere of 1917, new propaganda initiatives were required. Up till this point in time Liberals had been very much alone in cheering themselves upon such stirring visions as 'the emancipation of the German people' and 'the war that will end war', occasionally receiving a contemptuous glance from *The Times* which felt that there were sterner tasks on hand than consideration of the post-war settlement of Europe.[62] H. G. Wells received rather more encouragement since it was a concomitant of his theories that there should first be the *tabula rasa* of a war to the finish, and he was able to publicize openly his theories of a Peace League which would make future wars impossible. Other individuals and groups were working along similar lines, but felt it politic not to raise their voices too loudly. Of all discernible agencies of opinion probably the Fabian Society stands up best to close examination of its attitudes to the war, accepting that, because it was there, the war must be fought, but eschewing the glorification of the present one for the careful study of the avoidance of future ones. Its plans for international government were put before members and before the rather exclusive readership of the *New Statesman*. Other plans were worked out by a handful of dissident Liberals, who, along with Lord Bryce, the chairman of the Atrocities Committee, were known as the Bryce group; these plans were kept secret to avoid the charge of pacifism. Even when a League of Nations Society was formally constituted on 3 May 1915, under the chairmanship of the Liberal M.P. Sir Willoughby H. Dickinson, it carried on its propaganda in whispers, distributing its literature by personal contact. The *Manchester Guardian* was enthusiastic, but admitted the difficulties of promoting ideas generally associated with cranks and sentimentalists.[63]

Throughout 1917 and, indeed, 1918, the Conservative press remained unimpressed by, and sometimes hostile to, the concept of a League of Nations. But Lloyd George, whose vision hitherto of the ending of the war, as expressed in his war speeches, had been confined to the dealing of a 'knock-out' to Germany, or, more cryptically to the statement that 'this war will come to an end when the Allied Powers have reached the aims which they set out to attain when they accepted the challenge thrown down by Germany,'[64] recognized in it a good new plank with which to replace the shivering timbers of his propaganda wagon. Moreover, the entry into the war of America, where League of Nations sentiment, mustered by the unimpeachably patriotic League to Enforce Peace, and extolled by President Wilson, was strong, made the whole idea respectable, and in fact a necessity if amity between the new allies was to be maintained. The coming of Wilson, hailed by the *Daily News* on 3 April as 'the authentic voice of humanity', following so quickly upon the news of the Russian Revolution which seemed to herald the fall of the secret Liberal ogre, Russian autocracy, gave a tremendous boost to British Liberal idealism. Growing consciousness of the futility of the continuing slaughter moved that hardened reactionary, Lord Lansdowne, to circularize the Cabinet with a memorandum on a negotiated peace as early as November 1916, and he put forward his proposals publicly a year later. While other Conservatives referred to German feelers for a negotiated peace as 'peace plotting' or 'peace offensives', one of them, Lord Robert Cecil, to whom the latter phrase has been attributed, was becoming convinced by the horror around him that some sort of League of Nations must be formed at the end of the war. The Union of Democratic Control, whose main objectives were the early ending of the war and the establishment of parliamentary control over foreign policy rather than the sponsorship of a League of Nations, detected in the latter part of 1917 a 'turning of the tide', a greater willingness to listen to ideas which a year before would have been branded as 'defeatist' and pro-German.[65]

The new mood of the Labour movement has already been referred to; by making use of the work done by the I.L.P., which had long since produced its own plans for a 'League of Peoples', and by the U.D.C., whose war aims the Labour and Trade Union Conference of December 1917 took over *en bloc*, it now began to show a more sophisticated interest in the problems of war and peace. In August Arthur Henderson had been squeezed out of the War Cabinet because he favoured the holding of an international socialist conference at Stockholm, to be attended by German as well as Allied and Neutral delegates, but since Barnes moved into his place and G. J. Wardle into Barnes's place, Labour representation was undiminished. British Labour and the American President were the twin millstones which ground a declaration of war aims from Lloyd George. His first point was that Britain had no aggressive aims, no desire for 'the break-up of the German peoples or the disintegration of their State or Country'. To this he added three others: that 'the sanctity of treaties must be re-established', by which he meant that while there was 'no demand for war indemnity, such as that imposed on France by Germany in 1871', there must be 'complete restoration, political, territorial and economic, for the independence of Belgium, and such reparation as can be made for the devastation of its towns and provinces; . . . secondly, a territorial settlement must be secured, based on the right of self-determination or the consent of the governed'; lastly, Lloyd George said, 'we must seek by the creation of some international organization to limit the burden of armaments and diminish the probability of war,' a rather vague proposition which is glossed by the subheading inserted in the published version of the speech, 'A League of Nations.'[66]

That there was a change in public attitudes is made clear by the lessening hostility to such organizations as the U.D.C., and by the great success which attended the first mass meeting sponsored by the League of Nations Society once it dared to come out from under cover in the spring of 1917.[67] The old cries of honour and duty were wearing a little hoarse, the memories of the outrage inflicted upon Belgium rather hoary; it was becoming difficult for the human frame to bear all the slaughter and sacrifice and not believe that it was for something which was at the same time bigger, and more precise. Lloyd George sensed this in introducing his war aims speech:

When men by the million are being called upon to suffer and die, and vast populations are being subjected to the sufferings and privations of war on a scale unprecedented in the history of the world, they are entitled to know for what cause or causes they are making the sacrifice. It is only the clearest, greatest and justest of causes that can justify the continuance even for one day of this unspeakable agony of the Nations. And we ought to be able to state clearly and definitely not only the principles for which we are fighting but also their definite and concrete application to the war map of the World.

By adopting, at the instance of its most persuasive politicians, the phrases and slogans coined earlier by a minority of Liberals, largely to allay their own uneasiness, a whole nation was able to maintain the righteous quality of its war effort; unhappily the new righteousness went hand in hand with the old; a new world of virtue, yes, but punishment for the wickedness of Germany first.

[IV] THE ART OF DISENCHANTMENT

One area which became remarkably immune to anti-German hysteria was the front line: F. H. Keeling reported that few of the men around him felt much anger over, or sympathy for, Nurse Cavell; a similar detached scepticism towards other reported German activities in Belgium was reported by C. E. Montague and other front-line soldiers.[68] What deep hostility there was seemed rather to be directed towards the French, the allies with whom, to the misfortune of European peace, we were largely at odds throughout the inter-war years.[69] After the war there came a whole shoal of literature of disillusion written by ex-servicemen. In *Disenchantment* C. E. Montague movingly described the sordid tunnel existence which called

on all ranks of troops in the actual line to put up with a much diminished chance of survival, only the barest off-chance if they stayed there year after year. While they lived it was inflicting upon them in trenches a life squalid beyond precedent. And that same evolution had pressed back the chief seats of command into places where life was said to contrast itself in wonderful ways with that life of mud and stench and underground gloom.[70]

Those early volunteers who had a simple old-world religious faith were probably most immune to the numbing influence of trench life; but they and their faith were extinguished in the Battle of the Somme. Before going over the top Second Lieutenant J. S. Engall wrote to his parents that he had taken Communion the previous day with dozens of others who were going over with him, and that he had never attended a more impressive service:

I placed my soul and body in God's keeping, and I am going into battle with His name on my lips, full of confidence and trusting implicitly in Him. I have a strong feeling that I shall come through safely; but nevertheless should it be God's holy will to call me away, I am quite prepared to go: and ... I could not wish for a finer death; and you, dear Mother and Dad, will know that I died doing my duty to my God, my Country, and my King, I ask that you should look upon it as an honour that you have given a son for the sake of King and Country.[71]

Engall perished, as did thousands like him; for those who survived it was difficult not to doubt King, Country, or God. Another who fell had already written, 'Any faith in religion I ever had is most frightfully skaken by things I've seen.'[72] For a man whose enthusiasms had been social, not religious, one year was enough to turn enthusiasm sour: as F. H. Keeling put it to the Fabian historian, R. C. K. Ensor: 'I hope this bloody war is going to end soon – of course there is no chance of that, but the sooner the better.'[73]

Worst of all for the future of British society was the divide which yawned between, on the one side, the civilian fed on the sentimental mush of books like A. J. Dawson's *Somme Battle Stories* and the paper victories of the Press Bureau, aware of and almost inured to, colossal slaughter, but oblivious to the real tortures, physical and mental, of trench warfare, and on the other the soldier who was enduring them. At home there were air attacks, shortages; but these were the flickering of a match compared with the hell of the Western Front. At home there appeared to be affluence; there certainly was profiteering. As early as February 1916, F. H. Keeling pointed the bitter contrast:

Broadly speaking, the English either volunteer for this hell or else sit down and grow fat on big money at home. The contrast between the two fates is too great.[74]

Alienation of soldier from civilian is not the only cross-fissure which opened in British society. Lloyd George was borne to power on a justified reaction against the bungling of his predecessor; the bungling, exaggerated by the Northcliffe press in its constant reference to 'the old gang', seemed to be proven beyond doubt by the strictures of the Committee of Investigation into the

Dardanelles fiasco,[75] which were given the widest prominence in the same newspapers. In May 1918 Asquith associated himself with a bitter attack on the Lloyd George Ministry launched by Sir Frederick Maurice. Even more serious than the feuding among politicians was the feuding of politicians against generals, the hostility between Haig and Lloyd George being common knowledge. Curiously the Liberal press rallied to Haig, showing the same touching faith in him, as the expert in matters in which they themselves were inexpert, as they had shown in Kitchener.[76]

For the period of the war this is all rather nebulous, just a face at the window occasionally troubling the mind. It was the aftermath that brought disenchantment knocking boldly at the door; most of the bitterest words were reflected in the grim tranquillity of the post-war years. Contemporary records, such as Henry Williamson's War Diary[77] or the parts of Charles Edmonds's *A Subaltern's War* which were written in 1917, suggest that though by the end the soldier was wearied and sceptical, to call him disillusioned would be to add the sin of exaggeration to the folly of generalization. Looking back Edmonds's reflection was: 'The soldiers were not "disenchanted", for war had never offered them an enchanting prospect: they were just "fed up".'[78] Even Montague in 1917 was content to write the usual vacuous rubbish in introducing the war drawings of Muirhead Bone:

It is a trench to gladden the connoisseur's heart. How the men must have worked whenever they were not fighting – and digging is less dear than fighting in the soul of youth – in order to model this perfect line of defence and offence – its shapely firing-step and clean-cut vertical walls and massively squared traverses! Here is no gaping V-shaped ditch to collect the enemy's trench mortars and invite his wandering whizz-bangs in. And the men know it. You walk along the trench and see a just pride, as well as confidence, in their faces. It is noon now, and some of them are blowing on hot tea to cool it, or eating out of their dixies a hot stew of meat, potatoes and peas. It has not always been thus in an English firing-trench. The English only learn war, in each of their wars, by degrees. But now they have learnt it. The day is fine, and other men are asleep, basking like cats, in a state of beatitude, on little sunny shelves and bunks cunningly sculptured out of the trench's firm clay walls. One little knot of men off duty are bending over a comic paper at a corner . . .[79]

But from the rarer and more sensitive spirits, poets and artists, disillusionment, well before the ending of the war, was already bodying forth. While Rupert Brooke just lived long enough to hymn the heartfelt praises of a generation going to war, Wilfred Owen just lived long enough to utter the bitter despair of the same generation coming out of the same war. Nothing expresses more movingly the alienation of one generation from another than his *Parable of the Old Men and the Young*:

> So Abram rose, and clave the wood, and went,
> And took the fire with him, and a knife.
> And as they sojourned both of them together,
> Isaac the first-born spake and said, My Father,
> Behold the preparations, fire and iron,
> But where the lamb for this burnt-offering?
> Then Abram bound the youth with belts and straps,
> And builded parapets and trenches there,
> And stretched forth the knife to slay his son.
> When lo! an angel called him out of heaven,
> Saying, Lay not thy hand upon the lad,
> Neither do anything to him. Behold,
> A ram caught in a thicket by its horns;
> Offer the Ram of Pride instead of him.
> But the old man would not so, but slew his son . . .[80]

The War did not create a new movement in the arts, but it fostered what was barest and grimmest in 'modernism' and mocked the canons of the older schools. In Britain, as on the continent, the main characteristics of the modern movement were already established well before 1914; they were in a sense a product of the same restlessness and aspiration which led the peoples of Europe to welcome the war when it came. Britain had her futurists and her vorticists, her symbolists, and, in the theatre, her social realists. None the less there was a very strong tide of resistance apparent in the successes of the Georgian reaction in which poets such as Laurence Binyon stressed the traditional forms, and in the derision poured upon Roger Fry's attempt to mount an exhibition of Post Impressionist Art. But to deal with modern war only the techniques of modern art were adequate; what gilded Edwardian society had rejected, battered post-war society came slowly to accept. Not that there was complete continuity with pre-war developments in the arts any more than anywhere else; here too it was true that, where illusions had helped to ease the road to war, the war shattered these illusions. One of the major tenets of futurism was its faith in the dynamic of war; one of its younger British exponents, C. R. W. Nevinson, returned from the war with that faith destroyed.

It is in the latter part of 1917 that the letters of the young artist and serviceman, Paul Nash, begin to show intense anger against the war and its civilian proponents. One letter to his wife written in November 1917 is eloquent of the effect of the war upon him both as soldier and painter.

We all have a vague notion of the terrors of a battle, and can conjure up with the aid of some of the more inspired war correspondents and the pictures in the *Daily Mirror* some vision of a battlefield; but no pen or drawing can convey this country – the normal setting of the battles taking place day and night, month after month. Evil and the incarnate fiend alone can be master of this war, and no glimmer of God's hand is seen anywhere. Sunset and sunrise are blasphemous, they are mockeries to man, only the black rain out of the bruised and swollen clouds all through the bitter black of night is fit atmosphere in such a land. The rain drives on, the stinking mud becomes more evilly yellow, the shell holes fill up with green-white water, the roads and tracks are covered in inches of slime, the black dying trees ooze and sweat and the shells never cease. They alone plunge overhead, tearing away the rotting tree stumps, breaking the plank roads, striking down horses and mules, annihilating, maiming, maddening, they plunge into the grave which is this land; one huge grave, and cast up on it the poor dead. It is unspeakable, godless, hopeless. I am no longer an artist interested and curious, I am a messenger who will bring back word from the men who are fighting to those who want the war to go on for ever. Feeble, inarticulate, will be my message, but it will have a bitter truth, and may it burn their lousy souls.[81]

That the war was not entirely negative in its effects on the arts we saw when discussing developments in the world of music. The history of the British War Artists is one of the finest chapters in the war, and a true tribute to the genuineness of the conviction, so often voiced, that in fighting this war Britain was fighting on behalf of civilization. The idea of sending Muirhead Bone as the first War Artist emanated early in 1916 from a former literary agent employed in Wellington House. Bone's Exhibition of January 1917 became the first of a series given by the band of 'Official War Artists'.[82] It was during the darkest days of German victories in March 1918 that the Ministry of Information produced the massive and visionary scheme of a whole collection of war paintings, to be painted without hindrance or guidance by the best young talent then serving in the war. As Masterman – now head of the Literature and Art Department, as Wellington House had become upon the creation of the Ministry – later wrote:

We had to hunt the world to find the men we desired. We discovered Henry Lamb as Medical Officer in Palestine, Wyndham Lewis and D. P. Roberts in the Artillery in France, John and Paul Nash serving in the infantry in the battles round Ypres, Stanley Spencer a private (forbidden to sketch) in the hills round Salonika and his brother Gilbert as a Red Cross orderly in a hospital of Sinai.[83]

In putting opportunity before so many young men the scheme did immeasurable service to the future of British painting. That the resistance of the Treasury, which wanted to know 'how the painting of pictures which could only be exhibited after the war could be defined as British propaganda', was overcome was in large measure due to Masterman and Arnold Bennett, who had the powerful support of Lords Beaverbrook and Rothermere.[84] Thus laissez-faire in the arts was challenged as elsewhere, the State rising, in the words of the art critic P. G. Konody, 'to art patronage on an unprecedented scale'.[85] In return the State got as undeceived a view of the war as ever Goya's portraits were of his sitters. In an exhibition of 1917 entitled *Modern War*, Nevinson exhibited the subsequently famous, 'Illustration: Mitrailleuse', of which Sickert, a leader among the older generation of English artists, wrote:

Mr Nevinson's 'Mitrailleuse' will probably remain the most authoritative and concentrated utterance on the war in the history of painting.[86]

The scene depicted in bold simplified form is a grim and harrowing one, horror rather than heroism is the keynote. The Leicester Galleries Exhibition of May 1918, 'Void of War', by Paul Nash, was perceptively summarized by Arnold Bennett:

Lieutenant Nash has seen the Front simply and largely. He has found the essentials of it – that is to say, disfigurement, danger, desolation, ruin, chaos – and little figures of men creeping devotedly and tragically over the waste. The convention he uses is ruthlessly selective. The wave-like formations of shell-holes, the curves of shell-bursts, the straight lines and sharply defined angles of wooden causeways, decapitated trees, the fangs of obdurate masonry, the weight of heavy skies, the human pawns of battle – these things are repeated again and again, monotonously, endlessly. The artist cannot get away from them. They obsess him; and they obsess him because they are the obsession of trench-life.[87]

Of the most outstanding of the paintings on view, Konody wrote, 'I cannot think of a picture that interprets the whole terrible meaning of war as completely and convincingly as Lieutenant Paul Nash's little oil painting "Void"'.[88]

The highest product of a society, the products of its creative workers, are of the highest importance to the historian of that society. The art and poetry, tentative some of it still, of austerity and disillusionment appearing at the end of the war led on to some of the greatest creative work of the 1920's, to Eliot and his *Waste Land*, to Ben Nicolson and his nihilistic abstractions. But the vision of despair of the artist, the disenchantment of the literary soldier, are not necessarily representative of society as a whole, or even of all returning soldiers. Their attitudes, in so far as they had any, were only crystallized in the years which followed the ending of the war.

NOTES TO CHAPTER SIX

1. C. E. Montague, *Disenchantment*, 1922, p. 169.
2. Edmonds, *Short History of the First World War*, pp. 224–6.
3. *Report of British Association*, 1919, pp. 14, 273–4.
4. J. Terraine, *Douglas Haig, the Educated Soldier*, 1963.
5. The figures are for the period 31 July to 10 November, Edmonds, p. 252.
6. W. Beveridge, *British Food Control*, Oxford, 1928, p. 195.
7. ibid., pp. 33, 35, 36.
8. *The Times*, 3 February 1917.
9. Beveridge, *Food Control*, p. 37.
10. R. Smillie, *My Life for Labour*, 1925, p. 220. C. Addison, *Politics from Within*, p. 300.

11. McDonagh, *In London During the Great War*, p. 205.

12. Beveridge, pp. 172 ff.

13. ibid., pp. 196–7. A Briggs, *History of Birmingham*, II, 1955, p. 205.

14. Beveridge, p. 208.

15. *The Times*, 17 December 1917.

16. Beveridge, pp. 111, 155. *House of Commons Debates*, 25 July 1917.

17. Beveridge, pp. 142 ff., 205 ff.

18. *Report of Working Classes Cost of Living Committee* P.P., 1918, VII, Cd. 8980, p. 7. A. L. Bowley, *Prices and Wages in the United Kingdom, 1914–20*, Oxford 1921, pp. 32 ff.

19. *The Times*, 29 June 1917.

20. See esp. C. S. Peel, *The Eat-Less-Meat Book*, 1917, pp. 109–169.

21. ibid., p. 23.

22. Official figures, printed in *Observer*, 12 January 1919.

23. S. Coxon (ed.), *Dover during the Dark Days*, 1919, pp. 170–84.

24. *Report on the Administration of the National Relief Fund to 30 September 1918;* P.P., 1919, XXVI, Cmd. 16, p. 4.

25. McDonagh, p. 169 (20 January 1917).

26. P.P., 1918, VII, Cd. 8980.

27. E. M. H. Lloyd, *Experiments in State Control*, Oxford, 1924, p. 230.

28. Beveridge, *British Food Control*, p. 211.

29. Blumenfeld, *All in a Lifetime*, p. 81 (15 March 1917). Beveridge, p. 37.

30. C. Repington, *The First World War 1914–18*, 1920, Vol. II, p. 3 (21 July 1917).

31. C. Clark, *National Income and Outlay*, 1937, p. 94.

32. *The Times*, 21 April 1922.

33. For a wider perspective see W. L. Guttsman, 'The Changing Social Structure of the British Political Elite, 1886–1935' and 'Aristocracy and the Middle Classes in the British Political Elite, 1886–1916', in *British Journal of Sociology*, 1951 and 1954.

34. *Hist. Min. Mun.*, Vol. VII, pt. 1, p. 8.

35. Blumenfeld, p. 38: 'I looked up today at the tops of omnibuses, and counted fifteen omnibuses and not a single top hat.' (28 September 1915).

36. P.P., 1917–18, XIV, Cd. 8731, p. 4.

37. ibid., Cd. 8663, p. 31.

38. ibid., Cd. 8668, p. 23.

39. G. D. H. Cole, *Trade Unions and Munitions*, pp. 134, 142–4.

40. ibid., pp. 145–6.

41. P.P., 1917–18, XIV, Cd. 8662, p. 2.

42. ibid., pp. 2–6.

43. ibid., Cd. 8663, pp. 14, 16, 24, 25.

44. ibid., Cd. 8664, pp. 2–3, 6, 7.

45. ibid., Cd. 8665, pp. 3, 8; Cd. 8666, pp. 2–5; Cd. 8667, p. 4; Cd. 8668, *passim*; Cd. 8669, p. 3.

46. Cd. 8669, p. 3.

47. Cole, *Trade Unions and Munitions*, p. 151.

48. *Observer*, 21 October 1917.

49. Labour Party, *Report of Annual Conference 1918*, pp. 102, 140.

50. Cole, *Workshop Organization*, p. 71.

51. Cole, *Trade Unions and Munitions*, pp. 139–40, 155–6.

52. *Observer*, 30 June 1918.

53. H. D. Lasswell, *Propaganda Technique in the World War*, 1927, p. 9.

54. Hardie and Sabin, *War Posters*, p. 12.

55. McDonagh, *In London during the Great War*, p. 91.

56. *Bradford Pioneer*, 1 March 1918.

57. e.g., Blumenfeld, p. 62 (8 May 1916). McDonagh, p. 200.

58. *House of Commons Debates*, 5 August 1918. G. Bruntz, *Allied Propaganda and the Collapse of the German Empire in 1918*, 1938, pp. 22–4.

59. Bruntz, p. 19.

60. *A 'Corpse-Conversion' Factory*, n.d. (1917?). See L. Masterman, *C. F. G. Masterman*, pp. 292–3.

61. Lasswell, p. 45.

62. *The Times*, 2 July 1915, 4 December 1915.

63. H. Winkler, *The League of Nations Movement in Great Britain, 1914–1919*, New Brunswick, 1952, pp. 50 ff. *Manchester Guardian*, 31 October 1916.

64. Speech at Glasgow, 29 June 1917.

65. H. Hanak, 'The Union of Democratic Control during the First World War', in *Bulletin of Institute of Historical Research*, November 1963.

66. D. Lloyd George, *The Allied War-Aims*, 1918.

67. Winkler, p. 54.

68. Keeling, *Keeling Letters and Reminiscences*, p. 248 (11 November 1915). Montague, *Disenchantment*, p. 31. L. Housman (ed.), *Letters of Fallen Englishmen*, pp. 123, 128 ff.

69. See esp., R. Graves, *Goodbye to All That*.

70. Montague, p. 31.

71. J. S. Engall, *A Subaltern's Letters*, 1918, pp. 119–20.

72. *Letters of Fallen Englishmen*, p. 150 (March 1916).

73. Keeling, p. 238 (11 August 1915).

74. ibid., p. 290 (27 February 1916).

75. P.P., 1917–18, X, Cd. 8490.

76. e.g. *Daily News*, 5 October 1918.

77. H. Williamson, *A Soldier's Diary of the Great War*, 1929.

78. C. Edmonds, *A Subaltern's War*, 1929, p. 205.

79. C. E. Montague, *The Front Line*, 1917, pp. 4–5.

80. W. Owen, *Poems*, 1920, p. 9. c.p. Siegfried Sassoon's 'They' – *The War Poems of Siegfried Sassoon*, 1919, p. 47.

81. P. Nash, *Outline, an autobiography and other writings*, 1949, pp. 210–1.

82. L. Masterman, *C. F. G. Masterman*, p. 286.

83. ibid., p. 303.

84. ibid., pp. 303–4.

85. *Observer*, 14 December 1919.

86. C. R. W. Nevinson, *Modern War*, 1917, pp. 22–3.

87. Leicester Galleries, *Exhibition No. 258, May 1918*, pp. 4–5.

88. *Observer*, 19 January 1919.

CHAPTER SEVEN

Science and Collectivism

THE PROBLEMS of definition involved in a historical study of collectivism, socialism, nationalization, etc., are considerable; but they are nothing compared with the complex usage of words like science, technology and invention. Let it be understood first of all that by science is meant natural science, as does the plain man when he speaks of 'the wonders of science': he means television sets, not parliaments, though the systematic study of parliamentary institutions may be termed by its practitioners a social science. Science, as it is used here, then, is first defined by its subject matter: it is concerned with the phenomena of the physical universe. It is defined, secondly, by its method, which is empirical and systematic, and directed ultimately towards the establishment of general laws which state the relationship between different natural phenomena. The object of science thus described is simply knowledge: man's pursuit of the truth about his own environment. That this is a rarefied and detached pursuit is sometimes stressed by talking not of 'science', but of 'pure science'. But the product of this rarefied pursuit, knowledge of the workings of some aspect of the physical world, can clearly be of the utmost use to mankind. The man who applies his knowledge of scientific laws and his training in scientific empirical investigation with the aim of creating a precise material benefit is the applied scientist. The application, day in and day out, of the discoveries of the pure scientist and of the applied scientist to a particular economic use, to a particular industry or branch of an industry, gives rise to an important, but more limited, body of knowledge, technology. The skilled technologist may refine and develop the techniques of his own subject, but he will remain essentially orientated towards immediate use, rather than towards the establishment of abstract relationships or definitive truths.

There is an obvious line linking science to applied science to technology. In seeking a definition for invention we have to move on to a different track. The scientist or technologist is of necessity a man of some considerable acquired knowledge: invention is open to the most ignorant among us, though it is most likely to spring from someone with a scientific or technological background. George Stephenson, the pioneer of the steam locomotive, had no formal scientific or technological instruction, but he took good care that his son, who successfully developed this new means of traction, should be better prepared. It is still possible to conceive of a circumstance in which necessity might genuinely be the mother of invention; but more likely than not technology and science would be its father and grandfather. None the less, invention is essentially *ad hoc* and the laws governing it are chancy; it can make its own separate and direct contribution to technology and to industry.

Wars are not fought over the great truths of the universe, and, in immediate consequence at least, are more likely to hinder than help the progress of pure science. What a war will do, however, is to provide a stimulus to the development and application of existing ideas, that is to technology and to applied science; a war will release purse-strings and encourage politicians to found institutions for the practical applications of science; a war, itself the great creator of necessity, will foster an atmosphere favourable to invention. In the broad sweep of science history one can see that, while industry and technology owe an obvious debt to science, there is something of a two-way flow; that improvements at the level of technology and industry sometimes help to advance the frontiers of pure science – the laws of thermodynamics, for instance, owe something to the practical development of the steam engine. It is always possible, therefore, that in the flurry of wartime activity some advantage may rub off upon the pursuit of pure science.

Most of the governing advances in twentieth-century science had been made before the outbreak of war. In nuclear physics the discoveries of the great physicist J. J. Thomson in the nineties had led on to the construction of a model of the atom by his even greater protégé, Ernest Rutherford, just before the war. In theoretical physics the continental scientists, Einstein and Planck, had formulated the relativity and quantum theories respectively, though neither theory, as yet, had a very wide currency in Britain. The same was true for the new psychology, involving such concepts as the subconscious and the *libido*, pioneered by Sigmund Freud, though some knowledge of it had penetrated to bright young Edwardians, such as those one encounters on the early pages of Aldington's *Death of a Hero*. In biochemistry, the imperialist science of our own day which is fast invading the realms of anatomy, botany and genetics, the pioneer work was being done, in face of great obstacles, by Gowland Hopkins. The wartime food shortage, and the dietary problems which it involved, did bring the Government to some vague interest in this branch of science; it naturally had little interest in relativity, the subconscious, or the putative shape of the atom. Even the potential of the developments in applied science and technology, which in fact have revolutionized human life throughout the world, were scarcely appreciated in the Britain of 1914: the headship in chemicals, 'the central industry in modern civilization,'[1] had been allowed to pass to Germany; wireless telegraphy had had a popular coup in assisting the arrest at sea of Dr Crippen the murderer, but was otherwise scarcely exploited to the full; in manufacture and use of the internal combustion engine Britain lagged behind the European continent and America.

Government emergency action in other fields at the outbreak of war was paralleled by the setting up of a Government Chemical Products Supply Committee under Lord Haldane

to consider and advise as to the best means of obtaining for the use of British industries sufficient supplies of chemical products, colours and dye-stuffs of kinds hitherto largely imported from countries with which we are at present at war.[2]

From its labours there sprang the not very successful national dye company. Lack of urgency in scientific matters in the period of 'Business as Usual' is highlighted by the way in which one of Rutherford's most precious assistants, Lieutenant Moseley, was allowed to take part in the Gallipoli landings, where he was killed; it is difficult to imagine the nation today being quite so prodigal of its scientific brainpower. In May 1915 a deputation of professional scientists from the Royal Society and other learned

societies urged upon the Presidents of the Board of Trade and
Board of Education, the need for

Government assistance for scientific research for industrial purposes,
the establishment of closer relations between the manufacturers and
scientific workers and teachers, and the establishment of a National
Chemical Advisory Committee for these purposes.[3]

The Government was now very seriously worried by its 'embarrassment of . . . many necessities', its dangerous nakedness in the
production of optical glass, dye-stuffs, magnets, 'countless drugs
and pharmaceutical preparations', tungsten and zinc.[4] The President of the Board of Education, Pease, at once announced to
the Commons his plan for a central body of wider purpose and
powers than the proposed National Chemical Advisory Committee. Pease, like Haldane, was a casualty of the first Cabinet
crisis: both deserve credit for the White Paper issued in July by
Arthur Henderson, outlining a form of 'permanent organization
for the promotion of industrial and scientific research.'[5] This organization, formally established by an Order in Council of 28
July, took the traditional form of a Committee of the Privy Council
assisted by an Advisory Council, which, of course, did the work.
The Advisory Council met for the first time on 17 August; it was
allocated £25,000 for its first year's work, £40,000 for its second.
From 1 December 1916 the Committee of the Privy Council for
Scientific and Industrial Research was reorganized as a separate
government Department with a Minister, in the shape of the
Lord President of the Council, responsible to Parliament. (The
Lord President was, however, responsible for an awful lot of
other things as well.) A few months later a further step in the
consolidation of centralized control of scientific research was
taken when the National Physical Laboratory was transferred
from the Royal Society to this newly christened Department of
Scientific and Industrial Research (D.S.I.R.). One hundred years
before, Lord Liverpool's ministry had sought release from the
physical and spiritual ills which afflicted the country at the end of
the Napoleonic wars by providing one million pounds for the
building of new churches. Now in the latter part of another world
war Parliament again passed a 'Million Act', the money this time

to be devoted to scientific research. A new deity was being enthroned.[6]

While the original Privy Council committee was being formed, the Admiralty set up its own Board of Invention and Research. Although the presidency was given to the ex-First Sea Lord, Fisher, the Board contained some eminent scientists, including Professor J. J. Thomson, Sir Charles Parsons, and Dr G. T. Beilby, and had a consulting panel of twelve university science professors. Its functions were described thus:

(a) To concentrate expert scientific inquiry on certain definite problems, the solution of which is of importance to the naval service;

(b) To encourage research in directions in which it is probable that results of value to the navy may be made by organized scientific effort;

(c) To consider schemes or suggestions put forward by inventors and other members of the general public.

The Ministry of Munitions, too, had an Inventions Panel. The general public responded with enthusiasm, bombarding the panel with schemes for catching Zeppelins by magnetism, and for death rays powered by the mysterious agency of 'electricity'.[7]

Although the Medical Research Committee, an institution which under its later designation of Medical Research Council ranks more closely in importance with the D.S.I.R., had its origins in the 1911 National Insurance Act and was set up in August 1913, it was really the war which got it off the ground; it did not in fact present a report till the year 1914–15.[8] The reports thereafter are full of all the enthusiasm of writers who believe that not only civilization, but science is on the march; the war, they declare, is 'a great stimulus' providing 'unequalled opportunities for study and research, of which the outcome may bring lasting benefits to the whole future population'; diversion of resources to war problems, they claim, has meant no loss to medical science. Through the Medical Research Committee work of the utmost value on dysentery, typhoid, cerebro-spinal fever, and new antiseptics was indeed accomplished. Then the box of tricks, so useful in time of war, was banged shut. The first postwar report dolefully lamented that since the Armistice medical research had 'disintegrated' for lack of funds. None the less, although pruning of public expenditure was the order of the day, it was clear that the Government did not wish to chop the committee off completely: the will to permanence was expressed in the change of title, from 1 April 1920, to Medical Research Council.[9] On the whole, indeed, opinion at the end of the war was in favour of the further institutionalization of science, and a large number of committees on scientific problems were set up under the auspices of the Ministry of Munitions or the Ministry of Reconstruction.

Moving away from the more obvious forms of Government sponsorship of science, let us look at the way in which the war accelerated existing technological developments, or fostered invention. Before the war the motor vehicle was a luxury item, made, as likely as not, abroad; it was (apart from the motor bus) scarcely used at all commercially. The military had, however, long appreciated its potential, and, after the Boer War, Britain, like France and Germany, had adopted a subsidy plan to ensure supplies in time of war, while at the War Office there was a permanent Mechanical Transport Committee, subsequently the Mechanical Transport Branch, under the Director of Supplies and Transport. Starting with the subsidized vehicles and their drivers, the War Office finally, by a process which has already been exhaustively analysed in connection with the growth of collectivism, requisitioned the whole output of all factories able to produce suitable machines, of which a great variety, ranging from lorries and ambulances to, eventually, tanks, were developed.[10] The domestic motor car industry, as such, came to a standstill; but productive capacity was greatly increased and perceptive observers could see that the new developments were pregnant with possibilities for the future. This was especially true now that parturition could proceed behind the safe screen of the $33\frac{1}{3}$ per cent McKenna Duty.

The most famous of all the technological innovations of the First World War was the tank, to use the original code name which soon became universal. The idea rose with two different groups towards the end of 1914, one inspired by Winston Churchill at the Admiralty, the other centred on Sir William Tritton, Managing Director of the Lincoln firm of William Foster & Co., who had been asked by Admiral Bacon of the Admiralty to construct a tractor capable of laying its own bridge for crossing trenches.

In April 1915 the two groups came together, and in August the project was transferred to the Ministry of Munitions. By September, Foster's had produced the prototype of the first tank, called 'Little Willie'; this was replaced by 'Big Willie', which, when given different tracks, was renamed 'Mother'. 'Mother' was ready for tests in January 1916; secrecy was preserved by a deliberate policy of treating the whole matter as a joke.[11] The introduction of the tank was at first resisted by the War Office and by Kitchener, who called it 'a pretty mechanical toy', and its surprise value was thrown away in ineffective deployment on the Somme, but eventually the tank played an important part in breaking the frozen claw of trench warfare. The tank is a good example of an invention, spawned by many brains, nurtured in an environment of technology, but called forth by the necessity of war; what is in some ways an even more interesting one was the invention by Lieutenant-Colonel P. Nissen, a civil engineer with the Royal Engineers, of the Nissen hut, which went a long way to meeting the basic needs of shelter for the vast concentrations of troops behind the lines in France. Camouflage was a French idea, taken up in this country by the Royal Academician, Solomon J. Solomons.

As with land-bound motor vehicles before 1914 there was a certain limited apprehension of the military potential of aircraft, and the National Physical Laboratory, in addition to its regular grant of £7,000 per annum, received a special sum for aeronautical researches.[12] Both the army and the navy had their own air services, the Royal Flying Corps and the Royal Naval Air Service, with a Joint Air Committee under the Committee of Imperial Defence to secure co-operation. German air attacks in 1915 provoked demands for a unified policy of defence and retaliation, paraded in the Northcliffe press and focused on a by-election fought, and allegations made, by Mr Pemberton Billing. The curious division of labour, evolved in February 1916, that the navy was responsible for hostile aircraft till they reached the coast, and then the army thereafter, was scarcely satisfactory. A new Air Committee under Lord Derby was formed, but it was weakened from the start by internal rivalries and jealousies, and by its own lack of executive authority; a Committee of Investigation did, however, exonerate the Royal Flying Corps from the charges made against it by Billing and others. In May the Air Committee was succeeded by a stronger Air Board presided over by Lord Curzon, but, still short of executive powers, it failed, in particular, to pull the Admiralty into line. It was Lloyd George's New Ministries Act which reorganized the Board on a statutory basis, with a new President, Lord Cowdray, ranking as a minister. In November 1917, the Air Board became the Air Council, with a new Secretary of State for Air, in the person of Lord Rothermere, who had succeeded Lord Cowdray as President.[13]

In the early stages of the war, the main military function of aeroplanes was reconnaissance over the enemy lines, though a number of raids upon civilian centres were also undertaken. Such raids were greatly extended in 1917 while the defensive role of the air services was at all times constantly before the eye of the domestic population. By the end of the war there was widespread interest in the possible civilian uses of aircraft. In April 1918 the Government formed a Civil Aerial Transport Committee under Lord Northcliffe, and two leading manufacturers, Holt Thomas and Handley Page, anxious to exploit their new productive capacity, proclaimed their plans for the development of civil aviation.[14] The stimulus to what was virtually a new industry was enormous. At the outbreak of war the British air services had possessed a total of 272 machines; in October 1918 the R.A.F. had over 22,000 effective machines. During the first twelve months of war the average monthly delivery of aeroplanes was 50; in the last twelve months it was 2,700. Before the war Britain had been heavily dependent on other countries for aero-engines, so much so that in the Aerial Derby of 1911 only one of the eleven machines had a British engine. 'By the end of the war, however, British aero-engines had gained the foremost place in design and manufacture, and were well up to requirements as regards supply.' The total horse-power in the last twelve months of the war was 'comparable with the total horse-power of the marine engine output of the country'. Advances in performance were even more striking. The aeroplanes sent out with the B.E.F. in 1914 had a maximum speed of 80 miles per hour, a rate of climb from ground level of 300 or 400 feet per minute, and were equipped with engines of 60 to 100 horse-power. In 1918 the fastest machines could reach 140 miles per hour and had a rate of climb from ground level of 2,000 feet per minute. The Handley-Page V/1500, which had its first test flight in May 1918, was capable of developing over 1,300 horse power. The maximum flying height had been raised from 5,000 to 25,000 feet. Three days before the armistice two Handley Page bombers stood fully equipped awaiting the order to start for Berlin.[15]

Wireless likewise proclaimed its potential during the war: it was of especial use in maintaining communications along the far-spread front lines, though on the Eastern front the Russians so mishandled the medium that they provided a valuable intelligence service to their German enemy. In stressing the importance and future possibilities of wireless, the *Observer*, in January 1919, pointed out that but for this means of communication Germany would have been completely cut off from the outside world in the latter stages of the war. It was during the war that the first British valve transmitters, a big advance on the earlier disc, arc, or alternator transmission, were installed, mainly for wireless contact between the ground and planes on reconnaissance. As supplies from the main pioneer companies in this field, Marconi, Edison, Swan and A. C. Cossor, were insufficient, contracts for radio valves were given to the main manufacturers of electric light bulbs, the General Electric Company Ltd., the British Thomson-Houston Company, Ltd., and the British Westinghouse Electrical and Manufacturing Company Ltd. The commitment of these three companies to the nascent radio industry was, by the end of the war, so great that it was they who exerted some of the strongest pressure on the Government to permit broadcasting in the post-war years. The first actual broadcasters were in many cases men who had gained experience of wireless during the war: Arthur Burrows, employed by the Government to monitor the wireless transmissions of the Central Powers, H. J. Round, who operated wireless direction-finding stations on the East Coast, and Peter Eckersley, a wireless equipment officer in the Royal Flying Corps.[16] Burrows saw most clearly the future uses of wireless, for broadcasting of speech and music instead of merely for telegraphic communication: in 1918 he forecast 'the concert reproduction in all private residences of Albert Hall or Queen's Hall concerts, or the important recitals at the lesser *rendezvous* of the music world.'[17] The one important technological

advance in radio springing from the needs of war was the development of the thermionic valve: just as important were the
development of vested commercial interests in the future expansion of radio, the training of a small group of dedicated enthusiasts, and, on the other side, the firing of the public imagination
with the romantic possibilities of this medium of communication.

The same sort of impulses were at work in the other technologies affected by the war. The central importance of the chemicals
industry provoked the Government action which has already
been examined. The electrical industry benefited immensely
from the enormous power demands of the other war industries,
and between 1914 and 1919 the capacity of municipal and company generating stations nearly doubled.[18]

In the first fumblings of its food policy the Government made
little use of existing scientific knowledge, though Runciman, as
President of the Board of Trade, did, before the collapse of the
Asquith Ministry, invite a committee of the Royal Society to conduct a survey of British food supplies. The agricultural policy instituted at the beginning of 1917 was based on the principle that
the calorific value of grain is much higher if eaten direct rather
than fed to livestock and eaten as meat. Scientific evidence that
alcohol was at its deadliest when steadily accumulated through a
day's solid drinking was adduced in favour of the afternoon
closure of public houses. Full exploitation of scientific knowledge
only began after Lord Rhondda's appointment as Food Controller;
thereafter the Royal Society Committee acted 'practically as a
scientific consultative committee in all matters of food supply',
and Sir William Thompson was appointed Scientific Adviser to
the Food Ministry. A special Food Investigation Board of the
Department of Scientific and Industrial Research investigated
problems of food preservation.[19]

These various matters show the interaction between science
and the war effort, but the biggest scientific advance of the
whole war era, the artificial disintegration of the atom, had nothing whatever to do with the demands of the war. Rutherford had
for a time left his work on nuclear physics to devote his talents
to the problems of submarine detection – without any striking
success. Early in 1918 he returned to his laboratory in Manchester

to resume his own researches, and it was here that he brought about what has proved the most portentous scientific achievement of the century. Further investigations into Rutherford's discoveries required apparatus on a massive scale, so that nuclear physics, which had previously had no obvious social relation, was now brought into direct contact with the engineering industry. All of this added up to give a new scientific orientation to British society at the end of the war, just as economic developments gave an orientation towards collectivism.

It is an oversimplification, D. S. L. Cardwell has judiciously pointed out, to talk of the 'impact' of science on society: 'science is not an alien, external force like famine pestilence or conquest, it is a characteristic of our society.'[20] There are three sectors of society in which science is a particularly active characteristic: industry, education and thought (taking the last term to cover the highest philosophical speculations on the universe and its god or gods as well as every-day attitudes and prejudices). In the first sector, the war demonstrated more convincingly than ever before that science paid dividends – the dividend for the moment was national survival, but for the future it could be national or private profit. Before the war, science, one professor said, 'was a proper occupation for the leisure of an English gentleman'. The war unequivocally made it a proper full-time occupation for a growing professional and white-collar class: in the National Factories especially, the scientific worker enjoyed a marked rise in status.[21]

Science, religion and radicalism had been the three major forces behind such education as there was in the early nineteenth century. 'Britain's strength depends on sea power and school power,' Sir Michael Sadler had declared in the 1890s. But the lesson had constantly to be relearned; the Board of Education *Reports from Universities and University Colleges* for 1913–14 announced:

Among the many important national functions in which the university institutions will have a large share will be that of meeting the scientific needs of our industries on a scale which will enable this country to compete on equal terms with the best equipped of its rivals.[22]

In company with other committees on the teaching of modern

foreign languages, a committee on science teaching was a feature of the educational reconstruction programme of the last year of the war,[23] and it became very much the fashion to stress the role of education in a science-conscious society.[24]

Science in the mid-nineteenth century helped to foster the confident belief that man had the physical world at his feet, that the universe held no mysteries which could be withheld from him. The Darwinian thesis, though ultimately destructive of revealed religion, served at first to stimulate and highlight religious and philosophical disputation. Gladstone could happily integrate evolution into the existing framework of his religious belief; Disraeli nailed his colours to what became an enduring cliché:

What is this proposition now put before us with a glib assurance the most astounding? It is this: is man an ape or an angel? My Lord, I am on the side of the angels.

Men like John Stuart Mill rallied to the development of human reason as an alternative absolute to revealed religion. But in the early twentieth century Freudian psychology, with its revelation of the importance of the subconscious, and the quantum and relativity theories, involving what to the pedantic mind would seem to be contradictions and absurdities, took the stuffing out of Reason as well as of Religion. What was critical was the concatenation of these theories and the senseless havoc of war, which brought, as it were, a double-dose of Doubt. John Galsworthy, the novelist, put it jocularly:

Everything being now relative, there is no longer absolute dependence to be placed on God, Free Trade, Marriage, Consols, Coal or Caste.[25]

E. L. Woodward, the historian, put the matter more seriously:

Man was now left to himself, yet he was not even master of his own intelligence and will. It would appear that he was free only to laugh, and the echo of this laughter down the corridors of time was not a pleasant sound.[26]

So it seemed to a sensitive mind in the years after the war. For the less darkly sensitive the larger vision opened by scientific advance was the contrary one of developing material prosperity, tempered by that of ever more horrific weapons of war.

More relevant to the main purpose is the manner in which the advancement of science contributed to the growth of the collectivist idea. To the scientific mind the pre-1914 economic system (though it might be justified by other higher considerations) could scarcely be justified on grounds of efficiency, more especially since it had made so little provision for scientific research. By contrast the powers assumed by the State in 1917 did enable it for the first time to attempt a scientific allocation of the resources of the community. Developments in electricity supply, of its essence suited to large-scale production, and, later, in broadcasting, simply cried out for State action.[27] It would be nonsense to suggest that during the war all scientists became collectivists, or even that most of them had any thoughts on the subject, but certainly the most articulate of them, that is to say the scientists who played a part in opinion-forming, inclined in this direction. When the 1919 President of the British Association, the Hon. Sir Charles Parsons, asked whether the coal owners and, as he said, 'our masters the miners' were to remain free 'to waste or conserve at their own sweet will, or to exploit as they please, this necessity of the country's existence', he showed himself to be no socialist; yet he was in favour of nationalization of the coal mines. Left to themselves, he said business men produce 'slums and millionaires'.[28] Others, like Professor Frederick Soddy, went a good deal farther:

The uses already made of science show how necessary it is that a new social order be developed before a million times more awful powers are unleashed by man. So far the pearls of science have been cast before those who have given us in return the desolation of scientific warfare and the almost equal desolation of unscientific government. In the world that is to come the control of financiers, lawyers, politicians, and the merely possessive or acquisitive must give place to a system in which the creative elements must rule . . . Common ownership of the acquisitions of science is the only path of progress.[29]

As elsewhere, the reaction was a two-way one. The growth of science fostered the growth of the collectivist ideal; the establishment of collectivist policy in the last two years of the war fostered the growth of science. The founding of the Department of Scientific and Industrial Research was the symbol of collectivism applied to science just as the founding of the Ministry of Shipping was the symbol of collectivism applied to shipping. The new ministries of the war period, especially the first of them, the Ministry of Munitions, took a special interest in the techniques and potentialities of science.[30]

[II] RECONSTRUCTION

Many of the motive forces behind the wartime collectivism – egalitarianism in a time of high prices, the desire for scientific efficiency, the needs of self-defence, and the two great shortages of munitions and of food – have already been examined. Now a closer look must be taken at a word which was being bandied about in 1915, and which, from the summer of 1916, was on every politician's lips: 'reconstruction'. The idea of reconstruction rose naturally from the ideals of August 1914, and from such declarations as Lloyd George's 'Great War' speech of September 1914. It appeared early because, after all, the war was expected to end early. As the war went on and on it became more and more necessary to stress the radical nature of the reconstructed society which would arise from the carnage. Asquith had equipped his Government with a standing Reconstruction Committee of Cabinet ministers with a small Secretariat attached. In March 1917 the Cabinet Committee was replaced by a committee of experts with Lloyd George as nominal chairman and Edwin Montagu as vice-chairman and executive head, and this in turn was replaced, despite adverse comment in press and Parliament, by a Ministry of Reconstruction.[31] The scientific approach of the new Ministry was stressed:

The country is for the first time equipped with a Department not devoted to research in the field of the physical sciences, but to research into questions of political science and to the encouragement of action on the lines of the results ascertained.[32]

Reconstruction, in the words of the War Cabinet, was 'not so much a question of rebuilding society as it was before the war, but of moulding a better world out of the social and economic conditions which have come into being during the war.'³³

The first foreshadowing of social reconstruction, the extension of war pensions, grew directly out of the military war and its very high casualty rate, and the Act of November 1915 was more striking as evidence of the continued enshrinement of laissez-faire principles than of any dramatic shift in social policy. That shift comes only with the new Act of late 1916 and the creation of a Ministry of Pensions, both of which were concerned as much with the disruptions and flux in domestic employment as with the military situation, for the 1911 Act was now extended to cover all persons employed in trades relating to the war effort. On 26 February 1917 a more generous schedule of war disablement and widowhood pensions was introduced, with rates varying, for privates, from 27s 6d per week down to 5s 6d, with allowances for children.³⁴ The widely publicized reconstruction programmes of 1917, in which education and housing had star billing, were in part designed to allay war-weariness and discontent. All through 1917 and 1918 work continued on the most ambitious administrative reconstruction of all, the abolition of the Local Government Board and the creation of a Ministry of Health.

As with so many other reforms carried out by the Lloyd George Ministry, the idea of a Ministry of Health was already being discussed before the fall of Asquith. But it was the new President of the Local Government Board, Lord Rhondda, who put the shoulder of political purpose and enthusiasm to the idly turning wheel of vague speculation. Rhondda invited Dr Addison to take charge of an inquiry into the problem,³⁵ and himself, after two months' work, submitted an important Memorandum to the War Cabinet:

(1) Public opinion is now keenly aroused on the existing deficiency and inefficiency of our public medical services, especially for maternity and infant welfare. There is a widespread insistent demand for improvement. The working of the Insurance Act has shown what can be achieved by a systematic provision of medical services, but these are admittedly inadequate, particularly for the crucially important needs of women and children. . . .

(2) There are several other grave difficulties resulting from the existing chaos in our health services, e.g. in providing medical services for discharged soldiers and their widows and orphans, in the obstacles

hampering the development of the needed specialist services for in-
sured persons, large numbers of whom are discharged soldiers; in the
constant drag on the improvement of tuberculosis services; and in the
quarrelling over the maternity and infant welfare schemes ... These
and other crying evils can only be remedied by the immediate establishment of one Central Ministry of Health, in place of the two or three
separate and competing Government Departments, which at present
separately supervise various elements in the national health problem.

(3) ... All that is wanted is a three-clause Bill establishing a 'Ministry
of Health and of Local Government,' to supersede the Local Government Board and transferring to it the medical and sanatorium functions
(but, for the present, no others) of the English and Welsh Insurance
Commissions, and giving to it the necessary powers coupled with provisions of adequate Exchequer funds ...

(4) The Bill would be popular and would raise no party controversies.
It would be essentially a war emergency measure for making possible
the immediate development of the maternity and infant welfare and
other services above described, for which public opinion is already
clamouring, and which have become doubly needed by reason of the
war havoc, and doubly urgent if they are to be started before the difficulties of demobilization render such an initial step both too late and
impossible. It is, therefore, earnestly desired that this small but supremely useful step be sanctioned forthwith, so that the Bill may be
introduced in the House of Lords at once, with the promise of substantial Exchequer grants.[36]

Before succumbing to Lloyd George's pleas that he should take
over the Food Ministry, Rhondda extracted a promise from the
Prime Minister that a Ministry of Health would indeed be
brought into being.[37] Thereafter the project languished for a time,
but in 1918 it became one of the major preoccupations of the
Ministry of Reconstruction, now in the hands of Dr Addison.
In addition to the necessary inter-departmental communications,
Addison held a series of conferences with the local authorities,
members of the medical profession, and the insurance committees
and approved societies engaged in the administration of the
National Health Acts. After general agreement had been reached
upon the need for a Ministry of Health, discussion centred on the
problem of the Poor Law system administered by the Local
Government Board, the most troublesome aspects of which
were thrashed out by a Committee presided over by Sir Donald

Maclean. Eventually a draft Bill, introduced into the House of Commons four days before the Armistice, was drawn up by the Home Affairs Committee of the War Cabinet. Its purpose as explained by Addison was to bring together under one body of men and one Minister the chief government departments concerned in matters affecting the health of the people.[38]

Resistance to this great measure, especially from the mandarins of the Local Government Board, was strong enough to force its withdrawal. The new Bill, introduced early in 1919 and given a third reading in April, had the grave defect of leaving untouched the piecemeal health powers of the local authorities.[39] Yet in its modest way it did represent one important aspect of the positive effect of the war on social policy, well summed up by Addison in his speech on the second reading:

If we wanted an illustration of how necessary it was to bring our practice into accord with our knowledge, we have it before us at the present time, because in this matter our practice is far behind our knowledge. Somehow or other we hear of these things, they sink into our minds, and we go away and forget them. For years attention has been drawn to the fact that we have in our children, in our elementary schools, armies who are physically defective or have defective vision, etc. We have them of every age and in every year, not a company or a brigade or a division, but an army. Every year they go and lose themselves in the mass of the population. We forget them until suddenly some great national event occurs which brings it up to us in its reality. That was the case in the War. Then we saw those generations of children we had heard of so often who were represented in the military age by hundreds of thousands of men who were physically unfit and could not pass the very moderate standard of physical fitness which the army required. Then it was revealed as a source of national weakness, which is very great in time of emergency, but it is just as much a source of national weakness in time of peace.[40]

The war, Addison is saying, did not create a body of knowledge and theory which was not there before, but it brought a violent awareness of the need to apply it, especially through the revelation that about one recruit in three was medically unfit. The war, one might say, brought the level of social practice up to somewhere near that of social knowledge.

In education, nevertheless, the first effects of the war were far from favourable; Government plans for greatly increased expenditure on educational grants announced in the King's speeches of 10 March 1913 and 10 February 1914, were 'arrested by the outbreak of war'.[41] But in theory, if less obviously in practice, education benefited greatly from the notions of 'reconstruction' and the desire to improve national efficiency and competitiveness prevalent from the summer of 1916. The Board of Education Report for 1915–16 was prefaced by a panegyric on the importance and glorious future of education. The Report for 1917–18 declared that the war

has certainly brought a clearer and wider recognition of the value of education, and, while showing the defects and short-comings of our system, has produced the resolution to improve it.[42]

The implementation of this resolution was placed in the hands of H. A. L. Fisher, Vice-Chancellor of Sheffield University, and, in December 1916, the first professional teacher to hold political responsibility for education as President of the Board of Education. The actual realities of juvenile education were laid bare in March 1917 in the Final Report of the Departmental Committee on Juvenile Education in relation to Employment after the War (appointed in April 1916) which, however, after exposing the early withdrawal of children from school in order to employ them in strenuous and often futureless 'war work', went on to postulate the replacement of

the conception of the juvenile as primarily a little wage earner ... by the conception of the juvenile as primarily the workman and citizen in training.[43]

Fisher himself submitted a short, succinct report to the Cabinet calling for massive State subvention of education.[44] While theorizing abounded, war conditions did bring one practical advance: in those areas and amongst those families where greater employment had brought greater prosperity, there was a growing tendency to enroll children for secondary schools.[45]

In August 1917 Fisher put his proposals for the first major Education Act since 1902 before the House of Commons. It was the negative impulse of the war which he stressed: his Bill was prompted by deficiencies which have been revealed by the War; it is framed to repair the intellectual wastage which has been caused by the War; and should it pass into law before peace is struck it will put a prompt end to an evil which has grown to alarming proportions during the past three years – I allude to the industrial pressure upon the child life of this country – and it will greatly facilitate the solution of many problems of juvenile employment, which will certainly be affected by the transition of the country from a basis of war to a basis of peace.

On the positive side he referred to the 'increased feeling of social solidarity which has been created by the War' and remarked that the acceptance of conscription 'means that the boundaries of citizenship are not determined by wealth and that the same logic which leads us to desire an extension of the franchise points also to an extension of education'. State compulsion, he concluded, was essential for the protection of the rising generation against the 'injurious effects of industrial pressure'.[46] Fisher's proposals to consolidate the administration of education roused the hostility of the local authorities; his decision to prohibit completely the system of part-timers, and his intention of introducing compulsory continuation classes, were strongly opposed by industry, especially the coal owners and the farmers; it was also argued that his Bill involved the suppression of the individual and of the rights of parents, and, finally, that Parliament anyway had no mandate for such sweeping changes.[47] As with the Ministry of Health Bill, so too the Education Bill had to be withdrawn. Introduced in new form early in 1918, it passed its third reading in July.

As enacted, the measure called upon the local education authorities to formulate and submit to the Board of Education complete schemes covering all forms of education for their districts, combining where necessary with the authorities in adjoining districts. A universal minimum leaving age of fourteen was to be enforced, and there were to be compulsory day continuation schools for those between fourteen and eighteen not undergoing suitable alternative instruction. All fees in public elementary schools were to be abolished. Standards in higher classes were to be improved, physical training was to be encouraged, there was to be special provision for handicapped children and for nursery schools. The intention was to have a comprehensive system which would give all children and young persons the opportunity to enjoy the advantages of whatever form of education was best suited to their particular capacities.[48]

One of the gravest blows to education struck by the war was the loss of teachers in action. Fisher proposed that henceforth three-fifths of the cost of teachers' salaries should be met by the Board of Education, so that the earnings of elementary school teachers could be doubled. A separate Superannuation Act brought a trebling of teachers' pension benefits. Although the Board of Education still maintained the standard British doctrine that 'in material prospects the teaching profession can never hope to compete with other professions', elementary school teaching was now economically sufficiently attractive for it to become a middle-class rather than a working-class profession.[49] A shortage of graduates was another obvious consequence of the war: because of enlistment in the army, attendance at Oxford University, for instance, had fallen from 3,181 in 1914 to 491 in 1917.[50] Fisher was anxious to secure an expansion of university education in the post-war years, and again realized that this could only be achieved by direct provision of Government funds. Accordingly the University Grants Committee was appointed in 1919 as an autonomous agency for channelling State finance to the universities.[51] In 1920 two hundred State Scholarships were instituted.

Under the Ministry of Reconstruction, a Committee on Adult Education was appointed which reported that, after the obvious interruption to adult education work at the beginning of the war, the volume of educational activity in 1917 was larger than in pre-war years.

The awakened interest has been shown in the courses of lectures, study circles, and classes arranged by a large number of organizations. A large part of this activity has been directed towards the study of the historical background and causes of the war, but attention is now being turned to the problems of Reconstruction. We are informed that organizations find great difficulty in coping with the demand for knowledge on these questions.[52]

A subsequent report remarked that 'one of the most valuable fields of activity is the army itself'. The seeds of the awakened interest in learning, the committee reckoned, were to be found in the throwing together in closer association than had been usual in civilian life of men of varied antecedents, experience and outlook, whilst the war,

the issues involved, the changes it has precipitated, the problems which are arising out of it, have led many who previously thought but little about the larger problems of life and society to seek knowledge and understanding.[53]

The reasoning here is possibly a little specious; reading between the lines, one might rather say that the intense frustration and boredom of military training, the sense of vital years slipping fruitlessly by, gave the men an interest in the army educational facilities which they might otherwise have scorned. From the earliest stages of the war certain camps had provided such facilities, and by 1917 all eighteen-year-old recruits were given compulsory teaching of citizenship, history, elements of economics and natural science.[54] The committee recommended that the various bits and pieces of educational instruction should be organized into one unified educational service – a recommendation implemented in the Second World War.

[III] THE TURNING OF THE SCREW

Lloyd George's original proposal to Asquith had been that a smaller and more effective War Committee should have day-to-day executive authority over the conduct of the war. The traditional Cabinet would continue to exist, albeit in the administrative background rather than in the executive foreground. His final solution, facilitated by Asquith's refusal to co-operate, was to merge the War Committee and the Cabinet into a War Cabinet of five: Lloyd George, as Prime Minister, Lord Curzon, as Lord President of the Council, Lord Milner and Arthur Henderson, as Ministers without Portfolio, and Bonar Law, Chancellor of the Exchequer and Leader of the House of Commons. All but Bonar Law, therefore, were freed from departmental responsibilities. That the Prime Minister now ceased to hold the leadership of the House of Commons was a further sign of the declining influence of that House over government; Lloyd George's parliamentary attendances became extremely rare, and at one stage at the beginning of the following year it was indignantly pointed out that there was nobody on the front bench save a Junior Lord of the Treasury. To avoid the dangers of confused decisions ill-remembered afterwards, which had attended upon the old system, a minute-taking Cabinet Secretariat was established. While the executive was drastically weeded down in size, new offices sprouted in copious profusion, giving the ministry a total numerical strength of eighty-eight, which was nearly twice that of pre-war days. As about sixty of the new ministers and junior ministers were in the House of Commons, unkind parallels were drawn with the eighteenth century and the days of jobbery and placeholding.

We have already glanced at the way in which the new bureaucracy dealt with the pressing problem of food distribution. As a prelude to rationing meat retail price control had been introduced in September 1917. At the same date the Government took a 'long step in socialistic policy'[55] by instituting a flour subsidy at a rate of £50 million a year designed to bring down the price of bread to 9d. a quartern loaf. A potato subsidy followed in November. To hold down the prices of other commodities the Food Ministry ran the gamut of all possible expedients: complete control of the entire process of production and distribution, control of wholesale only, or control of retail only. Prices were determined by what Beveridge described as a mixture of 'costings, conference and compromise'. The tangible consequence was a constant stream of food control orders made under the authority of D.O.R.A. which, bound together, make a fat section of the Parliamentary Papers for the session 1917–1918.[56] The irrepressible individualist, Thomas Lough, declared to the House of Commons in February 1918 that, in despair of reading or counting the orders of the Ministry, he had taken to weighing them and had found that on one day alone he had received half a pound's worth. Vigorous action was taken against contravention of the food control orders, and in the last months of war and the first months of peace there was a total of 65,000 prosecutions, with penalties ranging from the £5,500 fine imposed upon a potato profiteer to the £10 fine imposed upon a man who expressed his dissatisfaction with his wife's cooking by throwing his dinner into the fire.[57]

Distribution was only one aspect of the food problem; production was another. It is very much to the credit of the Lloyd George Government that, after possessing itself of an energetic President of the Board of Agriculture, Rowland Prothero, it at once took up and put into practice the various projects which since 1915 had been floating in an administrative vacuum. First moves were made in December 1916, and these, a judicious mixture of carrot and stick, were consolidated in the Corn Production Act of April 1917: farmers were guaranteed minimum prices for wheat and oats for a period of five years; agricultural labourers were given a minimum wage; and the Board of Agriculture took to itself powers of entry and enforcement of proper cultivation. Within the Board, a Food Production Department (Food Production Committees in the case of the Scottish and Irish Boards) was established in January with special responsibility for increasing the productivity of existing arable land, and for bringing new land under cultivation by drainage and other methods.[58]

The existing and highly ineffective County War Agricultural Committees were called upon to appoint County Agricultural Executive Committees of not more than seven members, which were then stiffened by the inclusion of additional members appointed by the Board of Agriculture, and blessed, apart from minor reservations, with the Board's own emergency powers. In February and March 1917, the Executive Committees undertook a massive survey designed to reveal the amount of additional land which could be brought into cultivation in the spring: the total estimates amounted to 300,000 acres in England and Wales, and 50,000 acres in Scotland. They issued instructions to farmers on methods of cultivation, and, if these were not obeyed, dispossessed the recalcitrant occupier, either running the farms themselves or letting them to new tenants. The 1918 programme worked out by the central departments was a still more ambitious one, calling for an increase in arable of 2,700,000 acres in England and Wales, and 350,000 acres in Scotland, over the figures for 1916. To each Committee a quota of this was allocated, it being left to the Committee to give directions to individual farmers. In urban areas the Committees co-operated with the local town or urban district council in providing town-dwellers with allotments which they could cultivate in their leisure time. Allotments were a

characteristic feature of the First World War, as of the second and
the years which followed it; the allotments of 1917 and 1918
played their part in the universal blurring of class lines – the gar-
dening proletarian was well on the high road to middle-class
respectability.

Already in December 1916 there were, in the operations of the
Sugar Commission and the Wheat Commission, precedents for
the bulk-buying of imports. Under the Lloyd George ministry
this approach to the problem of food supply was vastly extended,
and, what is more, integrated into a buying machinery which
served not only Britain, but her West European Allies, all of
whom were by now largely dependent on the North American
continent. The basic co-ordinating agency was the Inter-Ally
Council of War Purchase and Finance,

the apex of a complex structure which, almost unnoticed, has effected
an unparalleled economic revolution by transferring the import of all
foodstuffs from private hands into Government control.[59]

Four main bodies, the Wheat Executive, the Sugar Commission,
the Meats and Fats Executive, and the Oil and Seed Executive,
each with their headquarters in London, and each linked to a
countervalent export body in America, undertook purchase and
allocation of food supplies to the Allies. At home the efforts to
stimulate farm production were followed up by the Ministry
entering the domestic agricultural market as a buyer on a similar
scale.[60]

Shortage of food had been one of the great pressures of necessity first making its weight felt in 1915; the other, shortage of
munitions, had been rather more competently dealt with before
December 1916. The extremely useful, though ill-written and
self-congratulatory *War Cabinet Report for the Year 1917*, published
in 1918, suggested that 'whilst no exact demarcation line can be
fixed,' a 'broad definition' would be that prior to the cabinet
crisis 'industries essential to war needs had been taken under
Government control', and that

In the same way 1917 may be described as a year in which State control
was extended until it covered not only national activities directly

affecting the military effort but every section of industry – production, transport and manufacture.[61]

The Ministry of Munitions was an upstart and an aggressionist: less set in its ways than such older departments of state as the War Office, it was an ideal instrument for direct Government action, and the aggrandisement of its spheres of interest after December 1916 is in itself symbolic of Government intention. The Ministry assumed responsibility for the supply of aircraft to both Army and Navy, the development of agricultural machinery, the supply of fuel oils, and the control of the manufacture, use and distribution of sulphuric acid. By October 1917 there were 143 National Factories in operation, all dealings in metals were under national control, and the Government was directly fostering the home production of tungsten from colonial ore and of iron and steel from British mines, which were themselves taken over in September. A special department, established in March 1917, was devoting its energies to the development of domestic sources of non-ferrous metals, such as tin, zinc, lead and wolfram.[62]

Coal, as a consumer commodity whose price rocketed in the early stages of the war, had been a subject for State interference in 1915. This apart, the supply of coal was central to the whole structure of Britain's industrial effort, and, indeed, was of great importance to Britain's military allies. Labour troubles in South Wales had brought Government control of the mines there. After a grim winter of domestic fuel shortages and further labour troubles, the Cabinet early in 1917, extended control to the entire coal industry, for this purpose creating at the Board of Trade a special Department under a Coal Controller. The financial arrangements were similar to those operating in regard to the railways, only more complicated: a levy on earnings above prewar created a fund used to compensate those owners whose earnings fell below prewar, or whose mines were closed altogether by the Coal Controller. Still not quite what a socialist would call nationalization, the arrangement did give the Government a stronger hand than it had in the railways; this it used with striking success in a scheme which, by ensuring that each community drew its needs from the nearest, rather than, as had happened under free enterprise, from a far coalfield, saved 700 million ton-miles per annum. Negotiating directly with the miners, the Coal Department conceded a wage increase of 1s. 6d. a day, operative from 17 September 1917.[63]

The War Office purchases in 1916 of the home and the Australian and New Zealand wool clips had been aimed at the specific problem of the provision of military clothing. But once it had established a monopoly or near-monopoly of purchase, the Government found itself implicated not only with military contractors, but with the ordinary textile manufacturers engaged in the home and export trade. To reconcile their needs with its own monopoly the Government evolved a complicated rationing scheme of quarterly allowances of wool based on former scales of consumption. In mitigation of the reality of Government control, supervision of the scheme was vested in a Board of Control sitting at Bradford, the heart of the wool and worsted trades, and composed of representatives of employers and employees, as well as of the Army Contracts Department; but the Board was chaired by a Government-appointed Director of Wool Textile Production. U. F. Wintour, Director of the Army Contracts Department, instituted a similar policy for hides and leather, while in August 1917 the Ministry of Munitions took possession of the year's flax crop. In the cotton industry, increasingly deprived of its raw material, crisis point was reached by June 1917. A Cotton Control Board was set up with the task of preserving the industry from total disruption through a policy of rationalization. A basic standard of 60 per cent of pre-war capacity was enforced; firms permitted to work above this contributed a levy to be used in the interests of the industry as a whole, and its workpeople. All this added up to a mechanism of economic planning and allocation of priorities of a sort never before possessed by a British Government.[64]

There was one other major sector of commercial enterprise which felt the tightening screw of state control after December 1916: shipping. Until December less than half the total British tonnage and practically none of the great liners had been requisitioned by the State; under the new Ministry of Shipping almost every ship was taken over, so that the Shipping Controller, working in conjunction with a committee of management of the big shipowners, was now able to organize and re-distribute the nation's ships in the most economical manner. For each consignment of freight the shipowners, whose high profits had been a known scandal, were paid Blue-Book rates, the basis determined early in the war which gave a fair margin over pre-war figures; any profit made on the transaction went to the Treasury. Control of shipbuilding, at first vested in the Shipping Controller, was tightened in May 1917, when a separate department under Sir Eric Geddes, who was given the title of Controller of the Navy, was made responsible for this.[65] Inland, a Canal Control Committee was appointed in March 1917 to run the more important canals not owned by the railway companies.

Who exactly thought up and carried out these experiments in State control? Lord Salter (Arthur Salter), Director of Ship Requisitioning at the Admiralty Transport Department, which provided the nucleus of the Ministry of Shipping, modestly deprecates any attempt to give credit to individuals and refers to 'the logic of events and the impelling necessity of the situation'.[66] At the top of the political tree Lloyd George was nothing of a theorist, very little of a planner; his concern was to get things done, his strength that he would give a hearing and a trial to all suggested means towards this end. From the summer of 1916 there were floods of suggestions from politicians and publicists of all descriptions. Most of the direct initiative however, came from men within the Civil Service. The real pioneers of bulk purchase in this country were the 'whirlwind trio' at the Army Contracts Department, E. M. H. Lloyd, 'the brains behind the throne', E. F. Wise, 'director of offensive and defensive operations' and U. F. Wintour.[67] Having done their good work in jute, textiles and leather, these three officials moved over to the Ministry of Food, where they were joined by one of the greatest administrators of the age, William Beveridge. Certainly the Civil Servants, like the politicians, were responding to implacable external pressures; but it is also important that the responses of men like Lloyd, Beveridge, Salter, Josiah Stamp at the Inland Revenue and Sir Hubert Llewellyn Smith at the Board of Trade, were the right ones. And many of them, having had first-hand experience of the operations of State collectivism in time of war, came to feel that these operations could with advantage be continued in time of peace.

In the end the experiments in State control triumphantly vindicated themselves, making an indispensable contribution to the
winning of the war, although some were conducted in a feeble
and half-hearted fashion. There was, too, an obvious tendency
to regard the creation of a new Ministry, or a new Department,
with its attendant bureaucracy, as in itself a panacea; the principle of the paramountcy of the national interest was at times
confused with the principle of jobs for the boys. One experiment
which notoriously failed was the establishment of a Ministry of
National Service with the simple purpose of making 'the best
use of all persons, whether men or women, able to work in any
industry, occupation or service'. The first Director-General of
National Service, Neville Chamberlain, formerly Lord Mayor
of Birmingham, was not lacking in energy: he had taken possession of a London hotel, assembled a large staff, and begun to
organize work before the Act establishing his Ministry was
passed. Although some connecting link between recruiting (the
responsibility of the War Office) and allocation of labour (mainly
the responsibility of the Ministry of Munitions) was obviously
desirable, it was difficult to see where the functions of National
Service differed from those of the recently-established Ministry
of Labour. Chamberlain found himself doing little more than
running an appeal for National Service Volunteers, who were
to take on civilian jobs and release more men for the forces.
This sudden burst of voluntaryism at a late stage in the war
simply added confusion to the problems of labour policy. 'What
National Service wants,' the *New Statesman* declared rudely, 'is
not a hotel, but a mortuary chamber and a post-mortem'.[68]
Chamberlain shortly resigned, 'because,' said one writer, 'he had
nothing to do.'[69] Upon the accession of Sir Auckland Geddes
the Ministry was reorganized and given a general responsibility
as 'the War Cabinet's General Staff on Man-Power'. With specific
tasks in regard to military recruiting, it had thereafter a more
obvious and respectable *raison-d'être*.

With over nine-tenths of the country's imports being bought
directly by the State, with 240 National Factories in operation and
large sectors of economic and social activity under direct State
supervision, people by 1918 were becoming inured to the idea of
State collectivism. 'As the war continued,' wrote Evelyn Wrench,

we became increasingly accustomed to restrictions of every sort. When the fourth anniversary came, Government control was so much part of our lives that we found it difficult to jump back in our minds to the pre-war world in which we lived in July 1914.[70]

Informed observers tended to the belief that some at least of the socialistic experiments would be worth maintaining after the war; making the best of a bad job the Anti-Socialist Union changed its name to the Reconstruction Society.[71] The leaders of private industry were remarkably silent while the war lasted, contenting themselves with singing the praises of large-scale industrial organization. The philosophy of the Federation of British Industries was that in modern conditions 'the group, the society, and the collective effort are authoritative'.[72] Overt hostility to State control did not burst out till October 1918 when the war looked to be all but won:

Among the business community there is practical unanimity of agreement that there should be as little interference as possible on the part of the State in the future Governance of Industry.[73]

At the same time the lessons so painfully learned over the previous years could not so suddenly be jettisoned, and the same writer recognized 'that the re-settlement of the industries of the country on a peace basis is a task so huge that it could not satisfactorily be left to unguided private effort'.[74] Officially the Government verdict was that the 'war has brought a transformation of the social and administrative structure of the state, much of which is bound to be permanent'.[75]

NOTES TO CHAPTER SEVEN

1. J. D. Bernal, *Science in History*, 1954, p. 569.
2. P.P., 1916, VIII, Cd. 8336, p. 8.
3. ibid.
4. ibid., pp. 7-8.
5. P.P., 1914-16, L. Cd. 8005.
6. Cd. 8336, pp. 3, 8-9, P.P., 1917-18, XI, Cd. 8718, pp. 3, 49. P.P., 1918, IX, Cd. 9144, p. 3.

7. *Report of British Association 1919*, p. 139. *House of Commons Debates*, 21 May 1917.

8. P.P., 1914–16, XXXI, Cd. 8101.

9. ibid. P.P., 1916, XIV, Cd. 8399; 1917–18, XVII, Cd. 8825; 1919, XXVI, Cmd. 412, pp. 5, 7; 1920, XXI, Cmd. 1088, p. 5.

10. *The Times History*, pp. 283–4. Fairlie, *British War Administration*, p. 89.

11. *Engineering*, 12 September 1919, p. 334. *Report of British Association 1919*, p. 263. Addison, *Politics from Within*, p. 133.

12. Cd. 8336, p. 6.

13. *Report of the War Cabinet for 1917;* P.P., 1918, XIV, Cd. 9005, pp. 56–66.

14. Fairlie, p. 119. *Observer*, 17 November 1918.

15. *Report of British Association 1919*, pp. 15, 258.

16. ibid., pp. 158, 269 270. S. G. Sturmey, *The Economic Development of Radio*, 1958, pp. 22–5, 34–5. A. Briggs, *The Birth of Broadcasting*, 1962, p. 37.

17. Quoted by Briggs, p. 38.

18. *Report of British Association 1919*, pp. 18, 165.

19. P.P., 1916, IX, Cd. 8421. Beveridge, pp. 99, 194 ff. P. Starling, *The Nation's Feeding*, 1919, pp. 12–13. Cd. 9144, p. 4.

20. D. S. L. Cardwell, *The Organisation of Science in England*, 1957, p. 2.

21. *Report of British Association 1919*, p. 166.

22. P.P., 1914–16, I, Cd. 8137.

23. P.P., 1918, IX, Cd. 9011 and Cd. 9036.

24. See e.g. *Bulletin of Federation of British Industries*, 14 February, 9 May and 12 September 1918.

25. J. Galsworthy, *A Modern Comedy*, 1929.

26. E. L. Woodward, *Short Journey*, 1941, p. 123.

27. *Report of British Association 1919*, p. 17. *Coal Conservation Sub-Committee Interim Report;* P.P., 1917–18, XVIII, Cd. 8880. *Departmental Committee on Electric Power Supply* (Williamson Committee); P.P., 1918, VIII, Cd. 9062. *Departmental Committee on Broadcasting;* P.P., 1923, X, Cmd. 1951.

28. *Report of British Association 1919*, p. 142.

29. *Daily Herald*, 30 January 1920.

30. Money, *Triumph of Nationalisation*, p. 53.

31. *Report of War Cabinet for 1917;* P.P., 1918, XIV, Cd. 9005, pp. 199 ff.

32. ibid., p. 202.

33. ibid., p. xix.

34. *House of Commons Debates*, 26 February 1917.

35. Viscountess Rhondda *et al.*, *D. A. Thomas, Viscount Rhondda*, 1921, p. 264. *House of Commons Debates*, 7 November 1918 (col. 2338).

36. Printed in Rhondda, pp. 266–7.

37. ibid., p. 268.

38. Cmd. 325, pp. 290 ff. *House of Commons Debates*, 7 November 1918.

39. A. Newsholme, *The Ministry of Health*, 1926, pp. 93, 137–8, 150–1. P. Abrams, 'The Failure of the Social Reform, 1918–1920' in *Past and Present*, April 1963, p. 51.

40. *House of Commons Debates*, 28 February 1919.

41. *Report of Board of Education 1914–15;* P.P., 1916, VIII, Cd. 8274, p. 1.

42. P.P., 1917–18, XI, Cd. 8594, pp. 1–4. P.P., 1919, XXI, Cmd. 165, p. 3.

43. P.P., 1917–18, XI, Cd. 8512, p. 5. See above p. 119.

44. H. A. L. Fisher, *An Unfinished Autobiography*, 1940, pp. 103–4.

45. *House of Commons Debates*, 19 April 1917.

46. ibid., 10 August 1917.

47. ibid., 13 March 1918. Fisher, pp. 106–8.

48. *Report of War Cabinet for 1918*, Cmd. 325, pp. 295 ff.

49. Cmd. 165, p. 2. Fisher, pp. 104–9. H. and M. Wickwar, *The Social Services*, 1949, p. 273.

50. Fairlie, *British War Administration*, p. 242.

51. Fisher, p. 116.

52. P.P., 1918, IX, Cd. 9107, p. 6.

53. P.P., 1918, IX, Cd. 9225, p. 3.

54. ibid.

55. Gray, *War Time Control of Industry*, p. 24.

56. Beveridge, *Food Control*, pp. 162–81. P.P., 1917–18, XXVI.

57. F. Coller, *A State Trading Adventure*, 1925, p. 75. Beveridge, pp. 237–8.

58. *Report of War Cabinet for 1917*, Cd. 9005, pp. 156–9, on which the next paragraphs are based.

59. ibid., p. 170.

60. Beveridge, pp. 162–81. Coller, pp. 59–152.

61. Cd. 9005, p. 130.

62. ibid., pp. 67–79.

63. On this paragraph see R. A. S. Redmayne, *The British Coal-Mining Industry during the War*, Oxford, 1923, pp. 257 ff.

64. H. D. Henderson, *The Cotton Control Board*, Oxford, 1922. *Economist*, 11 August 1917. *Memorandum on War Office Contracts;* P.P., 1917, XX, Cd. 8447, pp. 17–20.

65. A. Salter, *Allied Shipping Control*, Oxford, 1921, pp. 2 ff.

66. A. Salter, *Memoirs of a Public Servant*, 1961, p. 87.

67. Coller, *A State Trading Adventure*, pp. 66–7.

68. *New Statesman*, 21 July 1917.

69. Fairlie, p. 254.

70. E. Wrench, *Struggle 1914–20*, p. 333.

71. *Daily Express*, 20 May 1918.

72. Federation of British Industries, *What It Is and What It Does*, p. 3.

73. *Bulletin of Federation of British Industries*, 12 October 1918.

74. ibid.

75. *Report of War Cabinet for 1918*, Cmd. 325, pp. 214–15.

CHAPTER EIGHT

The End of the War

[I] ARMISTICE AND GENERAL ELECTION

THE SECOND Battle of the Marne of July 1918 was the first faint sign that the ascendancy had definitely passed to the Allies, and the news of the advances which followed brought a distinct lightening of domestic discontents, which had been exacerbated by the first wave of a drastic influenza epidemic. Earliest indications of the disease had appeared in the Grand Fleet at Scapa and Rosyth in April and May, and, at about the same time, among the British troops in France. In May there were a few civilian victims in Glasgow, but the massive simultaneous outbreak throughout the country did not come till the end of June. This first wave reached its crest in the second week of July, being shortly followed by a second wave which came to a peak in the first week of November. A final wave appeared towards the end of January 1919, and reached its crest in the last week of February. Total deaths were 151,446 (140,989 civilians), the highest relative to population for any epidemic since the cholera outbreak of 1849.

Virulent influenza appeared throughout the world in 1918–19, and attempts to relate it to British wartime privations are not completely satisfactory. In Britain, for the first time since the institution of public health records, the poor suffered no more than the rich. In the wealthy boroughs of Chelsea and Westminster the mortality rate ran at 6·1 per thousand and 5·2 per thousand respectively; in the poor boroughs of Bermondsey and Bethnal Green it ran at 5·6 and 5·1 per thousand respectively. The Scottish rate was 4·3 per thousand, with no significant variation between town and country, rich area or poor. If these statistics show anything, then, with a kind of sepulchral irony, they suggest that the conditions of resistance to disease as between social classes were now more equal than ever before. Where the epidemic was selective was in its high incidence among young adults – an unusual feature, which, however, was as true of neutral countries as of war-weary Britain.[1]

Two events demonstrated the high pitch which tensions had reached in the last summer of the war. In the fantastic Old Bailey trial, in which Pemberton Billing, M.P. was prosecuted for libelling a dancer, Maud Allan, as a sexual pervert, the egregious defendant secured acquittal and public acclaim by alleging the existence of a 'Black Book', compiled over twenty years by German agents, and containing the names of many prominent British men and women, with a catalogue of their sexual weaknesses. The other event was the strike of 12,000 policemen on 31 August over non-recognition of the newly-established National Union of Police and Prison Officers, the dismissal of a union official, and a demand for a wage rise of one pound a week, with an additional 12 per cent war bonus. By the end of the day, however, Lloyd George had wooed and won the men with the usual specious promises.[2]

By early October it was noted that:

London is more crowded today than at any time in the memory of the present generation, and now that the war news is so magnificently encouraging it is a brighter London too. . . . The hotels are full; there are queues at the best and most popular restaurants; the shops are reaping a rich harvest; and the theatres and music-halls are enjoying a boom.[3]

A week later McDonagh remarked that: 'All the talk is about the expected imminent collapse of the Germans'.[4] While the word 'Armistice' was being bandied in the press, the Bill completing the political emancipation of women was enacted: its single important clause read:

A woman shall not be disqualified by sex or marriage for being elected to or sitting or voting as a Member of the Commons House of Parliament.

On the evening of Saturday, 9 November, Lloyd George was guest at the Lord Mayor's Banquet; although the more ostentatious forms of gluttony were avoided, the feeding was lavish enough to provide the right setting for the knowledgeable rumours that the war was nearing a victorious close. Regretting that he had no more positive news, Lloyd George none the less confidently declared that, 'The issue is settled'. Even so, the announcement of the Armistice on Monday, 11 November, came with a certain unexpected suddenness.

This morning at eleven o'clock I was startled by the booming of maroons, fired from police and fire brigade stations, the loud reports of those near at hand being faintly re-echoed by others far off. As it is six months since these warnings of an air raid have been heard in London (our last bombardment by the enemy having occurred in May), I wondered what they could now imply, so early in the morning. Looking through my window I saw passers by stopping each other and exchanging remarks before hurrying on. They were obviously excited but unperturbed. I rushed out and inquired what was the matter. 'The Armistice!' they exclaimed, 'The War is over!'

I was stunned by the news, as if something highly improbable and difficult of belief had happened. It is not that what the papers have been saying about an Armistice had passed out of my mind, but that I had not expected the announcement of its success would have come so soon, and, above all, be proclaimed by the ill-omened maroons. Yet it was so. What is still more curious is that when I became fully seized of the tremendous nature of the event, though I was emotionally disturbed, I felt no joyous exultation. There was relief that the War was over, because it could not now end, as it might have done, in the crowning tragedy of the defeat of the Allies. I sorrowed for the millions of young men who had lost their lives; and perhaps more so for the living than for the dead – for the bereaved mothers and wives whose reawakened grief must in this hour of triumph be unbearably poignant. But what gave me the greatest shock was my feeling in regard to myself. A melancholy took possession of me when I came to realize, as I did quickly and keenly, that a great and unique episode in my life was past and gone, and, as I hoped as well as believed, would never be repeated. Our sense of the value of life and its excitements, so vividly heightened by the War, is, with one final leap of its flame today, about to expire in its ashes. Tomorrow we return to the monotonous and the humdrum. 'So sad, so strange, the days that are no more!'[5]

Many others undoubtedly shared this reflective frame of mind. Captain Henry Williamson, now based in England, included one last entry in his diary:

Thank God the end of the awful blind waste and brutality of war has come, and let us pray it may never return. . . . I am feeling rather ill and depressed, in spite of all the rejoicing around me; immeasurably relieved, glad to be alive, and glad we have won; but tired and a little sad.[6]

In that other society, the fighting line, there was even less enthusiasm.[7] But for the nation at home, Mrs Peel's fancy was a not impertinent one:

It seemed almost as if one heard a dead silence and then that the whole nation gave a sigh of relief. A few moments later the people had gone mad.[8]

On the packed tram on which McDonagh travelled in to town the passengers were 'obviously deeply moved, whether they were chattering and laughing or self-absorbed and silent', but another observer preferred Mrs Peel's epithet, 'London' he said, 'was a city gone mad'. Boy Scouts raced around on bicycles sounding the all clear; shops shut, schools released their children; Big Ben, silenced by the war, chimed: newspaper bills, banished by war economy, appeared to blazon the news, 'Fighting has ceased on all Fronts'. The grey November day turned to drizzle by the afternoon, but that could not abash what McDonagh described perceptively as 'the urge to do something ridiculous', to have, one might say, the last-but-one fling in a four-year intoxication.[9]

Not only did everyone seem bent on bursting their throats in an effort to contribute to the din, but everything that could be banged, blown and rattled seemed to have been pressed into service for a like purpose. I could distinguish the hooting of motors, the ringing of handbells, the banging of tea-trays, the shrilling of police whistles, and the screaming of toy trumpets in the resulting infernal orchestra. Among the many ludicrous incidents to be observed were a colonel in uniform squatted on the top of a motor-car sounding a dinner-gong and a parson marching at the head of a group of parishioners singing lustily with a Union Jack stuck in the top of his silk hat.[10]

The war seemed to be ending just as it had begun; it was like August 1914 all over again. A vast crowd gathered in front of Buckingham Palace chanting, 'We-want-King-George!' After being duly rewarded by the royal appearance, the concourse sang 'Land of Hope and Glory', followed by 'Tipperary'. Similar scenes of rejoicing took place throughout the country. At the same time Parliament's adjournment for a service of thanksgiving in Westminster Abbey was no mere formality, but a genuine expression of the religious element ever present in the war fever: in Birmingham people who had learned so patiently to queue for foodstuffs now queued outside the Cathedral for an opportunity to take part in one of the three separate services which had to be held there.[11] Optimism for the future was again as high as ever it had been among the Brookes, the Keelings, and the Gordon Carruthers's[12] of 1914. Asquith on 2 November had returned to an old theme in hailing the 'last act' in 'one of the greatest dramas in history':

It is not too much to say that it has cleansed and purged the whole atmosphere of the world.

Speeches everywhere elaborated the theme: addressing a meeting in Victoria Square, Birmingham, on the evening of Armistice Day, the Lord Mayor, Sir David Brooks, declared:

today is the greatest day in the history of our country, and it marks the beginning of a new era in human development. . . . We must take care to use this great opportunity aright so that the world may be better and not worse by reason of the overthrow of the old order.[13]

In the last entry in his war diary, McDonagh wrote of the inauguration of 'an era of peace and security, after years of care and worry'.[14]

The atmosphere was one of high hopes for a better world; but they went hand in hand with an inward-looking jubilation at the triumph of British arms. There was a real sense of religious dedication and thanksgiving; but it partnered a most unholy hatred of the defeated enemy. Not long before, A. J. Balfour had declared of them, 'Brutes they were when they began the war, and brutes they remain,' and this was an attitude the ruling politicians were happy to perpetuate, as thoughts turned towards the holding of a general election. The existing Parliament had been in being for very nearly ten full years; the recent Representation of the People Act had completely altered the basis of the electoral franchise; Liberals of independent mind had hankered after a general election even in the course of the war, and the Labour Party had begun flexing its muscles from the time of the ratification of its new constitution. But not only did Lloyd George decide upon an early election, he decided to fight it in concert with his allies in the war-time coalition. Sensing, apparently, that the days of the old Liberal Party were numbered, he ignored Asquith's speech of 2 November calling for Liberal reunion, and instead singled out a small group of amenable Liberals for the honour of endorsement as coalition candidates. These candidates, along with a balancing group of Conservatives, were granted what Asquith, with topical sarcasm, called the 'coupon', a joint letter of support signed by Lloyd George and Bonar Law. The coupon, as Mr. T. Wilson has pointed out, was simply the outcome of a tactical bargain between Lloyd George and the Conservatives, designed to secure for him a body of Liberal supporters at a time when he was 'declaring war on the greater number of Liberal candidates'; it was not, as is often said, determined on the basis of attitudes taken up in the Maurice debate .[15]

Labour members of the coalition were offered the opportunity of sharing in the political spoils of military victory, but a delegate conference on 14 November decided that the Party should withdraw from the Government and contest the election as a separate unit.[16] The argument for staying in was made most convincingly by J. R. Clynes, and on one view it is arguable that it might have been better had Labour remained in a position from which to exert some influence over immediate post-war policies. However, given the need to reintegrate completely the anti-war and pro-war elements, to establish the Party convincingly as the rallying point for progressive and internationalist opinion, and to assert its indisputable existence as a national political party, the decision, which Clynes, in contrast to a few time-servers like G. N. Barnes, loyally obeyed, was a wise one.

Parliament was dissolved on 25 November, and the election was scheduled for 14 December. The five major aims upon which Lloyd George and his associates campaigned chimed well with the many-belled tolling of public sentiment. They were: getting the soldier home as quickly as possible; fair treatment for soldier and sailor; punishment for the Kaiser; making Germany pay; better social conditions for the people of Britain. The first two aims and the last had been to the fore in a famous speech made by Lloyd George at Wolverhampton, two days before the dissolution of Parliament: in reply to his own question, 'What is our task?', he had declared: 'To make Britain a fit country for heroes to live in'. But as the campaign hotted up it was the frothy mischief of the other two aims which boiled over the top. The *Daily Mail* kept the flame high by publishing daily, in the same sort of black box it had used for hounding foreign waiters in the early part of the war, statistics of British casualties. Lloyd George declared that the Kaiser would be brought to trial; G. N. Barnes put the campaign firmly on the level of gutter-press apoplexy when, in reply to a questioner, he declared, 'Myself, I am in favour of hanging the Kaiser'. The fair reparation for war damage in France and Belgium of which Lloyd George had spoken in his war aims speech eleven months previously had now become the bubble demand for 'the whole cost of the war'; Sir Eric Geddes, one of the leaders of the generation of business experts and political incompetents of 1916, produced the delightful metaphor of 'squeezing Germany till the pips squeak'.[17]

Two other issues adorned the campaign. The Labour Party in its election manifesto went out of its way to stress its hostility to the institution of conscription. On 10 December, J. H. Thomas, railwayman's leader, pulled off a considerable dramatic success by reading out a letter written, he said, by a British general which advocated permanent conscription. Lloyd George urbanely replied (with his war-time experiences in mind he may well have meant every word he said) that he could not be held responsible for the opinions of every British general, but coalition candidates were subsequently subjected to strong heckling on this subject. When the *Daily News* came out with the claim that 'a vote for the Coalition is a vote for conscription', Lloyd George was forced to the categorical assertion that this was 'a calculated and characteristic falsehood'. In denouncing his opponents, especially the Labour Party, as being tainted with Bolshevism and Pacifism, the coalitionists gave more than they got. Russia could be pointed to as the dread warning when Lloyd George indicted the Labour Party as being 'run by the extreme pacifist, Bolshevist group': pacifist, to the earnest student of the popular press meant a 'funk-hole Cuthbert'; Bolshevist meant a bloodthirsty bearded cossack: but the contradiction apparently went unnoticed.[18] An especially bitter campaign was waged in East Leicester, where Ramsay MacDonald, despite the fact that the local I.L.P. was one of the two strongest in the country, lost his seat. The unpopularity of internationalist ideas, for all the talk of a League of Nations and of a better world, was driven home by the defeat in West Derbyshire of the Earl of Kerry, son of Lord Lansdowne: to lose a Unionist seat in this election was quite an achievement, shared by only seven others.[19] The strength of jingoistic fervour was most clearly demonstrated by the defeat of Asquith, although his Conservative opponent had not in fact been allotted a coupon.

From the first moment it became known that the coalition was going to fight an election as a unity, and in haste, the Liberal opponents of Lloyd George talked of the 'stampede election'. J. M. Keynes carved a permanent niche for this portraiture of the election in his *The Economic Consequences of the Peace,* published in 1919. Professor Mowat has stressed the quietness and sobriety of the contest and the appearance of rival candidates on common platforms, and concludes that 'it is probable that the temper of the campaign has been exaggerated'.[20] 107 out of 707 seats were in fact uncontested. None the less, contained in what Keynes intuitively grasped and so self-consciously embellished, there were profound truths: the general election of 1918 was probably the most critical, and certainly, in the Parliament it produced, the most unfortunate, in Britain's modern history. That the election was held in haste had one supremely important consequence – the failure, despite the parade of soldiers' voting rights and the holding up of the count till 28 December, to secure the suffrage of more than one soldier in four. To many soldiers, already bitten by the bug of disenchantment, the idea of voting, so the *Daily Mail* Parliamentary Bureau in Paris reported, was just a joke; the majority of the others, most of whom did not in practice get the opportunity, intended to vote Labour; the report, so obviously contrary to the political interests of the *Daily Mail*, seems reliable.[21] Altogether between fifty and sixty per cent of the electorate recorded their votes, and rather more than half of those – 5,091,528 in all – voted for the coalition, giving it 484 members, of whom 338 were Conservatives. The line between 'Coalition Unionist' and 'Unionist' *tout court* was not always a very distinct or a very valid one: there were at any rate yet another 44 Conservatives in the House so that, when it became clear that the Irish Sinn Fein candidates were not going to take their seats, the total Conservative contingent amounted to about three-fifths of the entire House of Commons. Labour, for the first time, became the largest opposition party with 59 members. The Asquith Liberals, or 'Wee Frees', secured only 26 seats, though polling more than a million and a quarter votes.

It is the dominant Conservative wall that most deserves analysis into its component bricks, and especial interest attaches to the 168 new members who had had 'something very much like a complimentary ticket to Westminster', as J. M. McEwen, whose brilliant statistical analysis of the election does much to demonstrate the validity of Keynes' flamboyant remarks, puts it.[22] The first remarkable point is that this election ratified and reinforced the changes in the political élite adumbrated in the ministerial appointments of 1916. Traditionally Unionist representation had been dominated by landowners or by businessmen of national eminence: thus of new members returned in January 1910, those in county constituencies were mainly (65 per cent) local men, while those sitting for boroughs were mainly (64 per cent) non-local. Among the new Conservative M.P.s of 1918 it was in the borough constituencies that local men predominated (82 per cent), while the counties now had a majority of outsiders (54 per cent). What these statistics represent is a great swelling in the number of local businessmen on the benches of the powerful Unionist Party; most of them had little or no experience of national politics. The other striking feature about the new Unionist members was that less than a quarter of them were under forty, whereas nearly one half of the re-elected Unionists had been under forty at the time of their own first entry into Parliament. The average age of the whole Parliament was 51 years, 7½ months. The Labour Party representation was not of much higher calibre. The tide of patriotic fervour was so high that MacDonald, Jowett and Henderson were each defeated by members of the jingoistic Labour splinter-group, the National Democratic Party. Only three I.L.P.-financed candidates were returned, all newcomers to Parliament, and the local Labour Parties, which were being formed under the terms of the new constitution, produced a mere seven successful candidates. The mass of the Parliamentary Labour Party consisted of trade union candidates of a solid and uninspiring cast: twenty-five of them were candidates of the Miners' Federation.[23]

266 THE END OF THE WAR

It was an old Parliament, and it was an inexperienced Parliament; it was not one with which men returning from the war would find any very close sense of identity. 'Only 68 of the newly elected Unionists,' J. M. McEwen points out, 'had been in uniform during the war, and it should not go unremarked that 27 of them held the rank at least of lieutenant-colonel or its equivalent.'²⁴ Yet it was still possible to see the election results, not as a massive triumph for reactionary and inexperienced Toryism, but as an overwhelming mandate for Lloyd George to proceed with his reconstruction plans for a better society. 'When the sweeping Election victories were announced in the closing days of 1918,' wrote Evelyn Wrench, 'I was convinced that we were about to witness the greatest constructive job of social reform carried out in our lifetime.'²⁵

[II] PLUS ÇA CHANGE...

However genuine Lloyd George's own hopes that he might fulfil his promises and carry through just such a job, he and his colleagues expected to be faced first with a hard battle against the industrial dislocation and unemployment likely to follow hot on the heels of the war. From the analogy of the Napoleonic and Boer wars it was argued that there must be no immediate or indiscriminate demobilization of Britain's vast armies. It was the same pessimism as had been evident in the first days of war, as much the product of an unbalanced insecure society as the hysterical enthusiasm which then, as now, went with it. The first serious planning for orderly demobilization was initiated in the pregnant summer of 1916 when Edwin Montagu was put at the head of a Demobilization Sub-committee of the Cabinet Reconstruction Committee. In August 1917 Montagu's Sub-committee came under the auspices of the new Ministry of Reconstruction, and it was here, with the co-operation of the War Office, the Admiralty, the Air Ministry and the Ministry of Labour, that the master plan was drawn up.²⁶ With the basic objective of averting mass unemployment it was decided that the priority of a man's release should be based, not on the length of his service, but on the ability of industry to absorb him. Individuals, not whole units, would be demobilized. Accordingly each serviceman was allotted to one of five categories, of which only two, and the Government stipulated that these should be numerically very small, were to be demobilized at once. Within each category, it was agreed, preference should be shown to married men, to those with long records of service, and to those who had served long in the firing line. When the Armistice did come, the Government had to bear in mind that, despite the popular upsurge of emotion, the war was not yet technically at an end, and that it might be desirable to maintain a considerable force in the field in order to secure an acceptable peace treaty; such a force would be less necessary if the Government intended to stand by its more idealistic utterances on the subject of war aims, but it did not; nor did public opinion seem to wish it to do so.

The two favoured categories of servicemen were the 'demobilizers' – those whose services were essential to expedite the demobilization of everybody else – and the 'pivotal men' – those who were vital to the industries of 'reconstruction' and whose employment, it was reckoned, would help to create further jobs. The Ministry of Labour made a selection of businesses and professions which might be regarded in this light, then special authorities within each occupation decided which individual men should be deemed 'pivotal'. To assist in determining allocation to the other three categories use was made of the labour exchanges, where employers seeking the return of specific men filled in a form giving the serviceman's full name, unit, regiment, and theatre of war or command. Each serviceman had to state on a civil employment form which was also filed at the labour exchange whether or not he had received an offer of employment; if he had not he was entitled to request that a particular employer be approached on his behalf. In those cases where the employer's form and the serviceman's form corresponded, a slip was torn from the latter and returned to the man's commanding officer. The relatively lucky individual concerned thus became a 'slip man' and entered the third category, those who were to be released after the start of general demobilization in accordance with priorities determined by the Ministry of Labour on the basis of the relative importance of each trade or profession to the national welfare. There remained a fourth category of those who, though without definite offers of jobs, were normally employed in industries which, being central

to the reconstruction effort, were likely to provide work immediately, and a fifth category of all other 'non-slip' men who would
be released in the order of importance of their normal civilian
occupation.[27]

Partial demobilization did not begin till 9 December, almost a
month after the Armistice. Each man now selected in accordance
with the grand plan was sent first to a camp behind the lines from
whence he proceeded across the Channel to a dispersal station in
his own home district. Here the various formalities took about
twenty-four hours, in the course of which he acquired a railway
warrant, a ration book, an out-of-work donation policy, a civilian
clothes allowance and 28 days home leave, together with pay and
ration allowances for that period. The out-of-work donation policy
was a considerable advance upon the original niggardly intention
to use the four-year-old charity-based National Relief Fund to sub-
vent those servicemen who, despite the Government's best-laid
demobilization schemes, might find themselves jobless. Without
being called upon to make any contribution himself, the ex-service-
man was entitled to benefits of 24s (raised to 29s four days before
the general election) for each week he was without employment,
with 6s for a first child under fifteen and 3s for each additional
child; payments however were restricted to a maximum of twenty
weeks out of the first fifty-two following upon demobilization.

At the end of the twenty-eight days furlough, the serviceman
became technically demobilized. He was not discharged but transferred to the Z Reserve, thus giving some colour to the conscription scare which arose during the election, and creating much
disquiet in the weeks which followed. More than that, the whole
scheme was grotesquely misconceived. At its root there was a
responsible desire to avoid mass misery and unemployment, but in
its effects it demonstrated power rather than responsibility, the
prerogative of unenlightened bureaucracy. There was no attempt
to deal positively with the problem of the provision of employment, that was left entirely to individual employers. The *Herald*
commented satirically on the lot of the serviceman:

We leave the matter of finding him employment to the owners and we
present him with cash and promises, which work out to an average of
about 9s a week for fifty-two weeks, provided he is unemployed for

twenty of them. It is superb, immense. None but an imperial people, victorious against its enemies, but overcome with emotion and thankfulness before its returning heroes could have done it.[28]

The negative endeavours of the scheme simply created a rising curve of unfairness: the man last in was the man most likely to have retained contacts with his civilian employment and therefore most likely to be first out; the man first in was likely to have lost all contact with former employers, and therefore likely to be last out. Even before the unfairness became apparent, the delay in beginning and continuing with demobilization seemed bad enough.

In calling for the men to be sent home at once the *Herald* was not alone:

Munition-making has stopped; motorists can joy ride; the King has a drink; society has had its victory ball and is settling down to its old job of pleasure making.[29]

The Government tried to meet the criticism with three distinct moves. On 13 December it introduced a scheme whereby a serviceman then on leave in Britain, though not yet demobilized, could take up an offer of employment from a pre-war employer if endorsed by the advisory committee of the local employment exchange, always provided that the soldier's service headquarters agreed that he was not indispensable to the armed forces. This 'contracts system', as it was called, though it might secure the release of a few more men, had the main consequence of adding yet another element of chance to the lottery of demobilization, and only served to inflame existing discontent. On 19 December it was announced that the payment of war gratuities would commence forthwith: each man was entitled to a lump sum, ranging from £5 for a private to £15 for a warrant officer, class I, with an additional 10s for each month after the first year of service overseas and 5s for each month after the first year of home service. On the same day Lloyd George appointed Sir Eric Geddes to co-ordinate the demobilization work then being administered by fourteen separate departments.[30]

The new year opened with the publication of the Government's explanation of the slow rate of demobilization: the needs of the army of occupation overseas, and the economic situation at home, it was explained, were paramount considerations; general demobilization had not yet been ordered and only 'pivotal' men, and coal miners, since the country had run into a serious coal crisis, were then being released; apart from this, French and British railway, shipping and port facilities were inadequate.[31] The explanations failed to satisfy those men who were in the most heart-rending position of all: on the point of re-embarkation for France at the termination of a period of leave. On Friday, 3 January, 10,000 soldiers at Folkestone demonstrated against this fate, and the following day 2,000 men demonstrated at Dover. Claiming that the trouble was mainly over the operation of the 'contracts system' the War Office decided to extend the facilities by which men on leave might procure or complete contracts. But the injustice of the system was merely underlined, for those who were not able to profit by the relaxation were ordered back to their units forthwith. At Brighton 8,000 soldiers took part in a mass meeting of complaint on 6 January, and on the same day and the day following, there were demonstrations in Whitehall. Soldiers appeared in lorries with placards which read: 'We won the war. Give us our tickets'; 'Get a move on Geddes'; 'No more red tape'; 'We want civvie suits'; and 'Promises are not piecrust'. Support for the servicemen was forthcoming from all sections of the press, from the *Daily Express* ('Get on or Get out, Geddes') as well as the *Herald*, and from many civic groups, including the Birmingham City Council, which denounced

the incapacity, circumlocution, and general disorder with which the question of demobilization is being dealt with by government departments, leading to general dislocation of business and great disadvantages to the men.[32]

The Army Council brought the contracts system to an abrupt end; then Winston Churchill, War Minister in the Government as it was recast after the election, announced what was in effect the jettisoning of the whole demobilization plan in favour of something nearer to a first-in first-out system, by which all but 900,000 men would be released. From 1 February, in a move to lessen the divide which every day was growing more bitter between soldier and citizen, pay rates in the army of occupation were increased. All this was more reasonable and more equitable, but it congealed into a solid spectre a number of uneasy shadows that had been flitting around for some time. First the fear of deeper military commitment in Russia – a fear, which, at a personal level, had almost certainly influenced the soldiers' demonstrations at the beginning of January; and second the fear of conscription. When the Government sought to give Parliamentary sanction to the retention of 900,000 conscripts beyond, if necessary, the conclusion of a peace treaty, it ran into an ingrained opposition which has endured for fifty years: in an intriguing debate, William Adamson, the Fifeshire miner who now led the Labour Party in the Commons, argued for a 'free' system in which voluntarily enlisted soldiers would be paid a wage on a par with the average earnings of the industrial worker.[33] The opposition of a few coalition members was not sufficient to prevent the measure passing on 6 March. Outside protests continued, both on the Russian and the conscription issue, but as the new demobilization plans were rapidly executed hostility faded. None the less the average serviceman could scarcely but have a feeling of resentment over the handling of his release from military duties; in February 1920 there were still 125,000 men awaiting demobilization.

While society waited for the men to come home, or ignored their very existence, there were a few modest fruits of victory upon which to sustain the joys of the Armistice.

The right to make cakes and pastries of every kind and to cover them with sugar or chocolate or both was restored to Britons on 7 December, 1918, as was the right to eat an unlimited quantity of these or other cakes at afternoon tea.[34]

Pre-war flour returned; street lights blazed again; there was a double meat ration for Christmas 1918. But rationing continued: for meat till November 1919, for butter till early 1920, and for sugar till November 1920. There were still many prosecutions for violation of the food control regulations, coal was in very short supply, and, worst of all, prices of nearly everything took a sharper upward turn than at any time since 1914.[35] Dislocation of trade prolonged scarcities, the burst of speculative investment which began shortly after the Armistice fostered inflation, the sanction of patriotism no longer restrained the would-be profiteer. Shortage of housing and pressure on urban centres brought an extreme rise in rents in 1920.

Wages rose rapidly too, giving rise again to the familiar paradox: a short-term sense of grievance in working-class households concealing a very real long-term gain. A bricklayer in full employment (he suffered, and continued to suffer, from the highly seasonal nature of his employment), earning an average weekly wage of 42s 10d in July 1914, was earning 79s 2d in July 1919, and 100s 7d in July 1920; his labourer's earnings at the same three points in time were 29s 1d, 65s 2d, and 87s 4d. In the engineering and shipbuilding trades a patternmaker's average wage rose from 42s 1d in August 1914, to 86s 8d in February 1920; a riveter earning 37s 9d in August 1914, earned 74s 9d in April 1919, and was earning 80s 5d a year later; the corresponding figures for a labourer were 22s 10d, 58s 3d, and 63s 11d. A compositor working in Sheffield (where wages were lower than in a larger town) was on average paid 36s a week in July 1914, 72s in 1918, and 89s 6d in July 1920. Engine-drivers, earning about 42s a week in 1914 were earning up to 90s in August 1919; firemen had risen from 26s to 66s. The trend towards greater proportionate increases in the poorer-paid employments can be clearly seen in the worst paid of all manual occupations: the agricultural worker who averaged 13s 4d in 1914 was by 1920–21 earning 46s a week. The average income of all working-class families between 1914 and 1920 rose by 100 per cent, which more than cancelled out a rise in the cost of living of 75 per cent. But there were pockets of extreme hardship; large families were hit all round, and above all by soaring milk prices which in the winter of 1919–20 reached 8½d a quart, twopence up on the first winter of peace. A special committee on milk prices reported that

numerous returns from Food Committees conclusively prove that consumption is being seriously reduced, and inquiries show that in the case of large families of young children the prices are proving a very great hardship.

Many hardships, real and imagined, combined to make 1919 a

year of strikes. As in the first year of war, so in the first year of peace: the watchdogs of the Clyde barked first. Acting in effective unity, the Clyde Workers' Committee and trade union leaders of the older type pressed their claim for a forty-hour week as the best method of absorbing the returning servicemen. A complex of circumstances contributed to the dramatic events which followed: on the labour side the syndicalist tradition kindled anew by revolution accomplished in Russia and attempted in other parts of the world; on the Government side a manifest fear of Bolshevism and its world-wide off-shoots, and a confirmed suspicion of Glasgow as an eternal trouble centre; on both sides the snapping of nerves tautly stretched, and now deprived of war's intoxication. The earlier Clyde strikes had been spontaneous and broad-based, but now, when the war was won and the peace in grave danger of being lost, there was greater working-class solidarity than ever. When the leaders of the forty-hours movement called a general strike on Monday, 27 January, they succeeded completely in all the principal factories: three mass demonstrations took place on the 27th, the 29th and the 31st. The third the Government anticipated by concentrating troops, tanks and machine guns on the city; the actual 'battle of George Square', however, was fought with policemen's truncheons – the police by all accounts being the aggressive party – fists, and bottles of fizzy lemonade. On 1 February the tanks moved in upon the deserted battlefield; the strike continued for a further ten days. A dozen of the leaders were arrested, but only against two could a successful charge be made out, and that scarcely implied any deep subversion of the established order: Willie Gallacher and Emanuel Shinwell were imprisoned for 'inciting to riot'. Looking back ruefully many years later Gallacher unwittingly exposed the whole situation: 'We were carrying on a strike when we ought to have been making a revolution', he wrote. All talk of the likelihood of revolution in Britain in 1919 is quite beside the point, as J. M. Keynes again perceptively observed.[36]

While agitation on Clydeside was met with a demonstration of force, the simultaneous threat of the Miners' Federation to call a strike was met by the appointment of a special statutory Commission with full miners' representation, to investigate the condition of the coal industry. The tanks had conquered a pitch from which the strikers had already retired; the Commission was to produce a report which the Government had no intention of implementing. But the miners were meantime prevailed upon not to strike. A Lancashire cotton-workers' strike in June passed off without great incident. A second London police strike on a rather small scale broke out in August, followed by a more serious one, accompanied by much rioting, in Liverpool: again the armed forces were called in. Most serious of all was the national railway strike which began on 29 September. Although the Government was able to deploy its wartime emergency powers, when the strike ended on 5 October the railwaymen had won their main point, abandonment of a proposed wage cut. From 20 September there was a major strike among the iron-moulders, and this was less easily disposed of – it continued in fact for four months.[37]

Strikes made the headlines, blown up by the press into windy extravaganzas about anarchism and Bolshevism. Since the other critical topic which came nearest home was that of Ireland where the internal war, so clearly presaged in 1914, had by January 1919 effectively begun, newspapers in this first post-war year presented a strikingly similar appearance to those of the last pre-war year. Society, believing itself launched on a voyage to a new and better world, seemed after all to have merely been on the Greenwich ferry.

[III] TYING UP THE LOOSE ENDS

For all that, there were developments of substance, a knitting up of loose threads which added another broad band to the unfolding pattern of social advancement. First in significance is the Housing and Town Planning Act of July 1919, the summation of wartime developments which can, more justly than in any other sector of the social services, be termed revolutionary. House-building had practically ceased during the war, creating a gap so vast that a mighty dynamo would be required to get a spark across it. Commissions of investigation had brought out the iniquity of existing housing conditions. The Government itself stood committed to building 'Homes fit for Heroes'. Heroes and others, in a time of galloping inflation, had become used to the idea of controlled rents. That private enterprise could provide the necessary 600,000 houses was dubious; that it could provide them at the sort of rents people expected to pay was out of the question. While the Salisbury Committee on *Housing in England and Wales*, which reported in October 1917, had tentatively canvassed the idea of intensified State action, the Royal Commission on Housing in Scotland had already indicated the only solution, a massive public initiative in house-building.[38]

The Act, therefore, called upon the local authorities to conduct within three months, and from time to time thereafter, surveys of the housing needs of their areas, to draw up plans for dealing with these needs, and to submit the plans for approval to the Ministry of Health. The first critical feature of the Act is the undertaking given that when these plans had been approved all losses incurred in carrying them out, save for the tiny driblet of a penny rate which the local authorities were to levy, would be borne by the Exchequer. The State, in other words, was assuming direct financial responsibility for a large sector of the future homes of the working classes. The second distinctive feature of the Act is the scheme drawn up for determining the rents to be charged in these new houses. The existing controlled rents of working-class houses were to be taken as a general guide but rents could be varied both above and below this line according to the amenities of the house and, more important, the tenant's capacity to pay. Though it was expected that by 1928 it would be possible in most cases to charge an economic rent, the principle of subsidized accommodation for those most in need was to be maintained. That costs under the Act were sometimes needlessly high was rather the fault of the way in which it was operated than of the Act itself: in providing for the building of local authority housing up till 1921 at a rate equivalent to 70,000 houses a year, let at rents ranging from about 5s a week in rural areas to about 12s a week in parts of London, the Act was not unsuccessful.[39] In that the Minister had powers to insist that the new houses should have fitted baths the Act did help, albeit modestly, to fuel the general movement towards the diffusion of a common material standard throughout society. This for the time being was more important than the long-term consideration that as long as there was both private and public housing, the boundary of the municipal housing estate would tend also to be a boundary of social class.

Aesthetically the houses were not always a great success, and in Scotland their construction marked a departure from the eminently sane, though grossly abused, tradition of tenement dwelling.

Dr Addison did not entirely circumvent private enterprise. The Housing (Additional Powers) Act, which followed rapidly behind the major Act, permitted a small lump sum subsidy for houses built by private enterprise, provided they conformed to certain conditions as to size. Although the finger which the State in 1915 had laid on fast-rising rents had opened out into two copious hands, the original problem had not disappeared. Acts of 1919 and 1920, while permitting substantial increases in controlled rents, extended the scope of control to cover houses built before the summer of 1919 which had rateable values of up to £105 in London, £90 in Scotland, and £78 elsewhere.

The Housing Act of 1919 and the Education Act of 1918 are the two major examples of the burgeoning of collectivist social action during the war era. A third is the Unemployment Insurance Act of 1920. The wartime additions to the rather limited 1911 Act have already been noted, as has the post-war 'out-of-work donation', which, despite the contempt of the *Herald*, had a certain significance – paid to both ex-service men and women, and war workers, and having no insurance basis whatever, it broke the tight bonds of the existing National Insurance structure. The principal Act of 1920 developed the idea of including nearly all wage-earners within its embrace, but sought to assert the strict insurance principle – the embrace was to be that of a Victorian father. Included were all wage-earners save for non-manual workers earning more than £250 per annum, Civil Servants, soldiers and schoolteachers, and farm labourers and domestic servants. A weekly contribution of 10d per week for men, shared, as in the 1911 Act, between employee, employer and the State, yielded an unemployment benefit of 15s per week for a maximum of 15 weeks in any one year, provided a minimum of twelve contributions had been made, and provided that though capable of work the applicant had been genuinely unable to find any. The confines of the scheme may seem more obvious than the breadth of commitment in fact assumed by the State; but when the melting snows of mass unemployment poured in after 1921, it was the confines which were easily swept away. It is true that the major extensions of social benefits in the twenties owed more to adverse economic circumstance than to the intentions of the framers of the 1920 Act; but the Act itself was very much the product of wartime developments, and of the desire to mitigate the economic dislocation expected as the aftermath of war.

The wartime experiment of running the railways as a consolidated national service rather than as a series of private profit-making agencies was widely held to have vindicated itself triumphantly, and in 1919 a Bill for the establishment of a Ministry of Ways and Communications with powers to buy up, by Order in Council, all railways, canals and docks, was introduced. But in the struggle between the Good Fairy Reconstruction and the Bad Fairy Bolshevism, the purchase clauses dropped off, and the putative Ministry of Ways and Communications shrank to a mere Ministry of Transport. When Government control finally expired in 1921, the 130-odd railway companies of pre-war days were grouped into the Big Four, the London and North Eastern, the London Midland and Scottish, the Great Western, and the Southern. Important safeguards for the community were preserved in the form of a new Railway Rates Tribunal, and in elaborate, though not very effective, conciliation machinery for dealing with labour disputes.

Even where there was no Government-imposed amalgamation, the phase of accelerated private industrial combination clearly detectable during the war reached its culmination at the end of the war. In the first half of 1919 the 43 chief banking concerns of 1914 became the Big Five, with a powerful hold on British trade and industry. Lever Brothers took a further gulp at their smaller competitors; Vickers Maxim amalgamated with Metropolitan Carriage Works; a group of financiers acquired and greatly extended Guest, Keen and Nettlefolds.[40] So manifest were these developments that the Government appointed a Committee on Trusts to investigate them.[41] A minority consisting of Ernest Bevin, the trade union leader, J. A. Hobson, W. H. Watkins, and Sidney Webb, the Fabian, concluded that in certain industries combination had gone so far as to render them ripe for public ownership. J. M. Rees, who wrote a study of the problem based on the report of the Committee, reached a similar conclusion.[42] The collectivists indeed were now happily having it both ways:

a highly fragmented industry had to be nationalized because it was inefficient; a highly concentrated one because it was a menace.

On the other side of industry there was a counterpart to industrial combination in the amalgamation and consolidation of trade unions which took place in the immediate post-war years. The Iron and Steel Trades Confederation had been established in 1917; the Amalgamated Engineering Union was established in 1920; and the Transport and General Workers' Union in 1921. In part these amalgamations, though they did not go anything like the length desired by the advocates of industrial unionism, marked a permanent triumph over the old sectionalism which had been submerged in the wartime 'unofficial' struggles. The new-found unity, purpose and confidence were expressed in the creation in 1921 of a permanent General Council to replace the old Parliamentary Committee of the T.U.C. Trade union membership figures which had reached 6½ million in 1918 soared to 8⅓ million by 1920.

After looking at the advances made by labour in the earlier part of the war, we turned to the advances made by women. The stop-go nature of the legislation of 1919 is illustrated in the last chapter of the story of the emancipation of women which falls within our purview. In November 1918, just before the election, an Act was rushed through making women eligible to stand for Parliament. After the election the Labour Party introduced a Women's Emancipation Bill to remove every remaining legal inequality between men and women. The Bill passed all stages in the Commons, but the Government had it defeated in the Lords, bringing in instead its own Sex Disqualification Bill which duly became law. This weaker measure opened jury service, the magistracy and the legal profession to women, and gave them qualified entry to the upper reaches of the Civil Service; it was made clear that there was in law no barrier to their full membership of the ancient Universities of Oxford and Cambridge. Political emancipation was indeed, as the suffragists had always said it would be, followed by a spate of social and economic legislation affecting women. But the new Affiliation Orders Act of 1918 was by no means abandoned in its generosity: it increased the five shillings maximum maintenance allowance of the Bastardy Laws Act of 1872 to ten shillings.

[IV] CUTTING THEM AGAIN

That the collectivist idea which had been applied so potently to the problems of housing and unemployment insurance would not be strong enough to secure the prolongation or extension of the wartime control of the major sectors of industry could not have been clearly foreseen at the time of the Armistice: indeed the very concept of reconstruction had seemed to imply some such control. However, with the return to peace, private enterprise recovered its voice. The day after the Armistice, Sir J. Walton unleashed in the House of Commons a tirade against the Government bureaucrats: 'every trade and industry that they have touched they have hampered and injured'.[43] One day later the Executive Committee of the F.B.I. turned its sights upon the National Factories and declared that they must not be used 'for the purpose of State trading under conditions which will inevitably be unfair to private enterprise'.[44] An impressive array of industrial chieftains gathered on 16 January 1919 in a joint meeting of the F.B.I., the Associated Chambers of Commerce of the United Kingdom, the Mansion House Association on Railway and Canal Traffic, the Traders' Traffic Conference, the Pressed Brick Manufacturers' Association, the Furniture Warehousemen and Removers' Association, the Horticultural Traders' Association of Great Britain and Ireland, the National Federation of Fruit and Potato Trades' Association, and Messrs. Butterley and Co. Ltd., to pass a unanimous resolution against nationalization of the railways.[45] As the war receded behind the golden horizon of the post-war boom the anti-collectivist sentiment of the employing class hardened, though there continued, in the light of recent experience, to be reservations and qualifications. Thus although the Executive of the F.B.I. at its meeting on 26 March 1919 was clearly worried by what it called 'the present strong efforts to commit the country to a policy of nationalization', and set up a special committee to watch the situation, it also remarked that 'some measure of national control might conceivably be a good thing in some industries'.[46] However, in the F.B.I. Report on Nationalization, published in 1919, the reservations were minimal, the old principles supreme:

We would begin by laying it down as a general proposition that centralized management by a Government Department is fatal to commercial efficiency and enterprise. . . . We desire to record our emphatic
opinion that in dealing with industries or public services of whatever
class, whether local or national, any further extension of state monopoly should be avoided. . . .[47]

The anxiety betrayed in these activities and resolutions was
justified, for from 3 March the Royal Commission on the coal
industry, appointed to avert a miners' strike, was effectively put-
ting private enterprise on trial. The Commission consisted of four
members appointed by the Government, the Hon. Justice Sankey
(Chairman), Arthur Balfour, Sir Arthur Duckham, and Sir
Thomas Royden; four members appointed by the Miners'
Federation of Great Britain, Robert Smillie, Herbert Smith, Frank
Hodges, and Sir Leo Chiozza Money; two members agreed between the Government and the miners, R. H. Tawney and Sidney
Webb; and three members appointed by the coal owners, R. W.
Cooper, J. T. Forgie, and Evan Williams. In an interim report
published at the end of March, the four Government nominees
declared:

Even upon the evidence already given, the present system of ownership
and working in the coal industry stands condemned, and some other
system must be substituted for it, either nationalization or a method of
unification by national purchase and /or by joint control.[48]

A separate interim report of the miners' representatives along with
Tawney and Webb, found that

in the interests of the consumers as much as in that of the miners,
nationalization ought to be, in principle, at once determined upon.[49]

The three coal-owners' representatives made no pronouncement
at this stage on these larger issues, confining themselves to the
more mundane question of wages.[50]
     In the second stage of the Commission's inquiries weighty
considerations were put forward both for and against nationalization; what is striking is the number of the former which were
based on the wartime experience. E. H. Davies of the Mines

Department of the Board of Trade was enthusiastic about the
Coal Transport Reorganization Scheme operated during the war;
Sir Richard Redmayne, Secretary to the Coal Controller, while
unsure about nationalization, favoured 'collective production'
and regarded the existing system as 'extravagant and wasteful';[51]
William Blane, a mining engineer and large-scale employer, who
worked in the War Office between 1915 and 1919 as Assistant
Director of Army Contracts, supported the principle of national-
ization, as did Arthur Greenwood,[52] successively Lecturer in
Economics at Leeds, Assistant Secretary to the Ministry of
Reconstruction, and Labour Parliamentary candidate, and A. E.
Davies, General Manager of the Banking Corporation. When A. J.
Hobson (not to be confused with J. A. Hobson, the economist,
who favoured nationalization[53]) on behalf of the Council of the
Associated Chambers of Commerce declared that the nationalization of the telephone had introduced what he called a 'forty per
cent factor of inefficiency' he was controverted by F. J. Pearson,[54]
Assistant Accountant-General for the Post Office, and Sir William
Slingo, Engineer-in-Chief to the Post Office.[55] The most illuminating remark of all was that of Sir Keith Price, a businessman who
had been brought into the War Office in November 1914, who
believed that in wartime Government control had worked well,
but 'in peace time the reverse would be the case'.[56]

The second stage concluded with the presentation by the
Commission of four separate reports.[57] First there was that of
Sankey alone,[58] which in advocating State ownership was fully
supported in the separate report presented by Money, Smillie,
Smith, Hodges, Tawney and Webb.[59] The third report, that of
Sir Adam Nimmo (who had replaced Forgie who became ill), Sir
Allan Smith (who replaced Royden), Balfour, Cooper, and Evan
Williams, was categorically opposed to nationalization.[60] A fourth
report was presented by Sir Arthur Duckham, who although
opposed to nationalization, advocated 'district unification'.[61] The
verdict was perhaps only a degree or two clearer than mud; it did
incline towards nationalization. That such a consummation was
devoutly to be rejected was announced to Parliament by Lloyd
George on 18 August. Coal Control ended on 31 March 1921,
though the Mining Industry Act of 1920 had meantime created
a special Mines Department of the Board of Trade with the powers

relating to mines and quarries formerly exercised by the Home Office and additional ones which permitted it to make schemes for the drainage of mines and to establish a welfare fund by a levy of 1d a ton on coal produced.

Controls now fell thick and fast as autumn leaves.[62] The Treasury waged a war of attrition against the Ministry of Food, whose continued existence was fully justified by the scarcity and inflationary conditions of the immediate post-war years. It and the Ministry of Munitions were abolished in March 1921. The liquor licensing situation was stabilized by the Licensing Act of August 1921, which, while ending the régime of the Liquor Control Board and returning full jurisdiction to the local justices, applied the new licensing hours to the whole country instead of just to the wartime controlled areas. The administration of the State schemes at Carlisle and Gretna was transferred to the Home Office. The permanent limitation on drinking implied in the 1921 Act was adventitiously reinforced by the coming into effect in 1920 of the 1913 Temperance (Scotland) Act, which permitted local option: polls were held in 584 out of 1,215 areas yielding the following results: 'no change' in 511 areas, limitation in 37, and 'no licence' in 36.

The return to economic orthodoxy was most completely demonstrated in the reports of the Balfour Committee and the Cunliffe Committee. The former, while divided on the question of free trade, with a strong minority advocating a general 10 per cent tariff, was firm in its advocacy of a rapid demolition of State control;[63] the latter cheerfully pinned its faith in the Bank Charter Act of 1844 and recommended an eventual return to the Gold Standard.[64] It recognized, however, that the internal circulation of gold sovereigns had gone for good, as indeed it had. In its decontrol policies the Government was actuated by the belief that it was doing the best thing for the stimulus of post-war industry. Exclusively wartime measures obviously had to go, and the sooner the better. However, the hope and encouragement stirred in collectivist breasts by the wartime innovations could not be permanently stilled; correspondingly the fears aroused among last-ditch individualists could not be allayed either. A Conservative Party leaflet of 1919 claimed to the credit of the Government in time of war that it had 'carried on war industries', 'controlled other industries', 'organized shipping' and 'organized food supplies'.[65] But a leaflet of 1920 declared:

Nationalization has never been tried on a large scale in this country, and where it has been tried – in Germany and Bolshevik Russia – it has proved a hopeless failure, compared with individual enterprise.[66]

The Federation of British Industries was able in the same year to bring home the full horror of nationalization by quoting M. Constantin Grunwald, General Secretary to the Russian Manufacturers' Association in London, as saying:

You cannot get nails in the Soviet shop, but a boy will be standing in the street offering you those same nails in a surreptitious way.[67]

Although on its final accounts the Ministry of Food actually made a small profit, *The Times*, whistling to keep its courage up, misleadingly reported the facts under such headings as 'State Trading Losses', 'Auditor's Strong Criticisms' and 'A Record of Waste'. Similarly the economic successes of the Carlisle experiment were grossly travestied.[68]

Till the late summer of 1920, Government, industry and society enjoyed boom conditions, then came the crash that led into the long inter-war depression. The index number of prices, standing at 192 in 1918, 206 in 1919, 265.1 at the peak in April 1920, collapsed to 155 in 1921 and 131 in 1922. The froth was off the pint, and what lay underneath was worse than anything purveyed under liquor control. Old markets had gone, others had shrunk; the world had too many ships, preferred oil to coal, was trying to operate the delicate nineteenth-century supply and demand mechanism when the conditions in which that had worked not too badly had been irreparably shattered. Unemployment, which averaged 3·1 per cent in the latter half of 1920 rose to 13·5 per cent in 1921 and 13·8 per cent in 1922. The Government reacted in the worst possible way: 'reconstruction, when not dropped into the dustbin, was put on the shelf'.[69] In the passion for economy of 1921, even the Fisher and Addison Acts were affected. It became clear that there was no prospect at all of the school-leaving age being raised to fifteen; such continuation

classes as had been formed were slowly strangled. Similarly the
Addison policy was effectively terminated in July 1921, when a
limit of about 170,000 was set on the number of houses to be
allotted a subsidy. Providing homes fit for heroes had become too
expensive; 'the heroes would have to go without'.[70] Heavy and
continuous unemployment certainly forced upon the Government greater and greater responsibility for providing unemployment benefits in which the insurance element was mere myth.
But for the man who would have preferred the Government to
create work for him this was no great boon.

Reconstruction turned to retrenchment, the land fit for heroes
became the waste land. What of the world outside, now that the
war to end war, the war to make the world safe for democracy,
was over? What of the cries for hanging the Kaiser, the promises
to make Germany pay? The Peace Treaty concluded at Versailles
on 28 June 1919 did as much as was humanly possible to reconcile these different objectives. Hanging the Kaiser was out of the
question as Lloyd George probably knew in advance of the
general election, since the Kaiser had fled to Holland where his
hosts were not willing to give him up. But Article 231 of the
Treaty declared that Germany was to pay reparations for the entire
cost of the war. Articles 1 to 26 established the dream of all pro-
gressives, and the noblest product of the war, a League of
Nations. Some men of the Left certainly were critical of what they
called a 'League of Victorious Allies' when what they wanted was
a 'League of Peoples', by which they meant a league representative of all shades of opinion within a country, not just of governments; but before long the whole Labour Party was united in its
championship of, to misquote what Mr R. A. Butler has said in a
different connexion, 'the best League we've got'. Within the
Conservative Party Lord Robert Cecil became an enthusiastic, and
eventually somewhat lonely, publicist for the League. But in 1919
a Conservative leaflet welcomed it in the words 'out of evil
cometh good'.[71]

There was a Peace, and there was a League of Nations. Yet
there was no peace, and the nations were divided. There were
revolutionary insurrections followed by reactionary repression
throughout the world. Allied forces were still involved in Russia.
The 'troubles' had broken out in Ireland. In the summer of 1920 it

appeared that the Government was about to intervene on the side of Poland in the Russo-Polish war: an extraordinary demonstration of labour hostility to such a 'crime against humanity', induced second thoughts.[72] If the country had not become pacifist it had certainly become war-weary. The desire to hang the Kaiser, never gratified, became a matter of shame, like an unsated debauch.

Three quarters of a million men were killed in the war, nearly two million wounded. That in itself was a serious physical loss and a deep wound in the social consciousness. Disillusionment had broken upon the more sensitive at various times during the war; the majority remained in a state of intoxication, or, for those in the armies, in a state of suspended judgement. On the whole hopes were high in 1918, and even in 1919, as to what great goals might now be achieved. Waiting for an interview in the Warden's lodgings of All Souls, E. L. Woodward, a good representative of the middle-class volunteer of 1914 (when he was in his mid-twenties), who later become a distinguished and level-headed historian, reckoned that the survivors of his generation,

would be able to use in peace their experience learned in war. I thought that the future was in our hands; that we should get the support of those immediately younger than ourselves; that our elders would listen to us, and, for very shame, be ready to give us a directing control over the management of affairs.[73]

In fact the election of 1918 had already entrenched the elderly in power, and the elderly enacted the policies of retrenchment. The grains of disillusionment were sown in the mudflats of war, but it was the post-war let-down which brought on the harvest of bitter rice. Woodward constructed moving words upon the bitterness he came to feel,

in the first few years after the war, about the hollow words used too often at the unveiling of war memorials. Glib words about the 'Great Sacrifice'. I know that in many cases these words were used with deep feeling by men who had lost their own sons. They became almost a cliché in the oratory of politicians. Laurence Binyon's noble words 'they shall not grow old as we who are left grow old' took on an ironic meaning in the mouths of speakers who were well content to grow old and fat, and who had never asked the dead whether they had chosen to die young in order to avoid old age. As time went on, I began to dislike more and more the celebration of Armistice Day. I wished that all the formal ceremonies might be abandoned, and that this commemoration of the dead could be left to those for whom it had some personal meaning. Darkness is not better than light, death is not better than life; no praise from comfortable men can bring the dead back to the sun they loved. It was too easy for the older generation to find a convenient anodyne in the formal politeness of a two-minutes' silence, in the weaving of wreaths, in the provision of adequate pensions for widows and orphans.[74]

This was a disillusionment which could not but be shared by men of all classes, as Government promises collapsed and industry went into stagnation. It marked the post-war decade. Yet it was only clearly and articulately expressed by a handful of middle-class poets and prose-writers. The working classes had always had their battles to fight. Owning so little in 1914, they had lost so much less over the war period. They and society as a whole had many gains to enter in the ledger along with the losses.

NOTES TO CHAPTER EIGHT

1. Local Government Board, *Report of Medical Department 1918–1919*; P.P., 1919, XXIV, Cmd. 462. *Report on Influenza Epidemic of 1918–1919*; P.P., 1920, X, Cmd. 700. *Report on Influenza Epidemic in Scotland 1918–1919*; P.P., 1919, X, Cmd. 282.

2. McDonagh, *In London During the Great War*, pp. 232 ff. *The Times,* 5 June 1918. R. Groves, 'When 12,000 London Policemen went on Strike' in *Socialist Outlook,* 22 January 1954.

3. *Daily News,* 10 October 1918.

4. McDonagh, p. 321 (17 October 1918).

5. ibid., p. 325 (9 November 1918), p. 327 (11 November 1918).

6. H. Williamson, *A Soldier's Diary of the Great War*, p. 252 (11 November 1918).

7. C. Edmonds, *A Subaltern's War*, p. 204. Montague, *Disenchantment*, p. 31. See the imaginative description in R. Aldington, *Roads to Glory*, 1930, pp. 35–45.

8. C. S. Peel, *How We Lived Then*, p. 173.

9. Wrench, *Struggle 1914–20*, p. 352. McDonagh, p. 328. See also C. E. Playne, *Britain Holds On, 1917–18*, 1933, pp. 392–5.

10. McDonagh, p. 329.

11. Briggs, *History of Birmingham*, p. 225.

12. In Alec Waugh's novel *The Loom of Youth*.

13. Quoted by Briggs, *History of Birmingham,* p. 225.

14. McDonagh, p. 333.

15. T. Wilson, 'The Coupon and the British General Election of 1918' in *Journal of Modern History*, March 1964.

16. G. D. H. Cole, *History of the Labour Party since 1914*, 1948, p. 83.

17. *The Times*, 24, 31 November, 10, 12 December 1918.

18. *Manchester Guardian*, 11, 13 December 1918. *Daily News*, 11, 12 December 1918. *The Times*, 14 December 1918.

19. See J. M. McEwan, 'The Coupon Election of 1918 and the Unionist Members of Parliament', *Journal of Modern History*, 1962, pp. 294 ff.

20. C. L. Mowat, *Britain Between the Wars*, 1955, p. 5.

21. *Daily Mail*, 30 December 1918.

22. McEwan, p. 295. The figures cited in the following sentences are taken from McEwan's valuable article.

23. Cole, *History*, pp. 83–8.

24. McEwan, p. 300.

25. Wrench, *Struggle 1914–20*, p. 423.

26. *Report of Ministry of Reconstruction to 31 December 1918*; P.P., 1918, XIII, Cd. 9231, p. 1. *Report of War Cabinet for 1918*; P.P., 1919, XXX, Cmd. 325, p. 301.

27. On these and the next two paragraphs see S. R. Graubard, 'Military Demobilisation in Britain following the First World War', in *Journal of Modern History*, 1947, pp. 297 ff., and sources there cited.

28. *The Herald*, 23 November 1918, quoted by Graubard.

29. ibid., 7 December 1918.

30. *The Times*, 20 December 1918.

31. ibid., 1 January 1919.

32. Quoted by Graubard (on whose article the preceding paragraph is based), p. 302.

33. *House of Commons Debates*, 27 February 1919 (cols. 677–8).

34. Beveridge, *British Food Control*, p. 269.

35. A. L. Bowley, *Prices and Incomes 1914–20*, p. 35.

36. Gallacher, *Revolt on the Clyde*, p. 221. J. M. Keynes, *The Economic Consequences of the Peace*, 1919, p. 237. Cp. 'Revolution Averted' in R. Graves and A. Hodge, *The Long Week End*, 1940.

37. Mowat, *Britain between the Wars*, pp. 38–40.

38. *Housing in England and Wales*; P.P., 1918, XXVI, Cmd. 9087. P.P., 1917–18, XIV, Cmd. 8731.

39. See esp. M. Bowley, *Housing and the State*, 1945, pp. 15–25.

40. *Report of Committee on Trusts*; P.P., 1918, XIII, Cmd. 9236.

41. ibid.

42. J. M. Rees, *Trusts in British Industry 1914–21*, 1922, pp. 252–5.

43. *House of Commons Debates*, 12 November 1918.

44. Federation of British Industries, *Annual Report 1918–19*, p. 12.

45. *Bulletin of the Federation of British Industries*, 16 January 1919.

46. ibid., 31 March 1919.

47. Federation of British Industries, *The Control of Industry: Nationalisation and Kindred Problems*, 1919, pp. 2, 4.

48. P.P., 1919, XI, Cmd. 84, p. 5.

49. P.P., 1919, XI, Cmd. 85, p. 3.

50. P.P., 1919, XI, Cmd. 86.

51. P.P., 1919, XI, Cmd. 359, pp. 79–89, 222–40.

52. P.P., 1919, XII, Cmd. 360, pp. 950, 545–8.

53. ibid., pp. 473–6.

54. Cmd. 359, pp. 174, 181–2.

55. Cmd. 360, p. 474.

56. ibid., p. 1001.

57. P.P., 1919, XI, Cmd. 210.

58. p. 5.

59. p. 27.

60. p. 35.

61. pp. 56–7.

62. See R. H. Tawney, 'The Abolition of Economic Controls 1918–21' in *Economic History Review*, 1943, on which this paragraph is based.

63. P.P., 1918, XIII, Cd. 9035, pp. 25–6, 44–53, 67–8.

64. P.P., 1919, XIII, Cmd. 464, p. 3.

65. National Union of Conservative Associations, *The Government Record in War and Peace*, 1919.

66. National Union of Conservative Associations, *Labour and the Labour Party*, 1920.

67. *Bulletin of Federation of British Industries*, 19 January 1920.

68. Beveridge, p. 330. Shadwell, *Drink in 1914–22*, pp. 127–8.

69. Tawney, p. 8.

70. M. Bowley, *Housing and the State*, pp. 22, 26.

71. National Union of Conservative Associations, *The League of Nations to prevent War*, 1919.

72. Cole, *History*, pp. 103–7.

73. Woodward, *Short Journey*, p. 114.

74. ibid., p. 116.

CHAPTER NINE
After the Deluge

[1] DADDY, WHAT DID THE GREAT WAR DO TO YOU?

WHERE HISTORY differs as a scholarly pursuit from a science is in the inability of the historian to conduct anything in the nature of a controlled experiment. In summarizing analytically the material presented chronologically in the course of this book, we find that there are not many topics in which we can say this or that was caused by the war, *and nothing but the war*. If we attempt to list the bed-rock direct consequences of the war, we shall find that we are dealing as much with the *method* by which the war affected society as with the actual effects in society.

The direct consequences, which we can limit to seven, reacted with a multiplicity of other forces creating a tremendous range of side effects and indirect consequences. First and second are the obvious tangibles, the loss of life and limb, and the destruction of what contemporary writers liked to call 'treasure'. Third is the wholesale disruption caused by the war in the old mechanism of international trade and finance. Fourth is the huge physical demand of the war for manpower and machines, which, given, of course, the deeper pressure of the will to survival, created an irresistible pressure for the reorganization and reorientation of society; what forms the reorganization took, what lessons were learned from it, depended on other circumstances, but the immediate and eventual ramifications were immense. Fifth is the way in which the war, in one sense the ultimate expression of the German challenge to British supremacy, brought to Britain a sharp sense of her deficiencies and a sharp determination to remedy them. Sixth is the mass of domestic problems piled up by the war's interruption of normal social development. Seventh is the scale, horror, and excitement of the war, calling forth all sorts of different responses from all sorts of different people, and necessitating the mobilization, not just of men and machines, but of minds, which in turn created all kinds of reactions and by-products.

The loss of 745,000 of the country's younger men (leaving aside the unknown proportion of the 1·6 million wounded who were gravely mutilated) amounting to about 9 per cent of all men under 45, meant a definite alteration in the population balance, which can be presented with reasonable statistical precision, but whose full emotional effects cannot be precisely assessed. In 1911 there were 155 males aged between 20 and 40 per thousand of the population in England and Wales; in 1921, for every thousand of the population, there were only 141. The balance of females over the age of 14, therefore (discounting any other minor factors involved), rose from 595 per thousand in 1911 to 638 per thousand in 1921, and the proportion of widows per thousand of the population rose from 38 to 43.[1] There is no exact measure of the quantity of personal agony concealed behind these figures, but society, in later years, exhibited all the signs of having suffered a deep mental wound, of having undergone a traumatic experience, to which the agony and the slaughter, as well as the more generalized horror over the destruction of an older civilization and its ways, which we shall consider in a moment, contributed. In the inter-war years the birth rate declined even further than it had in Edwardian times, but although the loss in the war of potential fathers was a contributory factor a later Royal Commission concluded that it was not in itself a significant one.[2] Other by-products of the war – the wider diffusion of contraceptives or the pruning of large family establishments for example – reacted within the broader trend. Already by 1921 the average number of children under 14 per family had declined from 1·29 to 1·12, bringing the important incidental consequence of a raising of living standards.[3]

Much was written in the years after 1918 on 'the lost generation'. We have seen the statistical basis – one in ten of the generation aged between 20 and 45 during the war, missing. What the figures do not make so clear, but what has often been pointed out, is that the missing were the cream of the generation, the first volunteers, the junior officers; out of Oxford University's total roll of service of 14,561, 2,680 were killed.[4] A faint touch of myth, perhaps, was mixed with the grim reality, which was mainly stressed by those articulate men who had themselves been Oxford men, junior officers, early volunteers. Society, very hesitantly, was turning towards the idea of choosing the occasional leader elsewhere than from the university officer class, but there is no doubt that much of the political weakness of Britain in the inter-war years can be attributed to the paucity of young talent of quality. To avoid getting one's generations hopelessly mixed, it is worth recalling that the survivors of the lost generation were men like Clement Attlee and Harold Macmillan, who reached political eminence in the forties and fifties, when they were not noticeably deficient in colleagues of high calibre. Where the loss of the tithe of a generation did also seem to make itself felt – this is problematical ground – was in the weakening of any possible mediatory agency between the old generation, entrenched in power by virtue of the Coupon Election, and the young generation which grew up in the maelstrom years of the war.

While the wartime damage to Britain's capital assets (with the notable exception of shipping) was not of great significance, the immense financial cost of the war, through the high taxation which it necessitated and the inflationary trend which it created, did have powerful social effects. First of all the trend towards the compression of disposable incomes intensified, drawing classes closer together, making it difficult for the upper classes, and very nearly impossible for the middle classes, to maintain the lavish standards of pre-war days. Secondly the landed classes received the final series of blows, which, in combination with other political developments, finally knocked them out of their political and social primacy. Thirdly, as the 'tax line' dropped to incomes of £130 at the same time as working-class earnings began to rise above this figure, it virtually ceased to exist as the sort of social demarcation that it had been in Edwardian times. The sale of War Savings Certificates was another financial expedient which contributed to this spreading of the pale of respectable citizenship.

The dislocations of the old international economic system were extremely serious for a trading nation such as Britain and created problems which helped to give rise to mass unemployment in the inter-war years. But the immediate effect was to demonstrate the falsity of many of the economic dogmas

associated with that system. Despite the effective departure from
gold, the economy not only survived, but was able to produce enormous sums of money for the prosecution of the war. It almost
began to look as though economics could be the servant of man,
rather than man the servant of economics. The same conclusion
could be drawn from the vast experiment in state control developed step by step to meet the needs of war. The lesson was
not immediately learned: what was wrong with Britain in the
twenties was that she suffered from what the war had done,
and failed to profit from what the war had taught – her governments were composed of sadder but not wiser men. But the story
does not end there. In the first place the precedents had been set,
establishing in fact a new measure of tolerance for large-scale
State intervention. Thus the collectivist measures which were
enacted at the end of the war, the big ones like the Housing Act
and the Unemployment Insurance Act, and, later, the setting up
of the B.B.C., and the little ones like the establishment of the
Forestry Commission in 1919, created little stir. In the second
place ideas which could in pre-war years be laughed off as Uto-
pian fantasies, denounced as contrary to economic law, or displayed as evidence of the sinister intentions of socialism, had been
put to work and had been seen to work. In the years after the
war, as the country entered upon economic depression and mass
unemployment, more and more political thinkers began to argue
that escape could only come through the revival of some of the
policies of the war years. In 1927 four young Conservatives,
Robert Boothby, Harold Macmillan, John de V. Loder and the
Hon. Oliver Stanley pointed out that:

The war period shattered preconceived economic notions, proved
possible theoretic impossibilities, removed irremovable barriers,
created new and undreamt-of situations. Yet by far the greater part of
the legislation which today governs trade and industry dates from
before that period. We are surely entitled to ask whether it is now
adequate to meet the vastly changed conditions of the modern economic era.[5]

Under the impact of the great crash of 1931 collectivist economic
policy was greatly extended in the thirties; it became dominant
in the nineteen-forties, and although there have been slight re-

laxations since then, no serious politician today, save perhaps Mr Enoch Powell, would contemplate a return to the orthodoxy of Edwardian Britain.

The shortage of manpower contributed along with the other shortages to the wartime extension of State control, but its main effects were more subtle. The working class as a social class, though suffering many hardships and grievances, derived a number of permanent advantages from their favourable market position – wage rates were doubled, the average working week was reduced from 55 hours to 48 – and, more important still, they got a taste of the better material comforts of modern civilization. That the working class made as much as it did of its favourable situation was in large measure due to the efforts of the organized labour movement, which was already developing in strength and cohesion before 1914; but the need of the Government for the co-operation of the leaders of the labour movement in maximizing the war effort meant that they also gained immensely in prestige and status, even to the extent of taking Cabinet office. The political side of the movement, the Labour Party, was strengthened sufficiently for it to be able to wring advantage from the divisions and weaknesses in the Liberal Party. The working man, in factory or mine, or conscripted into the army, not only was, but was seen to be, fully implicated in the country's survival. A handful at least of politicians and opinion-makers began to stress his claim upon a fuller citizenship, making this claim a major motivation behind the extension of the franchise in 1918, and one among several behind the social legislation of the same period.

The gaps in the home front left by men summoned to the fighting front had to be filled, and they could only be filled by women, and, to a lesser extent, by children. The manner in which the situation was exploited owed much to the experience the women's leaders had derived from the pre-war suffrage movements; it is also true that before the war the doors to a number of professions were already slowly opening. Yet it is difficult to see how women could have achieved so much in anything like a similar time-span without the unique circumstances arising from the war. Almost certainly when the time came for a further Reform Act in the great series extending back to 1832 they would, or some of them would, have been included in the new franchise, and the vote would no doubt have assisted the fight for further economic, social and civic freedoms. But the war brought opportunity in concentrated and varied form, and from the stock of patriotic bombast paid the women a valuable bonus: men and women joined together to praise women's contribution to the war effort, bringing a confidence in their new role to women, and an acceptance of it among men, which might otherwise not have been easy to create.

The straight demand for mighty weapons of offence and defence inevitably gave a great prestige to science and a stimulus to technological, if not scientific, research. At least as important an influence on public and private research, however, was the sense of insecurity and desperate challenge brought home to British society by the war. In the really major advances of twentieth-century science the war was totally irrelevant, and Sir Charles Parsons rightly pointed out that

the work of the scientists during the war has perforce been directed more to the application of known principles, trade knowledge, and the properties of matter to the waging of war than to the making of new and laborious discoveries.[6]

Yet even from such work there came developments – aviation and broadcasting being two of the most striking – of the utmost importance for society in time of peace. The two major features of the process were the desire of commercial companies to exploit the new technological potential they had developed for purposes of war, and the creation, through the drama of war, of a popular interest in, and appetite for, such developments. It must, however, always be borne well in mind that science is international, and that the influence of war was often very secondary to the influence of, in particular, the United States of America.

The interruption by the war of normal domestic, social and economic development undoubtedly contributed to the economic ailments of the inter-war years. At the same time by inflating such problems as housing and education to enormous size it brought them within the vision of the most myopic politician. The will to action was enhanced by the contemporary collectivist experience, by the need to appease the working class and the desire to accord its members some of the privileges of citizenship, and above all by the present supreme struggle which brought out Britain's defects in the physical well-being of her people, as it had exposed her weaknesses in scientific equipment. Here is part, the major part, of the explanation for the burst of social reform at the end of the war. We must qualify it by recollecting what the Wickwars[7] stress in discussing the Addison Housing Act, that the collectivist 'tendency was already at work before the war of 1914'. They then add that 'the end of the war gave an illusion of dramatic suddenness to what might otherwise have been a gradual and almost imperceptible process'. But in this book, following Miss Marion Bowley,[8] I have described the Housing Act in its scope and provisions as revolutionary. In reality, there is no conflict: the problem is the same as that involved in the new freedoms gained by women – no doubt they would have come eventually as an 'almost imperceptible process', but in fact, because of the war, they came in a sudden burst. Similarly, by an only slightly less direct train of causation, the Housing Act, and the other social legislation, in the form in which it actually came, was a consequence of the war.

But what were the consequences of these pieces of social legislation? Here we run up against the complicated chemistry of social improvement in modern society, which involves 'a rare and fascinating phenomenon, the rise of a new standard of living, the pursuit of which has made a profound difference to the poverty-stricken of all classes'.[9] Once it has started, this phenomenon is to some extent self-perpetuating, but at its centre are the material products of scientific advance and the extension of collectivist social welfare. The importance of the reconstruction legislation of the war period is that it forms the basis of this subsequent extension, and thus makes a large contribution to the overall process. Although the Addison Housing Act was stifled, half a million houses were built under its important successor, the Wheatley Act of 1924, which greatly extended the subsidy policy. Similarly, some of the ideals of the Fisher Education Act, destroyed in 1921, were restored after 1924. Many of the other wartime developments – the growth of women's spending power, for example – fit into the chain-reaction; by accelerating pre-war trends, they create still greater acceleration.

Our final direct consequence of the war is a multiple one. The war was exciting as well as horrible. Where the world was not really, as Blumenfeld put it, 'topsy-turvy', people tended to want to believe that it was; the wish became the father to the thought, and the thought became acceptable. Early twentieth-century Britain had been a disturbed society, but those who openly railed against its conventions were a small minority: the emotional excitement of this greatest of all wars gave a certain universality to the concept of change, gave a moral sanction to the disruptions and transformations demanded by the physical needs of war. When enthusiasm flagged, propaganda stepped in. For the ordinary citizen, despite dark liberal talk of truth being the first casualty of war, the poison did no more than prolong the emotional debauch a little longer than it might otherwise have lasted, leaving behind little but a bad taste and perhaps – among ex-soldiers at least – a certain healthy scepticism of the printed word: 'whatever your pastors and masters tell you had best be assumed to be just a bellyfull of east wind'.[10] Pastors indeed did their own cause great harm by their pulpit propaganda.

The havoc of the war, in the apt word of E. L. Woodward, had a 'scorching' effect on the minds of British intellectuals:

The novels and poems of D. H. Lawrence, the early novels of Aldous Huxley, Lytton Strachey's *Eminent Victorians*, Mr Keynes's *Economic Consequences of the Peace* bear evidence of minds 'scorched' by war, and reacting against a nervous strain which was almost unbearable. The strain was caused not by any doubt about the issue of the war, but by the very fact of a European war and the breakdown of accepted standards.[11]

Woodward obviously regretted the disappearance of old virtues; he obviously disliked the tone of, say, Lytton Strachey's closing description of the service of remembrance held for the martyred Victorian hero General Gordon:

The service was conducted by four chaplains – of the Catholic, Anglican, Presbyterian, and Methodist persuasions – and concluded with a performance of 'Abide with me' – the General's favourite hymn – by a select company of Sudanese buglers. Every one agreed that General Gordon had been avenged at last. Who could doubt it? General Gordon himself, possibly, fluttering, in some remote Nirvana, the pages of a phantasmal Bible, might have ventured on a satirical remark. But General Gordon had always been a contradictious person – even a little off his head perhaps, though a hero; and besides he was no longer there to contradict ... At any rate, it had all ended very happily – in a glorious slaughter of twenty thousand Arabs, a vast addition to the British Empire, and a step in the Peerage for Sir Evelyn Baring.[12]

To attribute the cynicism of Lytton Strachey or the mystical hatred for industrial civilization of D. H. Lawrence solely, or in any sizeable degree, to the experiences of the war would be ludicrous. The serious attack on Victorianism began in the 1890's and developed under the leadership of Shaw, Wells, Davidson, Fry and many others in the Edwardian period but it was in the nature of the war, murderous beyond all proportion to moral or material gains made, to foster scepticism, irony, irreverence.

Of religion not a great deal has been said so far, since no clear trend really emerges till the end of the war. It was in keeping with the exaltation of the times that the churches should be well patronized during the war, and they seemed a natural focal point of Armistice celebration and thanksgiving. Ministers of religion had embarked with enthusiasm upon the 'Holy War'. 'The Church', as the Minister of St Giles Cathedral, Edinburgh, recalled,

to an unfortunate degree, had become an instrument of the State and in too many pulpits the preacher had assumed the role of a recruiting sergeant. Almost every place of worship throughout the length and breadth of the land displayed the Union Jack, generally placed above the Holy Table, while some had great shields carrying the flags of all the allied nations. The first thing I did myself when I went to St Paul's, [Greenock] was to have a huge Union Jack and the national flag of Scotland displayed upon the east wall of the chancel. Being young, and owing to the inflamed feelings of the times, I said many things from my pulpit during the first six months of my ministry that I deeply regret. It is no excuse to say that many preachers were doing the same thing. I still feel ashamed when I recall declaiming on one occasion – about the time of Haig's 'Our Backs are to the Wall' message – that anyone who talked of initiating peace negotiations with the rulers of Germany was a moral and spiritual leper who ought to be shunned and cut by every decent-minded and honest man! This monstrous and stupid utterance, of which the Press got wind and duly lauded, so moved one of my patriotic hearers, the Manager of the Greenock Docks, that he startled the congregation by involuntarily shouting 'Hear, hear!'[13]

But sensitive believers were already secretly in revolt. C. F. G. Masterman, formerly a staunch Anglican, complained to his wife that a service at Westminster Abbey seemed like an activity at Wellington House, and remarked that the only religious leader who emerged with credit was the Pope, because of his appeal to the warring nations, and that the body which came through best was the Quakers.[14] After the war there was an immense reaction against the fervour and bigotry which had displayed itself in its most nauseating forms during the war. The brutal horror of the military war had a direct effect on religious belief: in February 1918 Masterman, in his diary, was musing upon the possibility that

God is a devil who rejoices in human suffering. He may be. There's no evidence to show He isn't.[15]

Many other long-term forces are involved in the decline of organized religion, not the least of them being the failure of the churches, from the time of the industrial revolution, to capture the interest of the proletariat. If anything, there did seem during the war to be a positive attempt to meet this situation, as Church-men asked 'why should it be the exception rather than the rule for the workers to feel that the Church is their home?'[16] In the social reorganizations of the war, the Churches, though they may have been assisted towards interdenominational unity through the sharing of ministers, were, on the whole, adversely affected, especially from the breaking-up by war-service of the old close-knit dissenting communities.[17] The extent to which, in the perspective of three decades of change, the Churches suffered, can be seen from Rowntree's 1935 survey of York:

the number of adults attending church has fallen from 17,060 in 1901 to 12,770 in 1935, notwithstanding the fact that during that period the adult population of the city has increased from 48,000 to 72,248. ...

In 1901 adult attendances amounted to 35.5 per cent of the adult population; in 1935 it amounted to only 17.7 per cent.[18]

The direct 'scorching' of the war reacted with the indirect consequences of the social transformations wrought by the war and with the broader trend of intellectual scepticism to create one great denominator, 'a widespread impatience of authority as such,'[19] which was both a part of, and an influence on, the social climate of the inter-war years. It could be seen in the 'new morality',[20] it could be seen in the decline of 'deference', it could be seen in religion. But, alas, it had only a negative influence on politics: that was the supreme equivocation bequeathed by the war, and the key to the tragic aspects of Britain's inter-war history.

[II] THE NEW SOCIETY

Geography, naturally, did not change much between 1914 and the 1920's (Southern Ireland gained independence at the end of 1921). In the twenties, however, a new population drift from the areas which in 1914 held the main concentrations of industrial power towards the Home Counties and the South East becomes apparent. While the population of London and the Home Counties increased by 18 per cent between 1921 and 1937, that of the Midland Counties increased by only 11 per cent, that of the West Riding, Notts and Derbyshire by only 6 per cent, the Lowlands of Scotland by only 4 per cent (although the Scottish birth rate was higher than the English) and that of Lancashire by less than 1 per cent. The population of South Wales declined by 9 per cent, and that of Northumberland and Durham by 1 per cent.[21] This trend was the geographical expression of the depression in coal mining and the old heavy industries, which accounted for the high and steady figure of $1\frac{1}{2}$ million unemployed throughout the decade, and of the growth (though insufficient growth) of the new light, science-based industries. London and its motorized traffic problem had already caused concern before the war, and it already had its extensive environs inhabited by 'suburbans'; but it was in the twenties that the great development of commuterland – Hendon, Morden, Wembley, etc. – began, so that the total population of Greater London rose to over eight millions. Before the war it was London with its sweated trades which housed the most notorious swamps of poverty while the miners and the skilled workers in the heavy industries had been the most prosperous members of the working classes.

Clearly the movement towards the new technologies was inevitable, and signs of it were apparent enough well before 1914. It can be argued that, apart from the wider interruption of international trade, the war had an adverse influence in that it brought a final intensive development and exploitation of the old industries, when there should instead have been a steady conversion to new industries.[22] There is some, but not a lot of, force in this, since the war did also bring a stimulus to the new industries. What was ironic about the wartime industrial experience was the great, and justified, sense of power and importance it gave to the miners and heavy engineering workers, who were then, after the war, to find themselves working in conditions of falling demand. And although that same experience demonstrated not just the value of science-based industry but also the uses of Government direction and control, no attempt in the twenties was made towards sending new industry where it was required to absorb unemployment. So the pattern established itself: a prosperous, bustling south producing a tremendous range of new consumer goods; a decaying north.

The war had a dissolving effect on the class structure of Britain, the elements working the change being both economic – taxation especially – and emotional: the sense of 'topsy-turvy-dom', the sense of common citizenship. But Britain was still, as it is today, very much a class-conscious society. At the top the landed class, which had been the dominant component of the political élite of Edwardian times, moved into political, though not so obviously into economic and social, eclipse. Much attention, in the first years of peace, was focused on the extensive land sales which took place: 'England is changing hands', became a stock remark. By March 1919 about half a million acres were on the market, and by the end of the year over a million acres had been sold. In 1920 sales were still greater, with the Duke of Rutland making the pace by selling off about half of his Belvoir estate, 28,000 acres in all, for £1½ million.[23] One firm of estate agents claimed that within a single year land equal in area to an English county had passed through their hands.[24] There were three main reasons for these sales. They could first of all be simply the continuation of a policy initiated at the beginning of the century whereby the landowner sought to consolidate his income by selling off outlying holdings; that is to say, financial impoverishment was not necessarily involved. Second, however, there was the question of high taxation, initiated as far as the landowner was concerned in the years before 1914, but greatly extended during and at the end of the war, when the 1919 budget raised death duties to 40 per cent on estates of £2 million and over. The frequent deaths in battle of young aristocrats made the burden of death duties even greater than it might otherwise have been. Third was the fact that, because of wartime exploitation of agriculture, land values had greatly risen, while rents had not; by selling, the landowner could put the increased value straight into his pocket. Economically, then, the position of the land-owners was not too serious: they

emerged into the inter-war period still in residence in their country seats, with their territorial empires considerably reduced, but with their incomes – once debts had been cleared and reinvestments made – probably much healthier than they had been for very many years.[25]

But their feudal dominance of the countryside was almost at an end, as their own tenants took the opportunity presented by the land-sales to set themselves up as owner-farmers. The sale of urban land, opening the door to the small domestic landlord, and to a new type of property developer, took place at the same time as the sale of landed estates. Town houses, now that the upkeep of large establishments was so difficult, were sold too, symboliz-ing the movement of aristocratic high society away from the centre of the London political stage.[26]

The new flow of political power within the topmost class was given its first big boost by the events of December 1916, and was ratified in the 1918 general election. It was expressed in the notorious energy with which Lloyd George created new peer-ages – 98 between 1917 and 1921, his fall from office unfortunately preventing him from completing his century – in the passing over of Lord Curzon in favour of the 'countrified businessman'

Stanley Baldwin for the Prime Ministership in 1922, and in the formation of the influential 1922 Committee of Conservative backbenchers – most of them businessmen. It was, naturally, a matter of deep regret to aristocrats like Lord Henry Bentinck who believed that the Conservative Party was being 'thoroughly commercialized and vulgarized', and Plutocracy 'ennobled, decorated, knighted and enriched'.[27] The upper class, then, is still, as in Edwardian times, a composite class, but the balance has moved definitely from the landed to the business interest. It was this class, or the younger members of it, which, drawing upon the hectic hedonism of the war, created the gay high-life associated with the ninteeen-twenties. It was this class which occupied the literary attentions of Aldous Huxley, and of John Galsworthy, the chronicler of the fortunes of a Victorian business family. Galsworthy, making a not very funny joke at the expense of social investigators who talked of the ten per cent below the poverty line, said that he was concerned only with the ten per cent above the property line.[28] Inequality in the division of income and wealth was still very marked, but not quite as marked as before the war: in 1910 1·1 per cent of the population took 30 per cent of the income; in 1929 1·5 per cent took 23 per cent of the income, and two thirds of the wealth was owned by 2½ per cent of the population. Bowley and Stamp, in their analysis of the national income as it was in 1924, pointed out that, while in 1911 individuals with incomes above £5,000 drew 8 per cent of the aggregate national income, in 1924 those earning £9,500 (the equivalent, given the rise in prices between 1914 and 1924) drew only 5½ per cent. They then proceeded to the very cautious summing up:

When the full effects of taxation are taken into account the real income available for saving or expenditure in the hands of the rich is definitely less than before the war. The sum devoted to luxurious expenditure is (allowing for the rise of prices) definitely less than in 1911, but it is still sufficient to bulk large in the eyes of the public, since it is concentrated in small areas, enlarged by the spending of visitors from overseas and advertised by the newspapers.[29]

When we move into the middle classes, the outstanding and incontrovertible statistical fact is the increase over the war period in the salaried class from under 1·7 millions in 1911 to over 2·7 millions in 1921, a rise from 12 per cent to 22 per cent of the occupied population.[30] The figures themselves are inflated because of the inclusion in this category of low-paid shop assistants, clerks, etc., and the expansion is exaggerated because the classification in 1921 was rather more rigorous. None the less the growth is striking. Itself a social phenomenon of outstanding importance, it reflects the expansion of four important groupings in the community: the professions, for whom rising material and welfare standards brought a new demand; the Civil Servants and clerical administrators, needed by the growing bureaucracy; the managerial class required for the running of large-scale modern industry; and those women who held on to the opportunities opened to them during the war (in 1931 there were $5\frac{1}{2}$ million women in employment, 37 per cent of the female population between 14 and 65).[31] The other important feature of note is the decline in servant-keeping among middle-class households. The total decrease in the number of servants in the country over the war period, about a third, is less than is sometimes suggested; despite what observers during the war thought, many women were forced back at the end of the war into this degrading occupation. Still, the decrease that did take place came largely out of the households of the middle classes. In the commuter areas of London the number of resident servants per 100 families declined from 24·1 to 12·4, whereas in the West End it only edged down from 57·3 to 41·3.[32] In the whole of Liverpool the decline was from 13·5 to 8·3; in suburban Wallasey from 22·4 to 14·5.[33]

The decline in servant-keeping helped to weaken the barriers between the middle and lower classes, though a comparison between John Galsworthy's Tony Bicket in *A Modern Comedy* and E. M. Forster's Leonard Bast do not suggest any great change in upper-middle-class attitudes. The 'tax line' had all but disappeared in 1919–20 when there were $7\frac{3}{4}$ million tax-paying citizens,[34] six times the number in 1914, though this total fell again when the exemption limit was shortly raised to £150 per annum. When Bowley conducted a second social survey in 1924 with the express purpose of finding out whether working-class poverty had diminished since 1913, the problems of deciding which were working-class households and which were not had subtly changed:

In general, our principle has been 'when in doubt, rule out.' In the previous inquiry the inclination seems rather to have been the other way.[35]

The lines of distinction between middle and working class, that is to say, have become much more blurred than before; the feeling is that the clearly definable working class has got a little smaller. This feeling is borne out by the figures in the 1921 census: the total number in the 'wage-earner' category, the main core of the working class, has fallen to under 15 millions,[36] other variables being at least cancelled out by the increase meantime in the population. Carr-Saunders and Caradog-Jones, in their inter-war studies of the social structure of England and Wales, it may be noted here, refused to use the language of social class, belligerently in the first study when they asserted that 'the belief in the existence of social classes . . . is the result of studying social theory of doubtful value and of neglecting social facts',[37] less belligerently in the second, when they merely inquired, 'is it not a misreading of the social structure of this country to dwell on class divisions when, in respect of dress, speech, and use of leisure, all members of the community are obviously coming to resemble one another?'[38]

The working class in 1914 was large and it was poor. In the early twenties it was not quite so large, and it was not quite so poor. Bowley referred to his earlier pronouncement that 'to raise the wages of the worst-paid workers is the most pressing social task with which the country is confronted today', and continued:

It has needed a war to do it, but that task has been accomplished, so far as rates of wages are concerned, though employment has not been permanently possible for all at those rates.[39]

There was the achievement, and there the qualification upon it. Real wages for full-time employment were up by 20 per cent, the average working week down from 55 hours to 48 hours. But there was also, in certain areas, continuous unemployment on an unprecedented scale. Where 11 per cent of the families in Bowley's previous survey had been in primary poverty, the new wage rates should have reduced this figure to 3·6 per cent; because of unemployment the actual figure was 6·5 per cent. In the mining village of Stanley, which had basked in the coal boom of 1913, conditions were actually slightly worse now that coal-mining was a depressed industry: 7·5 per cent in primary poverty in 1924 as opposed to 6 per cent in 1940. In the long view the achievement was much more important than the qualification; but in the meantime the qualification brought much misery.

The great flux in material conditions, mental attitudes, and leisure activities contributed to the blurring of social distinctions. The decline in drunkenness, in itself a most important social fact, also helped to bring working-class behaviour into the area of the middle-class norm. While mentioning 'the immense present-day volume of drinking which takes place', the *New Survey of London Life and Labour* stressed that 'the outstanding points are,

the decrease in the amount of drinking per head, as distinct from the amount spent on drink, and the decreased extent to which actual excess, and the economic and physical effects of excess, are found. The social status of drunkenness has steadily fallen in the eyes of the working-class population. Where once frequent drunkenness was half admired as a sign of virility, it is now regarded as, on the whole, rather squalid and ridiculous'.[41]

A levelling out in the opposite direction was suggested by Mary Agnes Hamilton, writing in 1935 of 'the new morality':

in this respect the practice of the middle classes now tends, with variations of its own, to resemble that previously common enough among what were then called the 'lower orders'.[42]

A similar sort of social communion was to be found in widespread religious non-observance.

The most potent force of all was the growth of the mass media of communication. This was at first treated by the politicians with something of the same fuddy-duddy obscurantism as brought the return of much of the old economic orthodoxy in 1920 and 1921, but was shortly made the occasion for the enlightened application of the wartime collectivist lesson. In March 1919 a wireless telephony (i.e. the broadcasting of speech and sound as distinct from code signals – wireless telegraphy) transmitter was set up at Ballybunion in Ireland by the Marconi Company, and, under the direction of H. J. Round, successful transmissions were made to America. This led to the installation of a more powerful 6-kilowatt transmitter at Chelmsford, where, in addition to the testing of speech and long-distance transmission, short transmissions of musical items were also made. The product of the experimental work at Chelmsford was a standard Marconi transmitter for commercial purposes. In February 1920 a new 15-kilowatt station at Chelmsford began broadcasting two half-hour daily programmes of news items and live and canned music, which were enthusiastically picked up by the owners of receiving sets. The *Daily Mail* gave a lead to popular interest and arranged the celebrated Melba broadcast from Chelmsford of 15 June 1920, which has been widely recognized as 'a turning-point in the public response to radio'. But many vested interests, particularly among the military, regarded these developments as entirely frivolous, and issued grave warnings on the plight of airmen seeking guidance in bad weather who received only musical entertainment. Accordingly the Chelmsford broadcasts were banned, though transmitting and receiving licences continued to be issued to those who could provide testimonials to the seriousness of their scientific interest. Serious or not, there was nothing to stop the owners of receivers listening to broadcasts from Paris and the Hague; from January 1922 the Marconi Company was again allowed to broadcast speech and music, and this it did at Writtle, and at 2 L O – Marconi House in the Strand – where broadcasts of one hour a day began on 11 May 1922. But the Post Office insisted that broadcasts must be broken off every seven minutes to allow a pause for the reception of official messages, a restriction which Professor Briggs has likened to the old prescription that motor cars must be preceded by a man with a red flag. The chief influence on 2 L O broadcasting was Arthur Burrows, who argued that although there should be a large number of items of 'a really popular character' the attempt should also be made to 'lift' the public above its 'present standard of musical appreciation'.[43]

The Marconi Company was not alone in its interest in broadcasting; other companies wished to exploit the new potential which they had developed for war purposes. At a meeting of the Wireless Society of London in 1920 the British Thomson-

Houston Company displayed a radio receiver which could be installed in the home for about £30. By the summer of 1922 both the Metropolitan-Vickers Electrical Company (now Associated Electrical Industries) and the Western Electric Company were preparing to make transmissions. Each had American associations, and it was indeed the tremendous radio boom which took place in the United States at the end of the war (demonstrating the international quality of technological advance), combined with the pressure of the British companies, which helped to bring about the next development, a 'treaty' between the Post Office and the 'Big Six' (the four companies already mentioned, plus the Radio Communications Company and the General Electric Company). The outcome was the British Broadcasting Company, which began operations at the end of 1922, and moved in April 1923 to the home always associated with it, at Savoy Hill.[44] With the Calvinistic Scot, John Reith, as General Manager, and, inside a year, Managing Director, and Arthur Burrows as Director of Programmes, standards were high, but the Company was in essence a commercial company working for private profit through expanding sales of radio sets. The State at first had shown a narrow suspiciousness of broadcasting; but from August 1923, when a Departmental Committee on Broadcasting presented a glowing appreciation of its potential as a medium of mass communication,[45] governmental attitudes began to change. A second Broadcasting Committee, reporting in 1925, declared:

Broadcasting has become so widespread, concerns so many people, and is fraught with so many far-reaching possibilities, that the organization laid down for the British Broadcasting Company no longer corresponds to national requirements or responsibility. Notwithstanding the progress which we readily acknowledge, and to the credit of which the Company is largely entitled, we are impelled to the conclusion that no company or body constituted on trade lines for the profit, direct or indirect, of those composing it can be regarded as adequate in view of the broader considerations now beginning to emerge.[46]

Acting on the Committee's recommendations, the Conservative Government of the day established a public corporation in place of the private company. The founding of the British Broadcasting Corporation, embodying the application of the collectivist method to one of the most potent of the social relations of science, symbolizes very neatly the union of two of the major forces discussed in this book.

A similar comment could be passed on the enactment of the British Cinematographic Films Bill in 1927, which, by instituting a system of quotas and subsidies, was designed to break the American monopoly and encourage the making of British films. The war had taught the value of propaganda and the after-glow of war flames up strongly in report of the Moyne Committee (1936), which described the cinema as

undoubtedly a most important factor in the education of all classes of the community, in the spread of national culture and in presenting national ideas and customs to the world. Its potentialities moreover in shaping the ideas of the very large numbers to whom it appeals are almost unlimited. The propaganda value of the film cannot be overemphasized.[47]

If it was the propaganda value of films which helped to bring about the necessary legislation for the protection and development of the native industry, it was their entertainment value which most affected British society in the early twenties. More than this, as the *New Survey of London Life and Labour* noted,

The influence of the films can be traced in the clothes and appearance of the women and in the furnishing of their houses. Girls copy the fashions of their favourite film star. At the time of writing [1934], girls in all classes of society wear 'Garbo' coats and wave their hair *à la* Norma Shearer or Lilian Harvey. It is impossible to measure the effect the films must have on the outlook and habits of the people. Undoubtedly they have great educational possibilities which have so far been very imperfectly attained. But the prime object aimed at is not to instruct or 'uplift', but to amuse, and in this object the cinema has proved very successful. It is estimated by the Cinematograph Exhibitors' Association that the aggregate weekly attendances at London cinemas now amount to a third of the population. Certainly today the cinema is *par excellence* the people's amusement.[48]

State intervention also took place in a third technological development greatly stimulated by the war, aviation, whose importance for society, however, was for the time being trivial compared with that of the cinema, or even radio. Holt Thomas's new Aircraft Transport and Travel Company began the first daily air service for passengers and goods between London and Paris in August 1919. Only two or three passengers were carried at a time:

One would walk into the little office where the clerk ... was seated and ask: 'How many have you got for today?' 'Two,' he would answer, with an air of satisfaction. 'And how many for tomorrow?' ... 'Three,' he would reply, with an even greater pride.[49]

The passengers, 'resigned but still apprehensive', would be packed into the 'small aeroplanes like sardines in a tin'.[50] By January 1920 three British companies were operating regular cross-channel services. But despite the Atlantic and Australian flights undertaken in the Vickers 'Vimy' (an adaptation of the wartime bomber) in 1919, which helped to preserve the romantic image which aviation alone brought untarnished from the war,[51] civil aviation simply did not pay. Temporary government subsidies to the three British companies were followed by the establishment in 1924 of Imperial Airways, with a government subsidy and certain government-appointed directors.[52] The major government ment assistance to the motor-car industry had come in the form of its wartime tariff policy. In 1920 there were 550,000 motor vehicles (including motor-bicycles) on British roads; in 1922, 952,000 and in 1930, 2,218,000.[53]

British society in 1914 was strongly jingoistic and showed marked enthusiasm at the outbreak of war. The strongest single popular sentiment on international politics after 1918 was 'It must never happen again'. There was doubtless nothing very heroic about this and indeed the envenomed European atmosphere of the early twenties suggested that, like it or not, it might very well happen again. Yet the 'war to end war' talk, the early Liberal idealism, the successful economic co-operation which had taken place between the Allies, and the realistic revolt against the possibility of another bloodbath, had produced the ideal represented by the League of Nations. The ideal was bedevilled by the bitter divisions and the cynicism also thrown up by the war, but there can be no doubt that, as represented by the League of Nations Union, it got stronger and stronger in Britain in the interwar years. Misguided and confused though it was, British society seemed to be seeking something at once finer and more rational than the emotional clap-trap which had led it into war in 1914: thus in October 1933 the electors in the safe Conservative constituency of East Fulham rejected the fire-eating blimp, Alderman W. J. Waldron, in favour of the young Labour candidate, J. C. Wilmot, fighting on a programme of, among other things, disarmament and international co-operation through the League of Nations; and in 1935 eleven million people expressed through the 'Peace Ballot' (or 'Blood Ballot' as the *Daily Express* wittily called it) their belief in the League of Nations.[54] Yet in 1939 this island paradox of Britain once again entered into a world war against Germany. It is to the political basis of the paradox that we must now turn.

[III] THE SAME OLD STATE

The political scientist draws a distinction between 'Society' and its political and administrative organization, 'the State'. A rough and ready way of explaining the paradoxical aftermath of the First World War would be to say that while society had changed, the State had not. Or one could say that the war had thrown the forces of social change and the forces of political change out of joint. A society of new ways and new attitudes had been created. New organs of government, sources of endless self-congratulation on the part of the War Cabinet, were elaborated, yet the Ministry of Reconstruction was denied any really effective executive authority, the Ministry of Health was a mere shadow of what it might have been, and the much-vaunted Haldane Committee on the Machinery of Government, presenting its Report a few days after the election, produced only a rigid and unrealistic blueprint which no one, in any case, made any attempt to put into force.[55] In economics important new lessons were learned, but in the end most of the old structure was restored. In politics old-style Liberalism was destroyed, but, despite the advances of Labour, the supremacy of Conservatism was established for two decades. Other countries had revolutions; Britain had a Coupon Election.

Not that a revolution in Britain was either likely (political and economic tensions were never sharp enough, there were no shattering blows of occupation or defeat) or desirable (Germany with its Weimar and then Nazi 'revolutions' fared far worse than did Britain). But the Coupon Election, in the size and calibre of the Conservative majority which it riveted on the country, was a misfortune. Equally unfortunate was Lloyd George's apparent acceptance that he was the captive rather than the leader of that majority. Thus votes given for Lloyd George and reconstruction, where they were given as such, became votes for Conservatism and reaction. But most votes were given as the last gesture in the long patriotic debauch (the defeat of Asquith is the most vivid piece of evidence of this): the Conservatives, after Lloyd George, 'the man who won the war', could, with justice, claim to be the best patriots; and many of them had the coalition coupon to prove it.

Over the war period there were changes in the composition of the Conservative Party. Ironically, these, if anything, were changes for the worse: Baldwin and Neville Chamberlain, businessmen both, had many admirable qualities, but neither had great gifts of political leadership. Why was there no successful challenge to the low-grade leadership of the inter-war years, even within the Conservative Party? Some of the men who might have raised it were dead. Many survivors, swept by the post-war tide of bitterness and disenchantment, conceived a healthy contempt for politics and all its ways. Men younger still, the generation too young to fight in the war, seemed completely remote from the ageing world of politics. The first inter-war decade was marked by a sceptical and bitter-sweet detachment from politics, the second by a firm and bitter, but utterly futile, commitment to violence and extra-parliamentary action.

These, however, are minor considerations compared with the key political fact at the end of the war, the absence of a strong party of the Left. Consider the Liberal and Labour Parties as two cars on a funicular railway: it was during the war that the Liberal Party, going down, met the Labour Party coming up. The image is not really very apt, since it implies that the Liberal Party was inevitably foredoomed, which was not so. What happened, as we saw, was that the Liberal Party was prevented by the war from gaining the necessary time in which it might have resolved its own internal contradictions. Prior to 1914 one or two Liberals like Arthur Ponsonby and C. P. Trevelyan who disagreed with the imperialistic trends in the Party, apparent after Lloyd George's Mansion House speech of 1911, were beginning to look with favour on the internationalist aspirations and keener devotion to social reform of the Labour Party; but their idea clearly was that Labour should be a subordinate partner to a radically-minded Liberal Party.[56] At the end of the war these same men flocked into the Labour Party, largely, they said, on the grounds that it, and especially its important component part, the I.L.P., was the only party with anything like a true internationalist spirit, but also because they now saw no hope of further social reform from any other party.[57] They were joined by others, enthusiastic upholders of the war effort, like Leo Chiozza Money, E. F. Wise, the live-wire Civil Servant from the Ministry of Food, and Christopher Addison, the Minister of Health whose attempt to build homes fit for heroes was frustrated by a Government whose concern turned to maintaining a land safe for investments. These men argued that socialistic theory had vindicated itself during the war, and re-gretted its abandonment.[58]

The Labour Party, then, strengthened and consolidated within itself by developments during the war, also benefited from an influx of new recruits; and this was just at the time that the Liberals were bitterly split between the majority trapped in the Lloyd George coalition, and the 'Wee Frees' who continued to follow Asquith. The long-term results were immense, but for the time being neither the twenty-six Asquithite Liberals returned in 1918 (actually, by an irony implicit in the 1916 crisis, the more reactionary section of the party) nor the 59 Labour M.P.s, inef-fectually led in the absence of their pre-war leaders, could present an effective opposition to a Coalition Government with a parlia-mentary strength of 474. In 1922 the Conservatives dropped Lloyd George; the election which followed gave Labour 142 seats, the Asquith Liberals 60 and the Lloyd George Liberals 57. By January 1924 Labour with 191 seats had taken office; arrayed against it were 259 Conservatives and a reunited (more or less) Liberal Party of 159.

As a new party regarded with the utmost suspicion in many quarters, Labour, once again under the able but not very adven-turous leadership of Ramsay MacDonald, set itself two tasks: to demonstrate its fitness to govern, and to establish its independent status as one of the two major parties of State. It was primarily for the latter reason that no attempt was made to strengthen the Government's parliamentary position by seeking an understanding with the Liberals (who were anyway, in many respects, more out-moded in their political ideas than the Conservatives, especially since their more radical members had joined the Labour Party). The upshot was that, apart from the Wheatley Housing Act, the first Labour Government hardly scratched the surface of the major problems of the day. The Conservatives under Baldwin then aggravated the economic situation by restoring the Gold Standard in 1925; at the same time their attempts to carry out the policies of 'Tory Socialism' roused the opposition of their own right-wing extremists. The ultimate expression of political confusion and economic failure came in the great crisis of 1931 which once again entrenched a solid Conservative majority in power. If there ever was an effective two-party system in Britain, it was not very apparent in the inter-war years; if ever a two-party system was needed, it was needed in the inter-war years. All attempts to form new groupings, planning groups, popular fronts, proved unsuccessful. Finally the Government and the country, determined to avoid the mistakes which had led to the First World War, blundered into the Second World War.

[IV] 1914–1918 AND ALL THAT

The First World War was, to borrow from *1066 And All That*, 'a bad thing', and no one but a callous rogue would wish to deny the validity of the bitterness which followed it; would wish, say, when talking of the emancipation of women to forget that a vote won might coincide with a husband or son lost. But no one but a romantic reactionary would wish to regret the world which disappeared in the deluge of 1914–18. In her *Testament of Youth,* one of the most moving of all descriptions of a private life shattered by the war, Vera Brittain incidentally brings out how the narrow conventions of provincial middle-class life by which girls were confined in pre-war days were also shattered. It is right to stress the hysteria, the phoney religion and the nauseating propaganda; but it is worth remembering that British Governments did at least have the conscience to make provision for conscientious objection, that Walter Long, the Tory squire at the Local Government Board, worked hard to see that conscientious objectors got their legal rights, and that a few crusty individualists did stand up for them.

Doubtless a new age in Britain would have been ushered in more slowly and more agreeably if there had been no war, if social and political forces, spared its distorting effects, had been left to march more closely in unison. But the war is a historical fact, whose consequences, in the end, can only be presented, not argued over. Its greatest significance is as a revelation, not so much of the folly of statesmen, but of the irrationality and love of violence bedded in human society.

NOTES TO CHAPTER NINE

1. The figures, drawn from the Census reports of 1911 and 1921, are presented in convenient form by A. L. Bowley and M. Hogg, *Has Poverty Diminished?*, 1925, p. 3.

2. *Report of Royal Commission on Population*; P.P., 1948–49, XIX, Cmd. 7695, p. 46.

3. Bowley and Hogg, p. 4.

4. Woodward, *Short Journey*, p. 115.

5. R. Boothby, *et al.*, *Industry and the State*, 1927, p. 35. See generally A. Marwick, 'Middle Opinion in the Thirties: Planning, Progress and Political Agreement', in *English Historical Review*, April 1964.

6. *Report of British Association 1919*, p. 10.

7. H. and M. Wickwar, *The Social Services*, 1949 edn., p. 137.

8. M. Bowley, *Housing and the State*, pp. 9–35.

9. H. and M. Wickwar, p. 289.

10. C. E. Montague, *Disenchantment*, p. 94.

11. Woodward, p. 122.

12. L. Strachey, *Eminent Victorians*, 1918, p. 309.

13. C. L. Warr, *The Glimmering Landscape*, 1960, pp. 118–19.

14. L. Masterman, *C. F. G. Masterman*, p. 290.

15. (14 February 1918) quoted in ibid., p. 305.

16. Society for Propagation of Christian Knowledge, *The Church and the People*, 1915.

17. G. Spinks (ed.), *Religion in Britain since 1900*, 1952, pp. 68, 75.

18. B. S. Rowntree, *Poverty and Progress*, 1940, p. 420.

19. National Council on Public Morals, *The Ethics of Birth Control*, 1925, pp. 2–3.

20. ibid.

21. P.P., 1939–40, IV, Cmd. 6153 (Barlow Report), pp. 36–7.

22. M. Abrams, *The Condition of the British People, 1911–45*, 1945, p. 21. Cp. Scott and Cunnison, *Industries of the Clyde Valley*, p. 185.

23. F. M. L. Thompson, *English Landed Society in the Nineteenth Century*, pp. 330–31.

24. C. F. G. Masterman, *England After the War*, 1922, pp. 45–6.

25. Thompson, p. 337.

26. ibid., pp. 335 ff.

27. H. Bentinck, *Tory Democracy*, 1918, pp. 2–3.

28. *A Modern Comedy*, p. x.

29. A. L. Bowley and J. Stamp, *The National Income 1924*, pp. 57–9.

30. ibid., pp. 11–12.

31. R. Strachey (ed.), *Our Freedom and its Results*, pp. 137–8.

32. *New Survey of London Life and Labour*, Vol. II, 1931, p. 465.

33. D. Caradog Jones (ed.), *Social Survey of Merseyside*, 1934, Vol. II, pp. 301, 306 ff.

34. D. C. Marsh, *Changing Social Structure of England and Wales*, 1955, pp. 216–17. Dr Marsh expresses this as one quarter of the population over twenty. It is, of course, a much higher proportion of heads of families.

35. Bowley and Hogg, *Has Poverty Diminished?*, p. 28.

36. Bowley and Stamp, p. 11.

37. A. M. Carr-Saunders and D. Caradog Jones, *Social Structure of England and Wales*, 1927, pp. 71–2.

38. ibid., 1937, p. 66.

39. Bowley and Hogg, p. 20.

40. ibid., p. 36.

41. *New Survey of London Life and Labour*, Vol. IX, 1935, p. 245.

42. *Our Freedom and Its Results*, p. 268.

43. A. Briggs, *The Birth of Broadcasting*, pp. 45, 47–53, 70–9.

44. ibid., pp. 53, 59–68, 82–3, 88, 93–142.

45. P.P., 1923, X, Cmd. 1951, pp. 5–7.

46. P.P., 1926, XX, Cmd. 2599, p. 240.

47. P.P., 1936–37, IX, Cmd. 5320.

48. *New Survey of London Life and Labour*, Vol. IX, p. 47.

49. R. Harper, *The Romance of a Modern Airway*, 1931, pp. 9–10.

50. ibid.

51. J. D. Scott, *Vickers*, 1962, pp. 174–6.

52. See esp. A. Plummer, *New British Industries in the Twentieth Century*, 1937, pp. 156 ff.

53. ibid., p. 103.

54. See Marwick, *Clifford Allen*, pp. 159, 200–1.

55. *Report of the Committee on the Machinery of Government*; P.P., 1918, XII, Cmd. 9230. P. Abrams in *Past and Present*, 1963, pp. 51–52.

56. See esp. A. Ponsonby, *Social Reform versus War*, 1912, and C. P. Trevelyan, *From Liberalism to Labour*, 1922.

57. Trevelyan, *op cit*.

58. C. Addison, *The Betrayal of the Slums*, 1922, *Practical Socialism*, 1926. L. C. Money, *The Triumph of Nationalisation*, 1921.

Bibliography

Place of publication is London unless otherwise stated

I. GOVERNMENT PUBLICATIONS AND OFFICIAL REPORTS

Public General Statutes, 1914–21 (8 vols.).

Sessional (or 'Parliamentary') Papers [cited as P.P.]: 1913 (82 vols.), 1914 (102 vols.), 1914–16 (85 vols.), 1916 (35 vols.), 1917–18 (27 vols.), 1919 (54 vols.), 1920 (52 vols.), 1921 (44 vols.), 1922 (28 vols.).

Report of Departmental Committee on Broadcasting, 1923, X, Cmd. 1951. *Report of Committee on Broadcasting,* 1926, VIII, Cmd. 2599. *Report of Committee on the Cinematographic Films Act* (Moyne Committee), 1936–37, IX, Cmd. 5320. *Report on the Distribution of the Industrial Population* (Barlow Report), 1939–40, IV, Cmd. 6153. *Report of Royal Commission on Population,* 1948–49, XIX, Cmd. 7695.

House of Commons Debates, 5 series, 1913–21.

House of Lords Debates, 5 series, 1913–21.

Official History of the Ministry of Munitions, 8 vols., 1918–22 [cited as *Hist. Min. Mun.*].

Annual Register, 1914–20.

Board of Trade, *Journal,* 1914–20.

Board of Trade (Ministry of Labour after December 1916), *Labour Gazette,* 1914–20.

British Association for the Advancement of Science, *Annual Reports,* 1914–20.

Federation of British Industries, *Annual Reports,* 1917–22.

Federation of British Industries, *Bulletin,* 1917–20.

General Federation of Trade Unions, *Annual Reports,* 1914–20.

Independent Labour Party, *Annual Reports,* 1910–22.

Labour Party, *Annual Reports,* 1910–22.

Labour Year Book, 1916.

Liberal Year Book, 1914–20.

Ministry of Reconstruction, *Reconstruction Problems,* 1918–19.

Trades Union Congress, *Annual Reports,* 1910–22.

War Office, *Women's War Work,* 1916.

II. NEWSPAPERS AND PERIODICALS

Bradford Pioneer

British Citizen and Empire Worker (1916–18)

Common Cause
Daily Chronicle
Daily Citizen (1912–15)
Daily Herald (1920)
Daily Mail
Daily Mirror
Daily News
Economist
Forward
The Herald (1915–19)
Manchester Guardian
Morning Post
Nation
New Statesman
Observer
Punch
Spectator
Suffragette
Sunday Pictorial (1915–18)
The Times
The Worker (1916)

III. OTHER CONTEMPORARY MATERIAL

(The propagandist literature issued during the war, of which there is a fine collection in the Edinburgh University Library, is too immense to be detailed here. Only a few of the most important pamphlets are mentioned.)

Addison, C., *British Workshops and the War*, 1917.
Addison, C., *The Betrayal of the Slums*, 1920.
Addison, C., *Practical Socialism*, 1926.
Aldington, R., *Death of a Hero*, 1929.
Andler, C., *'Frightfulness' in Theory and Practice*, 1916.
Angell, N., *The Great Illusion*, 1910.
Archer, W., *The Great Analysis*, 1911.
Barker, E., *et. al.*, *Why We are at War. Great Britain's Case*, 1914.
Bentinck, Lord H., *Tory Democracy*, 1918.
Booth, C., *Life and Labour of the People in London*, 17 vols., 1902–03.
Bowley, A. L., *The Division of the Product of Industry*, 1919.
Bowley, A. L., and Burnett-Hurst, A. R., *Livelihood and Poverty*, 1915.
Bowley, A. L., and Hogg, M., *Has Poverty Diminished?*, 1925.
Bowley, A. L., and Stamp, J., *The National Income, 1924*, 1927.
Brend, W. A., *Health and the State*, 1917.

Britain Transformed, n.d.
British Labour and the War, n.d.
British Universities and the War, 1917.
Brooke, R., *Collected Poems,* 1918.
Cable, B., *Doing Their Bit,* 1916.
Cable, B., *Between The Lines,* 1916.
Carr-Saunders, A. M., and Jones, D. C., *Social Structure of England and Wales,* 1927 and 1937.
Central Committee for National Patriotic Organisations, *Report,* 1914.
de Chair, Sir D., *How the British Blockade Works,* 1916.
Clifford, J., *Our Fight for Belgium and What It Means,* 1918.
Cole, G. D. H., *Labour in War Time,* 1915.
Cole, G. D. H., and Arnot, R. P., *Trade Unionism on the Railways,* 1917.
Commission on Educational and Cultural Films, *The Film in National Life,* 1932.
A 'Corpse-Conversion' Factory, n.d.
Cosens, M., *Lloyd George's Munitions Girls,* 1916.
Coxon, S. (ed.), *Dover During the Dark Days,* 1919.
Dawson, A. J., *Somme Battle Stories,* 1916.
Dawson, W. H. (ed.), *After War Problems,* 1917.
Donald, R., *Trade Control in War. Things which the British Government has done well,* 1916.
The Elements of Reconstruction, 1916.
Federation of British Industries, *The Control of Industry,* 1919.
Federation of British Industries, *What It Is and What It Does,* n.d.
Fisher, H. A. L., *Educational Reform,* 1917.
Gosling, H., *Peace: How to Get and Keep It,* 1916.
Henderson, A., *The League of Nations and Labour,* 1918.
H.M.S.O., *Great Britain and the European Crisis,* 1914.
H.M.S.O., *Report of Committee on Alleged German Outrages,* 1915.
Hirst, F. W., *The Political Economy of War,* 1915.
Horsfall, T. C., *National Service and the Welfare of the Community,* 1906.
Jones, D. C. (ed.), *Social Survey of Merseyside,* 1934.
Keynes, J. M., *The Economic Consequences of the Peace,* 1919.
Labour Party, *Report of Special Committee on Deportations in March 1916 in the Clyde District,* 1917.
Leeson, C., *The Child and the War,* 1917.
Leicester Galleries, *Catalogue of Exhibitions, 1917–1918.*
Lloyd, E. M. H., *Stabilisation,* 1923.
Lloyd George, D., *The Great War,* 1914.
Lloyd George, D., *When The War Will End,* 1917.
Lloyd George, D., *The Allied War Aims,* 1918.
McCurdy, C. A., *To Restore the Ten Commandments,* n.d.

Mackenzie, F. A., *British Railways and the War*, 1917.
Masterman, C. F. G., *The Condition of England*, 1909.
Masterman, C. F. G., *England After the War*, 1922.
Mathews, B., *We Must Go On To Victory*, n.d.
Metcalfe, A. E., *Woman's Effort*, 1917.
Money, L. C., *Riches and Poverty*, 1905 and 1913.
Money, L. C., *The Triumph of Nationalisation*, 1920.
Montague, C. E., *The Front Line*, 1917.
Moore, H. K., and Sayers, B., *Croydon and the Great War*, 1920.
Murray, G., *Ethical Problems of the War*, 1915.
Murray, G., 'The Pale Shade', 1917.
National Council on Public Morals, *The Declining Birthrate*, 1916.
National Council on Public Morals, *The Cinema*, 1917.
National Council on Public Morals, *The Ethics of Birth Control*, 1925.
National Housing and Town Planning Council, *The Housing Manual*, 1923.
National Union of Conservative Associations, *Leaflets*, 1911–21.
National Union of Women Workers, *Report of Reconstruction Conference October 1915*, 1915.
Nevinson, C. R. W., *Modern War*, 1917.
Nevinson, C. R. W., *The Roads of France*, 1918.
Nevinson, C. R. W., *The Great War – Fourth Year*, 1918.
Newton, A. P. (ed.), *The Empire and the Future*, 1916.
Northcliffe, Lord, *At the War*, 1916.
Oliver, F. S., *Ordeal by Battle*, 1915.
Owen, W., *Poems*, 1920.
Owen, W., *Collected Poems*, 1963.
The Oxford Pamphlets, 1914–15.
Pankhurst, C., *The War*, n.d.
Peel, C. S., *The Eat-Less-Meat Book*, 1917.
Ponsonby, A., *Democracy and the Control of Foreign Affairs*, 1912.
Ponsonby, A., *Social Reform Versus War*, 1912.
Proud, E. D., *Welfare Work*, 1916.
Reeves, Mrs P., *Round About a Pound a Week*, 1913.
Robertson, W. (ed.), *Middlesbrough's Effort in the Great War*, n.d.
Rowntree, B. S., *Poverty, a Study of Town Life*, 1901.
Rowntree, B. S., *Human Needs of Labour*, 1918.
Rowntree, B. S., *Poverty and Progress*, 1940.
Roxburgh, R. F., *The Prisoners of War Information Bureau in London*, 1915.
Sassoon, S., *War Poems*, 1919.
Scott, L., and Shaw, A., *Great Britain and the Neutral Countries*, 1915.
Seddon, J. A., *Why British Labour Supports the War*, n.d.
Selbie, W. B., *Christian Nationalism*, n.d.

Shaw, G. B., *Commonsense About the War*, 1915.
The Sinking of the 'Lusitania', n.d.
Smith, D. H., *The Industries of Greater London*, 1933.
Smith, H. L. (ed.), *New Survey of London Life and Labour*, 9 vols., 1930–35.
Society for the Propagation of Christian Knowledge, *War Time Tracts
    for the Workers*, 1915.
A Souvenir for Visitors to the British Front, n.d.
Starling, P., *The Nation's Feeding*, 1919.
Sprigg, W. S., *The British Blockade*, n.d.
Strachey, L., *Eminent Victorians*, 1918.
Tillett, B., *Who Was Responsible for the War – and Why?*, 1917.
The Times History of the War.
Trevelyan, C. P., *From Liberalism to Labour*, 1921.
The War Aims of the British People, n.d.
Ward, Mrs H., *England's Effort*, 1916.
Ward, Mrs H., *Towards the Goal*, 1917.
War Emergency: Workers' National Committee, *Report, August 1914–
    March 1916*.
Wells, H. G., *Mr Britling Sees It Through*, 1916.
Williams, J. E. H., *One Young Man*, 1917.
Worsfold, W. B., *The War and Social Reform*, 1919.
Yates, C., *The Women's Part*, 1918.

IV. LETTERS, JOURNALS AND MEMOIRS

Addison, C., *Four and a Half Years*, 2 vols., 1934.
Addison, C., *Politics from Within, 1911–1918*, 2 vols., 1924.
Asquith, H., *Moments of Memory*, 1937.
Asquith, M., *An Autobiography*, 4 vols., 1922.
Barnes, G. N., *From Workshop to War Cabinet*, 1924.
Beecham, Sir T., *A Mingled Chime*, 1944.
Bennett, A., *Journal 1896–1926*, 1933.
Bertie, Lord, *Diary, 1914–18*, 2 vols., 1924.
Beveridge, Lord, *Power and Influence*, 1953.
Blumenfeld, R. D., *All in a Lifetime*, 1931.
Blunden, E., *Undertones of War*, 1930.
Braithwaite, W. J., *Lloyd George's Ambulance Wagon*, 1957.
Brittain, V., *Testament of Youth*, 1936.
Brockway, F., *Inside the Left*, 1942.
Brownrigg, D., *Indiscretions of the Naval Censor*, 1920.
Buchan, J., *The King's Grace*, 1935.
Chamberlain, A., *Politics from Inside*, 1937.
Cecil, Viscount, *A Great Experiment*, 1941.

Childs, Sir W., *Episodes and Reflections*, 1930.
Clarke, T., *My Northcliffe Diary*, 1931.
Clynes, J. R., *Memoirs*, 2 vols., 1937.
Cockerill, Sir G., *What Fools We Were*, 1944.
Cole, M., *Growing Up into Revolution*, 1949.
Collingwood, R. G., *An Autobiography*, 1939.
Crozier, F. P., *Impressions and Recollections*, 1930.
Edmonds, C., *A Subaltern's War*, 1929.
Elton, Lord, *Among Others*, 1938.
Engall, J. S., *A Subaltern's Letters*, 1918.
Farrer, R., *The Void of War*, 1918.
Fawcett, M. G., *The Women's Victory and After: Personal Reminiscences 1911–1918*, 1920.
Fisher, H. A. L., *An Unfinished Autobiography*, 1940.
French, Lord, *1914*.
Gallacher, W., *Revolt on the Clyde*, 1936.
Gillespie, A. D., *Letters from Flanders*, 1916.
Graves, R., *Goodbye to All That*, 1929.
Grey of Fallodon, Viscount, *Twenty-five Years, 1892–1916*, 2 vols., 1925.
Gwynn, S., (ed.), *The Anvil of War: letters from F. S. Oliver to his brother*, 1936.
Haldane, R. B., *An Autobiography*, 1929.
Hamilton, M. A., *Remembering My Good Friends*, 1944.
Harper, R., *Romance of a Modern Airway*, 1931.
Henson, H. H., *Retrospect of an Unimportant Life*, 2 vols., 1942.
Hendrie, J., *Letters of a Durisdeer Soldier*, n.d.
Hitchcock, F. C., *Stand To: A Diary of the Trenches*, 1915–18, 1920.
Housman, L., *The Unexpected Years*, 1936.
Housman, L., (ed.), *Letters of Fallen Englishmen*, 1931.
Jones, P., *War Letters of a Public Schoolboy*, 1918.
Keeling, F. H., *Keeling Letters and Reminiscences*, 1918.
Kenney, A., *Memories of a Militant*, 1924.
Kirkwood, D., *My Life of Revolt*, 1935.
Lansbury, G., *My Life*, 1927.
Lloyd George, D., *War Memoirs*, 6 vols., 1933–36.
Lockhart, R. B., *Your England*, 1951.
Lucy, H., *Diary of a Journalist*, 1922.
McDonagh, M., *In London During the Great War*, 1935.
McKenna, S., *While I Remember*, 1921.
Montague, C. E., *Disenchantment*, 1922.
Mottram, R., Easton, J., and Partridge, E., *Three Personal Records of the War*, 1929.
Nash, P., *Outline, an Autobiography and other Writings*, 1949.

Nevinson, H. W., *More Changes, More Chances,* 1925.
Nevinson, H. W., *Last Changes, Last Chances,* 1928.
Newton, Lord, *Retrospection,* 1929.
Oxford and Asquith, Earl of, *Memories and Reflections,* 1928.
Pankhurst, S., *The Home Front,* 1932.
Priestley, J. B., *Margin Released,* 1962.
Repington, C., *The First World War, 1914–1918,* 1920.
Russell, Earl, *Portraits from Memory,* 1956.
Salter, Lord, *Memoirs of a Public Servant,* 1960.
Sassoon, S., *Memoirs of a Fox-Hunting Man,* 1928.
Sassoon, S., *Memoirs of an Infantry Officer,* 1930.
Smillie, R., *My Life for Labour,* 1924.
Steed, H. W., *Through Thirty Years, 1892–1922,* 1925.
Tawney, R. H., 'The Attack' and 'Some Reflections of a Soldier', in *The Attack and Other Papers,* 1953.
Warr, C. L., *The Glimmering Landscape,* 1960.
Beatrice Webb's Diaries, 1912–24 (ed. M. Cole), 1952.
Wells, H. G., *Experiment in Autobiography,* 1936.
Williamson, H., *A Soldier's Diary of the Great War,* 1929.
Willoughby de Broke, Lord, *The Passing Years,* 1924.
Woodward, E. L., *Short Journey,* 1942.
Woolf, L., *Beginning Again,* 1964.
Wrench, J. E., *Struggle 1914–1920,* 1935.

V. SECONDARY AUTHORITIES

Abrams, M., *The Condition of the British People 1911–1945,* 1945.
Abrams, P., 'The Failure of Social Reform: 1918–1920', in *Past and Present,* April 1963.
Andrews, I., and Hobbs, M., *Economic Effects of the War upon Women and Children in Great Britain,* New York, 1918.
Andrzejewski, S., *Military Organization and Society,* 1954.
Ashworth, W., *An Economic History of England 1870–1939,* 1960.
Baker, C. W., *Government Control and Operation of Industry in Great Britain and the United States During the World War,* New York, 1921.
Balfour, Lady F., *Dr Elsie Inglis,* 1918.
Barnett, C., *The Sword Bearers,* 1964.
Beaverbrook, Lord, *Politicians and the War, 1914–1916,* 1928.
Beaverbrook, Lord, *Men and Power 1917–1918,* 1956.
Beaverbrook, Lord, *Decline and Fall of Lloyd George,* 1963.
Bernal, J. D., *Science in History,* 1954.
Beveridge, W., *The Public Service in War and Peace,* 1920.
Beveridge, W., *British Food Control,* Oxford, 1928.

Beveridge, W., *Some Experiences of Economic Control in War Time*, 1940.

Beveridge, W., *War and Insurance*, Oxford, 1927.

Bolitho, H., *Alfred Mond, First Lord Melchett*, 1933.

Bowley, A. L., *Prices and Wages in the United Kingdom, 1914–1920*, New York, 1921.

Bowley, A. L., *Some Economic Consequences of the Great War*, 1930.

Bowley, A. L., *Wages and Income in the United Kingdom since 1860*, Cambridge, 1937.

Bowley, A. L., *Studies in the National Income*, 1942.

Bowley, M., *Housing and the State*, 1945.

Briggs, A., *History of Birmingham*, Vol. II, 1955.

Briggs, A., *Social Thought and Social Action. A Study of Seebohm Rowntree*, 1961.

Briggs, A., *Birth of Broadcasting*, 1962.

Bruce, M., *The Coming of the Welfare State*, 1961.

Bruntz, G., *Allied Propaganda and the Collapse of the German Empire in 1918*, 1938.

Bulkley, M. E., *Bibliographical Survey of Contemporary Sources for the Economic and Social History of the War*, New York, 1922.

Cardwell, D. S. L., *The Organisation of Science in England*, 1957.

Carter, H., *The Control of the Drink Trade in Great Britain*, New York, 1919.

Carver, T. N., *Government Control of the Liquor Business in Great Britain and the United States*, New York, 1919.

Chapman, G., *Vain Glory*, 1937.

Clark, C., *National Income and Outlay*, 1937.

Clarkson, J. D., and Cochran, T., *War as a Social Institution*, New York, 1941.

Clephane, I., *Towards Sex Freedom*, 1936.

Cole, G. D. H., *Labour in the Coal-Mining Industry 1914–21*, Oxford, 1923.

Cole, G. D. H., *Trade Unionism and Munitions*, Oxford, 1923.

Cole, G. D. H., *Workshop Organisation*, Oxford, 1927.

Cole, G. D. H., *History of the Labour Party since 1914*, 1948.

Cole, M., *The Story of Fabian Socialism*, 1961.

Coller, F., *A State Trading Adventure*, 1925.

Cook, Sir E., *The Press in War Time*, 1920.

Crowther, J. G., *British Scientists of the Twentieth Century*, 1952.

Curtis, S. J., *Education in Britain since 1900*, 1952.

Dearle, N. B., *A Dictionary of War Time Organisations*, Oxford, 1924.

Dearle, N. B., *An Economic Chronicle of the Great War for Great Britain and Ireland*, Oxford, 1929.

Dearle, N. B., *The Labour Cost of the World War to Great Britain, 1914–1922*, 1940.

Dewar, G. A. B., *The Great Munitions Feat 1914–1918*, 1921.

Dixon, F. H., and Parmelee, J. H., *War Administration of the Railways in the United States and Great Britain*, New York, 1918.

Edmonds, J. E., *Short History of World War I*, 1952.

Edwards, R. S., *Cooperative Industrial Research*, 1950.

Ensor, R. C. K., *England 1870–1914*, 1936.

Fairlie, J. A., *British War Administration*, New York, 1919.

Falls, C., *The First World War*, 1960.

Fayle, C. E., *The War and the Shipping Industry*, 1927.

Gaus, J. M., *Great Britain, A Study of Civic Loyalty*, Chicago, 1929.

Ginsberg, M. (ed.), *Law and Opinion in England in the Twentieth Century*, 1959.

Gollin, A. M., *Proconsul in Politics: a study of Lord Milner in Opposition and in Power*, 1964.

Gorham, M., *Broadcasting and Television Since 1900*, 1952.

Grady, H. F., *British War Finance 1914–1919*, New York, 1927.

Graham, J. W., *Conscription and Conscience*, 1922.

Graubard, S. R., 'Military Demobilisation in Britain following the First World War', in *Journal of Modern History*, 1947.

Graves, R., and Hodge, A., *The Long Week End*, 1940.

Gray, H. L., *War Time Control of Industry*, New York, 1918.

Grier, L., Ashley, A., and Kirkcaldy, A. W., *British Labour Replacement and Conciliation 1914–1921*, 1921.

Groves, R., 'When 12,000 London Policemen went on Strike', in *Socialist Outlook*, 22 January, 1954.

Guttsman, W. L., 'The Changing Social Structure of the British Political Elite, 1886–1935', in *British Journal of Sociology*, 1951.

Guttsman, W. L., 'Aristocracy and the Middle Classes in the British Political Elite, 1886–1916', in *British Journal of Sociology*, 1954.

Guttsman, W. L., *The British Political Elite*, 1963.

Hammond, J. L., *C. P. Scott of the Manchester Guardian*, 1934.

Hammond, M. B., *British Labour Conditions and Legislation during the War*, New York, 1919.

Hanak, H. H., 'The Union of Democratic Control during the First World War', in *Bulletin of Institute of Historical Research*, November 1963.

Hankey, Lord, *The Supreme Command 1914–1918*, 1961.

Hardie, M., and Sabin, A. K., *War Posters*, 1920.

Harrod, Sir R. F., *Life of John Maynard Keynes*, 1951.

Hassall, C., *Rupert Brooke*, 1964.

Havighurst, W., *Twentieth Century Britain*, New York, 1962.

Heath, H. F., and Hetherington, W., *Industrial Research and Development in the United Kingdom*, 1946.

Heard, G., *Morals since 1900*, 1955.

Henderson, H. D., *The Cotton Control Board*, Oxford, 1922.

Hibbard, B. H., *Effects of the Great War upon Agriculture in the United States and Great Britain*, New York, 1919.

Hirst, F. W., *The Consequences of the War to Great Britain*, 1934.

Hirst, F. W., and Allen, J. E., *British War Budgets*, Oxford, 1926.

Howard, M., 'Lest We Forget', in *Encounter*, December 1963.

Hurwitz, S. J., *State Intervention in Great Britain*, New York, 1949.

Jewkes, J., *et al.*, *The Sources of Invention*, 1958.

Jones, T., *Lloyd George*, 1951.

Kirkcaldy, A. W. (ed.), *British Finance During and After the War 1914–1921*, 1921.

Lasswell, H. D., *Propaganda Technique in the World War*, 1927.

Lee, J. M., *Social Leaders and Public Persons*, 1964.

Litman, S., *Price and Price Control in Great Britain and the United States During the World War*, New York, 1920.

Lloyd, E. M. H., *Experiments in State Control*, Oxford, 1924.

McDowall, R. B., *British Conservatism 1832–1914*, 1959.

McEwan, J. M., 'The Coupon Election of 1918 and the Unionist Members of Parliament', in *Journal of Modern History*, 1962.

Mackintosh, J. M., *Trends of Opinion about the Public Health, 1901–1951*, 1953.

Mackintosh, J. P., *The British Cabinet*, 1962.

McVey, F. L., *The Financial History of Great Britain 1914–18*, 1918.

Mantoux, E., *The Carthaginian Peace, or the Economic Consequences of Mr Keynes*, 1946.

Marchant, Sir J., *Dr John Clifford, Life, Letters, and Reminiscences*, 1922.

Marsh, D. C., *Changing Social Structure of England and Wales*, 1955.

Marshall, T. S., *Citizenship and Social Class*, 1950.

Marwick, A., *The Explosion of British Society, 1914–62*, 1963.

Marwick, A., *Clifford Allen: the Open Conspirator*, 1964.

Marwick, A., 'James Maxton, his Place in Scottish Labour History', in *Scottish Historical Review*, 1964.

Marwick, A., 'Middle Opinion in the Thirties: Planning, Progress and Political Agreement', in *English Historical Review*, 1964.

Masterman, L., *C. F. G. Masterman*, 1939.

Meech, T. C., *This Generation, 1900–1926*, 1927–28.

Middleton, T. H., *Food Production in War*, Oxford, 1923.

Morgan, E. V., *Studies in British Financial Policy, 1914–25*, 1952.

Mowat, C. L., *Britain Between the Wars*, 1955.

Nef, J. U., *War and Human Progress*, 1950.

Newsholme, Sir A., *The Last Thirty Years in Public Health*, 1936.
Newsholme, Sir A., *The Ministry of Health*, 1925.
Newsome, D., *Godliness and Good Learning*, 1961.
Nowell-Smith, F. (ed.), *Edwardian England*, 1964.
Ogilvie, V., *Our Times*, 1950.
Peel, C. S., *How We Lived Then 1914–1918*, 1929.
Pelling, H., *Modern Britain, 1885–1955*, 1960.
Playne, C. E., *The Pre-War Mind in Britain*, 1928.
Playne, C. E., *Society at War 1914–1916*, 1931.
Playne, C. E., *Britain Holds On 1917–1918*, 1933.
Plummer, A., *New British Industries in the Twentieth Century*, 1937.
Political and Economic Planning, *The British Film Industry*, 1952.
Pollard, S., *The Development of the British Economy 1914–1950*, 1960.
Ponsonby, A., *Falsehood in War Time*, 1926.
Pratt, E. A., *British Railways and the Great War*, 1921.
Pribicevik, B., *The Shop Stewards' Movement and Workers' Control 1910–1922*, Oxford, 1959.
Redmayne, Sir R. A. S., *The British Coal-Mining Industry During the War*, Oxford, 1923.
Rees, J. M., *Trusts in British Industry, 1914–21*, 1922.
Rhondda, Viscountess, *et al.*, *D. A. Thomas – Viscount Rhondda*, 1921.
Salter, J. A., *Allied Shipping Control*, Oxford, 1921.
Scott, J. D., *Vickers*, 1962.
Scott, W. R., and Cunnison J., *The Industries of the Clyde Valley During the War*, Oxford, 1924.
Scott, W. R., *et al.*, *Rural Scotland During the War*, Oxford, 1922.
Semmel, B., *Imperialism and Social Reform*, 1960.
Shadwell, A., *Drink in 1914–1922, A Lesson in Control*, 1923.
Smith, H. L., *The Board of Trade*, 1928.
Spinks, G. (ed.), *Religion in Britain since 1900*, 1952.
Squires, J. D., *British Propaganda at Home and in the United States from 1914 to 1917*, Cambridge, Mass., 1935.
Stamp, Sir J., *Taxation During the War*, Oxford, 1932.
Strachey, R. (ed.), *Our Victory and After*, 1936.
Sturmey, S. G., *The Economic Development of Radio*, 1958.
Tawney, R. H., 'The Abolition of Economic Controls 1918–21', in *Economic History Review*, 1943.
Taylor, A. J. P., *The First World War*, 1963.
Terraine, J., *Douglas Haig, the Educated Soldier*, 1963.
Thompson, F. M. L., *English Landed Society in the Nineteenth Century*, 1963.
Titmuss, R. M., *Essays on 'The Welfare State'*, 1958.
Welland, D., *Wilfred Owen*, 1960.

Wickwar, H. and M., *The Social Services,* 1949.

Williams, E. N., *Life in Georgian England,* 1962.

Willis, I. C., *England's Holy War,* New York, 1929.

Wilson, T., 'The Coupon and the British General Election of 1918', in *Journal of Modern History,* March 1964.

Winkler, H., *The League of Nations Movement in Great Britain, 1914–1919,* New Brunswick, 1952.

Wolfe, H., *British Labour Supply and Regulation,* Oxford, 1924.

Woolf, L., *After the Deluge,* Vol. I, 1931.

Index

Addison, Christopher (Minister of Reconstruction; Minister of Health), 181, 207, 241–2, 276, 312

advertising posters, 51–2

agriculture, 18; number of farmers in U.K., 22; women employed in, 90–1, 112; government directives on, 171–2; wage increases, 271

aircraft, development of, 232–3

air raids and air-raid precautions, 37, 44, 136–7; casualties in U.K., 197–8

air transport, 308–9

Aitken, Sir Max (later Lord Beaverbrook), 146, 182

alcohol: see liquor

Aliens Restriction Act (1914), 37–8

Allen, Clifford (pacifist leader), 80, 144

allotments scheme (land for food production), 248–9

allowances for servicemen's dependants: see pensions and allowances

amalgamations, combinations and co-operatives; industrial, 161, 174–6, 277–8; of trade unions, 278

America: see United States of America

amusements tax, 129

Angell, Norman, 28

Armistice, the, 259–62

Army, British: 1914 statistics and organization, 15, 41

art and literature, impact of the war on, 219–23, 296

art galleries and museums, wartime closing of, 145–6

Asquith, Herbert Henry, 24, 32; and Irish Home Rule, 40; and propaganda organizations, 45; and the shell shortage, 59; and conscientious objectors, 81; and women's suffrage, 101, 104; and the Dublin Easter rising, 181; background to resignation of, 181–5

atrocities, allegations of German, 48, 131–2, 214

Attlee, Clement, 291

Austria as object of race hatred, 50

Baldwin, Stanley, 302, 311

Balfour, A. J., and propaganda organizations, 45; and anti-German feeling, 261

banking: see finance and banking

Barnes, G. N. (labour leader), 201, 202, 262, 263

Beaverbrook, Lord: see Aitken, Sir Max

Beecham, Sir Thomas, 144–5

Belgium, Germans violate neutrality of, 31; refugees in Britain, 43–4; allegations of German atrocities in, 131–2

Bennett, Arnold, 38, 112, 180

Beveridge, William (later Lord Beveridge), 156

Billing, Pemberton, and the 'Black Book', 258

biochemistry, 228

Birmingham, expansion and population of, 17–18

Birrell, Augustine, and the Easter Rebellion in Ireland, 181

birth-control, increased availability of methods of, 107, 290

birth rate, decline in the, 290

'Black Book', Pemberton Billing and the, 258

Blatchford, Robert, 26–7

blockades by Britain and Germany, 52

Blumenfeld, R. D. (Editor, *Daily Express*), observations of, 41, 42, 133–4, 200, 296

Boer War, patriotic demonstrations in, 27

Bonar Law, Andrew, 40, 100, 124, 165, 182; becomes Prime Minister, 184, 246

Boothby, Robert (later Lord), 292

Bowley, A. L., social surveys of, 22–3

Brecht, Bertold, 152